WESTERN LEGENDS

WESTERN LEGENDS

To the Last Man

The Mysterious Rider

The Lone Star Ranger

ZANE GREY

A Tom Doherty Associates Book
New York

WESTERN LEGENDS

To the Last Man was first published in 1921; *The Mysterious Rider* was first published in 1921; *The Lone Star Ranger* was first published in 1915.

A Forge Book
Published by Tom Doherty Associates, LLC
175 Fifth Avenue
New York, NY 10010

www.tor-forge.com

Forge® is a registered trademark of Tom Doherty Associates, LLC.

Library of Congress Cataloging-in-Publication Data

Grey, Zane, 1872–1939.
Western legends / Zane Grey.
    p. cm.
"A Tom Doherty Associates book."
    ISBN-13: 978-0-7653-2065-0
    ISBN-10: 0-7653-2065-7
    1. Western stories. I. Title.
PS3513.R6545 W375 2008
813'.52—dc22

                      2008029742

First Edition: October 2008

Printed in the United States of America

0 9 8 7 6 5 4 3 2 1

CONTENTS

WESTERN LEGENDS

TO THE LAST MAN

FOREWORD

It was inevitable that in my efforts to write romantic history of the great West I should at length come to the story of a feud. For long I have steered clear of this rock. But at last I have reached it and must go over it, driven by my desire to chronicle the stirring events of pioneer days.

Even to-day it is not possible to travel into the remote corners of the West without seeing the lives of people still affected by a fighting past. How can the truth be told about the pioneering of the West if the struggle, the fight, the blood be left out? It cannot be done. How can a novel be stirring and thrilling, as were those times, unless it be full of sensation? My long labors have been devoted to making stories resemble the times they depict. I have loved the West for its vastness, its contrast, its beauty and color and life, for its wildness and violence, and for the fact that I have seen how it developed great men and women who died unknown and unsung.

In this materialistic age, this hard, practical, swift, greedy age of realism, it seems there is no place for writers of romance, no place for romance itself. For many years all the events leading up to the great war were realistic, and the war itself was horribly realistic, and the aftermath is likewise. Romance is only another name for idealism; and I contend that life without ideals is not worth living. Never in the history of the world were ideals needed so terribly as now. Walter Scott wrote romance;

so did Victor Hugo; and likewise Kipling, Hawthorne, Stevenson. It was
Stevenson, particularly, who wielded a bludgeon against the realists. People
live for the dream in their hearts. And I have yet to know anyone who
has not some secret dream, some hope, however dim, some storied wall
to look at in the dusk, some painted window leading to the soul. How
strange indeed to find that the realists have ideals and dreams! To read
them one would think their lives held nothing significant. But they
love, they hope, they dream, they sacrifice, they struggle on with that
dream in their hearts just the same as others. We all are dreamers, if not
in the heavy-lidded wasting of time, then in the meaning of life that
makes us work on.

It was Wordsworth who wrote, "The world is too much with us"; and
if I could give the secret of my ambition as a novelist in a few words it
would be contained in that quotation. My inspiration to write has always
come from nature. Character and action are subordinated to setting. In
all that I have done I have tried to make people see how the world is too
much with them. Getting and spending they lay waste their powers, with
never a breath of the free and wonderful life of the open!

So I come back to the main point of this foreword, in which I am trying to tell why and how I came to write the story of a feud notorious in
Arizona as the Pleasant Valley War.

Some years ago Mr. Harry Adams, a cattleman of Vermajo Park,
New Mexico, told me he had been in the Tonto Basin of Arizona and
thought I might find interesting material there concerning this Pleasant
Valley War. His version of the war between cattlemen and sheepmen certainly determined me to look over the ground. My old guide, Al Doyle of
Flagstaff, had led me over half of Arizona, but never down into that
wonderful wild and rugged basin between the Mogollon Mesa and the
Mazatzal Mountains. Doyle had long lived on the frontier and his version of the Pleasant Valley War differed markedly from that of Mr.
Adams. I asked other old timers about it, and their remarks further excited my curiosity.

Once down there, Doyle and I found the wildest, most rugged,
roughest, and most remarkable country either of us had visited; and the
few inhabitants were like the country. I went in ostensibly to hunt bear
and lion and turkey, but what I really was hunting for was the story of

that Pleasant Valley War. I engaged the services of a bear hunter who had three strapping sons as reserved and strange and aloof as he was. No wheel tracks of any kind had ever come within miles of their cabin. I spent two wonderful months hunting game and reveling in the beauty and grandeur of that Rim Rock country, but I came out knowing no more about the Pleasant Valley War. These Texans and their few neighbors, likewise from Texas, did not talk. But all I saw and felt only inspired me the more. This trip was in the fall of 1918.

The next year I went again with the best horses, outfit, and men the Doyles could provide. And this time I did not ask any questions. But I rode horses—some of them too wild for me—and packed a rifle many a hundred miles, riding sometimes thirty and forty miles a day, and I climbed in and out of the deep cañons, desperately staying at the heels of one of those long-legged Texans. I learned the life of those backwoodsmen, but I did not get the story of the Pleasant Valley War. I had, however, won the friendship of that hardy people.

In 1920 I went back with a still larger outfit, equipped to stay as long as I liked. And this time, without my asking it, different natives of the Tonto came to tell me about the Pleasant Valley War. No two of them agreed on anything concerning it, except that only one of the active participants survived the fighting. Whence comes my title, *To the Last Man*. Thus I was swamped in a mass of material out of which I could only flounder to my own conclusion. Some of the stories told me are singularly tempting to a novelist. But, though I believe them myself, I cannot risk their improbability to those who have no idea of the wildness of wild men at a wild time. There really was a terrible and bloody feud, perhaps the most deadly and least known in all the annals of the West. I saw the ground, the cabins, the graves, all so darkly suggestive of what must have happened.

I never learned the truth of the cause of the Pleasant Valley War, or if I did hear it I had no means of recognizing it. All the given causes were plausible and convincing. Strange to state, there is still secrecy and reticence all over the Tonto Basin as to the facts of this feud. Many descendents of those killed are living there now. But no one likes to talk about it. Assuredly many of the incidents told me really occurred, as, for example, the terrible one of the two women, in the face of relentless enemies, saving the bodies of their dead husbands from being devoured by wild hogs. Suffice it to say that this romance is true to my conception of the war, and I base it upon the setting I learned to know and love so well, upon the strange passions of primitive people, and upon my instinctive reaction to the facts and rumors that I gathered.

ZANE GREY
AVALON, CALIFORNIA,
April, 1921

CHAPTER 1

At the end of a dry, uphill ride over barren country Jean Isbel unpacked to camp at the edge of the cedars where a little rocky cañon, green with willow and cottonwood, promised water and grass.

His animals were tired, especially the pack mule that had carried a heavy load; and with slow heave of relief they knelt and rolled in the dust. Jean experienced something of relief himself as he threw off his chaps. He had not been used to hot, dusty, glaring days on the barren lands. Stretching his long length beside a tiny rill of clear water that tinkled over the red stones, he drank thirstily. The water was cool, but it had an acrid taste—an alkali bite that he did not like. Not since he had left Oregon had he tasted clear, sweet, cold water; and he missed it just as he longed for the stately shady forests he had loved. This wild, endless Arizona land bade fair to earn his hatred.

By the time he had leisurely completed his tasks twilight had fallen and coyotes had begun their barking. Jean listened to the yelps and to the moan of the cool wind in the cedars with a sense of satisfaction that these lonely sounds were familiar. This cedar wood burned into a pretty fire and the smell of its smoke was newly pleasant.

"Reckon maybe I'll learn to like Arizona," he mused, half aloud. "But I've a hankerin' for waterfalls an' dark-green forests. Must be the Indian in me. . . . Anyway, dad needs me bad, an' I reckon I'm here for keeps."

Jean threw some cedar branches on the fire, in the light of which he opened his father's letter, hoping by repeated reading to grasp more of its strange portent. It had been two months in reaching him, coming by traveler, by stage and train, and then by boat, and finally by stage again. Written in lead pencil on a leaf torn from an old ledger, it would have been hard to read even if the writing had been more legible.

"Dad's writin' was always bad, but I never saw it so shaky," said Jean, thinking aloud.

Grass Vally, Arizona.

SON JEAN,—Come home. Here is your home and here your needed. When we left Oregon we all reckoned you would not be long behind. But its years now. I am growing old, son, and you was always my steadiest boy. Not that you ever was so dam steady. Only your wildness seemed more for the woods. You take after mother, and your brothers Bill and Guy take after me. That is the red and white of it. Your part Indian, Jean, and that Indian I reckon I am going to need bad. I am rich in cattle and horses. And my range here is the best I ever seen. Lately we have been losing stock. But that is not all nor so bad. Sheepmen have moved into the Tonto and are grazing down on Grass Vally. Cattlemen and sheepmen can never bide in this country. We have bad times ahead. Reckon I have more reasons to worry and need you, but you must wait to hear that by word of mouth. Whatever your doing, chuck it and rustle for Grass Vally so to make here by spring. I am asking you to take pains to pack in some guns and a lot of shells. And hide them in your outfit. If you meet anyone when your coming down into the Tonto, listen more than you talk. And last, son, dont let anything keep you in Oregon. Reckon you have a sweetheart, and if so fetch her along. With love from your dad,

GASTON ISBEL.

Jean pondered over this letter. Judged by memory of his father, who had always been self-sufficient, it had been a surprise and somewhat of a shock. Weeks of travel and reflection had not helped him to grasp the meaning between the lines.

"Yes, dad's growin' old," mused Jean, feeling a warmth and a sadness stir in him. "He must be 'way over sixty. But he never looked old. . . . So he's rich now an' losin' stock, an' goin' to be sheeped off his range. Dad could stand a lot of rustlin', but not much from sheepmen."

The softness that stirred in Jean merged into a cold, thoughtful earnestness which had followed every perusal of his father's letter. A dark, full current seemed flowing in his veins, and at times he felt it swell and heat. It troubled him, making him conscious of a deeper, stronger self, opposed to his careless, free, and dreamy nature. No ties had bound him in Oregon, except love for the great, still forests and the thundering rivers; and this love came from his softer side. It had cost him a wrench to leave. And all the way by ship down the coast to San Diego and across the Sierra Madres by stage, and so on to this last overland travel by horseback, he had felt a retreating of the self that was tranquil and happy and a dominating of this unknown somber self, with its menacing possibilities. Yet despite a nameless regret and a loyalty to Oregon, when he lay in his blankets he had to confess a keen interest in his adventurous future, a keen enjoyment of this stark, wild Arizona. It appeared to be a different sky stretching in dark, star-spangled dome over him—closer, vaster, bluer. The strong fragrance of sage and cedar floated over him with the camp-fire smoke, and all seemed drowsily to subdue his thoughts.

At dawn he rolled out of his blankets and, pulling on his boots, began the day with a zest for the work that must bring closer his calling future. White, crackling frost and cold, nipping air were the same keen spurs to action that he had known in the uplands of Oregon, yet they were not wholly the same. He sensed an exhilaration similar to the effect of a strong, sweet wine. His horse and mule had fared well during the night, having been much refreshed by the grass and water of the little cañon. Jean mounted and rode into the cedars with gladness that at last he had put the endless leagues of barren land behind him.

The trail he followed appeared to be seldom traveled. It led, according to the meager information obtainable at the last settlement, directly to what was called the Rim, and from there Grass Valley could be seen down in the Basin. The ascent of the ground was so gradual that only in long, open stretches could it be seen. But the nature of the vegetation showed Jean how he was climbing. Scant, low, scraggy cedars gave place to more numerous, darker, greener, bushier ones, and these to high, full-foliaged, green-berried trees. Sage and grass in the open flats grew more luxuriously. Then came the piñons, and presently among them the checker-barked junipers. Jean hailed the first pine tree with a hearty slap on the brown, rugged bark. It was a small dwarf pine struggling to live. The next one was larger, and after that came several, and beyond them pines stood up everywhere above the lower trees. Odor of pine needles mingled with the other dry smells that made the wind pleasant to Jean. In an hour from the first line of pines he had ridden beyond the cedars and piñons into a slowly thickening and deepening forest. Underbrush appeared scarce except in ravines, and the ground in open patches held a bleached grass. Jean's eye roved for sight of squirrels, birds, deer, or any moving creature. It appeared to be a dry, uninhabited forest. About midday Jean halted at a pond of surface water, evidently melted snow, and gave his animals a drink. He saw a few old deer tracks in the mud and several huge bird tracks new to him which he concluded must have been made by wild turkeys.

The trail divided at this pond. Jean had no idea which branch he ought to take. "Reckon it doesn't matter," he muttered, as he was about to remount. His horse was standing with ears up, looking back along the trail. Then Jean heard a clip-clop of trotting hoofs, and presently espied a horseman.

Jean made a pretense of tightening his saddle girths while he peered over his horse at the approaching rider. All men in this country were going to be of exceeding interest to Jean Isbel. This man at a distance rode and looked like all the Arizonians Jean had seen, he had a superb seat in the saddle, and he was long and lean. He wore a huge black sombrero and a soiled red scarf. His vest was open and he was without a coat.

The rider came trotting up and halted several paces from Jean.

"Hullo, stranger!" he said, gruffly.

"Howdy yourself!" replied Jean. He felt an instinctive importance in the meeting with the man. Never had sharper eyes flashed over Jean and his outfit. He had a dust-colored, sun-burned face, long, lean, and hard, a huge sandy mustache that hid his mouth, and eyes of piercing light intensity. Not very much hard Western experience had passed by this man, yet he was not old, measured by years. When he dismounted Jean saw he was tall, even for an Arizonian.

"Seen your tracks back a ways," he said, as he slipped the bit to let his horse drink. "Where bound?"

"Reckon I'm lost, all right," replied Jean. "New country for me."

"Shore. I seen thet from your tracks an' your last camp. Wal, where was you headin' for before you got lost?"

The query was deliberately cool, with a dry, crisp ring. Jean felt the lack of friendliness or kindliness in it.

"Grass Valley. My name's Isbel," he replied, shortly.

The rider attended to his drinking horse and presently rebridled him; then with long swing of leg he appeared to step into the saddle.

"Shore I knowed you was Jean Isbel," he said. "Everybody in the Tonto has heerd old Gass Isbel sent fer his boy."

"Well then, why did you ask?" inquired Jean, bluntly.

"Reckon I wanted to see what you'd say."

"So? All right. But I'm not carin' very much for what *you* say."

Their glances locked steadily then and each measured the other by the intangible conflict of spirit.

"Shore thet's natural," replied the rider. His speech was slow, and the motions of his long, brown hands, as he took a cigarette from his vest, kept time with his words. "But seein' you're one of the Isbels, I'll hev my say whether you want it or not. My name's Colter an' I'm one of the sheepmen Gass Isbel's riled with."

"Colter. Glad to meet you," replied Jean. "An' I reckon who riled my father is goin' to rile me."

"Shore. If thet wasn't so you'd not be an Isbel," returned Colter, with a grim little laugh. "It's easy to see you ain't run into any Tonto Basin fellers yet. Wal, I'm goin' to tell you thet your old man gabbed like a woman down at Greaves's store. Bragged aboot you an' how you could fight an' how you could shoot an' how you could track a hoss or a man! Bragged how you'd chase every sheep herder back up on the Rim. . . . I'm tellin' you because we want you to git our stand right. We're goin' to run sheep down in Grass Valley."

"Ahuh! Well, who's we?" queried Jean, curtly.

"Wha-at? . . . We—I mean the sheepmen rangin' this Rim from Black Butte to the Apache country."

"Colter, I'm a stranger in Arizona," said Jean, slowly. "I know little about ranchers or sheepmen. It's true my father sent for me. It's true, I dare say, that he bragged, for he was given to bluster an' blow. An' he's old now. I can't help it if he bragged about me. But if he has, an' if he's justified in his stand against you sheepmen, I'm goin' to do my best to live up to his brag."

"I get your hunch. Shore we understand each other, an' thet's a powerful help. You take my hunch to your old man," replied Colter, as he turned his horse away toward the left. "Thet trail leadin' south is yours. When you come to the Rim you'll see a bare spot down in the Basin. Thet'll be Grass Valley."

He rode away out of sight into the woods. Jean leaned against his horse and pondered. It seemed difficult to be just to this Colter, not because of his claims, but because of a subtle hostility that emanated from him. Colter had the hard face, the masked intent, the turn of speech that Jean had come to associate with dishonest men. Even if Jean had not been prejudiced, if he had known nothing of his father's trouble with these sheepmen, and if Colter had met him only to exchange glances and greetings, still Jean would never have had a favorable impression. Colter grated upon him, roused an antagonism seldom felt.

"Heigho!" sighed the young man. "Good-by to huntin' an' fishin'! Dad's given me a man's job."

With that he mounted his horse and started the pack mule into the right-hand trail. Walking and trotting, he traveled all afternoon, toward sunset getting into heavy forest of pine. More than one snow bank showed white through the green, sheltered on the north slopes of shady ravines. And it was upon entering this zone of richer, deeper forestland that Jean sloughed off his gloomy forebodings. These stately pines were not the giant firs of Oregon, but any lover of the woods could be happy under them. Higher still he climbed until the forest spread before and around him like a level park, with thicketed ravines here and there on each side. And presently that deceitful level led to a higher bench upon which the pines towered, and were matched by beautiful trees he took for spruce. Heavily barked, with regular spreading branches, these conifers rose in symmetrical shape to spear the sky with silver plumes. A graceful gray-green moss, waved like veils from the branches. The air was not so dry and it was colder, with a scent and touch of snow. Jean made camp at the first likely site; taking the precaution to unroll his bed some little distance from his fire. Under the softly moaning pines he felt comfortable, having lost the sense of an immeasurable open space falling away from all around him.

The gobbling of wild turkeys awakened Jean, "Chug-a-lug, chug-a-lug, chug-a-lug-chug." There was not a great difference between the gobble of a wild turkey and that of a tame one. Jean got up, and taking his rifle went out into the gray obscurity of dawn to try to locate the turkeys. But it was too dark, and finally when daylight came they appeared to be gone. The mule had strayed, and, what with finding it and cooking breakfast and packing, Jean did not make a very early start. On this last lap of his long journey he had slowed down. He was weary of hurrying; the change from weeks in the glaring sun and dust-laden wind to this sweet cool darkly green and brown forest was very welcome; he wanted to linger along the shaded trail. This day he made sure would see him reach the Rim. By and by he lost the trail. It had just worn out from lack of use. Every now and then Jean would cross an old trail, and as he penetrated deeper into the forest every damp or dusty spot showed tracks of turkey, deer, and bear. The amount of bear sign surprised him. Presently his keen nostrils were assailed by a smell of sheep, and soon he rode into a broad sheep trail. From the tracks Jean calculated that the sheep had passed there the day before.

An unreasonable antipathy seemed born in him. To be sure he had been prepared to dislike sheep, and that was why he was unreasonable. But on the other hand this band of sheep had left a broad bare swath, weedless, grassless, flowerless, in their wake. Where sheep grazed they destroyed. That was what Jean had against them.

An hour later he rode to the crest of a long parklike slope, where new green grass was sprouting and flowers peeped everywhere. The pines appeared far apart; gnarled oak trees showed rugged and gray against the green wall of woods. A white strip of snow gleamed like a moving stream away down in the woods.

Jean heard the musical tinkle of bells and the baa-baa of sheep and the faint, sweet bleating of lambs. As he rode toward these sounds a dog ran out from an oak thicket and barked at him. Next Jean smelled a camp-fire and soon he caught sight of a curling blue column of smoke, and then a small peaked tent. Beyond the clump of oaks Jean encountered a Mexican lad carrying a carbine. The boy had a swarthy, pleasant face, and to Jean's greeting he replied, *"Buenos dias."* Jean understood little Spanish, and about all he gathered by his simple queries was that the lad was not alone—and that it was "lambing time."

This latter circumstance grew noisily manifest. The forest seemed shrilly full of incessant baas and plaintive bleats. All about the camp, on the slope, in the glades, and everywhere, were sheep. A few were grazing; many were lying down; most of them were ewes suckling white fleecy little lambs that staggered on their feet. Everywhere Jean saw tiny lambs just born. Their pin-pointed bleats pierced the heavier baa-baa of their mothers.

Jean dismounted and led his horse down toward the camp, where he rather expected to see another and older Mexican, from whom he might get information. The lad walked with him. Down this way the plaintive uproar made by the sheep was not so loud.

"Hello there!" called Jean, cheerfully, as he approached the tent. No answer was forthcoming. Dropping his bridle, he went on, rather slowly, looking for some one to appear. Then a voice from one side startled him.

"Mawnin', stranger."

A girl stepped out from beside a pine. She carried a rifle. Her face flashed richly brown, but she was not Mexican. This fact, and the sudden conviction that she had been watching him, somewhat disconcerted Jean.

"Beg pardon—miss," he floundered. "Didn't expect to see a— girl. . . . I'm sort of lost—lookin' for the Rim—an' thought I'd find a sheep herder who'd show me. I can't savvy this boy's lingo."

While he spoke it seemed to him an intentness of expression, a strain relaxed from her face. A faint suggestion of hostility likewise disappeared. Jean was not even sure that he had caught it, but there had been something that now was gone.

"Shore I'll be glad to show y'u," she said.

"Thanks, miss. Reckon I can breathe easy now," he replied. "It's a long ride from San Diego. Hot an' dusty! I'm pretty tired. An' maybe this woods isn't good medicine to achin' eyes!"

"San Diego! Y'u're from the coast?"

"Yes."

Jean had doffed his sombrero at sight of her and he still held it, rather deferentially, perhaps. It seemed to attract her attention.

"Put on y'ur hat, stranger. . . . Shore I can't recollect when any man bared his haid to me." She uttered a little laugh in which surprise and frankness mingled with a tint of bitterness.

Jean sat down with his back to a pine, and, laying the sombrero by his side, he looked full at her, conscious of a singular eagerness, as if he wanted to verify by close scrutiny a first hasty impression. If there had been an instinct in his meeting with Colter, there was more in this. The girl half sat, half leaned against a log, with the shiny little carbine across her knees. She had a level, curious gaze upon him, and Jean had never met one just like it. Her eyes were rather a wide oval in shape, clear and steady, with shadows of thought in their amber-brown depths. They seemed to look through Jean, and his gaze dropped first. Then it was he saw her ragged homespun skirt and a few inches of brown, bare ankles, strong and round, and crude worn-out moccasins that failed to hide the shapeliness of her feet. Suddenly she drew back her stockingless ankles and ill-shod little feet. When Jean lifted his gaze again he found her face half averted and a stain of red in the gold tan of her cheek. That touch of embarrassment somehow removed her from this strong, raw, wild woodland setting. It changed her poise. It detracted from the curious, unabashed, almost bold, look that he had encountered in her eyes.

"Reckon you're from Texas," said Jean, presently.

"Shore am," she drawled. She had a lazy Southern voice, pleasant to hear. "How'd y'u-all guess that?"

"Anybody can tell a Texan. Where I came from there were a good many pioneers an' ranchers from the old Lone Star State. I've worked for several. An', come to think of it, I'd rather hear a Texas girl talk than anybody."

"Did y'u know many Texas girls?" she inquired, turning again to face him.

"Reckon I did—quite a good many."

"Did y'u go with them?"

"Go with them? Reckon you mean keep company. Why, yes, I guess I did—a little," laughed Jean. "Sometimes on a Sunday or a dance once in a blue moon, an' occasionally a ride."

"Shore that accounts," said the girl, wistfully.

"For what?" asked Jean.

"Y'ur bein' a gentleman," she replied, with force. "Oh, I've not forgotten. I had friends when we lived in Texas. . . . Three years ago. Shore it seems longer. Three miserable years in this damned country!"

Then she bit her lip, evidently to keep back further unwitting utterance to a total stranger. And it was that biting of her lip that drew Jean's attention to her mouth. It held beauty of curve and fullness and color that could not hide a certain sadness and bitterness. Then the whole flashing brown face changed for Jean. He saw that it was young, full of passion and restraint, possessing a power which grew on him. This, with her shame and pathos and the fact that she craved respect, gave a leap to Jean's interest.

"Well, I reckon you flatter me," he said, hoping to put her at her ease again. "I'm only a rough hunter an' fisherman—woodchopper an' horse tracker. Never had all the school I needed—nor near enough company of nice girls like you."

"Am I nice?" she asked, quickly.

"You sure are," he replied, smiling.

"In these rags," she demanded, with a sudden flash of passion that thrilled him. "Look at the holes." She showed rips and worn-out places in the sleeves of her buckskin blouse, through which gleamed a round, brown arm. "I sew when I have anythin' to sew with. . . . Look at my skirt—a dirty rag. An' I have only one other to my name. . . . Look!" Again a color tinged her cheeks, most becoming, and giving the lie to her action. But shame could not check her violence now. A dammed-up resentment seemed to have broken out in flood. She lifted the ragged skirt almost to her knees. "No stockings! No shoes! . . . How can a girl be nice when she has no clean, decent woman's clothes to wear?"

"How—how can a girl . . ." began Jean. "See here, miss, I'm beggin' your pardon for—sort of stirrin' you to forget yourself a little. Reckon I understand. You don't meet many stranger an' I sort of hit you wrong—makin' you feel too much—an' talk too much. Who an' what you are is none of my business. But we met. . . . An' I reckon somethin' has happened—perhaps more to me than to you. . . . Now let me put you straight about clothes an' women. Reckon I know most women love nice things to wear an' think because clothes make them look pretty that they're nicer or better. But they're wrong. You're wrong. Maybe it 'd be too much for a girl like you to be happy without clothes. But you can be—you are just as nice, an'—an' fine—an', for all you know, a good deal more appealin' to some men."

"Stranger, y'u shore must excuse my temper an' the show I made of myself," replied the girl, with composure. "That, to say the least, was not nice. An' I don't want anyone thinkin' better of me than I deserve. My mother died in Texas, an' I've lived out heah in this wild country—a girl alone among rough men. Meetin' y'u to-day makes me see what a hard lot they are—an' what it's done to me."

Jean smothered his curiosity and tried to put out of his mind a growing sense that he pitied her, liked her.

"Are you a sheep herder?" he asked.

"Shore I am now an' then. My father lives back heah in a cañon. He's a sheepman. Lately there's been herders shot at. Just now we're short an' I have to fill in. But I like shepherdin' an' I love the woods, and the Rim Rock an' all the Tonto. If they were all, I'd shore be happy."

"Herders shot at!" exclaimed Jean, thoughtfully. "By whom? An' what for?"

"Trouble brewin' between the cattlemen down in the Basin an' the sheepmen up on the Rim. Dad says there'll shore be hell to pay. I tell him I hope the cattlemen chase him back to Texas."

"Then—Are you on the ranchers' side?" queried Jean, trying to pretend casual interest.

"No. I'll always be on my father's side," she replied, with spirit. "But I'm bound to admit I think the cattlemen have the fair side of the argument."

"How so?"

"Because there's grass everywhere. I see no sense in a sheepman goin' out of his way to surround a cattleman an' sheep off his range. That started the row. Lord knows how it 'll end. For most all of them heah are from Texas."

"So I was told," replied Jean. "An' I heard 'most all these Texans got run out of Texas. Any truth in that?"

"Shore I reckon there is," she replied, seriously. "But, stranger, it might not be healthy for y'u to say that anywhere. My dad, for one, was not run out of Texas. Shore I never can see why he came heah. He's accumulated stock, but he's not rich nor so well off as he was back home."

"Are you goin' to stay here always?" queried Jean, suddenly.

"If I do so it 'll be in my grave," she answered, darkly. "But what's the use of thinkin'? People stay places until they drift away. Y'u can never tell. . . . Well, stranger, this talk is keepin' y'u."

She seemed moody now, and a note of detachment crept into her voice. Jean rose at once and went for his horse. If this girl did not desire to talk further he certainly had no wish to annoy her. His mule had strayed off among the bleating sheep. Jean drove it back and then led his horse up to where the girl stood. She appeared taller and, though not of robust build, she was vigorous and lithe, with something about her that fitted the place. Jean was loath to bid her good-by.

"Which way is the Rim?" he asked, turning to his saddle girths.

"South," she replied, pointing. "It's only a mile or so. I'll walk down with y'u. . . . Suppose y'u're on the way to Grass Valley?"

"Yes; I've relatives there," he returned. He dreaded her next question, which he suspected would concern his name. But she did not ask. Taking up her rifle she turned away. Jean strode ahead to her side. "Reckon if you walk I won't ride."

So he found himself beside a girl with the free step of a mountaineer. Her bare, brown head came up nearly to his shoulder. It was a small, pretty head, graceful, well held, and the thick hair on it was a shiny, soft brown. She wore it in a braid, rather untidily and tangled, he thought, and it was tied with a string of buckskin. Altogether her apparel proclaimed poverty.

Jean let the conversation languish for a little. He wanted to think what to say presently, and then he felt a rather vague pleasure in stalking beside her. Her profile was straight cut and exquisite in line. From this side view the soft curve of lips could not be seen.

She made several attempts to start conversation, all of which Jean ignored, manifestly to her growing constraint. Presently Jean, having decided what he wanted to say, suddenly began: "I like this adventure. Do you?"

"Adventure! Meetin' me in the woods?" And she laughed the laugh of youth. "Shore you must be hard up for adventure, stranger."

"Do you like it?" he persisted, and his eyes searched the half-averted face.

"I might like it," she answered, frankly, "if—if my temper had not made a fool of me. I never meet any one I care to talk to. Why should it not be pleasant to run across some one new—some one strange in this heah wild country?"

"We are as we are," said Jean, simply. "I didn't think you made a fool of yourself. If I thought so, would I want to see you again?"

"Do y'u?" The brown face flashed on him with surprise, with a light he took for gladness. And because he wanted to appear calm and friendly, not too eager, he had to deny himself the thrill of meeting those changing eyes.

"Sure I do. Reckon I'm overbold on such short acquaintance. But I might not have another chance to tell you, so please don't hold it against me."

This declaration over, Jean felt relief and something of exultation. He had been afraid he might not have the courage to make it. She walked on as before, only with her head bowed a little and her eyes downcast. No color but the gold-brown tan and the blue tracery of veins showed in her cheeks. He noticed then a slight swelling quiver of her throat; and he became alive to its graceful contour, and to how full and pulsating it was, how nobly it set into the curve of her shoulder. Here in her quivering throat was the weakness of her, the evidence of her sex, the womanliness that belied the mountaineer stride and the grasp of strong brown hands on a rifle. It had an effect on Jean totally inexplicable to him, both in the strange warmth that stole over him and in the utterance he could not hold back.

"Girl, we're strangers, but what of that? We've met, an' I tell you it means somethin' to me. I've known girls for months an' never felt this way. I don't know who you are an' I don't care. You betrayed a good deal to me. You're not happy. You're lonely. An' if I didn't want to see you again for my own sake, I would for yours. Some things you said I'll not forget soon. I've got a sister, an' I know you have no brother. An' I reckon . . ."

At this juncture Jean in his earnestness and quite without thought grasped her hand. The contact checked the flow of his speech and suddenly made him aghast at his temerity. But the girl did not make any effort to withdraw it. So Jean, inhaling a deep breath and trying to see through his bewilderment, held on bravely. He imagined he felt a faint, warm, returning pressure. She was young, she was friendless, she was human. By this hand in his Jean felt more than ever the loneliness of her. Then, just as he was about to speak again, she pulled her hand free.

"Heah's the Rim," she said, in her quaint Southern drawl. "An' there's y'ur Tonto Basin."

Jean had been intent only upon the girl. He had kept step beside her without taking note of what was ahead of him. At her words he looked up expectantly, to be struck mute.

He felt a sheer force, a downward drawing of an immense abyss beneath him. As he looked afar he saw a black basin of timbered country, the darkest and wildest he had ever gazed upon, a hundred miles of blue distance across to an unflung mountain range, hazy purple against the sky. It seemed to be a stupendous gulf surrounded on three sides by bold, undulating lines of peaks, and on his side by a wall so high that he felt lifted aloft on the rim of the sky.

"Southeast y'u see the Sierra Anchas," said the girl, pointing. "That notch in the range is the pass where sheep are driven to Phoenix an' Maricopa. Those big rough mountains to the south are the Mazatzals. Round to the west is the Four Peaks Range. An' y'u're standin' on the Rim."

Jean could not see at first just what the Rim was, but by shifting his gaze westward he grasped this remarkable phenomenon of nature. For leagues and leagues a colossal red and yellow wall, a rampart, a mountain-faced cliff, seemed to zigzag westward. Grand and bold were the promontories reaching out over the void. They ran toward the westering sun. Sweeping and impressive were the long lines slanting away from them, sloping darkly spotted down to merge into the black timber. Jean had never seen such a wild and rugged manifestation of nature's depths and upheavals. He was held mute.

"Stranger, look down," said the girl.

Jean's sight was educated to judge heights and depths and distances. This wall upon which he stood sheered precipitously down, so far that it made him dizzy to look, and then the craggy broken cliffs merged into red-slided, cedar-greened slopes running down and down into gorges choked with forests, and from which soared up a roar of rushing waters. Slope after slope, ridge beyond ridge, cañon merging into cañon—so the tremendous bowl sunk away to its black, deceiving depths, a wilderness across which travel seemed impossible.

"Wonderful!" exclaimed Jean.

"Indeed it is!" murmured the girl. "Shore that is Arizona. I reckon I love *this*. The heights an' depths—the awfulness of its wilderness!"

"An' you want to leave it?"

"Yes an' no. I don't deny the peace that comes to me heah. But not often do I see the Basin, an' for that matter, one doesn't live on grand scenery."

"Child, even once in a while—this sight would cure any misery, if you only see. I'm glad I came. I'm glad you showed it to me first."

She too seemed under the spell of a vastness and loneliness and beauty and grandeur that could not but strike the heart.

Jean took her hand again. "Girl, say you will meet me here," he said, his voice ringing deep in his ears.

"Shore I will," she replied, softly, and turned to him. It seemed then that Jean saw her face for the first time. She was beautiful as he had never known beauty. Limned against that scene, she gave it life—wild, sweet, young life—the poignant meaning of which haunted yet eluded him. But she belonged there. Her eyes were again searching his, as if for some lost part of herself, unrealized, never known before. Wondering, wistful, hopeful, glad—they were eyes that seemed surprised, to reveal part of her soul.

Then her red lips parted. Their tremulous movement was a magnet to Jean. An invisible and mighty force pulled him down to kiss them. Whatever the spell had been, that rude, unconscious action broke it.

He jerked away, as if he expected to be struck. "Girl—I—I"—he gasped in amaze and sudden-dawning contrition—"I kissed you—but I swear it wasn't intentional—I never thought. . . ."

The anger that Jean anticipated failed to materialize. He stood, breathing hard, with a hand held out in unconscious appeal. By the same magic, perhaps, that had transfigured her a moment past, she was now invested again by the older character.

"Shore I reckon my callin' y'u a gentleman was a little previous," she said, with a rather dry bitterness. "But, stranger, y'u're sudden."

"You're not insulted?" asked Jean, hurriedly.

"Oh, I've been kissed before. Shore men are all alike."

"They're not," he replied, hotly, with a subtle rush of disillusion, a dulling of enchantment. "Don't you class me with other men who've kissed you. I wasn't myself when I did it an' I'd have gone on my knees to ask your forgiveness. . . . But now I wouldn't—an' I wouldn't kiss you again, either—even if you—you wanted it."

Jean read in her strange gaze what seemed to him a vague doubt, as if she was questioning him.

"Miss, I take that back," added Jean, shortly. "I'm sorry. I didn't mean to be rude. It was a mean trick for me to kiss you. A girl alone in the woods who's gone out of her way to be kind to me! I don't know why I forgot my manners. An' I ask your pardon."

She looked away then, and presently pointed far out and down into the Basin.

"There's Grass Valley. That long gray spot in the black. It's about fifteen miles. Ride along the Rim that way till y'u cross a trail. Shore y'u can't miss it. Then go down."

"I'm much obliged to you," replied Jean, reluctantly accepting what he regarded as his dismissal. Turning his horse, he put his foot in the stirrup, then, hesitating, he looked across the saddle at the girl. Her abstraction, as she gazed away over the purple depths, suggested loneliness and wistfulness. She was not thinking of that scene spread so wondrously before her. It struck Jean she might be pondering a subtle change in his feeling and attitude, something he was conscious of, yet could not define.

"Reckon this is good-by," he said, with hesitation.

"*Adios, señor,*" she replied, facing him again. She lifted the little carbine to the hollow of her elbow and, half turning, appeared ready to depart.

"Adios means good-by?" he queried.

"Yes, good-by till to-morrow or good-by forever. Take it as y'u like."

"Then you'll meet me here day after to-morrow?" How eagerly he spoke, on impulse, without a consideration of the intangible thing that had changed him!

"Did I say I wouldn't?"

"No. But I reckoned you'd not care to after—" he replied, breaking off in some confusion.

"Shore I'll be glad to meet y'u. Day after to-morrow about mid-afternoon. Right heah. Fetch all the news from Grass Valley."

"All right. Thanks. That 'll be—fine," replied Jean, and as he spoke he experienced a buoyant thrill, a pleasant lightness of enthusiasm, such as always stirred boyishly in him at a prospect of adventure. Before it passed he wondered at it and felt unsure of himself. He needed to think.

"Stranger, shore I'm not recollectin' that y'u told me who y'u are," she said.

"No, reckon I didn't tell," he returned. "What difference does that make? I said I didn't care who or what you are. Can't you feel the same about me?"

"Shore—I felt that way," she replied, somewhat nonplussed, with the level brown gaze steadily on his face. "But now y'u make me think."

"Let's meet without knowin' any more about each other than we do now."

"Shore. I'd like that. In this big wild Arizona a girl—an' I reckon a man—feels so insignificant. What's a name, anyhow? Still, people an' things have to be distinguished. I'll call y'u 'Stranger' an' be satisfied—if y'u say it's fair for y'u not to tell who y'u are."

"Fair! No, it's not," declared Jean, forced to confession. "My name's Jean—Jean Isbel."

"*Isbel!*" she exclaimed, with a violent start. "Shore y'u can't be son of old Gass Isbel. . . . I've seen both his sons."

"He has three," replied Jean, with relief, now the secret was out. "I'm the youngest. I'm twenty-four. Never been out of Oregon till now. On my way—"

The brown color slowly faded out of her face, leaving her quite pale, with eyes that began to blaze. The suppleness of her seemed to stiffen.

"My name's Ellen Jorth," she burst out, passionately. "Does it mean anythin' to y'u?"

"Never heard it in my life," protested Jean. "Sure I reckoned you belonged to the sheep raisers who 're on the outs with my father. That's why I had to tell you I'm Jean Isbel. . . . Ellen Jorth. It's strange an' pretty. . . . Reckon I can be just as good a—a friend to you—"

"No Isbel can ever be a friend to me," she said, with bitter coldness. Stripped of her ease and her soft wistfulness, she stood before him one instant, entirely another girl, a hostile enemy. Then she wheeled and strode off into the woods.

Jean, in amaze, in consternation, watched her swiftly draw away with her lithe, free step, wanting to follow her, wanting to call to her; but the resentment roused by her suddenly avowed hostility held him mute in his tracks. He watched her disappear, and when the brown-and-green wall of forest swallowed the slender gray form he fought against the insistent desire to follow her, and fought in vain.

CHAPTER 2

But Ellen Jorth's moccasined feet did not leave a distinguishable trail on the springy pine needle covering of the ground, and Jean could not find any trace of her.

A little futile searching to and fro cooled his impulse and called pride to his rescue. Returning to his horse, he mounted, rode out behind the pack mule to start it along, and soon felt the relief of decision and action. Clumps of small pines grew thickly in spots on the Rim, making it necessary for him to skirt them; at which times he lost sight of the purple basin. Every time he came back to an opening through which he could see the wild ruggedness and colors and distances, his appreciation of their nature grew on him. Arizona from Yuma to the Little Colorado had been to him an endless waste of wind-scoured, sun-blasted barrenness. This black-forested rock-rimmed land of untrodden ways was a world that in itself would satisfy him. Some instinct in Jean called for a lonely, wild land, into the fastnesses of which he could roam at will and be the other strange self that he had always yearned to be but had never been.

Every few moments there intruded into his flowing consciousness the flashing face of Ellen Jorth, the way she had looked at him, the things she had said. "Reckon I was a fool," he soliloquized, with an acute sense of humiliation. "She never saw how much in earnest I was." And Jean began to remember the circumstances with a vividness that disturbed and perplexed him.

The accident of running across such a girl in that lonely place might be out of the ordinary—but it had happened. Surprise had made him dull. The charm of her appearance, the appeal of her manner, must have drawn him at the very first, but he had not recognized that. Only at her words, "Oh, I've been kissed before," had his feelings been checked in their heedless progress. And the utterance of them had made a difference he now sought to analyze. Some personality in him, some voice, some idea had begun to defend her even before he was conscious that he had arraigned her before the bar of his judgment. Such defense seemed clamoring in him now and he forced himself to listen. He wanted, in his hurt pride, to justify his amazing surrender to a sweet and sentimental impulse.

He realized now that at first glance he should have recognized in her look, her poise, her voice the quality he called thoroughbred. Ragged and stained apparel did not prove her of a common sort. Jean had known a number of fine and wholesome girls of good family; and he remembered his sister. This Ellen Jorth was that kind of a girl irrespective of her present environment. Jean championed her loyally, even after he had gratified his selfish pride.

It was then—contending with an intangible and stealing glamour, unreal and fanciful, like the dream of a forbidden enchantment—that Jean arrived at the part in the little woodland drama where he had kissed Ellen Jorth and had been unrebuked. Why had she not resented his action? Dispelled was the illusion he had been dreamily and nobly constructing. "Oh, I've been kissed before!" The shock to him now exceeded his first dismay. Half bitterly she had spoken, and wholly scornful of herself, or of him, or of all men. For she had said all men were alike. Jean chafed under the smart of that, a taunt every decent man hated. Naturally every happy and healthy young man would want to kiss such red, sweet lips. But if those lips had been for others—never for him! Jean reflected that not since childish games had he kissed a girl—until this brown-faced Ellen Jorth came his way. He wondered at it. Moreover, he wondered at the significance he placed upon it. After all, was it not merely an accident? Why should he remember? Why should he ponder? What was the faint, deep, growing thrill that accompanied some of his thoughts?

Riding along with busy mind, Jean almost crossed a well-beaten trail, leading through a pine thicket and down over the Rim. Jean's pack mule led the way without being driven. And when Jean reached the edge of the bluff one look down was enough to fetch him off his horse. That trail was steep, narrow, clogged with stones, and as full of sharp corners as a crosscut saw. Once on the descent with a packed mule and a spirited horse, Jean had no time for mind wanderings and very little for occasional glimpses out over the cedar tops to the vast blue hollow asleep under a westering sun.

The stones rattled, the dust rose, the cedar twigs snapped, the little avalanches of red earth slid down, the iron-shod hoofs rang on the rocks. This slope had been narrow at the apex in the Rim where the trail led down a crack, and it widened in fan shape as Jean descended. He zigzagged down a thousand feet before the slope benched into dividing ridges. Here the cedars and junipers failed and pines once more hid the sun. Deep ravines were black with brush. From somewhere rose a roar of running water, most pleasant to Jean's ears. Fresh deer and bear tracks covered old ones made in the trail.

Those timbered ridges were but billows of that tremendous slope that now sheered above Jean, ending in a magnificent yellow wall of rock, greened in niches, stained by weather rust, carved and cracked and caverned. As Jean descended farther the hum of bees made melody, the roar of rapid water and the murmur of a rising breeze filled him with the content of the wild. Sheepmen like Colter and wild girls like Ellen Jorth and all that seemed promising or menacing in his father's letter could never change the Indian in Jean. So he thought. Hard upon that conclusion rushed another—one which troubled with its stinging revelation. Surely these influences he had defied were just the ones to bring out in him the Indian he had sensed but had never known. The eventful day had brought new and bitter food for Jean to reflect upon.

The trail landed him in the boulder-strewn bed of a wide cañon, where the huge trees stretched a canopy of foliage which denied the sunlight, and where a beautiful brook rushed and foamed. Here at last Jean tasted water that rivaled his Oregon springs. "Ah," he cried, "that sure is good!" Dark and shaded and ferny and mossy was this streamway; and everywhere were tracks of game, from the giant spread of a grizzly bear to the tiny, birdlike imprints of a squirrel. Jean heard familiar sounds of deer crackling the dead twigs; and the chatter of squirrels was incessant. This fragrant, cool retreat under the Rim brought back to him the dim recesses of Oregon forests. After all, Jean felt that he would not miss anything that he had loved in the Cascades. But what was the vague sense of all not being well with him—the essence of a faint regret—the insistence of a hovering shadow? And then flashed again, etched more vividly by the repetition in memory, a picture of eyes, of lips—of something he had to forget.

Wild and broken as this rolling Basin floor had appeared from the Rim, the reality of traveling over it made that first impression a deceit of distance. Down here all was on a big, rough, broken scale. Jean did not find even a few rods of level ground. Boulders as huge as houses obstructed the stream bed; spruce trees eight feet thick tried to lord it over the brawny pines; the ravine was a veritable cañon from which occasional glimpses through the foliage showed the Rim as a lofty red-tipped mountain peak.

Jean's pack mule became frightened at scent of a bear or lion and ran off down the rough trail, imperiling Jean's outfit. It was not an easy task to head him off nor, when that was accomplished, to keep him to a trot. But his fright and succeeding skittishness at least made for fast traveling. Jean calculated that he covered ten miles under the Rim before the character of ground and forest began to change.

The trail had turned southeast. Instead of gorge after gorge, red-walled and choked with forest, there began to be rolling ridges, some high; others were knolls; and a thick cedar growth made up for a falling off of pine. The spruce had long disappeared. Juniper thickets gave way more and more to the beautiful manzanita; and soon on the south slopes appeared cactus and a scrubby live oak. But for the well-broken trail, Jean would have fared ill through this tough brush.

Jean espied several deer, and again a coyote, and what he took to be a small herd of wild horses. No more turkey tracks showed in the dusty patches. He crossed a number of tiny brooklets, and at length came to a place where the trail ended or merged in a rough road that showed evidence of considerable travel. Horses, sheep, and cattle had passed along there that day. This road turned southward, and Jean began to have pleasurable expectations.

The road, like the trail, led down grade, but no longer at such steep angles, and was bordered by cedar and piñon, jack-pine and juniper, mescal and manzanita. Quite sharply, going around a ridge, the road led Jean's eye down to a small open flat of marshy, or at least grassy, ground. This green oasis in the wilderness of red and timbered ridges marked another change in the character of the Basin. Beyond that the country began to spread out and roll gracefully, its dark-green forest interspersed with grassy parks, until Jean headed into a long, wide gray-green valley surrounded by black-fringed hills. His pulses quickened here. He saw cattle dotting the expanse, and here and there along the edge log cabins and corrals.

As a village, Grass Valley could not boast of much, apparently, in the way of population. Cabins and houses were widely scattered, as if the inhabitants did not care to encroach upon one another. But the one store, built of stone, and stamped also with the characteristic isolation, seemed to Jean to be a rather remarkable edifice. Not exactly like a fort did it strike him, but if it had not been designed for defense it certainly gave that impression, especially from the long, low side with its dark eye-like windows about the height of a man's shoulder. Some rather fine horses were tied to a hitching rail. Otherwise dust and dirt and age and long use stamped this Grass Valley store and its immediate environment.

Jean threw his bridle, and, getting down, mounted the low porch and stepped into the wide open door. A face, gray against the background of gloom inside, passed out of sight just as Jean entered. He knew he had been seen. In front of the long, rather low-ceiled store were four men, all absorbed, apparently, in a game of checkers. Two were playing and two were looking on. One of these, a gaunt-faced man past middle age, casually looked up as Jean entered. But the moment of that casual glance afforded Jean time enough to meet eyes he instinctively distrusted. They masked their penetration. They seemed neither curious nor friendly. They saw him as if he had been merely thin air.

"Good evenin'," said Jean.

After what appeared to Jean a lapse of time sufficient to impress him with a possible deafness of these men, the gaunt-faced one said, "Howdy, Isbel!"

The tone was impersonal, dry, easy, cool, laconic, and yet it could not have been more pregnant with meaning. Jean's sharp sensibilities absorbed much. None of the slouch-sombreroed, long-mustached Texans—for so Jean at once classed them—had ever seen Jean, but they knew him and knew that he was expected in Grass Valley. All but the one who had spoken happened to have their faces in shadow under the wide-brimmed black hats. Motley-garbed, gun-belted, dusty-booted, they gave Jean the same impression of latent force that he had encountered in Colter.

"Will somebody please tell me where to find my father, Gaston Isbel?" inquired Jean, with as civil a tongue as he could command.

Nobody paid the slightest attention. It was the same as if Jean had not spoken. Waiting, half amused, half irritated, Jean shot a rapid glance around the store. The place had felt bare; and Jean, peering back through gloomy space, saw that it did not contain much. Dry goods and sacks littered a long rude counter; long rough shelves divided their length into stacks of canned foods and empty sections; a low shelf back of the counter held a generous burden of cartridge boxes, and next to it stood a rack of rifles. On the counter lay open cases of plug tobacco, the odor of which was second in strength only to that of rum.

Jean's swift-roving eye reverted to the men, three of whom were absorbed in the greasy checkerboard. The fourth man was the one who had spoken and he now deigned to look at Jean. Not much flesh was there stretched over his bony, powerful physiognomy. He stroked a lean chin with a big mobile hand that suggested more of bridle holding than familiarity with a bucksaw and plow handle. It was a lazy hand. The man looked lazy. If he spoke at all it would be with lazy speech. Yet Jean had not encountered many men to whom he would have accorded more potency to stir in him the instinct of self-preservation.

"Shore," drawled this gaunt-faced Texan, "old Gass lives aboot a mile down heah." With slow sweep of the big hand he indicated a general direction to the south; then, appearing to forget his questioner, he turned his attention to the game.

Jean muttered his thanks and, striding out, he mounted again, and drove the pack mule down the road. "Reckon I've run into the wrong folds to-day," he said. "If I remember dad right he was a man to make an' keep friends. Somehow I'll bet there's goin' to be hell." Beyond the store were some rather pretty and comfortable homes, little ranch houses back in the coves of the hills. The road turned west and Jean saw his first sunset in the Tonto Basin. It was a pageant of purple clouds with silver edges, and background of deep rich gold. Presently Jean met a lad driving a cow. "Hello, Johnny!" he said, genially, and with a double purpose. "My name's Jean Isbel. By Golly! I'm lost in Grass Valley. Will you tell me where my dad lives?"

"Yep. Keep right on, an' y'u cain't miss him," replied the lad, with a bright smile. "He's lookin' fer y'u."

"How do you know, boy?" queried Jean, warmed by that smile.

"Aw, I know. It's all over the valley thet y'u'd ride in ter-day. Shore I wus the one thet tole yer dad an' he give me a dollar."

"Was he glad to hear it?" asked Jean, with a queer sensation in his throat.

"Wal, he plumb was."

"An' who told you I was goin' to ride in to-day?"

"I heerd it at the store," replied the lad, with an air of confidence. "Some sheepmen was talkin' to Greaves. He's the storekeeper. I was settin' outside, but I heerd. A Mexican come down off the Rim ter-day an' he fetched the news." Here the lad looked furtively around, then whispered. "An' thet greaser was sent by somebody. I never heerd no more, but them sheepmen looked pretty plumb sour. An' one of them, comin' out, give me a kick, darn him. It shore is the luckedest day fer us cow-men."

"How's that, Johnny?"

"Wal, that's shore a big fight comin' to Grass Valley. My dad says so an' he rides fer yer dad. An' if it comes now y'u'll be heah."

"Ahuh!" laughed Jean. "An' what then, boy?"

The lad turned bright eyes upward. "Aw, now, y'u-all cain't come thet on me. Ain't y'u an Injun, Jean Isbel? Ain't y'u a hoss tracker thet rustlers cain't fool? Ain't y'u a plumb dead shot? Ain't y'u wuss'ern a grizzly bear in a rough-an'-tumble? . . . Now ain't y'u, shore?"

Jean bade the flattering lad a rather sober good day and rode on his way. Manifestly a reputation somewhat difficult to live up to had preceded his entry into Grass Valley.

Jean's first sight of his future home thrilled him through. It was a big, low, rambling log structure standing well out from a wooded knoll at the edge of the valley. Corrals and barns and sheds lay off at the back. To the fore stretched broad pastures where numberless cattle and horses grazed.

At sunset the scene was one of rich color. Prosperity and abundance and peace seemed attendant upon that ranch; lusty voices of burros braying and cows bawling seemed welcoming Jean. A hound bayed. The first cool touch of wind fanned Jean's cheek and brought a fragrance of wood smoke and frying ham.

Horses in the pasture romped to the fence and whistled at these new-comers. Jean espied a white-faced black horse that gladdened his sight. "Hello, Whiteface! I'll sure straddle you," called Jean. Then up the gentle slope he saw the tall figure of his father—the same as he had seen him thousands of times, bareheaded, shirt sleeved, striding with long step. Jean waved and called to him.

"Hi, you prodigal!" came the answer. Yes, the voice of his father—and Jean's boyhood memories flashed. He hurried his horse those last few rods. No—dad was not the same. His hair shone gray.

"Here I am, dad," called Jean, and then he was dismounting. A deep, quiet emotion settled over him, stilling the hurry, the eagerness, the pang in his breast.

"Son, I shore am glad to see you," said his father, and wrung his hand. "Wal, wal, the size of you! Shore you've grown, an' how you favor your mother."

Jean felt in the iron clasp of hand, in the uplifting of the handsome head, in the strong, fine light of piercing eyes that there was no differ-ence in the spirit of his father. But the old smile could not hide lines and shades strange to Jean.

"Dad, I'm as glad as you," replied Jean, heartily. "It seems long we've been parted, now I see you. Are you well, dad, an' all right?"

"Not complainin', son. I can ride all day same as ever," he said. "Come. Never mind your hosses. They'll be looked after. Come meet the folks. . . . Wal, wal, you got heah at last."

On the porch of the house a group awaited Jean's coming, rather silently, he thought. Wide-eyed children were there, very shy and watchful. The dark face of his sister corresponded with the image of her in his memory. She appeared taller, more womanly, as she embraced him. "Oh, Jean, Jean, I'm glad you've come!" she cried, and pressed him close. Jean felt in her a woman's anxiety for the present as well as affec-tion for the past. He remembered his aunt Mary, though he had not seen her for years. His half brothers, Bill and Guy, had changed but little except perhaps to grow lean and rangy. Bill resembled his father, though his aspect was jocular rather than serious. Guy was smaller, wiry, and hard as rock, with snapping eyes in a brown, still face, and he had the bow-legs of a cattleman. Both had married in Arizona. Bill's wife, Kate, was a stout, comely little woman, mother of three of the children. The other wife was young, a strapping girl, redheaded and freckled, with wonderful lines of pain and strength in her face. Jean remembered, as he looked at her, that some one had written him about the tragedy in her life. When she was only a child the Apaches had murdered all her family. Then next to greet Jean were the little children, all shy, yet all manifestly impressed by the occasion. A warmth and intimacy of forgotten home emotions flooded over Jean. Sweet it was to get home to these relatives who loved him and welcomed him with quiet gladness. But there seemed more. Jean was quick to see the shadow in the eyes of the women in that household and to sense a strange reliance which his presence brought.

"Son, this heah Tonto is a land of milk an' honey," said his father, as Jean gazed spellbound at the bounteous supper.

Jean certainly performed gastronomic feats on this occasion, to the delight of Aunt Mary and the wonder of the children. "Oh, he's starv-ved to death," whispered one of the little boys to his sister. They had begun to warm to this stranger uncle. Jean had no chance to talk, even had he been able to, for the meal-time showed a relaxation of restraint and they all tried to tell him things at once. In the bright lamplight his father looked easier and happier as he beamed upon Jean.

After supper the men went into an adjoining room that appeared most comfortable and attractive. It was long, and the width of the house, with a huge stone fireplace, low ceiling of hewn timbers and walls of the same, small windows with inside shutters of wood, and home-made table and chairs and rugs.

"Wal, Jean, do you recollect them shootin'-irons?" inquired the rancher, pointing above the fireplace. Two guns hung on the spreading deer antlers there. One was a musket Jean's father had used in the war of the rebellion and the other was a long, heavy, muzzle-loading flintlock Kentucky rifle with which Jean had learned to shoot.

"Reckon I do, dad," replied Jean, and with reverent hands and a rush of memory he took the old gun down.

"Jean, you shore handle thet old arm some clumsy," said Guy Isbel, dryly. And Bill added a remark to the effect that perhaps Jean had been leading a luxurious and tame life back there in Oregon, and then added, "But I reckon he's packin' that six-shooter like a Texan."

"Say, I fetched a gun or two along with me," replied Jean, jocularly. "Reckon I near broke my poor mule's back with the load of shells an' guns. Dad, what was the idea askin' me to pack out an arsenal?"

"Son, shore all shootin' arms an' such are at a premium in the Tonto," replied his father. "An' I was givin' you a hunch to come loaded."

His cool, drawling voice seemed to put a damper upon the pleasantries. Right there Jean sensed the charged atmosphere. His brothers were bursting with utterance about to break forth, and his father suddenly wore a look that recalled to Jean critical times of days long past. But the entrance of the children and the womenfolk put an end to confidences. Evidently the youngsters were laboring under subdued excitement. They preceded their mother, the smallest boy in the lead. For him this must have been both a dreadful and a wonderful experience, for he seemed to be pushed forward by his sister and brother and mother, and driven by yearnings of his own. "There now, Lee. Say, 'Uncle Jean, what did you fetch us?'" The lad hesitated for a shy, frightened look at Jean, and then, gaining something from his scrutiny of his uncle, he toddled forward and bravely delivered the question of tremendous importance.

"What did I fetch you, hey?" cried Jean, in delight, as he took the lad up on his knee. "Wouldn't you like to know? I didn't forget, Lee. I remembered you all. Oh! the job I had packin' your bundle of presents. . . . Now, Lee, make a guess."

"I dess you fetched a dun," replied Lee.

"A dun!—I'll bet you mean a gun," laughed Jean. "Well, you four-year-old Texas gunman! Make another guess."

That appeared too momentous and entrancing for the other two youngsters, and, adding their shrill and joyous voices to Lee's, they besieged Jean.

"Dad, where's my pack?" cried Jean. "These young Apaches are after my scalp."

"Reckon the boys fetched it onto the porch," replied the rancher.

Guy Isbel opened the door and went out. "By golly! heah's three packs," he called. "Which one do you want, Jean?"

"It's a long, heavy bundle all tied up," replied Jean.

Guy came staggering in under a burden that brought a whoop from the youngsters and bright gleams to the eyes of the women. Jean lost nothing of this. How glad he was that he had tarried in San Francisco because of a mental picture of this very reception in far-off wild Arizona.

When Guy deposited the bundle on the floor it jarred the room. It gave forth metallic and rattling and crackling sounds.

"Everybody stand back an' give me elbow room," ordered Jean, majestically. "My good folks, I want you all to know this is somethin' that doesn't happen often. The bundle you see here weighed about a hundred pounds when I packed it on my shoulder down Market Street in Frisco. It was stolen from me on shipboard. I got it back in San Diego an' licked the thief. It rode on a burro from San Diego to Yuma an' once I thought the burro was lost for keeps. It came up the Colorado River from Yuma to Ehrenberg an' there went on top of a stage. We got chased by bandits an' once when the horses were gallopin' hard it near rolled off. Then it went on the back of a pack horse an' helped wear him out. An' I reckon it would be somewhere else now if I hadn't fallen in with a freighter goin' north from Phoenix to the Santa Fe Trail. The last lap when it sagged the back of a mule was the riskiest an' full of the narrowest escapes. Twice my mule bucked off his pack an' left my outfit scattered. Worst of all, my precious bundle made the mule top heavy comin' down that place back here where the trail seems to drop off the earth. There I was hard put to keep sight of my pack. Sometimes it was on top an' other times the mule. But it got here at last. . . . An' now I'll open it."

After this long and impressive harangue, which at least augmented the suspense of the women and worked the children into a frenzy, Jean leisurely untied the many knots round the bundle and unrolled it. He had packed that bundle for just such travel as it had sustained. Three clothbound rifles he laid aside, and with them a long, very heavy package tied between two thin wide boards. From this came the metallic clink. "Oo, I know what dem is!" cried Lee, breaking the silence of suspense. Then Jean, tearing open a long flat parcel, spread before the mute, rapt-eyed

youngsters such magnificent things as they had never dreamed of—
picture books, mouthharps, dolls, a toy gun and a toy pistol, a wonderful
whistle and a fox horn, and last of all a box of candy. Before these treasures on the floor, too magical to be touched at first, the two little boys
and their sister simply knelt. That was a sweet, full moment for Jean; yet
even that was clouded by the something which shadowed these innocent
children fatefully born in a wild place at a wild time. Next Jean gave to
his sister the presents he had brought her—beautiful cloth for a dress,
ribbons and a bit of lace, handkerchiefs and buttons and yards of linen, a
sewing case and a whole box of spools of thread, a comb and brush and
mirror, and lastly a Spanish brooch inlaid with garnets. "There, Ann,"
said Jean, "I confess I asked a girl friend in Oregon to tell me some things
my sister might like." Manifestly there was not much difference in girls.
Ann seemed stunned by this munificence, and then awakening, she
hugged Jean in a way that took his breath. She was not a child any more,
that was certain. Aunt Mary turned knowing eyes upon Jean. "Reckon
you couldn't have pleased Ann more. She's engaged, Jean, an' where girls
are in that state these things mean a heap. . . . Ann, you'll be married in
that!" And she pointed to the beautiful folds of material that Ann had
spread out.

"What's this?" demanded Jean. His sister's blushes were enough to
convict her, and they were mightily becoming, too.

"Here, Aunt Mary," went on Jean, "here's yours, an' here's somethin'
for each of my new sisters." This distribution left the women as happy
and occupied, almost, as the children. It left also another package, the
last one in the bundle. Jean laid hold of it and, lifting it, he was about to
speak when he sustained a little shock of memory. Quite distinctly he saw
two little feet, with bare toes peeping out of worn-out moccasins, and
then round, bare, symmetrical ankles that had been scratched by brush.
Next he saw Ellen Jorth's passionate face as she looked when she had
made the violent action so disconcerting to him. In this happy moment
the memory seemed farther off than a few hours. It had crystallized. It
annoyed while it drew him. As a result he slowly laid this package aside
and did not speak as he had intended to.

"Dad, I reckon I didn't fetch a lot for you an' the boys," continued
Jean. "Some knives, some pipes an' tobacco. An' sure the guns."

"Shore, you're a regular Santa Claus, Jean," replied his father. "Wal, wal, look at the kids. An' look at Mary. An' for the land's sake look at Ann! Wal, wal, I'm gettin' old. I'd forgotten the pretty stuff an' gimcracks that mean so much to women. We're out of the world heah. It's just as well you've lived apart from us, Jean, for comin' back this way, with all that stuff, does us a lot of good. I cain't say, son, how obliged I am. My mind has been set on the hard side of life. An' it's shore good to forget—to see the smiles of the women an' the joy of the kids."

At this juncture a tall young man entered the open door. He looked a rider. All about him, even his face, except his eyes, seemed old, but his eyes were young, fine, soft, and dark.

"How do, y'u-all!" he said, evenly.

Ann rose from her knees. Then Jean did not need to be told who this newcomer was.

"Jean, this is my friend, Andrew Colmor."

Jean knew when he met Colmor's grip and the keen flash of his eyes that he was glad Ann had set her heart upon one of their kind. And his second impression was something akin to the one given him in the road by the admiring lad. Colmor's estimate of him must have been a monument built of Ann's eulogies. Jean's heart suffered misgivings. Could he live up to the character that somehow had forestalled his advent in Grass Valley? Surely life was measured differently here in the Tonto Basin.

The children, bundling their treasures to their bosoms, were dragged off to bed in some remote part of the house, from which their laughter and voices came back with happy significance. Jean forthwith had an interested audience. How eagerly these lonely pioneer people listened to news of the outside world! Jean talked until he was hoarse. In their turn his hearers told him much that had never found place in the few and short letters he had received since he had been left in Oregon. Not a word about sheepmen or any hint of rustlers! Jean marked the omission and thought all the more seriously of probabilities because nothing was said. Altogether the evening was a happy reunion of a family of which all living members were there present. Jean grasped that this fact was one of significant satisfaction to his father.

"Shore we're all goin' to live together heah," he declared. "I started this range. I call most of this valley mine. We'll run up a cabin for Ann soon as she says the word. An' you, Jean, where's your girl? I shore told you to fetch her."

"Dad, I didn't have one," replied Jean.

"Wal, I wish you had," returned the rancher. "You'll go courtin' one of these Tonto hussies that I might object to."

"Why, father, there's not a girl in the valley Jean would look twice at," interposed Ann Isbel, with spirit.

Jean laughed the matter aside, but he had an uneasy memory. Aunt Mary averred, after the manner of relatives, that Jean would play havoc among the women of the settlement. And Jean retorted that at least one member of the Isbels should hold out against folly and fight and love and marriage, the agents which had reduced the family to these few present. "I'll be the last Isbel to go under," he concluded.

"Son, you're talkin' wisdom," said his father. "An' shore that reminds me of the uncle you're named after. Jean Isbel! . . . Wal, he was my youngest brother an' shore a fire-eater. Our mother was a French creole from Louisiana, an' Jean must have inherited some of his fightin' nature from her. When the war of the rebellion started Jean an' I enlisted. I was crippled before we ever got to the front. But Jean went through three years before he was killed. His company had orders to fight to the last man. An' Jean fought an' lived long enough just to be that last man."

At length Jean was left alone with his father.

"Reckon you're used to bunkin' outdoors?" queried the rancher, rather abruptly.

"Most of the time," replied Jean.

"Wal, there's room in the house, but I want you to sleep out. Come get your beddin' an' gun. I'll show you."

They went outside on the porch, where Jean shouldered his roll of tarpaulin and blankets. His rifle, in its saddle sheath, leaned against the door. His father took it up and, half pulling it out, looked at it by the starlight. "Forty-four, eh? Wal, wal, there's shore no better, if a man can hold straight." At the moment a big gray dog trotted up to sniff at Jean. "An' heah's your bunkmate, Shepp. He's part lofer, Jean. His mother was a favorite shepherd dog of mine. His father was a big timber wolf that took us two years to kill. Some bad wolf packs runnin' this Basin."

The night was cold and still, darkly bright under moon and stars; the smell of hay seemed to mingle with that of cedar. Jean followed his father round the house and up a gentle slope of grass to the edge of the cedar line. Here several trees with low-sweeping thick branches formed a dense, impenetrable shade.

"Son, your uncle Jean was scout for Liggett, one of the greatest rebels the South had," said the rancher. "An' you're goin' to be scout for the Isbels of Tonto. Reckon you'll find it 'most as hot as your uncle did. . . . Spread your bed inside. You can see out, but no one can see you. Reckon there's been some queer happenin's 'round heah lately. If Shepp could talk he'd shore have lots to tell us. Bill an' Guy have been sleepin' out, trailin' strange hoss tracks, an' all that. But shore whoever's been prowlin' around heah was too sharp for them. Some bad, crafty, light-steppin' woodsmen 'round heah, Jean. . . . Three mawnin's ago, just after daylight, I stepped out the back door an' some one of these sneaks I'm talkin' aboot took a shot at me. Missed my head a quarter of an inch! To-morrow I'll show you the bullet hole in the doorpost. An' some of my gray hairs that're stickin' in it!"

"Dad!" ejaculated Jean, with a hand outstretched. "That's awful! You frighten me."

"No time to be scared," replied his father, calmly. "They're shore goin' to kill me. That's why I wanted you home. . . . In there with you, now! Go to sleep. You shore can trust Shepp to wake you if he gets scent or sound. . . . An' good night, my son. I'm sayin' that I'll rest easy to-night."

Jean mumbled a good night and stood watching his father's shining white head move away under the starlight. Then the tall, dark form vanished, a door closed, and all was still. The dog Shepp licked Jean's hand. Jean felt grateful for that warm touch. For a moment he sat on his roll of bedding, his thought still locked on the shuddering revelation of his father's words, "They're shore goin' to kill me." The shock of inaction passed. Jean pushed his pack in the dark opening and, crawling inside, he unrolled it and made his bed.

When at length he was comfortably settled for the night he breathed a long sigh of relief. What bliss to relax! A throbbing and burning of his muscles seemed to begin with his rest. The cool starlit night, the smell of cedar, the moan of wind, the silence—all were real to his senses. After long weeks of long, arduous travel he was home. The warmth of the welcome still lingered but it seemed to have been pierced by an icy thrust. What lay before him? The shadow in the eyes of his aunt, in the younger, fresher eyes of his sister—Jean connected that with the meaning of his father's tragic words. Far past was the morning that had been so keen, the breaking of camp in the sunlit forest, the riding down the brown aisles under the pines, the music of bleating lambs that had called him not to pass by. Thought of Ellen Jorth recurred. Had he met her only that morning? She was up there in the forest, asleep under the starlit pines. Who was she? What was her story? That savage fling of her skirt, her bitter speech and passionate flaming face—they haunted Jean. They were crystallizing into simpler memories, growing away from his bewilderment, and therefore at once sweeter and more doubtful. "Maybe she meant differently from what I thought," Jean soliloquized. "Anyway, she was honest." Both shame and thrill possessed him at the recall of an insidious idea—dare he go back and find her and give her the last package of gifts he had brought from the city? What might they mean to poor, ragged, untidy, beautiful Ellen Jorth? The idea grew on Jean. It could not be dispelled. He resisted stubbornly. It was bound to go to its fruition. Deep into his mind had sunk an impression of her need—a material need that brought spirit and pride to abasement. From one picture to another his memory wandered, from one speech and act of hers to another, choosing, selecting, casting aside, until clear and sharp as the stars shone the words, "Oh, I've been kissed before!" That stung him now. By whom? Not by one man, but by several, by many, she had meant. Pshaw! he had only been sympathetic and drawn by a strange girl in the woods. To-morrow he would forget. Work there was for him in Grass Valley. And he reverted uneasily to the remarks of his father until at last sleep claimed him.

A cold nose against his cheek, a low whine, awakened Jean. The big dog Shepp was beside him, keen, wary, intense. The night appeared far advanced toward dawn. Far away a cock crowed; the near-at-hand one answered in clarion voice. "What is it, Shepp?" whispered Jean, and he sat up. The dog smelled or heard something suspicious to his nature, but whether man or animal Jean could not tell.

CHAPTER 3

The morning star, large, intensely blue-white, magnificent in its dominance of the clear night sky, hung over the dim, dark valley ramparts. The moon had gone down and all the other stars were wan, pale ghosts.

Presently the strained vacuum of Jean's ears vibrated to a low roar of many hoofs. It came from the open valley, along the slope to the south. Shepp acted as if he wanted the word to run. Jean laid a hand on the dog. "Hold on, Shepp," he whispered. Then hauling on his boots and slipping into his coat, Jean took his rifle and stole out into the open. Shepp appeared to be well trained, for it was evident that he had a strong natural tendency to run off and hunt for whatever had roused him. Jean thought it more than likely that the dog scented an animal of some kind. If there were men prowling around the ranch Shepp might have been just as vigilant, but it seemed to Jean that the dog would have shown less eagerness to leave him, or none at all.

In the stillness of the morning it took Jean a moment to locate the direction of the wind, which was very light and coming from the south. In fact that little breeze had borne the low roar of trampling hoofs. Jean circled the ranch house to the right and kept along the slope at the edge of the cedars. It struck him suddenly how well fitted he was for work of this sort. All the work he had ever done, except for his few years in school, had been in the open. All the leisure he had ever been able to obtain had been given to his ruling passion for hunting and fishing. Love of the wild had been born in Jean. At this moment he experienced a grim assurance of what his instinct and his training might accomplish if directed to a stern and daring end. Perhaps his father understood this; perhaps the old Texan had some little reason for his confidence.

Every few paces Jean halted to listen. All objects, of course, were indistinguishable in the dark-gray obscurity, except when he came close upon them. Shepp showed an increasing eagerness to bolt out into the void. When Jean had traveled half a mile from the house he heard a scattered trampling of cattle on the run, and farther out a low strangled bawl of a calf. "Ahuh!" muttered Jean. "Cougar or some varmint pulled down that calf." Then he discharged his rifle in the air and yelled with all his might. It was necessary then to yell again to hold Shepp back.

Thereupon Jean set forth down the valley, and tramped out and across and around, as much to scare away whatever had been after the stock as to look for the wounded calf. More than once he heard cattle moving away ahead of him, but he could not see them. Jean let Shepp go, hoping the dog would strike a trail. But Shepp neither gave tongue nor came back. Dawn began to break, and in the growing light Jean searched around until at last he stumbled over a dead calf, lying in a little bare wash where water ran in wet seasons. Big wolf tracks showed in the soft earth. "Lofers," said Jean, as he knelt and just covered one track with his spread hand. "We had wolves in Oregon, but not as big as these. . . . Wonder where that half-wolf dog, Shepp, went. Wonder if he can be trusted where wolves are concerned. I'll bet not, if there's a she-wolf runnin' around."

Jean found tracks of two wolves, and he trailed them out of the wash, then lost them in the grass. But, guided by their direction, he went on and climbed a slope to the cedar line, where in the dusty patches he found the tracks again. "Not scared much," he muttered, as he noted the slow trotting tracks. "Well, you old gray lofers, we're goin' to clash." Jean knew from many a futile hunt that wolves were the wariest and most intelligent of wild animals in the quest. From the top of a low foothill he watched the sun rise; and then no longer wondered why his father waxed eloquent over the beauty and location and luxuriance of this grassy valley. But it was large enough to make rich a good many ranchers. Jean tried to restrain any curiosity as to his father's dealings in Grass Valley until the situation had been made clear.

Moreover, Jean wanted to love this wonderful country. He wanted to be free to ride and hunt and roam to his heart's content; and therefore he dreaded hearing his father's claims. But Jean threw off forebodings. Nothing ever turned out so badly as it presaged. He would think the best until certain of the worst. The morning was gloriously bright, and already the frost was glistening wet on the stones. Grass Valley shone like burnished silver dotted with innumerable black spots. Burros were braying their discordant messages to one another; the colts were romping in the fields; stallions were whistling; cows were bawling. A cloud of blue smoke hung low over the ranch house, slowly wafting away on the wind. Far out in the valley a dark group of horsemen were riding toward the village. Jean glanced thoughtfully at them and reflected that he seemed destined to harbor suspicion of all men new and strange to him. Above the distant village stood the darkly green foothills leading up to the craggy slopes, and these ending in the Rim, a red, black-fringed mountain front, beautiful in the morning sunlight, lonely, serene, and mysterious against the level skyline. Mountains, ranges, distances unknown to Jean, always called to him—to come, to seek, to explore, to find, but no wild horizon ever before beckoned to him as this one. And the subtle vague emotion that had gone to sleep with him last night awoke now hauntingly. It took effort to dispel the desire to think, to wonder.

Upon his return to the house, he went around on the valley side, so as to see the place by light of day. His father had built for permanence; and evidently there had been three constructive periods in the history of that long, substantial, picturesque log house. But few nails and little sawed lumber and no glass had been used. Strong and skillful hands, axes and a crosscut saw, had been the prime factors in erecting this habitation of the Isbels.

"Good mawnin', son," called a cheery voice from the porch. "Shore we-all heard you shoot; an' the crack of that forty-four was as welcome as May flowers."

Bill Isbel looked up from a task over a saddle girth and inquired pleasantly if Jean ever slept of nights. Guy Isbel laughed and there was warm regard in the gaze he bent on Jean.

"You old Indian!" he drawled, slowly. "Did you get a bead on anythin'?"

"No. I shot to scare away what I found to be some of your lofers," replied Jean. "I heard them pullin' down a calf. An' I found tracks of two whoppin' big wolves. I found the dead calf, too. Reckon the meat can be saved. Dad, you must lose a lot of stock here."

"Wal, son, you shore hit the nail on the haid," replied the rancher. "What with lions an' bears an' lofers—an' two-footed lofers of another breed—I've lost five thousand dollars in stock this last year."

"Dad! You don't mean it!" exclaimed Jean, in astonishment. To him that sum represented a small fortune.

"I shore do," answered his father.

Jean shook his head as if he could not understand such an enormous loss where there were keen able-bodied men about. "But that's awful, dad. How could it happen? Where were your herders an' cowboys? An' Bill an' Guy?"

Bill Isbel shook a vehement fist at Jean and retorted in earnest, having manifestly been hit in a sore spot. "Where was me an' Guy, huh? Wal, my Oregon brother, we was heah, all year, sleepin' more or less aboot three hours out of every twenty-four—ridin' our boots off—an' we couldn't keep down that loss."

"Jean, you-all have a mighty tumble comin' to you out heah," said Guy, complacently.

"Listen, son," spoke up the rancher. "You want to have some hunches before you figure on our troubles. There's two or three packs of lofers, an' in winter time they are hell to deal with. Lions thick as bees, an' shore bad when the snow's on. Bears will kill a cow now an' then. An' whenever an' old silvertip comes mozyin' across from the Mazatzals he kills stock. I'm in with half a dozen cattlemen. We all work together, an' the whole outfit cain't keep these vermints down. Then two years ago the Hash Knife Gang come into the Tonto."

"Hash Knife Gang? What a pretty name!" replied Jean. "Who're they?"

"Rustlers, son. An' shore the real old Texas brand. The old Lone Star State got too hot for them, an' they followed the trail of a lot of other Texans who needed a healthier climate. Some two hundred Texans around heah, Jean, an' maybe a matter of three hundred inhabitants in the Tonto all told, good an' bad. Reckon it's aboot half an' half."

A cheery call from the kitchen interrupted the conversation of the men.

"You come to breakfast."

During the meal the old rancher talked to Bill and Guy about the day's order of work; and from this Jean gathered an idea of what a big cattle business his father conducted. After breakfast Jean's brothers manifested keen interest in the new rifles. These were unwrapped and cleaned and taken out for testing. The three rifles were forty-four caliber Winchesters, the kind of gun Jean had found most effective. He tried them out first, and the shots he made were satisfactory to him and amazing to the others. Bill had used an old Henry rifle. Guy did not favor any particular rifle. The rancher pinned his faith to the famous old single-shot buffalo gun, mostly called *needle* gun. "Wal, reckon I'd better stick to mine. Shore you cain't teach an old dog new tricks. But you boys may do well with the forty-fours. Pack 'em on your saddles an' practice when you see a coyote."

Jean found it difficult to convince himself that this interest in guns and marksmanship had any sinister propulsion back of it. His father and brothers had always been this way. Rifles were as important to pioneers as plows, and their skillful use was an achievement every frontiersman tried to attain. Friendly rivalry had always existed among the members of the Isbel family: even Ann Isbel was a good shot. But such proficiency in the use of firearms—and life in the open that was correlative with it—had not dominated them as it had Jean. Bill and Guy Isbel were born cattlemen— chips of the old block. Jean began to hope that his father's letter was an exaggeration, and particularly that the fatalistic speech of last night, "they are goin' to kill me," was just a moody inclination to see the worst side. Still, even as Jean tried to persuade himself of this more hopeful view, he recalled many references to the peculiar reputation of Texans for gun-throwing, for feuds, for never-ending hatreds. In Oregon the Isbels had lived among industrious and peaceful pioneers from all over the States; to be sure, the life had been rough and primitive, and there had been fights on occasions, though no Isbel had ever killed a man. But now they had become fixed in a wilder and sparsely settled country among men of their own breed. Jean was afraid his hopes had only sentiment to foster them. Nevertheless, he forced back a strange, brooding, mental state and resolutely held up the brighter side. Whatever the evil conditions existing in

Grass Valley, they could be met with intelligence and courage, with an absolute certainty that it was inevitable they must pass away. Jean refused to consider the old, fatal law that at certain wild times and wild places in the West certain men had to pass away to change evil conditions.

"Wal, Jean, ride around the range with the boys," said the rancher. "Meet some of my neighbors, Jim Blaisdell, in particular. Take a look at the cattle. An' pick out some hosses for yourself."

"I've seen one already," declared Jean, quickly. "A black with white face. I'll take him."

"Shore you know a hoss. To my eye he's my pick. But the boys don't agree. Bill 'specially has degenerated into a fancier of pitchin' hosses. Ann can ride that black. You try him this mawnin'. . . . An', son, enjoy yourself."

True to his first impression, Jean named the black horse Whiteface and fell in love with him before ever he swung a leg over him. Whiteface appeared spirited, yet gentle. He had been trained instead of being broken. Of hard hits and quirts and spurs he had no experience. He liked to do what his rider wanted him to do.

A hundred or more horses grazed in the grassy meadow, and as Jean rode on among them it was a pleasure to see stallions throw heads and ears up and whistle or snort. Whole troops of colts and two-year-olds raced with flying tails and manes.

Beyond these pastures stretched the range, and Jean saw the gray-green expanse speckled by thousands of cattle. The scene was inspiring. Jean's brothers led him all around, meeting some of the herders and riders employed on the ranch, one of whom was a burly, grizzled man with eyes reddened and narrowed by much riding in wind and sun and dust. His name was Evarts and he was father of the lad whom Jean had met near the village. Evarts was busily skinning the calf that had been killed by the wolves. "See heah, y'u Jean Isbel," said Evarts, "it shore was aboot time y'u come home. We-all heahs y'u hev an eye fer tracks. Wal, mebbe y'u can kill Old Gray, the lofer thet did this job. He's pulled down nine calves an' yearlin's this last two months thet I know of. An' we've not hed the spring round-up."

Grass Valley widened to the southeast. Jean would have been backward about estimating the square miles in it. Yet it was not vast acreage so much as rich pasture that made it such a wonderful range. Several ranches lay along the western slope of this section. Jean was informed that open parks and swales, and little valleys nestling among the foothills, wherever there was water and grass, had been settled by ranchers. Every summer a few new families ventured in.

Blaisdell struck Jean as being a lionlike type of Texan, both in his broad, bold face, his huge head with its upstanding tawny hair like a mane, and in the speech and force that betokened the nature of his heart. He was not as old as Jean's father. He had a rolling voice, with the same drawling intonation characteristic of all Texans, and blue eyes that still held the fire of youth. Quite a marked contrast he presented to the lean, rangy, hard-jawed, intent-eyed men Jean had begun to accept as Texans.

Blaisdell took time for a curious scrutiny and study of Jean, that, frank and kindly as it was, and evidently the adjustment of impressions gotten from hearsay, yet bespoke the attention of one used to judging men for himself, and in this particular case having reasons of his own for so doing.

"Wal, you're like your sister Ann," said Blaisdell. "Which you may take as a compliment, young man. Both of you favor your mother. But you're an Isbel. Back in Texas there are men who never wear a glove on their right hands, an' shore I reckon if one of them met up with you sudden he'd think some graves had opened an' he'd go for his gun."

Blaisdell's laugh pealed out with deep, pleasant roll. Thus he planted in Jean's sensitive mind a significant thought-provoking idea about the past-and-gone Isbels.

His further remarks, likewise, were exceedingly interesting to Jean. The settling of the Tonto Basin by Texans was a subject often in dispute. His own father had been in the first party of adventurous pioneers who had traveled up from the south to cross over the Reno Pass of the Mazatzals into the Basin. "Newcomers from outside get impressions of the Tonto accordin' to the first settlers they meet," declared Blaisdell. "An' shore it's my belief these first impressions never change. Just so strong they are! Wal, I've heard my father say there were men in his wagon train that got run out of Texas, but he swore he wasn't one of them. So I reckon that sort of talk held good for twenty years, an' for all the Texans who emigrated, except, of course, such notorious rustlers as

Daggs an' men of his ilk. Shore we've got some bad men heah. There's no law. Possession used to mean more than it does now. Daggs an' his Hash Knife Gang have begun to hold forth with a high hand. No small rancher can keep enough stock to pay for his labor."

At the time of which Blaisdell spoke there were not many sheepmen and cattlemen in the Tonto, considering its vast area. But these, on account of the extreme wildness of the broken country, were limited to the comparatively open Grass Valley and its adjacent environs. Naturally, as the inhabitants increased and stock raising grew in proportion the grazing and water rights became matters of extreme importance. Sheepmen ran their flocks up on the Rim in summer time and down into the Basin in winter time. A sheepman could throw a few thousand sheep round a cattleman's ranch and ruin him. The range was free. It was as fair for sheepmen to graze their herds anywhere as it was for cattlemen. This of course did not apply to the few acres of cultivated ground that a rancher could call his own; but very few cattle could have been raised on such limited area. Blaisdell said that the sheepmen were unfair because they could have done just as well, though perhaps at more labor, by keeping to the ridges and leaving the open valley and little flats to the ranchers. Formerly there had been room enough for all; now the grazing ranges were being encroached upon by sheepmen newly come to the Tonto. To Blaisdell's way of thinking the rustler menace was more serious than the sheeping-off of the range, for the simple reason that no cattleman knew exactly who the rustlers were and for the more complex and significant reason that the rustlers did not steal sheep.

"Texas was overstocked with bad men an' fine steers," concluded Blaisdell. "Most of the first an' some of the last have struck the Tonto. The sheepmen have now got distributin' points for wool an' sheep at Maricopa an' Phoenix. They're shore waxin' strong an' bold."

"Ahuh! . . . An' what's likely to come of this mess?" queried Jean.

"Ask your dad," replied Blaisdell.

"I will. But I reckon I'd be obliged for your opinion."

"Wal, short an' sweet it's this: Texas cattlemen will never allow the range they stocked to be overrun by sheepmen."

"Who's this man Greaves?" went on Jean. "Never run into anyone like him."

"Greaves is hard to figure. He's a snaky customer in deals. But he seems to be good to the poor people 'round heah. Says he's from Missouri. Ha-ha! He's as much Texan as I am. He rode into the Tonto without even a pack to his name. An' presently he builds his stone house an' freights supplies in from Phoenix. Appears to buy an' sell a good deal of stock. For a while it looked like he was steerin' a middle course between cattlemen an' sheepmen. Both sides made a rendezvous of his store, where he heard the grievances of each. Laterly he's leanin' to the sheepmen. Nobody has accused him of that yet. But it's time some cattleman called his bluff."

"Of course there are honest an' square sheepmen in the Basin?" queried Jean.

"Yes, an' some of them are not unreasonable. But the new fellows that dropped in on us the last few years—they're the ones we're goin' to clash with."

"This—sheepman, Jorth?" went on Jean, in slow hesitation, as if compelled to ask what he would rather not learn.

"Jorth must be the leader of this sheep faction that's harryin' us ranchers. He doesn't make threats or roar around like some of them. But he goes on raisin' an' buyin' more an' more sheep. An' his herders have been grazin' down all around us this winter. Jorth's got to be reckoned with."

"Who is he?"

"Wal, I don't know enough to talk aboot. Your dad never said so, but I think he an' Jorth knew each other in Texas years ago. I never saw Jorth but once. That was in Greaves's barroom. Your dad an' Jorth met that day for the first time in this country. Wal, I've not known men for nothin'. They just stood stiff an' looked at each other. Your dad was aboot to draw. But Jorth made no sign to throw a gun."

Jean saw the growing and weaving and thickening threads of a tangle that had already involved him. And the sudden pang of regret he sustained was not wholly because of sympathies with his own people.

"The other day back up in the woods on the Rim I ran into a sheepman who said his name was Colter. Who is he?"

"Colter? Shore he's a new one. What'd he look like?"

Jean described Colter with a readiness that spoke volumes for the vividness of his impressions.

"I don't know him," replied Blaisdell. "But that only goes to prove my contention—any fellow runnin' wild in the woods can say he's a sheepman."

"Colter surprised me by callin' me by my name," continued Jean. "Our little talk wasn't exactly friendly. He said a lot about my bein' sent for to run sheep herders out of the country."

"Shore that's all over," replied Blaisdell, seriously. "You're a marked man already."

"What started such rumor?"

"Shore you cain't prove it by me. But it's not taken as rumor. It's got to the sheepmen as hard as bullets."

"Ahuh! That accounts for Colter's seemin' a little sore under the collar. Well, he said they were goin' to run sheep over Grass Valley, an' for me to take that hunch to my dad."

Blaisdell had his chair tilted back and his heavy boots against a post of the porch. Down he thumped. His neck corded with a sudden rush of blood and his eyes changed to blue fire.

"The hell he did!" he ejaculated, in furious amaze.

Jean gauged the brooding, rankling hurt of this old cattleman by his sudden break from the cool, easy Texan manner. Blaisdell cursed under his breath, swung his arms violently, as if to throw a last doubt or hope aside, and then relapsed to his former state. He laid a brown hand on Jean's knee.

"Two years ago I called the cards," he said, quietly. "It means a Grass Valley war."

Not until late that afternoon did Jean's father broach the subject uppermost in his mind. Then at an opportune moment he drew Jean away into the cedars out of sight.

"Son, I shore hate to make your home-comin' unhappy," he said, with evidence of agitation, "but so help me God I have to do it!"

"Dad, you called me Prodigal, an' I reckon you were right. I've shirked my duty to you. I'm ready now to make up for it," replied Jean, feelingly.

"Wal, wal, shore that's fine-spoken, my boy. . . . Let's set down heah an' have a long talk. First off, what did Jim Blaisdell tell you?"

Briefly Jean outlined the neighbor rancher's conversation. Then Jean recounted his experience with Colter and concluded with Blaisdell's reception of the sheepman's threat. If Jean expected to see his father rise up like a lion in his wrath he made a huge mistake. This news of Colter and his talk never struck even a spark from Gaston Isbel.

"Wal," he began, thoughtfully, "reckon there are only two points in Jim's talk I need touch on. There's shore goin' to be a Grass Valley war. An' Jim's idea of the cause of it seems to be pretty much the same as that of all the other cattlemen. It 'll go down a black blot on the history page of the Tonto Basin as a war between rival sheepmen an' cattlemen. Same old fight over water an' grass! . . . Jean, my son, that is wrong. It 'll not be a war between sheepmen an' cattlemen. But a war of honest ranchers against rustlers maskin' as sheep-raisers! . . . Mind you, I don't belittle the trouble between sheepmen an' cattlemen in Arizona. It's real an' it's vital an' it's serious. It 'll take law an' order to straighten out the grazin' question. Some day the government will keep sheep off of cattle ranges. . . . So get things right in your mind, my son. You can trust your dad to tell the absolute truth. In this fight that 'll wipe out some of the Isbels—maybe all of them—you're on the side of justice an' right. Knowin' that, a man can fight a hundred times harder than he who knows he is a liar an' a thief."

The old rancher wiped his perspiring face and breathed slowly and deeply. Jean sensed in him the rise of a tremendous emotional strain. Wonderingly he watched the keen lined face. More than material worries were at the root of brooding, mounting thoughts in his father's eyes.

"Now next take what Jim said aboot your comin' to chase these sheep herders out of the valley. . . . Jean, I started that talk. I had my tricky reasons. I know these greaser sheep herders an' I know the respect Texans have for a gunman. Some say I bragged. Some say I'm an old fool in his dotage, ravin' aboot a favorite son. But they are people who hate me an' are afraid. True, son, I talked with a purpose, but shore I was mighty cold an' steady when I did it. My feelin' was that you'd do what I'd do if I were thirty years younger. No, I reckoned you'd do more. For I figured on your blood. Jean, you're Indian, an' Texas an' French, an' you've trained yourself in the Oregon woods. When you were only a boy, few marksmen I ever knew could beat you, an' I never saw your equal for eye an' ear, for trackin' a hoss, for all the gifts that make a woodsman. . . . Wal, rememberin' this an' seein' the trouble ahaid for the Isbels, I just broke

out whenever I had a chance. I bragged before men I'd reason to believe
would take my words deep. For instance, not long ago I missed some
stock, an', happenin' into Greaves's place one Saturday night, I shore
talked loud. His barroom was full of men an' some of them were in my
black book. Greaves took my talk a little testy. He said. 'Wal, Gass,
mebbe you're right aboot some of these cattle thieves livin' among us,
but ain't they jest as liable to be some of your friends or relatives as Ted
Meeker's or mine or any one around heah?' That was where Greaves an'
me fell out. I yelled at him: 'No, by God, they're not! My record heah an'
that of my people is open. The least I can say for you, Greaves, an' your
crowd, is that your records fade away on dim trails.' Then he said, nasty-
like, 'Wal, if you could work out all the dim trails in the Tonto you'd
shore be surprised.' An' then I roared. Shore that was the chance I was
lookin' for. I swore the trails he hinted of would be tracked to the holes
of the rustlers who made them. I told him I had sent for you an' when
you got heah these slippery, mysterious thieves, whoever they were,
would shore have hell to pay. Greaves said he hoped so, but he was afraid
I was partial to my Indian son. Then we had hot words. Blaisdell got between us. When I was leavin' I took a partin' fling at him. 'Greaves, you
ought to know the Isbels, considerin' you're from Texas. Maybe you've
got reasons for throwin' taunts at my claims for my son Jean. Yes, he's got
Indian in him an' that 'll be the worse for the men who will have to meet
him. I'm tellin' you, Greaves, Jean Isbel is the black sheep of the family.
If you ride down his record you'll find he's shore in line to be another
Poggin, or Reddy Kingfisher, or Hardin', or any of the Texas gunmen
you ought to remember. . . . Greaves, there are men rubbin' elbows with
you right heah that my Indian son is goin' to track down!' "

Jean bent his head in stunned cognizance of the notoriety with which
his father had chosen to affront any and all Tonto Basin men who were
under the ban of his suspicion. What a terrible reputation and trust to have
saddled upon him! Thrills and strange, heated sensations seemed to rush
together inside Jean, forming a hot ball of fire that threatened to explode.
A retreating self made feeble protests. He saw his own pale face going
away from this older, grimmer man.

"Son, if I could have looked forward to anythin' but blood spillin' I'd
never have given you such a name to uphold," continued the rancher.

"What I'm goin' to tell you now is my secret. My other sons an' Ann have never heard it. Jim Blaisdell suspects there's somethin' strange, but he doesn't know. I'll shore never tell anyone else but you. An' you must promise to keep my secret now an' after I am gone."

"I promise," said Jean.

"Wal, an' now to get it out," began his father, breathing hard. His face twitched and his hands clenched. "The sheepman heah I have to reckon with is Lee Jorth, a lifelong enemy of mine. We were born in the same town, played together as children, an' fought with each other as boys. We never got along together. An' we both fell in love with the same girl. It was nip an' tuck for a while. Ellen Sutton belonged to one of the old families of the South. She was a beauty, an' much courted, an' I reckon it was hard for her to choose. But I won her an' we became engaged. Then the war broke out. I enlisted with my brother Jean. He advised me to marry Ellen before I left. But I would not. That was the blunder of my life. Soon after our partin' her letters ceased to come. But I didn't distrust her. That was a terrible time an' all was confusion. Then I got crippled an' put in a hospital. An' in aboot a year I was sent back home."

At this juncture Jean refrained from further gaze at his father's face.

"Lee Jorth had gotten out of goin' to war," went on the rancher, in lower, thicker voice. "He'd married my sweetheart, Ellen. . . . I knew the story long before I got well. He had run after her like a hound after a hare. . . . An' Ellen married him. Wal, when I was able to get aboot I went to see Jorth an' Ellen. I confronted them. I had to know why she had gone back on me. Lee Jorth hadn't changed any with all his good fortune. He'd made Ellen believe in my dishonor. . . . But, I reckon, lies or no lies, Ellen Sutton was faithless. In my absence he had won her away from me. An' I saw that she loved him as she never had me. I reckon that killed all my generosity. If she'd been imposed upon an' weaned away by his lies an' had regretted me a little I'd have forgiven, perhaps. But she worshiped him. She was his slave. An' I, wal, I learned what hate was.

"The war ruined the Suttons, same as so many Southerners. Lee Jorth went in for raisin' cattle. He'd gotten the Sutton range an' after a few years he began to accumulate stock. In those days every cattleman was a little bit of a thief. Every cattleman drove in an' branded calves he couldn't swear was his. Wal, the Isbels were the strongest cattle raisers in that country. An' I laid a trap for Lee Jorth, caught him in the act of brandin' calves of mine I'd marked, an' I proved him a thief. I made him a rustler. I ruined him. We met once. But Jorth was one Texan not strong on the draw, at least against an Isbel. He left the country. He had friends an' relatives an' they started him at stock raisin' again. But he began to gamble an' he got in with a shady crowd. He went from bad to worse an' then he came back home. When I saw the change in proud, beautiful Ellen Sutton, an' how she still worshiped Jorth, it shore drove me near mad between pity an' hate. . . . Wal, I reckon in a Texan hate outlives any other feelin'. There came a strange turn of the wheel an' my fortunes changed. Like most young bloods of the day, I drank an' gambled. An' one night I run across Jorth an' a card-sharp friend. He fleeced me. We quarreled. Guns were thrown. I killed my man. . . . Aboot that period the Texas Rangers had come into existence. . . . An', son, when I said I never was run out of Texas I wasn't holdin' to strict truth. I rode out on a hoss.

"I went to Oregon. There I married soon, an' there Bill an' Guy were born. Their mother did not live long. An' next I married your mother, Jean. She had some Indian blood, which, for all I could see, made her only the finer. She was a wonderful woman an' gave me the only happiness I ever knew. You remember her, of course, an' those home days in Oregon. I reckon I made another great blunder when I moved to Arizona. But the cattle country had always called me. I had heard of this wild Tonto Basin an' how Texans were settlin' there. An' Jim Blaisdell sent me word to come—that this shore was a garden spot of the West. Wal, it is. An' your mother was gone—

"Three years ago Lee Jorth drifted into the Tonto. An', strange to me, along aboot a year or so after his comin' the Hash Knife Gang rode up from Texas. Jorth went in for raisin' sheep. Along with some other sheepmen he lives up in the Rim cañons. Somewhere back in the wild brakes is the hidin' place of the Hash Knife Gang. Nobody but me, I reckon, associates Colonel Jorth, as he's called, with Daggs an' his gang. Maybe Blaisdell an' a few others have a hunch. But that's no matter. As a sheepman Jorth has a legitimate grievance with the cattlemen. But what could be settled by a square consideration for the good of all an' the future Jorth will never settle. He'll never settle because he is now no longer an honest man. He's in with Daggs. I cain't prove this, son, but I know it.

I saw it in Jorth's face when I met him that day with Greaves. I saw more. I shore saw what he is up to. He'd never meet me at an even break. He's dead set on usin' this sheep an' cattle feud to ruin my family an' me, even as I ruined him. But he means more, Jean. This will be a war between Texans, an' a bloody war. There are bad men in this Tonto—some of the worst that didn't get shot in Texas. Jorth will have some of these fellows. . . . Now, are we goin' to wait to be sheeped off our range an' to be murdered from ambush?"

"No, we are not," replied Jean, quietly.

"Wal, come down to the house." said the rancher, and led the way without speaking until he halted by the door. There he place his finger on a small hole in the wood at about the height of a man's head. Jean saw it was a bullet hole and that a few gray hairs stuck to its edges. The rancher stepped closer to the doorpost, so that his head was within an inch of the wood. Then he looked at Jean with eyes in which there glinted dancing specks of fire, like wild sparks.

"Son, this sneakin' shot at me was made three mawnin's ago. I recollect movin' my haid just when I heard the crack of a rifle. Shore was surprised. But I got inside quick."

Jean scarcely heard the latter part of this speech. He seemed doubled up inwardly, in hot and cold convulsions of changing emotion. A terrible hold upon his consciousness was about to break and let go. The first shot had been fired and he was an Isbel. Indeed, his father had made him ten times an Isbel. Blood was thick. His father did not speak to dull ears. This strife of rising tumult in him seemed the effect of years of calm, of peace in the woods, of dreamy waiting for he knew not what. It was the passionate primitive life in him that had awakened to the call of blood ties.

"That's aboot all, son," concluded the rancher. "You understand now why I feel they're goin' to kill me. I feel it heah." With solemn gesture he placed his broad hand over his heart. "An', Jean, strange whispers come to me at night. It seems like your mother was callin' or tryin' to warn me. I cain't explain these queer whispers. But I know what I know."

"Jorth has his followers. You must have yours." replied Jean, tensely.

"Shore, son, an' I can take my choice of the best men heah," replied the rancher, with pride. "But I'll not do that. I'll lay the deal before them an' let them choose. I reckon it 'll not be a long-winded fight. It 'll be short an bloody, after the way of Texans. I'm lookin' to you, Jean, to see that an Isbel is the last man!"

"My God—dad! is there no other way? Think of my sister Ann—of my brothers' wives—of—of other women! Dad, these damned Texas feuds are cruel, horrible!" burst out Jean, in passionate protest.

"Jean, would it be any easier for our women if we let these men shoot us down in cold blood?"

"Oh no—no, I see, there's no hope of—of. . . . But, dad. I wasn't thinkin' about myself. I don't care. Once started I'll—I'll be what you bragged I was. Only it's so hard to—to give in."

Jean leaned an arm against the side of the cabin and, bowing his face over it, he surrendered to the irresistible contention within his breast. And as if with a wrench that strange inward hold broke. He let down. He went back. Something that was boyish and hopeful—and in its place slowly rose the dark tide of his inheritance, the savage instinct of self-preservation bequeathed by his Indian mother, and the fierce, feudal blood lust of his Texan father.

Then as he raised himself, gripped by a sickening coldness in his breast, he remembered Ellen Jorth's face as she had gazed dreamily down off the Rim—so soft, so different, with tremulous lips, sad, musing, with far-seeing stare of dark eyes, peering into the unknown, the instinct of life still unlived. With confused vision and nameless pain Jean thought of her.

"Dad, it's hard on—the—the young folks," he said, bitterly. "The sins of the father, you know. An' the other side. How about Jorth? Has he any children?"

What a curious gleam of surprise and conjecture Jean encountered in his father's gaze!

"He has a daughter. Ellen Jorth. Named after her mother. The first time I saw Ellen Jorth I thought she was a ghost of the girl I had loved an' lost. Sight of her was like a blade in my side. But the looks of her an' what she is—they don't gibe. Old as I am, my heart—Bah! Ellen Jorth is a damned hussy!"

Jean Isbel went off alone into the cedars. Surrender and resignation to his father's creed should have ended his perplexity and worry. His instant and burning resolve to be as his father had represented him should have opened his mind to slow cunning, to the craft of the Indian, to the development of hate. But there seemed to be an obstacle. A cloud in the way of vision. A face limned on his memory.

Those damning words of his father's had been a shock—how little or great he could not tell. Was it only a day since he had met Ellen Jorth? What had made all the difference? Suddenly like a breath the fragrance of her hair came back to him. Then the sweet coolness of her lips! Jean trembled. He looked around him as if he were pursued or surrounded by eyes, by instincts, by fears, by incomprehensible things.

"Ahuh! That must be what ails me," he muttered. "The look of her—an' that kiss—they've gone hard with me. I should never have stopped to talk. An' I'm goin' to kill her father an' leave her to God knows what."

Something was wrong somewhere. Jean absolutely forgot that within the hour he had pledged his manhood, his life to a feud which could be blotted out only in blood. If he had understood himself he would have realized that the pledge was no more thrilling and unintelligible in its possibilities than this instinct which drew him irresistibly.

"Ellen Jorth! So—my dad calls her a damned hussy! So—that explains the—the way she acted—why she never hit me when I kissed her. An' her words, so easy an' cool-like. Hussy? That means she's bad—bad! Scornful of me—maybe disappointed because my kiss was innocent! It was, I swear. An' all she said: 'Oh, I've been kissed before.'"

Jean grew furious with himself for the spreading of a new sensation in his breast that seemed now to ache. Had he become infatuated, all in a day, with this Ellen Jorth? Was he jealous of the men who had the privilege of her kisses? No! But his reply was hot with shame, with uncertainty. The thing that seemed wrong was outside of himself. A blunder was no crime. To be attracted by a pretty girl in the woods—to yield to an impulse was no disgrace, nor wrong. He had been foolish over a girl before, though not to such a rash extent. Ellen Jorth had stuck in his consciousness, and with her a sense of regret.

Then swiftly rang his father's bitter words, the revealing: "But the looks of her an' what she is—they don't gibe!" In the import of these words hid the meaning of the wrong that troubled him. Broodingly he pondered over them.

"The looks of her. Yes, she was pretty. But it didn't dawn on me at first. I—I was sort of excited. I liked to look at her, but didn't think." And now consciously her face was called up, infinitely sweet and more impelling for the deliberate memory. Flash of brown skin, smooth and clear; level gaze of dark, wide eyes, steady, bold, unseeing; red curved lips, sad and sweet; her strong, clean, fine face rose before Jean, eager and wistful one moment, softened by dreamy musing thought, and the next stormily passionate, full of hate, full of longing, but the more mysterious and beautiful.

"She looks like that, but she's bad," concluded Jean, with bitter finality. "I might have fallen in love with Ellen Jorth if—if she'd been different."

But the conviction forced upon Jean did not dispel the haunting memory of her face nor did it wholly silence the deep and stubborn voice of his consciousness. Later that afternoon he sought a moment with his sister.

"Ann, did you ever meet Ellen Jorth?" he asked.

"Yes, but not lately," replied Ann.

"Well, I met her as I was ridin' along yesterday. She was herdin' sheep," went on Jean, rapidly. "I asked her to show me the way to the Rim. An' she walked with me a mile or so. I can't say the meetin' was not interestin', at least to me. . . . Will you tell me what you know about her?"

"Sure, Jean," replied his sister, with her dark eyes fixed wonderingly and kindly on his troubled face. "I've heard a great deal, but in this Tonto Basin I don't believe all I hear. What I know I'll tell you. I first met Ellen Jorth two years ago. We didn't know each other's names then. She was the prettiest girl I ever saw. I liked her. She liked me. She seemed unhappy. The next time we met was at a round-up. There were other girls with me and they snubbed her. But I left them and went around with her. That snub cut her to the heart. She was lonely. She had no friends. She talked about herself—how she hated the people, but loved Arizona. She had nothin' fit to wear. I didn't need to be told that she'd been used to better things. Just when it looked as if we were goin' to be friends she told me who she was and asked me my name. I told her. Jean, I couldn't have hurt her more if I'd slapped her face. She turned white. She gasped. And then she ran off. The last time I saw her was about a year ago. I was ridin' a shortcut trail to the ranch where a friend lived. And I met Ellen Jorth ridin' with a man I'd never seen. The trail was overgrown and shady. They were ridin' close and didn't see me right off. The man had his arm round her. She pushed him away. I saw her laugh. Then he got hold of her again and was kissin' her when his horse shied at sight of mine. They rode by me then. Ellen Jorth held her head high and never looked at me."

"Ann, do you think she's a bad girl?" demanded Jean, bluntly.

"Bad? Oh, Jean!" exclaimed Ann, in surprise and embarrassment.

"Dad said she was a damned hussy."

"Jean, dad hates the Jorths."

"Sister, I'm askin' you what you think of Ellen Jorth. Would you be friends with her if you could?"

"Yes."

"Then you don't believe she's bad."

"No. Ellen Jorth is lonely, unhappy. She has no mother. She lives alone among rough men. Such a girl can't keep men from handlin' her and kissin' her. Maybe she's too free. Maybe she's wild. But she's honest, Jean. You can trust a woman to tell. When she rode past me that day her face was white and proud. She was a Jorth and I was an Isbel. She hated herself—she hated me. But no bad girl could look like that. She knows what's said of her all around the valley. But she doesn't care. She'd encourage gossip."

"Thank you, Ann," replied Jean, huskily. "Please keep this—this meetin' of mine with her all to yourself, won't you?"

"Why, Jean, of course I will."

Jean wandered away again, peculiarly grateful to Ann for reviving and upholding something in him that seemed a wavering part of the best of him—a chivalry that had demanded to be killed by judgment of a righteous woman. He was conscious of an uplift, a gladdening of his spirit. Yet the ache remained. More than that, he found himself plunged deeper into conjecture, doubt. Had not the Ellen Jorth incident ended? He denied his father's indictment of her and accepted the faith of his sister. "Reckon that's aboot all, as dad says," he soliloquized. Yet was that all? He paced under the cedars. He watched the sun set. He listened to the coyotes. He lingered there after the call for supper; until out of the tumult of his conflicting emotions and ponderings there evolved the staggering consciousness that he must see Ellen Jorth again.

CHAPTER 4

Ellen Jorth hurried back into the forest, hotly resentful of the accident that had thrown her in contact with an Isbel.

Disgust filled her—disgust that she had been amiable to a member of the hated family that had ruined her father. The surprise of this meeting did not come to her while she was under the spell of stronger feeling. She walked under the trees, swiftly, with head erect, looking straight before her, and every step seemed a relief.

Upon reaching camp, her attention was distracted from herself. Pepe, the Mexican boy, with the two shepherd dogs, was trying to drive sheep into a closer bunch to save the lambs from coyotes. Ellen loved the fleecy, tottering little lambs, and at this season she hated all the prowling beast of the forest. From this time on for weeks the flock would be besieged by wolves, lions, bears, the last of which were often bold and dangerous. The old grizzlies that killed the ewes to eat only the milk-bags were particularly dreaded by Ellen. She was a good shot with a rifle, but had orders from her father to let the bears alone. Fortunately, such sheep-killing bears were but few, and were left to be hunted by men from the ranch. Mexican sheep herders could not be depended upon to protect their flocks from bears. Ellen helped Pepe drive in the stragglers, and she took several shots at coyotes skulking along the edge of the brush. The open glade in the forest was favorable for herding the sheep at night and the dogs could be depended upon to guard the flock, and in most cases to drive predatory beasts away.

After this task, which brought the time to sunset, Ellen had supper to cook and eat. Darkness came, and a cool night wind set in. Here and there a lamb bleated plaintively. With her work done for the day, Ellen sat before a ruddy camp-fire, and found her thoughts again centering around the singular adventure that had befallen her. Disdainfully she strove to think of something else. But there was nothing that could dispel the interest of her meeting with Jean Isbel. Thereupon she impatiently surrendered to it, and recalled every word and action which she could remember. And in the process of this meditation she came to an action of hers, recollection of which brought the blood tingling to her neck and cheeks, so unusually and burningly that she covered them with her hands. "What did he think of me?" she mused, doubtfully. It did not matter what he thought, but she could not help wondering. And when she came to the memory of his kiss she suffered more than the sensation of throbbing scarlet cheeks. Scornfully and bitterly she burst out, "Shore he couldn't have thought much good of me."

The half hour following this reminiscence was far from being pleasant. Proud, passionate, strong-willed Ellen Jorth found herself a victim of conflicting emotions. The event of the day was too close. She could not understand it. Disgust and disdain and scorn could not make this meeting with Jean Isbel as if it had never been. Pride could not efface it from her mind. The more she reflected, the harder she tried to forget, the stronger grew a significance of interest. And when a hint of this dawned upon her consciousness she resented it so forcibly that she lost her temper, scattered the camp fire, and went into the little teepee tent to roll in her blankets.

Thus settled snug and warm for the night, with a shepherd dog curled at the opening of her tent, she shut her eyes and confidently bade sleep end her perplexities. But sleep did not come at her invitation. She found herself wide awake, keenly sensitive to the sputtering of the camp fire, the tinkling of bells on the rams, the bleating of lambs, the sough of wind in the pines, and the hungry sharp bark of coyotes off in the distance. Darkness was no respecter of her pride. The lonesome night with its emphasis of solitude seemed to induce clamoring and strange thoughts, a confusing ensemble of all those that had annoyed her during the daytime. Not for long hours did sheer weariness bring her to slumber.

Ellen awakened late and failed of her usual alacrity. Both Pepe and the shepherd dog appeared to regard her with surprise and solicitude. Ellen's spirit was low this morning; her blood ran sluggishly; she had to fight a mournful tendency to feel sorry for herself. And at first she was not very successful. There seemed to be some kind of pleasure in reveling in melancholy which her common sense told her had no reason for existence. But states of mind persisted in spite of common sense.

"Pepe, when is Antonio comin' back?" she asked.

The boy could not give her a satisfactory answer. Ellen had willingly taken the sheep herder's place for a few days, but now she was impatient to go home. She looked down the green-and-brown aisles of the forest until she was tired. Antonio did not return. Ellen spent the day with the sheep; and in the manifold task of caring for a thousand new-born lambs she forgot herself. This day saw the end of lambing-time for that season. The forest resounded to a babel of baas and bleats. When night came she was glad to go to bed, for what with loss of sleep, and weariness she could scarcely keep her eyes open.

The following morning she awakened early, bright, eager, expectant, full of bounding life, strangely aware of the beauty and sweetness of the scented forest, strangely conscious of some nameless stimulus to her feelings.

Not long was Ellen in associating this new and delightful variety of sensations with the fact that Jean Isbel had set to-day for his ride up to the Rim to see her. Ellen's joyousness fled; her smiles faded. The spring morning lost its magic radiance.

"Shore there's no sense in my lyin' to myself," she soliloquized, thoughtfully. "It's queer of me—feelin' glad aboot him—without knowin'. Lord! I must be lonesome! To be glad of seein' an Isbel, even if he is different!"

Soberly she accepted the astounding reality. Her confidence died with her gayety; her vanity began to suffer. And she caught at her admission that Jean Isbel was different; she resented it in amaze; she ridiculed it; she laughed at her naïve confession. She could arrive at no conclusion other than that she was a weak-minded, fluctuating, inexplicable little fool.

But for all that she found her mind had been made up for her, without consent or desire, before her will had been consulted; and that inevitably and unalterably she meant to see Jean Isbel again. Long she battled with this strange decree. One moment she won a victory over this new curious self, only to lose it the next. And at last out of her conflict there emerged a few convictions that left her with some shreds of pride. She hated all Isbels, she hated any Isbel, and particularly she hated Jean Isbel. She was only curious—intensely curious to see if he would come back, and if he did come what he would do. She wanted only to watch him from some covert. She would not go near him, not let him see her or guess of her presence. Thus she assuaged her hurt vanity—thus she stifled her miserable doubts.

Long before the sun had begun to slant westward toward the mid-afternoon Jean Isbel had set as a meeting time Ellen directed her steps through the forest to the Rim. She felt ashamed of her eagerness. She had a guilty conscience that no strange thrills could silence. It would be fun to see him, to watch him, to let him wait for her, to fool him.

Like an Indian, she chose the soft pine-needle mats to tread upon, and her light-moccasined feet left no trace. Like an Indian also she made a wide detour, and reached the Rim a quarter of a mile west of the spot where she had talked with Jean Isbel; and here, turning east, she took care to step on the bare stones. This was an adventure, seemingly the first she had ever had in her life. Assuredly she had never before come directly to the Rim without halting to look, to wonder, to worship. This time she scarcely glanced into the blue abyss. All absorbed was she in hiding her tracks. Not one chance in a thousand would she risk. The Jorth pride burned even while the feminine side of her dominated her actions. She had some difficult rocky points to cross, then windfalls to round, and at length reached the covert she desired. A rugged yellow point of the Rim stood somewhat higher than the spot Ellen wanted to watch. A dense thicket of jack-pines grew to the very edge. It afforded an ambush that even the Indian eyes Jean Isbel was credited with could never penetrate. Moreover, if by accident she made a noise and excited suspicion, she could retreat unobserved and hide in the huge rocks below the Rim, where a ferret could not locate her.

With her plan decided upon, Ellen had nothing to do but wait, so she repaired to the other side of the pine thicket and to the edge of the Rim where she could watch and listen. She knew that long before she saw Isbel she would hear his horse. It was altogether unlikely that he would come on foot.

"Shore, Ellen Jorth, y'u're a queer girl," she mused. "I reckon I wasn't well acquainted with y'u."

Beneath her yawned a wonderful deep cañon, rugged and rocky with but few pines on the north slope, thick with dark green timber on the south slope. Yellow and gray crags, like turreted castles, stood up out of the sloping forest on the side opposite her. The trees were all sharp, spear pointed. Patches of light green aspens showed strikingly against the dense black. The great slope beneath Ellen was serrated with narrow, deep gorges, almost cañons in themselves. Shadows alternated with clear bright spaces. The mile-wide mouth of the cañon opened upon the Basin, down into a world of wild timbered ranges and ravines, valleys and hills, that rolled and tumbled in dark-green waves to the Sierra Anchas.

But for once Ellen seemed singularly unresponsive to this panorama of wildness and grandeur. Her ears were like those of a listening deer, and her eyes continually reverted to the open places along the Rim. At first, in her excitement, time flew by. Gradually, however, as the sun moved westward, she began to be restless. The soft thud of dropping pine cones, the rustling of squirrels up and down the shaggy-barked spruces, the cracking of weathered bits of rock, these caught her keen ears many times and brought her up erect and thrilling. Finally she heard a sound which resembled that of an unshod hoof on stone. Stealthily then she took her rifle and slipped back through the pine thicket to the spot she had chosen. The little pines were so close together that she had to crawl between their trunks. The ground was covered with a soft bed of pine needles, brown and fragrant. In her hurry she pricked her ungloved hand on a sharp pine cone and drew the blood. She sucked the tiny wound. "Shore I'm wonderin' if that's a bad omen," she muttered, darkly thoughtful. Then she resumed her sinuous approach to the edge of the thicket, and presently reached it.

Ellen lay flat a moment to recover her breath, then raised herself on her elbows. Through an opening in the fringe of buck brush she could plainly see the promontory where she had stood with Jean Isbel, and also the approaches by which he might come. Rather nervously she realized that her covert was hardly more than a hundred feet from the promontory. It was imperative that she be absolutely silent. Her eyes searched the openings along the Rim. The gray form of a deer crossed one of these, and she concluded it had made the sound she had heard. Then she lay down more comfortably and waited. Resolutely she held, as much as possible, to her sensorial perceptions. The meaning of Ellen Jorth lying in ambush just to see an Isbel was a conundrum she refused to ponder in the present. She was doing it, and the physical act had its fascination. Her ears, attuned to all the sounds of the lonely forest, caught them and arranged them according to her knowledge of woodcraft.

A long hour passed by. The sun had slanted to a point halfway between the zenith and the horizon. Suddenly a thought confronted Ellen Jorth: "He's not comin'," she whispered. The instant that idea presented itself she felt a blank sense of loss, a vague regret—something that must have been disappointment. Unprepared for this, she was held by surprise for a moment, and then she was stunned. Her spirit, swift and rebellious, had no time to rise in her defense. She was a lonely, guilty, miserable girl, too weak for pride to uphold, too fluctuating to know her real self. She stretched there, burying her face in the pine needles, digging her fingers into them, wanting nothing so much as that they might hide her. The moment was incomprehensible to Ellen, and utterly intolerable. The sharp pine needles, piercing her wrists and cheeks, and her hot heaving breast, seemed to give her exquisite relief.

The shrill snort of a horse sounded near at hand. With a shock Ellen's body stiffened. Then she quivered a little and her feelings underwent swift change. Cautiously and noiselessly she raised herself upon her elbows and peeped through the opening in the brush. She saw a man tying a horse to a bush somewhat back from the Rim. Drawing a rifle from its saddle sheath he threw it in the hollow of his arm and walked to the edge of the precipice. He gazed away across the Basin and appeared lost in contemplation or thought. Then he turned to look back into the forest, as if he expected some one.

Ellen recognized the lithe figure, the dark face so like an Indian's. It was Isbel. He had come. Somehow his coming seemed wonderful and terrible. Ellen shook as she leaned on her elbows. Jean Isbel, true to his word, in spite of her scorn, had come back to see her. The fact seemed monstrous. He was an enemy of her father. Long had range rumor been bandied from lip to lip—old Gass Isbel had sent for his Indian son to fight the Jorths. Jean Isbel—son of a Texan—unerring shot—peerless tracker—a bad and dangerous man! Then there flashed over Ellen a burning thought—if it were true, if he was an enemy of her father's, if a fight between Jorth and Isbel was inevitable, she ought to kill this Jean Isbel right there in his tracks as he boldly and confidently waited for her. Fool he was to think she would come. Ellen sank down and dropped her head until the strange tremor of her arms ceased. That dark and grim flash of thought retreated. She had not come to murder a man from ambush, but only to watch him, to try to see what he meant, what he thought, to allay a strange curiosity.

After a while she looked again. Isbel was sitting on an upheaved section of the Rim, in a comfortable position from which he could watch the openings in the forest and gaze as well across the west curve of the Basin to the Mazatzals. He had composed himself to wait. He was clad in a buckskin suit, rather new, and it certainly showed off to advantage, compared with the ragged and soiled apparel Ellen remembered. He did not look so large. Ellen was used to the long, lean, rangy Arizonians and Texans. This man was built differently. He had the widest shoulders of any man she had ever seen, and they made him appear rather short. But his lithe, powerful limbs proved he was not short. Whenever he moved the muscles rippled. His hands were clasped round a knee—brown, sinewy hands, very broad, and fitting the thick muscular wrists. His collar was open, and he did not wear a scarf, as did the men Ellen knew. Then her intense curiosity at last brought her steady gaze to Jean Isbel's head and face. He wore a cap, evidently of some thin fur. His hair was straight and short, and in color a dead raven black. His complexion was dark, clear tan, with no trace of red. He did not have the prominent cheek bones nor the high-bridged nose usual with white men who were part Indian. Still he had the Indian look. Ellen caught that in the dark, intent, piercing eyes, in the wide, level, thoughtful brows, in the stern impassiveness of his smooth face. He had a straight, sharp-cut profile.

Ellen whispered to herself: "I saw him right the other day. Only, I'd not admit it. . . . The finest-lookin' man I ever saw in my life is a damned Isbel! . . . Was that what I come out heah for?"

She lowered herself once more and, folding her arms under her breast, she reclined comfortably on them, and searched out a smaller peephole from which she could spy upon Isbel. And as she watched him the new and perplexing side of her mind waxed busier. Why had he come back? What did he want of her? Acquaintance, friendship, was impossible for them. He had been respectful, deferential toward her, in a way that had strangely pleased, until the surprising moment when he had kissed her. That had only disrupted her rather dreamy pleasure in a situation she had not experienced before. All the men she had met in this wild country were rough and bold; most of them had wanted to marry her, and, failing that, they had persisted in amorous attentions not particularly flattering or honorable. They were a bad lot. And contact with them had dulled some of her sensibilities. But this Jean Isbel had seemed a gentleman. She struggled to be fair, trying to forget her antipathy, as much to understand herself as to give him due credit. True, he had kissed her, crudely and forcibly. But that kiss had not been an insult. Ellen's finer feeling forced her to believe this. She remembered the honest amaze and shame and contrition with which he had faced her, trying awkwardly to explain his bold act. Likewise she recalled the subtle swift change in him at her words, "Oh, I've been kissed before!" She was glad she had said that. Still—was she glad, after all?

She watched him. Every little while he shifted his gaze from the blue gulf beneath him to the forest. When he turned thus the sun shone on his face and she caught the piercing gleam of his dark eyes. She saw, too, that he was listening. Watching and listening for her! Ellen had to still a tumult within her. It made her feel very young, very shy, very strange. All the while she hated him because he manifestly expected her to come. Several times he rose and walked a little way into the woods. The last time he looked at the westering sun and shook his head. His confidence had gone. Then he sat and gazed down into the void. But Ellen knew he did not see anything there. He seemed an image carved in the stone of the Rim, and he gave Ellen a singular impression of loneliness and sadness. Was he thinking of the miserable battle his father had summoned him to lead—of what it would cost—of its useless pain and hatred? Ellen seemed to divine his thoughts. In that moment she softened toward him, and in her soul quivered and stirred an intangible something that was like pain, that was too deep for her understanding. But she felt sorry for an Isbel until the old pride resurged. What if he admired her? She remembered his interest, the wonder and admiration, the growing light in his eyes. And it had not been repugnant to her until he disclosed his name. "What's in a name?" she mused, recalling poetry learned in her girlhood. " 'A rose by any other name would smell as sweet.' . . . He's an Isbel—yet he might be splendid—noble. . . . Bah! he's not—and I'd hate him anyhow."

All at once Ellen felt cold shivers steal over her. Isbel's piercing gaze was directed straight at her hiding place. Her heart stopped beating. If he discovered her there she felt that she would die of shame. Then she became aware that a blue jay was screeching in a pine above her, and a red squirrel somewhere near was chattering his shrill annoyance. These two denizens of the woods could be depended upon to espy the wariest hunter and make known his presence to their kind. Ellen had a moment of more than dread. This keen-eyed, keen-eared Indian might see right through her brushy covert, might hear the throbbing of her heart. It relieved her immeasurably to see him turn away and take to pacing the promontory, with his head bowed and his hands behind his back. He had stopped looking off into the forest. Presently he wheeled to the west, and by the light upon his face Ellen saw that the time was near sunset. Turkeys were beginning to gobble back on the ridge.

Isbel walked to his horse and appeared to be untying something from the back of his saddle. When he came back Ellen saw that he carried a small package apparently wrapped in paper. With this under his arm he strode off in the direction of Ellen's camp and soon disappeared in the forest.

For a little while Ellen lay there in bewilderment. If she had made conjectures before, they were now multiplied. Where was Jean Isbel going? Ellen sat up suddenly. "Well, shore this heah beats me," she said. "What did he have in that package? What was he goin' to do with it?"

It took no little will power to hold her there when she wanted to steal after him through the woods and find out what he meant. But his reputation influenced even her and she refused to pit her cunning in the forest against his. It would be better to wait until he returned to his horse. Thus decided, she lay back again in her covert and gave her mind over to pondering curiosity. Sooner than she expected she espied Isbel approaching through the forest, empty handed. He had not taken his rifle. Ellen averted her glance a moment and thrilled to see the rifle leaning against a rock. Verily Jean Isbel had been far removed from hostile intent that day. She watched him stride swiftly up to his horse, untie the halter, and mount. Ellen had an impression of his arrowlike straight figure, and sinuous grace and ease. Then he looked back at the promontory, as if to fix a picture of it in his mind, and rode away along the Rim. She watched him out of sight. What ailed her? Something was wrong with her, but she recognized only relief.

When Isbel had been gone long enough to assure Ellen that she might safely venture forth she crawled through the pine thicket to the Rim on the other side of the point. The sun was setting behind the Black Range, shedding a golden glory over the Basin. Westward the zigzag Rim reached like a streamer of fire into the sun. The vast promontories jutted out with blazing beacon lights upon their stone-walled faces. Deep down, the Basin was turning shadowy dark blue, going to sleep for the night.

Ellen bent swift steps toward her camp. Long shafts of gold preceded her through the forest. Then they paled and vanished. The tips of pines and spruces turned gold. A hoarse-voiced old turkey gobbler was booming his chug-a-lug from the highest ground, and the softer chick of hen turkeys answered him. Ellen was almost breathless when she arrived. Two packs and a couple of lop-eared burros attested to the fact of Antonio's return. This was good news for Ellen. She heard the bleat of lambs and tinkle of bells coming nearer and nearer. And she was glad to feel that if Isbel had visited her camp, most probably it was during the absence of the herders.

The instant she glanced into her tent she saw the package Isbel had carried. It lay on her bed. Ellen stared blankly. "The—the impudence of him!" she ejaculated. Then she kicked the package out of the tent. Words and action seemed to liberate a dammed-up hot fury. She kicked the package again, and thought she would kick it into the smoldering campfire. But somehow she stopped short of that. She left the thing there on the ground.

Pepe and Antonio hove in sight, driving in the tumbling woolly flock. Ellen did not want them to see the package, so with contempt for herself, and somewhat lessening anger, she kicked it back into the tent. What was in it? She peeped inside the tent, devoured by curiosity. Neat, well wrapped and tied packages like that were not often seen in the Tonto Basin. Ellen decided she would wait until after supper, and at a favorable moment lay it unopened on the fire. What did she care what it contained? Manifestly it was a gift. She argued that she was highly incensed with this insolent Isbel who had the effrontery to approach her with some sort of present.

It developed that the usually cheerful Antonio had returned taciturn and gloomy. All Ellen could get out of him was that the job of sheep herder had taken on hazards inimical to peace-loving Mexicans. He had heard something he would not tell. Ellen helped prepare the supper and she ate in silence. She had her own brooding troubles. Antonio presently told her that her father had said she was not to start back home after dark. After supper the herders repaired to their own tents, leaving Ellen the freedom of her camp-fire. Wherewith she secured the package and brought it forth to burn. Feminine curiosity rankled strong in her breast. Yielding so far as to shake the parcel and press it, and finally tear a corner off the paper, she saw some words written in lead pencil. Bending nearer the blaze, she read, "For my sister Ann." Ellen gazed at the big, bold hand-writing, quite legible and fairly well done. Suddenly she tore the outside wrapper completely off. From printed words on the inside she gathered that the package had come from a store in San Francisco. "Reckon he fetched home a lot of presents for his folks—the kids—and his sister," muttered Ellen. "That was nice of him. Whatever this is he shore meant it for sister Ann. . . . Ann Isbel. Why, she must be that black-eyed girl I met and liked so well before I knew she was an Isbel. . . . His sister!"

Whereupon for the second time Ellen deposited the fascinating package in her tent. She could not burn it up just then. She had other emotions besides scorn and hate. And memory of that soft-voiced, kind-hearted, beautiful Isbel girl checked her resentment. "I wonder if he is like his sister," she said, thoughtfully. It appeared to be an unfortunate thought. Jean Isbel certainly resembled his sister. "Too bad they belong to the family that ruined dad."

Ellen went to bed without opening the package or without burning it. And to her annoyance, whatever way she lay she appeared to touch this strange package. There was not much room in the little tent. First she put it at her head beside her rifle, but when she turned over her cheek came in contact with it. Then she felt as if she had been stung. She moved it again, only to touch it presently with her hand. Next she flung it to the bottom of her bed, where it fell upon her feet, and whatever way she moved them she could not escape the pressure of this undesirable and mysterious gift.

By and by she fell asleep, only to dream that the package was a caressing hand stealing about her, feeling for hers, and holding it with soft, strong clasp. When she awoke she had the strangest sensation in her right palm. It was moist, throbbing, hot, and the feel of it on her cheek was strangely thrilling and comforting. She lay awake then. The night was dark and still. Only a low moan of wind in the pines and the faint tinkle of a sheep bell broke the serenity. She felt very small and lonely lying there in the deep forest, and, try how she would, it was impossible to think the same then as she did in the clear light of day. Resentment, pride, anger—these seemed abated now. If the events of the day had not changed her, they had at least brought up softer and kinder memories and emotions than she had known for long. Nothing hurt and saddened her so much as to remember the gay, happy days of her childhood, her sweet mother, her old home. Then her thought returned to Isbel and his gift. It had been years since anyone had made her a gift. What could this one be? It did not matter. The wonder was that Jean Isbel should bring it to her and that she could be perturbed by its presence. "He meant it for his sister and so he thought well of me," she said, in finality.

Morning brought Ellen further vacillation. At length she rolled the obnoxious package inside her blankets, saying that she would wait until she got home and then consign it cheerfully to the flames. Antonio tied her pack on a burro. She did not have a horse, and therefore had to walk the several miles to her father's ranch.

She set off at a brisk pace, leading the burro and carrying her rifle. And soon she was deep in the fragrant forest. The morning was clear and cool, with just enough frost to make the sunlit grass sparkle as if with diamonds. Ellen felt fresh, buoyant, singularly full of life. Her youth would not be denied. It was pulsing, yearning. She hummed an old

Southern tune and every step seemed one of pleasure in action, of advance toward some intangible future happiness. All the unknown of life before her called. Her heart beat high in her breast and she walked as one in a dream. Her thoughts were swift-changing, intimate, deep, and vague, not of yesterday or to-day, nor of reality.

The big, gray, white-tailed squirrels crossed ahead of her on the trail, scampered over the piny ground to hop on tree trunks, and there they paused to watch her pass. The vociferous little red squirrels barked and chattered at her. From every thicket sounded the gobble of turkeys. The blue jays squalled in the treetops. A deer lifted its head from browsing and stood motionless, with long ears erect, watching her go by.

Thus happily and dreamily absorbed, Ellen covered the forest miles and soon reached the trail that led down into the wild brakes of Chevelon Cañon. It was rough going and less conducive to sweet wanderings of mind. Ellen slowly lost them. And then a familiar feeling assailed her, one she never failed to have upon returning to her father's ranch—a reluctance, a bitter dissatisfaction with her home, a loyal struggle against the vague sense that all was not as it should be.

At the head of this cañon in a little, level, grassy meadow stood a rude one-room log shack, with a leaning red-stone chimney on the outside. This was the abode of a strange old man who had long lived there. His name was John Sprague and his occupation was raising burros. No sheep or cattle or horses did he own, not even a dog. Rumor had said Sprague was a prospector, one of the many who had searched that country for the Lost Dutchman gold mine. Sprague knew more about the Basin and Rim than any of the sheepmen or ranchers. From Black Butte to the Cibique and from Chevelon Butte to Reno Pass he knew every trail, cañon, ridge, and spring, and could find his way to them on the darkest night. His fame, however, depended mostly upon the fact that he did nothing but raise burros, and would raise none but black burros with white faces. These burros were the finest bred in all the Basin and were in great demand. Sprague sold a few every year. He had made a present of one to Ellen, although he hated to part with them. This old man was Ellen's one and only friend.

Upon her trip out to the Rim with the sheep, Uncle John, as Ellen called him, had been away on one of his infrequent visits to Grass Valley.

It pleased her now to see a blue column of smoke lazily lifting from the old chimney and to hear the discordant bray of burros. As she entered the clearing Sprague saw her from the door of his shack.

"Hello, Uncle John!" she called.

"Wal, if it ain't Ellen!" he replied, heartily. "When I seen thet white-faced Jinny I knowed who was leadin' her. Where you been, girl?"

Sprague was a little, stoop-shouldered old man, with grizzled head and face, and shrewd gray eyes that beamed kindly on her over his ruddy cheeks. Ellen did not like the tobacco stain on his grizzled beard nor the dirty, motley, ragged, ill-smelling garb he wore, but she had ceased her useless attempts to make him more cleanly.

"I've been herdin' sheep," replied Ellen. "And where have y'u been, uncle? I missed y'u on the way over."

"Been packin' in some grub. An' I reckon I stayed longer in Grass Valley than I recollect. But thet was only natural, considerin'—"

"What?" asked Ellen, bluntly, as the old man paused.

Sprague took a black pipe out of his vest pocket and began rimming the bowl with his fingers. The glance he bent on Ellen was thoughtful and earnest, and so kind that she feared it was pity. Ellen suddenly burned for news from the village.

"Wal, come in an' set down, won't you?" he asked.

"No, thanks," replied Ellen, and she took a seat on the chopping block. "Tell me, uncle, what's goin' on down in the Valley?"

"Nothin' much yet—except talk. An' there's a heap of thet."

"Humph! There always was talk," declared Ellen, contemptuously. "A nasty, gossipy, catty hole, that Grass Valley!"

"Ellen, thar's goin' to be war—a bloody war in the ole Tonto Basin," went on Sprague, seriously.

"War! . . . Between whom?"

"The Isbels an' their enemies. I reckon most people down thar, an' sure all the cattlemen, air on old Gass's side. Blaisdell, Gordon, Fredericks, Blue—they'll all be in it."

"Who are they goin' to fight?" queried Ellen, sharply.

"Wal, the open talk is thet the sheepmen are forcin' this war. But thar's talk not so open, an' I reckon not very healthy for any man to whisper hyarbouts."

"Uncle John, y'u needn't be afraid to tell me anythin'," said Ellen. "I'd never give y'u away. Y'u've been a good friend to me."

"Reckon I want to be, Ellen," he returned, nodding his shaggy head. "It ain't easy to be fond of you as I am an' keep my mouth shet. . . . I'd like to know somethin'. Hev you any relatives away from hyar thet you could go to till this fight's over?"

"No. All I have, so far as I know, are right heah."

"How aboot friends?"

"Uncle John, I have none," she said, sadly, with bowed head.

"Wal, wal, I'm sorry. I was hopin' you might git away."

She lifted her face. "Shore y'u don't think I'd run off if my dad got in a fight?" she flashed.

"I hope you will."

"I'm a Jorth," she said, darkly, and dropped her head again.

Sprague nodded gloomily. Evidently he was perplexed and worried, and strongly swayed by affection for her.

"Would you go away with me?" he asked. "We could pack over to the Mazatzals an' live thar till this blows over."

"Thank y'u, Uncle John. Y'u're kind and good. But I'll stay with my father. His troubles are mine."

"Ahuh! . . . Wal, I might hev reckoned so. . . . Ellen, how do you stand on this hyar sheep an' cattle question?"

"I think what's fair for one is fair for another. I don't like sheep as much as I like cattle. But that's not the point. The range is free. Suppose y'u had cattle and I had sheep. I'd feel as free to run my sheep anywhere as y'u were to run your cattle."

"Right. But what if you throwed your sheep round my range an' sheeped off the grass so my cattle would hev to move or starve?"

"Shore I wouldn't throw my sheep round y'ur range," she declared, stoutly.

"Wal, you've answered half of the question. An' now supposin' a lot of my cattle was stolen by rustlers, but not a single one of your sheep. What 'd you think then?"

"I'd shore think rustlers chose to steal cattle because there was no profit in stealin' sheep."

"Egzactly. But wouldn't you hev a queer idee aboot it?"

"I don't know. Why queer? What 're y'u drivin' at, Uncle John?"

"Wal, wouldn't you git kind of a hunch thet the rustlers was—say a leetle friendly toward the sheepmen?"

Ellen felt a sudden vibrating shock. The blood rushed to her temples. Trembling all over, she rose.

"Uncle John!" she cried.

"Now, girl, you needn't fire up thet way. Set down an' don't—"

"Dare y'u insinuate my father has—"

"Ellen, I ain't insinuatin' nothin'," interrupted the old man. "I'm jest askin' you to think. Thet's all. You're 'most grown into a young woman now. An' you've got sense. Thar's bad times ahead, Ellen. An' I hate to see you mix in them."

"Oh, y'u do make me think," replied Ellen, with smarting tears in her eyes. "Y'u make me unhappy. Oh, I know my dad is not liked in this cattle country. But it's unjust. He happened to go in for sheep raising. I wish he hadn't. It was a mistake. Dad always was a cattleman till we came heah. He made enemies—who—who ruined him. And everywhere misfortune crossed his trail. . . . But, oh, Uncle John, my dad is an honest man."

"Wal, child, I—I didn't mean to—to make you cry," said the old man, feelingly, and he averted his troubled gaze. "Never mind what I said. I'm an old meddler. I reckon nothin' I could do or say would ever change what's goin' to happen. If only you wasn't a girl! . . . Thar I go ag'in. Ellen, face your future an' fight your way. All youngsters hev to do thet. An' it's the right kind of fight thet makes the right kind of man or woman. Only you must be sure to find yourself. An' by thet I mean to find the real, true, honest-to-God best in you an' stick to it an' die fightin' for it. You're a young woman, almost, an' a blamed handsome one. Which means you'll hev more trouble an' a harder fight. This country ain't easy on a woman when once slander has marked her."

"What do I care for the talk down in that Basin?" returned Ellen. "I know they think I'm a hussy. I've let them think it. I've helped them to."

"You're wrong, child," said Sprague, earnestly. "Pride an' temper! You must never let anyone think bad of you, much less help them to."

"I hate everybody down there," cried Ellen, passionately. "I hate them so I'd glory in their thinkin' me bad. . . . My mother belonged to the best blood in Texas. I am her daughter. I know *who and what I am*. That uplifts me whenever I meet the sneaky, sly suspicions of these Basin people. It shows me the difference between them and me. That's what I glory in."

"Ellen, you're a wild, headstrong child," rejoined the old man, in severe tones. "Word has been passed ag'in' your good name—your honor. . . . An' hevn't you given cause fer thet?"

Ellen felt her face blanch and all her blood rush back to her heart in sickening force. The shock of his words was like a stab from a cold blade. If their meaning and the stern, just light of the old man's glance did not kill her pride and vanity they surely killed her girlishness. She stood mute, staring at him, with her brown, trembling hands stealing up toward her bosom, as if to ward off another and a mortal blow.

"Ellen!" burst out Sprague, hoarsely. "You mistook me. Aw, I didn't mean—what you think, I swear. . . . Ellen, I'm old an' blunt. I ain't used to wimmen. But I've love for you, child, an' respect, jest the same as if you was my own. . . . An' I *know* you're good. . . . Forgive me. . . . I meant only hevn't you been, say, sort of—careless?"

"Care-less?" queried Ellen, bitterly and low.

"An' powerful thoughtless an'—an' blind—lettin' men kiss you an' fondle you—when you're really a growed-up woman now?"

"Yes—I have," whispered Ellen.

"Wal, then, why did you let them?"

"I—I don't know. . . . I didn't think. The men never let me alone—never—never! I got tired everlastingly pushin' them away. And sometimes—when they were kind—and I was lonely for something I—I didn't mind if one or another fooled round me. I never thought. It never looked as y'u have made it look. . . . Then—those few times ridin' the trail to Grass Valley—when people saw me—then I guess I encouraged such attentions. . . . Oh, I must be—I am a shameless little hussy!"

"Hush thet kind of talk," said the old man, as he took her hand. "Ellen, you're only young an' lonely an' bitter. No mother—no friends—no one but a lot of rough men! It's a wonder you hev kept yourself good. But now your eyes are open, Ellen. They're brave an' beautiful eyes, girl, an' if you stand by the light in them you will come through any trouble. An' you'll be happy. Don't ever forget that. Life is hard enough, God knows, but it's unfailin' true in the end to the man or woman who finds the best in them an' stands by it."

"Uncle John, y'u talk so—so kindly. Y'u make me have hope. There seemed really so little for me to live for—hope for. . . . But I'll never be a coward again—nor a thoughtless fool. I'll find some good in me—or make some—and never fail it, come what will. I'll remember your words. I'll believe the future holds wonderful things for me. . . . I'm only eighteen. Shore all my life won't be lived heah. Perhaps this threatened fight over sheep and cattle will blow over. . . . Somewhere there must be some nice girl to be a friend—a sister to me. . . . And maybe some man who'd believe, in spite of all they say—that I'm not a hussy."

"Wal, Ellen, you remind me of what I was wantin' to tell you when you just got here. . . . Yestiddy I heard you called thet name in a barroom. An' thar was a fellar thar who raised hell. He near killed one man an' made another plumb eat his words. An' he scared thet crowd stiff."

Old John Sprague shook his grizzled head and laughed, beaming upon Ellen as if the memory of what he had seen had warmed his heart.

"Was it—y'u?" asked Ellen, tremulously.

"Me? Aw, I wasn't nowhere. Ellen, this fellar was quick as a cat in his actions an' his words was like lightnin'."

"Who?" she whispered.

"Wal, no one else but a stranger jest come to these parts—an Isbel, too. Jean Isbel."

"Oh!" exclaimed Ellen, faintly.

"In a barroom full of men—almost all of them in sympathy with the sheep crowd—most of them on the Jorth side—this Jean Isbel resented an insult to Ellen Jorth."

"No!" cried Ellen. Something terrible was happening to her mind or her heart.

"Wal, he sure did," replied the old man, "an' it's goin' to be good fer you to hear all about it."

CHAPTER 5

Old John Sprague launched into his narrative with evident zest.

"I hung round Greaves's store most of two days. An' I heerd a heap. Some of it was jest plain ole men's gab, but I reckon I got the drift of things concernin' Grass Valley. Yestiddy mornin' I was packin' my burros in Greaves's back yard, takin' my time carryin' out supplies from the store. An' as last when I went in I seen a strange fellar was thar. Strappin' young man—not so young, either—an' he had on buckskin. Hair black as my burros, dark face, sharp eyes—you'd took him fer an Injun. He carried a rifle—one of them new forty-fours—an' also somethin' wrapped in paper thet he seemed partickler careful about. He wore a belt round his middle an' thar was a bowie knife in it, carried like I've seen scouts an' Injun fighters hev on the frontier in the 'seventies. That looked queer to me, an' I reckon to the rest of the crowd thar. No one overlooked the big six-shooter he packed Texas fashion. Wal, I didn't hev no idee this fellar was an Isbel until I heard Greaves call him thet.

" 'Isbel,' said Greaves, 'reckon your money's counterfeit hyar. I cain't sell you anythin'.'

" 'Counterfeit? Not much,' spoke up the young fellar, an' he flipped some gold twenties on the bar, where they rung like bells. 'Why not? Ain't this a store? I want a cinch strap.'

"Greaves looked particular sour thet mornin'. I'd been watchin' him fer two days. He hedn't hed much sleep fer I hed my bed back of the store, an' I heerd men come in the night an' hev long confabs with him. Whatever was in the wind hedn't pleased him none. An' I calkilated thet young Isbel wasn't a sight good fer Greaves's sore eyes, anyway. But he paid no more attention to Isbel. Acted jest as if he hedn't heerd Isbel say he wanted a cinch strap.

"I stayed inside the store then. Thar was a lot of fellars I'd seen, an' some I knowed. Couple of card games goin', an' drinkin', of course. I soon gathered thet the general atmosphere wasn't friendly to Jean Isbel. He seen thet quick enough, but he didn't leave. Between you an' me I sort of took a likin' to him. An' I sure watched him as close as I could, not seemin' to, you know. Reckon they all did the same, only you couldn't see it. It got jest about the same as if Isbel hedn't been in thar, only you knowed it wasn't really the same. Thet was how I got the hunch the crowd was all sheepmen or their friends. The day before I'd heerd a lot of talk about this young Isbel, an' what he'd come to Grass Valley fer, an' what a bad hombre he was. An' when I seen him I was bound to admit he looked his reputation.

"Wal, pretty soon in come two more fellars, an' I knowed both of them. You know them, too, I'm sorry to say. Fer I'm comin' to facts now thet will shake you. The first fellar was your father's Mexican foreman, Lorenzo, and the other was Simm Bruce. I reckon Bruce wasn't drunk, but he'd sure been lookin' on red licker. When he seen Isbel darn me if he didn't swell an' bustle all up like a mad ole turkey gobbler.

" 'Greaves,' he said, 'if thet fellar's Jean Isbel I ain't hankerin' fer the company y'u keep.' An' he made no bones of pointin' right at Isbel. Greaves looked up dry an' sour an' he bit out spiteful-like: 'Wal, Simm, we ain't hed a hell of a lot of choice in this heah matter. Thet's Jean Isbel shore enough. Mebbe you can persuade him thet his company an' his custom ain't wanted round heah!'

"Jean Isbel set on the counter an' took it all in, but he didn't say nothin'. The way he looked at Bruce was sure enough fer me to see thet thar might be a surprise any minnit. I've looked at a lot of men in my day, an' can sure feel events comin'. Bruce got himself a stiff drink an' then he straddles over the floor in front of Isbel.

" 'Air you Jean Isbel, son of the ole Gass Isbel?' asked Bruce, sort of lolling back an' givin' a hitch to his belt.

" 'Yes sir, you've identified me,' said Isbel, nice an' polite.

" 'My name's Bruce. I'm rangin' sheep heahaboots, an' I hev interest in Kurnel Lee Jorth's bizness.'

" 'Hod do, Mister Bruce,' replied Isbel, very civil an' cool as you please. Bruce hed an eye fer the crowd thet was now listenin' an' watchin'. He swaggered closer to Isbel.

" 'We heerd y'u come into the Tonto Basin to run us sheepmen off the range. How aboot thet?'

" 'Wal, you heerd wrong,' said Isbel, quietly. 'I came to work fer my father. Thet work depends on what happens.'

"Bruce began to git redder of face, an' he shook a husky hand in front of Isbel. 'I'll tell y'u this heah, my Nez Perce Isbel—' an' when he sort of choked fer more wind Greaves spoke up, 'Simm, I shore reckon thet Nez Perce handle will stick.' An' the crowd haw-hawed. Then Bruce got goin' ag'in. 'I'll tell y'u this heah, Nez Perce. Thar's been enough happen already to run y'u out of Arizona.'

" 'Wal, you don't say! What, fer instance?' asked Isbel, quick an' sarcastic.

"Thet made Bruce bust out puffin' an' spittin': 'Wha-tt, fer instance? Huh! Why, y'u dam half-breed, y'u'll git run out fer makin' up to Ellen Jorth. Thet won't go in this heah country. Not fer any Isbel.'

" 'You're a liar,' called Isbel, an' like a big cat he dropped off the counter. I heerd his moccasins pat soft on the floor. An' I bet to myself thet he was as dangerous as he was quick. But his voice an' his looks didn't change even a leetle.

" 'I'm not a liar,' yelled Bruce. 'I'll make y'u eat thet. I can prove what I say. . . . Y'u was seen with Ellen Jorth—up on the Rim—day before yestiddy. Y'u was watched. Y'u was with her. Y'u made up to her. Y'u grabbed her an' kissed her! . . . An' I'm heah to say. Nez Perce, thet y'u're a marked man on this range.'

" 'Who saw me?' asked Isbel, quiet an' cold. I seen then thet he'd turned white in the face.

" 'Yu cain't lie out of it,' hollered Bruce, wavin' his hands. 'We got y'u daid to rights. Lorenzo saw y'u—follered y'u—watched y'u.' Bruce pointed at the grinnin' greaser. 'Lorenzo is Kurnel Jorth's foreman. He seen y'u maulin' of Ellen Jorth. An' when he tells the Kurnel an' Tad

Jorth an Jackson Jorth! . . . Haw! Haw! Why, hell 'd be a cooler place fer y'u then this heah Tonto.'

"Greaves an' his gang hed come round, sure tickled clean to thar gizzards at this mess. I noticed, howsomever, thet they was Texans enough to keep back to one side in case this Isbel started any action. . . . Wal, Isbel took a look at Lorenzo. Then with one swift grab he jerked the little greaser off his feet an' pulled him close. Lorenzo stopped grinnin'. He began to look a leetle sick. But it was plain he hed right on his side.

" 'You say you saw me?' demanded Isbel.

" '*Si*, señor,' replied Lorenzo.

" 'What did you see?'

" 'I see señor an' señorita. I hide by manzanita. I see señorita like grande señor ver mooch. She like señor keese. She—'

"Then Isbel hit the little greaser a back-handed crack in the mouth. Sure it was a crack! Lorenzo went over the counter backward an' landed like a pack load of wood. An' he didn't git up.

" 'Mister Bruce,' said Isbel, 'an' you fellars who heerd thet lyin' greaser, I did meet Ellen Jorth. An' I lost my head. I—I kissed her. . . . But it was an accident. I meant no insult. I apologized—I tried to explain my crazy action. . . . Thet was all. The greaser lied. Ellen Jorth was kind enough to show me the trail. We talked a little. Then—I suppose—because she was young an' pretty an' sweet—I lost my head. She was absolutely innocent. Thet damned greaser told a bare-faced lie when he said she liked me. The fact was she despised me. She said so. An' when she learned I was Jean Isbel she turned her back on me an' walked away.' "

At this point of his narrative the old man halted as if to impress Ellen not only with what just had been told, but particularly with what was to follow. The reciting of this tale had evidently given Sprague an unconscious pleasure. He glowed. He seemed to carry the burden of a secret that he yearned to divulge. As for Ellen, she was deadlocked in breathless suspense. All her emotions waited for the end. She begged Sprague to hurry.

"Wal, I wish I could skip the next chapter an' hev only the last to tell," rejoined the old man, and he put a heavy, but solicitous, hand upon hers. . . . "Simm Bruce haw-hawed loud an' loud. . . . 'Say, Nez Perce,' he calls out, most insolent-like, 'we air too good sheepmen heah to hev the wool pulled over our eyes. We shore know what y'u meant by Ellen Jorth. But y'u wasn't smart when y'u told her y'u was Jean Isbel! . . . Haw-haw!'

"Isbel flashed a strange, surprised look from the red-faced Bruce to Greaves and to the other men. I take it he was wonderin' if he'd heerd right or if they'd got the same hunch thet 'd come to him. An' I reckon he determined to make sure.

"'Why wasn't I smart?' he asked.

"'Shore y'u wasn't smart if y'u was aimin' to be one of Ellen Jorth's lovers,' said Bruce, with a leer. 'Fer if y'u hedn't give y'urself away y'u could hev been easy enough.'

"Thar was no mistakin' Bruce's meanin' an' when he got it out some of the men thar laughed. Isbel kept lookin' from one to another of them. Then facin' Greaves, he said, deliberately: 'Greaves, this drunken Bruce is excuse enough fer a show-down. I take it that you are sheepmen, an' you're goin' on Jorth's side of the fence in the matter of this sheep rangin'.'

"'Wal, Nez Perce, I reckon you hit plumb center,' said Greaves, dryly. He spread wide his big hands to the other men, as if to say they'd might as well own the jig was up.

"'All right. You're Jorth's backers. Have any of you a word to say in Ellen Jorth's defense? I tell you the Mexican lied. Believin' me or not doesn't matter. But this vile-mouthed Bruce hinted against thet girl's honor.'

"Ag'in some of the men laughed, but not so noisy, an' there was a nervous shufflin' of feet. Isbel looked sort of queer. His neck had a bulge round his collar. An' his eyes was like black coals of fire. Greaves spread his big hands again, as if to wash them of this part of the dirty argument.

"'When it comes to any wimmen I pass—much less play a hand fer a wildcat like Jorth's gurl,' said Greaves, sort of cold an' thick. 'Bruce shore ought to know her. Accordin' to talk heahaboots an' what *he* says, Ellen Jorth has been his gurl fer two years.'

"Then Isbel turned his attention to Bruce an' I fer one begun to shake in my boots.

"'Say thet to me!' he called.

"'Shore she's my gurl, an' thet's why I'm a-goin' to hev y'u run off this range.'

"Isbel jumped at Bruce. 'You damned drunken cur! You vile-mouthed liar! . . . I may be an Isbel, but by God you cain't slander thet girl to my face!' . . . Then he moved so quick I couldn't see what he did. But I heerd his fist hit Bruce. It sounded like an ax ag'in' a beef. Bruce fell clear across the room. An' by Jinny when he landed Isbel was thar. As Bruce staggered up, all bloody-faced, bellowin' an' spittin' out teeth Isbel eyed Greaves's crowd an' said: 'If any of y'u make a move it 'll mean gun-play.' Nobody moved, thet's sure. In fact, none of Greaves's outfit was packin' guns, at least in sight. When Bruce got all the way up—he's a tall fellar— why Isbel took a full swing at him an' knocked him back across the room ag'in' the counter. Y'u know when a fellar's hurt by the way he yells. Bruce got thet second smash right on his big red nose. . . . I never seen any one so quick as Isbel. He vaulted over that counter jest the second Bruce fell back on it, an' then with Greaves's gang in front so he could catch any moves of theirs, he jest slugged Bruce right an' left, an' banged his head on the counter. Then as Bruce sunk limp an' slipped down, lookin' like a bloody sack, Isbel let him fall to the floor. Then he vaulted back over the counter. Wipin' the blood off his hands, he throwed his kerchief down in Bruce's face. Bruce wasn't dead or bad hurt. He'd jest been beaten bad. He was moanin' an' slobberin'. Isbel kicked him, not hard, but jest sort of disgustful. Then he faced thet crowd. 'Greaves, thet's what I think of your Simm Bruce. Tell him next time he sees me to run or pull a gun. 'An' then Isbel grabbed his rifle an' package off the counter an' went out. He didn't even look back. I seen him mount his horse an' ride away. . . . Now, girl, what hev you to say?"

Ellen could only say good-by and the word was so low as to be almost inaudible. She ran to her burro. She could not see very clearly through tear-blurred eyes, and her shaking fingers were all thumbs. It seemed she had to rush away—somewhere, anywhere—not to get away from old John Sprague, but from herself—this palpitating, bursting self whose feet stumbled down the trail. All—all seemed ended for her. That interminable story! It had taken so long. And every minute of it she had been helplessly torn asunder by feelings she had never known she possessed. This Ellen Jorth was an unknown creature. She sobbed now as she dragged the burro down the cañon trail. She sat down only to rise. She hurried only to stop. Driven, pursued, barred, she had no way to escape the flaying thoughts, no time or will to repudiate them. The death of her girlhood, the rending aside of a veil of maiden mystery only vaguely instinctively guessed, the barren, sordid truth of her life as seen by her enlightened eyes, the bitter realization of the vileness of men of her clan in contrast to the manliness and chivalry of an enemy, the hard facts of unalterable repute as created by slander and fostered by low minds, all these were forces in a cataclysm that had suddenly caught her heart and whirled her through changes immense and agonizing, to bring her face to face with reality, to force upon her suspicion and doubt of all she had trusted, to warn her of the dark, impending horror of a tragic bloody feud, and lastly to teach her the supreme truth at once so glorious and so terrible—that she could not escape the doom of womanhood.

About noon that day Ellen Jorth arrived at the Knoll, which was the location of her father's ranch. Three cañons met there to form a larger one. The Knoll was a symmetrical hill situated at the mouth of the three cañons. It was covered with brush and cedars, with here and there lichened rocks showing above the bleached grass. Below the Knoll was a wide, grassy flat or meadow through which a willow-bordered stream cut its rugged boulder-strewn bed. Water flowed abundantly at this season, and the deep washes leading down from the slopes attested to the fact of cloudbursts and heavy storms. This meadow valley was dotted with horses and cattle, and meandered away between the timbered slopes to lose itself in a green curve. A singular feature of this cañon was that a heavy growth of spruce trees covered the slope facing northwest; and the opposite slope, exposed to the sun and therefore less snowbound in winter, held a sparse growth of yellow pines. The ranch house of Colonel Jorth stood round the rough corner of the largest of the three cañons, and rather well hidden, it did not obtrude its rude and broken-down log cabins, its squalid surroundings, its black mud-holes of corrals upon the beautiful and serene meadow valley.

Ellen Jorth approached her home slowly, with dragging, reluctant steps; and never before in the three unhappy years of her existence there had the ranch seemed so bare, so uncared for, so repugnant to her. As she had seen herself with clarified eyes, so now she saw her home. The cabin that Ellen lived in with her father was a single-room structure with one door and no windows. It was about twenty feet square. The huge, ragged, stone chimney had been built on the outside, with the wide open fireplace set inside the logs. Smoke was rising from the chimney. As Ellen halted at the door and began unpacking her burro she heard the loud, lazy laughter of men. An adjoining log cabin had been built in two sections, with a wide roofed hall or space between them. The door in each cabin faced the other, and there was a tall man standing in one. Ellen recognized Daggs, a neighbor sheepman, who evidently spent more time with her father than at his own home, wherever that was. Ellen had never seen it. She heard this man drawl, "Jorth, heah's your kid come home."

Ellen carried her bed inside the cabin, and unrolled it upon a couch built of boughs in the far corner. She had forgotten Jean Isbel's package, and now it fell out under her sight. Quickly she covered it. A Mexican woman, relative of Antonio, and the only servant about the place, was squatting Indian fashion before the fireplace, stirring a pot of beans. She and Ellen did not get along well together, and few words ever passed between them. Ellen had a canvas curtain stretched upon a wire across a small triangular corner, and this afforded her a little privacy. Her possessions were limited in number. The crude square table she had constructed herself. Upon it was a little old-fashioned walnut-framed mirror, a brush and comb, and a dilapidated ebony cabinet which contained odds and ends the sight of which always brought a smile of derisive self-pity to her lips. Under the table stood an old leather trunk. It had come with her from Texas, and contained clothing and belongings of her mother's. Above the couch on pegs hung her scant wardrobe. A tiny shelf held several worn-out books.

When her father slept indoors, which was seldom except in winter, he occupied a couch in the opposite corner. A rude cupboard had been built against the logs next to the fireplace. It contained supplies and utensils. Toward the center, somewhat closer to the door, stood a crude table and two benches. The cabin was dark and smelled of smoke, of the stale odors of past cooked meals, of the mustiness of dry, rotting timber. Streaks of light showed through the roof where the rough-hewn shingles had split or weathered. A strip of bacon hung upon one side of the cupboard, and upon the other a haunch of venison. Ellen detested the Mexican woman because she was dirty. The inside of the cabin presented the same unkempt appearance usual to it after Ellen had been away for a few days. Whatever Ellen had lost during the retrogression of the Jorths, she had kept her habits of cleanliness, and straightway upon her return she set to work.

The Mexican woman sullenly slouched away to her own quarters outside and Ellen was left to the satisfaction of labor. Her mind was as busy as her hands. As she cleaned and swept and dusted she heard from time to time the voices of men, the clip-clop of shod horses, the bellow of cattle. And a considerable time elapsed before she was disturbed.

A tall shadow darkened the doorway.

"Howdy, little one!" said a lazy, drawling voice. "So y'u-all got home?"

Ellen looked up. A superbly built man leaned against the doorpost. Like most Texans, he was light haired and light eyed. His face was lined and hard. His long, sandy mustache hid his mouth and drooped with a curl. Spurred, booted, belted, packing a heavy gun low down on his hip, he gave Ellen an entirely new impression. Indeed, she was seeing everything strangely.

"Hello, Daggs!" replied Ellen. "Where's my dad?"

"He's playin' cairds with Jackson an' Colter. Shore's playin' bad, too, an' it's gone to his haid."

"Gamblin'?" queried Ellen.

"Mah child, when'd Kurnel Jorth ever play for fun?" said Daggs, with a lazy laugh. "There's a stack of gold on the table. Reckon yo' uncle Jackson will win it. Colter's shore out of luck."

Daggs stepped inside. He was graceful and slow. His long spurs clinked. He laid a rather compelling hand on Ellen's shoulder.

"Heah, mah gal, give us a kiss," he said.

"Daggs, I'm not your girl," replied Ellen as she slipped out from under his hand.

Then Daggs put his arm round her, not with violence or rudeness, but with an indolent, affectionate assurance, at once bold and self-contained. Ellen, however, had to exert herself to get free of him, and when she had placed the table between them she looked him square in the eyes.

"Daggs, y'u keep your paws off me," she said.

"Aw, now, Ellen, I ain't no bear," he remonstrated. "What's the matter, kid?"

"I'm not a kid. And there's nothin' the matter. Y'u're to keep your hands to yourself, that's all."

He tried to reach her across the table, and his movements were lazy and slow, like his smile. His tone was coaxing.

"Mah dear, shore you set on my knee just the other day, now, didn't you?"

Ellen felt the blood sting her cheeks.

"I was a child," she returned.

"Wal, listen to this heah grown-up young woman. All in a few days! . . . Doon't be in a temper, Ellen. . . . Come, give us a kiss."

She deliberately gazed into his eyes. Like the eyes of an eagle, they were clear and hard, just now warmed by the dalliance of the moment, but there was no light, no intelligence in them to prove he understood her. The instant separated Ellen immeasurably from him and from all of his ilk.

"Daggs, I was a child," she said. "I was lonely—hungry for affection—I was innocent. Then I was careless, too, and thoughtless when I should have known better. But I hardly understood y'u men. I put such thoughts out of my mind. I know now—know what y'u mean—what y'u have made people believe I am."

"Ahuh! Shore I get your hunch," he returned, with a change of tone. "But I asked you to marry me?"

Yes y'u did. The first day y'u got heah to my dad's house. And y'u asked me to marry y'u after y'u found y'u couldn't have your way with me. To y'u the one didn't mean any more than the other."

"Shore I did more than Simm Bruce an' Colter," he retorted. "They never asked you to marry."

"No, they didn't. And if I could respect them at all I'd do it because they didn't ask me."

"Wal, I'll be doggoned!" ejaculated Daggs, thoughtfully, as he stroked his long mustache.

"I'll say to them what I've said to y'u," went on Ellen. "I'll tell dad to make y'u let me alone. I wouldn't marry one of y'u—y'u loafers to save my life. I've my suspicions about y'u. Y'u're a bad lot."

Daggs changed subtly. The whole indolent nonchalance of the man vanished in an instant.

"Wal, Miss Jorth, I reckon you mean we're a bad lot of sheepmen?" he queried, in the cool, easy speech of a Texan.

"No," flashed Ellen. "Shore I don't say sheepmen. I say y'u're a *bad lot.*"

"Oh, the hell you say!" Daggs spoke as he might have spoken to a man; then turning swiftly on his heel he left her. Outside he encountered Ellen's father. She heard Daggs speak: "Lee, your little wildcat is shore heah. An' take mah hunch. Somebody has been talkin' to her."

"Who has?" asked her father, in his husky voice. Ellen knew at once that he had been drinking.

"Lord only knows," replied Daggs. "But shore it wasn't any friends of ours."

"We cain't stop people's tongues," said Jorth, resignedly.

"Wal, I ain't so shore," continued Daggs, with his slow, cool laugh. "Reckon I never yet heard any daid men's tongues wag."

Then the musical tinkle of his spurs sounded fainter. A moment later Ellen's father entered the cabin. His dark, moody face brightened at sight of her. Ellen knew she was the only person in the world left for him to love. And she was sure of his love. Her very presence always made him different. And through the years, the darker their misfortunes, the farther he slipped away from better days, the more she loved him.

"Hello, my Ellen!" he said, and he embraced her. When he had been drinking he never kissed her. "Shore I'm glad you're home. This heah hole is bad enough any time, but when you're gone it's black. . . . I'm hungry."

Ellen laid food and drink on the table; and for a little while she did not look directly at him. She was concerned about this new searching power of her eyes. In relation to him she vaguely dreaded it.

Lee Jorth had once been a singularly handsome man. He was tall, but did not have the figure of a horseman. His dark hair was streaked with gray, and was white over his ears. His face was sallow and thin, with deep lines. Under his round, prominent, brown eyes, like deadened furnaces, were blue swollen welts. He had a bitter mouth and weak chin, not wholly concealed by gray mustache and pointed beard. He wore a long frock coat and a wide-brimmed sombrero, both black in color, and so old and stained and frayed that along with the fashion of them they betrayed that they had come from Texas with him. Jorth always persisted in wearing a white linen shirt, likewise a relic of his Southern prosperity, and today it was ragged and soiled as usual.

Ellen watched her father eat and waited for him to speak. It occurred to her strangely that he never asked about the sheep or the new-born lambs. She divined with a subtle new woman's intuition that he cared nothing for his sheep.

"Ellen, what riled Daggs?" inquired her father, presently. "He shore had fire in his eye."

Long ago Ellen had betrayed an indignity she had suffered at the hands of a man. Her father had nearly killed him. Since then she had taken care to keep her troubles to herself. If her father had not been blind and absorbed in his own brooding he would have seen a thousand things sufficient to inflame his Southern pride and temper.

"Daggs asked me to marry him again and I said he belonged to a bad lot," she replied.

Jorth laughed in scorn. "Fool! . . . My God! Ellen, I must have dragged you low—that every damned ru—er—sheepman—who comes along thinks he can marry you."

At the break in his words, the incompleted meaning, Ellen dropped her eyes. Little things once never noted by her were now come to have a fascinating significance.

"Never mind, dad," she replied. "They cain't marry me."

"Daggs said somebody had been talkin' to you. How aboot that?"

"Old John Sprague has just gotten back from Grass Valley," said Ellen. "I stopped in to see him. Shore he told me all the village gossip."

"Anythin' to interest me?" he queried, darkly.

"Yes, dad, I'm afraid a good deal," she said, hesitatingly. Then in accordance with a decision Ellen had made she told him of the rumored war between sheepmen and cattlemen; that old Isbel had Blaisdell, Gordon, Fredericks, Blue, and other well-known ranchers on his side; that his son Jean Isbel had come from Oregon with a wonderful reputation as fighter and scout and tracker; that it was no secret how Colonel Lee Jorth was at the head of the sheepmen; that a bloody war was sure to come.

"Hah!" exclaimed Jorth, with a stain of red in his sallow cheek. "Reckon none of that is news to me. I knew all that."

Ellen wondered if he had heard of her meeting with Jean Isbel. If not he would hear as soon as Simm Bruce and Lorenzo came back. She decided to forestall them.

"Dad, I met Jean Isbel. He came into my camp. Asked the way to the Rim. I showed him. We—we talked a little. And shore were gettin' acquainted when—when he told me who he was. Then I left him—hurried back to camp."

"Colter met Isbel down in the woods," replied Jorth, ponderingly. "Said he looked like an Indian—a hard an' slippery customer to reckon with."

"Shore I guess I can indorse what Colter said," returned Ellen, dryly. She could have laughed aloud at her deceit. Still she had not lied.

"How'd this heah young Isbel strike you?" queried her father, suddenly glancing up at her.

Ellen felt the slow, sickening, guilty rise of blood in her face. She was helpless to stop it. But her father evidently never saw it. He was looking at her without seeing her.

"He—he struck me as different from men heah," she stammered.

"Did Sprague tell you aboot this half-Indian Isbel—aboot his reputation?"

"Yes."

"Did he look to you like a real woodsman?"

"Indeed he did. He wore buckskin. He stepped quick and soft. He acted at home in the woods. He had eyes black as night and sharp as lightnin'. They shore saw about all there was to see."

Jorth chewed at his mustache and lost himself in brooding thought.

"Dad, tell me, is there goin' to be a war?" asked Ellen, presently.

What a red, strange, rolling flash blazed in his eyes! His body jerked.

"Shore. You might as well know."

"Between sheepmen and cattlemen?"

"Yes."

"With y'u, dad, at the haid of one faction and Gaston Isbel the other?"

"Daughter, you have it correct, so far as you go."

"Oh! . . . Dad, can't this fight be avoided?"

"You forget you're from Texas," he replied.

"Cain't it be helped?" she repeated, stubbornly.

"No!" he declared, with deep, hoarse passion.

"Why not?"

"Wal, we sheepmen are goin' to run sheep anywhere we like on the range. An' cattlemen won't stand for that."

"But, dad, it's so foolish," declared Ellen, earnestly. "Y'u sheepmen do not have to run sheep over the cattle range."

"I reckon we do."

"Dad, that argument doesn't go with me. I know the country. For years to come there will be room for both sheep and cattle without over-runnin'. If some of the range is better in water and grass, then whoever got there first should have it. That shore is only fair. It's common sense, too."

"Ellen, I reckon some cattle people have been prejudicin' you," said Jorth, bitterly.

"Dad!" she cried, hotly.

This had grown to be an ordeal for Jorth. He seemed a victim of contending tides of feeling. Some will or struggle broke within him and the change was manifest. Haggard, shifty-eyed, with wabbling chin, he burst into speech.

"See heah, girl. You listen. There's a clique of ranchers down in the Basin, all those you named, with Isbel at their haid. They have resented sheepmen comin' down into the valley. They want it all to themselves. That's the reason. Shore there's another. All the Isbels are crooked. They're cattle an' horse thieves—have been for years. Gaston Isbel always was a maverick rustler. He's gettin' old now an' rich, so he wants to cover his tracks. He aims to blame this cattle rustlin' an' horse stealin' on to us sheepmen, an' run us out of the country."

Gravely Ellen Jorth studied her father's face, and the newly found truth-seeing power of her eyes did not fail her. In part, perhaps in all, he was telling lies. She shuddered a little, loyally battling against the insidious convictions being brought to fruition. Perhaps in his brooding over his failures and troubles he leaned toward false judgments. Ellen could not attach dishonor to her father's motives or speeches. For long, however, something about him had troubled her, perplexed her. Fearfully she believed she was coming to some revelation, and, despite her keen determination to know, she found herself shrinking.

"Dad, mother told me before she died that the Isbels had ruined you," said Ellen, very low. It hurt her so to see her father cover his face that she could hardly go on. "If they ruined you they ruined all of us. I know what we had once—what we lost again and again—and I see what we are come to now. Mother hated the Isbels. She taught me to hate the very name. But I never knew how they ruined you—or why—or when. And I want to know now."

Then it was not the face of a liar that Jorth disclosed. The present was forgotten. He lived in the past. He even seemed younger in the re- vivifying flash of hate that made his face radiant. The lines burned out. Hate gave him back the spirit of his youth.

"Gaston Isbel an' I were boys together in Weston, Texas," began Jorth, in swift, passionate voice. "We went to school together. We loved the same girl—your mother. When the war broke out she was engaged to Isbel. His family was rich. They influenced her people. But she loved me. When Isbel went to war she married me. He came back an' faced us. God! I'll never forget that. Your mother confessed her unfaithfulness— by Heaven! She taunted him with it. Isbel accused me of winnin' her by lies. But she took the sting out of that. . . . Isbel never forgave her an' he hounded me to ruin. He made me out a card-sharp, cheatin' my best friends. I was disgraced. Later he tangled me in the courts—he beat me out of property—an' last by convictin' me of rustlin' cattle he run me out of Texas."

Black and distorted now, Jorth's face was a spectacle to make Ellen sick with a terrible passion of despair and hate. The truth of her father's ruin and her own were enough. What mattered all else? Jorth beat the table with fluttering, nerveless hands that seemed all the more significant for their lack of physical force.

"An' so help me God, it's got to be wiped out in blood!" he hissed.

That was his answer to the wavering and nobility of Ellen. And she in her turn had no answer to make. She crept away into the corner behind the curtain, and there on her couch in the semidarkness she lay with strained heart, and a resurging, unconquerable tumult in her mind. And she lay there from the middle of that afternoon until the next morning.

When she awakened she expected to be unable to rise—she hoped she could not—but life seemed multiplied in her, and inaction was impossible. Something young and sweet and hopeful that had been in her did not greet the sun this morning. In their place was a woman's passion to learn for herself, to watch events, to meet what must come, to survive.

After breakfast, at which she sat alone, she decided to put Isbel's package out of the way, so that it would not be subjecting her to continual annoyance. The moment she picked it up the old curiosity assailed her.

"Shore I'll see what it is, anyway," she muttered, and with swift hands she opened the package. The action disclosed two pairs of fine, soft shoes, of a style she had never seen, and four pairs of stockings, two of strong, serviceable wool, and the others of a finer texture. Ellen looked at them in amaze. Of all things in the world, these would have been the last she expected to see. And, strangely, they were what she wanted and needed most. Naturally, then, Ellen made the mistake of taking them in her hands to feel their softness and warmth.

"Shore! He saw my bare legs! And he brought me these presents he'd intended for his sister. . . . He was ashamed for me—sorry for me. . . . And I thought he looked at me bold-like, as I'm used to be looked at heah! Isbel or not, he's shore . . ."

But Ellen Jorth could not utter aloud the conviction her intelligence tried to force upon her.

"It'd be a pity to burn them," she mused. "I cain't do it. Sometime I might send them to Ann Isbel."

Whereupon she wrapped them up again and hid them in the bottom of the old trunk, and slowly, as she lowered the lid, looking darkly, blankly at the wall, she whispered: "Jean Isbel! . . . I hate him!"

Later when Ellen went outdoors she carried her rifle, which was unusual for her, unless she intended to go into the woods.

The morning was sunny and warm. A group of shirt-sleeved men lounged in the hall and before the porch of the double cabin. Her father was pacing up and down, talking forcibly. Ellen heard his hoarse voice. As she approached he ceased talking and his listeners relaxed their attention. Ellen's glance ran over them swiftly—Daggs, with his superb head, like that of a hawk, uncovered to the sun; Colter with his lowered, secretive looks, his sand-gray lean face; Jackson Jorth, her uncle, huge, gaunt, hulking, with white in his black beard and hair, and the fire of a ghoul in his hollow eyes; Tad Jorth, another brother of her father's, younger, red of eye and nose, a weak-chinned drinker of rum. Three other limber-legged Texans lounged there, partners of Daggs, and they were sun-browned, light-haired, blue-eyed men singularly alike in appearance, from their dusty high-heeled boots to their broad black sombreros. They claimed to be sheepmen. All Ellen could be sure of was that Rock Wells spent most of his time there, doing nothing but look for a chance to way-lay her; Springer was a gambler; and the third, who answered to the strange name of Queen, was a silent, lazy, watchful-eyed man who never wore a glove on his right hand and who never was seen without a gun within easy reach of that hand.

"Howdy, Ellen. Shore you ain't goin' to say good mawnin' to this heah bad lot?" drawled Daggs, with good-natured sarcasm.

"Why, shore! Good morning, y'u hard-working industrious *mañana* sheep-raisers," replied Ellen, coolly.

Daggs stared. The others appeared taken back by a greeting so for-eign from any to which they were accustomed from her. Jackson Jorth let out a gruff haw-haw. Some of them doffed their sombreros, and Rock Wells managed a lazy, polite good morning. Ellen's father seemed most significantly struck by her greeting, and the least amused.

"Ellen, I'm not likin' your talk," he said, with a frown.

"Dad, when y'u play cards don't y'u call a spade a spade?"

"Why, shore I do."

"Well, I'm calling spades spades."

"Ahuh!" grunted Jorth, furtively dropping his eyes. "Where you goin' with your gun? I'd rather you hung round heah now."

"Reckon I might as well get used to packing my gun all the time," replied Ellen. "Reckon I'll be treated more like a man."

Then the event Ellen had been expecting all morning took place. Simm Bruce and Lorenzo rode around the slope of the Knoll and trotted toward the cabin. Interest in Ellen was relegated to the background.

"Shore they're bustin' with news," declared Daggs.

"They been ridin' some, you bet," remarked another.

"Huh!" exclaimed Jorth. "Bruce shore looks queer to me."

"Red liquor," said Tad Jorth, sententiously. "You-all know the brand Greaves hands out."

"Naw, Simm ain't drunk," said Jackson Jorth. "Look at his bloody shirt."

The cool, indolent interest of the crowd vanished at the red color pointed out by Jackson Jorth. Daggs rose in a single springy motion to his lofty height. The face Bruce turned to Jorth was swollen and bruised, with unhealed cuts. Where his right eye should have been showed a puffed dark purple bulge. His other eye, however, gleamed with hard and sullen light. He stretched a big shaking hand toward Jorth.

"Thet Nez Perce Isbel beat me half to death," he bellowed.

Jorth stared hard at the tragic, almost grotesque figure, at the battered face. But speech failed him. It was Daggs who answered Bruce.

"Wal, Simm, I'll be damned if you don't look it."

"Beat you! What with?" burst out Jorth, explosively.

"I thought he was swingin' an ax, but Greaves swore it was his fists," bawled Bruce, in misery and fury.

"Where was your gun?" queried Jorth, sharply.

"Gun? Hell!" exclaimed Bruce, flinging wide his arms. "Ask Lorenzo. He had a gun. An' he got a biff in the jaw before my turn come. Ask him?"

Attention thus directed to the Mexican showed a heavy discolored swelling upon the side of his olive-skinned face. Lorenzo looked only serious.

"Hah! Speak up," shouted Jorth, impatiently.

"Señor Isbel heet me ver quick," replied Lorenzo, with expressive gesture. "I see thousand stars—then moocho black—all like night."

At that some of Daggs's men lolled back with dry crisp laughter. Daggs's hard face rippled with a smile. But there was no humor in anything for Colonel Jorth.

"Tell us what come off. Quick!" he ordered. "Where did it happen? Why? Who saw it? What did you do?"

Bruce lapsed into a sullen impressiveness. "Wal, I happened in Greaves's store an' run into Jean Isbel. Shore was lookin' fer him. I had my mind made up what to do, but I got to shootin' off my gab instead of my gun. I called him Nez Perce—an' I throwed all thet talk in his face about old Gass Isbel sendin' fer him—an' I told him he'd git run out of the Tonto. Reckon I was jest warmin' up. . . . But then it all happened.

He slugged Lorenzo jest one. An' Lorenzo slid peaceful-like to bed behind the counter. I hadn't time to think of throwin' a gun before he whaled into me. He knocked out two of my teeth. An' I swallered one of them."

Ellen stood in the background behind three of the men and in the shadow. She did not join in the laugh that followed Bruce's remarks. She had known that he would lie. Uncertain yet of her reaction to this, but more bitter and furious as he revealed his utter baseness, she waited for more to be said.

"Wal, I'll be doggoned," drawled Daggs.

"What do you make of this kind of fightin'?" queried Jorth.

"Darn if I know," replied Daggs in perplexity. "Shore an' sartin it's not the way of a Texan. Mebbe this young Isbel really is what old Gass swears he is. Shore Bruce ain't nothin' to give an edge to a real gun fighter. Looks to me like Isbel bluffed Greaves an' his gang an' licked your men without throwin' a gun."

"Maybe Isbel doesn't want the name of drawin' first blood," suggested Jorth.

"That 'd be like Gass," spoke up Rock Wells, quietly. "I once rode fer Gass in Texas."

"Say, Bruce," said Daggs, "was this heah palaverin' of yours an' Jean Isbel's aboot the old stock dispute? Aboot his father's range an' water? An' partickler aboot sheep?"

"Wal—I—I yelled a heap," declared Bruce, haltingly, "but I don't recollect all I said—I was riled. . . . Shore, though it was the same old argyment thet's been fetchin' us closer an' closer to trouble."

Daggs removed his keen hawklike gaze from Bruce. "Wal, Jorth, all I'll say is this. If Bruce is tellin' the truth we ain't got a hell of a lot to fear from this young Isbel. I've known a heap of gun fighters in my day. An' Jean Isbel don't run true to class. Shore there never was a gunman who'd risk cripplin' his right hand by sluggin' anybody."

"Wal," broke in Bruce, sullenly. "You-all can take it daid straight or not. I don't give a damn. But you've shore got my hunch thet Nez Perce Isbel is liable to handle any of you fellars jest as he did me, an' jest as easy. What's more, he's got Greaves figgered. An' you-all know thet Greaves is as deep in—"

"Shut up that kind of gab," demanded Jorth, stridently. "An' answer me. Was the row in Greaves's barroom aboot sheep?"

"Aw, hell! I said so, didn't I?" shouted Bruce, with a fierce uplift of his distorted face.

Ellen strode out from the shadow of the tall men who had obscured her.

"Bruce, y'u're a liar," she said, bitingly.

The surprise of her sudden appearance seemed to root Bruce to the spot. All but the discolored places on his face turned white. He held his breath a moment, then expelled it hard. His effort to recover from the shock was painfully obvious. He stammered incoherently.

"Shore y'u're more than a liar, too," cried Ellen, facing him with blazing eyes. And the rifle, gripped in both hands, seemed to declare her intent of menace. "That row was not about sheep. . . . Jean Isbel didn't beat y'u for anythin' about sheep. . . . Old John Sprague was in Greaves's store. He heard y'u. He saw Jean Isbel beat y'u as y'u deserved. . . . An' he told *me!*"

Ellen saw Bruce shrink in fear of his life; and despite her fury she was filled with disgust that he could imagine she would have his blood on her hands. Then she divined that Bruce saw more in the gathering storm in her father's eyes than he had to fear from her.

"Girl, what the hell are y'u sayin'?" hoarsely called Jorth, in dark amaze.

"Dad, y'u leave this to me," she retorted.

Daggs stepped beside Jorth, significantly on his right side. "Let her alone, Lee," he advised, coolly. "She's shore got a hunch on Bruce."

"Simm Bruce, y'u cast a dirty slur on my name," cried Ellen, passionately.

It was then that Daggs grasped Jorth's right arm and held it tight. "Jest what I thought," he said. "Stand still, Lee. Let's see the kid make him show-down."

"That's what Jean Isbel beat y'u for," went on Ellen. "For slandering a girl who wasn't there. . . . Me! Y'u rotten liar!"

"But, Ellen, it wasn't all lies," said Bruce, huskily. "I was half drunk— an' horrible jealous. . . . You know Lorenzo seen Isbel kissin' you. I can prove thet."

Ellen threw up her head and a scarlet wave of shame and wrath flooded her face.

"Yes," she cried, ringingly. "He saw Jean Isbel kiss me. Once! . . . An' it was the only decent kiss I've had in years. He meant no insult. I didn't know who he was. An' through his kiss I learned a difference between men. . . . Y'u made Lorenzo lie. An' if I had a shred of good name left in Grass Valley you dishonored it. . . . Y'u made *him* think I was your girl! Damn y'u! I ought to kill y'u. . . . Eat your words now—take them back—or I'll cripple y'u for life!"

Ellen lowered the cocked rifle toward his feet.

"Shore, Ellen, I take back—all I said," gulped Bruce. He gazed at the quivering rifle barrel and then into the face of Ellen's father. Instinct told him where his real peril lay.

Here the cool and tactful Daggs showed himself master of the situation.

"Heah, listen!" he called. "Ellen, I reckon Bruce was drunk an' out of his haid. He's shore ate his words. Now, we don't want any cripples in this camp. Let him alone. Your dad got me heah to lead the Jorths, an' that's my say to you. . . . Simm, you're shore a low-down, lyin' rascal. Keep away from Ellen after this or I'll bore you myself. . . . Jorth, it won't be a bad idee for you to forget you're a Texan till you cool off. Let Bruce stop some Isbel lead. Shore the Jorth-Isbel war is aboot on, an' I reckon we'd be smart to believe old Gass's talk aboot his Nez Perce son."

CHAPTER 6

From this hour Ellen Jorth bent all of her lately awakened intelligence and will to the only end that seemed to hold possible salvation for her. In the crisis sure to come she did not want to be blind or weak. Dreaming and indolence, habits born in her which were often a comfort to one as lonely as she, would ill fit her for the hard test she divined and dreaded. In the matter of her father's fight she must stand by him whatever the issue or the outcome; in what pertained to her own principles, her womanhood, and her soul she stood absolutely alone.

Therefore, Ellen put dreams aside, and indolence of mind and body behind her. Many tasks she found, and when these were done for a day she kept active in other ways, thus earning the poise and peace of labor.

Jorth rode off every day, sometimes with one or two of the men, often with a larger number. If he spoke of such trips to Ellen it was to give an impression of visiting the ranches of his neighbors or the various sheep camps. Often he did not return the day he left. When he did get back he smelled of rum and appeared heavy from need of sleep. His horses were always dust and sweat covered. During his absences Ellen fell victim to anxious dread until he returned. Daily he grew darker and more haggard of face, more obsessed by some impending fate. Often he stayed up late, haranguing with the men in the dim-lit cabin, where they drank and smoked, but seldom gambled any more. When the men did not gamble something immediate and perturbing was on their minds.

Ellen had not yet lowered herself to the deceit and suspicion of eaves-dropping, but she realized that there was a climax approaching in which she would deliberately do so.

In those closing May days Ellen learned the significance of many things that previously she had taken as a matter of course. Her father did not run a ranch. There was absolutely no ranching done, and little work. Often Ellen had to chop wood herself. Jorth did not possess a plow. Ellen was bound to confess that the evidence of this lack dumfounded her. Even old John Sprague raised some hay, beets, turnips. Jorth's cattle and horses fared ill during the winter. Ellen remembered how they used to clean up four-inch oak saplings and aspens. Many of them died in the snow. The flocks of sheep, however, were driven down into the Basin in the fall, and across the Reno Pass to Phoenix and Maricopa.

Ellen could not discover a fence post on the ranch, nor a piece of salt for the horses and cattle, nor a wagon, nor any sign of a sheep-shearing outfit. She had never seen any sheep sheared. Ellen could never keep track of the many and different horses running loose and hobbled round the ranch. There were droves of horses in the woods, and some of them wild as deer. According to her long-established understanding, her father and her uncles were keen on horse trading and buying.

Then the many trails leading away from the Jorth ranch—these grew to have a fascination for Ellen; and the time came when she rode out on them to see for herself where they led. The sheep ranch of Daggs, sup-posed to be only a few miles across the ridges, down in Bear Cañon, never materialized at all for Ellen. This circumstance so interested her that she went up to see her friend Sprague and got him to direct her to Bear Cañon, so that she would be sure not to miss it. And she rode from the narrow, maple-thicketed head of it near the Rim down all its length. She found no ranch, no cabin, not even a corral in Bear Cañon. Sprague said there was only one cañon by that name. Daggs had assured her of the exact location on his place, and so had her father. Had they lied? Were they mistaken in the cañon? There were many cañons, all heading up near the Rim, all running and widening down for miles through the wooded mountain, and vastly different from the deep, short, yellow-walled gorges that cut into the Rim from the Basin side. Ellen investi-gated the cañons within six or eight miles of her home, both to east and to west. All she discovered was a couple of old log cabins, long deserted. Still, she did not follow out all the trails to their ends. Several of them led far into the deepest, roughest, wildest brakes of gorge and thicket that she had seen. No cattle or sheep had ever been driven over these trails.

This riding around of Ellen's at length got to her father's ears. Ellen expected that a bitter quarrel would ensue, for she certainly would refuse to be confined to the camp; but her father only asked her to limit her riding to the meadow valley, and straightway forgot all about it. In fact, his abstraction one moment, his intense nervousness the next, his harder drinking and fiercer harangues with the men, grew to be distressing for Ellen. They presaged his further deterioration and the ever-present evil of the growing feud.

One day Jorth rode home in the early morning, after an absence of two nights. Ellen heard the clip-clop of horses long before she saw them.

"Hey, Ellen! Come out heah," called her father.

Ellen left her work and went outside. A stranger had ridden in with her father, a young giant whose sharp-featured face appeared marked by ferret-like eyes and a fine, light, fuzzy beard. He was long, loose jointed, not heavy of build, and he had the largest hands and feet Ellen had ever seen. Next Ellen espied a black horse they had evidently brought with them. Her father was holding a rope halter. At once the black horse struck Ellen as being a beauty and a thoroughbred.

"Ellen, heah's a horse for you," said Jorth with something of pride. "I made a trade. Reckon I wanted him myself, but he's too gentle for me an' maybe a little small for my weight."

Delight visited Ellen for the first time in many days. Seldom had she owned a good horse, and never one like this.

"Oh, dad!" she exclaimed, in her gratitude.

"Shore he's yours on one condition," said her father.

"What's that?" asked Ellen, as she laid caressing hands on the restless horse.

"You're not to ride him out of the cañon."

"Agreed. . . . All daid black, isn't he, except that white face? What's his name, dad?"

"I forgot to ask," replied Jorth, as he began unsaddling his own horse. "Slater, what's this heah black's name?"

The lanky giant grinned. "I reckon it was Spades."

"Spades?" ejaculated Ellen, blankly. "What a name! . . . Well, I guess it's as good as any. He's shore black."

"Ellen, keep him hobbled when you're not ridin' him," was her father's parting advice as he walked off with the stranger.

Spades was wet and dusty and his satiny skin quivered. He had fine, dark, intelligent eyes that watched Ellen's every move. She knew how her father and his friends dragged and jammed horses through the woods and over the rough trails. It did not take her long to discover that this horse had been a pet. Ellen cleaned his coat and brushed him and fed him. Then she fitted her bridle to suit his head and saddled him. His evident response to her kindness assured her that he was gentle, so she mounted and rode him, to discover he had the easiest gait she had ever experienced. He walked and trotted to suit her will, but when left to choose his own gait he fell into a graceful little pace that was very easy for her. He appeared quite ready to break into a run at her slightest bidding, but Ellen satisfied herself on this first ride with his slower gaits.

"Spades, y'u've shore cut out my burro Jinny," said Ellen, regretfully. "Well, I reckon women are fickle."

Next day she rode up the cañon to show Spades to her friend John Sprague. The old burro breeder was not at home. As his door was open, however, and a fire smoldering, Ellen concluded he would soon return. So she waited. Dismounting, she left Spades free to graze on the new green grass that carpeted the ground. The cabin and little level clearing accentuated the loneliness and wildness of the forest. Ellen always liked it here and had once been in the habit of visiting the old man often. But of late she had stayed away, for the reason that Sprague's talk and his news and his poorly hidden pity depressed her.

Presently she heard hoof beats on the hard, packed trail leading down the cañon in the direction from which she had come. Scarcely likely was it that Sprague should return from this direction. Ellen thought her father had sent one of the herders for her. But when she caught a glimpse of the approaching horseman, down in the aspens, she failed to recognize him. After he had passed one of the openings she heard his horse stop. Probably the man had seen her; at least she could not otherwise account for his stopping. The glimpse she had of him had given her the impression that he was bending over, peering ahead in the trail, looking for tracks. Then she heard the rider come on again, more slowly this time. At length the horse trotted out into the opening, to be hauled up short. Ellen recognized the buckskin-clad figure, the broad shoulders, the dark face of Jean Isbel.

Ellen felt prey to the strangest quaking sensation she had ever suffered. It took violence of her new-born spirit to subdue that feeling.

Isbel rode slowly across the clearing toward her. For Ellen his approach seemed singularly swift—so swift that her surprise, dismay, conjecture, and anger obstructed her will. The outwardly calm and cold Ellen Jorth was a travesty that mocked her—that she felt he would discern.

The moment Isbel drew close enough for Ellen to see his face she experienced a strong, shuddering repetition of her first shock of recognition. He was not the same. The light, the youth was gone. This, however, did not cause her emotion. Was it not a sudden transition of her nature to the dominance of hate? Ellen seemed to feel the shadow of her unknown self standing with her.

Isbel halted his horse. Ellen had been standing near the trunk of a fallen pine and she instinctively backed against it. How her legs trembled! Isbel took off his cap and crushed it nervously in his bare, brown hand.

"Good mornin', Miss Ellen!" he said.

Ellen did not return his greeting, but queried, almost breathlessly, "Did y'u come by our ranch?"

"No. I circled," he replied.

"Jean Isbel! What do y'u want heah?" she demanded.

"Don't you know?" he returned. His eyes were intensely black and piercing. They seemed to search Ellen's very soul. To meet their gaze was an ordeal that only her rousing fury sustained.

Ellen felt on her lips a scornful allusion to his half-breed Indian traits and the reputation that had preceded him. But she could not utter it.

"No" she replied.

"It's hard to call a woman a liar," he returned, bitterly. "But you must be—seein' you're a Jorth."

"Liar! Not to y'u, Jean Isbel," she retorted. "I'd not lie to y'u to save my life."

He studied her with keen, sober, moody intent. The dark fire of his eyes thrilled her.

"If that's true, I'm glad," he said.

"Shore it's true. I've no idea why y'u came heah."

Ellen did have a dawning idea that she could not force into oblivion. But if she ever admitted it to her consciousness, she must fail in the contempt and scorn and fearlessness she chose to throw in this man's face.

"Does old Sprague live here?" asked Isbel.

"Yes. I expect him back soon. . . . Did y'u come to see him?"

"No. . . . Did Sprague tell you anythin' about the row he saw me in?"

"He—did not," replied Ellen, lying with stiff lips. She who had sworn she could not lie! She felt the hot blood leaving her heart, mounting in a wave. All her conscious will seemed impelled to deceive. What had she to hide from Jean Isbel? And a still, small voice replied that she had to hide the Ellen Jorth who had waited for him that day, who had spied upon him, who had treasured a gift she could not destroy, who had hugged to her miserable heart the fact that he had fought for her name.

"I'm glad of that," Isbel was saying, thoughtfully.

"Did you come heah to see me?" interrupted Ellen. She felt that she could not endure this reiterated suggestion of fineness, of consideration in him. She would betray herself—betray what she did not even realize herself. She must force other footing—and that should be the one of strife between the Jorths and Isbels.

"No—honest. I didn't, Miss Ellen," he rejoined, humbly. "I'll tell you, presently, why I came. But it wasn't to see you. . . . I don't deny I wanted . . . but that's no matter. You didn't meet me that day on the Rim."

"Meet y'u!" she echoed, coldly. "Shore y'u never expected me?"

"Somehow I did," he replied, with those penetrating eyes on her. "I put somethin' in your tent that day. Did you find it?"

"Yes," she replied, with the same casual coldness.

"What did you do with it?"

"I kicked it out, of course," she replied.

She saw him flinch.

"And you never opened it?"

"Certainly not," she retorted, as if forced. "Doon't y'u know anythin' about—about people? . . . Shore even if y'u are an Isbel y'u never were born in Texas."

"Thank God I wasn't!" he replied. "I was born in a beautiful country of green meadows and deep forests and white rivers, not in a barren desert where men live dry and hard as the cactus. Where I come from men don't live on hate. They can forgive."

"Forgive! . . . Could y'u forgive a Jorth?"

"Yes, I could."

"Shore that's easy to say—with the wrongs all on your side," she declared, bitterly.

"Ellen Jorth, the first wrong was on your side," retorted Jean, his voice full. "Your father stole my father's sweetheart—by lies, by slander, by dishonor, by makin' terrible love to her in his absence."

"It's a lie," cried Ellen, passionately.

"It is not," he declared, solemnly.

"Jean Isbel, I say y'u lie!"

"No! *I* say you've been lied to," he thundered.

The tremendous force of his spirit seemed to fling truth at Ellen. It weakened her.

"But—mother loved dad—best."

"Yes, afterward. No wonder, poor woman! . . . But it was the action of your father and your mother that ruined all these lives. You've got to know the truth, Ellen Jorth. . . . All the years of hate have borne their fruit. God Almighty can never save us now. Blood must be spilled. The Jorths and the Isbels can't live on the same earth. . . . And you've got to know the truth because the worst of this hell falls on you and me."

The hate that he spoke of alone upheld her.

"Never, Jean Isbel!" she cried. "I'll never know truth from y'u. . . . I'll never share anythin' with y'u—not even hell."

Isbel dismounted and stood before her, still holding his bridle reins. The bay horse champed his bit and tossed his head.

"Why do you hate me so?" he asked. "I just happen to be my father's son. I never harmed you or any of your people. I met you . . . fell in love with you in a flash—though I never knew it till after. . . . Why do you hate me so terribly?"

Ellen felt a heavy, stifling pressure within her breast. "Y'u're an Isbel. . . . Doon't speak of love to me."

"I didn't intend to. But your—your hate seems unnatural. And we'll probably never meet again. . . . I can't help it. I love you. Love at first sight! Jean Isbel and Ellen Jorth! Strange, isn't it? . . . It was all so strange. My meetin' you so lonely and unhappy, my seein' you so sweet and beautiful, my thinkin' you so good in spite of—"

"Shore it was strange," interrupted Ellen, with scornful laugh. She had found her defense. In hurting him she could hide her own hurt. "Thinking me so good in spite of—Ha-ha! And I said I'd been kissed before!"

"Yes, in spite of everything," he said.

Ellen could not look at him as he loomed over her. She felt a wild tumult in her heart. All that crowded to her lips for utterance was false.

"Yes—kissed before I met you—and since," she said, mockingly. "And I laugh at what y'u call love, Jean Isbel."

"Laugh if you want—but believe it was sweet, honorable—the best in me," he replied, in deep earnestness.

"Bah!" cried Ellen, with all the force of her pain and shame and hate.

"By Heaven, you must be different from what I thought!" exclaimed Isbel, huskily.

"Shore if I wasn't, I'd make myself. . . . Now, Mister Jean Isbel, get on your horse an' go!"

Something of composure came to Ellen with these words of dismissal, and she glanced up at him with half-veiled eyes. His changed aspect prepared her for some blow.

"That's a pretty black horse."

"Yes," replied Ellen, blankly.

"Do you like him?"

"I—I love him."

"All right, I'll give him to you then. He'll have less work and kinder treatment than if I used him. I've got some pretty hard rides ahead of me."

"Y'u—y'u give—" whispered Ellen, slowly stiffening.

"Yes. He's mine," replied Isbel. With that he turned to whistle. Spades threw up his head, snorted, and started forward at a trot. He came faster the closer he got, and if ever Ellen saw the joy of a horse at sight of a beloved master she saw it then. Isbel laid a hand on the animal's neck and caressed him, then, turning back to Ellen, he went on speaking: "I picked him from a lot of fine horses of my father's. We got along well. My sister Ann rode him a good deal. . . . He was stolen from our pasture day before yesterday. I took his trail and tracked him up here. Never lost his trail till I got to your ranch, where I had to circle till I picked it up again."

"Stolen—pasture—tracked him up heah?" echoed Ellen without any evidence of emotion whatever. Indeed, she seemed to have been turned to stone.

"Trackin' him was easy. I wish for your sake it'd been impossible," he said, bluntly.

"For my sake?" she echoed, in precisely the same tone.

Manifestly that tone irritated Isbel, beyond control. He misunderstood it. With a hand far from gentle he pushed her bent head back so he could look into her face.

"Yes, for your sake!" he declared, harshly. "Haven't you sense enough to see that? . . . What kind of a game do you think you can play with me?"

"Game! . . . Game of what?" she asked.

"Why, a—a game of ignorance—innocence—any old game to fool a man who's tryin' to be decent."

This time Ellen mutely looked her dull, blank questioning. And it inflamed Isbel.

"You know your father's a horse thief!" he thundered.

Outwardly Ellen remained the same. She had been prepared for an unknown and a terrible blow. It had fallen. And her face, her body, her hands, locked with the supreme fortitude of pride and sustained by hate, gave no betrayal of the crashing, thundering ruin within her mind and soul. Motionless she leaned there, meeting the piercing fire of Isbel's eyes, seeing in them a righteous and terrible scorn. In one flash the naked truth seemed blazed at her. The faith she had fostered died a sudden death. A thousand perplexing problems were solved in a second of whirling, revealing thought.

"Ellen Jorth, you know your father's in with this Hash Knife Gang of rustlers," thundered Isbel.

"Shore," she replied, with the cool, easy, careless defiance of a Texan.

"You know he's got this Daggs to lead his faction against the Isbels?"

"Shore."

"You know this talk of sheepmen buckin' the cattlemen is all a blind?"

"Shore," reiterated Ellen.

Isbel gazed darkly down upon her. With his anger spent for the moment, he appeared ready to end the interview. But he seemed fascinated by the strange look of her, by the incomprehensible something she emanated. Havoc gleamed in his pale, set face. He shook his dark head and his broad hand went to his breast.

"To think I fell in love with such as you!" he exclaimed, and his other hand swept out in a tragic gesture of helpless pathos and impotence.

The hell Isbel had hinted at now possessed Ellen—body, mind, and soul. Disgraced, scorned by an Isbel! Yet loved by him! In that divination there flamed up a wild, fierce passion to hurt, to rend, to flay, to fling back upon him a stinging agony. Her thought flew upon her like whips. Pride of the Jorths! Pride of the old Texan blue blood! It lay dead at her feet, killed by the scornful words of the last of that family to whom she owed her degradation. Daughter of a horse thief and rustler! Dark and evil and grim set the forces within her, accepting her fate, damning her enemies, true to the blood of the Jorths. The sins of the father must be visited upon the daughter.

"Shore y'u might have had me—that day on the Rim—if y'u hadn't told your name," she said, mockingly, and she gazed into his eyes with all the mystery of a woman's nature.

Isbel's powerful frame shook as with an ague. "Girl, what do you mean?"

"Shore, I'd have been plumb fond of havin' y'u make up to me," she drawled. It possessed her now with irresistible power, this fact of the love he could not help. Some fiendish woman's satisfaction dwelt in her consciousness of her power to kill the noble, the faithful, the good in him.

"Ellen Jorth, you lie!" he burst out, hoarsely.

"Jean, shore I'd been a toy and a rag for these rustlers long enough. I was tired of them. . . . I wanted a new lover. . . . And if y'u hadn't give yourself away—"

Isbel moved so swiftly that she did not realize his intention until his hard hand smote her mouth. Instantly she tasted the hot, salty blood from a cut lip.

"Shut up, you hussy!" he ordered, roughly. "Have you no shame? . . . My sister Ann spoke well of you. She made excuses—she pitied you."

That for Ellen seemed the culminating blow under which she almost sank. But one moment longer could she maintain this unnatural and terrible poise.

"Jean Isbel—go along with y'u," she said, impatiently. "I'm waiting heah for Simm Bruce!"

At last it was as if she struck his heart. Because of doubt of himself and a stubborn faith in her, his passion and jealousy were not proof against this last stab. Instinctive subtlety inherent in Ellen had prompted the speech that tortured Isbel. How the shock to him rebounded on her! She gasped as he lunged for her, too swift for her to move a hand. One arm crushed round her like a steel band; the other, hard across her breast and neck, forced her head back. Then she tried to wrestle away. But she was utterly powerless. His dark face bent down closer and closer. Suddenly Ellen ceased trying to struggle. She was like a stricken creature paralyzed by the piercing, hypnotic eyes of a snake. Yet in spite of her terror, if he meant death by her, she welcomed it.

"Ellen Jorth, I'm thinkin' yet—you lie!" he said, low and tense between his teeth.

"No! No!" she screamed, wildly. Her nerve broke there. She could no longer meet those terrible black eyes. Her passionate denial was not only the last of her shameful deceit; it was the woman of her, repudiating herself and him, and all this sickening, miserable situation.

Isbel took her literally. She had convinced him. And the instant held blank horror for Ellen.

"By God—then I'll have somethin'—of you anyway!" muttered Isbel, thickly.

Ellen saw the blood bulge in his powerful neck. She saw his dark, hard face, strange now, fearful to behold, come lower and lower, till it blurred and obstructed her gaze. She felt the swell and ripple and stretch—then the bind of his muscles, like huge coils of elastic rope. Then with savage rude force his mouth closed on hers. All Ellen's senses reeled, as if she were swooning. She was suffocating. The spasm passed, and a bursting spurt of blood revived her to acute and terrible consciousness. For the endless period of one moment he held her so that her breast seemed crushed. His kisses burned and bruised her lips. And then, shifting violently to her neck, they pressed so hard that she choked under them. It was as if a huge bat had fastened upon her throat.

Suddenly the remorseless binding embraces—the hot and savage kisses—fell away from her. Isbel had let go. She saw him throw up his hands, and stagger back a little, all the while with his piercing gaze on her. His face had been dark purple: now it was white.

"No—Ellen Jorth," he panted, "I don't—want any of you—that way." And suddenly he sank on the log and covered his face with his hands. "What I loved in you—was what I thought—you were."

Like a wildcat Ellen sprang upon him, beating him with her fists, tearing at his hair, scratching his face, in a blind fury. Isbel made no move to stop her, and her violence spent itself with her strength. She swayed back from him, shaking so that she could scarcely stand.

"Y'u—damned—Isbel!" she gasped, with hoarse passion. "Y'u insulted me!"

"Insulted you? . . ." laughed Isbel, in bitter scorn. "It couldn't be done."

"Oh! . . . I'll *kill* y'u!" she hissed.

Isbel stood up and wiped the red scratches on his face. "Go ahead. There's my gun," he said, pointing to his saddle sheath. "Somebody's got to begin this Jorth-Isbel feud. It'll be a dirty business. I'm sick of it already. . . . Kill me! . . . First blood for Ellen Jorth!"

Suddenly the dark grim tide that had seemed to engulf Ellen's very soul cooled and receded, leaving her without its false strength. She began to sag. She stared at Isbel's gun. "Kill him," whispered the retreating voices of her hate. But she was as powerless as if she were still held in Jean Isbel's giant embrace.

"I—I want to—kill y'u," she whispered, "but I cain't. . . . Leave me."

"You're no Jorth—the same as I'm no Isbel. We oughtn't be mixed in this deal," he said, somberly. "I'm sorrier for you than I am for myself. . . . You're a girl. . . . You once had a good mother—a decent home. And this life you've led here—mean as it's been—is nothin' to what you'll face now. Damn the men that brought you to this! I'm goin' to kill some of them."

With that he mounted and turned away. Ellen called out for him to take his horse. He did not stop nor look back. She called again, but her voice was fainter, and Isbel was now leaving at a trot. Slowly she sagged against the tree, lower and lower. He headed into the trail leading up the cañon. How strange a relief Ellen felt! She watched him ride into the aspens and start up the slope, at last to disappear in the pines. It seemed at the moment that he took with him something which had been hers. A pain in her head dulled the thoughts that wavered to and fro. After he had gone she could not see so well. Her eyes were tired. What had happened to her? There was blood on her hands. Isbel's blood! She shuddered. Was it an omen? Low she sank against the tree and closed her eyes.

Old John Sprague did not return. Hours dragged by—dark hours for Ellen Jorth lying prostrate beside the tree, hiding the blue sky and golden sunlight from her eyes. At length the lethargy of despair, the black dull misery wore away; and she gradually returned to a condition of coherent thought.

What had she learned? Sight of the black horse grazing near seemed to prompt the trenchant replies. Spades belonged to Jean Isbel. He had been stolen by her father or by one of her father's accomplices. Isbel's vaunted cunning as a tracker had been no idle boast. Her father was a horse thief, a rustler, a sheepman only as a blind, a consort of Daggs, leader of the Hash Knife Gang. Ellen well remembered the ill repute of that gang, way back in Texas, years ago. Her father had gotten in with this famous band of rustlers to serve his own ends—the extermination of the Isbels. It was all very plain now to Ellen.

"Daughter of a horse thief an' rustler!" she muttered.

And her thoughts sped back to the days of her girlhood. Only the very early stage of that time had been happy. In the light of Isbel's revelation the many changes of residence, the sudden moves to unsettled parts of Texas, the periods of poverty and sudden prosperity, all leading to the final journey to this God-forsaken Arizona—these were now seen in their true significance. As far back as she could remember her father had been a crooked man. And her mother had known it. He had dragged her to her ruin. That degradation had killed her. Ellen realized that with poignant sorrow, with a sudden revolt against her father. Had Gaston Isbel truly and dishonestly started her father on his downhill road? Ellen wondered. She hated the Isbels with unutterable and growing hate, yet she had it in her to think, to ponder, to weigh judgments in their behalf. She owed it to something in herself to be fair. But what did it matter who was to blame for the Jorth-Isbel feud? Somehow Ellen was forced to confess that deep in her soul it mattered terribly. To be true to herself—the self that she alone knew—she must have right on her side. If the Jorths were guilty, and she clung to them and their creed, then she would be one of them.

"But I'm not," she mused, aloud. "My name's Jorth, an' I reckon I have bad blood. . . . But it never came out in me till to-day. I've been honest. I've been good—yes, *good*, as my mother taught me to be—in spite of all. . . . Shore my pride made me a fool. . . . An' now have I any choice to make? I'm a Jorth. I must stick to my father."

All this summing up, however, did not wholly account for the pang in her breast.

What had she done that day? And the answer beat in her ears like a great throbbing hammer-stroke. In an agony of shame, in the throes of hate, she had perjured herself. She had sworn away her honor. She had basely made herself vile. She had struck ruthlessly at the great heart of a man who loved her. Ah! That thrust had rebounded to leave this dreadful pang in her breast. Loved her? Yes, the strange truth, the insupportable truth! She had to contend now, not with her father and her disgrace, not with the baffling presence of Jean Isbel, but with the mysteries of her own soul. Wonder of all wonders was it that such love had been born for her. Shame worse than all other shame was it that she should kill it by a poisoned lie. By what monstrous motive had she done that? To sting Isbel as he had stung her! But that had been base. Never could she have stooped so low except in a moment of tremendous tumult. If she had done sore injury to Isbel what had she done to herself? How strange, how tenacious had been his faith in her honor! Could she ever forget? She must forget it. But she could never forget the way he had scorned those vile men in Greaves's store—the way he had beaten Bruce for defiling her name—the way he had stubbornly denied her own insinuations. She was a woman now. She had learned something of the complexity of a woman's heart. She could not change nature. And all her passionate being thrilled to the manhood of her defender. But even while she thrilled she acknowledged her hate. It was the contention between the two that caused the pang in her breast. "An' now what's left for me?" murmured Ellen. She did not analyze the significance of what had prompted that query. The most incalculable of the day's disclosures was the wrong she had done herself. "Shore I'm done for, one way or another. . . . I must stick to Dad. . . . or kill myself?"

Ellen rode Spades back to the ranch. She rode like the wind. When she swung out of the trail into the open meadow in plain sight of the ranch her appearance created a commotion among the loungers before the cabin. She rode Spades at a full run.

"Who's after you?" yelled her father, as she pulled the black to a halt. Jorth held a rifle. Daggs, Colter, the other Jorths were there, likewise armed, and all watchful, strung with expectancy.

"Shore nobody's after me," replied Ellen. "Cain't I run a horse round heah without being chased?"

Jorth appeared both incensed and relieved.

"Hah! . . . What you mean, girl, runnin' like a streak right down on us? You're actin' queer these days, an' you look queer. I'm not likin' it."

"Reckon these are queer times—for the Jorths," replied Ellen, sarcastically.

"Daggs found strange horse tracks crossin' the meadow," said her father. "An' that worried us. Some one's been snoopin' round the ranch. An' when we seen you runnin' so wild we shore thought you was bein' chased."

"No. I was only trying out Spades to see how fast he could run," returned Ellen. "Reckon when we do get chased it'll take some running to catch me."

"Haw! Haw!" roared Daggs. "It shore will, Ellen."

"Girl, it's not only your runnin' an' your looks that's queer," declared Jorth, in dark perplexity. "You talk queer."

"Shore, dad, y'u're not used to hearing spades called spades," said Ellen, as she dismounted.

"Humph!" ejaculated her father, as if convinced of the uselessness of trying to understand a woman. "Say, did you see any strange horse tracks?"

"I reckon I did. And I know who made them."

Jorth stiffened. All the men behind him showed a sudden intensity of suspense.

"Who?" demanded Jorth.

"Shore it was Jean Isbel," replied Ellen, coolly. "He came up heah tracking his black horse."

"Jean—Isbel—trackin'—his—black horse," repeated her father.

"Yes. He's not overrated as a tracker, that's shore."

Blank silence ensued. Ellen cast a slow glance over her father and the others, then she began to loosen the cinches of her saddle. Presently Jorth burst the silence with a curse, and Daggs followed with one of his sardonic laughs.

"Wal, boss, what did I tell you?" he drawled.

Jorth strode to Ellen, and, whirling her around with a strong hand, he held her facing him.

"Did y'u see Isbel?"

"Yes," replied Ellen, just as sharply as her father had asked.

"Did y'u talk to him?"

"Yes."

"What did he want up heah?"

"I told y'u. He was tracking the black horse y'u stole."

Jorth's hand and arm dropped limply. His sallow face turned a livid hue. Amaze merged into discomfiture and that gave place to rage. He raised a hand as if to strike Ellen. And suddenly Daggs's long arm shot out to clutch Jorth's wrist. Wrestling to free himself, Jorth cursed under his breath. "Let go, Daggs," he shouted, stridently. "Am I drunk that you grab me?"

"Wal, y'u ain't drunk, I reckon," replied the rustler, with sarcasm. "But y'u're shore some things I'll reserve for your private ear."

Jorth gained a semblance of composure. But it was evident that he labored under a shock.

"Ellen, did Jean Isbel see this black horse?"

"Yes. He asked me how I got Spades an' I told him."

"Did he say Spades belonged to him?"

"Shore I reckon he proved it. Y'u can always tell a horse that loves its master."

"Did y'u offer to give Spades back?"

"Yes. But Isbel wouldn't take him."

"Hah! . . . An' why not?"

"He said he'd rather I kept him. He was about to engage in a dirty, blood-spilling deal, an' he reckoned he'd not be able to care for a fine horse. . . . I didn't want Spades. I tried to make Isbel take him. But he rode off. . . . And that's all there is to that."

"Maybe it's not," replied Jorth, chewing his mustache and eying Ellen with dark, intent gaze. "Y'u've met this Isbel twice."

"It wasn't any fault of mine," retorted Ellen.

"I heah he's sweet on y'u. How aboot that?"

Ellen smarted under the blaze of blood that swept to neck and cheek and temple. But it was only memory which fired this shame. What her father and his crowd might think were matters of supreme indifference. Yet she met his suspicious gaze with truthful blazing eyes.

"I heah talk from Bruce an' Lorenzo," went on her father. "An' Daggs heah—"

"Daggs nothin'!" interrupted that worthy. "Don't fetch me in. I said nothin' an' I think nothin'.'"

"Yes, Jean Isbel *was* sweet on me, dad . . . but he will never be again," returned Ellen, in low tones. With that she pulled her saddle off Spades and, throwing it over her shoulder, she walked off to her cabin.

Hardly had she gotten indoors when her father entered.

"Ellen, I didn't know that horse belonged to Isbel," he began, in the swift, hoarse, persuasive voice so familiar to Ellen. "I swear I didn't. I bought him—traded with Slater for him. . . . Honest to God, I never had any idea he was stolen! . . . Why, when y'u said 'that horse y'u stole,' I felt as if y'u'd knifed me. . . ."

Ellen sat at the table and listened while her father paced to and fro and, by his restless action and passionate speech, worked himself into a frenzy. He talked incessantly, as if her silence was condemnatory and as if eloquence alone could convince her of his honesty. It seemed that Ellen saw and heard with keener faculties than ever before. He had a terrible thirst for her respect. Not so much for her love, she divined, but that she would not see how he had fallen!

She pitied him with all her heart. She was all he had, as he was all the world to her. And so, as she gave ear to his long, illogical rigmarole of argument and defense, she slowly found that her pity and her love were making vital decisions for her. As of old, in poignant moments, her father lapsed at last into a denunciation of the Isbels and what they had brought him to. His sufferings were real, at least, in Ellen's presence. She was the only link that bound him to long-past happier times. She was her mother over again—the woman who had betrayed another man for him and gone with him to her ruin and death.

"Dad, don't go on so," said Ellen, breaking in upon her father's rant. "I will be true to y'u—as my mother was. . . . I am a Jorth. Your place is my place—your fight is my fight. . . . Never speak of the past to me again. If God spares us through this feud we will go away and begin all over again, far off where no one ever heard of a Jorth. . . . If we're not spared we'll at least have had our whack at these damned Isbels."

CHAPTER 7

During June Jean Isbel did not ride far away from Grass Valley. Another attempt had been made upon Gaston Isbel's life. Another cowardly shot had been fired from ambush, this time from a pine thicket bordering the trail that led to Blaisdell's ranch. Blaisdell heard this shot, so near his home was it fired. No trace of the hidden foe could be found. The ground all around that vicinity bore a carpet of pine needles which showed no trace of footprints. The supposition was that this cowardly attempt had been perpetrated, or certainly instigated, by the Jorths. But there was no proof. And Gaston Isbel had other enemies in the Tonto Basin besides the sheep clan. The old man raged like a lion about this sneaking attack on him. And his friend Blaisdell urged an immediate gathering of their kin and friends. "Let's quit ranchin' till this trouble's settled," he declared. "Let's arm an' ride the trails an' meet these men half-way. . . . It won't help our side any to wait till you're shot in the back." More than one of Isbel's supporters offered the same advice.

"No; we'll wait till we know for shore," was the stubborn cattleman's reply to all these promptings.

"Know! Wal, hell! Didn't Jean find the black hoss up at Jorth's ranch?" demanded Blaisdell. "What more do we want?"

"Jean couldn't swear Jorth stole the black."

"Wal, by thunder, I can swear to it!" growled Blaisdell.

"An' we're losin' cattle all the time. Who's stealin' 'em?"

"We've always lost cattle ever since we started ranchin' heah."

"Gas, I reckon y'u want Jorth to start this fight in the open."

"It'll start soon enough," was Isbel's gloomy reply.

Jean had not failed altogether in his tracking of lost or stolen cattle. Circumstances had been against him, and there was something baffling about this rustling. The summer storms set in early, and it had been his luck to have heavy rains wash out fresh tracks that he might have followed. The range was large and cattle were everywhere. Sometimes a loss was not discovered for weeks. Gaston Isbel's sons were now the only men left to ride the range. Two of his riders had quit because of the threatened war, and Isbel had let another go. So that Jean did not often learn that cattle had been stolen until their tracks were old. Added to that was the fact that this Grass Valley country was covered with horse tracks and cattle tracks. The rustlers, whoever they were, had long been at the game, and now that there was reason for them to show their cunning they did it.

Early in July the hot weather came. Down on the red ridges of the Tonto it was hot desert. The nights were cool, the early mornings were pleasant, but the day was something to endure. When the white cumulus clouds rolled up out of the southwest, growing larger and thicker and darker, here and there coalescing into a black thundercloud, Jean welcomed them. He liked to see the gray streamers of rain hanging down from a canopy of black, and the roar of rain on the trees as it approached like a trampling army was always welcome. The grassy flats, the red ridges, the rocky slopes, the thickets of manzanita and scrub oak and cactus were dusty, glaring, throat-parching places under the hot summer sun. Jean longed for the cool heights of the Rim, the shady pines, the dark sweet verdure under the silver spruces, the tinkle and murmur of the clear rills. He often had another longing, too, which he bitterly stifled.

Jean's ally, the keen-nosed shepherd dog, had disappeared one day, and had never returned. Among men at the ranch there was a difference of opinion as to what had happened to Shepp. The old rancher thought he had been poisoned or shot; Bill and Guy Isbel believed he had been stolen by sheep herders, who were always stealing dogs; and Jean inclined to the conviction that Shepp had gone off with the timber wolves. The fact was that Shepp did not return, and Jean missed him.

One morning at dawn Jean heard the cattle bellowing and trampling out in the valley; and upon hurrying to a vantage point he was amazed to see upward of five hundred steers chasing a lone wolf. Jean's father had seen such a spectacle as this, but it was a new one for Jean. The wolf was a big gray and black fellow, rangy and powerful, and until he got the steers all behind him he was rather hard put to it to keep out of their way. Probably he had dogged the herd, trying to sneak in and pull down a yearling, and finally the steers had charged him. Jean kept along the edge of the valley in the hope they would chase him within range of a rifle. But the wary wolf saw Jean and sheered off, gradually drawing away from his pursuers.

Jean returned to the house for his breakfast, and then set off across the valley. His father owned one small flock of sheep that had not yet been driven up on the Rim, where all the sheep in the country were run during the hot, dry summer down on the Tonto. Young Evarts and a Mexican boy named Bernardino had charge of this flock. The regular Mexican herder, a man of experience, had given up his job; and these boys were not equal to the task of risking the sheep up in the enemies' stronghold.

This flock was known to be grazing in a side draw, well up from Grass Valley, where the brush afforded some protection from the sun, and there was good water and a little feed. Before Jean reached his destination he heard a shot. It was not a rifle shot, which fact caused Jean a little concern. Evarts and Bernardino had rifles, but, to his knowledge, no small arms. Jean rode up on one of the black-brushed conical hills that rose on the south side of Grass Valley, and from there he took a sharp survey of the country. At first he made out only cattle, and bare meadowland, and the low encircling ridges and hills. But presently up toward the head of the valley he descried a bunch of horsemen riding toward the village. He could not tell their number. That dark moving mass seemed to Jean to be instinct with life, mystery, menace. Who were they? It was too far for him to recognize horses, let alone riders. They were moving fast, too.

Jean watched them out of sight, then turned his horse downhill again, and rode on his quest. A number of horsemen like that was a very unusual sight around Grass Valley at any time. What then did it portend now? Jean experienced a little shock of uneasy dread that was a new sensation for him. Brooding over this he proceeded on his way, at length to turn into the draw where the camp of the sheep herders was located. Upon coming in sight of it he heard a hoarse shout. Young Evarts appeared running frantically out of the brush. Jean urged his horse into a run and soon covered the distance between them. Evarts appeared beside himself with terror.

"Boy! what's the matter?" queried Jean, as he dismounted, rifle in hand, peering quickly from Evarts's white face to the camp, and all around.

"Ber-nardino! Ber-nardino!" gasped the boy, wringing his hands and pointing.

Jean ran the few remaining rods to the sheep camp. He saw the little teepee, a burned-out fire, a half-finished meal—and then the Mexican lad lying prone on the ground, dead, with a bullet hole in his ghastly face. Near him lay an old six-shooter.

"Whose gun is that?" demanded Jean, as he picked it up.

"Ber-nardino's," replied Evarts, huskily. "He—he jest got it—the other day."

"Did he shoot himself accidentally?"

"Oh no! No! He didn't do it—at all."

"Who did, then?"

"The men—they rode up—a gang—they did it," panted Evarts.

"Did you know who they were?"

"No. I couldn't tell. I saw them comin' an' I was skeered. Bernardino had gone fer water. I run an' hid in the brush. I wanted to yell, but they come too close. . . . Then I heerd them talkin'. Bernardino come back. They 'peared friendly-like. Thet made me raise up to look. An' I couldn't see good. I heerd one of them ask Bernardino to let him see his gun. An' Bernardino handed it over. He looked at the gun an' haw-hawed, an' flipped it up in the air, an' when it fell back in his hand it—it went off bang! . . . An' Bernardino dropped. . . . I hid down close. I was skeered stiff. I heerd them talk more, but not what they said. Then they rode away. . . . An' I hid there till I seen y'u comin'."

"Have you got a horse?" queried Jean, sharply.

"No. But I can ride one of Bernardino's burros."

"Get one. Hurry over to Blaisdell. Tell him to send word to Blue and Gordon and Fredericks to ride like the devil to my father's ranch. Hurry now!"

Young Evarts ran off without reply. Jean stood looking down at the limp and pathetic figure of the Mexican boy. "By Heaven!" he exclaimed, grimly, "the Jorth-Isbel war is on! . . . Deliberate, cold-blooded murder! I'll gamble Daggs did this job. He's been given the leadership. He's started it. . . . Bernardino, greaser or not, you were a faithful lad, and you won't go long unavenged."

Jean had no time to spare. Tearing a tarpaulin out of the teepee he covered the lad with it and then ran for his horse. Mounting, he galloped down the draw, over the little red ridges, out into the valley, where he put his horse to a run.

Action changed the sickening horror that sight of Bernardino had engendered. Jean even felt a strange, grim relief. The long, dragging days of waiting were over. Jorth's gang had taken the initiative. Blood had begun to flow. And it would continue to flow now till the last man of one faction stood over the dead body of the last man of the other. Would it be a Jorth or an Isbel? "My instinct was right," he muttered, aloud. "That bunch of horses gave me a queer feelin'." Jean gazed all around the grassy, cattle-dotted valley he was crossing so swiftly, and toward the village, but he did not see any sign of the dark group of riders. They had gone on to Greaves's store, there, no doubt, to drink and to add more enemies of the Isbels to their gang. Suddenly across Jean's mind flashed a thought of Ellen Jorth. "What 'll become of her? . . . What 'll become of all the women? My sister? . . . The little ones?"

No one was in sight around the ranch. Never had it appeared more peaceful and pastoral to Jean. The grazing cattle and horses in the foreground, the haystack half eaten away, the cows in the fenced pasture, the column of blue smoke lazily ascending, the cackle of hens, the solid, well-built cabins—all these seemed to repudiate Jean's haste and his darkness of mind. This place was his father's farm. There was not a cloud in the blue, summer sky.

As Jean galloped up the lane some one saw him from the door, and then Bill and Guy and their gray-headed father came out upon the porch.

Jean saw how he waved the womenfolk back, and then strode out into the lane. Bill and Guy reached his side as Jean pulled his heaving horse to a halt. They all looked at Jean, swiftly and intently, with a little, hard, fiery gleam strangely identical in the eyes of each. Probably before a word was spoken they knew what to expect.

"Wal, you shore was in a hurry," remarked the father.

"What the hell's up?" queried Bill, grimly.

Guy Isbel remained silent and it was he who turned slightly pale. Jean leaped off his horse.

"Bernardino has just been killed—murdered with his own gun."

Gaston Isbel seemed to exhale a long-dammed, bursting breath that let his chest sag. A terrible deadly glint, pale and cold as sunlight on ice, grew slowly to dominate his clear eyes.

"A-huh!" ejaculated Bill Isbel, hoarsely.

Not one of the three men asked who had done the killing. They were silent a moment, motionless, locked in the secret seclusion of their own minds. Then they listened with absorption to Jean's brief story.

"Wal, that lets us in," said his father. "I wish we had more time. Reckon I'd done better to listen to you boys an' have my men close at hand. Jacobs happened to ride over. That makes five of us besides the women."

"Aw, dad, you don't reckon they'll round us up heah?" asked Guy Isbel.

"Boys, I always feared they might," replied the old man. "But I never really believed they'd have the nerve. Shore I ought to have figgered Daggs better. This heah secret bizness an' shootin' at us from ambush looked aboot Jorth's size to me. But I reckon now we'll have to fight without our friends."

"Let them come," said Jean. "I sent for Blaisdell, Blue, Gordon, and Fredericks. Maybe they'll get here in time. But if they don't it needn't worry us much. We can hold out here longer than Jorth's gang can hang around. We'll want plenty of water, wood, and meat in the house."

"Wal, I'll see to that," rejoined his father. "Jean, you go out close by, where you can see all around, an' keep watch."

"Who's goin' to tell the women?" asked Guy Isbel.

The silence that momentarily ensued was an eloquent testimony to the hardest and saddest aspect of this strife between men. The inevitableness of it in no wise detracted from its sheer uselessness. Men from time immemorial had hated, and killed one another, always to the misery and degradation of their women. Old Gaston Isbel showed this tragic realization in his lined face.

"Wal, boys, I'll tell the women," he said. "Shore you needn't worry none aboot them. They'll be game."

Jean rode away to an open knoll a short distance from the house, and here he stationed himself to watch all points. The cedared ridge back of the ranch was the one approach by which Jorth's gang might come close without being detected, but even so, Jean could see them and ride to the house in time to prevent a surprise. The moments dragged by, and at the end of an hour Jean was in hopes that Blaisdell would soon come. These hopes were well founded. Presently he heard a clatter of hoofs on hard ground to the south, and upon wheeling to look he saw the friendly neighbor coming fast along the road, riding a big white horse. Blaisdell carried a rifle in his hand, and the sight of him gave Jean a glow of warmth. He was one of the Texans who would stand by the Isbels to the last man. Jean watched him ride to the house—watched the meeting between him and his lifelong friend. There floated out to Jean old Blaisdell's roar of rage.

Then out on the green of Grass Valley, where a long, swelling plain swept away toward the village, there appeared a moving dark patch. A bunch of horses! Jean's body gave a slight start—the shock of sudden propulsion of blood through all his veins. Those horses bore riders. They were coming straight down the open valley, on the wagon road to Isbel's ranch. No subterfuge nor secrecy nor sneaking in that advance! A hot thrill ran over Jean.

"By Heaven! They mean business!" he muttered. Up to the last moment he had unconsciously hoped Jorth's gang would not come boldly like that. The verifications of all a Texan's inherited instincts left no doubts, no hopes, no illusions—only a grim certainty that this was not conjecture nor probability, but fact. For a moment longer Jean watched the slowly moving dark patch of horsemen against the green background, then he hurried back to the ranch. His father saw him coming—strode out as before.

"Dad—Jorth is comin'," said Jean, huskily. How he hated to be forced to tell his father that! The boyish love of old had flashed up.

"Whar?" demanded the old man, his eagle gaze sweeping the horizon.

"Down the road from Grass Valley. You can't see from here."

"Wal, come in an' let's get ready."

Isbel's house had not been constructed with the idea of repelling an attack from a band of Apaches. The long living room of the main cabin was the one selected for defense and protection. This room had two windows and a door facing the lane, and a door at each end, one of which opened into the kitchen and the other into an adjoining and later-built cabin. The logs of this main cabin were of large size, and the doors and window coverings were heavy, affording safer protection from bullets than the other cabins.

When Jean went in he seemed to see a host of white faces lifted to him. His sister Ann, his two sisters-in-law, the children, all mutely watched him with eyes that would haunt him.

"Wal, Blaisdell, Jean says Jorth an' his precious gang of rustlers are on the way heah," announced the rancher.

"Damn me if it's not a bad day fer Lee Jorth!" declared Blaisdell.

"Clear off that table," ordered Isbel, "an' fetch out all the guns an' shells we got."

Once laid upon the table these presented a formidable arsenal, which consisted of the three new .44 Winchesters that Jean had brought with him from the coast; the enormous buffalo, or so-called "needle" gun, that Gaston Isbel had used for years; a Henry rifle which Blaisdell had brought, and half a dozen six-shooters. Piles and packages of ammunition littered the table.

"Sort out these heah shells," said Isbel. "Everybody wants to get hold of his own."

Jacobs, the neighbor who was present, was a thick-set, bearded man, rather jovial among those lean-jawed Texans. He carried a .44 rifle of an old pattern. "Wal, boys, if I'd knowed we was in fer some fun I'd hev fetched more shells. Only got one magazine full. Mebbe them new .44's will fit my gun."

It was discovered that the ammunition Jean had brought in quantity fitted Jacobs's rifle, a fact which afforded peculiar satisfaction to all the men present.

"Wal, shore we're lucky," declared Gaston Isbel.

The women sat apart, in the corner toward the kitchen, and there seemed to be a strange fascination for them in the talk and action of the men. The wife of Jacobs was a little woman, with homely face and very bright eyes. Jean thought that she would be a help in that household during the next doubtful hours.

Every moment Jean would go to the window and peer out down the road. His companions evidently relied upon him, for no one else looked out. Now that the suspense of days and weeks was over, these Texans faced the issue with talk and act not noticeably different from those of ordinary moments.

At last Jean espied the dark mass of horsemen out in the valley road. They were close together, walking their mounts, and evidently in earnest conversation. After several ineffectual attempts Jean counted eleven horses, every one of which he was sure bore a rider.

"Dad, look out!" called Jean.

Gaston Isbel strode to the door and stood looking, without a word.

The other men crowded to the windows. Blaisdell cursed under his breath. Jacobs said: "By Golly! Come to pay us a call!" The women sat motionless, with dark, strained eyes. The children ceased their play and looked fearfully to their mother.

When just out of rifle shot of the cabins the band of horsemen halted and lined up in a half circle, all facing the ranch. They were close enough for Jean to see their gestures, but he could not recognize any of their faces. It struck him singularly that not one of them wore a mask.

"Jean, do you know any of them?" asked his father.

"No, not yet. They're too far off."

"Dad, I'll get your old telescope," said Guy Isbel, and he ran out toward the adjoining cabin.

Blaisdell shook his big, hoary head and rumbled out of his bull-like neck, "Wal, now you're heah, you sheep fellars, what are you goin' to do aboot it?"

Guy Isbel returned with a yard-long telescope, which he passed to his father. The old man took it with shaking hands and leveled it. Suddenly it was as if he had been transfixed; then he lowered the glass, shaking violently, and his face grew gray with an exceeding bitter wrath.

"Jorth!" he swore, harshly.

Jean had only to look at his father to know that recognition had been like a mortal shock. It passed. Again the rancher leveled the glass.

"Wal, Blaisdell, there's our old Texas friend, Daggs," he drawled, dryly. "An' Greaves, our honest storekeeper of Grass Valley. An' there's Stonewall Jackson Jorth. An' Tad Jorth, with the same old red nose! . . . An', say, damn if one of that gang isn't Queen, as bad a gun fighter as Texas ever bred. Shore I thought he'd been killed in the Big Bend country. So I heard. . . . An' there's Craig, another respectable sheepman of Grass Valley. Haw-haw! . . . An', wal, I don't recognize any more of them."

Jean forthwith took the glass and moved it slowly across the faces of that group of horsemen. "Simm Bruce," he said, instantly. "I see Colter. And, yes, Greaves is there. I've seen the man next to him—face like a ham. . . ."

"Shore that is Craig," interrupted his father.

Jean knew the dark face of Lee Jorth by the resemblance it bore to Ellen's, and the recognition brought a twinge. He thought, too, that he could tell the other Jorths. He asked his father to describe Daggs and then Queen. It was not likely that Jean would fail to know these several men in the future. Then Blaisdell asked for the telescope and, when he got through looking and cursing, he passed it on to others, who, one by one, took a long look, until finally it came back to the old rancher.

"Wal, Daggs is wavin' his hand heah an' there, like a general aboot to send out scouts. Haw-haw! . . . An' 'pears to me he's not overlookin' our hosses. Wal, that's natural for a rustler. He'd have to steal a hoss or a steer before goin' into a fight or to dinner or to a funeral."

"It 'll be his funeral if he goes to foolin' 'round them hosses," declared Guy Isbel, peering anxiously out of the door.

"Wal, son, shore it 'll be somebody's funeral," replied his father.

Jean paid but little heed to the conversation. With sharp eyes fixed upon the horsemen, he tried to grasp at their intention. Daggs pointed to the horses in the pasture lot that lay between him and the house. These animals were the best on the range and belonged mostly to Guy Isbel, who was the horse fancier and trader of the family. His horses were his passion.

"Looks like they'd do some horse stealin'," said Jean.

"Lend me that glass," demanded Guy, forcefully. He surveyed the band of men for a long moment, then he handed the glass back to Jean.

"I'm goin' out there after my hosses," he declared.

"No!" exclaimed his father.

"That gang come to steal an' not to fight. Can't you see that? If they meant to fight they'd do it. They're out there arguin' about my hosses."

Guy picked up his rifle. He looked sullenly determined and the gleam in his eye was one of fearlessness.

"Son, I know Daggs," said his father. "An' I know Jorth. They've come to kill us. It 'll be shore death for y'u to go out there."

"I'm goin', anyhow. They can't steal my hosses out from under my eyes. An' they ain't in range."

"Wal, Guy, you ain't goin' alone," spoke up Jacobs, cheerily, as he came forward.

The red-haired young wife of Guy Isbel showed no change of her grave face. She had been reared in a stern school. She knew men in times like these. But Jacobs's wife appealed to him, "Bill, don't risk your life for a horse or two."

Jacobs laughed and answered, "Not much risk," and went out with Guy. To Jean their action seemed foolhardy. He kept a keen eye on them and saw instantly when the band became aware of Guy's and Jacob's entrance into the pasture. It took only another second then to realize that Daggs and Jorth had deadly intent. Jean saw Daggs slip out of his saddle, rifle in hand. Others of the gang did likewise, until half of them were dismounted.

"Dad, they're goin' to shoot," called out Jean, sharply. "Yell for Guy and Jacobs. Make them come back."

The old man shouted; Bill Isbel yelled; Blaisdell lifted his stentorian voice.

Jean screamed piercingly: "Guy! Run! Run!"

But Guy Isbel and his companion strode on into the pasture, as if they had not heard, as if no menacing horse thieves were within miles. They had covered about a quarter of the distance across the pasture, and were nearing the horses, when Jean saw red flashes and white puffs of smoke burst out from the front of that dark band of rustlers. Then followed the sharp, rattling crack of rifles.

Guy Isbel stopped short, and, dropping his gun, he threw up his arms and fell headlong. Jacobs acted as if he had suddenly encountered an invisible blow. He had been hit. Turning, he began to run and ran fast for a few paces. There were more quick, sharp shots. He let go of his rifle. His running broke. Walking, reeling, staggering, he kept on. A hoarse cry came from him. Then a single rifle shot pealed out. Jean heard the bullet strike. Jacobs fell to his knees, then forward on his face.

Jean Isbel felt himself turned to marble. The suddenness of this tragedy paralyzed him. His gaze remained riveted on those prostrate forms.

A hand clutched his arm—a shaking woman's hand, slim and hard and tense.

"Bill's—killed!" whispered a broken voice. "I was watchin'. . . . They're both dead!"

The wives of Jacobs and Guy Isbel had slipped up behind Jean and from behind him they had seen the tragedy.

"I asked Bill—not to—go," faltered the Jacobs woman, and, covering her face with her hands, she groped back to the corner of the cabin, where the other women, shaking and white, received her in their arms. Guy Isbel's wife stood at the window, peering over Jean's shoulder. She had the nerve of a man. She had looked out upon death before.

"Yes, they're dead," she said, bitterly. "An' how are we goin' to get their bodies?"

At this Gaston Isbel seemed to rouse from the cold spell that had transfixed him.

"God, this is hell for our women," he cried out, hoarsely. "My son—my son! . . . Murdered by the Jorths!" Then he swore a terrible oath.

Jean saw the remainder of the mounted rustlers get off, and then all of them leading their horses, they began to move around to the left.

"Dad, they're movin' round," said Jean.

"Up to some trick," declared Bill Isbel.

"Bill, you make a hole through the back wall, say aboot the fifth log up," ordered the father. "Shore we've got to look out."

The elder son grasped a tool and, scattering the children, who had been playing near the back corner, he began to work at the point designated. The little children backed away with fixed, wondering, grave eyes.

The women moved their chairs, and huddled together as if waiting and listening.

Jean watched the rustlers until they passed out of his sight. They had moved toward the sloping, brushy ground to the north and west of the cabins.

"Let me know when you get a hole in the back wall," said Jean, and he went through the kitchen and cautiously out another door to slip into a low-roofed, shed-like end of the rambling cabin. This small space was used to store winter firewood. The chinks between the walls had not been filled with adobe clay, and he could see out on three sides. The rustlers were going into the juniper brush. They moved out of sight, and presently reappeared without their horses. It looked to Jean as if they intended to attack the cabins. Then they halted at the edge of the brush and held a long consultation. Jean could see them distinctly, though they were too far distant for him to recognize any particular man. One of them, however, stood and moved apart from the closely massed group. Evidently, from his strides and gestures, he was exhorting his listeners. Jean concluded this was either Daggs or Jorth. Whoever it was had a loud, coarse voice, and this and his actions impressed Jean with a suspicion that the man was under the influence of the bottle.

Presently Bill Isbel called Jean in a low voice. "Jean, I got the hole made, but we can't see any one."

"I see them," Jean replied. "They're havin' a powwow. Looks to me like either Jorth or Daggs is drunk. He's arguin' to charge us, an' the rest of the gang are holdin' back. . . . Tell dad, an' all of you keep watchin'. I'll let you know when they make a move."

Jorth's gang appeared to be in no hurry to expose their plan of battle. Gradually the group disintegrated a little; some of them sat down; others walked to and fro. Presently two of them went into the brush, probably back to the horses. In a few moments they reappeared, carrying a pack. And when this was deposited on the ground all the rustlers sat down around it. They had brought food and drink. Jean had to utter a grim laugh at their coolness; and he was reminded of many dare-devil deeds known to have been perpetrated by the Hash Knife Gang. Jean was glad of a reprieve. The longer the rustlers put off an attack the more time the allies of the Isbels would have to get here. Rather hazardous, however, would it be now for anyone to attempt to get to the Isbel cabins in the daytime. Night would be more favorable.

Twice Bill Isbel came through the kitchen to whisper to Jean. The strain in the large room, from which the rustlers could not be seen, must have been great. Jean told him all he had seen and what he thought about it. "Eatin' an' drinkin'!" ejaculated Bill. "Well, I'll be—! That 'll jar the old man. He wants to get the fight over."

"Tell him I said it 'll be over too quick—for us—unless we are mighty careful," replied Jean, sharply.

Bill went back muttering to himself. Then followed a long wait, fraught with suspense, during which Jean watched the rustlers regale themselves. The day was hot and still. And the unnatural silence of the cabin was broken now and then by the gay laughter of the children. The sound shocked and haunted Jean. Playing children! Then another sound, so faint he had to strain to hear it, disturbed and saddened him—his father's slow tread up and down the cabin floor, to and fro, to and fro. What must be in his father's heart this day!

At length the rustlers rose and, with rifles in hand, they moved as one man down the slope. They came several hundred yards closer, until Jean, grimly cocking his rifle, muttered to himself that a few more rods closer would mean the end of several of that gang. They knew the range of a rifle well enough, and once more sheered off at right angles with the cabin. When they got even with the line of corrals they stooped down and were lost to Jean's sight. This fact caused him alarm. They were, of course, crawling up on the cabins. At the end of that line of corrals ran a ditch, the bank of which was high enough to afford cover. Moreover, it ran along in front of the cabins, scarcely a hundred yards, and it was covered with grass and little clumps of brush, from behind which the rustlers could fire into the windows and through the clay chinks without any considerable risk to themselves. As they did not come into sight again, Jean concluded he had discovered their plan. Still, he waited awhile longer, until he saw faint, little clouds of dust rising from behind the far end of the embankment. That discovery made him rush out, and through the kitchen to the large cabin, where his sudden appearance startled the men.

"Get back out of sight!" he ordered, sharply, and with swift steps he reached the door and closed it. "They're behind the bank out there by the corrals. An' they're goin' to crawl down the ditch closer to us. . . . It looks bad. They'll have grass an' brush to shoot from. We've got to be mighty careful how we peep out."

"Ahuh! All right," replied his father. "You women keep the kids with you in that corner. An' you all better lay down flat."

Blaisdell, Bill Isbel, and the old man crouched at the large window, peeping through cracks in the rough edges of the logs. Jean took his post beside the small window, with his keen eyes vibrating like a compass needle. The movement of a blade of grass, the flight of a grasshopper could not escape his trained sight.

"Look sharp now!" he called to the other men. "I see dust. . . . They're workin' along almost to that bare spot on the bank. . . . I saw the tip of a rifle . . . a black hat . . . more dust. They're spreadin' along behind the bank."

Loud voices, and then thick clouds of yellow dust, coming from behind the highest and brushiest line of the embankment, attested to the truth of Jean's observation, and also to a reckless disregard of danger.

Suddenly Jean caught a glint of moving color through the fringe of brush. Instantly he was strung like a whipcord.

Then a tall, hatless and coatless man stepped up in plain sight. The sun shone on his fair, ruffled hair. Daggs!

"Hey, you —— —— Isbels!" he bawled, in magnificent derisive boldness. "Come out an' fight!"

Quick as lightning Jean threw up his rifle and fired. He saw tufts of fair hair fly from Daggs's head. He saw the squirt of red blood. Then quick shots from his comrades rang out. They all hit the swaying body of the rustler. But Jean knew with a terrible thrill that his bullet had killed Daggs before the other three struck. Daggs fell forward, his arms and half his body resting over the embankment. Then the rustlers dragged him back out of sight. Hoarse shouts rose. A cloud of yellow dust drifted away from the spot.

"Daggs!" burst out Gaston Isbel. "Jean, you knocked off the top of his haid. I seen that when I was pullin' trigger. Shore we over heah wasted our shots."

"God! he must have been crazy or drunk—to pop up there—an' brace us that way," said Blaisdell, breathing hard.

"Arizona is bad for Texans," replied Isbel, sardonically. "Shore it's been too peaceful heah. Rustlers have no practice at fightin'. An' I reckon Daggs forgot."

"Daggs made as crazy a move as that of Guy an' Jacobs," spoke up Jean. "They were overbold, an' he was drunk. Let them be a lesson to us."

Jean had smelled whisky upon his entrance to this cabin. Bill was a hard drinker, and his father was not immune. Blaisdell, too, drank heavily upon occasions. Jean made a mental note that he would not permit their chances to become impaired by liquor.

Rifles began to crack, and puffs of smoke rose all along the embankment for the space of a hundred feet. Bullets whistled through the rude window casing and spattered on the heavy door, and one split the clay between the logs before Jean, narrowly missing him. Another volley followed, then another. The rustlers had repeating rifles and they were emptying their magazines. Jean changed his position. The other men profited by his wise move. The volleys had merged into one continuous rattling roar of rifle shots. Then came a sudden cessation of reports, with silence of relief. The cabin was full of dust, mingled with the smoke from the shots of Jean and his companions. Jean heard the stifled breaths of the children. Evidently they were terror-stricken, but they did not cry out. The women uttered no sound.

A loud voice pealed from behind the embankment.

"Come out an' fight! Do you Isbels want to be killed like sheep?"

This sally gained no reply. Jean returned to his post by the window and his comrades followed his example. And they exercised extreme caution when they peeped out.

"Boys, don't shoot till you see one," said Gaston Isbel. "Maybe after a while they'll get careless. But Jorth will never show himself."

The rustlers did not again resort to volleys. One by one, from different angles, they began to shoot, and they were not firing at random. A few bullets came straight in at the windows to pat into the walls; a few others ticked and splintered the edges of the windows; and most of them broke through the clay chinks between the logs. It dawned upon Jean that these dangerous shots were not accident. They were well aimed, and most of them hit low down. The cunning rustlers had some unerring riflemen and they were picking out the vulnerable places all along the front of the cabin. If Jean had not been lying flat he would have been hit twice. Presently he conceived the idea of driving pegs between the logs, high up, and, kneeling on these, he managed to peep out from the upper edge of the window. But this position was awkward and difficult to hold for long.

He heard a bullet hit one of his comrades. Whoever had been struck never uttered a sound. Jean turned to look. Bill Isbel was holding his shoulder, where red splotches appeared on his shirt. He shook his head at Jean, evidently to make light of the wound. The women and children were lying face down and could not see what was happening. Plain it was that Bill did not want them to know. Blaisdell bound up the bloody shoulder with a scarf.

Steady firing from the rustlers went on, at the rate of one shot every few minutes. The Isbels did not return these. Jean did not fire again that afternoon. Toward sunset, when the besiegers appeared to grow restless or careless, Blaisdell fired at something moving behind the brush; and Gaston Isbel's huge buffalo gun boomed out.

"Wal, what 're they goin' to do after dark, an' what 're *we* goin' to do?" grumbled Blaisdell.

"Reckon they'll never charge us," said Gaston.

"They might set fire to the cabins," added Bill Isbel. He appeared to be the gloomiest of the Isbel faction. There was something on his mind.

"Wal, the Jorths are bad, but I reckon they'd not burn us alive," replied Blaisdell.

"Hah!" ejaculated Gaston Isbel. "Much you know aboot Lee Jorth. He would skin me alive an' throw red-hot coals on my raw flesh."

So they talked during the hour from sunset to dark. Jean Isbel had little to say. He was revolving possibilities in his mind. Darkness brought a change in the attack of the rustlers. They stationed men at four points around the cabins; and every few minutes one of these outposts would fire. These bullets embedded themselves in the logs, causing but little anxiety to the Isbels.

"Jean, what you make of it?" asked the old rancher.

"Looks to me this way," replied Jean. "They're set for a long fight. They're shootin' just to let us know they're on the watch."

"Ahuh! Wal, what 're you goin' to do aboot it?"

"I'm goin' out there presently."

Gaston Isbel grunted his satisfaction at this intention of Jean's.

All was pitch dark inside the cabin. The women had water and food at hand. Jean kept a sharp lookout from his window while he ate his supper of meat, bread, and milk. At last the children, worn out by the long day, fell asleep. The women whispered a little in their corner.

About nine o'clock Jean signified his intention of going out to reconnoitre.

"Dad, they've got the best of us in the daytime," he said, "but not after dark."

Jean buckled on a belt that carried shells, a bowie knife, and revolver, and with rifle in hand he went out through the kitchen to the yard. The night was darker than usual, as some of the stars were hidden by clouds. He leaned against the log cabin, waiting for his eyes to become perfectly adjusted to the darkness. Like an Indian. Jean could see well at night. He knew every point around cabins and sheds and corrals, every post, log, tree, rock, adjacent to the ranch. After perhaps a quarter of an hour watching, during which time several shots were fired from behind the embankment and one each from the rustlers at the other locations. Jean slipped out on his quest.

He kept in the shadow of the cabin walls, then the line of orchard trees, then a row of currant bushes. Here, crouching low, he halted to look and listen. He was now at the edge of the open ground, with the gently rising slope before him. He could see the dark patches of cedar and juniper trees. On the north side of the cabin a streak of fire flashed in the blackness, and a shot rang out. Jean heard the bullet hit the cabin. Then silence enfolded the lonely ranch and the darkness lay like a black blanket. A low hum of insects pervaded the air. Dull sheets of lightning illumined the dark horizon to the south. Once Jean heard voices, but could not tell from which direction they came. To the west of him then flared out another rifle shot. The bullet whistled down over Jean to thud into the cabin.

Jean made a careful study of the obscure, gray-black open before him and then the background to his rear. So long as he kept the dense shadows behind him he could not be seen. He slipped from behind his covert and, gliding with absolutely noiseless footsteps, he gained the first clump of junipers. Here he waited patiently and motionlessly for another round of shots from the rustlers. After the second shot from the west side Jean sheered off to the right. Patches of brush, clumps of juniper, and isolated cedars covered this slope, affording Jean a perfect means for his purpose, which was to make a detour and come up behind the rustler who was firing from that side. Jean climbed to the top of the ridge, descended the opposite slope, made his turn to the left, and slowly worked up behind the point near where he expected to locate the rustler. Long habit in the open, by day and night, rendered his sense of direction almost as perfect as sight itself. The first flash of fire he saw from this side proved that he had come straight up toward his man. Jean's intention was to crawl up on this one of the Jorth gang and silently kill him with a knife. If the plan worked successfully, Jean meant to work round to the next rustler. Laying aside his rifle, he crawled forward on hands and knees, making no more sound than a cat. His approach was slow. He had to pick his way, be careful not to break twigs nor rattle stones. His buckskin garments made no sound against the brush. Jean located the rustler sitting on the top of the ridge in the center of an open space. He was alone. Jean saw the dull-red end of the cigarette he was smoking. The ground on the ridge top was rocky and not well adapted for Jean's purpose. He had to abandon the idea of crawling up on the rustler. Whereupon, Jean turned back, patiently and slowly, to get his rifle.

Upon securing it he began to retrace his course, this time more slowly than before, as he was hampered by the rifle. But he did not make the slightest sound, and at length he reached the edge of the open ridge top, once more to espy the dark form of the rustler silhouetted against the sky. The distance was not more than fifty yards.

As Jean rose to his knee and carefully lifted his rifle round to avoid the twigs of a juniper he suddenly experienced another emotion besides the one of grim, hard wrath at the Jorths. It was an emotion that sickened him, made him weak internally, a cold, shaking, ungovernable sensation. Suppose this man was Ellen Jorth's father. Jean lowered the rifle. He felt it shake over his knee. He was trembling all over. The astounding discovery that he did not want to kill Ellen's father—that he could not do it— awakened Jean to the despairing nature of his love for her. In this grim moment of indecision, when he knew his Indian subtlety and ability gave him a great advantage over the Jorths, he fully realized his strange, hopeless, and irresistible love for the girl. He made no attempt to deny it any longer. Like the night and the lonely wilderness around him, like the inevitableness of this Jorth-Isbel feud, this love of his was a thing, a fact, a reality. He breathed to his own inward ear, to his soul—he could not kill Ellen Jorth's father. Feud or no feud, Isbel or not, he could not deliberately do it. And why not? There was no answer. Was he not faithless to his father? He had no hope of ever winning Ellen Jorth. He did not want the love of a girl of her character. But he loved her. And his struggle must be against the insidious and mysterious growth of that passion. It swayed him already. It made him a coward. Through his mind and heart swept the memory of Ellen Jorth, her beauty and charm, her boldness and pathos, her shame and her degradation. And the sweetness of her outweighed the boldness. And the mystery of her arrayed itself in unquenchable protest against her acknowledged shame. Jean lifted his face to the heavens, to the pitiless white stars, to the infinite depths of the dark-blue sky. He could sense the fact of his being an atom in the universe of nature. What was he, what was his revengeful father, what were hate and passion and strife in comparison to the nameless something, immense and everlasting, that he sensed in this dark moment?

But the rustlers—Daggs—the Jorths—they had killed his brother Guy—murdered him brutally and ruthlessly. Guy had been a playmate of Jean's—a favorite brother. Bill had been secretive and selfish. Jean had never loved him as he did Guy. Guy lay dead down there on the meadow. This feud had begun to run its bloody course. Jean steeled his nerve. The hot blood crept back along his veins. The dark and masterful tide of revenge waved over him. The keen edge of his mind then cut out sharp and trenchant thoughts. He must kill when and where he could. This man could hardly be Ellen Jorth's father. Jorth would be with the main crowd, directing hostilities. Jean could shoot this rustler guard and his shot would be taken by the gang as the regular one from their comrade. Then swiftly Jean leveled his rifle, covered the dark form, grew cold and set, and pressed the trigger. After the report he rose and wheeled away. He did not look nor listen for the result of his shot. A clammy sweat wet his face, the hollow of his hands, his breast. A horrible, leaden, thick sensation oppressed his heart. Nature had endowed him with Indian gifts, but the exercise of them to this end caused a revolt in his soul.

Nevertheless, it was the Isbel blood that dominated him. The wind blew cool on his face. The burden upon his shoulders seemed to lift. The clamoring whispers grew fainter in his ears. And by the time he had retraced his cautious steps back to the orchard all his physical being was strung to the task at hand. Something had come between his reflective self and this man of action.

Crossing the lane, he took to the west line of sheds, and passed beyond them into the meadow. In the grass he crawled silently away to the right, using the same precaution that had actuated him on the slope, only here he did not pause so often, nor move so slowly. Jean aimed to go far enough to the right to pass the end of the embankment behind which the rustlers had found such efficient cover. This ditch had been made to keep water, during spring thaws and summer storms, from pouring off the slope to flood the corrals.

Jean miscalculated and found he had come upon the embankment somewhat to the left of the end, which fact, however, caused him no uneasiness. He lay there awhile to listen. Again he heard voices. After a time a shot pealed out. He did not see the flash, but he calculated that it had come from the north side of the cabins.

The next quarter of an hour discovered to Jean that the nearest guard was firing from the top of the embankment, perhaps a hundred yards distant, and a second one was performing the same office from a point apparently only a few yards farther on. Two rustlers close together! Jean had not calculated upon that. For a little while he pondered on what was best to do, and at length decided to crawl round behind them, and as close as the situation made advisable.

He found the ditch behind the embankment a favorable path by which to stalk these enemies. It was dry and sandy, with borders of high weeds. The only drawback was that it was almost impossible for him to keep from brushing against the dry, invisible branches of the weeds. To offset this he wormed his way like a snail, inch by inch, taking a long time before he caught sight of the sitting figure of a man, black against the dark-blue sky. This rustler had fired his rifle three times during Jean's slow approach. Jean watched and listened a few moments, then wormed himself closer and closer, until the man was within twenty steps of him.

Jean smelled tobacco smoke, but could see no light of pipe or cigarette, because the fellow's back was turned.

"Say, Ben," said this man to his companion sitting hunched up a few yards distant, "shore it strikes me queer thet Somers ain't shootin' any over thar."

Jean recognized the dry, drawling voice of Greaves, and the shock of it seemed to contract the muscles of his whole thrilling body, like that of a panther about to spring.

CHAPTER 8

I was shore thinkin' thet same," said the other man. "An', say, didn't thet last shot sound too sharp fer Somers's forty-five?"

"Come to think of it, I reckon it did," replied Greaves.

"Wal, I'll go around over thar an' see."

The dark form of the rustler slipped out of sight over the embankment.

"Better go slow an' careful," warned Greaves. "An' only go close enough to call Somers. . . . Mebbe thet damn half-breed Isbel is comin' some Injun on us."

Jean heard the soft swish of footsteps through wet grass. Then all was still. He lay flat, with his cheek on the sand, and he had to look ahead and upward to make out the dark figure of Greaves on the bank. One way or another he meant to kill Greaves, and he had the will power to resist the strongest gust of passion that had ever stormed his breast. If he arose and shot the rustler, that act would defeat his plan of slipping on around upon the other outposts who were firing at the cabins. Jean wanted to call softly to Greaves, "You're right about the half-breed!" and then, as he wheeled aghast, to kill him as he moved. But it suited Jean to risk leaping upon the man. Jean did not waste time in trying to understand the strange, deadly instinct that gripped him at the moment. But he realized then he had chosen the most perilous plan to get rid of Greaves.

Jean drew a long, deep breath and held it. He let go of his rifle. He rose, silently as a lifting shadow. He drew the bowie knife. Then with light, swift bounds he glided up the bank. Greaves must have heard a rustling—a soft, quick pad of moccasin, for he turned with a start. And that instant Jean's left arm darted like a striking snake round Greaves's neck and closed tight and hard. With his right hand free, holding the knife, Jean might have ended the deadly business in just one move. But when his bared arm felt the hot, bulging neck something terrible burst out of the depths of him. To kill this enemy of his father's was not enough! Physical contact had unleashed the savage soul of the Indian. Yet there was more, and as Jean gave the straining body a tremendous jerk backward, he felt the same strange thrill, the dark joy that he had known when his fist had smashed the face of Simm Bruce. Greaves had leered— he had corroborated Bruce's vile insinuation about Ellen Jorth. So it was more than hate that actuated Jean Isbel.

Greaves was heavy and powerful. He whirled himself, feet first, over backward, in a lunge like that of a lassoed steer. But Jean's hold held. They rolled down the bank into the sandy ditch, and Jean landed upper- most, with his body at right angles with that of his adversary.

"Greaves, your hunch was right," hissed Jean. "It's the half-breed. . . . An' I'm goin' to cut you—first for Ellen Jorth—an' then for Gaston Isbel!"

Jean gazed down into the gleaming eyes. Then his right arm whipped the big blade. It flashed. It fell. Low down, as far as Jean could reach, it entered Greaves's body.

All the heavy, muscular frame of Greaves seemed to contract and burst. His spring was that of an animal in terror and agony. It was so tremendous that it broke Jean's hold. Greaves let out a strangled yell that cleared, swelling wildly, with a hideous mortal note. He wrestled free. The big knife came out. Supple and swift, he got to his knees. He had his gun out when Jean reached him again. Like a bear Jean enveloped him. Greaves shot, but he could not raise the gun, nor twist it far enough. Then Jean, letting go with his right arm, swung the bowie. Greaves's strength went out in an awful, hoarse cry. His gun boomed again, then dropped from his hand. He swayed. Jean let go. And that enemy of the Isbels sank limply in the ditch. Jean's eyes roved for his rifle and caught the starlit gleam of it. Snatching it up, he leaped over the embankment and ran straight for the cabins. From all around yells of the Jorth faction attested to their excitement and fury.

A fence loomed up gray in the obscurity. Jean vaulted it, darted across the lane into the shadow of the corral, and soon gained the first cabin. Here he leaned to regain his breath. His heart pounded high and seemed too large for his breast. The hot blood beat and surged all over his body. Sweat poured off him. His teeth were clenched tight as a vise, and it took effort on his part to open his mouth so he could breathe more freely and deeply. But these physical sensations were as nothing compared to the tumult of his mind. Then the instinct, the spell, let go its grip and he could think. He had avenged Guy, he had depleted the ranks of the Jorths, he had made good the brag of his father, all of which afforded him satisfaction. But these thoughts were not accountable for all that he felt, especially for the bittersweet sting of the fact that death to the defiler of Ellen Jorth could not efface the doubt, the regret which seemed to grow with the hours.

Groping his way into the woodshed, he entered the kitchen and, calling low, he went on into the main cabin.

"Jean! Jean!" came his father's shaking voice.

"Yes, I'm back," replied Jean.

"Are—you—all right?"

"Yes. I think I've got a bullet crease on my leg. I didn't know I had it till now. . . . It's bleedin' a little. But it's nothin'."

Jean heard soft steps and some one reached shaking hands for him. They belonged to his sister Ann. She embraced him. Jean felt the heave and throb of her breast.

"Why, Ann, I'm not hurt," he said, and held her close. "Now you lie down an' try to sleep."

In the black darkness of the cabin Jean led her back to the corner and his heart was full. Speech was difficult, because the very touch of Ann's hands had made him divine that the success of his venture in no wise changed the plight of the women.

"Wal, what happened out there?" demanded Blaisdell.

"I got two of them," replied Jean. "That fellow who was shootin' from the ridge west. An' the other was Greaves."

"Hah!" exclaimed his father.

"Shore then it was Greaves yellin'," declared Blaisdell. "By God, I never heard such yells! What'd you do, Jean?"

"I knifed him. You see, I'd planned to slip up on one after another. An' I didn't want to make noise. But I didn't get any farther than Greaves."

"Wal, I reckon that 'll end their shootin' in the dark," muttered Gaston Isbel. "We've got to be on the lookout for somethin' else—fire, most likely."

The old rancher's surmise proved to be partially correct. Jorth's faction ceased the shooting. Nothing further was seen or heard from them. But this silence and apparent break in the siege were harder to bear than deliberate hostility. The long, dark hours dragged by. The men took turns watching and resting, but none of them slept. At last the blackness paled and gray dawn stole out of the east. The sky turned rose over the distant range and daylight came.

The children awoke hungry and noisy, having slept away their fears. The women took advantage of the quiet morning hour to get a hot breakfast.

"Maybe they've gone away," suggested Guy Isbel's wife, peering out of the window. She had done that several times since daybreak. Jean saw her somber gaze search the pasture until it rested upon the dark, prone shape of her dead husband, lying face down in the grass. Her look worried Jean.

"No, Esther, they've not gone yet," replied Jean. "I've seen some of them out there at the edge of the brush."

Blaisdell was optimistic. He said Jean's night work would have its effect and that the Jorth contingent would not renew the siege very determinedly. It turned out, however, that Blaisdell was wrong. Directly after sunrise they began to pour volleys from four sides and from closer range. During the night Jorth's gang had thrown earth banks and constructed log breastworks, from behind which they were now firing. Jean and his comrades could see the flashes of fire and streaks of smoke to such good advantage that they began to return the volleys.

In half an hour the cabin was so full of smoke that Jean could not see the womenfolk in their corner. The fierce attack then abated somewhat, and the firing became more intermittent, and therefore more carefully aimed. A glancing bullet cut a furrow in Blaisdell's hoary head, making a painful, though not serious wound. It was Esther Isbel who stopped the flow of blood and bound Blaisdell's head, a task which she performed skillfully and without a tremor. The old Texan could not sit still during this operation. Sight of the blood on his hands, which he tried to rub off, appeared to inflame him to a great degree.

"Isbel, we got to go out thar," he kept repeating, "an' kill them all."

"No, we're goin' to stay heah," replied Gaston Isbel. "Shore I'm lookin' for Blue an' Fredericks an' Gordon to open up out there. They ought to be heah, an' if they are y'u shore can bet they've got the fight sized up."

Isbel's hopes did not materialize. The shooting continued without any lull until about midday. Then the Jorth faction stopped.

"Wal, now what's up?" queried Isbel. "Boys, hold your fire an' let's wait."

Gradually the smoke wafted out of the windows and doors, until the room was once more clear. And at this juncture Esther Isbel came over to take another gaze out upon the meadows. Jean saw her suddenly start violently, then stiffen, with a trembling hand outstretched.

"Look!" she cried.

"Esther, get back," ordered the old rancher. "Keep away from that window."

"What the hell!" muttered Blaisdell. "She sees somethin', or she's gone dotty."

Esther seemed turned to stone. "Look! The hogs have broken into the pasture! . . . They'll eat Guy's body!"

Everyone was frozen with horror at Esther's statement. Jean took a swift survey of the pasture. A bunch of big black hogs had indeed appeared on the scene and were rooting around in the grass not far from where lay the bodies of Guy Isbel and Jacobs. This herd of hogs belonged to the rancher and was allowed to run wild.

"Jane, those hogs—" stammered Esther Isbel, to the wife of Jacobs. "Come! Look! . . . Do y'u know anythin' about hogs?"

The woman ran to the window and looked out. She stiffened as had Esther.

"Dad, will those hogs—eat human flesh?" queried Jean, breathlessly.

The old man stared out of the window. Surprise seemed to hold him. A completely unexpected situation had staggered him.

"Jean—can you—can you shoot that far?" he asked, huskily.

"To those hogs? No, it's out of range."

"Then, by God, we've got to stay trapped in heah an' watch an awful sight," ejaculated the old man, completely unnerved. "See that break in the fence! . . . Jorth's done that. . . . To let in the hogs!"

"Aw, Isbel, it's not so bad as all that," remonstrated Blaisdell, wagging his bloody head. "Jorth wouldn't do such a hell-bent trick."

"It's shore done."

"Wal, mebbe the hogs won't find Guy an Jacobs," returned Blaisdell, weakly. Plain it was that he only hoped for such a contingency and certainly doubted it.

"Look!" cried Esther Isbel, piercingly. "They're workin' straight up the pasture!"

Indeed, to Jean it appeared to be the fatal truth. He looked blankly, feeling a little sick. Ann Isbel came to peer out of the window and she uttered a cry. Jacobs's wife stood mute, as if dazed.

Blaisdell swore a mighty oath. "—— ——! Isbel, we cain't stand heah an' watch them hogs eat our people!"

"Wal, we'll have to. What else on earth can we do?"

Esther turned to the men. She was white and cold, except her eyes, which resembled gray flames.

"Somebody can run out there an' bury our dead men," she said.

"Why, child, it'd be shore death. Y'u saw what happened to Guy an' Jacobs. . . . We've jest got to bear it. Shore nobody needn't look out—an' see."

Jean wondered if it would be possible to keep from watching. The thing had a horrible fascination. The big hogs were rooting and tearing in the grass, some of them lazy, others nimble, and all were gradually working closer and closer to the bodies. The leader, a huge, gaunt boar, that had fared ill all his life in this barren country, was scarcely fifty feet away from where Guy Isbel lay.

"Ann, get me some of your clothes, an' a sunbonnet—quick," said Jean, forced out of his lethargy. "I'll run out there disguised. Maybe I can go through with it."

"No!" ordered his father, positively, and with dark face flaming. "Guy an' Jacobs are dead. We cain't help them now."

"But, dad—" pleaded Jean. He had been wrought to a pitch by Esther's blaze of passion, by the agony in the face of the other woman.

"I tell y'u no!" thundered Gaston Isbel, flinging his arms wide.

"*I will go!*" cried Esther, her voice ringing.

"You won't go alone!" instantly answered the wife of Jacobs, repeating unconsciously the words her husband had spoken.

"You stay right heah," shouted Gaston Isbel, hoarsely.

"I'm goin'," replied Esther. "You've no hold over me. My husband is dead. No one can stop me. I'm goin' out there to drive those hogs away an' bury him."

"Esther, for Heaven's sake, listen," replied Isbel. "If y'u show yourself outside, Jorth an' his gang will kill y'u."

"They may be mean, but no white men could be so low as that."

Then they pleaded with her to give up her purpose. But in vain! She pushed them back and ran out through the kitchen with Jacobs's wife following her. Jean turned to the window in time to see both women run out into the lane. Jean looked fearfully, and listened for shots. But only a loud, "Haw! Haw!" came from the watchers outside. That coarse laugh relieved the tension in Jean's breast. Possibly the Jorths were not as black as his father painted them. The two women entered an open shed and came forth with a shovel and spade.

"Shore they've got to hurry," burst out Gaston Isbel.

Shifting his gaze, Jean understood the import of his father's speech. The leader of the hogs had no doubt scented the bodies. Suddenly he espied them and broke into a trot.

"Run, Esther, run!" yelled Jean, with all his might.

That urged the women to flight. Jean began to shoot. The hog reached the body of Guy. Jean's shots did not reach nor frighten the beast. All the hogs now had caught a scent and went ambling toward their leader. Esther and her companion passed swiftly out of sight behind a corral. Loud and piercingly, with some awful note, rang out their screams. The hogs appeared frightened. The leader lifted his long snout, looked, and turned away. The others had halted. Then they, too, wheeled and ran off.

All was silent then in the cabin and also outside wherever the Jorth faction lay concealed. All eyes manifestly were fixed upon the brave wives. They spaded up the sod and dug a grave for Guy Isbel. For a shroud Esther wrapped him in her shawl. Then they buried him. Next they hurried to the side of Jacobs, who lay some yards away. They dug a grave for him. Mrs. Jacobs took off her outer skirt to wrap round him. Then the two women labored hard to lift him and lower him. Jacobs was a heavy man. When he had been covered his widow knelt beside his grave. Esther went back to the other. But she remained standing and did not look as if she prayed. Her aspect was tragic—that of a woman who had lost father, mother, sisters, brother, and now her husband, in this bloody Arizona land.

The deed and the demeanor of these wives of the murdered men surely must have shamed Jorth and his followers. They did not fire a shot during the ordeal nor give any sign of their presence.

Inside the cabin all were silent, too. Jean's eyes blurred so that he continually had to wipe them. Old Isbel made no effort to hide his tears. Blaisdell nodded his shaggy head and swallowed hard. The women sat staring into space. The children, in round-eyed dismay, gazed from one to the other of their elders.

"Wal, they're comin' back," declared Isbel, in immense relief. "An' so help me—Jorth let them bury their daid!"

The fact seemed to have been monstrously strange to Gaston Isbel. When the women entered the old man said, brokenly: "I'm shore glad. . . . An' I reckon I was wrong to oppose you . . . an' wrong to say what I did aboot Jorth."

No one had any chance to reply to Isbel, for the Jorth gang, as if to make up for lost time and surcharged feelings of shame, renewed the attack with such a persistent and furious volleying that the defenders did not risk a return shot. They all had to lie flat next to the lowest log in order to keep from being hit. Bullets rained in through the window. And all the clay between the logs low down was shot away. This fusillade lasted for more than an hour, then gradually the fire diminished on one side and then on the other until it became desultory and finally ceased.

"Ahuh! Shore they've shot their bolt," declared Gaston Isbel.

"Wal, I doon't know aboot that," returned Blaisdell, "but they've shot a hell of a lot of shells."

"Listen," suddenly called Jean. "Somebody's yellin'."

"Hey, Isbel!" came in loud, hoarse voice. "Let your women fight for you."

Gaston Isbel sat up with a start and his face turned livid. Jean needed no more to prove that the derisive voice from outside had belonged to Jorth. The old rancher lunged up to his full height and with reckless disregard of life he rushed to the window. "Jorth," he roared, "I dare you to meet me—man to man!"

This elicited no answer. Jean dragged his father away from the window. After that a waiting silence ensued, gradually less fraught with suspense. Blaisdell started conversation by saying he believed the fight was over for that particular time. No one disputed him. Evidently Gaston Isbel was loath to believe it. Jean, however, watching at the back of the kitchen, eventually discovered that the Jorth gang had lifted the siege. Jean saw them congregate at the edge of the brush, somewhat lower down than they had been the day before. A team of mules, drawing a wagon, appeared on the road, and turned toward the slope. Saddled horses were led down out of the junipers. Jean saw bodies, evidently of dead men, lifted into the wagon, to be hauled away toward the village. Seven mounted men, leading four riderless horses, rode out into the valley and followed the wagon.

"Dad, they've gone," declared Jean. "We had the best of this fight. . . . If only Guy an' Jacobs had listened!"

The old man nodded moodily. He had aged considerably during these two trying days. His hair was grayer. Now that the blaze and glow of the fight had passed he showed a subtle change, a fixed and morbid sadness, a resignation to a fate he had accepted.

The ordinary routine of ranch life did not return for the Isbels. Blaisdell returned home to settle matters there, so that he could devote all his time to this feud. Gaston Isbel sat down to wait for the members of his clan.

The male members of the family kept guard in turn over the ranch that night. And another day dawned. It brought word from Blaisdell that Blue, Fredericks, Gordon, and Colmor were all at his house, on the way to join the Isbels. This news appeared greatly to rejuvenate Gaston Isbel.

But his enthusiasm did not last long. Impatient and moody by turns, he paced or moped around the cabin, always looking out, sometimes toward Blaisdell's ranch, but mostly toward Grass Valley.

It struck Jean as singular that neither Esther Isbel nor Mrs. Jacobs suggested a reburial of their husbands. The two bereaved women did not ask for assistance, but repaired to the pasture, and there spent several hours working over the graves. They raised mounds, which they sodded, and then placed stones at the heads and feet. Lastly, they fenced in the graves.

"I reckon I'll hitch up an' drive back home," said Mrs. Jacobs, when she returned to the cabin. "I've much to do an' plan. Probably I'll go to my mother's home. She's old an' will be glad to have me."

"If I had any place to go to I'd sure go," declared Esther Isbel, bitterly.

Gaston Isbel heard this remark. He raised his face from his hands, evidently both nettled and hurt.

"Esther, shore that's not kind," he said.

The red-haired woman—for she did not appear to be a girl any more—halted before his chair and gazed down at him, with a terrible flare of scorn in her gray eyes.

"Gaston Isbel, all I've got to say to you is this," she retorted, with the voice of a man. "Seein' that you an' Lee Jorth hate each other, why couldn't you act like men? . . . You damned Texans, with your bloody feuds, draggin' in every relation, every friend to murder each other! That's not the way of Arizona men. . . . We've all got to suffer—an' we women be ruined for life—because *you* had differences with Jorth. If you were half a man you'd go out an' kill him yourself, an' not leave a lot of widows an' orphaned children!"

Jean himself writhed under the lash of her scorn. Gaston Isbel turned a dead white. He could not answer her. He seemed stricken with merciless truth. Slowly dropping his head, he remained motionless, a pathetic and tragic figure; and he did not stir until the rapid beat of hoofs denoted the approach of horsemen. Blaisdell appeared on his white charger, leading a pack animal. And behind rode a group of men, all heavily armed, and likewise with packs.

"Get down an' come in," was Isbel's greeting. "Bill—you look after their packs. Better leave the hosses saddled."

The booted and spurred riders trooped in, and their demeanor fitted their errand. Jean was acquainted with all of them. Fredericks was a lanky Texan, the color of dust, and he had yellow, clear eyes, like those of a hawk. His mother had been an Isbel. Gordon, too, was related to Jean's family, though distantly. He resembled an industrious miner more than a prosperous cattleman. Blue was the most striking of the visitors, as he was the most noted. A little, shrunken gray-eyed man, with years of cowboy written all over him, he looked the quiet, easy, cool, and deadly Texan he was reputed to be. Blue's Texas record was shady, and was seldom alluded to, as unfavorable comment had turned out to be hazardous. He was the only one of the group who did not carry a rifle. But he packed two guns, a habit not often noted in Texans, and almost never in Arizonians.

Colmor, Ann Isbel's fiancé, was the youngest member of the clan, and the one closest to Jean. His meeting with Ann affected Jean powerfully, and brought to a climax an idea that had been developing in Jean's mind. His sister devotedly loved this lean-faced, keen-eyed Arizonian; and it took no great insight to discover that Colmor reciprocated her affection. They were young. They had long life before them. It seemed to Jean a pity that Colmor should be drawn into this war. Jean watched them, as they conversed apart; and he saw Ann's hands creep up to Colmor's breast, and he saw her dark eyes, eloquent, hungry, fearful, lifted with queries her lips did not speak. Jean stepped beside them, and laid an arm over both their shoulders.

"Colmor, for Ann's sake you'd better back out of this Jorth-Isbel fight," he whispered.

Colmor looked insulted. "But, Jean, it's Ann's father," he said. "I'm almost one of the family."

"You're Ann's sweetheart, an', by Heaven, I say you oughtn't to go with us!" whispered Jean.

"Go—with—you," faltered Ann.

"Yes. Dad is goin' straight after Jorth. Can't you tell that? An' there'll be one hell of a fight."

Ann looked up into Colmor's face with all her soul in her eyes, but she did not speak. Her look was noble. She yearned to guide him right, yet her lips were sealed. And Colmor betrayed the trouble of his soul.

The code of men held him bound, and he could not break from it, though he divined in that moment how truly it was wrong.

"Jean, your dad started me in the cattle business," said Colmor, earnestly. "An' I'm doin' well now. An' when I asked him for Ann he said he'd be glad to have me in the family. . . . Well, when this talk of fight come up, I asked your dad to let me go in on his side. He wouldn't hear of it. But after a while, as the time passed an' he made more enemies, he finally consented. I reckon he needs me now. An' I can't back out, not even for Ann."

"I would if I were you," replied Jean, and knew that he lied.

"Jean, I'm gamblin' to come out of the fight," said Colmor, with a smile. He had no morbid fears nor presentiments, such as troubled Jean.

"Why, sure—you stand as good a chance as any one," rejoined Jean. "It wasn't that I was worryin' about so much."

"What was it, then?" asked Ann, steadily.

"If Andrew *does* come through alive he'll have blood on his hands," returned Jean, with passion. "He can't come through without it. . . . I've begun to feel what it means to have killed my fellow men. . . . An' I'd rather your husband an' the father of your children never felt that."

Colmor did not take Jean as subtly as Ann did. She shrunk a little. Her dark eyes dilated. But Colmor showed nothing of her spiritual reaction. He was young. He had wild blood. He was loyal to the Isbels.

"Jean, never worry about my conscience," he said, with a keen look. "Nothin' would tickle me any more than to get a shot at every damn one of the Jorths."

That established Colmor's status in regard to the Jorth-Isbel feud. Jean had no more to say. He respected Ann's friend and felt poignant sorrow for Ann.

Gaston Isbel called for meat and drink to be set on the table for his guests. When his wishes had been complied with the women took the children into the adjoining cabin and shut the door.

"Hah! Wal, we can eat an' talk now."

First the newcomers wanted to hear particulars of what had happened. Blaisdell had told all he knew and had seen, but that was not sufficient. They plied Gaston Isbel with questions. Laboriously and ponderously he rehearsed the experiences of the fight at the ranch, according to his impressions. Bill Isbel was exhorted to talk, but he had of late manifested a sullen and taciturn disposition. In spite of Jean's vigilance Bill had continued to imbibe red liquor. Then Jean was called upon to relate all he had seen and done. It had been Jean's intention to keep his mouth shut, first for his own sake and, secondly, because he did not like to talk of his deeds. But when thus appealed to by these somber-faced, intent-eyed men he divined that the more carefully he described the cruelty and baseness of their enemies, and the more vividly he presented his participation in the first fight of the feud the more strongly he would bind these friends to the Isbel cause. So he talked for an hour, beginning with his meeting with Colter up on the Rim and ending with an account of his killing Greaves. His listeners sat through this long narrative with unabated interest and at the close they were leaning forward, breathless and tense.

"Ah! So Greaves got his desserts at last," exclaimed Gordon.

All the men around the table made comments, and the last, from Blue, was the one that struck Jean forcibly.

"Shore thet was a strange an' a hell of a way to kill Greaves. Why'd you do thet, Jean?"

"I told you. I wanted to avoid noise an' I hoped to get more of them."

Blue nodded his lean, eagle-like head and sat thoughtfully, as if not convinced of anything save Jean's prowess. After a moment Blue spoke again.

"Then, goin' back to Jean's tellin' aboot trackin' rustled cattle, I've got this to say. I've long suspected thet somebody livin' right heah in the valley has been drivin' off cattle an' dealin' with rustlers. An' now I'm shore of it."

This speech did not elicit the amaze from Gaston Isbel that Jean expected it would.

"You mean Greaves or some of his friends?"

"No. They wasn't none of them in the cattle business, like we are. Shore we all knowed Greaves was crooked. But what I'm figgerin' is thet some so-called honest man in our settlement has been makin' crooked deals."

Blue was a man of deeds rather than words, and so much strong speech from him, whom everybody knew to be remarkably reliable and keen, made a profound impression upon most of the Isbel faction. But, to Jean's surprise, his father did not rave. It was Blaisdell who supplied the rage and invective. Bill Isbel, also, was strangely indifferent to this new element in the condition of cattle dealing. Suddenly Jean caught a vague flash of thought, as if he had intercepted the thought of another's mind, and he wondered—could his brother Bill know anything about this crooked work alluded to by Blue? Dismissing the conjecture, Jean listened earnestly.

"An' if it's true it shore makes this difference—we cain't blame all the rustlin' on to Jorth," concluded Blue.

"Wal, it's not true," declared Gaston Isbel, roughly. "Jorth an' his Hash Knife Gang are at the bottom of all the rustlin' in the valley for years back. An' they've got to be wiped out!"

"Isbel, I reckon we'd all feel better if we talk straight," replied Blue, coolly. "I'm heah to stand by the Isbels. An' y'u know what thet means. But I'm not heah to fight Jorth because he may be a rustler. The others may have their own reasons, but mine is this—you once stood by me in Texas when I was needin' friends. Wal, I'm standin' by y'u now. Jorth is your enemy, an' so he is mine."

Gaston Isbel bowed to this ultimatum, scarcely less agitated than when Esther Isbel had denounced him. His rabid and morbid hate of Jorth had eaten into his heart to take possession there, like the parasite that battened upon the life of its victim. Blue's steely voice, his cold, gray eyes, showed the unbiased truth of the man, as well as his fidelity to his creed. Here again, but in a different manner, Gaston Isbel had the fact flung at him that other men must suffer, perhaps die, for his hate. And the very soul of the old rancher apparently rose in passionate revolt against the blind, headlong, elemental strength of his nature. So it seemed to Jean, who, in love and pity that hourly grew, saw through his father. Was it too late? Alas! Gaston Isbel could never be turned back! Yet something was altering his brooding, fixed mind.

"Wal," said Blaisdell, gruffly, "let's get down to business. . . . I'm for havin' Blue be foreman of this heah outfit, an' all of us to do as he says."

Gaston Isbel opposed this selection and indeed resented it. He intended to lead the Isbel faction.

"All right, then. Give us a hunch what we're goin' to do," replied Blaisdell.

"We're goin' to ride off on Jorth's trail—an' one way or another—kill him—*kill him!* . . . I reckon that'll end the fight."

What did old Isbel have in his mind? His listeners shook their heads.

"No," asserted Blaisdell. "Killin' Jorth might be the end of your desires, Isbel, but it'd never end *our* fight. We'll have gone too far. . . . If we take Jorth's trail from heah it means we've got to wipe out that rustler gang, or stay to the last man."

"Yes, by God!" exclaimed Fredericks.

"Let's drink to thet!" said Blue. Strangely they all turned to this Texas gunman, instinctively recognizing in him the brain and heart, and the past deeds, that fitted him for the leadership of such a clan. Blue had all in life to lose, and nothing to gain. Yet his spirit was such that he could not lean to all the possible gain of the future, and leave a debt unpaid. Then his voice, his look, his influence were those of a fighter. They all drank with him, even Jean, who hated liquor. And this act of drinking seemed the climax of the council. Preparations were at once begun for their departure on Jorth's trail.

Jean took but little time for his own needs. A horse, a blanket, a knapsack of meat and bread, a canteen, and his weapons, with all the ammunition he could pack, made up his outfit. He wore his buckskin suit, leggings, and moccasins. Very soon the cavalcade was ready to depart. Jean tried not to watch Bill Isbel say good-by to his children, but it was impossible not to. Whatever Bill was, as a man, he was father of those children, and he loved them. How strange that the little ones seemed to realize the meaning of this good-by! They were grave, somber-eyed, pale up to the last moment, then they broke down and wept. Did they sense that their father would never come back? Jean caught that dark, fatalistic presentiment. Bill Isbel's convulsed face showed that he also caught it. Jean did not see Bill say good-by to his wife. But he heard her. Old Gaston Isbel forgot to speak to the children, or else could not. He never looked at them. And his good-by to Ann was as if he were only riding to the village for a day. Jean saw woman's love, woman's intuition, woman's grief in her eyes. He could not escape her. "Oh, Jean! oh, brother!" she whispered as she enfolded him. "It's awful! It's wrong! Wrong! Wrong! . . . Good-by! . . . If killing *must* be—see that y'u kill the Jorths! . . . Good-by!"

Even in Ann, gentle and mild, the Isbel blood spoke at the last. Jean gave Ann over to the pale-faced Colmor, who took her in his arms. Then Jean fled out to his horse. This cold-blooded devastation of a home was almost more than he could bear. There was love here. What would be left?

Colmor was the last one to come out to the horses. He did not walk erect, nor as one whose sight was clear. Then, as the silent, tense, grim men mounted their horses, Bill Isbel's eldest child, the boy, appeared in the door. His little form seemed instinct with a force vastly different from grief. His face was the face of an Isbel.

"Daddy—kill 'em all!" he shouted, with a passion all the fiercer for its incongruity to the treble voice.

So the poison had spread from father to son.

CHAPTER 9

Half a mile from the Isbel ranch the cavalcade passed the log cabin of Evarts, father of the boy who had tended sheep with Bernardino.

It suited Gaston Isbel to halt here. No need to call! Evarts and his son appeared so quickly as to convince observers that they had been watching.

"Howdy, Jake!" said Isbel. "I'm wantin' a word with y'u alone."

"Shore, boss, git down an' come in," replied Evarts.

Isbel led him aside, and said something forcible that Jean divined from the very gesture which accompanied it. His father was telling Evarts that he was not to join in the Isbel-Jorth war. Evarts had worked for the Isbels a long time, and his faithfulness, along with something stronger and darker, showed in his rugged face as he stubbornly opposed Isbel. The old man raised his voice: "No, I tell you. An' that settles it."

They returned to the horses, and, before mounting, Isbel, as if he remembered something, directed his somber gaze on young Evarts.

"Son, did you bury Bernardino?"

"Dad an' me went over yestiddy," replied the lad. "I shore was glad the coyotes hadn't been round."

"How aboot the sheep?"

"I left them there. I was goin' to stay, but bein' all alone—I got skeered. . . . The sheep was doin' fine. Good water an' some grass. An' this ain't time fer varmints to hang round."

"Jake, keep your eye on that flock," returned Isbel. "An' if I shouldn't happen to come back y'u can call them sheep yours. . . . I'd like your boy to ride up to the village. Not with us, so anybody would see him. But afterward. We'll be at Abel Meeker's."

Again Jean was confronted with an uneasy premonition as to some idea or plan his father had not shared with his followers. When the cavalcade started on again Jean rode to his father's side and asked him why he had wanted the Evarts boy to come to Grass Valley. And the old man replied that, as the boy could run to and fro in the village without danger, he might be useful in reporting what was going on at Greaves's store, where undoubtedly the Jorth gang would hold forth. This appeared reasonable enough, therefore Jean smothered the objection he had meant to make.

The valley road was deserted. When, a mile farther on, the riders passed a group of cabins, just on the outskirts of the village, Jean's quick eye caught sight of curious and evidently frightened people trying to see while they avoided being seen. No doubt the whole settlement was in a state of suspense and terror. Not unlikely this dark, closely grouped band of horsemen appeared to them as Jorth's gang had looked to Jean. It was an orderly, trotting march that manifested neither hurry nor excitement. But any Western eye could have caught the singular aspect of such a group, as if the intent of the riders was a visible thing.

Soon they reached the outskirts of the village. Here their approach had been watched for or had been already reported. Jean saw men, women, children peeping from behind cabins and from half-opened doors. Farther on Jean espied the dark figures of men, slipping out the back way through orchards and gardens and running north, toward the center of the village. Could these be friends of the Jorth crowd, on the way with warnings of the approach of the Isbels? Jean felt convinced of it. He was learning that his father had not been absolutely correct in his estimation of the way Jorth and his followers were regarded by their neighbors. Not improbably there were really many villagers who, being more interested in sheep raising than in cattle, had an honest leaning toward the Jorths. Some, too, no doubt, had leanings that were dishonest in deed if not in sincerity.

Gaston Isbel led his clan straight down the middle of the wide road of Grass Valley until he reached a point opposite Abel Meeker's cabin. Jean espied the same curiosity from behind Meeker's door and windows as had been shown all along the road. But presently, at Isbel's call, the door opened and a short, swarthy man appeared. He carried a rifle.

"Howdy, Gass!" he said. "What's the good word?"

"Wal, Abel, it's not good, but bad. An' it's shore started," replied Isbel. "I'm askin' y'u to let me have your cabin."

"You're welcome. I'll send the folks 'round to Jim's," returned Meeker. "An' if y'u want me, I'm with y'u, Isbel."

"Thanks, Abel, but I'm not leadin' any more kin an' friends into this heah deal."

"Wal, jest as y'u say. But I'd like damn bad to jine with y'u. . . . My brother Ted was shot last night."

"Ted! Is he daid?" ejaculated Isbel, blankly.

"We can't find out," replied Meeker. "Jim says thet Jeff Campbell said thet Ted went into Greaves's place last night. Greaves allus was friendly to Ted, but Greaves wasn't thar—"

"No, he shore wasn't," interrupted Isbel, with a dark smile, "an' he never will be there again."

Meeker nodded with slow comprehension and a shade crossed his face.

"Wal, Campbell claimed he'd heerd from some one who was thar. Anyway, the Jorths were drinkin' hard, an' they raised a row with Ted— same old sheep talk—an' somebody shot him. Campbell said Ted was thrown out back, an' he was shore he wasn't killed."

"Ahuh! Wal, I'm sorry, Abel, your family had to lose in this. Maybe Ted's not bad hurt. I shore hope so. . . . An' y'u an' Jim keep out of the fight, anyway."

"All right, Isbel. But I reckon I'll give y'u a hunch. If this heah fight lasts long the whole damn Basin will be in it, on one side or t'other."

"Abe, you're talkin' sense," broke in Blaisdell. "An' that's why we're up heah for quick action."

"I heerd y'u got Daggs," whispered Meeker, as he peered all around.

"Wal, y'u heerd correct," drawled Blaisdell.

Meeker muttered strong words into his beard. "Say, was Daggs in thet Jorth outfit?"

"He *was*. But he walked right into Jean's forty-four. . . . An' I reckon his carcass would show some more."

"An' whar's Guy Isbel?" demanded Meeker.

"Daid an' buried, Abel," repled Gaston Isbel. "An' now I'd be obliged if y'u'll hurry your folks away, an' let us have your cabin an' corral. Have y'u got any hay for the hosses?"

"Shore. The barn's half full," replied Meeker, as he turned away. "Come on in."

"No. We'll wait till you've gone."

When Meeker had gone, Isbel and his men sat their horses and looked about them and spoke low. Their advent had been expected, and the little town awoke to the imminence of the impending battle. Inside Meeker's house there was the sound of indistinct voices of women and the bustle incident to a hurried vacating.

Across the wide road people were peering out on all sides, some hiding, others walking to and fro, from fence to fence, whispering in little groups. Down the wide road, at the point where it turned, stood Greaves's fort-like stone house. Low, flat, isolated, with its dark, eye-like windows, it presented a forbidding and sinister aspect. Jean distinctly saw the forms of men, some dark, others in shirt sleeves, come to the wide door and look down the road.

"Wal, I reckon only aboot five hundred good hoss steps are separatin' us from that outfit," drawled Blaisdell.

No one replied to his jocularity. Gaston Isbel's eyes narrowed to a slit in his furrowed face and he kept them fastened upon Greaves's store. Blue, likewise, had a somber cast of countenance, not, perhaps, any darker nor grimmer than those of his comrades, but more representative of intense preoccupation of mind. The look of him thrilled Jean, who could sense its deadliness, yet could not grasp any more. Altogether, the manner of the villagers and the watchful pacing to and fro of the Jorth followers and the silent, boding front of Isbel and his men summed up for Jean the menace of the moment that must very soon change to a terrible reality.

At a call from Meeker, who stood at the back of the cabin, Gaston Isbel rode into the yard, followed by the others of his party. "Somebody look after the hosses," ordered Isbel, as he dismounted and took his rifle and pack. "Better leave the saddles on, leastways till we see what's comin' off."

Jean and Bill Isbel led the horses back to the corral. While watering and feeding them, Jean somehow received the impression that Bill was trying to speak, to confide in him, to unburden himself of some load. This peculiarity of Bill's had become marked when he was perfectly sober. Yet he had never spoken or even begun anything unusual. Upon the present occasion, however, Jean believed that his brother might have gotten rid of his emotion, or whatever it was, had they not been interrupted by Colmor.

"Boys, the old man's orders are for us to sneak round on three sides of Greaves's store, keepin' out of gunshot till we find good cover, an' then crawl closer an' to pick off any of Jorth's gang who shows himself."

Bill Isbel strode off without a reply to Colmor.

"Well, I don't think so much of that," said Jean, ponderingly. "Jorth has lots of friends here. Somebody might pick us off."

"I kicked, but the old man shut me up. He's not to be bucked ag'in' now. Struck me as powerful queer. But no wonder."

"Maybe he knows best. Did he say anythin' about what he an' the rest of them are goin' to do?"

"Nope. Blue taxed him with that an' got the same as me. I reckon we'd better try it out, for a while, anyway."

"Looks like he wants us to keep out of the fight," replied Jean, thoughtfully. "Maybe, though . . . Dad's no fool. Colmor, you wait here till I get out of sight. I'll go round an' come up as close as advisable behind Greaves's store. You take the right side. An' keep hid."

With that Jean strode off, going around the barn, straight out the orchard lane to the open flat, and then climbing a fence to the north of the village. Presently he reached a line of sheds and corrals, to which he held until he arrived at the road. This point was about a quarter of a mile from Greaves's store, and around the bend. Jean sighted no one. The road, the fields, the yards, the backs of the cabins all looked deserted. A blight had settled down upon the peaceful activities of Grass Valley. Crossing the road, Jean began to circle until he came close to several cabins, around which he made a wide detour. This took him to the edge of the slope, where brush and thickets afforded him a safe passage to a line directly back of Greaves's store. Then he turned toward it. Soon he was again approaching a cabin of that side, and some of its inmates descried him.

Their actions attested to their alarm. Jean half expected a shot from this quarter, such were his growing doubts, but he was mistaken. A man, unknown to Jean, closely watched his guarded movements and then waved a hand, as if to signify to Jean that he had nothing to fear. After this act he disappeared. Jean believed that he had been recognized by some one not antagonistic to the Isbels. Therefore he passed the cabin and, coming to a thick scrub-oak tree that offered shelter, he hid there to watch. From this spot he could see the back of Greaves's store, at a distance probably too far for a rifle bullet to reach. Before him, as far as the store, and on each side, extended the village common. In front of the store ran the road. Jean's position was such that he could not command sight of this road down toward Meeker's house, a fact that disturbed him. Not satisfied with this stand, he studied his surroundings in the hope of espying a better. And he discovered what he thought would be a more favorable position, although he could not see much farther down the road. Jean went back around the cabin and, coming out into the open to the right, he got the corner of Greaves's barn between him and the window of the store. Then he boldly hurried into the open, and soon reached an old wagon, from behind which he proposed to watch. He could not see either window or door of the store, but if any of the Jorth contingent came out the back way they would be within reach of his rifle. Jean took the risk of being shot at from either side.

So sharp and roving was his sight that he soon espied Colmor slipping along behind the trees some hundred yards to the left. All his efforts to catch a glimpse of Bill, however, were fruitless. And this appeared strange to Jean, for there were several good places on the right from which Bill could have commanded the front of Greaves's store and the whole west side.

Colmor disappeared among some shrubbery, and Jean seemed left alone to watch a deserted, silent village. Watching and listening, he felt that the time dragged. Yet the shadows cast by the sun showed him that, no matter how tense he felt and how the moments seemed hours, they were really flying.

Suddenly Jean's ears rang with the vibrant shock of a rifle report. He jerked up, strung and thrilling. It came from in front of the store. It was followed by revolver shots, heavy, booming. Three he counted, and the rest were too close together to enumerate. A single hoarse yell pealed out, somehow trenchant and triumphant. Other yells, not so wild and strange, muffled the first one. Then silence clapped down on the store and the open square.

Jean was deadly certain that some of the Jorth clan would show themselves. He strained to still the trembling those sudden shots and that significant yell had caused him. No man appeared. No more sounds caught Jean's ears. The suspense, then, grew unbearable. It was not that he could not wait for an enemy to appear, but that he could not wait to learn what had happened. Every moment that he stayed there, with hands like steel on his rifle, with eyes of a falcon, but added to a dreadful, dark certainty of disaster. A rifle shot swiftly followed by revolver shots! What could they mean? Revolver shots of different caliber, surely fired by different men! What could they mean? It was not these shots that accounted for Jean's dread, but the yell which had followed. All his intelligence and all his nerve were not sufficient to fight down the feeling of calamity. And at last, yielding to it, he left his post, and ran like a deer across the open, through the cabin yard, and around the edge of the slope to the road. Here his caution brought him to a halt. Not a living thing crossed his vision. Breaking into a run, he soon reached the back of Meeker's place and entered, to hurry forward to the cabin.

Colmor was there in the yard, breathing hard, his face working, and in front of him crouched several of the men with rifles ready. The road, to Jean's flashing glance, was apparently deserted. Blue sat on the doorstep, lighting a cigarette. Then on the moment Blaisdell strode to the door of the cabin. Jean had never seen him look like that.

"Jean—look—down the road," he said, brokenly, and with big hand shaking he pointed down toward Greaves's store.

Like lightning Jean's glance shot down—down—down—until it stopped to fix upon the prostrate form of a man, lying in the middle of the road. A man of lengthy build, shirt-sleeved arms flung wide, white head in the dust—dead! Jean's recognition was as swift as his sight. His father! They had killed him! The Jorths! It was done. His father's premonition of death had not been false. And then, after these flashing thoughts, came a sense of blankness, momentarily almost oblivion, that gave place to a rending of the heart. That pain Jean had known only at the death of his mother. It passed, this agonizing pang, and its icy pressure yielded to a rushing gust of blood, fiery as hell.

"Who—did it?" whispered Jean.

"Jorth!" replied Blaisdell, huskily. "Son, we couldn't hold your dad back. . . . We couldn't. He was like a lion. . . . An' he throwed his life away! Oh, if it hadn't been for that it 'd not be so awful. Shore, we come heah to shoot an' be shot. But not like that. . . . By God, it was murder—murder!"

Jean's mute lips framed a query easily read.

"Tell him, Blue. I cain't," continued Blaisdell, and he tramped back into the cabin.

"Set down, Jean, an' take things easy," said Blue, calmly. "You know we all reckoned we'd git plugged one way or another in this deal. An' shore it doesn't matter much how a fellar gits it. All thet ought to bother us is to make shore the other outfit bites the dust—same as your dad had to."

Under this man's tranquil presence, all the more quieting because it seemed to be so deadly sure and cool, Jean felt the uplift of his dark spirit, the acceptance of fatality, the mounting control of faculties that must wait. The little gunman seemed to have about his inert presence something that suggested a rattlesnake's inherent knowledge of its destructiveness. Jean sat down and wiped his clammy face.

"Jean, your dad reckoned to square accounts with Jorth, an' save us all," began Blue, puffing out a cloud of smoke. "But he reckoned too late. Mebbe years ago—or even not long ago—if he'd called Jorth out man to man there'd never been any Jorth-Isbel war. Gaston Isbel's conscience woke too late. That's how I figger it."

"Hurry! Tell me—how it—happened," panted Jean.

"Wal, a little while after y'u left I seen your dad writin' on a leaf he tore out of a book—Meeker's Bible, as y'u can see. I thought thet was funny. An' Blaisdell gave me a hunch. Pretty soon along comes young Evarts. The old man calls him out of our hearin' an' talks to him. Then I seen him give the boy somethin' which I afterward figgered was what he wrote on the leaf out of the Bible. Me an' Blaisdell both tried to git out of him what thet meant. But not a word. I kept watchin' an' after a while I seen young Evarts slip out the back way. Mebbe half an hour I seen a bare-legged kid cross the road an' go into Greaves's store. . . . Then shore I tumbled to your dad. He'd sent a note to Jorth to come out an' meet him face to face, man to man! . . . Shore it was like readin' what your dad had wrote. But I didn't say nothin' to Blaisdell. I jest watched."

Blue drawled these last words, as if he enjoyed remembrance of his keen reasoning. A smile wreathed his thin lips. He drew twice on the cigarette and emitted another cloud of smoke. Quite suddenly then he changed. He made a rapid gesture—the whip of a hand, significant and passionate. And swift words followed:

"Colonel Lee Jorth stalked out of the store—out into the road— mebbe a hundred steps. Then he halted. He wore his long black coat an' his wide black hat, an' he stood like a stone.

" 'What the hell!' burst out Blaisdell, comin' out of his trance.

"The rest of us jest looked. I'd forgot your dad, for the minnit. So had all of us. But we remembered soon enough when we seen him stalk out. Everybody had a hunch then. I called him. Blaisdell begged him to come back. All the fellars had a say. No use! Then I shore cussed him an' told him it was plain as day thet Jorth didn't hit me like an honest man. I can sense such things. I knew Jorth had a trick up his sleeve. I've not been a gun fighter fer nothin'.

"Your dad had no rifle. He packed his gun at his hip. He jest stalked down thet road like a giant, goin' faster an' faster, holdin' his head high. It shore was fine to see him. But I was sick. I heerd Blaisdell groan, an' Fredericks thar cussed somethin' fierce. . . . When your dad halted—I reckon aboot fifty steps from Jorth—then we all went numb. I heerd your dad's voice—then Jorth's. They cut like knives. Y'u could shore heah the hate they hed fer each other."

Blue had become a little husky. His speech had grown gradually to denote his feeling. Underneath his serenity there was a different order of man.

"I reckon both your dad an' Jorth went fer their guns at the same time—an even break. But jest as they drew, some one shot a rifle from the store. Must hev been a forty-five seventy. A big gun! The bullet must have hit your dad low down, aboot the middle. He acted thet way, sinkin' to his knees. An' he was wild in shootin'—so wild thet he must hev missed. Then he wabbled—an' Jorth run in a dozen steps, shootin' fast, till your dad fell over. . . . Jorth run closer, bent over him, an' then straightened up with an Apache yell, if I ever heerd one. . . . An' then Jorth backed slow—lookin' all the time—backed to the store, an' went in."

Blue's voice ceased. Jean seemed suddenly released from an impelling magnet that now dropped him to some numb, dizzy depth. Blue's lean face grew hazy. Then Jean bowed his head in his hands, and sat there, while a slight tremor shook all his muscles at once. He grew deathly cold and deathly sick. This paroxysm slowly wore away, and Jean grew conscious of a dull amaze at the apparent deadness of his spirit. Blaisdell placed a huge, kindly hand on his shoulder.

"Brace up, son!" he said, with voice now clear and resonant. "Shore it's what your dad expected—an' what we all must look for. . . . If y'u was goin' to kill Jorth before—think how ——— ——— shore y'u're goin' to kill him now."

"Blaisdell's talkin'," put in Blue, and his voice had a cold ring. "Lee Jorth will never see the sun rise ag'in!"

These calls to the primitive in Jean, to the Indian, were not in vain. But even so, when the dark tide rose in him, there was still a haunting consciousness of the cruelty of this singular doom imposed upon him. Strangely Ellen Jorth's face floated back in the depths of his vision, pale, fading, like the face of a spirit floating by.

"Blue," said Blaisdell, "let's get Isbel's body soon as we dare, an' bury it. Reckon we can, right after dark."

"Shore," replied Blue. "But y'u fellers figger thet out. I'm thinkin' hard. I've got somethin' on my mind."

Jean grew fascinated by the looks and speech and action of the little gunman. Blue, indeed, had something on his mind. And it boded ill to the men in that dark square stone house down the road. He paced to and fro in the yard, back and forth on the path to the gate, and then he entered the cabin to stalk up and down, faster and faster, until all at once he halted as if struck, to upfling his right arm in a singular fierce gesture.

"Jean, call the men in," he said, tersely.

They all filed in, sinister and silent, with eager faces turned to the little Texan. His dominance showed markedly.

"Gordon, y'u stand in the door an' keep your eye peeled," went on

Blue. . . . "Now, boys, listen! I've thought it all out. This game of man huntin' is the same to me as cattle raisin' is to y'u. An' my life in Texas all comes back to me, I reckon, in good stead fer us now. I'm goin' to kill Lee Jorth! Him first, an' mebbe his brothers. I had to think of a good many ways before I hit on one I reckon will be shore. It's got to be *shore*. Jorth has got to die! Wal, heah's my plan. . . . Thet Jorth outfit is drinkin' some, we can gamble on it. They're not goin' to leave thet store. An' of course they'll be expectin' us to start a fight. I reckon they'll look fer some such siege as they held round Isbel's ranch. But we shore ain't goin' to do thet. I'm goin' to surprise thet outfit. There's only one man among them who is dangerous, an' thet's Queen. I know Queen. But he doesn't know me. An' I'm goin' to finish my job before he gets acquainted with me. After thet, all right!"

Blue paused a moment, his eyes narrowing down, his whole face setting in hard cast of intense preoccupation, as if he visualized a scene of extraordinary nature.

"Wal, what's your trick?" demanded Blaisdell.

"Y'u all know Greaves's store," continued Blue. "How them winders have wooden shutters thet keep a light from showin' outside? Wal, I'm gamblin' thet as soon as it's dark Jorth's gang will be celebratin'. They'll be drinkin' an' they'll have a light, an' the winders will be shut. They're not goin' to worry none aboot us. Thet store is like a fort. It won't burn. An' shore they'd never think of us chargin' them in there. Wal, as soon as it's dark, we'll go round behind the lots an' come up jest acrost the road from Greaves's. I reckon we'd better leave Isbel where he lays till this fight's over. Mebbe y'u'll have more 'n him to bury. We'll crawl behind them bushes in front of Coleman's yard. An' heah's where Jean comes in. He'll take an ax, an' his guns, of course, an' do some of his Injun sneakin' round to the back of Greaves's store. . . . An', Jean, y'u must do a slick job of this. But I reckon it 'll be easy fer you. Back there it 'll be dark as pitch, fer anyone lookin' out of the store. An' I'm figgerin' y'u can take your time an' crawl right up. Now if y'u don't remember how Greaves's back yard looks I'll tell y'u."

Here Blue dropped on one knee to the floor and with a finger he traced a map of Greaves's barn and fence, the back door and window, and especially a break in the stone foundation which led into a kind of cellar where Greaves stored wood and other things that could be left outdoors.

"Jean, I take particular pains to show y'u where this hole is," said Blue, "because if the gang runs out y'u could duck in there an' hide. An' if they run out into the yard—wal, y'u'd make it a sorry run fer them. . . . Wal, when y'u've crawled up close to Greaves's back door, an' waited long enough to see an' listen—then you're to run fast an' swing your ax smash ag'in' the winder. Take a quick peep in if y'u want to. It might help. Then jump quick an' take a swing at the door. Y'u'll be standin' to one side, so if the gang shoots through the door they won't hit y'u. Bang thet door good an' hard. . . . Wal, now's where I come in. When y'u swing thet ax I'll shore run fer the front of the store. Jorth an' his outfit will be some attentive to thet poundin' of yours on the back door. So I reckon. An' they'll be *lookin'* thet way. I'll run in—yell—an' throw my guns on Jorth."

"Humph! Is that all?" ejaculated Blaisdell.

"I reckon thet's all an' I'm figgerin' it's a hell of a lot," responded Blue, dryly. "Thet's what Jorth will think."

"Where do we come in?"

"Wal, y'u all can back me up," replied Blue, dubiously. "Y'u see, my plan goes as far as killin' Jorth—an' mebbe his brothers. Mebbe I'll get a crack at Queen. But I'll be shore of Jorth. After thet all depends. Mebbe it 'll be easy fer me to get out. An' if I do y'u fellars will know it an' can fill thet storeroom full of bullets."

"Wal, Blue, with all due respect to y'u, I shore don't like your plan," declared Blaisdell. "Success depends upon too many little things any one of which might go wrong."

"Blaisdell, I reckon I know this heah game better than y'u," replied Blue. "A gun fighter goes by instinct. This trick will work."

"But suppose that front door of Greaves's store is barred," protested Blaisdell.

"It hasn't got any bar," said Blue.

"Y'u're shore?"

"Yes, I reckon," replied Blue.

"Hell, man! Aren't y'u takin' a terrible chance?" queried Blaisdell.

Blue's answer to that was a look that brought the blood to Blaisdell's face. Only then did the rancher really comprehend how the little gunman had taken such desperate chances before, and meant to take them now, not with any hope or assurance of escaping with his life, but to live up to his peculiar code of honor.

"Blaisdell, did y'u ever heah of me in Texas?" he queried, dryly.

"Wal, no, Blue, I cain't swear I did," replied the rancher, apologetically. "An' Isbel was always sort of mysterious aboot his acquaintance with you."

"My name's not Blue."

"Ahuh! Wal, what is it, then—if I'm safe to ask?" returned Blaisdell, gruffly.

"It's King Fisher," replied Blue.

The shock that stiffened Blaisdell must have been communicated to the others. Jean certainly felt amaze, and some other emotion not fully realized, when he found himself face to face with one of the most notorious characters ever known in Texas—an outlaw long supposed to be dead.

"Men, I reckon I'd kept my secret if I'd any idee of comin' out of this Isbel-Jorth war alive," said Blue. "But I'm goin' to cash. I feel it heah. . . . Isbel was my friend. He saved me from bein' lynched in Texas. An' so I'm goin' to kill Jorth. Now I'll take it kind of y'u—if any of y'u come out of this alive—to tell who I was an' why I was on the Isbel side. Because this sheep an' cattle war—this talk of Jorth an' the Hash Knife Gang—it makes me sick. I *know* there's been crooked work on Isbel's side, too. An' I never want it on record thet I killed Jorth because he was a rustler."

"By God, Blue! it's late in the day for such talk," burst out Blaisdell, in rage and amaze. "But I reckon y'u know what y'u're talkin' aboot. . . . Wal, I shore don't want to heah it."

At this juncture Bill Isbel quietly entered the cabin, too late to hear any of Blue's statement. Jean was positive of that, for as Blue was speaking those last revealing words Bill's heavy boots had resounded on the gravel path outside. Yet something in Bill's look or in the way Blue averted his lean face or in the entrance of Bill at that particular moment, or all these together, seemed to Jean to add further mystery to the long secret causes leading up to the Jorth-Isbel war. Did Bill know what Blue knew? Jean had an inkling that he did. And on the moment, so perplexing and bitter, Jean gazed out the door, down the deserted road to where his dead father lay, white-haired and ghastly in the sunlight.

"Blue, you could have kept that to yourself, as well as your real name," interposed Jean, with bitterness. "It's too late now for either to do any good. . . . But I appreciate your friendship for dad, an' I'm ready to help carry out your plan."

That decision of Jean's appeared to put an end to protest or argument from Blaisdell or any of the others. Blue's fleeting dark smile was one of satisfaction. Then upon most of this group of men seemed to settle a grim restraint. They went out and walked and watched; they came in again, restless and somber. Jean thought that he must have bent his gaze a thousand times down the road to the tragic figure of his father. That sight roused all emotions in his breast, and the one that stirred there most was pity. The pity of it! Gaston Isbel lying face down in the dust of the village street! Patches of blood showed on the back of his vest and one white-sleeved shoulder. He had been shot through. Every time Jean saw this blood he had to stifle a gathering of wild, savage impulses.

Meanwhile the afternoon hours dragged by and the village remained as if its inhabitants had abandoned it. Not even a dog showed on the side road. Jorth and some of his men came out in front of the store and sat on the steps, in close convening groups. Every move they made seemed significant of their confidence and importance. About sunset they went back into the store, closing door and window shutters. Then Blaisdell called the Isbel faction to have food and drink. Jean felt no hunger. And Blue, who had kept apart from the others, showed no desire to eat. Neither did he smoke, though early in the day he had never been without a cigarette between his lips.

Twilight fell and darkness came. Not a light showed anywhere in the blackness.

"Wal, I reckon it's aboot time," said Blue, and he led the way out of the cabin to the back of the lot. Jean strode behind him, carrying his rifle and an ax. Silently the other men followed. Blue turned to the left and led through the field until he came within sight of a dark line of trees.

"Thet's where the road turns off," he said to Jean. "An' heah's the back of Coleman's place. . . . Wal, Jean, good luck!"

Jean felt the grip of a steel-like hand, and in the darkness he caught the gleam of Blue's eyes. Jean had no response in words for the laconic Blue, but he wrung the hard, thin hand and hurried away in the darkness.

Once alone, his part of the business at hand rushed him into eager thrilling action. This was the sort of work he was fitted to do. In this instance it was important, but it seemed to him that Blue had coolly taken the perilous part. And this cowboy with gray in his thin hair was in reality the great King Fisher! Jean marveled at the fact. And he shivered all over for Jorth. In ten minutes—fifteen, more or less, Jorth would lie gasping bloody froth and sinking down. Something in the dark, lonely, silent, oppressive summer night told Jean this. He strode on swiftly. Crossing the road at a run, he kept on over the ground he had traversed during the afternoon, and in a few moments he stood breathing hard at the edge of the common behind Greaves's store.

A pin point of light penetrated the blackness. It made Jean's heart leap. The Jorth contingent were burning the big lamp that hung in the center of Greaves's store. Jean listened. Loud voices and coarse laughter sounded discord on the melancholy silence of the night. What Blue had called his instinct had surely guided him aright. Death of Gaston Isbel was being celebrated by revel.

In a few moments Jean had regained his breath. Then all his faculties set intensely to the action at hand. He seemed to magnify his hearing and his sight. His movements made no sound. He gained the wagon, where he crouched a moment.

The ground seemed a pale, obscure medium, hardly more real than the gloom above it. Through this gloom of night, which looked thick like a cloud, but was really clear, shone the thin, bright point of light, accentuating the black square that was Greaves's store. Above this stood a gray line of tree foliage, and then the intensely dark-blue sky studded with white, cold stars.

A hound bayed lonesomely somewhere in the distance. Voices of men sounded more distinctly, some deep and low, others loud, unguarded, with the vacant note of thoughtlessness.

Jean gathered all his forces, until sense of sight and hearing were in exquisite accord with the suppleness and lightness of his movements. He glided on about ten short, swift steps before he halted. That was as far as his piercing eyes could penetrate. If there had been a guard stationed outside the store Jean would have seen him before being seen. He saw the fence, reached it, entered the yard, glided in the dense shadow of the barn until the black square began to loom gray—the color of stone at night. Jean peered through the obscurity. No dark figure of a man showed against that gray wall—only a black patch, which must be the hole in the foundation mentioned. A ray of light now streaked out from the little black window. To the right showed the wide, black door.

Farther on Jean glided silently. Then he halted. There was no guard outside. Jean heard the clink of a cup, the lazy drawl of a Texan, and then a strong, harsh voice—Jorth's. It strung Jean's whole being tight and vibrating. Inside he was on fire while cold thrills rippled over his skin. It took tremendous effort of will to hold himself back another instant to listen, to look, to feel, to make sure. And that instant charged him with a mighty current of hot blood, straining, throbbing, damming.

When Jean leaped this current burst. In a few swift bounds he gained his point halfway between door and window. He leaned his rifle against the stone wall. Then he swung the ax. Crash! The window shutter split and rattled to the floor inside. The silence then broke with a hoarse, "What's thet?"

With all his might Jean swung the heavy ax on the door. Smash! The lower half caved in and banged to the floor. Bright light flared out the hole.

"Look out!" yelled a man, in loud alarm. "They're batterin' the back door!"

Jean swung again, high on the splintered door. Crash! Pieces flew inside.

"They've got axes," hoarsely shouted another voice. "Shove the counter ag'in' the door."

"No!" thundered a voice of authority that denoted terror as well. "Let them come in. Pull your guns an' take to cover!"

"They ain't comin' in," was the hoarse reply. "They'll shoot in on us from the dark."

"Put out the lamp!" yelled another.

Jean's third heavy swing caved in part of the upper half of the door. Shouts and curses intermingled with the sliding of benches across the floor and the hard shuffle of boots. This confusion seemed to be split and silenced by a piercing yell, of different caliber, of terrible meaning. It stayed Jean's swing—caused him to drop the ax and snatch up his rifle.

"Don't anybody move!"

Like a steel whip this voice cut the silence. It belonged to Blue. Jean swiftly bent to put his eye to a crack in the door. Most of those visible seemed to have been frozen into unnatural positions. Jorth stood rather in front of his men, hatless and coatless, one arm outstretched, and his dark profile set toward a little man just inside the door. This man was Blue. Jean needed only one flashing look at Blue's face, at his leveled, quivering guns, to understand why he had chosen this trick.

"Who 're—you?" demanded Jorth, in husky pants.

"Reckon I'm Isbel's right-hand man," came the biting reply. "Once tolerable well known in Texas. . . . *King Fisher!*"

The name must have been a guarantee of death. Jorth recognized this outlaw and realized his own fate. In the lamplight his face turned a pale greenish white. His outstretched hand began to quiver down.

Blue's left gun seemed to leap up and flash red and explode. Several heavy reports merged almost as one. Jorth's arm jerked limply, flinging his gun. And his body sagged in the middle. His hands fluttered like crippled wings and found their way to his abdomen. His death-pale face never changed its set look nor position toward Blue. But his gasping utterance was one of horrible mortal fury and terror. Then he began to sway, still with that strange, rigid set of his face toward his slayer, until he fell.

His fall broke the spell. Even Blue, like the gunman he was, had paused to watch Jorth in his last mortal action. Jorth's followers began to draw and shoot. Jean saw Blue's return fire bring down a huge man, who fell across Jorth's body. Then Jean, quick as the thought that actuated him, raised his rifle and shot at the big lamp. It burst in a flare. It crashed to the floor. Darkness followed—a blank, thick, enveloping mantle. Then red flashes of guns emphasized the blackness. Inside the store there broke loose a pandemonium of shots, yells, curses, and thudding boots. Jean shoved his rifle barrel inside the door and, holding it low down, he moved it to and fro while he worked lever and trigger until the magazine was empty. Then, drawing his six-shooter, he emptied that. A roar of rifles from the front of the store told Jean that his comrades had entered the fray. Bullets zipped through the door he had broken. Jean ran swiftly round the corner, taking care to sheer off a little to the left, and when he got clear of the building he saw a line of flashes in the middle of the road. Blaisdell and the others were firing into the door of the store. With nimble fingers Jean reloaded his rifle. Then swiftly he ran across the road and down to get behind his comrades. Their shooting had slackened. Jean saw dark forms coming his way.

"Hello, Blaisdell!" he called, warningly.

"That y'u, Jean?" returned the rancher, looming up. "Wal, we wasn't worried aboot y'u."

"Blue?" queried Jean, sharply.

A little, dark figure shuffled past Jean. "Howdy, Jean!" said Blue, dryly. "Y'u shore did your part. Reckon I'll need to be tied up, but I ain't hurt much."

"Colmor's hit," called the voice of Gordon, a few yards distant. "Help me, somebody!"

Jean ran to help Gordon uphold the swaying Colmor. "Are you hurt—bad?" asked Jean, anxiously. The young man's head rolled and hung. He was breathing hard and did not reply. They had almost to carry him.

"Come on, men!" called Blaisdell, turning back toward the others who were still firing. "We'll let well enough alone. . . . Fredericks, y'u an' Bill help me find the body of the old man. It's heah somewhere."

Farther on down the road the searchers stumbled over Gaston Isbel. They picked him up and followed Jean and Gordon, who were supporting the wounded Colmor. Jean looked back to see Blue dragging himself along in the rear. It was too dark to see distinctly; nevertheless, Jean got the impression that Blue was more severely wounded than he had claimed to be. The distance to Meeker's cabin was not far, but it took what Jean felt to be a long and anxious time to get there. Colmor apparently rallied somewhat. When this procession entered Meeker's yard, Blue was lagging behind.

"Blue, how air y'u?" called Blaisdell, with concern.

"Wal, I got—my boots—on—anyhow," replied Blue, huskily.

He lurched into the yard and slid down on the grass and stretched out.

"Man! Y'u're hurt bad!" exclaimed Blaisdell. The others halted in their slow march and, as if by tacit, unspoken word, lowered the body of

Isbel to the ground. Then Blaisdell knelt beside Blue. Jean left Colmor to Gordon and hurried to peer down into Blue's dim face.

"No, I ain't—hurt," said Blue, in a much weaker voice. "I'm—jest killed! . . . It was Queen! . . . Y'u all heerd me—Queen was—only bad man in that lot. I knowed it. . . . I could—hev killed him. . . . But I was—after Lee Jorth—an' his brothers. . . ."

Blue's voice failed there.

"Wal!" ejaculated Blaisdell.

"Shore was funny—Jorth's face—when I said—King Fisher," whispered Blue. "Funnier—when I bored—him through. . . . But it—was—Queen—"

His whisper died away.

"Blue!" called Blaisdell, sharply. Receiving no answer, he bent lower in the starlight and placed a hand upon the man's breast.

"Wal, he's gone. . . . I wonder if he really was the old Texas King Fisher. No one would ever believe it. . . . But if he killed the Jorths, I'll shore believe him."

CHAPTER 10

Two weeks of lonely solitude in the forest had worked incalculable change in Ellen Jorth.

Late in June her father and her two uncles had packed and ridden off with Daggs, Colter, and six other men, all heavily armed, some somber with drink, others hard and grim with a foretaste of fight. Ellen had not been given any orders. Her father had forgotten to bid her good-by or had avoided it. Their dark mission was stamped on their faces.

They had gone and, keen as had been Ellen's pang, nevertheless, their departure was a relief. She had heard them bluster and brag so often that she had her doubts of any great Jorth-Isbel war. Barking dogs did not bite. Somebody, perhaps on each side, would be badly wounded, possibly killed, and then the feud would go on as before, mostly talk. Many of her former impressions had faded. Development had been so rapid and continuous in her that she could look back to a day-by-day transformation. At night she had hated the sight of herself and when the dawn came she would rise, singing.

Jorth had left Ellen at home with the Mexican woman and Antonio. Ellen saw them only at meal times, and often not then, for she frequently visited old John Sprague or came home late to do her own cooking.

It was but a short distance up to Sprague's cabin, and since she had stopped riding the black horse, Spades, she walked. Spades was accustomed to having grain, and in the mornings he would come down to the ranch and whistle. Ellen had vowed she would never feed the horse and bade Antonio do it. But one morning Antonio was absent. She fed Spades herself. When she laid a hand on him and when he rubbed his nose against her shoulder she was not quite so sure she hated him. "Why should I?" she queried. "A horse cain't help it if he belongs to—to—" Ellen was not sure of anything except that more and more it grew good to be alone.

A whole day in the lonely forest passed swiftly, yet it left a feeling of long time. She lived by her thoughts. Always the morning was bright, sunny, sweet and fragrant and colorful, and her mood was pensive, wistful, dreamy. And always, just as surely as the hours passed, thought intruded upon her happiness, and thought brought memory, and memory brought shame, and shame brought fight. Sunset after sunset she had dragged herself back to the ranch, sullen and sick and beaten. Yet she never ceased to struggle.

The July storms came, and the forest floor that had been so sear and brown and dry and dusty changed as if by magic. The green grass shot up, the flowers bloomed, and along the cañon beds of lacy ferns swayed in the wind and bent their graceful tips over the amber-colored water. Ellen haunted these cool dells, these pine-shaded, mossy-rocked ravines where the brooks tinkled and the deer came down to drink. She wandered alone. But there grew to be company in the aspens and the music of the little waterfalls. If she could have lived in that solitude always, never returning to the ranch home that reminded her of her name, she could have forgotten and have been happy.

She loved the storms. It was a dry country and she had learned through years to welcome the creamy clouds that rolled from the southwest. They came sailing and clustering and darkening at last to form a great, purple, angry mass that appeared to lodge against the mountain rim and burst into dazzling streaks of lightning and gray palls of rain. Lightning seldom struck near the ranch, but up on the Rim there was never a storm that did not splinter and crash some of the noble pines. During the storm season sheep herders and woodsmen generally did not camp under the pines. Fear of lightning was inborn in the natives, but for Ellen the dazzling white streaks or the tremendous splitting, crackling shock, or the thunderous boom and rumble along the battlements of the

Rim had no terrors. A storm eased her breast. Deep in her heart was a hidden gathering storm. And somehow, to be out when the elements were warring, when the earth trembled and the heavens seemed to burst asunder, afforded her strange relief.

The summer days became weeks, and farther and farther they carried Ellen on the wings of solitude and loneliness until she seemed to look back years at the self she had hated. And always, when the dark memory impinged upon peace, she fought and fought until she seemed to be fighting hatred itself. Scorn of scorn and hate of hate! Yet even her battles grew to be dreams. For when the inevitable retrospect brought back Jean Isbel and his love and her cowardly falsehood she would shudder a little and put an unconscious hand to her breast and utterly fail in her fight and drift off down to vague and wistful dreams. The clean and healing forest, with its whispering wind and imperious solitude, had come between Ellen and the meaning of the squalid sheep ranch, with its travesty of home, its tragic owner. And it was coming between her two selves, the one that she had been forced to be and the other that she did not know—the thinker, the dreamer, the romancer, the one who lived in fancy the life she loved.

The summer morning dawned that brought Ellen strange tidings. They must have been created in her sleep, and now were realized in the glorious burst of golden sun, in the sweep of creamy clouds across the blue, in the solemn music of the wind in the pines, in the wild screech of the blue jays and the noble bugle of a stag. These heralded the day as no ordinary day. Something was going to happen to her. She divined it. She felt it. And she trembled. Nothing beautiful, hopeful, wonderful could ever happen to Ellen Jorth. She had been born to disaster, to suffer, to be forgotten, and die alone. Yet all nature about her seemed a magnificent rebuke to her morbidness. The same spirit that came out there with the thick, amber light was in her. She lived, and something in her was stronger than mind.

Ellen went to the door of her cabin, where she flung out her arms, driven to embrace this nameless purport of the morning. And a well-known voice broke in upon her rapture.

"Wal, lass, I like to see you happy an' I hate myself fer comin'. Because I've been to Grass Valley fer two days an' I've got news."

Old John Sprague stood there, with a smile that did not hide a troubled look.

"Oh! Uncle John! You startled me," exclaimed Ellen, shocked back to reality. And slowly she added: "Grass Valley! News?"

She put out an appealing hand, which Sprague quickly took in his own, as if to reassure her.

"Yes, an' not bad so far as you Jorths are concerned," he replied. "The first Jorth-Isbel fight has come off. . . . Reckon you remember makin' me promise to tell you if I heerd anythin'. Wal, I didn't wait fer you to come up."

"So," Ellen heard her voice calmly saying. What was this lying calm when there seemed to be a stone hammer at her heart? The first fight—not so bad for the Jorths! Then it had been bad for the Isbels. A sudden, cold stillness fell upon her senses.

"Let's sit down—outdoors," Sprague was saying. "Nice an' sunny this—mornin'. I declare—I'm out of breath. Not used to walkin'. An' besides, I left Grass Valley in the night—an' I'm tired. But excoose me from hangin' round thet village last night! There was shore—"

"Who—who was killed?" interrupted Ellen, her voice breaking low and deep.

"Guy Isbel an' Bill Jacobs on the Isbel side, an' Daggs, Craig, an' Greaves on your father's side," stated Sprague, with something of awed haste.

"Ah!" breathed Ellen, and she relaxed to sink back against the cabin wall.

Sprague seated himself on the log beside her, turning to face her, and he seemed burdened with grave and important matters.

"I heerd a good many conflictin' stories," he said, earnestly. "The village folks is all skeered an' there's no believin' their gossip. But I got what happened straight from Jake Evarts. The fight come off day before yestiddy. Your father's gang rode down to Isbel's ranch. Daggs was seen to be wantin' some of the Isbel hosses, so Evarts says. An' Guy Isbel an' Jacobs run out in the pasture. Daggs an' some others shot them down . . ."

"Killed them—that way?" put in Ellen, sharply.

"So Evarts says. He was on the ridge an' swears he seen it all. They killed Guy an' Jacobs in cold blood. No chance fer their lives—not even to fight! . . . Wal, then they surrounded the Isbel cabin. The fight lasted all thet day an' all night an' the next day. Evarts says Guy an' Jacobs laid out thar all this time. An' a herd of hogs broke in the pasture an' was eatin' the dead bodies . . ."

"My God!" burst out Ellen. "Uncle John, y'u shore cain't mean my father wouldn't stop fightin' long enough to drive the hogs off an' bury those daid men?"

"Evarts says they stopped fightin', all right, but it was to watch the hogs," declared Sprague. "An' then, what d' ye think? The wimminfolks come out—the redheaded one, Guy's wife, an' Jacobs's wife—they drove the hogs away an' buried their husbands right there in the pasture. Evarts says he seen the graves."

"It is the women who can teach these bloody Texans a lesson," declared Ellen, forcibly.

"Wal, Daggs was drunk, an' he got up from behind where the gang was hidin', an' dared the Isbels to come out. They shot him to pieces. An' thet night some one of the Isbels shot Craig, who was alone on guard. . . . An' last—this here's what I come to tell you—Jean Isbel slipped up in the dark on Greaves an' knifed him."

"Why did y'u want to tell me that particularly?" asked Ellen, slowly.

"Because I reckon the facts in the case are queer—an' because, Ellen, your name was mentioned," announced Sprague, positively.

"My name—mentioned?" echoed Ellen. Her horror and disgust gave way to a quickening process of thought, a mounting astonishment. "By whom?"

"Jean Isbel," replied Sprague, as if the name and the fact were momentous.

Ellen sat still as a stone, her hands between her knees. Slowly she felt the blood recede from her face, prickling her skin down below her neck. That name locked her thought.

"Ellen, it's a mighty queer story—too queer to be a lie," went on Sprague. "Now you listen! Evarts got this from Ted Meeker. An' Ted Meeker heerd it from Greaves, who didn't die till the next day after Jean Isbel knifed him. An' your dad shot Ted fer tellin' what he heerd. . . . No, Greaves wasn't killed outright. He was cut somethin' turrible—in two places. They wrapped him all up an' next day packed him in a wagon back to Grass Valley. Evarts says Ted Meeker was friendly with Greaves an' went to see him as he was layin' in his room next to the store. Wal, accordin' to Meeker's story, Greaves came to an' talked. He said he was sittin' there in the dark, shootin' occasionally at Isbel's cabin, when he heerd a rustle behind him in the grass. He knowed some one was crawlin' on him. But before he could get his gun around he was jumped by what he thought was a grizzly bear. But it was a man. He shut off Greaves's wind an' dragged him back in the ditch. An' he said: 'Greaves, it's the half-breed. An' he's goin' to cut you—*first for Ellen Jorth!* an' then for Gaston Isbel!' . . . Greaves said Jean ripped him with a bowie knife. . . . An' thet was all Greaves remembered. He died soon after tellin' this story. He must hev fought awful hard. Thet second cut Isbel gave him went clear through him. . . . Some of the gang was thar when Greaves talked, an' naturally they wondered why Jean Isbel had said 'first for Ellen Jorth.' . . . Somebody remembered thet Greaves had cast a slur on your good name, Ellen. An' then they had Jean Isbel's reason fer sayin' thet to Greaves. It caused a lot of talk. An' when Simm Bruce busted in some of the gang haw-hawed him an' said as how he'd get the third cut from Jean Isbel's bowie. Bruce was half drunk an' he began to cuss an' rave about Jean Isbel bein' in love with his girl. . . . As bad luck would have it, a couple of more fellars come in an' asked Meeker questions. He jest got to thet part, 'Greaves, it's the half-breed, an' he's goin' to cut you—*first for Ellen Jorth,*' when in walked your father! . . . Then it all had to come out—what Jean Isbel had said an' done—an' why. How Greaves had backed Simm Bruce in slurrin' you!"

Sprague paused to look hard at Ellen.

"Oh! Then—what did dad do?" whispered Ellen.

"He said, 'By God! half-breed or not, there's one Isbel who's a man!' An' he killed Bruce on the spot an' gave Meeker a nasty wound. Somebody grabbed him before he could shoot Meeker again. They threw Meeker out an' he crawled to a neighbor's house, where he was when Evarts seen him."

Ellen felt Sprague's rough but kindly hand shaking her. "An' now what do you think of Jean Isbel?" he queried.

A great, unsurmountable wall seemed to obstruct Ellen's thought. It seemed gray in color. It moved toward her. It was inside her brain.

"I tell you, Ellen Jorth," declared the old man, "thet Jean Isbel loves you—loves you turribly—an' he believes you're good."

"Oh no—he doesn't!" faltered Ellen.

"Wal, he jest does."

"Oh, Uncle John, he cain't believe that!" she cried.

"Of course he can. He does. You are good—good as gold, Ellen, an' he knows it. . . . What a queer deal it all is! Poor devil! To love you thet turribly an' hev to fight your people! Ellen, your dad had it correct. Isbel or not he's a man. . . . An' I say what a shame you two are divided by hate. Hate thet you hed nothin' to do with." Sprague patted her head and rose to go. "Mebbe thet fight will end the trouble. I reckon it will. Don't cross bridges till you come to them, Ellen. . . . I must hurry back now. I didn't take time to unpack my burros. Come up soon. . . . An', say, Ellen, don't think hard any more of thet Jean Isbel."

Sprague strode away, and Ellen neither heard nor saw him go. She sat perfectly motionless, yet had a strange sensation of being lifted by invisible and mighty power. It was like movement felt in a dream. She was being impelled upward when her body seemed immovable as stone. When her blood beat down this deadlock of all her physical being and rushed on and on through her veins it gave her an irresistible impulse to fly, to sail through space, to run and run and run.

And on the moment the black horse, Spades, coming from the meadow, whinnied at sight of her. Ellen leaped up and ran swiftly, but her feet seemed to be stumbling. She hugged the horse and buried her hot face in his mane and clung to him. Then just as violently she rushed for her saddle and bridle and carried the heavy weight as easily as if it had been an empty sack. Throwing them upon him, she buckled and strapped with strong, eager hands. It never occurred to her that she was not dressed to ride. Up she flung herself. And the horse, sensing her spirit, plunged into strong, free gait down the cañon trail.

The ride, the action, the thrill, the sensations of violence were not all she needed. Solitude, the empty aisles of the forest, the far miles of lonely wilderness—were these the added all? Spades took a swinging, rhythmic lope up the winding trail. The wind fanned her hot face. The sting of whipping aspen branches was pleasant. A deep rumble of thunder shook the sultry air. Up beyond the green slope of the cañon massed the creamy clouds, shading darker and darker. Spades loped on the levels, leaped the washes, trotted over the rocky ground, and took to a walk up the long slope. Ellen dropped the reins over the pommel. Her hands could not stay set on anything. They pressed her breast and flew out to caress the white aspens and to tear at the maple leaves, and gather the lavender juniper berries, and came back again to her heart. Her heart that was going to burst or break! As it had swelled, so now it labored. It could not keep pace with her needs. All that was physical, all that was living in her had to be unleashed.

Spades gained the level forest. How the great, brown-green pines seemed to bend their lofty branches over her, protectively, understandingly. Patches of azure-blue sky flashed between the trees. The great white clouds sailed along with her, and shafts of golden sunlight, flecked with gleams of falling pine needles, shone down through the canopy overhead. Away in front of her, up the slow heave of forest land, boomed the heavy thunderbolts along the battlements of the Rim.

Was she riding to escape from herself? For no gait suited her until Spades was running hard and fast through the glades. Then the pressure of dry wind, the thick odor of pine, the flashes of brown and green and gold and blue, the soft, rhythmic thuds of hoofs, the feel of the powerful horse under her, the whip of spruce branches on her muscles contracting and expanding in hard action—all these sensations seemed to quell for the time the mounting cataclysm in her heart.

The oak swales, the maple thickets, the aspen groves; the pine-shaded aisles, and the miles of silver spruce all sped by her, as if she had ridden the wind; and through the forest ahead shone the vast open of the Basin, gloomed by purple and silver cloud, shadowed by gray storm, and in the west brightened by golden sky.

Straight to the Rim she had ridden, and to the point where she had watched Jean Isbel that unforgettable day. She rode to the promontory behind the pine thicket and beheld a scene which stayed her restless hands upon her heaving breast.

The world of sky and cloud and earthly abyss seemed one of storm-sundered grandeur. The air was sultry and still, and smelled of the peculiar burnt-wood odor caused by lightning striking trees. A few heavy drops of rain were pattering down from the thin, gray edge of clouds overhead. To the east hung the storm—a black cloud lodged against the Rim, from which long, misty veils of rain streamed down into the gulf. The roar of rain sounded like the steady roar of the rapids of a river. Then a blue-white, piercingly bright, ragged streak of lightning shot down out of the black cloud. It struck with a splitting report that shocked the very wall of rock under Ellen. Then the heavens seemed to burst open with thundering crash and close with mighty thundering boom. Long roar and longer rumble rolled away to the eastward. The rain poured down in roaring cataracts.

The south held a panorama of purple-shrouded range and cañon, cañon and range, on across the rolling leagues to the dim, lofty peaks, all canopied over with angry, dusky, low-drifting clouds, horizon-wide, smoky, and sulphurous. And as Ellen watched, hands pressed to her breast, feeling incalculable relief in sight of this tempest and gulf that resembled her soul, the sun burst out from behind the long bank of purple cloud in the west and flooded the world there with golden lightning.

"It is for me!" cried Ellen. "My mind—my heart—my very soul. . . . Oh, I know! I know now! . . . I love him—love him—love him!"

She cried it out to the elements. "Oh, I love Jean Isbel—an' my heart will burst or break!"

The might of her passion was like the blaze of the sun. Before it all else retreated, diminished. The suddenness of the truth dimmed her sight. But she saw clearly enough to crawl into the pine thicket, through the clutching, dry twigs, over the mats of fragrant needles to the covert where she had once spied upon Jean Isbel. And here she lay face down for a while, hands clutching the needles, breast pressed hard upon the ground, stricken and spent. But vitality was exceeding strong in her. It passed, that weakness of realization, and she awakened to the consciousness of love.

But in the beginning it was not consciousness of the man. It was new, sensorial life, elemental, primitive, a liberation of a million inherited instincts, quivering and physical, over which Ellen had no more control than she had over the glory of the sun. If she thought at all it was of her need to be hidden, like an animal, low down near the earth, covered by green thicket, lost in the wildness of nature. She went to nature, unconsciously seeking a mother. And love was a birth from the depths of her, like a rushing spring of pure water, long underground, and at last propelled to the surface by a convulsion.

Ellen gradually lost her tense rigidity and relaxed. Her body softened. She rolled over until her face caught the lacy, golden shadows cast by sun and bough. Scattered drops of rain pattered around her. The air was hot, and its odor was that of dry pine and spruce fragrance penetrated by brimstone from the lightning. The nest where she lay was warm and sweet. No eye save that of nature saw her in her abandonment. An ineffable and exquisite smile wreathed her lips, dreamy, sad, sensuous, the supremity of unconscious happiness. Over her dark and eloquent eyes, as Ellen gazed upward, spread a luminous film, a veil. She was looking intensely, yet she did not see. The wilderness enveloped her with its secretive, elemental sheaths of rock, of tree, of cloud, of sunlight. Through her thrilling skin poured the multiple and nameless sensations of the living organism stirred to supreme sensitiveness. She could not lie still, but all her movements were gentle, involuntary. The slow reaching out of her hand, to grasp at nothing visible, was similar to the lazy stretching of her limbs, to the heave of her breast, to the ripple of muscle.

Ellen knew not what she felt. To live that sublime hour was beyond thought. Such happiness was like the first dawn of the world to the sight of man. It had to do with bygone ages. Her heart, her blood, her flesh, her very bones were filled with instincts and emotions common to the race before intellect developed, when the savage lived only with his sensorial perceptions. Of all happiness, joy, bliss, rapture to which man was heir, that of intense and exquisite preoccupation of the senses, unhindered and unburdened by thought, was the greatest. Ellen felt that which life meant with its inscrutable design. Love was only the realization of her mission on the earth.

The dark storm cloud with its white, ragged ropes of lightning and down-streaming gray veils of rain, the purple gulf rolling like a colored sea to the dim mountains, the glorious golden light of the sun—these had enchanted her eyes with the beauty of the universe. They had burst the windows of her blindness. When she crawled into the green-brown covert it was to escape too great perception. She needed to be encompassed by close tangible things. And there her body paid the tribute to the realization of life. Shock, convulsion, pain, relaxation, and then unutterable and insupportable sensing of her environment and the heart! In one way she was a wild animal alone in the woods, forced into the mating that meant reproduction of its kind. In another she was an infinitely higher being shot through and through with the most resistless and mysterious transport that life could give to flesh.

And when that spell slackened its hold there wedged into her mind a consciousness of the man she loved—Jean Isbel. Then emotion and thought strove for mastery over her. It was not herself or love that she loved, but a living man. Suddenly he existed so clearly for her that she could see him, hear him, almost feel him. Her whole soul, her very life cried out to him for protection, for salvation, for love, for fulfillment. No denial, no doubt marred the white blaze of her realization. From the instant that she had looked up into Jean Isbel's dark face she had loved him. Only she had not known. She bowed now, and bent, and humbly quivered under the mastery of something beyond her ken. Thought clung to the beginnings of her romance—to the three times she had seen him. Every look, every word, every act of his returned to her now in the light of the truth. Love at first sight! He had sworn it, bitterly, eloquently, scornful of her doubts. And now a blind, sweet, shuddering ecstasy swayed her. How weak and frail seemed her body—too small, too slight for this monstrous and terrible engine of fire and lightning and fury and glory—her heart! It must burst or break. Relentlessly memory pursued Ellen, and her thoughts whirled and emotion conquered her. At last she quivered up to her knees as if lashed to action. It seemed that first kiss of Isbel's, cool and gentle and timid, was on her lips. And her eyes closed and hot tears welled from under her lids. Her groping hands found only the dead twigs and the pine boughs of the trees. Had she reached out to clasp him? Then hard and violent on her mouth and cheek and neck burned those other kisses of Isbel's, and with the flashing, stinging memory came the truth that now she would have bartered her soul for them. Utterly she surrendered to the resistlessness of this love. Her loss of mother and friends, her wandering from one wild place to another, her lonely life among bold and rough men, had developed her for violent love. It overthrew all pride, it engendered humility, it killed hate. Ellen wiped the tears from her eyes, and as she knelt there she swept to her breast a fragrant spreading bough of pine needles. "I'll go to him," she whispered. "I'll tell him of—of my—my love. I'll tell him to take me away—away to the end of the world—away from heah—before it's too late!"

It was a solemn, beautiful moment. But the last spoken words lingered hauntingly. "Too late?" she whispered.

And suddenly it seemed that death itself shuddered in her soul. Too late! It was too late. She had killed his love. That Jorth blood in her—that poisonous hate—had chosen the only way to strike this noble Isbel to the heart. Basely, with an abandonment of womanhood, she had mockingly perjured her soul with a vile lie. She writhed, she shook under the whip of this inconceivable fact. Lost! Lost! She wailed her misery. She might as well be what she had made Jean Isbel think she was. If she had been shamed before, she was now abased, degraded, lost in her own sight. And if she would have given her soul for his kisses, she now would have killed herself to earn back his respect. Jean Isbel had given her at sight the deference that she had unconsciously craved, and the love that would have been her salvation. What a horrible mistake she had made of her life! Not her mother's blood, but her father's—the Jorth blood—had been her ruin.

Again Ellen fell upon the soft pine-needle mat, face down, and she groveled and burrowed there, in an agony that could not bear the sense of light. All she had suffered was as nothing to this. To have awakened to a splendid and uplifting love for a man whom she had imagined she hated, who had fought for her name and had killed in revenge for the dishonor she had avowed—to have lost his love and what was infinitely more precious to her now in her ignominy—his faith in her purity—this broke her heart.

CHAPTER 11

When Ellen, utterly spent in body and mind, reached home that day a melancholy, sultry twilight was falling. Fitful flares of sheet lightning swept across the dark horizon to the east. The cabins were deserted. Antonio and the Mexican woman were gone. The circumstances made Ellen wonder, but she was too tired and too sunken in spirit to think long about it or to care. She fed and watered her horse and left him in the corral. Then, supperless and without removing her clothes, she threw herself upon the bed, and at once sank into heavy slumber.

Sometime during the night she awoke. Coyotes were yelping, and from that sound she concluded it was near dawn. Her body ached; her mind seemed dull. Drowsily she was sinking into slumber again when she heard the rapid clip-clop of trotting horses. Startled, she raised her head to listen. The men were coming back. Relief and dread seemed to clear her stupor.

The trotting horses stopped across the lane from her cabin, evidently at the corral where she had left Spades. She heard him whistle. From the sound of hoofs she judged the number of horses to be six or eight. Low voices of men mingled with thuds and cracking of straps and flopping of saddles on the ground. After that the heavy tread of boots sounded on the porch of the cabin opposite. A door creaked on its hinges. Next a slow footstep, accompanied by clinking of spurs, approached Ellen's door, and a heavy hand banged upon it. She knew this person could not be her father.

"Hullo, Ellen!"

She recognized the voice as belonging to Colter. Somehow its tone, or something about it, sent a little shiver down her spine. It acted like a revivifying current. Ellen lost her dragging lethargy.

"Hey, Ellen, are y'u there?" added Colter, in louder voice.

"Yes. Of course I'm heah," she replied. "What do y'u want?"

"Wal—I'm shore glad y'u're home," he replied. "Antonio's gone with his squaw. An' I was some worried aboot y'u."

"Who's with y'u, Colter?" queried Ellen, sitting up.

"Rock Wells an' Springer. Tad Jorth was with us, but we had to leave him over heah in a cabin."

"What's the matter with him?"

"Wal, he's hurt tolerable bad," was the slow reply.

Ellen heard Colter's spurs jangle, as if he had uneasily shifted his feet.

"Where's dad an' Uncle Jackson?" asked Ellen.

A silence pregnant enough to augment Ellen's dread finally broke to Colter's voice, somehow different. "Shore they're back on the trail. An' we're to meet them where we left Tad."

"Are y'u goin' away again?"

"I reckon. . . . An', Ellen, y'u're goin' with us."

"I am not," she retorted.

"Wal, y'u are, if I have to pack y'u," he replied, forcibly. "It's not safe heah any more. That damned half-breed Isbel with his gang are on our trail."

That name seemed like a red-hot blade at Ellen's leaden heart. She wanted to fling a hundred queries on Colter, but she could not utter one.

"Ellen, we've got to hit the trail an' hide," continued Colter, anxiously. "Y'u mustn't stay heah alone. Suppose them Isbels would trap y'u! . . . They'd tear your clothes off an' rope y'u to a tree. Ellen, shore y'u're goin'. . . . Y'u heah me!"

"Yes—I'll go," she replied, as if forced.

"Wal—that's good," he said, quickly. "An' rustle tolerable lively. We've got to pack."

The slow jangle of Colter's spurs and his slow steps moved away out of Ellen's hearing. Throwing off the blankets, she put her feet to the floor and sat there a moment staring at the blank nothingness of the cabin interior in the obscure gray of dawn. Cold, gray, dreary, obscure—like her life, her future! And she was compelled to do what was hateful to her. As a Jorth she must take to the unfrequented trails and hide like a rabbit in the thickets. But the interest of the moment, a premonition of events to be, quickened her into action.

Ellen unbarred the door to let in the light. Day was breaking with an intense, clear, steely light in the east through which the morning star still shone white. A ruddy flare betokened the advent of the sun. Ellen unbraided her tangled hair and brushed and combed it. A queer, still pang came to her at sight of pine needles tangled in her brown locks. Then she washed her hands and face. Breakfast was a matter of considerable work and she was hungry.

The sun rose and changed the gray world of forest. For the first time in her life Ellen hated the golden brightness, the wonderful blue of sky, the scream of the eagle and the screech of the jay; and the squirrels she had always loved to feed were neglected that morning.

Colter came in. Either Ellen had never before looked attentively at him or else he had changed. Her scrutiny of his lean, hard features accorded him more Texan attributes than formerly. His gray eyes were as light, as clear, as fierce as those of an eagle. And the sand gray of his face, the long, drooping, fair mustache hid the secrets of his mind, but not its strength. The instant Ellen met his gaze she sensed a power in him that she instinctively opposed. Colter had not been so bold nor so rude as Daggs, but he was the same kind of man, perhaps the more dangerous for his secretiveness, his cool, waiting inscrutableness.

"Mawnin', Ellen!" he drawled. "Y'u shore look good for sore eyes."

"Don't pay me compliments, Colter," replied Ellen. "An' your eyes are not sore."

"Wal, I'm shore sore from fightin' an' ridin' an' layin' out," he said, bluntly.

"Tell me—what's happened," returned Ellen.

"Girl, it's a tolerable long story," replied Colter. "An' we've no time now. Wait till we get to camp."

"Am I to pack my belongin's or leave them heah?" asked Ellen.

"Reckon y'u'd better leave—them heah."

"But if we did not come back—"

"Wal, I reckon it's not likely we'll come—soon," he said, rather evasively.

"Colter, I'll not go off into the woods with just the clothes I have on my back."

"Ellen, we shore got to pack all the grub we can. This shore ain't goin' to be a visit to neighbors. We're shy pack hosses. But y'u make up a bundle of belongin's y'u care for, an' the things y'u'll need bad. We'll throw it on somewhere."

Colter stalked away across the lane, and Ellen found herself dubiously staring at his tall figure. Was it the situation that struck her with a foreboding perplexity or was her intuition steeling her against this man? Ellen could not decide. But she had to go with him. Her prejudice was unreasonable at this portentous moment. And she could not yet feel that she was solely responsible to herself.

When it came to making a small bundle of her belongings she was in a quandary. She discarded this and put in that, and then reversed the order. Next in preciousness to her mother's things were the long-hidden gifts of Jean Isbel. She could part with neither.

While she was selecting and packing this bundle Colter again entered and, without speaking, began to rummage in the corner where her father kept his possessions. This irritated Ellen.

"What do y'u want there?" she demanded.

"Wal, I reckon your dad wants his papers—an' the gold he left heah—an' a change of clothes. Now doesn't he?" returned Colter, coolly.

"Of course. But I supposed y'u would have me pack them."

Colter vouchsafed no reply to this, but deliberately went on rummaging, with little regard for how he scattered things. Ellen turned her back on him. At length, when he left, she went to her father's corner and found that, as far as she was able to see, Colter had taken neither papers nor clothes, but only the gold. Perhaps, however, she had been mistaken, for she had not observed Colter's departure closely enough to know whether or not he carried a package. She missed only the gold. Her father's papers, old and musty, were scattered about, and these she gathered up to slip in her own bundle.

Colter, or one of the men, had saddled Spades, and he was now tied to the corral fence, champing his bit and pounding the sand. Ellen wrapped bread and meat inside her coat, and after tying this behind her saddle she was ready to go. But evidently she would have to wait, and, preferring to remain outdoors, she stayed by her horse. Presently, while watching the men pack, she noticed that Springer wore a bandage round his head under the brim of his sombrero. His motions were slow and lacked energy. Shuddering at the sight, Ellen refused to conjecture. All too soon she would learn what had happened, and all too soon, perhaps, she herself would be in the midst of another fight. She watched the men. They were making a hurried slipshod job of packing food supplies from both cabins. More than once she caught Colter's gray gleam of gaze on her, and she did not like it.

"I'll ride up an' say good-by to Sprague," she called to Colter.

"Shore y'u won't do nothin' of the kind," he called back.

There was authority in his tone that angered Ellen, and something else which inhibited her anger. What was there about Colter with which she must reckon? The other two Texans laughed aloud, to be suddenly silenced by Colter's harsh and lowered curses. Ellen walked out of hearing and sat upon a log, where she remained until Colter hailed her.

"Get up an' ride," he called.

Ellen complied with this order and, riding up behind the three mounted men, she soon found herself leaving what for years had been her home. Not once did she look back. She hoped she would never see the squalid, bare pretension of a ranch again.

Colter and the other riders drove the pack horses across the meadow, off of the trails, and up the slope into the forest. Not very long did it take Ellen to see that Colter's object was to hide their tracks. He zigzagged through the forest, avoiding the bare spots of dust, the dry, sun-baked flats of clay where water lay in spring, and he chose the grassy, open glades, the long, pine-needle matted aisles. Ellen rode at their heels and it pleased her to watch for their tracks. Colter manifestly had been long practiced in this game of hiding his trail, and he showed the skill of a rustler. But Ellen was not convinced that he could ever elude a real woodsman. Not improbably, however, Colter was only aiming to leave a trail difficult to follow and which would allow him and his confederates ample time to forge ahead of pursuers. Ellen could not accept a certainty of pursuit. Yet Colter must have expected it, and Springer and Wells also, for they had a dark, sinister, furtive demeanor that strangely contrasted with the cool, easy manner habitual to them.

They were not seeking the level routes of the forestland, that was sure. They rode straight across the thick-timbered ridge down into another cañon, up out of that, and across rough, rocky bluffs, and down again. These riders headed a little to the northwest and every mile brought them into wilder, more rugged country, until Ellen, losing count of cañons and ridges, had no idea where she was. No stop was made at noon to rest the laboring, sweating pack animals.

Under circumstances where pleasure might have been possible Ellen would have reveled in this hard ride into a wonderful forest ever thickening and darkening. But the wild beauty of glade and the spruce slopes and the deep, bronze-walled cañons left her cold. She saw and felt, but had no thrill, except now and then a thrill of alarm when Spades slid to his haunches down some steep, damp, piny declivity.

All the woodland, up and down, appeared to be richer, greener as they traveled farther west. Grass grew thick and heavy. Water ran in all ravines. The rocks were bronze and copper and russet, and some had green patches of lichen.

Ellen felt the sun now on her left cheek and knew that the day was waning and that Colter was swinging farther to the northwest. She had never before ridden through such heavy forest and down and up such wild cañons. Toward sunset the deepest and ruggedest cañon halted their advance. Colter rode to the right, searching for a place to get down through a spruce thicket that stood on end. Presently he dismounted and the others followed suit. Ellen found she could not lead Spades because he slid down upon her heels, so she looped the end of her reins over the pommel and left him free. She herself managed to descend by holding to branches and sliding all the way down that slope. She heard the horses cracking the brush, snorting and heaving. One pack slipped and had to be removed from the horse, and rolled down. At the bottom of this deep, green-walled notch roared a stream of water. Shadowed, cool, mossy, damp, this narrow gulch seemed the wildest place Ellen had ever seen. She could just see the sunset-flushed, gold-tipped spruces far above her. The men repacked the horse that had slipped his burden, and once more resumed their progress ahead, now turning up this cañon. There was no horse trail, but deer and bear trails were numerous. The sun sank and the sky darkened, but still the men rode on; and the farther they traveled the wilder grew the aspect of the cañon.

At length Colter broke a way through a heavy thicket of willows and entered a side cañon, the mouth of which Ellen had not even descried. It turned and widened, and at length opened out into a round pocket, apparently inclosed, and as lonely and isolated a place as even pursued rustlers could desire. Hidden by jutting wall and thicket of spruce were two old log cabins joined together by roof and attic floor, the same as the double cabin at the Jorth ranch.

Ellen smelled wood smoke, and presently, on going round the cabins, saw a bright fire. One man stood beside it gazing at Colter's party, which evidently he had heard approaching.

"Hullo, Queen!" said Colter. "How's Tad?"

"He's holdin' on fine," replied Queen, bending over the fire, where he turned pieces of meat.

"Where's father?" suddenly asked Ellen, addressing Colter.

As if he had not heard her, he went on wearily loosening a pack.

Queen looked at her. The light of the fire only partially shone on his face. Ellen could not see its expression. But from the fact that Queen did not answer her question she got further intimation of an impending catastrophe. The long, wild ride had helped prepare her for the secrecy and taciturnity of men who had resorted to flight. Perhaps her father had been delayed or was still off on the deadly mission that had obsessed him; or there might, and probably was, darker reason for his absence. Ellen shut her teeth and turned to the needs of her horse. And presently, returning to the fire, she thought of her uncle.

"Queen, is my uncle Tad heah?" she asked.

"Shore. He's in there," replied Queen, pointing at the nearer cabin.

Ellen hurried toward the dark doorway. She could see how the logs of the cabin had moved awry and what a big, dilapidated hovel it was. As she looked in, Colter loomed over her—placed a familiar and somehow masterful hand upon her. Ellen let it rest on her shoulder a moment. Must she forever be repulsing these rude men among whom her lot was cast? Did Colter mean what Daggs had always meant? Ellen felt herself weary, weak in body, and her spent spirit had not rallied. Yet, whatever Colter meant by his familiarity, she could not bear it. So she slipped out from under his hand.

"Uncle Tad, are y'u heah?" she called into the blackness. She heard the mice scamper and rustle and she smelled the musty, old, woody odor of a long-unused cabin.

"Hello, Ellen!" came a voice she recognized as her uncle's, yet it was strange. "Yes. I'm heah—bad luck to me! . . . How 're y'u buckin' up, girl?"

"I'm all right, Uncle Tad—only tired an' worried. I—"

"Tad, how's your hurt?" interrupted Colter.

"Reckon I'm easier," replied Jorth, wearily, "but shore I'm in bad shape. I'm still spittin' blood. I keep tellin' Queen that bullet lodged in my lungs—but he says it went through."

"Wal, hang on, Tad!" replied Colter, with a cheerfulness Ellen sensed was really indifferent.

"Oh, what the hell's the use!" exclaimed Jorth. "It's all—up with us—Colter!"

"Wal, shut up, then," tersely returned Colter. "It ain't doin' y'u or us any good to holler."

Tad Jorth did not reply to this. Ellen heard his breathing and it did not seem natural. It rasped a little—came hurriedly—then caught in his throat. Then he spat. Ellen shrunk back against the door. He was breathing through blood.

"Uncle, are y'u in pain?" she asked.

"Yes, Ellen—it burns like hell," he said.

"Oh! I'm sorry. . . . Isn't there something I can do?"

"I reckon not. Queen did all anybody could do for me—now—unless it's pray."

Colter laughed at this—the slow, easy, drawling laugh of a Texan. But Ellen felt pity for this wounded uncle. She had always hated him. He had been a drunkard, a gambler, a waster of her father's property; and now he was a rustler and a fugitive, lying in pain, perhaps mortally hurt.

"Yes, uncle—I will pray for y'u," she said, softly.

The change in his voice held a note of sadness that she had been quick to catch.

"Ellen, y'u're the only good Jorth—in the whole damned lot," he said. "God! I see it all now. . . . We've dragged y'u to hell!"

"Yes, Uncle Tad, I've shore been dragged some—but not yet—to hell," she responded, with a break in her voice.

"Y'u will be—Ellen—unless—"

"Aw, shut up that kind of gab, will y'u?" broke in Colter, harshly.

It amazed Ellen that Colter should dominate her uncle, even though he was wounded. Tad Jorth had been the last man to take orders from anyone, much less a rustler of the Hash Knife Gang. This Colter began to loom up in Ellen's estimate as he loomed physically over her, a lofty figure, dark, motionless, somehow menacing.

"Ellen, has Colter told y'u yet—aboot—aboot Lee an' Jackson?" inquired the wounded man.

The pitch-black darkness of the cabin seemed to help fortify Ellen to bear further trouble.

"Colter told me dad an' Uncle Jackson would meet us heah," she rejoined, hurriedly.

Jorth could be heard breathing in difficulty, and he coughed and spat again, and seemed to hiss.

"Ellen, he lied to y'u. They'll never meet us—heah!"

"Why not?" whispered Ellen.

"Because—Ellen—" he replied, in husky pants, "your dad an'—uncle Jackson—are daid—an' buried!"

If Ellen suffered a terrible shock it was a blankness, a deadness, and a slow, creeping failure of sense in her knees. They gave way under her and she sank on the grass against the cabin wall. She did not faint nor grow dizzy nor lose her sight, but for a while there was no process of thought in her mind. Suddenly then it was there—the quick, spiritual rending of her heart—followed by a profound emotion of intimate and irretrievable loss—and after that grief and bitter realization.

An hour later Ellen found strength to go to the fire and partake of the food and drink her body sorely needed.

Colter and the men waited on her solicitously, and in silence, now and then stealing furtive glances at her from under the shadow of their black sombreros. The dark night settled down like a blanket. There were no stars. The wind moaned fitfully among the pines, and all about that lonely, hidden recess was in harmony with Ellen's thoughts.

"Girl, y'u're shore game," said Colter, admiringly. "An' I reckon y'u never got it from the Jorths."

"Tad in there—he's game," said Queen, in mild protest.

"Not to my notion," replied Colter. "Any man can be game when he's croakin', with somebody around. . . . But Lee Jorth an' Jackson—they always was yellow clear to their gizzards. They was born in Louisiana—not Texas. . . . Shore they're no more Texans than I am. Ellen heah, she must have got another strain in her blood."

To Ellen their words had no meaning. She rose and asked, "Where can I sleep?"

"I'll fetch a light presently an' y'u can make your bed in there by Tad," replied Colter.

"Yes, I'd like that."

"Wal, if y'u reckon y'u can coax him to talk you're shore wrong," declared Colter, with that cold timbre of voice that struck like steel on Ellen's nerves. "I cussed him good an' told him he'd keep his mouth shut. Talkin' makes him cough an' that fetches up the blood. . . . Besides, I reckon I'm the one to tell y'u how your dad an' uncle got killed. Tad didn't see it done, an' he was bad hurt when it happened. Shore all the fellars left have their idee aboot it. But I've got it straight."

"Colter—tell me now," cried Ellen.

"Wal, all right. Come over heah," he replied, and drew her away from the camp-fire, out in the shadow of gloom. "Poor kid! I shore feel bad aboot it." He put a long arm around her waist and drew her against him. Ellen felt it, yet did not offer any resistance. All her faculties seemed absorbed in a morbid and sad anticipation.

"Ellen, y'u shore know I always loved y'u—now don't y'u?" he asked, with suppressed breath.

"No, Colter. It's news to me—an' not what I want to heah."

"Wal, y'u may as well heah it right now," he said. "It's true. An' what's more—your dad gave y'u to me before he died."

"What! Colter, y'u must be a liar."

"Ellen, I swear I'm not lyin'," he returned, in eager passion. "I was with your dad last an' heard him last. He shore knew I'd loved y'u for years. An' he said he'd rather y'u be left in my care than anybody's."

"My father gave me to y'u in marriage!" ejaculated Ellen, in bewilderment.

Colter's ready assurance did not carry him over this point. It was evident that her words somewhat surprised and disconcerted him for the moment.

"To let me marry a rustler—one of the Hash Knife Gang!" exclaimed Ellen, with weary incredulity.

"Wal, your dad belonged to Daggs's gang, same as I do," replied Colter, recovering his cool ardor.

"No!" cried Ellen.

"Yes, he shore did, for years," declared Colter, positively. "Back in Texas. An' it was your dad that got Daggs to come to Arizona."

Ellen tried to fling herself away. But her strength and her spirit were ebbing, and Colter increased the pressure of his arm. All at once she sank limp. Could she escape her fate? Nothing seemed left to fight with or for.

"All right—don't hold me—so tight." she panted. "Now tell me how dad was killed . . . an' who—who—"

Colter bent over so he could peer into her face. In the darkness Ellen just caught the gleam of his eyes. She felt the virile force of the man in the strain of his body as he pressed her close. It all seemed unreal—a hideous dream—the gloom, the moan of the wind, the weird solitude, and this rustler with hand and will like cold steel.

"We'd come back to Greaves's store," Colter began. "An' as Greaves was daid we all got free with his liquor. Shore some of us got drunk. Bruce was drunk, an' Tad in there—he was drunk. Your dad put away more 'n I ever seen him. But shore he wasn't exactly drunk. He got one of them weak an' shaky spells. He cried an' he wanted some of us to get the Isbels to call off the fightin'. . . . He shore was ready to call it quits. I reckon the killin' of Daggs—an' then the awful way Greaves was cut up by Jean Isbel—took all the fight out of your dad. He said to me, 'Colter, we'll take Ellen an' leave this heah country—an' begin life all over again—where no one knows us.'"

"Oh, did he really say that? . . . . Did he—really mean it?" murmured Ellen, with a sob.

"I'll swear it by the memory of my daid mother," protested Colter. "Wal, when night come the Isbels rode down on us in the dark an' began to shoot. They smashed in the door—tried to burn us out—an' hollered around for a while. Then they left an' we reckoned there'd be no more trouble that night. All the same we kept watch. I was the soberest one an' I bossed the gang. We had some quarrels aboot the drinkin'. Your dad said if we kept it up it 'd be the end of the Jorths. An' he planned to send word to the Isbels next mawnin' that he was ready for a truce. An' I was to go fix it up with Gaston Isbel. Wal, your dad went to bed in Greaves's room, an' a little while later your uncle Jackson went in there, too. Some of the men laid down in the store an' went to sleep. I kept guard till aboot three in the mawnin'. An' I got so sleepy I couldn't hold my eyes open. So I waked up Wells an' Slater an' set them on guard, one at each end of the store. Then I laid down on the counter to take a nap."

Colter's low voice, the strain and breathlessness of him, the agitation with which he appeared to be laboring, and especially the simple, matter-of-fact detail of his story, carried absolute conviction to Ellen Jorth. Her vague doubt of him had been created by his attitude toward her. Emotion dominated her intelligence. The images, the scenes called up by Colter's words, were as true as the gloom of the wild gulch and the loneliness of the night solitude—as true as the strange fact that she lay passive in the arm of a rustler.

"Wal, after a while I woke up," went on Colter, clearing his throat. "It was gray dawn. All was as still as death. . . . An' somethin' shore was wrong. Wells an' Slater had got to drinkin' again an' now laid daid drunk or asleep. Anyways, when I kicked them they never moved. Then I heard a moan. It came from the room where your dad an' uncle was. I went in. It was just light enough to see. Your uncle Jackson was layin' on the floor—cut half in two—daid as a door nail. . . . Your dad lay on the bed. He was alive, breathin' his last. . . . He says, 'That half-breed Isbel—knifed us—while we slept' . . . The winder shutter was open. I seen where Jean Isbel had come in an' gone out. I seen his moccasin tracks in the dirt outside an' I seen where he'd stepped in Jackson's blood an' tracked it to the winder. Y'u shore can see them bloody tracks yourself, if y'u go back to Greaves's store. . . . Your dad was goin' fast. . . . He said, 'Colter—take care of Ellen,' an' I reckon he meant a lot by that. He kept sayin', 'My God! if I'd only seen Gaston Isbel before it was too late!' an' then he raved a little, whisperin' out of his haid. . . . An' after that he died. . . . I woke up the men, an' aboot sunup we carried your dad an' uncle out of town an' buried them. . . . An' them Isbels shot at us while we were buryin' our daid! That's where Tad got his hurt. . . . Then we hit the trail for Jorth's ranch. . . . An now, Ellen, that's all my story. Your dad was ready to bury the hatchet with his old enemy. An' that Nez Perce Jean Isbel, like the sneakin' savage he is, murdered your uncle an' your dad. . . . Cut him horrible—made him suffer tortures of hell—all for Isbel revenge!"

When Colter's husky voice ceased Ellen whispered through lips as cold and still as ice, "Let me go . . . leave me—heah—alone!"

"Why, shore! I reckon I understand," replied Colter. "I hated to tell y'u. But y'u had to heah the truth aboot that half-breed. . . . I'll carry your pack in the cabin an' unroll your blankets."

Releasing her, Colter strode off in the gloom. Like a dead weight, Ellen began to slide until she slipped down full length beside the log. And then she lay in the cool, damp shadow, inert and lifeless so far as outward physical movement was concerned. She saw nothing and felt nothing of the night, the wind, the cold, the falling dew. For the moment or hour she was crushed by despair, and seemed to see herself sinking down and down into a black, bottomless pit, into an abyss where murky tides of blood and furious gusts of passion contended between her body and her soul. Into the stormy blast of hell! In her despair she longed, she ached for death. Born of infidelity, cursed by a taint of evil blood, further cursed by higher instinct for good and happy life, dragged from one lonely and wild and sordid spot to another, never knowing love or peace or joy or home, left to the companionship of violent and vile men, driven by a strange fate to love with unquenchable and insupportable love a half-breed, a savage, an Isbel, the hereditary enemy of her people, and at last the ruthless murderer of her father—what in the name of God had she left to live for? Revenge! An eye for an eye! A life for a life! But she could not kill Jean Isbel. Woman's love could turn to hate, but not the love of Ellen Jorth. He could drag her by the hair in the dust, beat her, and make her a thing to loathe, and cut her mortally in his savage and implacable thirst for revenge—but with her last gasp she would whisper she loved him and that she had lied to him to kill his faith. It was that—his strange faith in her purity—which had won her love. Of all men, that he should be the one to recognize the truth of her, the womanhood yet unsullied—how strange, how terrible, how overpowering! False, indeed, was she to the Jorths! False as her mother had been to an Isbel! This agony and destruction of her soul was the bitter Dead Sea fruit—the sins of her parents visited upon her.

"I'll end it all," she whispered to the night shadows that hovered over her. No coward was she—no fear of pain or mangled flesh or death or the mysterious hereafter could ever stay her. It would be easy, it would be a last thrill, a transport of self-abasement and supreme self-proof of her love for Jean Isbel to kiss the Rim rock where his feet had trod and then fling herself down into the depths. She was the last Jorth. So the wronged Isbels would be avenged.

"But he would never know—never know—I lied to him!" she wailed to the night wind.

She was lost—lost on earth and to hope of heaven. She had right neither to live nor to die. She was nothing but a little weed along the trail of life, trampled upon, buried in the mud. She was nothing but a single rotten thread in a tangled web of love and hate and revenge. And she had broken.

Lower and lower she seemed to sink. Was there no end to this gulf of despair? If Colter had returned he would have found her a rag and a toy— a creature degraded, fit for his vile embrace. To be thrust deeper into the mire—to be punished fittingly for her betrayal of a man's noble love and her own womanhood—to be made an end of, body, mind, and soul.

But Colter did not return.

The wind mourned, the owls hooted, the leaves rustled, the insects whispered their melancholy night song, the camp-fire flickered and faded. Then the wild forestland seemed to close imponderably over Ellen. All that she wailed in her despair, all that she confessed in her abasement, was true, and hard as life could be—but she belonged to nature. If nature had not failed her, had God failed her? It was there—the lonely land of tree and fern and flower and brook, full of wild birds and beasts, where the mossy rocks could speak and the solitude had ears, where she had always felt herself unutterably a part of creation. Thus a wavering spark of hope quivered through the blackness of her soul and gathered light.

The gloom of the sky, the shifting clouds of dull shade, split asunder to show a glimpse of a radiant star, piercingly white, cold, pure, a steadfast eye of the universe, beyond all understanding and illimitable with its meaning of the past and the present and the future. Ellen watched it until the drifting clouds once more hid it from her strained sight.

What had that star to do with hell? She might be crushed and destroyed by life, but was there not something beyond? Just to be born, just to suffer, just to die—could that be all? Despair did not loose its hold on Ellen, the strife and pang of her breast did not subside. But with the long hours and the strange closing in of the forest around her and the fleeting glimpse of that wonderful star, with a subtle divination of the meaning of her beating heart and throbbing mind, and, lastly, with a voice thundering at her conscience that a man's faith in a woman must not be greater, nobler, than her faith in God and eternity—with these she checked the dark flight of her soul toward destruction.

CHAPTER 12

A chill, gray, somber dawn was breaking when Ellen dragged herself into the cabin and crept under her blankets, there to sleep the sleep of exhaustion.

When she awoke the hour appeared to be late afternoon. Sun and sky shone through the sunken and decayed roof of the old cabin. Her uncle, Tad Jorth, lay upon a blanket bed upheld by a crude couch of boughs. The light fell upon his face, pale, lined, cast in a still mold of suffering. He was not dead, for she heard his respiration.

The floor underneath Ellen's blankets was bare clay. She and Jorth were alone in this cabin. It contained nothing besides their beds and a rank growth of weeds along the decayed lower logs. Half of the cabin had a rude ceiling of rough-hewn boards which formed a kind of loft. This attic extended through to the adjoining cabin, forming the ceiling of the porch-like space between the two structures. There was no partition. A ladder of two aspen saplings, pegged to the logs, and with braces between for steps, led up to the attic.

Ellen smelled wood smoke and the odor of frying meat, and she heard the voices of men. She looked out to see that Slater and Somers had joined their party—an addition that might have strengthened it for defense, but did not lend her own situation anything favorable. Somers had always appeared the one best to avoid.

Colter espied her and called her to "Come an' feed your pale face."

His comrades laughed, not loudly, but guardedly, as if noise was something to avoid. Nevertheless, they awoke Tad Jorth, who began to toss and moan on the bed.

Ellen hurried to his side and at once ascertained that he had a high fever and was in a critical condition. Every time he tossed he opened a wound in his right breast, rather high up. For all she could see, nothing had been done for him except the binding of a scarf round his neck and under his arm. This scant bandage had worked loose. Going to the door, she called out:

"Fetch me some water." When Colter brought it, Ellen was rummaging in her pack for some clothing or towel that she could use for bandages.

"Weren't any of y'u decent enough to look after my uncle?" she queried.

"Huh! Wal, what the hell!" rejoined Colter. "We shore did all we could. I reckon y'u think it wasn't a tough job to pack him up the Rim. He was done for then an' I said so."

"I'll do all I can for him," said Ellen.

"Shore. Go ahaid. When I get plugged or knifed by that half-breed I shore hope y'u'll be round to nurse me."

"Y'u seem to be pretty shore of your fate, Colter."

"Shore as hell!" he bit out, darkly. "Somers saw Isbel an' his gang trailin' us to the Jorth ranch."

"Are y'u goin' to stay heah—an' wait for them?"

"Shore I've been quarrelin' with the fellars out there over that very question. I'm for leavin' the country. But Queen, the damn gun fighter, is daid set to kill that cowman, Blue, who swore he was King Fisher, the old Texas outlaw. None but Queen are spoilin' for another fight. All the same they won't leave Tad Jorth heah alone."

Then Colter leaned in at the door and whispered: "Ellen, I can't boss this outfit. So let's y'u an' me shake 'em. I've got your dad's gold. Let's ride off to-night an' shake this country."

Colter, muttering under his breath, left the door and returned to his comrades. Ellen had received her first intimation of his cowardice; and his mention of her father's gold started a train of thought that persisted in spite of her efforts to put all her mind to attending her uncle. He grew conscious enough to recognize her working over him, and thanked her with a look that touched Ellen deeply. It changed the direction of her mind. His suffering and imminent death, which she was able to alleviate and retard somewhat, worked upon her pity and compassion so that she forgot her own plight. Half the night she was tending him, cooling his fever, holding him quiet. Well she realized that but for her ministrations he would have died. At length he went to sleep.

And Ellen, sitting beside him in the lonely, silent darkness of that late hour, received again the intimation of nature, those vague and nameless stirrings of her innermost being, those whisperings out of the night and the forest and the sky. Something great would not let go of her soul. She pondered.

Attention to the wounded man occupied Ellen; and soon she redoubled her activities in this regard, finding in them something of protection against Colter.

He had waylaid her as she went to a spring for water, and with a lunge like that of a bear he had tried to embrace her. But Ellen had been too quick.

"Wal, are y'u goin' away with me?" he demanded.

"No. I'll stick by my uncle," she replied.

That motive of hers seemed to obstruct his will. Ellen was keen to see that Colter and his comrades were at a last stand and disintegrating under a severe strain. Nerve and courage of the open and the wild they possessed, but only in a limited degree. Colter seemed obsessed by his passion for her, and though Ellen in her stubborn pride did not yet fear him, she realized she ought to. After that incident she watched closely, never leaving her uncle's bedside except when Colter was absent. One or more of the men kept constant lookout somewhere down the cañon.

Day after day passed on the wings of suspense, of watching, of ministering to her uncle, of waiting for some hour that seemed fixed.

Colter was like a hound upon her trail. At every turn he was there to importune her to run off with him, to frighten her with the menace of the Isbels, to beg her to give herself to him. It came to pass that the only relief she had was when she ate with the men or barred the cabin door at night. Not much relief, however, was there in the shut and barred door. With one thrust of his powerful arm Colter could have caved it in. He knew this as well as Ellen. Still she did not have the fear she should have had. There was her rifle beside her, and though she did not allow her mind to run darkly on its possible use, still the fact of its being there at hand somehow strengthened her. Colter was a cat playing with a mouse, but not yet sure of his quarry.

Ellen came to know hours when she was weak—weak physically, mentally, spiritually, morally—when under the sheer weight of this frightful and growing burden of suspense she was not capable of fighting her misery, her abasement, her low ebb of vitality, and at the same time wholly withstanding Colter's advances.

He would come into the cabin and, utterly indifferent to Tad Jorth, he would try to make bold and unrestrained love to Ellen. When he caught her in one of her unresisting moments and was able to hold her in his arms and kiss her he seemed to be beside himself with the wonder of her. At such moments, if he had any softness or gentleness in him, they expressed themselves in his sooner or later letting her go, when apparently she was about to faint. So it must have become fascinatingly fixed in Colter's mind that at times Ellen repulsed him with scorn and at others could not resist him.

Ellen had escaped two crises in her relation with this man, and as a morbid doubt, like a poisonous fungus, began to strangle her mind, she instinctively divined that there was an approaching and final crisis. No uplift of her spirit came this time—no intimations—no whisperings. How horrible it all was! To long to be good and noble—to realize that she was neither—to sink lower day by day! Must she decay there like one of these rotting logs? Worst of all, then, was the insinuating and ever-growing hopelessness. What was the use? What did it matter? Who would ever think of Ellen Jorth? "O God!" she whispered in her distraction, "is there nothing left—nothing at all?"

A period of several days of less torment to Ellen followed. Her uncle apparently took a turn for the better and Colter let her alone. This last circumstance nonplussed Ellen. She was at a loss to understand it unless the Isbel menace now encroached upon Colter so formidably that he had forgotten her for the present.

Then one bright August morning, when she had just began to relax her eternal vigilance and breathe without oppression, Colter encountered her and, darkly silent and fierce, he grasped her and drew her off her feet. Ellen struggled violently, but the total surprise had deprived her of strength. And that paralyzing weakness assailed her as never before. Without apparent effort Colter carried her, striding rapidly away from the cabins into the border of spruce trees at the foot of the cañon wall.

"Colter—where—oh, where are y'u takin' me?" she found voice to cry out.

"By God! I don't know," he replied, with strong, vibrant passion. "I was a fool not to carry y'u off long ago. But I waited. I was hopin' y'u'd love me! . . . An' now that Isbel gang has corralled us. Somers seen the half-breed up on the rocks. An' Springer seen the rest of them sneakin' around. I run back after my horse an' y'u."

"But Uncle Tad! . . . We mustn't leave him alone," cried Ellen.

"We've got to," replied Colter, grimly. "Tad shore won't worry y'u no more—soon as Jean Isbel gets to him."

"Oh, let me stay," implored Ellen. "I will save him."

Colter laughed at the utter absurdity of her appeal and claim. Suddenly he set her down upon her feet. "Stand still," he ordered. Ellen saw his big bay horse, saddled, with pack and blanket, tied there in the shade of a spruce. With swift hands Colter untied him and mounted him, scarcely moving his piercing gaze from Ellen. He reached to grasp her. "Up with y'u! . . . Put your foot in the stirrup!" His will, like his powerful arm, was irresistible for Ellen at that moment. She found herself swung up behind him. Then the horse plunged away. What with the hard motion and Colter's iron grasp on her Ellen was in a painful position. Her knees and feet came into violent contact with branches and snags. He galloped the horse, tearing through the dense thicket of willows that served to hide the entrance to the side cañon, and when out in the larger and more open cañon he urged him to a run. Presently when Colter put the horse to a slow rise of ground, thereby bringing him to a walk, it was just in time to save Ellen a serious bruising. Again the sunlight appeared to shade over. They were in the pines. Suddenly with backward lunge Colter halted the horse. Ellen heard a yell. She recognized Queen's voice.

"Turn back, Colter! Turn back!"

With an oath Colter wheeled his mount. "If I didn't run plump into them," he ejaculated, harshly. And scarcely had the goaded horse gotten a start when a shot rang out. Ellen felt a violent shock, as if her momentum had suddenly met with a check, and then she felt herself wrenched from Colter, from the saddle, and propelled into the air. She alighted on soft ground and thick grass, and was unhurt save for the violent wrench and shaking that had rendered her breathless. Before she could rise Colter was pulling at her, lifting her to her feet. She saw the horse lying with bloody head. Tall pines loomed all around. Another rifle cracked. "Run!" hissed Colter, and he bounded off, dragging her by the hand. Another yell pealed out. "Here we are, Colter!" Again it was Queen's shrill voice. Ellen ran with all her might, her heart in her throat, her sight failing to record more than a blur of passing pines and a blank green wall of spruce. Then she lost her balance, was falling, yet could not fall because of that steel grip on her hand, and was dragged, and finally carried, into a dense shade. She was blinded. The trees whirled and faded. Voices and shots sounded far away. Then something black seemed to be wiped across her feeling.

It turned to gray, to moving blankness, to dim, hazy objects, spectral and tall, like blanketed trees, and when Ellen fully recovered consciousness she was being carried through the forest.

"Wal, little one, that was a close shave for y'u," said Colter's hard voice, growing clearer. "Reckon your keelin' over was natural enough."

He held her lightly in both arms, her head resting above his left elbow. Ellen saw his face as a gray blur, then taking sharper outline, until it stood out distinctly, pale and clammy, with eyes cold and wonderful in their intense flare. As she gazed upward Colter turned his head to look back through the woods, and his motion betrayed a keen, wild vigilance. The veins of his lean, brown neck stood out like whipcords. Two comrades were stalking beside him. Ellen heard their stealthy steps, and she felt Colter sheer from one side or the other. They were proceeding cautiously, fearful of the rear, but not wholly trusting to the fore.

"Reckon we'd better go slow an' look before we leap," said one whose voice Ellen recognized as Springer's.

"Shore. That open slope ain't to my likin', with our Nez Perce friend prowlin' round," drawled Colter, as he set Ellen down on her feet.

Another of the rustlers laughed. "Say, can't he twinkle through the forest? I had four shots at him. Harder to hit than a turkey runnin' cross-ways."

This facetious speaker was the evil-visaged, sardonic Somers. He carried two rifles and wore two belts of cartridges.

"Ellen, shore y'u ain't so daid white as y'u was," observed Colter, and he chucked her under the chin with familiar hand. "Set down heah. I don't want y'u stoppin' any bullets. An' there's no tellin'."

Ellen was glad to comply with his wish. She had begun to recover wits and strength, yet she still felt shaky. She observed that their position then was on the edge of a well-wooded slope from which she could see the grassy cañon floor below. They were on a level bench, projecting out from the main cañon wall that loomed gray and rugged and pine fringed. Somers and Colter and Springer gave careful attention to all points of the compass, especially in the direction from which they had come. They evidently anticipated being trailed or circled or headed off, but did not manifest much concern. Somers lit a cigarette; Springer wiped his face with a grimy hand and counted the shells in his belt, which appeared to be half empty. Colter stretched his long neck like a vulture and peered down the slope and through the aisles of the forest up toward the cañon rim.

"Listen!" he said, tersely, and bent his head a little to one side, ear to the slight breeze.

They all listened. Ellen heard the beating of her heart, the rustle of leaves, the tapping of a woodpecker, and faint, remote sounds that she could not name.

"Deer, I reckon," spoke up Somers.

"Ahuh! Wal, I reckon they ain't trailin' us yet," replied Colter. "We gave them a shade better 'n they sent us."

"Short an' sweet!" ejaculated Springer, and he removed his black sombrero to poke a dirty forefinger through a bullet hole in the crown. "Thet's how close I come to cashin'. I was lyin' behind a log, listenin' an' watchin', an' when I stuck my head up a little—zam! Somebody made my bonnet leak."

"Where's Queen?" asked Colter.

"He was with me fust off," replied Somers. "An' then when the shootin' slacked—after I'd plugged thet big, red-faced, white-haired pal of Isbel's—"

"Reckon thet was Blaisdell," interrupted Springer.

"Queen—he got tired layin' low," went on Somers. "He wanted action. I heerd him chewin' to himself, an' when I asked him what was eatin' him he up an' growled he was goin' to quit this Injun fightin'. An' he slipped off in the woods."

"Wal, that's the gun fighter of it," declared Colter, wagging his head. "Ever since that cowman, Blue, braced us an' said he was King Fisher, why Queen has been sulkier an' sulkier. He cain't help it. He'll do the same trick as Blue tried. An' shore he'll get his everlastin'. But he's the Texas breed all right."

"Say, do you reckon Blue really is King Fisher?" queried Somers.

"Naw!" ejaculated Colter, with downward sweep of his hand. "Many a would-be gun slinger has borrowed Fisher's name. But Fisher is daid these many years."

"Ahuh! Wal, mebbe, but don't you fergit it—thet Blue was no would-be," declared Somers. "He was the genuine article."

"I should smile!" affirmed Springer.

The subject irritated Colter, and he dismissed it with another forcible gesture and a counter question.

"How many left in that Isbel outfit?"

"No tellin'. There shore was enough of them," replied Somers. "Anyhow, the woods was full of flyin' bullets. . . . Springer, did you account for any of them?"

"Nope—not thet I noticed," responded Springer, dryly. "I had my chance at the half-breed. . . . Reckon I was nervous."

"Was Slater near you when he yelled out?"

"No. He was lyin' beside Somers."

"Wasn't thet a queer way fer a man to act?" broke in Somers. "A bullet hit Slater, cut him down the back as he was lyin' flat. Reckon it wasn't bad. But it hurt him so thet he jumped right up an' staggered around. He made a target big as a tree. An' mebbe them Isbels didn't riddle him!"

"That was when I got my crack at Bill Isbel," declared Colter, with grim satisfaction. "When they shot my horse out from under me I had

Ellen to think of an' couldn't get my rifle. Shore had to run, as y'u seen. Wal, as I only had my six-shooter, there was nothin' for me to do but lay low an' listen to the sping of lead. Wells was standin' up behind a tree aboot thirty yards off. He got plugged, an' fallin' over he began to crawl my way, still holdin' to his rifle. I crawled along the log to meet him. But he dropped aboot half-way. I went on an' took his rifle an' belt. When I peeped out from behind a spruce bush then I seen Bill Isbel. He was shootin' fast, an' all of them was shootin' fast. That was when they had the open shot at Slater. . . . Wal, I bored Bill Isbel right through his middle. He dropped his rifle an', all bent double, he fooled around in a circle till he flopped over the Rim. I reckon he's layin' right up there somewhere below that daid spruce. I'd shore like to see him."

"Wal, you'd be as crazy as Queen if you tried thet," declared Somers. "We're not out of the woods yet."

"I reckon not," replied Colter. "An' I've lost my horse. Where'd y'u leave yours?"

"They're down the cañon, below thet willow brake. An' saddled an' none of them tied. Reckon we'll have to look them up before dark."

"Colter, what 're we goin' to do?" demanded Springer.

"Wait heah a while—then cross the cañon an' work round up under the bluff, back to the cabin."

"An' then what?" queried Somers, doubtfully eying Colter.

"We've got to eat—we've got to have blankets," rejoined Colter, testily. "An' I reckon we can hide there an' stand a better show in a fight than runnin' for it in the woods."

"Wal, I'm givin' you a hunch thet it looked like you was runnin' fer it," retorted Somers.

"Yes, an' packin' the girl," added Springer. "Looks funny to me."

Both rustlers eyed Colter with dark and distrustful glances. What he might have replied never transpired, for the reason that his gaze, always shifting around, had suddenly fixed on something.

"Is that a wolf?" he asked, pointing to the Rim.

Both his comrades moved to get in line with his finger. Ellen could not see from her position.

"Shore thet's a big lofer," declared Somers. "Reckon he scented us."

"There he goes along the Rim," observed Colter. "He doesn't act leary. Looks like a good sign to me. Mebbe the Isbels have gone the other way."

"Looks bad to me," rejoined Springer, gloomily.

"An' why?" demanded Colter.

"I seen thet animal. Fust time I reckoned it was a lofer. Second time it was right near them Isbels. An' I'm damned now if I don't believe it's thet half-lofer sheep dog of Gass Isbel's."

"Wal, what if it is?"

"Ha! . . . Shore we needn't worry about hidin' out," replied Springer, sententiously. "With thet dog Jean Isbel could trail a grasshopper."

"The hell y'u say!" muttered Colter. Manifestly such a possibility put a different light upon the present situation. The men grew silent and watchful, occupied by brooding thoughts and vigilant surveillance of all points. Somers slipped off into the brush, soon to return, with intent look of importance.

"I heerd somethin'," he whispered, jerking his thumb backward. "Rollin' gravel—crackin' of twigs. No deer! . . . Reckon it 'd be a good idee for us to slip round acrost this bench."

"Wal, y'u fellars go, an' I'll watch heah," returned Colter.

"Not much," said Somers, while Springer leered knowingly.

Colter became incensed, but he did not give way to it. Pondering a moment, he finally turned to Ellen. "Y'u wait heah till I come back. An' if I don't come in reasonable time y'u slip across the cañon an' through the willows to the cabins. Wait till aboot dark." With that he possessed himself of one of the extra rifles and belts and silently joined his comrades. Together they noiselessly stole into the brush.

Ellen had no other thought than to comply with Colter's wishes. There was her wounded uncle who had been left unattended, and she was anxious to get back to him. Besides, if she had wanted to run off from Colter, where could she go? Alone in the woods, she would get lost and die of starvation. Her lot must be cast with the Jorth faction until the end. That did not seem far away.

Her strained attention and suspense made the moments fly. By and by several shots pealed out far across the side cañon on her right, and they were answered by reports sounding closer to her. The fight was on again. But these shots were not repeated. The flies buzzed, the hot sun beat down and sloped to the west, the soft, warm breeze stirred the aspens, the ravens croaked, the red squirrels and blue jays chattered.

Suddenly a quick, short, yelp electrified Ellen, brought her upright with sharp, listening rigidity. Surely it was not a wolf and hardly could it be a coyote. Again she heard it. The yelp of a sheep dog! She had heard that often enough to know. And she rose to change her position so she could command a view of the rocky bluff above. Presently she espied what really appeared to be a big timber wolf. But another yelp satisfied her that it really was a dog. She watched him. Soon it became evident that he wanted to get down over the bluff. He ran to and fro, and then out of sight. In a few moments his yelp sounded from lower down, at the base of the bluff, and it was now the cry of an intelligent dog that was trying to call some one to his aid. Ellen grew convinced that the dog was near where Colter had said Bill Isbel had plunged over the declivity. Would the dog yelp that way if the man was dead? Ellen thought not.

No one came, and the continuous yelping of the dog got on Ellen's nerves. It was a call for help. And finally she surrendered to it. Since her natural terror when Colter's horse was shot from under her and she had been dragged away, she had not recovered from fear of the Isbels. But calm consideration now convinced her that she could hardly be in a worse plight in their hands than if she remained in Colter's. So she started out to find the dog.

The wooded bench was level for a few hundred yards, and then it began to heave in rugged, rocky bulges up toward the Rim. It did not appear far to where the dog was barking, but the latter part of the distance proved to be a hard climb over jumbled rocks and through thick brush. Panting and hot, she at length reached the base of the bluff, to find that it was not very high.

The dog espied her before she saw him, for he was coming toward her when she discovered him. Big, shaggy, grayish white and black, with wild, keen face and eyes he assuredly looked the reputation Springer had accorded him. But sagacious, guarded as was his approach, he appeared friendly.

"Hello—doggie!" panted Ellen. "What's—wrong—up heah?"

He yelped, his ears lost their stiffness, his body sank a little, and his bushy tail wagged to and fro. What a gray, clear, intelligent look he gave her! Then he trotted back.

Ellen followed him around a corner of bluff to see the body of a man lying on his back. Fresh earth and gravel lay about him, attesting to his fall from above. He had on neither coat nor hat, and the position of his body and limbs suggested broken bones. As Ellen hurried to his side she saw that the front of his shirt, low down, was a bloody blotch. But he could lift his head; his eyes were open; he was perfectly conscious. Ellen did not recognize the dusty, skinned face, yet the mold of features, the look of the eyes, seemed strangely familiar.

"You're—Jorth's—girl," he said, in faint voice of surprise.

"Yes, I'm Ellen Jorth," she replied. "An' are y'u Bill Isbel?"

"All thet's left of me. But I'm thankin' God somebody come—even a Jorth."

Ellen knelt beside him and examined the wound in his abdomen. A heavy bullet had indeed, as Colter had avowed, torn clear through his middle. Even if he had not sustained other serious injury from the fall over the cliff, that terrible bullet wound meant death very shortly. Ellen shuddered. How inexplicable were men! How cruel, bloody, mindless!

"Isbel, I'm sorry—there's no hope," she said, low voiced. "Y'u've not long to live. . . . I cain't help y'u. God knows I'd do so if I could."

"All over!" he sighed, with his eyes looking beyond her. "I reckon—I'm glad. . . . But y'u can—do somethin' for me. Will y'u?"

"Indeed, yes. Tell me," she replied, lifting his dusty head on her knee. Her hands trembled as she brushed his wet hair back from his clammy brow.

"I've somethin'—on my conscience," he whispered.

The woman, the sensitive in Ellen, understood and pitied him then.

"Yes," she encouraged him.

"I stole cattle—my dad's an' Blaisdell's—an' made deals—with Daggs. . . . All the crookedness—wasn't on—Jorth's side. . . . I want—my brother Jean—to know."

"I'll try—to tell him," whispered Ellen, out of her great amaze.

"We were all—a bad lot—except Jean," went on Isbel. "Dad wasn't fair. . . . God! how he hated Jorth! Jorth, yes, who was—your father. . . . Wal, they're even now."

"How—so?" faltered Ellen.

"Your father killed dad. . . . At the last—dad wanted to—save us. He sent word—he'd meet him—face to face—an' let thet end the feud. They met out in the road. . . . But some one shot dad down—with a rifle—an' then your father finished him."

"An' then, Isbel," added Ellen, with unconscious mocking bitterness, "your brother murdered my dad!"

"What!" whispered Bill Isbel. "Shore y'u've got—it wrong. I reckon Jean—could have killed—your father. . . . But he didn't. Queer, we all thought."

"Ah! . . . Who did kill my father?" burst out Ellen, and her voice rang like great hammers at her ears.

"It was Blue. He went in the store—alone—faced the whole gang alone. Bluffed them—taunted them—told them he was King Fisher. . . . Then he killed—your dad—an' Jackson Jorth. . . . Jean was out—back of the store. We were out—front. There was shootin'. Colmor was hit. Then Blue ran out—bad hurt. . . . Both of them—died in Meeker's yard."

"An' so Jean Isbel has not killed a Jorth!" said Ellen, in strange, deep voice.

"No," replied Isbel, earnestly, "I reckon this feud—was hardest on Jean. He never lived heah. . . . An' my sister Ann said—he got sweet on y'u. . . . Now did he?"

Slow, stinging tears filled Ellen's eyes, and her head sank low and lower.

"Yes—he did," she murmured, tremulously.

"Ahuh! Wal, thet accounts," replied Isbel, wonderingly. "Too bad! . . . It might have been. . . . A man always sees—different when—he's dyin'. . . . If I had—my life—to live over again! . . . My poor kids—deserted in their babyhood—ruined for life! All for nothin'. . . . May God forgive—"

Then he choked and whispered for water.

Ellen laid his head back and, rising, she took his sombrero and started hurriedly down the slope, making dust fly and rocks roll. Her mind was a seething ferment. Leaping, bounding, sliding down the weathered slope, she gained the bench, to run across that, and so on down into the open cañon to the willow-bordered brook. Here she filled the sombrero with water and started back, forced now to walk slowly and carefully. It was then, with the violence and fury of intense muscular activity denied her, that the tremendous import of Bill Isbel's revelation burst upon her very flesh and blood and transfiguring the very world of golden light and azure sky and speaking forestland that encompassed her.

Not a drop of the precious water did she spill. Not a misstep did she make. Yet so great was the spell upon her that she was not aware she had climbed the steep slope until the dog yelped his welcome. Then with all the flood of her emotion surging and resurging she knelt to allay the parching thirst of this dying enemy whose words had changed frailty to strength, hate to love, and the gloomy hell of despair to something unutterable. But she had returned too late. Bill Isbel was dead.

CHAPTER 13

Jean Isbel, holding the wolf-dog Shepp in leash, was on the trail of the most dangerous of Jorth's gang, the gunman Queen. Dark drops of blood on the stones and plain tracks of a rider's sharp-heeled boots behind coverts indicated the trail of a wounded, slow-traveling fugitive. Therefore, Jean Isbel held in the dog and proceeded with the wary eye and watchful caution of an Indian.

Queen, true to his class, and emulating Blue with the same magnificent effrontery and with the same paralyzing suddenness of surprise, had appeared as if by magic at the last night camp of the Isbel faction. Jean had seen him first, in time to leap like a panther into the shadow. But he carried in his shoulder Queen's first bullet of that terrible encounter. Upon Gordon and Fredericks fell the brunt of Queen's fusillade. And they, shot to pieces, staggering and falling, held passionate grip on life long enough to draw and still Queen's guns and send him reeling off into the darkness of the forest.

Unarmed, and hindered by a painful wound, Jean had kept a vigil near camp all that silent and menacing night. Morning disclosed Gordon and Fredericks stark and ghastly beside the burned-out camp-fire, their guns clutched immovably in stiffened hands. Jean buried them as best he could, and when they were under ground with flat stones on their graves he knew himself to be indeed the last of the Isbel clan. And all that was wild and savage in his blood and desperate in his spirit rose to make him more than man and less than human. Then for the third time during these tragic last days the wolf-dog Shepp came to him.

Jean washed the wound Queen had given him and bound it tightly. The keen pang and burn of the lead was a constant and all-powerful reminder of the grim work left for him to do. The whole world was no longer large enough for him and whoever was left of the Jorths. The heritage of blood his father had bequeathed him, the unshakable love for a worthless girl who had so dwarfed and obstructed his will and so bitterly defeated and reviled his poor, romantic, boyish faith, the killing of hostile men, so strange in its after effects, the pursuits and fights, and loss of one by one of his confederates—these had finally engendered in Jean Isbel a wild, unslakable thirst, these had been the cause of his retrogression, these had unalterably and ruthlessly fixed in his darkened mind one fierce passion—to live and die the last man of that Jorth-Isbel feud.

At sunrise Jean left this camp, taking with him only a small knapsack of meat and bread, and with the eager, wild Shepp in leash he set out on Queen's bloody trail.

Black drops of blood on the stones and an irregular trail of footprints proved to Jean that the gunman was hard hit. Here he had fallen, or knelt, or sat down, evidently to bind his wounds. Jean found strips of scarf, red and discarded. And the blood drops failed to show on more rocks. In a deep forest of spruce, under silver-tipped spreading branches, Queen had rested, perhaps slept. Then laboring with dragging steps, not improbably with a lame leg, he had gone on, up out of the dark-green ravine to the open, dry, pine-tipped ridge. Here he had rested, perhaps waited to see if he were pursued. From that point his trail spoke an easy language for Jean's keen eye. The gunman knew he was pursued. He had seen his enemy. Therefore Jean proceeded with a slow caution, never getting within revolver range of ambush, using all his woodcraft to trail this man and yet save himself. Queen traveled slowly, either because he was wounded or else because he tried to ambush his pursuer, and Jean accommodated his pace to that of Queen. From noon of that day they were never far apart, never out of hearing of a rifle shot.

The contrast of the beauty and peace and loneliness of the surroundings to the nature of Queen's flight often obtruded its strange truth into the somber turbulence of Jean's mind, into that fixed columnar idea around which fleeting thoughts hovered and gathered like shadows.

Early frost had touched the heights with its magic wand. And the forest seemed a temple in which man might worship nature and life rather than steal through the dells and under the arched aisles like a beast of prey. The green-and-gold leaves of aspens quivered in the glades; maples in the ravines fluttered their red-and-purple leaves. The needle-matted carpet under the pines vied with the long lanes of silvery grass, alike enticing to the eye of man and beast. Sunny rays of light, flecked with dust and flying insects, slanted down from the overhanging brown-limbed, green-massed foliage. Roar of wind in the distant forest alternated with soft breeze close at hand. Small dove-gray squirrels ran all over the woodland, very curious about Jean and his dog, rustling the twigs, scratching the bark of trees, chattering and barking, frisky, saucy, and bright-eyed. A plaintive twitter of wild canaries came from the region above the treetops—first voices of birds in their pilgrimage toward the south. Pine cones dropped with soft thuds. The blue jays followed these intruders in the forest, screeching their displeasure. Like rain pattered the dropping seeds from the spruces. A woody, earthy, leafy fragrance, damp with the current of life, mingled with a cool, dry, sweet smell of withered grass and rotting pines.

Solitude and lonesomeness, peace and rest, wild life and nature, reigned there. It was a golden-green region, enchanting to the gaze of man. An Indian would have walked there with his spirits.

And even as Jean felt all this elevating beauty and inscrutable spirit his keen eye once more fastened upon the blood-red drops Queen had again left on the gray moss and rock. His wound had reopened. Jean felt the thrill of the scenting panther.

The sun set, twilight gathered, night fell. Jean crawled under a dense, low-spreading spruce, ate some bread and meat, fed the dog, and lay down to rest and sleep. His thoughts burdened him, heavy and black as the mantle of night. A wolf mourned a hungry cry for a mate. Shepp quivered under Jean's hand. That was the call which had lured him from the ranch. The wolf blood in him yearned for the wild. Jean tied the cowhide leash to his wrist. When this dark business was at an end Shepp could be free to join the lonely mate mourning out there in the forest. Then Jean slept.

Dawn broke cold, clear, frosty, with silvered grass sparkling, with a soft, faint rustling of falling aspen leaves. When the sun rose red Jean was again on the trail of Queen. By a frosty-ferned brook, where water tinkled and ran clear as air and cold as ice, Jean quenched his thirst, leaning on a stone that showed drops of blood. Queen, too, had to quench his thirst. What good, what help, Jean wondered, could the cold, sweet, granite water, so dear to woodsmen and wild creatures, do this wounded, hunted rustler? Why did he not wait in the open to fight and face the death he had meted? Where was that splendid and terrible daring of the gunman? Queen's love of life dragged him on and on, hour by hour, through the pine groves and spruce woods, through the oak swales and aspen glades, up and down the rocky gorges, around the windfalls and over the rotting logs.

The time came when Queen tried no more ambush. He gave up trying to trap his pursuer by lying in wait. He gave up trying to conceal his tracks. He grew stronger or, in desperation, increased his energy, so that he redoubled his progress through the wilderness. That, at best, would count only a few miles a day. And he began to circle to the northwest, back toward the deep cañon where Blaisdell and Bill Isbel had reached the end of their trails. Queen had evidently left his comrades, had lonehanded it in his last fight, but was now trying to get back to them. Somewhere in these wild, deep forest brakes the rest of the Jorth faction had found a hiding place. Jean let Queen lead him there.

Ellen Jorth would be with them. Jean had seen her. It had been his shot that killed Colter's horse. And he had withheld further fire because Colter had dragged the girl behind him, protecting his body with hers. Sooner or later Jean would come upon their camp. She would be there. The thought of her dark beauty, wasted in wantonness upon these rustlers, added a deadly rage to the blood lust and righteous wrath of his vengeance. Let her again flaunt her degradation in his face and, by the God she had forsaken, he would kill her, and so end the race of Jorths!

Another night fell, dark and cold, without starlight. The wind moaned in the forest. Shepp was restless. He sniffed the air. There was a step on his trail. Again a mournful, eager, wild, and hungry wolf cry broke the silence. It was deep and low, like that of a baying hound, but infinitely wilder. Shepp strained to get away. During the night, while Jean slept, he managed to chew the cowhide leash apart and run off.

Next day no dog was needed to trail Queen. Fog and low-drifting clouds in the forest and a misty rain had put the rustler off his bearings. He was lost, and showed that he realized it. Strange how a matured man, fighter of a hundred battles, steeped in bloodshed, and on his last stand, should grow panic-stricken upon being lost! So Jean Isbel read the signs of the trail.

Queen circled and wandered through the foggy, dripping forest until he headed down into a cañon. It was one that notched the Rim and led down and down, mile after mile into the Basin. Not soon had Queen discovered his mistake. When he did do so, night overtook him.

The weather cleared before morning. Red and bright the sun burst out of the east to flood that low basin land with light. Jean found that Queen had traveled on and on, hoping, no doubt, to regain what he had lost. But in the darkness he had climbed to the manzanita slopes instead of back up the cañon. And here he had fought the hold of that strange brush of Spanish name until he fell exhausted.

Surely Queen would make his stand and wait somewhere in this devilish thicket for Jean to catch up with him. Many and many a place Jean would have chosen had he been in Queen's place. Many a rock and dense thicket Jean circled or approached with extreme care. Manzanita grew in patches that were impenetrable except for a small animal. The brush was a few feet high, seldom so high that Jean could not look over it, and of a beautiful appearance, having glossy, small leaves, a golden berry, and branches of dark-red color. These branches were tough and unbendable. Every bush, almost, had low branches that were dead, hard as steel, sharp as thorns, as clutching as cactus. Progress was possible only by endless detours to find the half-closed aisles between patches, or else by crashing through with main strength or walking right over the tops. Jean preferred this last method, not because it was the easiest, but for the reason that he could see ahead so much farther. So he literally walked across the tips of the manzanita brush. Often he fell through and had to step up again; many a branch broke with him, letting him down; but for the most part he stepped from fork to fork, on branch after branch, with balance of an Indian and the patience of a man whose purpose was sustaining and immutable.

On that south slope under the Rim the sun beat down hot. There was no breeze to temper the dry air. And before midday Jean was laboring, wet with sweat, parching with thirst, dusty and hot and tiring. It amazed him, the doggedness and tenacity of life shown by this wounded rustler. The time came when under the burning rays of the sun he was compelled to abandon the walk across the tips of the manzanita bushes and take to the winding, open threads that ran between. It would have been poor sight indeed that could not have followed Queen's labyrinthine and broken passage through the brush. Then the time came when Jean espied Queen, far ahead and above, crawling like a black bug along the bright-green slope. Sight then acted upon Jean as upon a hound in the chase. But he governed his actions if he could not govern his instincts. Slowly but surely he followed the dusty, hot trail, and never a patch of blood failed to send a thrill along his veins.

Queen, headed up toward the Rim, finally vanished from sight. Had he fallen? Was he hiding? But the hour disclosed that he was crawling. Jean's keen eye caught the slow moving of the brush and enabled him to keep just so close to the rustler, out of range of the six-shooters he carried. And so all the interminable hours of the hot afternoon that snail-pace flight and pursuit kept on.

Half-way up the Rim the growth of manzanita gave place to open, yellow, rocky slope dotted with cedars. Queen took to a slow-ascending ridge and left his bloody tracks all the way to the top, where in the gathering darkness the weary pursuer lost them.

Another night passed. Daylight was relentless to the rustler. He could not hide his trail. But somehow in a desperate last rally of strength he reached a point on the heavily timbered ridge that Jean recognized as being near the scene of the fight in the cañon. Queen was nearing the rendezvous of the rustlers. Jean crossed tracks of horses, and then more tracks that he was certain had been made days past by his own party. To the left of this ridge must be the deep cañon that had frustrated his efforts to catch up with the rustlers on the day Blaisdell lost his life, and probably Bill Isbel, too. Something warned Jean that he was nearing the end of the trail, and an unaccountable sense of imminent catastrophe seemed foreshadowed by vague dreads and doubts in his gloomy mind.

Jean felt the need of rest, of food, of ease from the strain of the last weeks. But his spirit drove him implacably.

Queen's rally of strength ended at the edge of an open, bald ridge that was bare of brush or grass and was surrounded by a line of forest on three sides, and on the fourth by a low bluff which raised its gray head above the pines. Across this dusty open Queen had crawled, leaving unmistakable signs of his condition. Jean took long survey of the circle of trees and of the low, rocky eminence, neither of which he liked. It might be wiser to keep to cover, Jean thought, and work around to where Queen's trail entered the forest again. But he was tired, gloomy, and his eternal vigilance was failing. Nevertheless, he stilled for the thousandth time that bold prompting of his vengeance and, taking to the edge of the forest, he went to considerable pains to circle the open ground. And suddenly sight of a man sitting back against a tree halted Jean.

He stared to make sure his eyes did not deceive him. Many times stumps and snags and rocks had taken on strange resemblance to a standing or crouching man. This was only another suggestive blunder of the mind behind his eyes—what he wanted to see he imagined he saw. Jean glided on from tree to tree until he made sure that this sitting image indeed was that of a man. He sat bolt upright, facing back across the open, hands resting on his knees—and closer scrutiny showed Jean that he held a gun in each hand.

Queen! At the last his nerve had revived. He could not crawl any farther, he could never escape, so with the courage of fatality he chose the open, to face his foe and die. Jean had a thrill of admiration for the rustler. Then he stalked out from under the pines and strode forward with his rifle ready.

A watching man could not have failed to espy Jean. But Queen never made the slightest move. Moreover, his stiff, unnatural position struck Jean so singularly that he halted with a muttered exclamation. He was now about fifty paces from Queen, within range of those small guns. Jean called, sharply, *"Queen!"* Still the figure never relaxed in the slightest.

Jean advanced a few more paces, rifle up, ready to fire the instant Queen lifted a gun. The man's immobility brought the cold sweat to Jean's brow. He stopped to bend the full intense power of his gaze upon this inert figure. Suddenly over Jean flashed its meaning. Queen was dead. He had backed up against the pine, ready to face his foe, and he had died there. Not a shadow of a doubt entered Jean's mind as he started forward again. He knew. After all, Queen's blood would not be on his hands. Gordon and Fredericks in their death throes had given the rustler mortal wounds. Jean kept on, marveling the while. How ghastly thin and hard! Those four days of flight had been hell for Queen.

Jean reached him—looked down with staring eyes. The guns were tied to his hands. Jean started violently as the whole direction of his mind shifted. A lightning glance showed that Queen had been propped against the tree—another showed boot tracks in the dust.

"By Heaven, they've fooled me!" hissed Jean, and quickly as he leaped behind the pine he was not quick enough to escape the cunning rustlers who had waylaid him thus. He felt the shock, the bite and burn of lead before he heard a rifle crack. A bullet had ripped through his left forearm. From behind the tree he saw a puff of white smoke along the face of the bluff—the very spot his keen and gloomy vigilance had descried as one of menace. Then several puffs of white smoke and ringing reports betrayed the ambush of the tricksters. Bullets barked the pine and whistled by. Jean saw a man dart from behind a rock and, leaning over, run for another. Jean's swift shot stopped him midway. He fell, got up, and floundered behind a bush scarcely large enough to conceal him. Into that bush Jean shot again and again. He had no pain in his wounded arm, but the sense of the shock clung in his consciousness, and this, with the tremendous surprise of the deceit, and sudden release of long-dammed overmastering passion, caused him to empty the magazine of his Winchester in a terrible haste to kill the man he had hit.

These were all the loads he had for his rifle. Blood passion had made him blunder. Jean cursed himself, and his hand moved to his belt. His six-shooter was gone. The sheath had been loose. He had tied the gun fast. But the strings had been torn apart. The rustlers were shooting again. Bullets thudded into the pine and whistled by. Bending carefully, Jean reached one of Queen's guns and jerked it from his hand. The weapon was empty. Both of his guns were empty. Jean peeped out again to get the line in which the bullets were coming and, marking a course from his position to the cover of the forest, he ran with all his might. He gained the shelter. Shrill yells behind warned him that he had been seen, that his reason for flight had been guessed. Looking back, he saw two or three men scrambling down the bluff. Then the loud neigh of a frightened horse pealed out.

Jean discarded his useless rifle, and headed down the ridge slope, keeping to the thickest line of pines and sheering around the clumps of spruce. As he ran, his mind whirled with grim thoughts of escape, of his necessity to find the camp where Gordon and Fredericks were buried, there to procure another rifle and ammunition. He felt the wet blood dripping down his arm, yet no pain. The forest was too open for good cover. He dared not run uphill. His only course was ahead, and that soon ended in an abrupt declivity too precipitous to descend. As he halted, panting for breath, he heard the ring of hoofs on stone, then the thudding beat of running horses on soft ground. The rustlers had sighted the direction he had taken. Jean did not waste time to look. Indeed, there was no need, for as he bounded along the cliff to the right a rifle cracked and a bullet whizzed over his head. It lent wings to his feet. Like a deer he sped along, leaping cracks and logs and rocks, his ears filled by the rush of wind, until his quick eye caught sight of thick-growing spruce foliage close to the precipice. He sprang down into the green mass. His weight precipitated him through the upper branches. But lower down his spread arms broke his fall, then retarded it until he caught. A long, swaying limb let him down and down, where he grasped another and a stiffer one that held his weight. Hand over hand he worked toward the trunk of this spruce and, gaining it, he found other branches close together down which he hastened, hold by hold and step by step, until all above him was black, dense foliage, and beneath him the brown, shady slope. Sure of being unseen from above, he glided noiselessly down under the trees, slowly regaining freedom from that constriction of his breast.

Passing on to a gray-lichened cliff, overhanging and gloomy, he paused there to rest and to listen. A faint crack of hoof on stone came to him from above, apparently farther on to the right. Eventually his pursuers would discover that he had taken to the cañon. But for the moment he felt safe. The wound in his forearm drew his attention. The bullet had gone clear through without breaking either bone. His shirt sleeve was soaked with blood. Jean rolled it back and tightly wrapped his scarf around the wound, yet still the dark-red blood oozed out and dripped down into his hand. He became aware of a dull, throbbing pain.

Not much time did Jean waste in arriving at what was best to do. For the time being he had escaped, and whatever had been his peril, it was past. In dense, rugged country like this he could not be caught by rustlers. But he had only a knife left for a weapon, and there was very little meat in the pocket of his coat. Salt and matches he possessed. Therefore the imperative need was for him to find the last camp, where he could get rifle and ammunition, bake bread, and rest up before taking again the trail of the rustlers. He had reason to believe that this cañon was the one where the fight on the Rim, and later, on a bench of woodland below, had taken place.

Thereupon he arose and glided down under the spruces toward the level, grassy open he could see between the trees. And as he proceeded, with the slow step and wary eye of an Indian, his mind was busy.

Queen had in his flight unerringly worked in the direction of this cañon until he became lost in the fog; and upon regaining his bearings he had made a wonderful and heroic effort to surmount the manzanita slope and the Rim and find the rendezvous of his comrades. But he had failed up there on the ridge. In thinking it over Jean arrived at a conclusion that Queen, finding he could go no farther, had waited, guns in hands, for his pursuer. And he had died in this position. Then by strange coincidence his comrades had happened to come across him and, recognizing the situation, they had taken the shells from his guns and propped him up with the idea of luring Jean on. They had arranged a cunning trick and ambush, which had all but snuffed out the last of the Isbels. Colter probably had been at the bottom of this crafty plan. Since the fight at the Isbel ranch, now seemingly far back in the past, this man Colter had loomed up more and more as a stronger and more dangerous antagonist then either Jorth or Daggs. Before that he had been little known to any of the Isbel faction. And it was Colter now who controlled the remnant of the gang and who had Ellen Jorth in his possession.

The cañon wall above Jean, on the right, grew more rugged and loftier, and the one on the left began to show wooded slopes and brakes, and at last a wide expanse with a winding, willow border on the west and long, low, pine-dotted bench on the east. It took several moments of study for Jean to recognize the rugged bluff above this bench. On up that cañon several miles was the site where Queen had surprised Jean and his comrades at their camp-fire. Somewhere in this vicinity was the hiding place of the rustlers.

Thereupon Jean proceeded with the utmost stealth, absolutely certain that he would miss no sound, movement, sign, or anything unnatural to the wild peace of the cañon. And his first sense to register something was his keen smell. Sheep! He was amazed to smell sheep. There must be a flock not far away. Then from where he glided along under the trees he saw down to open places in the willow brake and noticed sheep tracks in the dark, muddy bank of the brook. Next he heard faint tinkle of bells, and at length, when he could see farther into the open enlargement of the cañon, his surprised gaze fell upon an immense gray, woolly patch that blotted out acres and acres of grass. Thousands of sheep were grazing there. Jean knew there were several flocks of Jorth's sheep on the mountain in the care of herders, but he had never thought of them being so far west, more than twenty miles from Chevelon Cañon. His roving eyes could not descry any herders or dogs. But he knew there must be dogs close to that immense flock. And, whatever his cunning, he could not hope to elude the scent and sight of shepherd dogs. It would be best to go back the way he had come, wait for darkness, then cross the cañon and climb out, and work around to his objective point. Turning at once, he started to glide back. But almost immediately he was brought stock-still and thrilling by the sound of hoofs.

Horses were coming in the direction he wished to take. They were close. His swift conclusion was that the men who had pursued him up on the Rim had worked down into the cañon. One circling glance showed him that he had no sure covert near at hand. It would not do to risk their passing him there. The border of woodland was narrow and not dense enough for close inspection. He was forced to turn back up the cañon, in the hope of soon finding a hiding place or a break in the wall where he could climb up.

Hugging the base of the wall, he slipped on, passing the point where he had espied the sheep, and gliding on until he was stopped by a bend in the dense line of willows. It sheered to the west there and ran close to the high wall. Jean kept on until he was stooping under a curling border of

willow thicket, with branches slim and yellow and masses of green foliage that brushed against the wall. Suddenly he encountered an abrupt
corner of rock. He rounded it, to discover that it ran at right angles with
the one he had just passed. Peering up through the willows, he ascertained that there was a narrow crack in the main wall of the cañon. It had
been concealed by willows low down and leaning spruces above. A wild,
hidden retreat! Along the base of the wall there were tracks of small animals. The place was odorous like all dense thickets, but it was not dry.
Water ran through there somewhere. Jean drew easier breath. All sounds
except the rustling of birds or mice in the willows had ceased. The brake
was pervaded by a dreamy emptiness. Jean decided to steal on a little farther, then wait till he felt he might safely dare go back.

The golden-green gloom suddenly brightened. Light showed ahead,
and parting the willows, he looked out into a narrow, winding cañon,
with an open, grassy, willow-streaked lane in the center and on each side
a thin strip of woodland.

His surprise was short lived. A crashing of horses back of him in the
willows gave him a shock. He ran out along the base of the wall, back of
the trees. Like the strip of woodland in the main cañon, this one was
scant and had but little underbrush. There were young spruces growing
with thick branches clear to the grass, and under these he could have
concealed himself. But, with a certainty of sheep dogs in the vicinity, he
would not think of hiding except as a last resource. These horsemen,
whoever they were, were as likely to be sheep herders as not. Jean slackened his pace to look back. He could not see any moving objects, but he
still heard horses, though not so close now. Ahead of him this narrow
gorge opened out like the neck of a bottle. He would run on to the head
of it and find a place to climb to the top.

Hurried and anxious as Jean was, he yet received an impression of
singular, wild nature of this side gorge. It was a hidden, pine-fringed
crack in the rock-ribbed and cañon-cut tableland. Above him the sky
seemed a winding stream of blue. The walls were red and bulged out in
spruce-greened shelves. From wall to wall was scarcely a distance of a
hundred feet. Jumbles of rock obstructed his close holding to the wall.
He had to walk at the edge of the timber. As he progressed, the gorge
widened into wilder, ruggeder aspect. Through the trees ahead he saw

where the wall circled to meet the cliff on the left, forming an oval depression, the nature of which he could not ascertain. But it appeared to be a small opening surrounded by dense thickets and the overhanging walls. Anxiety augmented to alarm. He might not be able to find a place to scale those rough cliffs. Breathing hard, Jean halted again. The situation was growing critical again. His physical condition was worse. Loss of sleep and rest, lack of food, the long pursuit of Queen, the wound in his arm, and the desperate run for his life—these had weakened him to the extent that if he undertook any strenuous effort he would fail. His cunning weighed all chances.

The shade of wall and foliage above, and another jumble of ruined cliff, hindered his survey of the ground ahead, and he almost stumbled upon a cabin, hidden on three sides, with a small, bare clearing in front. It was an old, ramshackle structure like others he had run across in the cañons. Cautiously he approached and peeped around the corner. At first swift glance it had all the appearance of long disuse. But Jean had no time for another look. A clip-clop of trotting horses on hard ground brought the same pell-mell rush of sensations that had driven him to wild flight scarcely an hour past. His body jerked with its instinctive impulse, then quivered with his restraint. To turn back would be risky, to run ahead would be fatal, to hide was his one hope. No covert behind! And the clip-clop of hoofs sounded closer. One moment longer Jean held mastery over his instincts of self-preservation. To keep from running was almost impossible. It was the sheer primitive animal sense to escape. He drove it back and glided along the front of the cabin.

Here he saw that the cabin adjoined another. Reaching the door, he was about to peep in when the thud of hoofs and voices close at hand transfixed him with a grim certainty that he had not an instant to lose. Through the thin, black-streaked line of trees he saw moving red objects. Horses! He must run. Passing the door, his keen nose caught a musty, woody odor and the tail of his eye saw bare dirt floor. This cabin was unused. He halted—gave a quick look back. And the first thing his eye fell upon was a ladder, right inside the door, against the wall. He looked up. It led to a loft that, dark and gloomy, stretched halfway across the cabin. An irresistible impulse drove Jean. Slipping inside, he climbed up the ladder to the loft. It was like night up there. But he crawled on the rough-hewn rafters and, turning with his head toward the opening, he stretched out and lay still.

What seemed an interminable moment ended with a trample of hoofs outside the cabin. It ceased. Jean's vibrating ears caught the jingle of spurs and a thud of boots striking the ground.

"Wal, sweetheart, heah we are home again," drawled a slow, cool, mocking Texas voice.

"Home! I wonder, Colter—did y'u ever have a home—a mother—a sister—much less a sweetheart?" was the reply, bitter and caustic.

Jean's palpitating, hot body suddenly stretched still and cold with intensity of shock. His very bones seemed to quiver and stiffen into ice. During the instant of realization his heart stopped. And a slow, contracting pressure enveloped his breast and moved up to constrict his throat. That woman's voice belonged to Ellen Jorth. The sound of it had lingered in his dreams. He had stumbled upon the rendezvous of the Jorth faction. Hard indeed had been the fates meted out to those of the Isbels and Jorths who had passed to their deaths. But no ordeal, not even Queen's, could compare with this desperate one Jean must endure. He had loved Ellen Jorth, strangely, wonderfully, and he had scorned evil repute to believe her good. He had spared her father and her uncle. He had weakened or lost the cause of the Isbels. He loved her now, desperately, deathlessly, knowing from her own lips that she was worthless—loved her the more because he had felt her terrible shame. And to him—the last of the Isbels—had come the cruelest of dooms—to be caught like a crippled rat in a trap; to be compelled to lie helpless, wounded, without a gun; to listen, and perhaps to see Ellen Jorth enact the very truth of her mocking insinuation. His will, his promise, his creed, his blood must hold him to the stern decree that he should be the last man of the Jorth-Isbel war. But could he lie there to hear—to see—when he had a knife and an arm?

CHAPTER 14

Then followed the leathery flop of saddles to the soft turf and the stamp of loosened horses.

Jean heard a noise at the cabin door, a rustle, and then a knock of something hard against wood. Silently he moved his head to look down through a crack between the rafters. He saw the glint of a rifle leaning against the sill. Then the doorstep was darkened. Ellen Jorth sat down with a long, tired sigh. She took off her sombrero and the light shone on the rippling, dark-brown hair, hanging in a tangled braid. The curved nape of her neck showed a warm tint of golden tan. She wore a gray blouse, soiled and torn, that clung to her lissome shoulders.

"Colter, what are y'u goin' to do?" she asked, suddenly. Her voice carried something Jean did not remember. It thrilled into the icy fixity of his senses.

"We'll stay heah," was the response, and it was followed by a clinking step of spurred boot.

"Shore I won't stay heah," declared Ellen. "It makes me sick when I think of how Uncle Tad died in there alone—helpless—sufferin'. The place seems haunted."

"Wal, I'll agree that it's tough on y'u. . . . But what the hell *can* we do?"

A long silence ensued which Ellen did not break.

"Somethin' has come off round heah since early mawnin'," declared

Colter. "Somers an' Springer haven't got back. An' Antonio's gone. . . .
Now, honest, Ellen, didn't y'u heah rifle shots off somewhere?"

"I reckon I did," she responded, gloomily.

"An' which way?"

"Sounded to me up on the bluff, back pretty far."

"Wal, shore that's my idee. An' it makes me think hard. Y'u know
Somers come across the last camp of the Isbels. An' he dug into a grave to
find the bodies of Jim Gordon an' another man he didn't know. Queen
kept good his brag. He braced that Isbel gang an' killed those fellars. But
either him or Jean Isbel went off leavin' bloody tracks. If it was Queen's
y'u can bet Isbel was after him. An' if it was Isbel's tracks, why shore
Queen would stick to them. Somers an' Springer couldn't follow the trail.
They're shore not much good at trackin'. But for days they've been ridin'
the woods, hopin' to run across Queen. . . . Wal now, mebbe they run
across Isbel instead. An' if they did an' got away from him they'll be heah
sooner or later. If Isbel was too many for them he'd hunt for my trail. I'm
gamblin' that either Queen or Jean Isbel is daid. I'm hopin' it's Isbel. Because if he ain't daid he's the last of the Isbels, an' mebbe I'm the last of
Jorth's gang. . . . Shore I'm not hankerin' to meet the half-breed. That's
why I say we'll stay heah. This is as good a hidin' place as there is in the
country. We've grub. There's water an' grass."

"Me—stay heah with y'u—alone!"

The tone seemed a contradiction to the apparently accepted sense of
her words. Jean held his breath. But he could not still the slowly mounting and accelerating faculties within that were involuntarily rising to
meet some strange, nameless import. He felt it. He imagined it would be
the catastrophe of Ellen Jorth's calm acceptance of Colter's proposition.
But down in Jean's miserable heart lived something that would not die.
No mere words could kill it. How poignant that moment of her silence!
How terribly he realized that if his intelligence and his emotion had believed her betraying words, his soul had not!

But Ellen Jorth did not speak. Her brown head hung thoughtfully.
Her supple shoulders sagged a little.

"Ellen, what's happened to y'u?" went on Colter.

"All the misery possible to a woman," she replied, dejectedly.

"Shore I don't mean that way," he continued, persuasively. "I ain't gainsayin' the hard facts of your life. It's been bad. Your dad was no good. . . . But I mean I can't figger the change in y'u."

"No, I reckon y'u cain't," she said. "Whoever was responsible for your make-up left out a mind—not to say feeling."

Colter drawled a low laugh.

"Wal, have that your own way. But how much longer are y'u goin' to be like this heah?"

"Like what?" she rejoined, sharply.

"Wal, this stand-offishness of yours?"

"Colter, I told y'u to let me alone," she said, sullenly.

"Shore. An' y'u did that before. But this time y'u're different. . . . An' wal, I'm gettin' tired of it."

Here the cool, slow voice of the Texan sounded an inflexibility before absent, a timber that hinted of illimitable power.

Ellen Jorth shrugged her lithe shoulders and, slowly rising, she picked up the little rifle and turned to step into the cabin.

"Colter," she said, "fetch my pack an' my blankets in heah."

"Shore," he returned, with good nature.

Jean saw Ellen Jorth lay the rifle lengthwise in a chink between two logs and then slowly turn, back to the wall. Jean knew her then, yet did not know her. The brown flash of her face seemed that of an older, graver woman. His strained gaze, like his waiting mind, had expected something, he knew not what—a hardened face, a ghost of beauty, a recklessness, a distorted, bitter, lost expression in keeping with her fortunes. But he had reckoned falsely. She did not look like that. There was incalculable change, but the beauty remained, somehow different. Her red lips were parted. Her brooding eyes, looking out straight from under the level, dark brows, seemed sloe black and wonderful with their steady, passionate light.

Jean, in his eager, hungry devouring of the beloved face, did not on the first instant grasp the significance of its expression. He was seeing the features that had haunted him. But quickly he interpreted her expression as the somber, hunted look of a woman who would bear no more. Under the torn blouse her full breast heaved. She held her hands clenched at her sides. She was listening, waiting for that jangling, slow step. It came, and with the sound she subtly changed. She was a woman hiding her true feelings. She relaxed, and that strong, dark look of fury seemed to fade back into her eyes.

Colter appeared at the door, carrying a roll of blankets and a pack.

"Throw them heah," she said. "I reckon y'u needn't bother coming in."

That angered the man. With one long stride he stepped over the doorsill, down into the cabin, and flung the blankets at her feet and then the pack after it. Whereupon he deliberately sat down in the door, facing her. With one hand he slid off his sombrero, which fell outside, and with the other he reached in his upper vest pocket for the little bag of tobacco that showed there. All the time he looked at her. By the light now unobstructed Jean descried Colter's face; and sight of it then sounded the roll and drum of his passions.

"Wal, Ellen, I reckon we'll have it out right now an' heah," he said, and with tobacco in one hand, paper in the other he began the operations of making a cigarette. However, he scarcely removed his glance from her.

"Yes?" queried Ellen Jorth.

"I'm goin' to have things the way they were before—an' more," he declared. The cigarette paper shook in his fingers.

"What do y'u mean?" she demanded.

"Y'u know what I mean," he retorted. Voice and action were subtly unhinging this man's control over himself.

"Maybe I don't. I reckon y'u'd better talk plain."

The rustler had clear gray-yellow eyes, flawless, like crystal, and suddenly they danced with little fiery flecks.

"The last time I laid my hand on y'u I got hit for my pains. An' shore that's been ranklin'."

"Colter, y'u'll get hit again if y'u put your hands on me," she said, dark, straight glance on him. A frown wrinkled the level brows.

"Y'u mean that?" he asked, thickly.

"I shore do."

Manifestly he accepted her assertion. Something of incredulity and bewilderment, that had vied with his resentment, utterly disappeared from his face.

"Heah I've been waitin' for y'u to love me," he declared, with a gesture not without dignified emotion. "Your givin' in without that wasn't so much to me."

And at these words of the rustler's Jean Isbel felt an icy, sickening shudder creep into his soul. He shut his eyes. The end of his dream had been long in coming, but at last it had arrived. A mocking voice, like a hollow wind, echoed through that region—that lonely and ghost-like hall of his heart which had harbored faith.

She burst into speech, louder and sharper, the first words of which Jean's strangely throbbing ears did not distinguish.

"————— ————— you! . . . I never gave in to y'u an' I never will."

"But, girl—I kissed y'u—hugged y'u—handled y'u—" he expostulated, and the making of the cigarette ceased.

"Yes, y'u did—y'u brute—when I was so downhearted and weak I couldn't lift my hand," she flashed.

"Ahuh! Y'u mean I couldn't do that now?"

"I should smile I do, Jim Colter!" she replied.

"Wal, mebbe—I'll see—presently," he went on, straining with words. "But I'm shore curious. . . . Daggs, then—he was nothin' to y'u?"

"No more than y'u," she said, morbidly. "He used to run after me—long ago, it seems. . . . I was only a girl then—innocent—an' I'd not known any but rough men. I couldn't all the time—every day, every hour—keep him at arm's length. Sometimes before I knew—I didn't care. I was a child. A kiss meant nothing to me. But after I knew—"

Ellen dropped her head in brooding silence.

"Say, do y'u expect me to believe that?" he queried with a derisive leer.

"Bah! What do I care what y'u believe?" she cried, with lifting head.

"How aboot Simm Bruce?"

"That coyote! . . . He lied aboot me, Jim Colter. And any man half a man would have known he lied."

"Wal, Simm always bragged aboot y'u bein' his girl," asserted Colter. "An' he wasn't over-particular aboot details of your love-makin'."

Ellen gazed out of the door, over Colter's head, as if the forest out there was a refuge. She evidently sensed more about the man than appeared in his slow talk, in his slouching position. Her lips shut in a firm line, as if to hide their trembling and to still her passionate tongue. Jean, in his absorption, magnified his perceptions. Not yet was Ellen Jorth afraid of this man, but she feared the situation. Jean's heart was at bursting pitch. All within him seemed chaos—a wreck of beliefs and convictions. Nothing was true. He would wake presently out of a nightmare. Yet, as surely as he quivered there, he felt the imminence of a great moment—a lightning flash—a thunderbolt—a balance struck.

Colter attended to the forgotten cigarette. He rolled it, lighted it, all the time with lowered, pondering head, and when he had puffed a cloud of smoke he suddenly looked up with face as hard as flint, eyes as fiery as molten steel.

"Wal, Ellen—how aboot Jean Isbel—our half-breed Nez Perce friend—who was shore seen handlin' y'u familiar?" he drawled.

Ellen Jorth quivered as under a lash, and her brown face turned a dusty scarlet, that slowly receding left her pale.

"Damn y'u, Jim Colter!" she burst out, furiously. "I wish Jean Isbel would jump in that door—or down out of that loft! . . . He killed Greaves for defiling my name! . . . He'd kill *y'u* for your dirty insult. . . . And I'd like to watch him do it. . . . Y'u cold-blooded Texan! Y'u thieving rustler! Y'u liar! . . . Y'u lied aboot my father's death. And I know why. Y'u stole my father's gold. . . . An' now y'u want me—y'u expect me to fall into your arms. . . . My Heaven! cain't y'u tell a decent woman? Was your mother decent? Was your sister decent? . . . Bah! I'm appealing to deafness. But y'u'll *heah* this, Jim Colter! . . . I'm not what y'u think I am! I'm not the—the damned hussy y'u liars have made me out. . . . I'm a Jorth, alas! I've no home, no relatives, no friends! I've been forced to live my life with rustlers—vile men like y'u an' Daggs an' the rest of your like. . . . But I've been good! Do y'u heah that? . . . I *am* good—an', so help me God, y'u an' all your rottenness cain't make me bad!"

Colter lounged to his tall height and the laxity of the man vanished.

Vanished also was Jean Isbel's suspended icy dread, the cold clogging of his fevered mind—vanished in a white, living, leaping flame.

Silently he drew his knife and lay there watching with the eyes of a wildcat. The instant Colter stepped far enough over toward the edge of the loft Jean meant to bound erect and plunge down upon him. But Jean could wait now. Colter had a gun at his hip. He must never have a chance to draw it.

"Ahuh! So y'u wish Jean Isbel would hop in heah, do y'u?" queried Colter. "Wal, if I had any pity on y'u, that's done for it."

A sweep of his long arm, so swift Ellen had no time to move, brought his hand in clutching contact with her. And the force of it flung her half across the cabin room, leaving the sleeve of her blouse in his grasp. Pantingly she put out that bared arm and her other to ward him off as he took long, slow strides toward her.

Jean rose half to his feet, dragged by almost ungovernable passion to risk all on one leap. But the distance was too great. Colter, blind as he was to all outward things, would hear, would see in time to make Jean's effort futile. Shaking like a leaf, Jean sank back, eye again to the crack between the rafters.

Ellen did not retreat, nor scream, nor move. Every line of her body was instinct with fight, and the magnificent blaze of her eyes would have checked a less callous brute.

Colter's big hand darted between Ellen's arms and fastened in the front of her blouse. He did not try to hold her or draw her close. The unleashed passion of the man required violence. In one savage pull he tore off her blouse, exposing her white, rounded shoulders and heaving bosom, where instantly a wave of red burned upward.

Overcome by the tremendous violence and spirit of the rustler, Ellen sank to her knees, with blanched face and dilating eyes, trying with folded arms and trembling hand to hide her nudity.

At that moment the rapid beat of hoofs on the hard trail outside halted Colter in his tracks.

"Hell!" he exclaimed. "An' who's that?" With a fierce action he flung the remnants of Ellen's blouse in her face and turned to leap out the door.

Jean saw Ellen catch the blouse and try to wrap it around her, while she sagged against the wall and stared at the door. The hoof beats pounded to a solid thumping halt just outside.

"Jim—thar's hell to pay!" rasped out a panting voice.

"Wal, Springer, I reckon I wished y'u'd paid it without spoilin' my deals," retorted Colter, cool and sharp.

"Deals? Ha! Y'u'll be forgettin'—your lady love—in a minnit," replied Springer. "When I catch—my breath."

"Where's Somers?" demanded Colter.

"I reckon he's all shot up—if my eyes didn't fool me."

"Where is he?" yelled Colter.

"Jim—he's layin' up in the bushes round thet bluff. I didn't wait to see how he was hurt. But he shore stopped some lead. An' he flopped like a chicken with its—haid cut off."

"Where's Antonio?"

"He run like the greaser he is," declared Springer, disgustedly.

"Ahuh! An' where's Queen?" queried Colter, after a significant pause.

"Dead!"

The silence ensuing was fraught with a suspense that held Jean in cold bonds. He saw the girl below rise from her knees, one hand holding the blouse to her breast, the other extended, and with strange, repressed, almost frantic look she swayed toward the door.

"Wal, talk," ordered Colter, harshly.

"Jim, there ain't a hell of a lot," replied Springer, drawing a deep breath, "but what there is is shore interestin'. . . . Me an' Somers took Antonio with us. He left his woman with the sheep. An' we rode up the cañon, clumb out on top, an' made a circle back on the ridge. That's the way we've been huntin' fer tracks. Up thar in a bare spot we run plump into Queen sittin' against a tree, right out in the open. Queerest sight y'u ever seen! The damn gun fighter had set down to wait for Isbel, who was trailin' him, as we suspected—an' he died thar. He wasn't cold when we found him. . . . Somers was quick to see a trick. So he propped Queen up an' tied the guns to his hands—an', Jim, the queerest thing aboot that deal was this—Queen's guns was empty! Not a shell left! It beat us holler. . . . We left him thar, an' hid up high on the bluff, mebbe a hundred yards off. The hosses we left back of a thicket. An' we waited thar a long time. But, sure enough, the half-breed come. He was too smart. Too much Injun! He would not cross the open, but went around. An' then he seen Queen. It was great to watch him. After a little he shoved his rifle out an' went right fer Queen. This is when I wanted to shoot. I could have plugged him. But Somers says wait an' make it sure. When Isbel got up to Queen he was sort of half hid by the tree. An' I couldn't wait no longer, so I shot. I hit him, too. We all begun to shoot. Somers showed himself, an' that's when Isbel opened up. He used up a whole magazine on Somers an' then, suddenlike, he quit. It didn't take me long to figger mebbe he was out of shells. When I seen him run I was certain of it. Then we made for the hosses an' rode after Isbel. Pretty soon I seen him runnin' like a deer down the ridge. I yelled an' spurred after him. There is where Antonio quit me. But I kept on. An' I got a shot at Isbel. He ran out of sight. I follered him by spots of blood on the stones an' grass until I couldn't trail him no more. He must have gone down over the cliffs. He couldn't have done nothin' else without me seein' him. I found his rifle, an' here it is to prove what I say. I had to go back to climb down off the Rim, an' I rode fast down the cañon. He's somewhere along that west wall, hidin' in the brush, hard hit if I know anythin' aboot the color of blood."

"Wal! . . . that beats me holler, too," ejaculated Colter.

"Jim, what's to be done?" inquired Springer, eagerly. "If we're sharp we can corral that half-breed. He's the last of the Isbels."

"More, pard. He's the last of the Isbel outfit," declared Colter. "If y'u can show me blood in his tracks I'll trail him."

"Y'u can bet I'll show y'u," rejoined the other rustler. "But listen! Wouldn't it be better for us first to see if he crossed the cañon? I reckon he didn't. But let's make sure. An' if he didn't we'll have him somewhar along that west cañon wall. He's not got no gun. He'd never run thet way if he had. . . . Jim, he's our meat!"

"Shore, he'll have that knife," pondered Colter.

"We needn't worry about thet." said the other, positively. "He's hard hit, I tell y'u. All we got to do is find thet bloody trail again an' stick to it—goin' careful. He's layin' low like a crippled wolf."

"Springer, I want the job of finishin' that half-breed," hissed Colter. "I'd give ten years of my life to stick a gun down his throat an' shoot it off."

"All right. Let's rustle. Mebbe y'u'll not have to give much more 'n ten minnits. Because I tell y'u I can find him. It'd been easy—but, Jim, I reckon I was afraid."

"Leave your hoss for me an' go ahaid," the rustler then said, brusquely. "I've a job in the cabin heah."

"Haw-haw! . . . Wal, Jim, I'll rustle a bit down the trail an' wait. No huntin' Jean Isbel alone—not fer me. I've had a queer feelin' about thet knife he used on Greaves. An' I reckon y'u'd oughter let thet Jorth hussy alone long enough to—"

"Springer, I reckon I've got to hawg-tie her—" His voice became indistinguishable, and footfalls attested to a slow moving away of the men.

Jean had listened with ears acutely strung to catch every syllable while his gaze rested upon Ellen who stood beside the door. Every line of her body denoted a listening intensity. Her back was toward Jean, so that he could not see her face. And he did not want to see, but could not help seeing her naked shoulders. She put her head out of the door. Suddenly she drew it in quickly and half turned her face, slowly raising her white arm. This was the left one and bore the marks of Colter's hard fingers.

She gave a little gasp. Her eyes became large and staring. They were bent on the hand that she had removed from a step on the ladder. On hand and wrist showed a bright-red smear of blood.

Jean, with a convulsive leap of his heart, realized that he had left his bloody tracks on the ladder as he had climbed. That moment seemed the supremely terrible one of his life.

Ellen Jorth's face blanched and her eyes darkened and dilated with exceeding amaze and flashing thought to become fixed with horror. That instant was the one in which her reason connected the blood on the ladder with the escape of Jean Isbel.

One moment she leaned there, still as a stone except for her heaving breast, and then her fixed gaze changed to a swift, dark blaze, comprehending, yet inscrutable, as she flashed it up the ladder to the loft. She could see nothing, yet she knew and Jean knew that she knew he was there. A marvelous transformation passed over her features and even over her form. Jean choked with the ache in his throat. Slowly she put the bloody hand behind her while with the other she still held the torn blouse to her breast.

Colter's slouching, musical step sounded outside. And it might have been a strange breath of infinitely vitalizing and passionate life blown into the well-springs of Ellen Jorth's being. Isbel had no name for her then. The spirit of a woman had been to him a thing unknown.

She swayed back from the door against the wall in singular, softened poise, as if all the steel had melted out of her body. And as Colter's tall shadow fell across the threshold Jean Isbel felt himself staring with eyeballs that ached—straining incredulous sight at this woman who in a few seconds had bewildered his senses with her transfiguration. He saw but could not comprehend.

"Jim—I heard—all Springer told y'u," she said. The look of her dumfounded Colter and her voice seemed to shake him visibly.

"Suppose y'u did. What then?" he demanded, harshly, as he halted with one booted foot over the threshold. Malignant and forceful, he eyed her darkly, doubtfully.

"I'm afraid," she whispered.

"What of? Me?"

"No. Of—of Jean Isbel. He might kill y'u and—then where would I be?"

"Wal, I'm damned!" ejaculated the rustler. "What's got into y'u?" He moved to enter, but a sort of fascination bound him.

"Jim, I hated y'u a moment ago," she burst out. "But now—with that Jean Isbel somewhere near—hidin'—watchin' to kill y'u—an' maybe me, too—I—I don't hate y'u any more. . . . Take me away."

"Girl, have y'u lost your nerve?" he demanded.

"My God! Colter—cain't y'u see?" she implored. "Won't y'u take me away?"

"I shore will—presently," he replied, grimly. "But y'u'll wait till I've shot the lights out of this Isbel."

"No!" she cried. "Take me away now. . . . An' I'll give in—I'll be what y'u—want. . . . Y'u can do with me—as y'u like."

Colter's lofty frame leaped as if at the release of bursting blood. With a lunge he cleared the threshold to loom over her.

"Am I out of my haid, or are y'u?" he asked, in low, hoarse voice. His darkly corded face expressed extremest amaze.

"Jim, I mean it," she whispered, edging an inch nearer him, her white face uplifted, her dark eyes unreadable in their eloquence and mystery. "I've no friend but y'u. . . . I'll be—yours. . . . I'm lost. . . . What does it matter? . . . If y'u want me—take me *now*—before I kill myself."

"Ellen Jorth, there's somethin' wrong aboot y'u," he responded. "Did y'u tell the truth—when y'u denied ever bein' a sweetheart of Simm Bruce?"

"Yes, I told y'u the truth."

"Ahuh! An' how do y'u account for layin' me out with every dirty name y'u could give tongue to?"

"Oh, it was temper. I wanted to be let alone."

"Temper! Wal, I reckon y'u've got one," he retorted, grimly. An' I'm not shore y'u're not crazy or lyin'. An hour ago I couldn't touch y'u."

"Y'u may now—if y'u promise to take me away—at once. This place has got on my nerves. I couldn't sleep heah with that Isbel hidin' around. Could y'u?"

"Wal, I reckon I'd not sleep very deep."

"Then let us go."

He shook his lean, eagle-like head in slow, doubtful vehemence, and his piercing gaze studied her distrustfully. Yet all the while there was manifest in his strung frame an almost irrepressible violence, held in abeyance to his will.

"That aboot your bein' so good?" he inquired, with a return of the mocking drawl.

"Never mind what's past," she flashed, with passion dark as his. "I've made my offer."

"Shore there's a lie aboot y'u somewhere," he muttered, thickly.

"Man, could I do more?" she demanded, in scorn.

"No. But it's a lie," he returned. "Y'u'll get me to take y'u away an' then fool me—run off—God knows what. Women are all liars."

Manifestly he could not believe in her strange transformation. Memory of her wild and passionate denunciation of him and his kind must have seared even his calloused soul. But the ruthless nature of him had not weakened nor softened in the least as to his intentions. This weather-vane veering of hers bewildered him, obsessed him with its possibilities. He had the look of a man who was divided between love of her and hate, whose love demanded a return, but whose hate required a proof of her abasement. Not proof of surrender, but proof of her shame! The ignominy of him thirsted for its like. He could grind her beauty under his heel, but he could not soften to this feminine inscrutableness.

And whatever was the truth of Ellen Jorth in this moment, beyond Colter's gloomy and stunted intelligence, beyond even the love of Jean Isbel, it was something that held the balance of mastery. She read Colter's mind. She dropped the torn blouse from her hand and stood there, unashamed, with the wave of her white breast pulsing, eyes black as night and full of hell, her face white, tragic, terrible, yet strangely lovely.

"Take me away," she whispered, stretching one white arm toward him, then the other.

Colter, even as she moved, had leaped with inarticulate cry and radiant face to meet her embrace. But it seemed, just as her left arm flashed up toward his neck, that he saw her bloody hand and wrist. Strange how that checked his ardor—threw up his lean head like that of a striking bird of prey.

"Blood! What the hell!" he ejaculated, and in one sweep he grasped her. "How'd y'u do that? Are y'u cut? . . . Hold still."

Ellen could not release her hand.

"I scratched myself," she said.

"Where? . . . All that blood!" And suddenly he flung her hand back with fierce gesture, and the gleams of his yellow eyes were like the points of leaping flames. They pierced her—read the secret falsity of her. Slowly he stepped backward, guardedly his hand moved to his gun, and his glance circled and swept the interior of the cabin. As if he had the nose of a hound and sight to follow scent, his eyes bent to the dust of the ground before the door. He quivered, grew rigid as stone, and then moved his head with exceeding slowness as if searching through a microscope in the dust—farther to the left—to the foot of the ladder—and up one step—another—a third—all the way up to the loft. Then he whipped out his gun and wheeled to face the girl.

"Ellen, y'u've got your half-breed heah!" he said, with a terrible smile.

She neither moved nor spoke. There was a suggestion of collapse, but it was only a change where the alluring softness of her hardened into a strange, rapt glow. And in it seemed the same mastery that had characterized her former aspect. Herein the treachery of her was revealed. She had known what she meant to do in any case.

Colter, standing at the door, reached a long arm toward the ladder, where he laid his hand on a rung. Taking it away he held it palm outward for her to see the dark splotch of blood.

"See?"

"Yes, I see," she said, ringingly.

Passion wrenched him, transformed him. "All that—aboot leavin' heah—with me—aboot givin' in—was a lie!"

"No, Colter. It was the truth. I'll go—yet—now—if y'u'll spare—
him!" She whispered the last word and made a slight movement of her
hand toward the loft.

"Girl!" he exploded, incredulously. "Y'u love this half-breed—this
Isbel? . . . Y'u *love* him!"

"With all my heart! . . . Thank God! It has been my glory. . . . It
might have been my salvation. . . . But now I'll go to hell with y'u—if
y'u'll spare him."

"Damn my soul!" rasped out the rustler, as if something of respect
was wrung from that sordid deep of him. "Y'u—y'u woman! . . . Jorth
will turn over in his grave. He'd rise out of his grave if this Isbel got y'u,"

"Hurry! Hurry!" implored Ellen. "Springer may come back. I think
I heard a call."

"Wal, Ellen Jorth, I'll not spare Isbel—nor y'u," he returned, with
dark and meaning leer, as he turned to ascend the ladder.

Jean Isbel, too, had reached the climax of his suspense. Gathering all
his muscles in a knot he prepared to leap upon Colter as he mounted the
ladder. But Ellen Jorth screamed piercingly and snatched her rifle from
its resting place and, cocking it, she held it forward and low.

"*Colter!*"

Her scream and his uttered name stiffened him.

"Y'u will spare Jean Isbel!" she rang out. "Drop that gun—drop it!"

"Shore, Ellen. . . . Easy now. Remember your temper. . . . I'll let Isbel off," he panted, huskily, and all his body sank quiveringly to a crouch.

"Drop your gun! Don't turn round. . . . Colter!—*I'll kill y'u!*"

But even then he failed to divine the meaning and the spirit of her.

"Aw, now, Ellen," he entreated, in louder, huskier tones, and as if
dragged by fatal doubt of her still, he began to turn.

Crash! The rifle emptied its contents in Colter's breast. All his body
sprang up. He dropped the gun. Both hands fluttered toward her. And an
awful surprise flashed over his face.

"So—help—me—God!" he whispered, with blood thick in his voice.
Then darkly, as one groping, he reached for her with shaking hands.
"Y'u—y'u white-throated hussy! . . . I'll . . ."

He grasped the quivering rifle barrel. Crash! She shot him again. As
he swayed over her and fell she had to leap aside, and his clutching hand

tore the rifle from her grasp. Then in convulsion he writhed, to heave on his back, and stretch out—a ghastly spectacle. Ellen backed away from it, her white arms wide, a slow horror blotting out the passion of her face.

Then from without came a shrill call and the sound of rapid footsteps. Ellen leaned against the wall, staring still at Colter. "Hey, Jim—what's the shootin'?" called Springer, breathlessly.

As his form darkened the doorway Jean once again gathered all his muscular force for a tremendous spring.

Springer saw the girl first and he appeared thunderstruck. His jaw dropped. He needed not the white gleam of her person to transfix him. Her eyes did that and they were riveted in unutterable horror upon something on the ground. Thus instinctively directed, Springer espied Colter.

"Y'u—y'u shot him!" he shrieked. "What for—y'u hussy? . . . Ellen Jorth, if y'u've killed him, I'll . . ."

He strode toward where Colter lay.

Then Jean, rising silently, took a step and like a tiger he launched himself into the air, down upon the rustler. Even as he leaped Springer gave a quick, upward look. And he cried out. Jean's moccasined feet struck him squarely and sent him staggering into the wall, where his head hit hard. Jean fell, but bounded up as the half-stunned Springer drew his gun. Then Jean lunged forward with a single sweep of his arm—and looked no more.

Ellen ran swaying out of the door, and, once clear of the threshold, she tottered out on the grass, to sink to her knees. The bright, golden sunlight gleamed upon her white shoulders and arms. Jean had one foot out of the door when he saw her and he whirled back to get her blouse. But Springer had fallen upon it. Snatching up a blanket, Jean ran out.

"Ellen! Ellen! Ellen!" he cried. "It's over!" And reaching her, he tried to wrap her in the blanket.

She wildly clutched his knees. Jean was conscious only of her white, agonized face and the dark eyes with their look of terrible strain.

"Did y'u—did y'u . . ." she whispered.

"Yes—it's over," he said, gravely. "Ellen, the Isbel-Jorth feud is ended."

"Oh, thank—God!" she cried, in breaking voice. "Jean—y'u are wounded . . . the blood on the step!"

"My arm. See. It's not bad. . . . Ellen, let me wrap this round you."

Folding the blanket around her shoulders, he held it there and entreated her to get up. But she only clung the closer. She hid her face on his knees. Long shudders rippled over her, shaking the blanket, shaking Jean's hands. Distraught, he did not know what to do. And his own heart was bursting.

"Ellen, you must not kneel—there—that way," he implored.

"Jean! Jean!" she moaned, and clung the tighter.

He tried to lift her up, but she was a dead weight, and with that hold on him seemed anchored at his feet.

"I killed Colter," she gasped. "I *had* to—kill him! . . . I offered—to fling myself away. . . ."

"For me!" he cried, poignantly. "Oh, Ellen! Ellen! the world has come to an end! . . . Hush! don't keep sayin' that. Of course you killed him. You saved my life. For I'd never have let you go off with him. . . . Yes, you killed him. . . . You're a Jorth an' I'm an Isbel . . . We've blood on our hands—both of us—I for you an' you for me!"

His voice of entreaty and sadness strengthened her and she raised her white face, loosening her clasp to lean back and look up. Tragic, sweet, despairing, the loveliness of her—the significance of her there on her knees—thrilled him to his soul.

"Blood on my hands!" she whispered. "Yes. It was awful—killing him. . . . But—all I care for in this world is for your forgiveness—and your faith that saved my soul!"

"Child, there's nothin' to forgive," he responded. "Nothin' . . . Please, Ellen . . ."

"I lied to y'u!" she cried. "I lied to y'u!"

"Ellen, listen—darlin'." And the tender epithet brought her head and arms back close-pressed to him. "I know—now," he faltered on. "I found out to-day what I believed. An' I swear to God—by the memory of my dead mother—down in my heart I never, never, never believed what they—what y'u tried to make me believe. *Never!*"

"Jean—I love y'u—love y'u—love y'u!" she breathed with exquisite, passionate sweetness. Her dark eyes burned up into his.

"Ellen, I can't lift you up," he said, in trembling eagerness, signifying his crippled arm. "But I can kneel with you! . . ."

THE MYSTERIOUS RIDER

CHAPTER 1

A September sun, losing some of its heat if not its brilliance, was dropping low in the west over the black Colorado range. Purple haze began to thicken in the timbered notches. Gray foothills, round and billowy, rolled down from the higher country. They were smooth, sweeping, with long velvety slopes and isolated patches of aspens that blazed in autumn gold. Splotches of red vine colored the soft gray of sage. Old White Slides, a mountain scarred by avalanche, towered with bleak rocky peak above the valley, sheltering it from the north.

A girl rode along the slope, with gaze on the sweep and range and color of the mountain fastness that was her home. She followed an old trail which led to a bluff overlooking an arm of the valley. Once it had been a familiar lookout for her, but she had not visited the place of late. It was associated with serious hours of her life. Here seven years before, when she was twelve, she had made a hard choice to please her guardian—the old rancher whom she loved and called father, who had indeed been a father to her. That choice had been to go to school in Denver. Four years she had lived away from her beloved gray hills and black mountains. Only once since her return had she climbed to this height, and that occasion, too, was memorable as an unhappy hour. It had been three years ago. To-day girlish ordeals and griefs seemed back in the past: she was a woman at nineteen and face to face with the first great problem in her life.

The trail came up back of the bluff, through a clump of aspens with white trunks and yellow fluttering leaves, and led across a level bench of luxuriant grass and wild flowers to the rocky edge.

She dismounted and threw the bridle. Her mustang, used to being petted, rubbed his sleek, dark head against her and evidently expected like demonstration in return, but as none was forthcoming he bent his nose to the grass and began grazing. The girl's eyes were intent upon some waving, slender, white-and-blue flowers. They smiled up wanly, like pale stars, out of the long grass that had a tinge of gold.

"Columbines," she mused, wistfully, as she plucked several of the flowers and held them up to gaze wonderingly at them, as if to see in them some revelation of the mystery that shrouded her birth and her name. Then she stood with dreamy gaze upon the distant ranges.

"Columbine! . . . So they named me—those miners who found me— a baby—lost in the woods—asleep among the columbines." She spoke aloud, as if the sound of her voice might convince her.

So much of the mystery of her had been revealed that day by the man she had always called father. Vaguely she had always been conscious of some mystery, something strange about her childhood, some relation never explained.

"No name but Columbine," she whispered, sadly, and now she understood a strange longing of her heart.

Scarcely an hour back, as she ran down the wide porch of White Slides ranch-house, she had encountered the man who had taken care of her all her life. He had looked upon her as kindly and fatherly as of old, yet with a difference. She seemed to see him as old Bill Belllounds, pioneer and rancher, of huge frame and broad face, hard and scarred and grizzled, with big eyes of blue fire.

"Collie," the old man had said, "I reckon hyar's news. A letter from Jack. . . . He's comin' home."

Belllounds had waved the letter. His huge hand trembled as he reached to put it on her shoulder. The hardness of him seemed strangely softened. Jack was his son. Buster Jack, the range had always called him, with other terms, less kind, that never got to the ears of his father. Jack had been sent away three years ago, just before Columbine's return from school. Therefore she had not seen him for over seven years. But she remembered him well—a big, rangy boy, handsome and wild, who had made her childhood almost unendurable.

"Yes—my son—Jack—he's comin' home," said Belllounds, with a break in his voice. "An', Collie—now I must tell you somethin'."

"Yes, dad," she had replied, with strong clasp of the heavy hand on her shoulder.

"Thet's just it, lass. I ain't your dad. I've tried to be a dad to you an' I've loved you as my own. But you're not flesh an' blood of mine. An' now I must tell you."

The brief story followed. Seventeen years ago miners working a claim of Belllounds's in the mountains above Middle Park had found a child asleep in the columbines along the trail. Near that point Indians, probably Arapahoes coming across the mountains to attack the Utes, had captured or killed the occupants of a prairie-schooner. There was no other clue. The miners took the child to their camp, fed and cared for it, and, after the manner of their kind, named it Columbine. Then they brought it to Belllounds.

"Collie," said the old rancher, "it needn't never have been told, an' wouldn't but fer one reason. I'm gettin' old. I reckon I'd never split my property between you an' Jack. So I mean you an' him to marry. You always steadied Jack. With a wife like you'll be—wal, mebbe Jack'll—"

"Dad!" burst out Columbine. "Marry Jack! . . . Why I—I don't even remember him!"

"Haw! Haw!" laughed Belllounds. "Wal, you dog-gone soon will. Jack's in Kremmlin', an' he'll be hyar to-night or to-morrow."

"But—I—I don't l-love him," faltered Columbine.

The old man lost his mirth; the strong-lined face resumed its hard cast; the big eyes smoldered. Her appealing objection had wounded him. She was reminded of how sensitive the old man had always been to any reflection cast upon his son.

"Wal, thet's onlucky," he replied, gruffly. "Mebbe you'll change. I reckon no girl could help a boy much, unless she cared for him. Anyway, you an' Jack will marry."

He had stalked away and Columbine had ridden her mustang far up the valley slope where she could be alone. Standing on the verge of the bluff, she suddenly became aware that the quiet and solitude of her lonely resting-place had been disrupted. Cattle were bawling below her and along the slope of Old White Slides and on the grassy uplands above. She had forgotten that the cattle were being driven down into the lowlands for the fall round-up. A great red-and-white-spotted herd was milling in the park just beneath her. Calves and yearlings were making the dust fly along the mountain slope; wild old steers were crashing in the sage, holding level, unwilling to be driven down; cows were running and lowing for their lost ones. Melodious and clear rose the clarion calls of the cowboys. The cattle knew those calls and only the wild steers kept up-grade.

Columbine also knew each call and to which cowboy it belonged. They sang and yelled and swore, but it was all music to her. Here and there along the slope, where the aspen groves clustered, a horse would flash across an open space; the dust would fly, and a cowboy would peal out a lusty yell that rang along the slope and echoed under the bluff and lingered long after the daring rider had vanished in the steep thickets.

"I wonder which is Wils," murmured Columbine, as she watched and listened, vaguely conscious of a little difference, a strange check in her remembrance of this particular cowboy. She felt the change, yet did not understand. One after one she recognized the riders on the slopes below, but Wilson Moore was not among them. He must be above her, then, and she turned to gaze across the grassy bluff, up the long, yellow slope, to where the gleaming aspens half hid a red bluff of mountain, towering aloft. Then from far to her left, high up a scrubby ridge of the slope, rang down a voice that thrilled her: "Go—aloong—you—ooooo." Red cattle dashed pell-mell down the slope, raising the dust, tearing the brush, rolling rocks, and letting out hoarse bawls.

"Whoop-ee!" High-pitched and pealing came a clearer yell.

Columbine saw a white mustang flash out on top of the ridge, silhouetted against the blue, with mane and tail flying. His gait on that edge of steep slope proved his rider to be a reckless cowboy for whom no heights or depths had terrors. She would have recognized him from the way he rode, if she had not known the slim, erect figure. The cowboy saw her instantly. He pulled the mustang, about to plunge down the slope and lifted him, rearing and wheeling. Then Columbine waved her hand. The cowboy spurred his horse along the crest of the ridge, disappeared behind the grove of aspens, and came in sight again around to the right, where on the grassy bench he slowed to a walk in descent to the bluff.

The girl watched him come, conscious of an unfamiliar sense of uncertainty in this meeting, and of the fact that she was seeing him differently from any other time in the years he had been a playmate, a friend almost like a brother. He had ridden for Belllounds for years, and was a cowboy because he loved cattle well and horses better, and above all a life in the open. Unlike most cowboys, he had been to school; he had a family in Denver that objected to his wild range life, and often importuned him to come home; he seemed aloof sometimes and not readily understood.

While many thoughts whirled through Columbine's mind she watched the cowboy ride slowly down to her, and she became more concerned with a sudden restraint. How was Wilson going to take the news of this forced change about to come in her life? That thought leaped up. It gave her a strange pang. But she and he were only good friends. As to that, she reflected, of late they had not been the friends and comrades they formerly were. In the thrilling uncertainty of this meeting she had forgotten his distant manner and the absence of little attentions she had missed.

By this time the cowboy had reached the level, and with the lazy grace of his kind slipped out of the saddle. He was tall, slim, round-limbed, with the small hips of a rider, and square, though not broad shoulders. He stood straight like an Indian. His eyes were hazel, his features regular, his face bronzed. All men of the open had still, lean, strong faces, but added to this in him was a steadiness of expression, a restraint that seemed to hide sadness.

"Howdy, Columbine!" he said. "What are you doing up here? You might get run over."

"Hello, Wils!" she replied, slowly. "Oh, I guess I can keep out of the way."

"Some bad steers in that bunch. If any of them run over here Pronto will leave you to walk home. That mustang hates cattle. And he's only half broke, you know."

"I forgot you were driving to-day," she replied, and looked away from him. There was a moment's pause—long, it seemed to her.

"What'd you come for?" he asked, curiously.

"I wanted to gather columbines. See." She held out the nodding flowers toward him. "Take one. . . . Do you like them?"

"Yes. I like columbine," he replied, taking one of them. His keen hazel eyes, softened, darkened. "Colorado's flower."

"Columbine! . . . It is my name."

"Well, could you have a better? It sure suits you."

"Why?" she asked, and she looked at him again.

"You're slender—graceful. You sort of hold your head high and proud. Your skin is white. Your eyes are blue. Not bluebell blue, but columbine blue—and they turn purple when you're angry."

"Compliments! Wilson, this is new kind of talk for you," she said.

"You're different to-day."

"Yes, I am." She looked across the valley toward the westering sun, and the slight flush faded from her cheeks. "I have no right to hold my head proud. No one knows who I am—where I came from."

"As if that made any difference!" he exclaimed.

"Belllounds is not my dad. I have no dad. I was a waif. They found me in the woods—a baby—lost among the flowers. Columbine Belllounds I've always been. But that is not my name. No one can tell what my name really is."

"I knew your story years ago, Columbine," he replied, earnestly. "Everybody knows. Old Bill ought to have told you long before this. But he loves you. So does—everybody. You must not let this knowledge sadden you. . . . I'm sorry you've never known a mother or a sister. Why, I could tell you of many orphans who—whose stories were different."

"You don't understand. I've been happy. I've not longed for any—any one except a mother. It's only—"

"What don't I understand?"

"I've not told you all."

"No? Well, go on," he said, slowly.

Meaning of the hesitation and the restraint that had obstructed her thought now flashed over Columbine. It lay in what Wilson Moore might think of her prospective marriage to Jack Belllounds. Still she could not guess why that should make her feel strangely uncertain of the ground she stood on or how it could cause a constraint she had to fight herself to hide.

Moreover, to her annoyance, she found that she was evading his direct request for the news she had withheld.

"Jack Belllounds is coming home to-night or to-morrow," she said. Then, waiting for her companion to reply, she kept an unseeing gaze upon the scanty pines fringing Old White Slides. But no reply appeared to be forthcoming from Moore. His silence compelled her to turn to him. The cowboy's face had subtly altered; it was darker with a tinge of red under the bronze; and his lower lip was released from his teeth, even as she looked. He had his eyes intent upon the lasso he was coiling. Suddenly he faced her and the dark fire of his eyes gave her a shock.

"I've been expecting that shorthorn back for months." he said, bluntly.

"You—never—liked Jack?" queried Columbine, slowly. That was not what she wanted to say, but the thought spoke itself.

"I should smile I never did."

"Ever since you and he fought—long ago—all over—"

His sharp gesture made the coiled lasso loosen.

"Ever since I licked him good—don't forget that," interrupted Wilson. The red had faded from the bronze.

"Yes, you licked him," mused Columbine. "I remember that. And Jack's hated you ever since."

"There's been no love lost."

"But, Wils, you never before talked this way—spoke out so—against Jack," she protested.

"Well, I'm not the kind to talk behind a fellow's back. But I'm not mealy-mouthed, either, and—and—"

He did not complete the sentence and his meaning was enigmatic. Altogether Moore seemed not like himself. The fact disturbed Columbine. Always she had confided in him. Here was a most complex situation—she burned to tell him, yet somehow feared to—she felt an incomprehensible satisfaction in his bitter reference to Jack—she seemed to realize that she valued Wilson's friendship more than she had known, and now for some strange reason it was slipping from her.

"We—we were such good friends—pards," said Columbine, hurriedly and irrelevantly.

"Who?" He stared at her.

"Why, you—and me."

"Oh!" His tone softened, but there was still disapproval in his glance. "What of that?"

"Something has happened to make me think I've missed you—lately—that's all."

"Ahuh!" His tone held finality and bitterness, but he would not commit himself. Columbine sensed a pride in him that seemed the cause of his aloofness.

"Wilson, why have you been different lately?" she asked, plaintively.

"What's the good to tell you now?" he queried, in reply.

That gave her a blank sense of actual loss. She had lived in dreams and he in realities. Right now she could not dispel her dream—see and understand all that he seemed to. She felt like a child, then, growing old swiftly. The strange past longing for a mother surged up in her like a strong tide. Some one to lean on, some one who loved her, some one to help her in this hour when fatality knocked at the door of her youth—how she needed that!

"It might be bad for me—to tell me, but tell me, anyhow," she said, finally, answering as some one older than she had been an hour ago—to something feminine that leaped up. She did not understand this impulse, but it was in her.

"No!" declared Moore, with dark red staining his face. He slapped the lasso against his saddle, and tied it with clumsy hands. He did not look at her. His tone expressed anger and amaze.

"Dad says I must marry Jack," she said, with a sudden return to her natural simplicity.

"I heard him tell that months ago," snapped Moore.

"You did! Was that—why?" she whispered.

"It was," he answered, ringingly.

"But that was no reason for you to be—be—to stay away from me," she declared, with rising spirit.

He laughed shortly.

"Wils, didn't you like me any more after dad said that?" she queried.

"Columbine, a girl nineteen years and about to—to get married—ought not be a fool," he replied, with sarcasm.

"I'm not a fool," she rejoined, hotly.

"You ask fool questions."

"Well, you *didn't* like me afterward or you'd never have mistreated me."

"If you say I mistreated you—you say what's untrue," he replied, just as hotly.

They had never been so near a quarrel before. Columbine experienced a sensation new to her—a commingling of fear, heat, and pang, it seemed, all in one throb. Wilson was hurting her. A quiver ran all over her, along her veins, swelling and tingling.

"You mean I lie?" she flashed.

"Yes, I do—if—"

But before he could conclude she slapped his face. It grew pale then, while she began to tremble.

"Oh—I didn't intend that. Forgive me," she faltered.

He rubbed his cheek. The hurt had not been great, so far as the blow was concerned. But his eyes were dark with pain and anger.

"Oh, don't distress yourself," he burst out. "You slapped me before— once, years ago—for kissing you. I—I apologize for saying you lied. You're only out of your head. So am I."

That poured oil upon the troubled waters. The cowboy appeared to be hesitating between sudden flight and the risk of staying longer.

"Maybe that's it," replied Columbine, with a half-laugh. She was not far from tears and fury with herself. "Let us make up—be friends again."

Moore squared around aggressively. He seemed to fortify himself against something in her. She felt that. But his face grew harder and older than she had ever seen it.

"Columbine, do *you* know where Jack Belllounds has been for these three years?" he asked, deliberately, entirely ignoring her overtures of friendship.

"No. Somebody said Denver. Some one else said Kansas City. I never asked dad, because I knew Jack had been sent away. I've supposed he was working—making a man of himself."

"Well, I hope to Heaven—for your sake—what you suppose comes true," returned Moore, with exceeding bitterness.

"Do *you* know where he has been?" asked Columbine. Some strange feeling prompted that. There was a mystery here. Wilson's agitation seemed strange and deep.

"Yes, I do." The cowboy bit that out through closing teeth, as if locking them against an almost overmastering temptation.

Columbine lost her curiosity. She was woman enough to realize that there might well be facts which would only make her situation harder.

"Wilson," she began, hurriedly, "I owe all I am to dad. He has cared for me—sent me to school. He has been so good to me. I've loved him always. It would be a shabby return for all his protection and love if—if I refused—"

"Old Bill is the best man ever," interrupted Moore, as if to repudiate any hint of disloyalty to his employer. "Everybody in Middle Park and all over owes Bill something. He's sure good. There never was anything wrong with him except his crazy blindness about his son. Buster Jack—the—the—"

Columbine put a hand over Moore's lips.

"The man I must marry," she said, solemnly.

"You must—you will?" he demanded.

"Of course. What else could I do? I never thought of refusing."

"Columbine!" Wilson's cry was so poignant, his gesture so violent, his dark eyes so piercing that Columbine sustained a shock that held her trembling and mute. "How can you love Jack Belllounds? You were twelve years old when you saw him last. How can you love him?"

"I don't," replied Columbine.

"Then how could you marry him?"

"I owe dad obedience. It's his hope that I can steady Jack."

"*Steady Jack!*" exclaimed Moore, passionately. "Why, you girl—you white-faced flower! *You* with your innocence and sweetness steady that damned pup! My Heavens! He was a gambler and a drunkard. He—"

"Hush!" implored Columbine.

"He cheated at cards," declared the cowboy, with a scorn that placed that vice as utterly base.

"But Jack was only a wild boy," replied Columbine, trying with brave words to champion the son of the man she loved as her father. "He has been sent away to work. He'll have outgrown that wildness. He'll come home a man."

"Bah!" cried Moore, harshly.

Columbine felt a sinking within her. Where was her strength? She, who could walk and ride so many miles, to become sick with an inward quaking! It was childish. She struggled to hide her weakness from him.

"It's not like you to be this way," she said. "You used to be generous. Am I to blame? Did I choose my life?"

Moore looked quickly away from her, and, standing with a hand on his horse, he was silent for a moment. The squaring of his shoulders bore testimony to his thought. Presently he swung up into the saddle. The mustang snorted and champed the bit and tossed his head, ready to bolt.

"Forget my temper," begged the cowboy, looking down upon Columbine. "I take it all back. I'm sorry. Don't let a word of mine worry you. I was only jealous."

"Jealous!" exclaimed Columbine, wonderingly.

"Yes. That makes a fellow see red and green. Bad medicine! You never felt it."

"What were you jealous of?" asked Columbine.

The cowboy had himself in hand now and he regarded her with a grim amusement.

"Well, Columbine, it's like a story," he replied. "I'm the fellow disowned by his family—a wanderer of the wilds—no good—and no prospects. . . . Now our friend Jack, he's handsome and rich. He has a doting old dad. Cattle, horses—ranches! He wins the girl. See!"

Spurring his mustang, the cowboy rode away. At the edge of the slope he turned in the saddle. "I've got to drive in this bunch of cattle. It's late. You hurry home." Then he was gone. The stones cracked and rolled down under the side of the bluff.

Columbine stood where he had left her: dubious, yet with the blood still hot in her cheeks.

"Jealous? . . . He wins the girl?" she murmured in repetition to herself. "What ever could he have meant? He didn't mean—he didn't—"

The simple, logical interpretation of Wilson's words opened Columbine's mind to a disturbing possibility of which she had never dreamed. That he might love her! If he did, why had he not said so? Jealous, maybe, but he did not love her! The next throb of thought was like a knock at a door of her heart—a door never yet opened, inside which seemed a mystery of feeling, of hope, despair, unknown longing, and clamorous voices. The woman just born in her, instinctive and self-preservative, shut that door before she had more than a glimpse inside. But then she felt her heart swell with its nameless burdens.

Pronto was grazing near at hand. She caught him and mounted. It struck her then that her hands were numb with cold. The wind had ceased fluttering the aspens, but the yellow leaves were falling, rustling. Out on the brow of the slope she faced home and the west.

A glorious Colorado sunset had just reached the wonderful height of its color and transformation. The sage slopes below her seemed rosy velvet; the golden aspens on the farther reaches were on fire at the tips; the foothills rolled clear and mellow and rich in the light; the gulf of distance on to the great black range was veiled in mountain purple; and the dim peaks beyond the range stood up, sunset-flushed and grand. The narrow belt of blue sky between crags and clouds was like a river full of fleecy sails and wisps of silver. Above towered a pall of dark cloud, full of the shades of approaching night.

"Oh, beautiful!" breathed the girl, with all her worship of nature. That wild world of sunset grandeur and loneliness and beauty was hers. Over there, under a peak of the black range, was the place where she had been found, baby, lost in the forest. She belonged to that, and so belonged to her. Strength came to her from the glory light on the hills.

Pronto shot up his ears and checked his trot.

"What is it, boy?" called Columbine. The trail was getting dark. Shadows were creeping up the slope as she rode down to meet them. The mustang had keen sight and scent. She reined him to a halt.

All was silent. The valley had begun to shade on the far side and the rose and gold seemed fading from the nearer. Below, on the level floor of the valley, lay the rambling old ranch-house, with the cabins nestling around, and the corrals leading out to the soft hay-fields, misty and gray in the twilight. A single light gleamed. It was like a beacon.

The air was cold with a nip of frost. From far on the other side of the ridge she had descended came the bawls of the last straggling cattle of the round-up. But surely Pronto had not shot up his ears for them. As if in answer a wild sound pealed down the slope, making the mustang jump. Columbine had heard it before.

"Pronto, it's only a wolf," she soothed him.

The peal was loud, rather harsh at first, then softened to a mourn, wild, lonely, haunting. A pack of coyotes barked in angry answer, a sharp, staccato, yelping chorus, the more piercing notes biting on the cold night air. These mountain mourns and yelps were music to Columbine. She rode on down the trail in the gathering darkness, less afraid of the night and its wild denizens than of what awaited her at White Slides Ranch.

CHAPTER 2

Darkness settled down like a black mantle over the valley. Columbine rather hoped to find Wilson waiting to take care of her horse, as used to be his habit, but she was disappointed. No light showed from the cabin in which the cowboys lived; he had not yet come in from the round-up. She unsaddled, and turned Pronto loose in the pasture.

The windows of the long, low ranch-house were bright squares in the blackness, sending cheerful rays afar. Columbine wondered in trepidation if Jack Belllounds had come home. It required effort of will to approach the house. Yet since she must meet him, the sooner the ordeal was over the better. Nevertheless she tiptoed past the bright windows, and went all the length of the long porch, and turned around and went back, and then hesitated, fighting a slow drag of her spirit, an oppression upon her heart. The door was crude and heavy. It opened hard.

Columbine entered a big room lighted by a lamp on the upper table and by blazing logs in a huge stone fireplace. This was the living-room, rather gloomy in the corners, and bare, but comfortable, for all simple needs. The logs were new and the chinks between them filled with clay, still white, showing that the house was of recent build.

The rancher, Belllounds, sat in his easy-chair before the fire, his big, horny hands extended to the warmth. He was in his shirt-sleeves, a gray, bold-faced man, of over sixty years, still muscular and rugged.

At Columbine's entrance he raised his drooping head, and so removed the suggestion of sadness in his posture.

"Wal, lass, hyar you are," was his greeting. "Jake has been hollerin' thet chuck was ready. Now we can eat."

"Dad—did—did your son come?" asked Columbine.

"No. I got word jest at sundown. One of Baker's cowpunchers from up the valley. He rode up from Kremmlin' an' stopped to say Jack was celebratin' his arrival by too much red liquor. Reckon he won't be home to-night. Mebbe to-morrow."

Belllounds spoke in an even, heavy tone, without any apparent feeling. Always he was mercilessly frank and never spared the truth. But Columbine, who knew him well, felt how this news flayed him. Resentment stirred in her toward the wayward son, but she knew better than to voice it.

"Natural like, I reckon, fer Jack to feel gay on gettin' home. I ain't holdin' thet ag'in' him. These last three years must have been gallin' to thet boy."

Columbine stretched her hands to the blaze.

"It's cold, dad," she averred. "I didn't dress warmly, so I nearly froze. Autumn is here and there's frost in the air. Oh, the hills were all gold and red—the aspen leaves were falling. I love autumn, but it means winter is so near."

"Wal, wal, time flies," sighed the old man. "Where'd you ride?"

"Up the west slope to the bluff. It's far. I don't go there often."

"Meet any of the boys? I sent the outfit to drive stock down from the mountain. I've lost a good many head lately. They're eatin' some weed thet poisons them. They swell up an' die. Wuss this year than ever before."

"Why, that is serious, dad! Poor things! That's worse than eating loco. . . . Yes, I met Wilson Moore driving down the slope."

"Ahuh! Wal, let's eat."

They took seats at the table which the cook, Jake, was loading with steaming victuals. Supper appeared to be a rather sumptuous one this evening, in honor of the expected guest, who had not come. Columbine helped the old man to his favorite dishes, stealing furtive glances at his lined and shadowed face. She sensed a subtle change in him since the afternoon, but could not see any sign of it in his look or demeanor. His appetite was as hearty as ever.

"So you met Wils. Is he still makin' up to you?" asked Belllounds, presently.

"No, he isn't. I don't see that he ever did—that—dad," she replied.

"You're a kid in mind an' a woman in body. Thet cowpuncher has been lovesick over you since you were a little girl. It's what kept him hyar ridin' fer me."

"Dad, I don't believe it," said Columbine, feeling the blood at her temples. "You always imagined such things about Wilson, and the other boys as well."

"Ahuh! I'm an old fool about wimmen, hey? Mebbe I was years ago. But I can see now. . . . Didn't Wils always get ory-eyed when any of the other boys shined up to you?"

"I can't remember that he did," replied Columbine. She felt a desire to laugh, yet the subject was anything but amusing to her.

"Wal, you've always been innocent-like. Thank the Lord you never leaned to tricks of most pretty lasses, makin' eyes at all the men. Anyway, a matter of three months ago I told Wils to keep away from you—thet you were not fer any poor cowpuncher."

"You never liked him. Why? Was it fair, taking him as boys come?"

"Wal, I reckon it wasn't," replied Belllounds, and as he looked up his broad face changed to ruddy color. "Thet boy's the best rider an' roper I've had in years. He ain't the bronco-bustin' kind. He never drank. He was honest an' willin'. He saves his money. He's good at handlin' stock. Thet boy will be a rich rancher some day."

"Strange, then, you never liked him," murmured Columbine. She felt ashamed of the good it did her to hear Wilson praised.

"No, it ain't strange. I have my own reasons," replied Belllounds, gruffly, as he resumed eating.

Columbine believed she could guess the cause of the old rancher's unreasonable antipathy for this cowboy. Not improbably it was because Wilson had always been superior in every way to Jack Belllounds. The boys had been natural rivals in everything pertaining to life on the range. What Bill Belllounds admired most in men was paramount in Wilson and lacking in his own son.

"Will you put Jack in charge of your ranches, now?" asked Columbine.

"Not much. I reckon I'll try him hyar at White Slides as foreman. An' if he runs the outfit, then I'll see."

"Dad, he'll never run the White Slides outfit," asserted Columbine.

"Wal, it is a hard bunch, I'll agree. But I reckon the boys will stay, exceptin', mebbe, Wils. An' it'll be jest as well fer him to leave."

"It's not good business to send away your best cowboy. I've heard you complain lately of lack of men."

"I sure do need men," replied Belllounds, seriously. "Stock gettin' more 'n we can handle. I sent word over the range to Meeker, hopin' to get some men there. What I need most jest now is a fellar who knows dogs an' who'll hunt down the wolves an' lions an' bears thet're livin' off my cattle."

"Dad, you need a whole outfit to handle the packs of hounds you've got. Such an assortment of them! There must be a hundred. Only yesterday some man brought a lot of mangy, long-eared canines. It's funny. Why, dad, you're the laughing-stock of the range!"

"Yes, an' the range'll be thankin' me when I rid it of all these varmints," declared Belllounds. "Lass, I swore I'd buy every dog fetched to me, until I had enough to kill off the coyotes an' lofers an' lions. I'll do it, too. But I need a hunter."

"Why not put Wilson Moore in charge of the hounds? He's a hunter."

"Wal, lass, thet might be a good idee," replied the rancher, nodding his grizzled head. "Say, you're sort of wantin' me to keep Wils on."

"Yes, dad."

"Why? Do you like him so much?"

"I like him—of course. He has been almost a brother to me."

"Ahuh! Wal, are you sure you don't like him more'n you ought—considerin' what's in the wind?"

"Yes, I'm sure I don't," replied Columbine, with tingling cheeks.

"Wal, I'm glad of thet. Reckon it'll be no great matter whether Wils stays or leaves. If he wants to I'll give him a job with the hounds."

That evening Columbine went to her room early. It was a cozy little blanketed nest which she had arranged and furnished herself. There was a little square window cut through the logs and through which many a night the snow had blown in upon her bed. She loved her little isolated refuge. This night it was cold, the first time this autumn, and the lighted lamp, though brightening the room, did not make it appreciably warmer. There was a stone fireplace, but as she had neglected to bring in wood she could not start a fire. So she undressed, blew out the lamp, and went to bed.

Columbine was soon warm, and the darkness of her little room seemed good to her. Sleep she felt never would come that night. She wanted to think; she could not help but think; and she tried to halt the whirl of her mind. Wilson Moore occupied the foremost place in her varying thoughts—a fact quite remarkable and unaccountable. She tried to change it. In vain! Wilson persisted—on his white mustang flying across the ridgetop—coming to her as never before—with his anger and disapproval—his strange, poignant cry, "Columbine!" that haunted her— with his bitter smile and his resignation and his mocking talk of jealousy. He persisted and grew with the old rancher's frank praise.

"I must not think of him," she whispered. "Why, I'll be—be married soon. . . . Married!"

That word transformed her thought, and where she had thrilled she now felt cold. She revolved the fact in mind.

"It's true, I'll be married, because I ought—I must," she said, half aloud. "Because I can't help myself. I ought to want to—for dad's sake. . . . But I don't—I don't."

She longed above all things to be good, loyal, loving, helpful, to show her gratitude for the home and the affection that had been bestowed upon a nameless waif. Bill Belllounds had not been under any obligation to succor a strange, lost child. He had done it because he was big, noble. Many splendid deeds had been laid at the old rancher's door. She was not of an ungrateful nature. She meant to pay. But the significance of the price began to dawn upon her.

"It will change my whole life," she whispered, aghast.

But how? Columbine pondered. She must go over the details of that change. No mother had ever taught her. The few women that had been in the Belllounds home from time to time had not been sympathetic or had not stayed long enough to help her much. Even her school life in Denver had left her still a child as regarded the serious problems of women.

"If I'm his wife," she went on, "I'll have to be with him—I'll have to give up this little room—I'll never be free—alone—happy, any more."

That was the first detail she enumerated. It was also the last. Realization came with a sickening little shudder. And that moment gave birth to the nucleus of an unconscious revolt.

The coyotes were howling. Wild, sharp, sweet notes! They soothed her troubled, aching head, lulled her toward sleep, reminded her of the gold-and-purple sunset, and the slopes of sage, the lonely heights, and the beauty that would never change. On the morrow, she drowsily thought, she would persuade Wilson not to kill all the coyotes; to leave a few, because she loved them.

Bill Belllounds had settled in Middle Park in 1860. It was wild country, a home of the Ute Indians, and a natural paradise for elk, deer, antelope, buffalo. The mountain ranges harbored bear. These ranges sheltered the rolling valley land which some explorer had named Middle Park in earlier days.

Much of this inclosed table-land was prairie, where long grass and wild flowers grew luxuriantly. Belllounds was a cattleman, and he saw the possibilities there. To which end he sought the friendship of Piah, chief of the Utes. This noble red man was well disposed toward the white settlers, and his tribe, during those troublous times, kept peace with these invaders of their mountain home.

In 1868 Belllounds was instrumental in persuading the Utes to relinquish Middle Park. The slopes of the hills were heavily timbered; gold and silver had been found in the mountains. It was a country that attracted prospectors, cattlemen, lumbermen. The summer season was not long enough to grow grain, and the nights too frosty for corn; otherwise Middle Park would have increased rapidly in population.

In the years that succeeded the departure of the Utes Bill Belllounds developed several cattle-ranches and acquired others. White Slides Ranch lay some twenty-odd miles from Middle Park, being a winding arm of the main valley land. Its development was a matter of later years, and Belllounds lived there because the country was wilder. The rancher, as he advanced in years, seemed to want to keep the loneliness that had been his in earlier days. At the time of the return of his son to White

Slides Belllounds was rich in cattle and land, but he avowed frankly that he had not saved any money, and probably never would. His hand was always open to every man and he never remembered an obligation. He trusted every one. A proud boast of his was that neither white man nor red man had ever betrayed his trust. His cowboys took advantage of him, his neighbors imposed upon him, but none were there who did not make good their debts of service or stock. Belllounds was one of the great pioneers of the frontier days to whom the West owed its settlement; and he was finer than most, because he proved that the Indians, if not robbed or driven, would respond to friendliness.

Belllounds was not seen at his customary tasks on the day he expected his son. He walked in the fields and around the corrals; he often paced up and down the porch, scanning the horizon below, where the road from Kremmling showed white down the valley; and part of the time he stayed indoors.

It so happened that early in the afternoon he came out in time to see a buckboard, drawn by dust-and-lather-stained horses, pull into the yard. And then he saw his son. Some of the cowboys came running. There were greetings to the driver, who appeared well known to them.

Jack Belllounds did not look at them. He threw a bag out of the buckboard and then clambered down slowly, to go toward the porch.

"Wal, Jack—my son—I'm sure glad you're back home," said the old rancher, striding forward. His voice was deep and full, singularly rich. But that was the only sign of feeling he showed.

"Howdy—dad!" replied the son, not heartily, as he put out his hand to his father's.

Jack Belllounds's form was tall, with a promise of his father's bulk. But he did not walk erect; he slouched a little. His face was pale, showing he had not of late been used to sun and wind. Any stranger would have seen the resemblance of boy to man, would have granted the handsome boldness, but denied the strength. The lower part of Jack Belllounds's face was weak.

The constraint of this meeting was manifest mostly in the manner of the son. He looked ashamed, almost sullen. But if he had been under the influence of liquor at Kremmling, as reported the day before, he had entirely recovered.

"Come on in," said the rancher.

When they got into the big living-room, and Belllounds had closed the doors, the son threw down his baggage and faced his father aggressively.

"Do they all know where I've been?" he asked, bitterly. Broken pride and shame flamed in his face.

"Nobody knows. The secret's been kept." replied Belllounds.

Amaze and relief transformed the young man. "Aw, now, I'm— glad—" he exclaimed, and he sat down, half covering his face with shaking hands.

"Jack, we'll start over," said Belllounds, earnestly, and his big eyes shone with a warm and beautiful light. "Right hyar. We'll never speak of where you've been these three years. Never again!"

Jack gazed up, then, with all the sullenness and shadow gone.

"Father, you were wrong about—doing me good. It's done me harm. But now, if nobody knows—why, I'll try to forget it."

"Mebbe I blundered," replied Belllounds, pathetically. "Yet, God knows I meant well. You sure were—But thet's enough palaver. . . . You'll go to work as foreman of White Slides. An' if you make a success of it I'll be only too glad to have you boss the ranch. I'm gettin' along in years, son. An' the last year has made me poorer. Hyar's a fine range, but I've less stock this year than last. There's been some rustlin' of cattle, an' a big loss from wolves an' lions an' poison-weed. . . . What d'you say, son?"

"I'll run White Slides," replied Jack, with a wave of his hand. "I hadn't hoped for such a chance. But it's due me. Who's in the outfit I know?"

"Reckon no one, except Wils Moore."

"Is that cowboy here yet? I don't want him."

"Wal, I'll put him to chasin' varmints with the hounds. An' say, son, this outfit is bad. You savvy—it's bad. You can't run that bunch. The only way you can handle them is to get up early an' come back late. Sayin' little, but sawin' wood. Hard work."

Jack Belllounds did not evince any sign of assimilating the seriousness of his father's words.

"I'll show them," he said. "They'll find out who's boss. Oh, I'm aching to get into boots and ride and tear around."

Belllounds stroked his grizzled beard and regarded his son with mingled pride and doubt. Not at this moment, most assuredly, could he get away from the wonderful fact that his only son was home.

"Thet's all right, son. But you've been off the range for three years. You'll need advice. Now listen. Be gentle with hosses. You used to be mean with a hoss. Some cowboys jam their hosses around an' make 'em pitch an' bite. But it ain't the best way. A hoss has got sense. I've some fine stock, an' don't want it spoiled. An' be easy an' quiet with the boys. It's hard to get help these days. I'm short on hands now. . . . You'd do best, son, to stick to your dad's ways with hosses an' men."

"Dad, I've seen you kick horses an' shoot at men" replied Jack.

"Right, you have. But them was particular bad cases. I'm not advisin' thet way. . . . Son, it's close to my heart—this hope I have thet you'll—"

The full voice quavered and broke. It would indeed have been a hardened youth who could not have felt something of the deep and unutterable affection in the old man. Jack Belllounds put an arm around his father's shoulder.

"Dad, I'll make you proud of me yet. Give me a chance. And don't be sore if I can't do wonders right at first."

"Son, you shall have every chance. An' thet reminds me. Do you remember Columbine?"

"I should say so," replied Jack, eagerly. "They spoke of her in Kremmling. Where is she?"

"I reckon somewheres about. Jack, you an' Columbine are to marry."

"Marry! Columbine and me?" he ejaculated.

"Yes. You're my son an' she's my adopted daughter. I won't split my property. An' it's right she had a share. A fine, strong, quiet, pretty lass, Jack, an' she'll make a good wife. I've set my heart on the idee."

"But Columbine always hated me."

"Wal, she was a kid then an' you teased her. Now she's a woman, an' willin' to please me. Jack, you'll not buck ag'in' this deal?"

"That depends," replied Jack. "I'd marry 'most any girl you wanted me to. But if Columbine were to flout me as she used to—why, I'd buck sure enough. . . . Dad, are you sure she knows nothing, suspects nothing of where you—you sent me?"

"Son, I swear she doesn't."

"Do you mean you'd want us to marry soon?"

"Wal, yes, as soon as Collie would think reasonable. Jack, she's shy an' strange, an' deep, too. If you ever win her heart you'll be richer than if you owned all the gold in the Rockies. I'd say go slow. But contrariwise, it'd mebbe be surer to steady you, keep you home, if you married right off."

"Married right off!" echoed Jack, with a laugh. "It's like a story. But wait till I see her."

At that very moment Columbine was sitting on the topmost log of a high corral, deeply interested in the scene before her.

Two cowboys were in the corral with a saddled mustang. One of them carried a canvas sack containing tools and horseshoes. As he dropped it with a metallic clink the mustang snorted and jumped and rolled the whites of his eyes. He knew what that clink meant.

"Miss Collie, air you-all goin' to sit up thar?" inquired the taller cowboy, a lean, supple, and powerful fellow, with a rough, red-blue face, hard as a rock, and steady, bright eyes.

"I sure am, Jim," she replied, imperturbably.

"But we've gotta hawg-tie him," protested the cowboy.

"Yes, I know. And you're going to be gentle about it."

Jim scratched his sandy head and looked at his comrade, a little gnarled fellow, like the bleached root of a tree. He seemed all legs.

"You hear, you Wyomin' galoot," he said to Jim. "Them shoes goes on Whang right gentle."

Jim grinned, and turned to speak to his mustang. "Whang, the law's laid down an' we wanta see how much hoss sense you hev."

The shaggy mustang did not appear to be favorably impressed by this speech. It was a mighty distrustful look he bent upon the speaker.

"Jim, seein' as how this here job's aboot the last Miss Collie will ever boss us on, we gotta do it without Whang turnin' a hair," drawled the other cowboy.

"Lem, why is this the last job I'll ever boss you boys?" demanded Columbine, quickly.

Jim gazed quizzically at her, and Lem assumed that blank, innocent face Columbine always associated with cowboy deviltry.

"Wal, Miss Collie, we reckon the new boss of White Slides rode in to-day."

"You mean Jack Belllounds came home," said Columbine. "Well, I'll boss you boys the same as always."

"Thet'd be mighty fine for us, but I'm feared it ain't writ in the fatal history of White Slides," replied Jim.

"Buster Jack will run over the ole man an' marry you," added Lem.

"Oh, so that's your idea," rejoined Columbine, lightly. "Well, if such a thing did come to pass I'd be your boss more than ever."

"I reckon no, Miss Collie, for we'll not be ridin' fer White Slides," said Jim, simply.

Columbine had sensed this very significance long before when the possibility of Buster Jack's return had been rumored. She knew cowboys. As well try to change the rocks of the hills!

"Boys, the day you leave White Slides will be a sad one for me," sighed Columbine.

"Miss Collie, we ain't gone yet," put in Lem, with awkward softness. "Jim has long hankered fer Wyomin' an' he jest talks thet way."

Then the cowboys turned to the business in hand. Jim removed the saddle, but left the bridle on. This move, of course, deceived Whang. He had been broken to stand while his bridle hung, and, like a horse that would have been good if given a chance, he obeyed as best he could, shaking in every limb. Jim, apparently to hobble Whang, roped his forelegs together, low down, but suddenly slipped the rope over the knees. Then Whang knew he had been deceived. He snorted fire, let out a scream, and, rearing on his hind legs, he pawed the air savagely. Jim hauled on the rope while Whang screamed and fought with his forefeet high in the air. Then Jim, with a powerful jerk, pulled Whang down and threw him, while Lem, seizing the bridle, hauled him over on his side and sat upon his head. Whereupon Jim slipped the loop off one front hoof and pulled the other leg back across one of the hind ones, where both were secured by a quick hitch. Then the lasso was wound and looped around front and back hoofs together. When this had been done the mustang was rolled over on his other side, his free front hoof lassoed and pulled back to the hind one, where both were secured, as had been the others. This rendered the mustang powerless, and the shoeing proceeded.

Columbine hated to sit by and watch it, but she always stuck to her post, when opportunity afforded, because she knew the cowboys would not be brutal while she was there.

"Wal, he'll step high to-morrer," said Lem, as he got up from his seat on the head of Whang.

"Ahuh! An', like a mule, he'll be my friend fer twenty years jest to get a chance to kick me," replied Jim.

For Columbine, the most interesting moment of this incident was when the mustang raised his head to look at his legs, in order to see what had been done to them. There was something almost human in that look. It expressed intelligence and fear and fury.

The cowboys released his legs and let him get up. Whang stamped his iron-shod hoofs.

"It was a mean trick, Whang," said Columbine. "If I owned you that'd never be done to you."

"I reckon you can have him fer the askin'," said Jim, as he threw on the saddle. "Nobody but me can ride him. Do you want to try?"

"Not in these clothes," replied Columbine, laughing.

"Wal, Miss Collie, you're shore dressed up fine to-day, fer some reason or other," said Lem, shaking his head, while he gathered up the tools from the ground.

"Ahuh! An' here comes the reason," exclaimed Jim, in low, hoarse whisper.

Columbine heard the whisper and at the same instant a sharp footfall on the gravel road. She quickly turned, almost losing her balance. And she recognized Jack Belllounds. The boy Buster Jack she remembered so well was approaching, now a young man, taller, heavier, older, with paler face and bolder look. Columbine had feared this meeting, had prepared herself for it. But all she felt when it came was annoyance at the fact that he had caught her sitting on top of the corral fence, with little regard for dignity. It did not occur to her to jump down. She merely sat straight, smoothed down her skirt, and waited.

Jim led the mustang out of the corral and Lem followed. It looked as if they wanted to avoid the young man, but he prevented that.

"Howdy, boys! I'm Jack Belllounds," he said, rather loftily. But his manner was nonchalant. He did not offer to shake hands.

Jim mumbled something, and Lem said, "Hod do."

"That's an ornery-looking bronc," went on Belllounds, and he reached with careless hand for the mustang. Whang jerked so hard that he pulled Jim half over.

"Wal, he ain't a bronc, but I reckon he's all the rest." drawled Jim.

Both cowboys seemed slow, careless. They were neither indifferent nor responsive. Columbine saw their keen, steady glances go over Belllounds. Then she took a second and less hasty look at him. He wore high-heeled, fancy-topped boots, tight-fitting trousers of dark material, a heavy belt with silver buckle, and a white, soft shirt, with wide collar, open at the neck. He was bareheaded.

"I'm going to run White Slides," he said to the cowboys. "What're your names?"

Columbine wanted to giggle, which impulse she smothered. The idea of any one asking Jim his name! She had never been able to find out.

"My handle is Lemuel Archibawld Billings," replied Lem, blandly. The middle name was an addition no one had ever heard.

Belllounds then directed his glance and steps toward the girl. The cowboys dropped their heads and shuffled on their way.

"There's only one girl on the ranch," said Belllounds, "so you must be Columbine."

"Yes. And you're Jack," she replied, and slipped off the fence. "I'm glad to welcome you home."

She offered her hand, and he held it until she extricated it. There was genuine surprise and pleasure in his expression.

"Well, I'd never have known you," he said, surveying her from head to foot. "It's funny. I had the clearest picture of you in mind. But you're not at all like I imagined. The Columbine I remember was thin, white-faced, and all eyes."

"It's been a long time. Seven years," she replied. "But I knew you. You're older, taller, bigger, but the same Buster Jack."

"I hope not," he said, frankly condemning that former self. "Dad needs me. He wants me to take charge here—to be a man. I'm back now.

It's good to be home. I never was worth much. Lord! I hope I don't disappoint him again."

"I hope so, too," she murmured. To hear him talk frankly, seriously, like this counteracted the unfavorable impression she had received. He seemed earnest. He looked down at the ground, where he was pushing little pebbles with the toe of his boot. She had a good opportunity to study his face, and availed herself of it. He did look like his father, with his big, handsome head, and his blue eyes, bolder perhaps from their prominence than from any direct gaze or fire. His face was pale, and shadowed by worry or discontent. It seemed as though a repressed character showed there. His mouth and chin were undisciplined. Columbine could not imagine that she despised anything she saw in the features of this young man. Yet there was something about him that held her aloof. She had made up her mind to do her part unselfishly. She would find the best in him, like him for it, be strong to endure and to help. Yet she had no power to control her vague and strange perceptions. Why was it that she could not feel in him what she liked in Jim Montana or Lem or Wilson Moore?

"This was my second long stay away from home," said Belllounds. "The first was when I went to school in Kansas City. I liked that. I was sorry when they turned me out—sent me home. . . . But the last three years were hell."

His face worked, and a shade of dark blood rippled over it.

"Did you work?" queried Columbine.

"Work! It was worse than work. . . . Sure I worked," he replied.

Columbine's sharp glance sought his hands. They looked as soft and unscarred as her own. What kind of work had he done, if he told the truth?

"Well, if you work hard for dad, learn to handle the cowboys, and never take up those old bad habits—"

"You mean drink and cards? I swear I'd forgotten them for three years—until yesterday. I reckon I've the better of them."

"Then you'll make dad and me happy. You'll be happy, too."

Columbine thrilled at the touch of fineness coming out in him. There was good in him, whatever the mad, wild pranks of his boyhood.

"Dad wants us to marry," he said, suddenly, with shyness and a strange, amused smile. "Isn't that funny? You and me—who used to fight like cat and dog! Do you remember the time I pushed you into the old mudhole? And you lay in wait for me, behind the house, to hit me with a rotten cabbage?"

"Yes, I remember," replied Columbine, dreamily. "It seems so long ago."

"And the time you ate my pie, and how I got even by tearing off your little dress, so you had to run home almost without a stitch on?"

"Guess I've forgotten that," replied Columbine, with a blush. "I must have been very little then."

"You were a little devil. . . . Do you remember the fight I had with Moore—about you?"

She did not answer, for she disliked the fleeting expression that crossed his face. He remembered too well.

"I'll settle that score with Moore," he went on. "Besides, I won't have him on the ranch."

"Dad needs good hands," she said, with her eyes on the gray sage slopes. Mention of Wilson Moore augmented the aloofness in her. An annoyance pricked along her veins.

"Before we get any farther I'd like to know something. Has Moore ever made love to you?"

Columbine felt that prickling augment to a hot, sharp wave of blood. Why was she at the mercy of strange, quick, unfamiliar sensations? Why did she hesitate over that natural query from Jack Belllounds?

"No. He never has," she replied, presently.

"That's damn queer. You used to like him better than anybody else. You sure hated me. . . . Columbine, have you outgrown that?"

"Yes, of course," she answered. "But I hardly hated you."

"Dad said you were willing to marry me. Is that so?"

Columbine dropped her head. His question, kindly put, did not affront her, for it had been expected. But his actual presence, the meaning of his words, stirred in her an unutterable spirit of protest. She had already in her will consented to the demand of the old man; she was learning now, however, that she could not force her flesh to consent to a surrender it did not desire.

"Yes, I'm willing," she replied, bravely.

"Soon?" he flashed, with an eager difference in his voice.

"If I had my way it'd not be—too soon," she faltered. Her downcast eyes had seen the stride he had made closer to her, and she wanted to run.

"Why? Dad thinks it'd be good for me," went on Belllounds, now, with strong, self-centered thought. "It'd give me responsibility. I reckon I need it. Why not soon?"

"Wouldn't it be better to wait awhile?" she asked. "We do not know each other—let alone care—"

"Columbine, I've fallen in love with you," he declared, hotly.

"Oh, how could you!" cried Columbine, incredulously.

"Why, I always was moony over you—when we were kids," he said. "And now to meet you grown up like this—so pretty and sweet—such a—a healthy, blooming girl. . . . And dad's word that you'd be my wife soon—*mine*—why, I just went off my head at sight of you."

Columbine looked up at him and was reminded of how, as a boy, he had always taken a quick, passionate longing for things he must and would have. And his father had not denied him. It might really be that Jack had suddenly fallen in love with her.

"Would you want to take me without my—my love?" she asked, very low. "I don't love you now. I might some time, if you were good—if you made dad happy—if you conquered—"

"Take you! I'd take you if you—if you hated me," he replied, now in the grip of passion.

"I'll tell dad how I feel," she said, faintly, "and—and marry you when he says."

He kissed her, would have embraced her had she not put him back.

"Don't! Some—some one will see."

"Columbine, we're engaged," he asserted, with a laugh of possession. "Say, you needn't look so white and scared. I won't eat you. But I'd like to. . . . Oh, you're a sweet girl! Here I was hating to come home. And look at my luck!"

Then with a sudden change, that seemed significant of his character, he lost his ardor, dropped the half-bold, half-masterful air, and showed the softer side.

"Collie, I never was any good," he said. "But I want to be better. I'll prove it. I'll make a clean breast of everything. I won't marry you with any secret between us. You might find out afterward and hate me. . . . Do you have any idea where I've been these last three years?"

"No," answered Columbine.

"I'll tell you right now. But you must promise never to mention it to any one—or throw it up to me—ever."

He spoke hoarsely, and had grown quite white. Suddenly Columbine thought of Wilson Moore! He had known where Jack had spent those years. He had resisted a strong temptation to tell her. That was as noble in him as the implication of Jack's whereabouts had been base.

"Jack, that is big of you," she replied, hurriedly. "I respect you—like you for it. But you needn't tell me. I'd rather you didn't. I'll take the will for the deed."

Belllounds evidently experienced a poignant shock of amaze, of relief, of wonder, of gratitude. In an instant he seemed transformed.

"Collie, if I hadn't loved you before I'd love you now. That was going to be the hardest job I ever had—to tell you my—my story. I meant it. And now I'll not have to feel your shame for me and I'll not feel I'm a cheat or a liar. . . . But I will tell you this—if you love me you'll make a man of me!"

CHAPTER 3

The rancher thought it best to wait till after the round-up before he turned over the foremanship to his son. This was wise, but Jack did not see it that way. He showed that his old, intolerant spirit had, if anything, grown during his absence. Belllounds patiently argued with him, explaining what certainly should have been clear to a young man brought up in Colorado. The fall round-up was the most important time of the year, and during the strenuous drive the appointed foreman should have absolute control. Jack gave in finally with a bad grace.

It was unfortunate that he went directly from his father's presence out to the corrals. Some of the cowboys who had ridden all the day before and stood guard all night had just come in. They were begrimed with dust, weary, and sleepy-eyed.

"This hyar outfit won't see my tracks no more," said one, disgustedly. "I never kicked on doin' two men's work. But when it comes to rustlin' day and night, all the time, I'm agoin' to pass."

"Turn in, boys, and sleep till we get back with the chuck-wagon," said Wilson Moore. "We'll clean up that bunch to-day."

"Ain't you tired, Wils?" queried Bludsoe, a squat, bow-legged cow-puncher who appeared to be crippled or very lame.

"Me? Naw!" grunted Moore, derisively. "Blud, you sure ask fool questions. . . . Why, you—mahogany-colored, stump-legged biped of a cowpuncher, I've had three hours' sleep in four nights!"

"What's a biped?" asked Bludsoe, dubiously.

Nobody enlightened him.

"Wils, you-all air the only eddicated cowman I ever loved, but I'm a son-of-a-gun if we ain't agoin' to come to blows some day," declared Bludsoe.

"He shore can sling English," drawled Lem Billings. "I reckon he swallowed a dictionary onct."

"Wal, he can sling a rope, too, an' thet evens up," added Jim Montana.

Just at this moment Jack Belllounds appeared upon the scene. The cowboys took no notice of him. Jim was bandaging a leg of his horse; Bludsoe was wearily gathering up his saddle and trappings; Lem was giving his tired mustang a parting slap that meant much. Moore evidently awaited a fresh mount. A Mexican lad had come in out of the pasture leading several horses, one of which was the mottled white mustang that Moore rode most of the time.

Belllounds lounged forward with interest as Moore whistled, and the mustang showed his pleasure. Manifestly he did not like the Mexican boy and he did like Moore.

"Spottie, it's drag yearlings around for you to-day," said the cowboy, as he caught the mustang. Spottie tossed his head and stepped high until the bridle was on. When the saddle was thrown and strapped in place the mustang showed to advantage. He was beautiful, but not too graceful or sleek or fine-pointed or prancing to prejudice any cowboy against his qualities for work.

Jack Belllounds admiringly walked all around the mustang, a little too close to please Spottie.

"Moore, he's a fair-to-middling horse," said Belllounds, with the air of judge of horseflesh. "What's his name?"

"Spottie," replied Moore, shortly, as he made ready to mount.

"Hold on, will you!" ordered Jack, peremptorily. "I like this horse. I want to look him over."

When he grasped the bridle-reins out of the cowboy's hand Spottie jumped as if he had been shot at. Belllounds jerked at him and went closer. The mustang reared, snorting, plunging to get loose. Then Jack Belllounds showed the sudden temper for which he was noted. Red stained his pale cheeks.

"Damn you—come down!" he shouted, infuriated at the mustang, and with both hands he gave a powerful lunge. Spottie came down, and stood there, trembling all over, his ears laid back, his eyes showing fright and pain. Blood dripped from his mouth where the bit had cut him.

"I'll teach you to stand," said Belllounds, darkly. "Moore, lend me your spurs. I want to try him out."

"I don't lend my spurs—or my horse, either," replied the cowboy, quietly, with a stride that put him within reach of Spottie.

The other cowboys had dropped their trappings and stood at attention, with intent gaze and mute lips.

"Is he your horse?" demanded Jack, with a quick flush.

"I reckon so," replied Moore, slowly. "No one but me ever rode him."

"Does my father own him or do you own him?"

"Well, if that's the way you figure—he belongs to White Slides," returned the cowboy. "I never bought him. I only raised him from a colt, broke him, and rode him."

"I thought so. Moore, he's mine, and I'm going to ride him now. Lend me spurs, one of you cowpunchers."

Nobody made any motion to comply. There seemed to be a suspense at hand that escaped Belllounds.

"I'll ride him without spurs," he declared, presently, and again he turned to mount the mustang.

"Belllounds, it'd be better for you not to ride him now," said Moore, coolly.

"Why, I'd like to know?" demanded Belllounds, with the temper of one who did not tolerate opposition.

"He's the only horse left for me to ride," answered the cowboy. "We're branding to-day. Hudson was hurt yesterday. He was foreman, and he appointed me to fill his place. I've got to rope yearlings. Now, if you get up on Spottie you'll excite him. He's high-strung, nervous. That'll be bad for him, as he hates cutting-out and roping."

The reasonableness of this argument was lost upon Belllounds.

"Moore, maybe it'd interest you to know that I'm foreman of White Slides," he asserted, not without loftiness.

His speech manifestly decided something vital for the cowboy.

"Ahuh! . . . I'm sure interested this minute," replied Moore, and then, stepping to the side of the mustang, with swift hands he unbuckled the cinch, and with one sweep he drew saddle and blanket to the ground.

The action surprised Belllounds. He stared. There seemed something boyish in his lack of comprehension. Then his temper flamed.

"What do you mean by that?" he demanded, with a strident note in his voice. "Put that saddle back."

"Not much. It's my saddle. Cost sixty dollars at Kremmling last year. Good old hard-earned saddle! . . . And you can't ride it. Savvy?"

"Yes, I savvy," replied Belllounds, violently. "Now you'll savvy what I say. I'll have you discharged."

"Nope. Too late," said Moore, with cool, easy scorn. "I figured that. And I quit a minute ago—when you showed what little regard you had for a horse."

"You quit! . . . Well, it's damned good riddance. I wouldn't have you in the outfit."

"You couldn't have kept me, Buster Jack."

The epithet must have been an insult to Belllounds. "Don't you dare call me that," he burst out, furiously.

Moore pretended surprise. "Why not? It's your range name. We all get a handle, whether we like it or not. There's Montana and Blud and Lemme Two Bits. They call me Professor. Why should you kick on yours?"

"I won't stand it now. Not from any one—especially not you."

"Ahuh! Well, I'm afraid it'll stick," replied Moore, with sarcasm. "It sure suits you. Don't you bust everything you monkey with? Your old dad will sure be glad to see you bust the round-up to-day—and I reckon the outfit to-morrow."

"You insolent cowpuncher!" shouted Belllounds, growing beside himself with rage. "If you don't shut up I'll bust your face."

"Shut up! . . . Me? Nope. It can't be did. This is a free country, Buster Jack." There was no denying Moore's cool, stinging repetition of the epithet that had so affronted Belllounds.

"I always hated you!" he rasped out, hoarsely. Striking hard at Moore, he missed, but a second effort landed a glancing blow on the cowboy's face.

Moore staggered back, recovered his balance, and, hitting out shortly, he returned the blow. Belllounds fell against the corral fence, which upheld him.

"Buster Jack—you're crazy!" cried the cowboy, his eyes flashing. "Do you think you can lick me—after where you've been these three years?"

Like a maddened boy Belllounds leaped forward, this time his increased violence and wildness of face expressive of malignant rage. He swung his arms at random. Moore avoided his blows and planted a fist squarely on his adversary's snarling mouth. Belllounds fell with a thump. He got up with clumsy haste, but did not rush forward again. His big, prominent eyes held a dark and ugly look. His lower jaw wabbled as he panted for breath and speech at once.

"Moore—I'll kill—you!" he hissed, with glance flying everywhere for a weapon. From ground to cowboys he looked. Bludsoe was the only one packing a gun. Belllounds saw it, and he was so swift in bounding forward that he got a hand on it before Bludsoe could prevent.

"Let go! Give me—that gun! By God! I'll fix him!" yelled Belllounds, as Bludsoe grappled with him.

There was a sharp struggle. Bludsoe wrenched the other's hands free, and, pulling the gun, he essayed to throw it. But Belllounds blocked his action and the gun fell at their feet.

"Grab it!" sang out Bludsoe, ringingly. "Quick, somebody! The damned fool'll kill Wils."

Lem, running in, kicked the gun just as Belllounds reached for it. When it rolled against the fence Jim was there to secure it. Lem likewise grappled with the struggling Belllounds.

"Hyar, you Jack Belllounds," said Lem, "couldn't you see Wils wasn't packin' no gun? A-r'arin' like thet! . . . Stop your rantin' or we'll sure handle you rough."

"The old man's comin'," called Jim, warningly.

The rancher appeared. He strode swiftly, ponderously. His gray hair waved. His look was as stern as that of an eagle.

"What the hell's goin' on?" he roared.

The cowboys released Jack. That worthy, sullen and downcast, muttering to himself, stalked for the house.

"Jack, stand your ground," called old Belllounds.

But the son gave no heed. Once he looked back over his shoulder, and his dark glance saw no one save Moore.

"Boss, thar's been a little argyment," explained Jim, as with swift hand he hid Bludsoe's gun. "Nuthin' much."

"Jim, you're a liar," replied the old rancher.

"Aw!" exclaimed Jim, crestfallen.

"What're you hidin'? . . . You've got somethin' there. Gimme thet gun."

Without more ado Jim handed the gun over.

"It's mine, boss," put in Bludsoe.

"Ahuh? Wal, what was Jim hidin' it fer?" demanded Belllounds.

"Why, I jest tossed it to him—when I—sort of j'ined in with the argyment. We was tusslin' some an' I didn't want no gun."

How characteristic of cowboys that they lied to shield Jack Belllounds! But it was futile to attempt to deceive the old rancher. Here was a man who had been forty years dealing with all kinds of men and events.

"Bludsoe, you can't fool me," said old Bill, calmly. He had roared at them, and his eyes still flashed like blue fire, but he was calm and cool. Returning the gun to its owner, he continued: "I reckon you'd spare my feelin's an' lie about some trick of Jack's. Did he bust out?"

"Wal, tolerable like," replied Bludsoe, dryly.

"Ahuh! Tell me, then—an' no lies."

Belllounds's shrewd eyes had rested upon Wilson Moore. The cowboy's face showed the red marks of battle and the white of passion.

"I'm not going to lie, you can bet on that," he declared, forcefully.

"Ahuh! I might hev knowed you an' Jack'd clash," said Belllounds, gruffly. "What happened?"

"He hurt my horse. If it hadn't been for that there'd been no trouble."

A light leaped up in the old man's bold eyes. He was a lover of horses. Many hard words, and blows, too, he had dealt cowboys for being brutal.

"What'd he do?"

"Look at Spottie's mouth."

The rancher's way of approaching a horse was singularly different from his son's, notwithstanding the fact that Spottie knew him and showed no uneasiness. The examination took only a moment.

"Tongue cut bad. Thet's a damn shame. Take thet bridle off. . . . There. If it'd been an ornery hoss, now. . . . Moore, how'd this happen?"

"We just rode in," replied Wilson, hurriedly. "I was saddling Spottie when Jack came up. He took a shine to the mustang and wanted to ride him. When Spottie reared—he's shy with strangers—why, Jack gave a hell of a jerk on the bridle. The bit cut Spottie. . . . Well, that made me mad, but I held in. I objected to Jack riding Spottie. You see, Hudson was hurt yesterday and he appointed me foreman for to-day. I needed Spottie. But your son couldn't see it, and that made me sore. Jack said the mustang was his—"

"His?" interrupted Belllounds.

"Yes. He claimed Spottie. Well, he wasn't really mine, so I gave in. When I threw off the saddle, which *was* mine, Jack began to roar. He said he was foreman and he'd have me discharged. But I said I'd quit already. We both kept getting sorer and I called him Buster Jack. . . . He hit me first. Then we fought. I reckon I was getting the best of him when he made a dive for Bludsoe's gun. And that's all."

"Boss, as sure as I'm a born cowman," put in Bludsoe, "he'd hev plugged Wils if he'd got my gun. At thet he damn near got it!"

The old man stroked his scant gray beard with his huge, steady hand, apparently not greatly concerned by the disclosure.

"Montana, what do you say?" he queried, as if he held strong store by that quiet cowboy's opinion.

"Wal, boss," replied Jim, reluctantly, "Buster Jack's temper was bad onct, but now it's plumb wuss."

Whereupon Belllounds turned to Moore with a gesture and a look of a man who, in justice to something in himself, had to speak.

"Wils, it's onlucky you clashed with Jack right off," he said. "But thet was to be expected. I reckon Jack was in the wrong. Thet hoss was yours by all a cowboy holds right an' square. Mebbe by law Spottie belonged to White Slides Ranch—to me. But he's yours now, fer I give him to you."

"Much obliged, Belllounds. I sure do appreciate that," replied Moore, warmly. "It's what anybody'd gamble Bill Belllounds would do."

"Ahuh! An' I'd take it as a favor if you'd stay on to-day an' get thet brandin' done."

"All right, I'll do that for you," replied Moore. "Lem, I guess you won't get your sleep till to-night. Come on."

"Aw!" sighed Lem, as he picked up his bridle.

Late that afternoon Columbine sat upon the porch, watching the sunset. It had been a quiet day for her, mostly indoors. Once only had she seen Jack, and then he was riding by, toward the pasture, whirling a lasso round his head. Jack could ride like one born to the range, but he was not adept in the use of a rope. Nor had Columbine seen the old rancher since breakfast. She had heard his footsteps, however, pacing slowly up and down his room.

She was watching the last rays of the setting sun rimming with gold the ramparts of the mountain eastward, and burning a crown for Old White Slides peak. A distant bawl and bellow of cattle had died away. The branding was over for that fall. How glad she felt! The wind, beginning to grow cold as the sun declined, cooled her hot face. In the solitude of her room Columbine had cried enough that day to scald her cheeks.

Presently, down the lane between the pastures, she saw a cowboy ride into view. Very slowly he came, leading another horse. Columbine recognized Lem a second before she saw that he was leading Pronto. That struck her as strange. Another glance showed Pronto to be limping. Apparently he could just get along, and that was all. Columbine ran out in dismay, reaching the corral gate before Lem did. At first she had eyes only for her beloved mustang.

"Oh, Lem—Pronto's hurt!" she cried.

"Wal, I should smile he is," replied Lem.

But Lem was not smiling. And when he wore a serious face for Columbine something had indeed happened. The cowboy was the color of dust and so tired that he reeled.

"Lem, he's all bloody!" exclaimed Columbine, as she ran toward Pronto.

"Hyar, you jest wait," ordered Lem, testily. "Pronto's all cut up, an' you gotta hustle some linen an' salve."

Columbine flew away to do his bidding, and so quick and violent was she that when she got back to the corral she was out of breath. Pronto whinnied as she fell, panting, on her knees beside Lem, who was examining bloody gashes on the legs of the mustang.

"Wal, I reckon no great harm did," said Lem, with relief. "But he shore hed a close shave. Now you help me doctor him up."

"Yes—I'll help," panted Columbine. "I've done this kind—of thing often—but never—to Pronto. . . . Oh, I was afraid—he'd been gored by a steer."

"Wal, he come damn near bein'," replied Lem, grimly. "An' if it hedn't been fer ridin' you don't see every day, why thet ornery Texas steer'd hev got him."

"Who was riding? Lem, was it you? Oh, I'll never be able to do enough for you!"

"Wuss luck, it weren't me," said Lem.

"No? Who, then?"

"Wal, it was Wils, an' he made me swear to tell you nuthin'—leastways about him."

"Wils! Did *he* save Pronto? . . . And didn't want you to tell me? Lem, something has happened. You're not like yourself."

"Miss Collie, I reckon I'm nigh all in," replied Lem, wearily. "When I git this bandagin' done I'll fall right off my hoss."

"But you're on the ground now, Lem," said Columbine, with a nervous laugh. "What happened?"

"Did you hear about the argyment this mawnin'?"

"No. What—who—"

"You can ask Ole Bill about thet. The way Pronto was hurt come off like this. Buster Jack rode out to where we was brandin' an' jumped his hoss over a fence into the pasture. He hed a rope an' he got to chasin' some hosses over thar. One was Pronto, an' the son-of-a-gun somehow did git the noose over Pronto's head. But he couldn't hold it, or didn't want to, fer Pronto broke loose an' jumped the fence. This wasn't so bad as far as it went. But one of them bad steers got after Pronto. He run an' sure stepped on the rope, an' fell. The big steer nearly piled on him. Pronto broke some records then. He shore was scared. Howsoever he picked out rough ground an' run plumb into some dead brush. Reckon thar he got cut up. We was all a good ways off. The steer went bawlin' an' plungin' after Pronto. Wils yelled fer a rifle, but nobody hed one. Nor a six-shooter, either. . . . I'm goin' back to packin' a gun. Wal, Wils did some ridin' to git over thar in time to save Pronto."

"Lem, that is not all," said Columbine, earnestly, as the cowboy concluded. Her knowledge of the range told her that Lem had narrated nothing so far which could have been cause for his cold, grim, evasive manner; and her woman's intuition divined a catastrophe.

"Nope. . . . Wils's hoss fell on him."

Lem broke that final news with all a cowboy's bluntness.

"Was he hurt—*Lem!*" cried Columbine.

"Say, Miss Collie," remonstrated Lem, "we're doctorin' up your hoss. You needn't drop everythin' an' grab me like thet. An' you're white as a sheet, too. It ain't nuthin' much fer a cowboy to hev a hoss fall on him."

"Lem Billings, I'll hate you if you don't tell me quick," flashed Columbine, fiercely.

"Ahuh! So thet's how the land lays," replied Lem, shrewdly. "Wal, I'm sorry to tell you thet Wils was bad hurt. Now, not *real* bad! . . . The hoss fell on his leg an' broke it. I cut off his boot. His foot was all smashed. But thar wasn't any other hurt—honest! They're takin' him to Kremmlin'."

"Ah!" Columbine's low cry sounded strangely in her ears, as if some one else had uttered it.

"Buster Jack made two bursts this hyar day," concluded Lem, reflectively. "Miss Collie, I ain't shore how you're regardin' that individool, but I'm tellin' you this, fer your own good. He's bad medicine. He has his old man's temper thet riles up at nuthin' an' never felt a halter. Wusser'n thet, he's spoiled an' he acts like a colt thet'd tasted loco. The idee of his ropin' Pronto right thar near the round-up! Any one would think he jest come West. Old Bill is no fool. But he wears blinders when he looks at his son. I'm predictin' bad days fer White Slides Ranch."

CHAPTER 4

Only one man at Meeker appeared to be attracted by the news that Rancher Bill Belllounds was offering employment. This was a little cadaverous-looking fellow, apparently neither young nor old, who said his name was Bent Wade. He had drifted into Meeker with two poor horses and a pack.

"Whar you from?" asked the innkeeper, observing how Wade cared for his horses before he thought of himself. The query had to be repeated.

"Cripple Creek. I was cook for some miners an' I panned gold between times," was the reply.

"Humph! Thet oughter been a better-payin' job than any to be hed hereabouts."

"Yes, got big pay there," said Wade, with a sigh.

"What'd you leave fer?"

"We hed a fight over the diggin's an' I was the only one left. I'll tell you. . . ." Whereupon Wade sat down on a box, removed his old sombrero, and began to talk. An idler sauntered over, attracted by something. Then a miner happened by to halt and join the group.

Next, old Kemp, the patriarch of the village, came and listened attentively. Wade seemed to have a strange magnetism, a magic tongue.

He was small of stature, but wiry and muscular. His garments were old, soiled, worn. When he removed the wide-brimmed sombrero he exposed a remarkable face. It was smooth except for a drooping mustache, and pallid, with drops of sweat standing out on the high, broad forehead; gaunt and hollow-cheeked, with an enormous nose, and cavernous eyes set deep under shaggy brows. These features, however, were not so striking in themselves. Long, sloping, almost invisible lines of pain, the shadow of mystery and gloom in the deepset, dark eyes, a sad harmony between features and expression, these marked the man's face with a record no keen eye could miss.

Wade told a terrible tale of gold and blood and death. It seemed to relieve him. His face changed, and lost what might have been called its tragic light, its driven intensity.

His listeners shook their heads in awe. Hard tales were common in Colorado, but this one was exceptional. Two of the group left without comment. Old Kemp stared with narrow, half-recognizing eyes at the newcomer.

"Wal! Wal!" ejaculated the innkeeper. "It do beat hell what can happen! . . . Stranger, will you put up your hosses an' stay?"

"I'm lookin' for work," replied Wade.

It was then that mention was made of Belllounds sending to Meeker for hands.

"Old Bill Belllounds thet settled Middle Park an' made friends with the Utes," said Wade, as if certain of his facts.

"Yep, you have Bill to rights. Do you know him?"

"I seen him once twenty years ago."

"Ever been to Middle Park? Belllounds owns ranches there," said the innkeeper.

"He ain't livin' in the Park now," interposed Kemp. "He's at White Slides, I reckon, these last eight or ten years. Thet's over the Gore Range."

"Prospected all through that country," said Wade.

"Wal, it's a fine part of Colorado. Hay an' stock country—too high fer grain. Did you mean you'd been through the Park?"

"Once—long ago," replied Wade, staring with his great, cavernous eyes into space. Some memory of Middle Park haunted him.

"Wal, then, I won't be steerin' you wrong," said the innkeeper. "I like thet country. Some people don't. An' I say if you can cook or pack or punch cows or 'most anythin' you'll find a bunk with Old Bill. I under-stand he was needin' a hunter most of all. Lions an' wolves bad! Can you hunt?"

"Hey?" queried Wade, absently, as he inclined his ear. "I'm deaf on one side."

"Are you a good man with dogs an' guns?" shouted his questioner.

"Tolerable," replied Wade.

"Then you're sure of a job."

"I'll go. Much obliged to you."

"Not a-tall. I'm doin' Belllounds a favor. Reckon you'll put up here to-night?"

"I always sleep out. But I'll buy feed an' supplies," replied Wade, as he turned to his horses.

Old Kemp trudged down the road, wagging his gray head as if he was contending with a memory sadly failing him. An hour later when Bent Wade rode out of town he passed Kemp, and hailed him. The old-timer suddenly slapped his leg: "By Golly! I knowed I'd met him before!"

Later, he said with a show of gossipy excitement to his friend the innkeeper, "Thet fellar was Bent Wade!"

"So he told me," returned the other.

"But didn't you never hear of him? *Bent Wade?*"

"Now you tax me, thet name do 'pear familiar. But dash take it, I can't remember. I knowed he was somebody, though. Hope I didn't wish a gun-fighter or outlaw on Old Bill. Who was he, anyhow?"

"They call him Hell-Bent Wade. I seen him in Wyomin', whar he were a stage-driver. But I never heerd who he was an' what he was till years after. Thet was onct I dropped down into Boulder. Wade was thar, all shot up, bein' nussed by Sam Coles. Sam's dead now. He was a friend of Wade's an' knowed him fer long. Wal, I heerd all thet anybody ever heerd about him, I reckon. Accordin' to Coles this hyar Hell-Bent Wade was a strange, wonderful sort of fellar. He had the most amazin' ways. He could do anythin' under the sun better 'n any one else. Bad with guns! He never stayed in one place fer long. He never hunted trouble, but trouble follered him. As I remember Coles, thet was Wade's queer idee—he couldn't shake trouble. No matter whar he went, always thar was hell. Thet's what gave him the name Hell-Bent. . . . An' Coles swore thet Wade was the whitest man he ever knew. Heart of gold, he said. Always savin' somebody, helpin' somebody, givin' his money or time— never thinkin' of himself a-tall. . . . When he began to tell thet story about Cripple Creek then my ole head begun to ache with remem- berin'. Fer I'd heerd Bent Wade talk before. Jest the same kind of story he told hyar, only wuss. Lordy! but thet fellar has seen times. An' queerest of all is thet idee he has how hell's on his trail an' everywhere he roams it ketches up with him, an' thar he meets the man who's got to hear his tale!"

Sunset found Bent Wade far up the valley of White River under the shadow of the Flat Top Mountains.

It was beautiful country. Grassy hills, with colored aspen groves, swelled up on his left, and across the brawling stream rose a league-long slope of black spruce, above which the bare red-and-gray walls of the range towered, glorious with the blaze of sinking sun. White patches of snow showed in the sheltered nooks. Wade's gaze rested longest on the colored heights.

By and by the narrow valley opened into a park, at the upper end of which stood a log cabin. A few cattle and horses grazed in an inclosed pasture. The trail led by the cabin. As Wade rode up a bushy-haired man came out of the door, rifle in hand. He might have been going out to hunt, but his scrutiny of Wade was that of a lone settler in a wild land.

"Howdy, stranger!" he said.

"Good evenin'," replied Wade. "Reckon you're Blair an' I'm nigh the headwaters of this river?"

"Yep, a matter of three miles to Trapper's Lake."

"My name's Wade. I'm packin' over to take a job with Bill Bell- lounds."

"Git down an' come in," returned Blair. "Bill's man stopped with me some time ago."

"Obliged, I'm sure, but I'll be goin' on," responded Wade. "Do you happen to have a hunk of deer meat? Game powerful scarce comin' up this valley."

"Lots of deer an' elk higher up. I chased a bunch of more 'n thirty, I reckon, right out of my pasture this mornin'."

Blair crossed to an open shed near by and returned with half a deer haunch, which he tied upon Wade's pack-horse.

"My ole woman's ailin'. Do you happen to hev some terbaccer?"

"I sure do—both smokin' an' chewin', an' I can spare more chewin'. A little goes a long ways with me."

"Wal, gimme some of both, most chewin'," replied Blair, with evident satisfaction.

"You acquainted with Belllounds?" asked Wade, as he handed over the tobacco.

"Wal, yes, everybody knows Bill. You'd never find a whiter boss in these hills."

"Has he any family?"

"Now, I can't say as to thet," replied Blair. "I heerd he lost a wife years ago. Mebbe he married ag'in. But Bill's gittin' along."

"Good day to you, Blair," said Wade, and took up his bridle.

"Good day an' good luck. Take the right-hand trail. Better trot up a bit, if you want to make camp before dark."

Wade soon entered the spruce forest. Then he came to a shallow, roaring river. The horses drank the water, foaming white and amber around their knees, and then with splash and thump they forded it over the slippery rocks. As they cracked out upon the trail a covey of grouse whirred up into the low branches of spruce-trees. They were tame.

"That's somethin' like," said Wade. "First birds I've seen this fall. Reckon I can have stew any day."

He halted his horse and made a move to dismount, but with his eyes on the grouse he hesitated. "Tame as chickens, an' they sure are pretty."

Then he rode on, leading his pack-horse. The trail was not steep, although in places it had washed out, thus hindering a steady trot. As he progressed the forest grew thick and darker, and the fragrance of pine and spruce filled the air. A dreamy roar of water rushing over rocks rang in the traveler's ears. It receded at times, then grew louder. Presently the forest shade ahead lightened and he rode out into a wide space where green moss and flags and flowers surrounded a wonderful spring-hole. Sunset gleams shone through the trees to color the wide, round pool. It was shallow all along the margin, with a deep, large green hole in the middle, where the water boiled up. Trout were feeding on gnats and playing on the surface, and some big ones left wakes behind them as they sped to deeper water. Wade had an appreciative eye for all this beauty, his gaze lingering longest upon the flowers.

"Wild woods is the place for me," he soliloquized, as the cool wind fanned his cheeks and the sweet tang of evergreen tingled his nostrils. "But sure I'm most haunted in these lonely, silent places."

Bent Wade had the look of a haunted man. Perhaps the consciousness he confessed was part of his secret.

Twilight had come when again he rode out into the open. Trapper's Lake lay before him, a beautiful sheet of water, mirroring the black slopes and the fringed spruces and the flat peaks. Over all its gray, twilight-softened surface showed little swirls and boils and splashes where the myriads of trout were rising. The trail led out over open grassy shores, with a few pines straggling down to the lake, and clumps of spruces raising dark blurs against the background of gleaming lake. Wade heard a sharp crack of hoofs on rock, and he knew he had disturbed deer at their drinking; also he heard a ring of horns on the branch of a tree, and was sure an elk was slipping off through the woods. Across the lake he saw a camp-fire and a pale, sharp-pointed object that was a trapper's tent or an Indian's tepee.

Selecting a camp-site for himself, he unsaddled his horse, threw the pack off the other, and, hobbling both animals, he turned them loose. His roll of bedding, roped in canvas tarpaulin, he threw under a spruce-tree. Then he opened his oxhide-covered packs and laid out utensils and bags, little and big. All his movements were methodical, yet swift, accurate, habitual. He was not thinking about what he was doing. It took him some little time to find a suitable log to split for firewood, and when he had started a blaze night had fallen, and the light as it grew and brightened played fantastically upon the isolating shadows.

Lid and pot of the little Dutch oven he threw separately upon the sputtering fire, and while they heated he washed his hands, mixed the biscuits, cut slices of meat off the deer haunch, and put water on to boil. He broiled his meat on the hot, red coals, and laid it near on clean pine chips, while he waited for bread to bake and coffee to boil. The smell of wood-smoke and odorous steam from pots and the fragrance of spruce mingled together, keen, sweet, appetizing. Then he ate his simple meal hungrily, with the content of the man who had fared worse.

After he had satisfied himself he washed his utensils and stowed them away, with the bags. Whereupon his movements acquired less dexterity and speed. The rest hour had come. Still, like the long-experienced man in the open, he looked around for more to do, and his gaze fell upon his weapons, lying on his saddle. His rifle was a Henry—shiny and smooth from long service and care. His small gun was a Colt's .45. It had been carried in a saddle holster. Wade rubbed the rifle with his hands, and then with a greasy rag which he took from the sheath. After that he held the rifle to the heat of the fire. A squall of rain had overtaken him that day, wetting his weapons. A subtle and singular difference seemed to show in the way he took up the Colt's. His action was slow, his look reluctant. The small gun was not merely a thing of steel and powder and ball. He dried it and rubbed it with care, but not with love, and then he stowed it away.

Next Wade unrolled his bed under the spruce, with one end of the tarpaulin resting on the soft mat of needles. On top of that came the two woolly sheepskins, which he used to lie upon, then his blankets, and over all the other end of the tarpaulin.

This ended his tasks for the day. He lighted his pipe and composed himself beside the camp-fire to smoke and rest awhile before going to bed. The silence of the wilderness enfolded lake and shore; yet presently it came to be a silence accentuated by near and distant sounds, faint, wild, lonely—the low hum of falling water, the splash of tiny waves on the shore, the song of insects, and the dismal hoot of owls.

"Bill Belllounds—an' he needs a hunter," soliloquized Bent Wade, with gloomy, penetrating eyes, seeing far through the red embers. "That will suit me an' change my luck, likely. Livin' in the woods, away from people—I could stick to a job like that. . . . But if this White Slides is close to the old trail I'll never stay."

He sighed, and a darker shadow, not from flickering fire, overspread his cadaverous face. Eighteen years ago he had driven the woman he loved away from him, out into the world with her baby girl. Never had he rested beside a camp-fire that that old agony did not recur! Jealous fool!

Too late he had discovered his fatal blunder; and then had begun a search over Colorado, ending not a hundred miles across the wild mountains from where he brooded that lonely hour—a search ended by news of the massacre of a wagon-train by Indians.

That was Bent Wade's secret.

And no earthly sufferings could have been crueler than his agony and remorse, as through the long years he wandered on and on. The very good that he tried to do seemed to foment evil. The wisdom that grew out of his suffering opened pitfalls for his wandering feet. The wildness of men and the passion of women somehow waited with incredible fatality for that hour when chance led him into their lives. He had toiled, he had given, he had fought, he had sacrificed, he had killed, he had endured for the human nature which in his savage youth he had betrayed. Yet out of his supreme and endless striving to undo, to make reparation, to give his life, to find God, had come, it seemed to Wade in his abasement, only a driving torment.

But though his thought and emotion fluctuated, varying, wandering, his memory held a fixed and changeless picture of a woman, fair and sweet, with eyes of nameless blue, and face as white as a flower.

"Baby would have been—let's see—'most nineteen years old now—if she'd lived," he said. "A big girl, I reckon, like her mother. . . . Strange how, as I grow older, I remember better!"

The night wind moaned through the spruces; dark clouds scudded across the sky, blotting out the bright stars; a steady, low roar of water came from the outlet of the lake. The camp-fire flickered and burned out, so that no sparks blew into the blackness, and the red embers glowed and paled and crackled. Wade at length got up and made ready for bed. He threw back tarpaulin and blankets, and laid his rifle alongside where he could cover it. His coat served for a pillow and he put the Colt's gun under that; then pulling off his boots, he slipped into bed, dressed as he was, and, like all men in the open, at once fell asleep.

For Wade, and for countless men like him, who for many years had roamed the West, this sleeping alone in wild places held both charm and peril. But the fascination of it was only a vague realization, and the danger was laughed at.

Over Bent Wade's quiet form the shadows played, the spruce boughs waved, the piny needles rustled down, the wind moaned louder as the night advanced. By and by the horses rested from their grazing; the insects ceased to hum; and the continuous roar of water dominated the solitude. If wild animals passed Wade's camp they gave it a wide berth.

S unrise found Wade on the trail, climbing high up above the lake, making for the pass over the range. He walked, leading his horses up a zigzag trail that bore the tracks of recent travelers. Although this country was sparsely settled, yet there were men always riding from camp to camp or from one valley town to another. Wade never tarried on a well-trodden trail.

As he climbed higher the spruce-trees grew smaller, no longer forming a green aisle before him, and at length they became dwarfed and stunted, and at last failed altogether. Soon he was above timber-line and out upon a flat-topped mountain range, where in both directions the land rolled and dipped, free of tree or shrub, colorful with grass and flowers. The elevation exceeded eleven thousand feet. A whipping wind swept across the plain-land. The sun was pale-bright in the east, slowly being obscured by gray clouds. Snow began to fall, first in scudding, scanty flakes, but increasing until the air was full of a great, fleecy swirl. Wade rode along the rim of a mountain wall, watching a beautiful snow-storm falling into the brown gulf beneath him. Once as he headed round a break he caught sight of mountain-sheep cuddled under a protecting shelf. The snow-squall blew away, like a receding wall, leaving grass and flowers wet. As the dark clouds parted, the sun shone warmer out of the blue. Gray peaks, with patches of white, stood up above their black-timbered slopes.

Wade soon crossed the flat-topped pass over the range and faced a descent, rocky and bare at first, but yielding gradually to the encroachment of green. He left the cold winds and bleak trails above him. In an hour, when he was half down the slope, the forest had become warm and dry, fragrant and still. At length he rode out upon the brow of a last wooded bench above a grassy valley, where a bright, winding stream gleamed in the sun. While the horses rested Wade looked about him. Nature never tired him. If he had any peace it emanated from the silent places, the solemn hills, the flowers and animals of the wild and lonely land.

A few straggling pines shaded this last low hill above the valley. Grass grew luxuriantly there in the open, but not under the trees, where the brown needle-mats jealously obstructed the green. Clusters of columbines waved their graceful, sweet, pale-blue flowers that Wade felt a joy in seeing. He loved flowers—columbines, the glory of Colorado, came first, and next the many-hued purple asters, and then the flaunting spikes of paint-brush, and after them the nameless and numberless wild flowers that decked the mountain meadows and colored the grass of the aspen groves and peeped out of the edge of snowfields.

"Strange how it seems good to live—when I look at a columbine—or watch a beaver at his work—or listen to the bugle of an elk!" mused Bent Wade. He wondered why, with all his life behind him, he could still find comfort in these things.

Then he rode on his way. The grassy valley, with its winding stream, slowly descended and widened, and left foothill and mountain far behind. Far across a wide plain rose another range, black and bold against the blue. In the afternoon Wade reached Elgeria, a small hamlet, but important by reason of its being on the main stage line, and because here miners and cattlemen bought supplies. It had one street, so wide it appeared to be a square, on which faced a line of bold board houses with high, flat fronts. Wade rode to the inn where the stagecoaches made headquarters. It suited him to feed and rest his horses there, and partake of a meal himself, before resuming his journey.

The proprietor was a stout, pleasant-faced little woman, loquacious and amiable, glad to see a stranger for his own sake rather than from considerations of possible profit. Though Wade had never before visited Elgeria, he soon knew all about the town, and the miners up in the hills, and the only happenings of moment—the arrival and departure of stages.

"Prosperous place," remarked Wade. "I saw that. An' it ought to be growin'."

"Not so prosperous fer me as it uster be," replied the lady. "We did well when my husband was alive, before our competitor come to town. He runs a hotel where miners can drink an' gamble. I don't . . . But I reckon I've no cause to complain. I live."

"Who runs the other hotel?"

"Man named Smith. Reckon thet's not his real name. I've had people here who—but it ain't no matter."

"Men change their names," replied Wade.

"Stranger, air you packin' through or goin' to stay?"

"On my way to White Slides Ranch, where I'm goin' to work for Bell-lounds. Do you know him?"

"Know Bill Belllounds? Me? Wal, he's the best friend I ever had when I was at Kremmlin'. I lived there several years. My husband had stock there. In fact, Bill started us in the cattle business. But we got out of there an' come here, where Bob died, an' I've been stuck ever since."

"Everybody has a good word for Belllounds," observed Wade.

"You'll never hear a bad one," replied the woman, with cheerful warmth. "Bill never had but one fault, an' people loved him fer thet."

"What was it?"

"He's got a wild boy thet he thinks the sun rises an' sets in. Buster Jack, they call him. He used to come here often. But Bill sent him away somewhere. The boy was spoiled. I saw his mother years ago—she's dead this long time—an' she was no wife fer Bill Belllounds. Jack took after her. An' Bill was thet woman's slave. When she died all his big heart went to the son, an' thet accounts. Jack will never be any good."

Wade thoughtfully nodded his head, as if he understood, and was pondering other possibilities.

"Is he the only child?"

"There's a girl, but she's not Bill's kin. He adopted her when she was a baby. An' Jack's mother hated this child—jealous, we used to think, because it might grow up an' get some of Bill's money."

"What's the girl's name?" asked Wade.

"Columbine. She was over here last summer with Old Bill. They stayed with me. It was then Bill had hard words with Smith across the street. Bill was resentin' somethin' Smith put in my way. Wal, the lass 's the prettiest I ever seen in Colorado, an' as good as she's pretty. Old Bill hinted to me he'd likely make a match between her an' his son Jack. An' I ups an' told him, if Jack hadn't turned over a new leaf when he come home, thet such a marriage would be tough on Columbine. Whew but Old Bill was mad. He jest can't stand a word ag'in' thet Buster Jack."

"Columbine Belllounds," mused Wade. "Queer name."

"Oh, I've knowed three girls named Columbine. Don't you know the flower? It's common in these parts. Very delicate, like a sago lily, only paler."

"Were you livin' in Kremmlin' when Belllounds adopted the girl?" asked Wade.

"Laws no!" was the reply. "Thet was long before I come to Middle Park. But I heerd all about it. The baby was found by gold-diggers up in the mountains. Must have got lost from a wagon-train thet Indians set on soon after—so the miners said. Anyway, Old Bill took the baby an' raised her as his own."

"How old is she now?" queried Wade, with a singular change in his tone.

"Columbine's around nineteen."

Bent Wade lowered his head a little, hiding his features under the old, battered, wide-brimmed hat. The amiable innkeeper did not see the tremor that passed over him, nor the slight stiffening that followed, nor the gray pallor of his face. She went on talking until some one called her.

Wade went outdoors, and with bent head walked down the street, across a little river, out into green pasture-land. He struggled with an amazing possibility. Columbine Belllounds might be his own daughter. His heart leaped with joy. But the joy was short-lived. No such hope in this world for Bent Wade! This coincidence, however, left him with a strange, prophetic sense in his soul of a tragedy coming to White Slides Ranch. Wade possessed some power of divination, some strange gift to pierce the veil of the future. But he could not exercise this power at will; it came involuntarily, like a messenger of trouble in the dark night. Moreover, he had never yet been able to draw away from the fascination of this knowledge. It lured him on. Always his decision had been to go on, to meet this boding circumstance, or to remain and meet it, in the hope that he might take some one's burden upon his shoulders. He sensed it now, in the keen, poignant clairvoyance of the moment—the tangle of life that he was about to enter. Old Bill Belllounds, big and fine, victim of love for a wayward son; Buster Jack, the waster, the tearer-down, the destroyer, the wild youth at a wild time; Columbine, the girl of unknown birth, good and loyal, subject to a condition sure to ruin her. Wade's strange mind revolved a hundred outcomes to this conflict of characters, but not one of them was the one that was written. That remained dark. Never had he received so strong a call out of the unknown, nor had he ever felt such intense curiosity. Hope had long been dead in him, except the one that he might atone in some way for the wrong he had done his wife. So the pangs of emotion that recurred, in spite of reason and bitterness, were not recognized by him as lingering hopes. Wade denied the human in him, but he thrilled at the thought of meeting Columbine Belllounds. There was something here beyond all his comprehension.

"It *might*—be true!" he whispered. "I'll know when I see her."

Then he walked back toward the inn. On the way he looked into the barroom of the hotel run by Smith. It was a hard-looking place, half full of idle men, whose faces were as open pages to Bent Wade. Curiosity did not wholly control the impulse that made him wait at the door till he could have a look at the man Smith. Somewhere, at some time, Wade had met most of the veterans of western Colorado. So much he had traveled! But the impulse that held him was answered and explained when Smith came in—a burly man, with an ugly scar marring one eye. Bent Wade recognized Smith. He recognized the scar. For that scar was his own mark, dealt to this man, whose name was not Smith, and who had been as evil as he looked, and whose nomadic life was not due to remorse or love of travel.

Wade passed on without being seen. This recognition meant less to him than it would have ten years ago, as he was not now the kind of man who hunted old enemies for revenge or who went to great lengths to keep out of their way. Men there were in Colorado who would shoot at him on sight. There had been more than one that had shot to his cost.

That night Wade camped in the foothills east of Elgeria, and upon the following day, at sunrise, his horses were breaking the frosty grass and ferns of the timbered range. This he crossed, rode down into a valley where a lonely cabin nestled, and followed an old, blazed trail that wound up the course of a brook. The water was of a color that made rock and sand and moss seem like gold. He saw no signs or tracks of game. A gray jay now and then screeched his approach to unseen denizens of the woods. The stream babbled past him over mossy ledges, under the dark shade of clumps of spruces, and it grew smaller as he progressed toward its source. At length it was lost in a swale of high, rank grass, and the blazed trail led on through heavy pine woods. At noon he reached the crest of the divide, and, halting upon an open, rocky eminence, he gazed down over a green and black forest, slow-descending to a great irregular park that was his destination for the night.

Wade needed meat, and to that end, as he went on, he kept a sharp lookout for deer, especially after he espied fresh tracks crossing the trail. Slipping along ahead of his horses, that followed him almost too closely to permit of his noiseless approach to game, he hunted all the way down to the great open park without getting a shot.

This park was miles across and miles long, covered with tall, waving grass, and it had straggling arms that led off into the surrounding belt of timber. It sloped gently toward the center, where a round, green acreage of grass gave promise of water. Wade rode toward this, keeping somewhat to the right, as he wanted to camp at the edge of the woods. Soon he rode out beyond one of the projecting peninsulas of forest to find the park spreading wider in that direction. He saw horses grazing with elk, and far down at the notch, where evidently the park had outlet in a narrow valley, he espied the black, hump-shaped, shaggy forms of buffalo. They bobbed off out of sight. Then the elk saw or scented him, and they trotted away, the antlered bulls ahead of the cows. Wade wondered if the horses were wild. They showed great interest, but no fear. Beyond them was a rising piece of ground, covered with pine, and it appeared to stand aloft from the forest on the far side as well as upon that by which he was approaching. Riding a mile or so farther he ascertained that this bit of wooded ground resembled an island in a lake. Presently he saw smoke arising above the treetops.

A tiny brook welled out of the green center of the park and meandered around to pass near the island of pines. Wade saw unmistakable signs of prospecting along this brook, and farther down, where he crossed it, he found tracks made that day.

The elevated plot of ground appeared to be several acres in extent, covered with small-sized pines, and at the far edge there was a little log cabin. Wade expected to surprise a lone prospector at his evening meal. As he rode up a dog ran out of the cabin, barking furiously. A man, dressed in fringed buckskin, followed. He was tall, and had long, iron-gray hair over his shoulders. His bronzed and weather-beaten face was a mass of fine wrinkles where the grizzled hair did not hide them, and his shining, red countenance proclaimed an honest, fearless spirit.

"Howdy, stranger!" he called, as Wade halted several rods distant.

His greeting was not welcome, but it was civil. His keen scrutiny, however, attested to more than his speech.

"Evenin', friend," replied Wade. "Might I throw my pack here?"

"Sure. Get down," answered the other. "I calkilate I never seen you in these diggin's."

"No. I'm Bent Wade, an' on my way to White Slides to work for Belllounds."

"Glad to meet you. I'm new hereabouts, myself, but I know Belllounds. My name's Lewis. I was jest cookin' grub. An' it'll burn, too, if I don't rustle. Turn your hosses loose an' come in."

Wade presented himself with something more than his usual methodical action. He smelled buffalo steak, and he was hungry. The cabin had been built years ago, and was a ramshackle shelter at best. The stone fireplace, however, appeared well preserved. A bed of red coals glowed and cracked upon the hearth.

"Reckon I sure smelled buffalo meat," observed Wade, with much satisfaction. "It's long since I chewed a hunk of that."

"All ready. Now pitch in . . . Yes, thar's some buffalo left in here. Not hunted much. Thar's lots of elk an' herds of deer. After a little snow you'd think a drove of sheep had been trackin' around. An' some bear."

Wade did not waste many words until he had enjoyed that meal. Later, while he helped his host, he recurred to the subject of game.

"If there's so many deer then there's lions an' wolves."

"You bet. I see tracks every day. Had a shot at a lofer not long ago. Missed him. But I reckon thar's more varmints over in the Troublesome country back of White Slides."

"Troublesome! Do they call it that?" asked Wade, with a queer smile.

"Sure. An' it *is* troublesome. Belllounds has been tryin' to hire a hunter. Offered me big wages to kill off the wolves an' lions."

"That's the job I'm goin' to take."

"Good!" exclaimed Lewis. "I'm sure glad. Belllounds is a nice fellar. I felt sort of cheap till I told him I wasn't really a hunter. You see, I'm prospectin' up here, an' pretendin' to be a hunter."

"What do you make that bluff for?" queried Wade. "You couldn't fool any one who'd ever prospected for gold. I saw your signs out here."

"Wal, you've sharp eyes, thet's all. Wade, I've some ondesirable neighbors over here. I'd just as lief they didn't see me diggin' gold. Lately I've had a hunch they're rustlin' cattle. Anyways, they've sold cattle in Kremmlin' thet came from over around Elgeria."

"Wherever there's cattle there's sure to be some stealin'," observed Wade.

"Wal, you needn't say anythin' to Belllounds, because mebbe I'm wrong. An' if I found out I was right I'd go down to White Slides an' tell it myself. Belllounds done me some favors."

"How far to White Slides?" asked Wade, with a puff on his pipe.

"Roundabout trail, an' rough, but you'll make it in one day, easy. Beautiful country. Open, big peaks an' ranges, with valleys an' lakes. Never seen such grass!"

"Did you ever see Belllounds's son?"

"No. Didn't know he hed one. But I seen his gal the fust day I was thar. She was nice to me. I went thar to be fixed up a bit. Nearly chopped my hand off. The gal—Columbine, she's called—doctored me up. Fact is, I owe considerable to thet White Slides Ranch. There's a cowboy, Wils somethin', who rode up here with some medicine fer me—some they didn't have when I was thar. You'll like thet boy. I seen he was sweet on the gal an' I sure couldn't blame him."

Bent Wade removed his pipe and let out a strange laugh, significant with its little note of grim confirmation.

"What's funny about thet?" demanded Lewis, rather surprised.

"I was only laughin'," replied Wade. "What you said about the cowboy bein' sweet on the girl popped into my head before you told it. Well, boys will be boys. I was young once an' had my day."

Lewis grunted as he bent over to lift a red coal to light his pipe, and as he raised his head he gave Wade a glance of sympathetic curiosity.

"Wal, I hope I'll see more of you," he said, as his guest rose, evidently to go.

"Reckon you will, as I'll be chasin' hounds all over. An' I want a look at them neighbors you spoke of that might be rustlers. . . . I'll turn in now. Good night."

CHAPTER 5

Bent Wade rode out of the forest to look down upon the White Slides country at the hour when it was most beautiful.

"Never seen the beat of that!" he exclaimed, as he halted.

The hour was sunset, with the golden rays and shadows streaking ahead of him down the rolling sage hills, all rosy and gray with rich, strange softness. Groves of aspens stood isolated from one another— here crowning a hill with blazing yellow, and there fringing the brow of another with gleaming gold, and lower down reflecting the sunlight with brilliant red and purple. The valley seemed filled with a delicate haze, almost like smoke. White Slides Ranch was hidden from sight, as it lay in the bottomland. The gray old peak towered proud and aloof, clear-cut and sunset-flushed against the blue. The eastern slope of the valley was a vast sweep of sage and hill and grassy bench and aspen bench, on fire with the colors of autumn made molten by the last flashing of the sun. Great black slopes of forest gave sharp contrast, and led up to the red-walled ramparts of the mountain range.

Wade watched the scene until the fire faded, the golden shafts paled and died, the rosy glow on sage changed to cold steel gray. Then he rode out upon the foothills. The trail led up and down slopes of sage. Grass grew thicker as he descended. Once he startled a great flock of prairie-chickens, or sage-hens, large gray birds, lumbering, swift fliers, that whirred up, and soon plumped down again into the sage. Twilight found him on a last long slope of the foothills, facing the pasture-land of the valley, with the ranch still five miles distant, now showing misty and dim in the gathering shadows.

Wade made camp where a brook ran near an aspen thicket. He had no desire to hurry to meet events at White Slides Ranch, although he longed to see this girl that belonged to Belllounds. Night settled down over the quiet foothills. A pack of roving coyotes visited Wade, and sat in a half-circle in the shadows back of the camp-fire. They howled and barked. Nevertheless sleep visited Wade's tired eyelids the moment he lay down and closed them.

Next morning, rather late, Wade rode down to White Slides Ranch. It looked to him like the property of a rich rancher who held to the old and proven customs of his generation. The corrals were new, but their style was old. Wade reflected that it would be hard for rustlers or horse-thieves to steal out of those corrals. A long lane led from the pasture-land, following the brook that ran through the corrals and by the back door of the rambling, comfortable-looking cabin. A cowboy was leading horses across a wide square between the main ranch-house and a cluster of cabins and sheds. He saw the visitor and waited.

"Mornin'," said Wade, as he rode up.

"Hod do," replied the cowboy.

Then these two eyed each other, not curiously nor suspiciously, but with that steady, measuring gaze common to Western men.

"My name's Wade," said the traveler. "Come from Meeker way. I'm lookin' for a job with Belllounds."

"I'm Lem Billings," replied the other. "Ridin' fer White Slides fer years. Reckon the boss'll be glad to take you on."

"Is he around?"

"Sure. I jest seen him," replied Billings, as he haltered his horses to a post. "I reckon I ought to give you a hunch."

"I'd take that as a favor."

"Wal, we're short of hands," said the cowboy. "Jest got the round-up over. Hudson was hurt an' Wils Moore got crippled. Then the boss's son has been put on as foreman. Three of the boys quit. Couldn't stand him. This hyar son of Belllounds is a son-of-a-gun! Me an' pards of mine,

Montana an' Bludsoe, are stickin' on—wal, fer reasons thet ain't egzactly love fer the boss. But Old Bill's the best of bosses. . . . Now the hunch is—thet if you git on hyar you'll hev to do two or three men's work."

"Much obliged," replied Wade. "I don't shy at that."

"Wal, git down an' come in," added Billings, heartily.

He led the way across the square, around the corner of the ranch-house, and up on a long porch, where the arrangement of chairs and blankets attested to the hand of a woman. The first door was open, and from it issued voices; first a shrill, petulant boy's complaint, and then a man's deep, slow, patient reply.

Lem Billings knocked on the door-jamb.

"Wal, what's wanted?" called Belllounds.

"Boss, thar's a man wantin' to see you," replied Lem.

Heavy steps approached the doorway and it was filled with the large figure of the rancher. Wade remembered Belllounds and saw only a gray difference in years.

"Good mornin', Lem, an' good mornin' to you, stranger," was the rancher's greeting, his bold, blue glance, honest and frank and keen, with all his long experience of men, taking Wade in with one flash.

Lem discreetly walked to the end of the porch as another figure, that of the son who resembled the father, filled the doorway, with eyes less kind, bent upon the visitor.

"My name's Wade. I'm over from Meeker way, hopin' to find a job with you," said Wade.

"Glad to meet you," replied Belllounds, extending his huge hand to shake Wade's. "I need you, sure bad. What's your special brand of work?"

"I reckon any kind."

"Set down, stranger," replied Belllounds, pulling up a chair. He seated himself on a bench and leaned against the log wall. "Now, when a boy comes an' says he can do anythin', why I jest haw! haw! at him. But you're a man, Wade, an' one as has been there. Now I'm hard put fer hands. Jest speak out now fer yourself. No one else can speak fer you, thet's sure. An' this is bizness."

"Any work with stock, from punchin' steers to doctorin' horses," replied Wade, quietly. "Am fair carpenter an' mason. Good packer. Know farmin'. Can milk cows an' make butter. I've been cook in many outfits.

Read an' write an' not bad at figures. Can do work on saddles an' harness, an—"

"Hold on!" yelled Belllounds, with a hearty laugh. "I ain't imposin' on no man, no matter how I need help. You're sure a jack of all range trades. An' I wish you was a hunter."

"I was comin' to that. You didn't give me time."

"Say, do you know hounds?" queried Belllounds, eagerly.

"Yes. Was raised where everybody had packs. I'm from Kentucky. An' I've run hounds off an' on for years. I'll tell you—"

Belllounds interrupted Wade.

"By all that's lucky! An' last, can you handle guns? We ain't had a good shot on this range fer Lord knows how long. I used to hit plumb center with a rifle. My eyes are pore now. An' my son can't hit a flock of haystacks. An' the cowpunchers are 'most as bad. Sometimes right hyar where you could hit elk with a club we're out of fresh meat."

"Yes, I can handle guns," replied Wade, with a quiet smile and a lowering of his head. "Reckon you didn't catch my name."

"Wal—no, I didn't," slowly replied Belllounds, and his pause, with the keener look he bestowed upon Wade, told how the latter's query had struck home.

"Wade—Bent Wade," said Wade, with quiet distinctness.

"*Not Hell-Bent Wade!*" ejaculated Belllounds.

"The same. . . . I ain't proud of the handle, but I never sail under false colors."

"Wal, I'll be damned!" went on the rancher. "Wade, I've heerd of you fer years. Some bad, but most good, an' I reckon I'm jest as glad to meet you as if you'd been somebody else."

"You'll give me the job?"

"I should smile."

"I'm thankin' you. Reckon I was some worried. Jobs are hard for me to get an' harder to keep."

"Thet's not onnatural, considerin' the hell which's said to camp on your trail," replied Belllounds, dryly. "Wade, I can't say I take a hell of a lot of stock in such talk. Fifty years I've been west of the Missouri. I know the West an' I know men. Talk flies from camp to ranch, from diggin's to town, an' always some one adds a little more. Now I trust my judgment an' I trust men. No one ever betrayed me yet."

"I'm that way, too," replied Wade. "But it doesn't pay, an' yet I still kept on bein' that way. . . . Belllounds, my name's as bad as good all over western Colorado. But as man to man I tell you—I never did a low-down trick in my life. . . . Never but once."

"An' what was thet?" queried the rancher, gruffly.

"I killed a man who was innocent," replied Wade, with quivering lips, "an'—an' drove the woman I loved to her death."

"Aw! we all make mistakes some time in our lives," said Belllounds, hurriedly. "I made 'most as big a one as yours—so help me God! . . ."

"I'll tell you—" interrupted Wade.

"You needn't tell me anythin'," said Belllounds, interrupting in his turn. "But at thet some time I'd like to hear about the Lascelles outfit over on the Gunnison. I knowed Lascelles. An' a pardner of mine down in Middle Park came back from the Gunnison with the dog-gondest story I ever heerd. Thet was five years ago this summer. Of course I knowed your name long before, but this time I heerd it powerful strong. You got in thet mix-up to your neck. . . . Wal, what consarns me now is this. Is there any sense in the talk thet wherever you land there's hell to pay?"

"Belllounds, there's no sense in it, but a lot of truth," confessed Wade, gloomily.

"Ahuh! . . . Wal, Hell-Bent Wade, I'll take a chance on you," boomed the rancher's deep voice, rich with the intent of his big heart. "I've gambled all my life. An' the best friends I ever made were men I'd helped. . . . What wages do you ask?"

"I'll take what you offer."

"I'm payin' the boys forty a month, but thet's not enough fer you."

"Yes, that'll do."

"Good, it's settled," concluded Belllounds, rising. Then he saw his son standing inside the door. "Say, Jack, shake hands with Bent Wade, hunter an' all-around man. Wade, this's my boy. I've jest put him on as foreman of the outfit, an' while I'm at it I'll say thet you'll take orders from me an' not from him."

Wade looked up into the face of Jack Belllounds, returned his brief greeting, and shook his limp hand. The contact sent a strange chill over Wade. Young Belllounds's face was marred by a bruise and shaded by a sullen light.

"Get Billin's to take you out to thet new cabin an' sheds I jest had put up," said the rancher. "You'll bunk in the cabin. . . . Aw, I know. Men like you sleep in the open. But you can't do thet under Old White Slides in winter. Not much! Make yourself to home, an' I'll walk out after a bit an' we'll look over the dog outfit. When you see thet outfit you'll holler fer help."

Wade bowed his thanks, and, putting on his sombrero, he turned away. As he did so he caught a sound of light, quick footsteps on the far end of the porch.

"Hello, you-all!" cried a girl's voice, with melody in it that vibrated piercingly upon Wade's sensitive ears.

"Mornin', Columbine," replied the rancher.

Bent Wade's heart leaped up. This girlish voice rang upon the chord of memory. Wade had not the strength to look at her then. It was not that he could not bear to look, but that he could not bear the disillusion sure to follow his first glimpse of this adopted daughter of Belllounds. Sweet to delude himself! Ah! the years were bearing sterner upon his head! The old dreams persisted, sadder now for the fact that from long use they had become half-realities! Wade shuffled slowly across the green square to where the cowboy waited for him. His eyes were dim, and a sickness attended the sinking of his heart.

"Wade, I ain't a bettin' fellar, but I'll bet Old Bill took you up," vouchsafed Billings, with interest.

"Glad to say he did," replied Wade. "You're to show me the new cabin where I'm to bunk."

"Come along," said Lem, leading off. "Air you agoin' to handle stock or chase coyotes?"

"My job's huntin'."

"Wal, it may be thet from sunup to sundown, but betweentimes you'll be sure busy otherwise, I opine," went on Lem. "Did you meet the boss's son?"

"Yes, he was there. An' Belllounds made it plain I was to take orders from him an' not from his son."

"Thet'll make your job a million times easier," declared Lem, as if to make up for former hasty pessimism. He led the way past some log cabins, and sheds with dirt roofs, and low, flat-topped barns, out across another brook where willow-trees were turning yellow. Then the new cabin came into view. It was small, with one door and one window, and a porch across the front. It stood on a small elevation, near the swift brook, and overlooking the ranch-house perhaps a quarter of a mile below. Above it, and across the brook, had been built a high fence constructed of aspen poles laced closely together. The sounds therefrom proclaimed this stockade to be the dog-pen.

Lem helped Wade unpack and carry his outfit into the cabin. It contained one room, the corner of which was filled with blocks and slabs of pine, evidently left there after the construction of the cabin, and meant for firewood. The ample size of the stone fireplace attested to the severity of the winters.

"Real sawed boards on the floor!" exclaimed Lem, meaning to impress the newcomer. "I call this a plumb good bunk."

"Much too good for me," replied Wade.

"Wal, I'll look after your hosses," said Lem. "I reckon you'll fix up your bunk. Take my hunch an' ask Miss Collie to find you some furniture an' sich like. She's Ole Bill's daughter, an' she makes up fer—fer—wal, fer a lot we hev to stand. I'll fetch the boys over later."

"Do you smoke?" asked Wade. "I've somethin' fine I fetched up from Leadville."

"Smoke! Me? I'll give you a hoss right now for a cigar. I git one onct a year, mebbe."

"Here's a box I've been packin' for long," replied Wade, as he handed it up to Billings. "They're Spanish, all right. Too rich for my blood!"

A box of gold could not have made that cowboy's eyes shine any brighter.

"*Whoop-ee!*" he yelled. "Why, man, you're like the fairy in the kid's story! Won't I make the outfit wild? Aw, I forgot. Thar's only Jim an' Blud left. Wal, I'll divvy with them. Sure, Wade, you hit me right. I was dyin' fer a real smoke. An' I reckon what's mine is yours."

Then he strode out of the cabin, whistling a merry cowboy tune.

Wade was left sitting in the middle of the room on his roll of bedding, and for a long time he remained there motionless, with his head bent, his worn hands idly clasped. A heavy footfall outside aroused him from his meditation.

"Hey, Wade!" called the cheery voice of Belllounds. Then the rancher appeared at the door. "How's this bunk suit you?"

"Much too fine for an old-timer like me," replied Wade.

"Old-timer! Say, you're young yet. Look at me. Sixty-eight last birthday! Wal, every dog has his day. . . . What're you needin' to fix this bunk comfortable like?"

"Reckon I don't need much."

"Wal, you've beddin' an' cook outfit. Go get a table, an' a chair an' a bench from thet first cabin. The boys thet had it are gone. Somethin' with a back to it, a rockin'-chair, if there's one. You'll find tools, an' boxes, an' stuff in the workshop, if you want to make a cupboard or anythin'."

"How about a lookin'-glass?" asked Wade. "I had a piece, but I broke it."

"Haw! Haw! Mebbe we can rustle thet, too. My girl's good on helpin' the boys fix up. Woman-like, you know. An' she'll fetch you some decorations on her own hook. Now let's take a look at the hounds."

Belllounds led the way out toward the crude dog-corral, and the way he leaped the brook bore witness to the fact that he was still vigorous and spry. The door of the pen was made of boards hung on wire. As Belllounds opened it there came a pattering rush of many padded feet, and a chorus of barks and whines. Wade's surprised gaze took in forty or fifty dogs, mostly hounds, browns and blacks and yellows, all sizes—a motley, mangy, hungry pack, if he had ever seen one.

"I swore I'd buy every hound fetched to me, till I'd cleaned up the varmints around White Slides. An' sure I was imposed on," explained the rancher.

"Some good-lookin' hounds in the bunch," replied Wade. "An' there's hardly too many. I'll train two packs, so I can rest one when the other's huntin'."

"Wal, I'll be dog-goned!" ejaculated Belllounds, with relief. "I sure thought you'd roar. All this rabble to take care of!"

"No trouble after I've got acquainted," said Wade. "Have they been hunted any?"

"Some of the boys took out a bunch. But they split on deer tracks an' elk tracks an' Lord knows what all. Never put up a lion! Then again Billings took some out after a pack of coyotes, an' gol darn me if the coyotes didn't lick the hounds. An' wuss! Jack, my son, got it into his head thet he was a hunter. The other mornin' he found a fresh lion track back of the corral. An' he ups an' puts the whole pack of hounds on the trail. I had a good many more hounds in the pack than you see now. Wal, anyway, it was great to hear the noise thet pack made. Jack lost every blamed hound of them. Thet night an' next day an' the followin' they straggled in. But twenty some never did come back."

Wade laughed. "They may come yet. I reckon, though, they've gone home where they came from. Are any of these hounds recommended?"

"Every consarned one of them," declared Belllounds.

"That's funny. But I guess it's natural. Do you know for sure whether you bought any good dogs?"

"Yes, I gave fifty dollars for two hounds. Got them of a friend in Middle Park whose pack killed off the lions there. They're good dogs, trained on lion, wolf, an' bear."

"Pick 'em out," said Wade.

With a throng of canines crowding and fawning round him, and snapping at one another, it was difficult for the rancher to draw the two particular ones apart so they could be looked over. At length he succeeded, and Wade drove back the rest of the pack.

"The big fellar's Sampson an' the other's Jim," said Belllounds.

Sampson was a huge hound, gray and yellow, with mottled black marks, very long ears, and big, solemn eyes. Jim, a good-sized dog, but small in comparison with the other, was black all over, except around the nose and eyes. Jim had many scars. He was old, yet not past a vigorous age, and he seemed a quiet, dignified, wise hound, quite out of his element in that mongrel pack.

"If they're as good as they look we're lucky," said Wade, as he tied the ends of his rope round their necks. "Now are there any more you know are good?"

"Denver, come hyar!" yelled Belllounds. A white, yellow-spotted hound came wagging his tail. "I'll swear by Denver. An' there's one more—Kane. He's half bloodhound, a queer, wicked kind of dog. He keeps to himself. . . . Kane! Come hyar!"

Belllounds tramped around the corral, and finally found the hound in question, asleep in a dusty hole. Kane was the only beautiful dog in the lot. If half of him was bloodhound the other half was shepherd, for his black and brown hair was inclined to curl, and his head had the fine thoroughbred contour of the shepherd. His ears, long and drooping and thin, betrayed the hound in him. Kane showed no disposition to be friendly. His dark eyes, sad and mournful, burned with the fires of doubt.

Wade haltered Kane, Jim, and Sampson, which act almost precipitated a fight, and led them out of the corral. Denver, friendly and glad, followed at the rancher's heels.

"I'll keep them with me an' make lead dogs out of them," said Wade. "Belllounds, that bunch hasn't had enough to eat. They're half starved."

"Wal, thet's worried me more'n you'll guess," declared Belllounds, with irritation. "What do a lot of cow-punchin' fellers know about dogs? Why, they nearly ate Bludsoe up. He wouldn't feed 'em. An' Wils, who seemed good with dogs, was taken off bad hurt the other day. Lem's been tryin' to rustle feed fer them. Now we'll give back the dogs you don't want to keep, an' thet way thin out the pack."

"Yes, we won't need 'em all. An' I reckon I'll take the worry of this dog-pack off your mind."

"Thet's your job, Wade. My orders are fer you to kill off the varmints. Lions, wolves, coyotes. An' every fall some ole silvertip gits bad, an' now an' then other bears. Whatever you need in the way of supplies jest ask fer. We send regular to Kremmlin'. You can hunt fer two months yet, barrin' an onusual early winter. . . . I'm askin' you—if my son tramps on your toes—I'd take it as a favor fer you to be patient. He's only a boy yet, an' coltish."

Wade divined that was a favor difficult for Belllounds to ask. The old rancher, dominant and forceful and self-sufficient all his days, had begun to feel an encroachment of opposition beyond his control. If he but realized it, the favor he asked of Wade was an appeal.

"Belllounds, I get along with everybody," Wade assured him. "An' maybe I can help your son. Before I'd reached here I'd heard he was wild, an' so I'm prepared."

"If you'd do thet—wal, I'd never forgit it," replied the rancher, slowly. "Jack's been away fer three years. Only got back a week or so ago. I calkilated he'd be sobered, steadied, by—thet—thet work I put him to. But I'm not sure. He's changed. When he gits his own way he's all I could ask. But thet way he wants ain't always what it ought to be. An' so thar's been clashes. But Jack's a fine young man. An' he'll outgrow his temper an' crazy notions. Work'll do it."

"Boys will be boys," replied Wade, philosophically. "I've not forgotten when I was a boy."

"Neither hev I. Wal, I'll be goin', Wade. I reckon Columbine will be up to call on you. Bein' the only woman-folk in my house, she sort of runs it. An' she's sure interested in thet pack of hounds."

Belllounds trudged away, his fine old head erect, his gray hair shining in the sun.

Wade sat down upon the step of his cabin, pondering over the rancher's remarks about his son. Recalling the young man's physiognomy, Wade began to feel that it was familiar to him. He had seen Jack Belllounds before. Wade never made mistakes in faces, though he often had a task to recall names. And he began to go over the recent past, recalling all that he could remember of Meeker, and Cripple Creek, where he had worked for several months, and so on, until he had gone back as far as his last trip to Denver.

"Must have been there," mused Wade, thoughtfully, and he tried to recall all the faces he had seen. This was impossible, of course, yet he remembered many. Then he visualized the places in Denver that for one reason or another had struck him particularly. Suddenly into one of these flashed the pale, sullen, bold face of Jack Belllounds.

"It was *there*!" he exclaimed, incredulously. "Well! . . . If thet's not the strangest yet! Could I be mistaken? No. I saw him. . . . Belllounds must have known it—must have let him stay there. . . . Maybe put him there! He's just the kind of a man to go to extremes to reform his son."

Singular as was this circumstance, Wade dwelt only momentarily on it. He dismissed it with the conviction that it was another strange happening in the string of events that had turned his steps toward White Slides Ranch. Wade's mind stirred to the probability of an early sight of Columbine Belllounds. He would welcome it, both as interesting and pleasurable, and surely as a relief. The sooner a meeting with her was over the better. His life had been one long succession of shocks, so that it seemed nothing the future held could thrill him, amaze him, torment him. And yet how well he knew that his heart was only the more responsive for all it had withstood! Perhaps here at White Slides he might meet with an experience dwarfing all others. It was possible; it was in the nature of events. And though he repudiated such a possibility, he fortified himself against a subtle divination that he might at last have reached the end of his long trail, where anything might happen.

Three of the hounds lay down at Wade's feet. Kane, the bloodhound, stood watching this new master, after the manner of a dog who was a judge of men. He sniffed at Wade. He grew a little less surly.

Wade's gaze, however, was on the path that led down along the border of the brook to disappear in the willows. Above this clump of yellowing trees could be seen the ranch-house. A girl with fair hair stepped off the porch. She appeared to be carrying something in her arms, and shortly disappeared behind the willows. Wade saw her and surmised that she was coming to his cabin. He did not expect any more or think any more. His faculties condensed to the objective one of sight.

The girl, when she reappeared, was perhaps a hundred yards distant. Wade bent on her one keen, clear glance. Then his brain and his blood beat wildly. He saw a slender girl in riding-costume, lithe and strong, with the free step of one used to the open. It was this form, this step that struck Wade. "My—God! how like Lucy!" he whispered, and he tried to pierce the distance to see her face. It gleamed in the sunshine. Her fair hair waved in the wind. She was coming, but so slowly! All of Wade that was physical and emotional seemed to wait—clamped. The moment was agelong, with nothing beyond it. While she was still at a distance her face became distinct. And Wade sustained a terrible shock. . . . Then, as one in a dream, as in a blur of strained peering into a maze, he saw the face of his sweetheart, his wife, the Lucy of his early manhood. It moved him out of the past. Closer! Pang on pang quivered in his heart. Was this only a nightmare? Or had he at last gone mad! This girl raised her head. She was looking—she saw him. Terror mounted upon Wade's consciousness.

"That's Lucy's face!" he gasped. "So help—me, God! . . . It's for this— I wandered here! She's my flesh an' blood—my Lucy's child—my own!"

Fear and presentiment and blank amaze and stricken consciousness left him in the lightning-flash of divination that was recognition as well. A shuddering cataclysm enveloped him, a passion so stupendous that it almost brought oblivion.

The three hounds leaped up with barks and wagging tails. They welcomed this visitor. Kane lost still more of his canine aloofness.

Wade's breast heaved. The blue sky, the gray hills, the green willows, all blurred in his sight, that seemed to hold clear only the face floating closer.

"I'm Columbine Belllounds," said a voice.

It stilled the storm in Wade. It was real. It was a voice of twenty years ago. The burden on his breast lifted. Then flashed the spirit, the old self-control of a man whose life had held many terrible moments.

"Mornin', miss. I'm glad to meet you," he replied, and there was no break, no tone unnatural in his greeting.

So they gazed at each other, she with that instinctive look peculiar to women in its intuitive powers, but common to all persons who had lived far from crowds and to whom a newcomer was an event. Wade's gaze, intense and all-embracing, found that face now closer in resemblance to the imagined Lucy's—a pretty face, rather than beautiful, but strong and sweet—its striking qualities being a colorless fairness of skin that yet held a rose and golden tint, and the eyes of a rare and exquisite shade of blue.

"Oh! Are you feeling ill?" she asked. "You look so—so pale."

"No. I'm only tuckered out," replied Wade, easily, as he wiped the clammy drops from his brow. "It was a long ride to get here."

"I'm the lady of the house," she said, with a smile. "I'm glad to welcome you to White Slides, and hope you'll like it."

"Well, Miss Columbine, I reckon I will," he replied, returning the smile. "Now if I was younger I'd like it powerful much."

She laughed at that. "Men are all alike, young or old."

"Don't ever think so," said Wade, earnestly.

"No? I guess you're right about that. I've fetched you up some things for your cabin. May I peep in?"

"Come in," replied Wade, rising. "You must excuse my manners. It's long indeed since I had a lady caller."

She went in, and Wade, standing on the threshold, saw her survey the room with a woman's sweeping glance.

"I told dad to put some—"

"Miss, your dad told me to go get them, an' I've not done it yet. But I will presently."

"Very well. I'll leave these things and come back later," she replied, depositing a bundle upon the floor. "You won't mind if I try to—to make you a little comfortable. It's dreadful the way outdoor men live when they do get indoors."

"I reckon I'll be slow in lettin' you see what a good housekeeper I am," he replied. "Because then, maybe, I'll see more of you."

"Weren't you a sad flatterer in your day?" she queried, archly.

Her intonation, the tilt of her head, gave Wade such a pang that he could not answer. And to hide his momentary restraint he turned back to the hounds. Then she came out upon the porch.

"I love hounds," she said, patting Denver, which caress immediately made Jim and Sampson jealous. "I've gotten on pretty well with these, but that Kane won't make up. Isn't he splendid? But he's afraid—no, not afraid of me, but he doesn't like me."

"It's mistrust. He's been hurt. I reckon he'll get over that after a while."

"You don't beat dogs?" she asked, eagerly.

"No, miss. That's not the way to get on with hounds or horses."

Her glance was a blue flash of pleasure.

"How glad that makes me! Why, I quit coming here to see and feed the dogs because somebody was always kicking them around."

Wade handed the rope to her. "You hold them, so when I come out with some meat they won't pile over me." He went inside, took all that was left of the deer haunch out of his pack, and, picking up his knife, returned to the porch. The hounds saw the meat and yelped. They pulled on the rope.

"You hounds behave," ordered Wade, as he sat down on the step and began to cut the meat. "Jim, you're the oldest an' hungriest. Here. . . . Now you, Sampson. Here!" . . . The big hound snapped at the meat. Whereupon Wade slapped him. "Are you a pup or a wolf that you grab for it? Here." Sampson was slower to act, but he snapped again. Whereupon Wade hit him again, with open hand, not with violence or rancor, but a blow that meant Sampson must obey.

Next time the hound did not snap. Denver had to be cuffed several times before he showed deference to this new master. But the blood-hound Kane refused to take any meat out of Wade's hand. He growled and showed his teeth, and sniffed hungrily.

"Kane will have to be handled carefully," observed Wade. "He'd bite pretty quick."

"But he's so splendid," said the girl. "I don't like to think he's mean. You'll be good to him—try to win him?"

"I'll do my best with him."

"Dad's full of glee that he has a real hunter at White Slides at last. Now I'm glad, and sorry, too. I hate to think of little calves being torn and killed by lions and wolves. And it's dreadful to know bears eat grown-up cattle. But I love the mourn of a wolf and the yelp of a coyote. I can't help hoping you don't kill them all—quite."

"It's not likely, miss," he replied. "I'll be pretty sure to clean out the lions an' drive off the bears. But the wolf family can't be exterminated. No animal so cunnin' as a wolf! . . . I'll tell you. . . . Some years ago I went to cook on a ranch north of Denver, on the edge of the plains. An' right off I began to hear stories about a big lobo—a wolf that was an old residenter. He'd been known for long, an' he got meaner an' wiser as he was hunted. His specialty got to be yearlings, an' the ranchers all over rose up in arms against him. They hired all the old hunters an' trappers in the country to kill him. No good! Old Lobo went right on pullin' down yearlings. Every night he'd get one or more. An' he was so cute an' so swift that he'd work on different ranches on different nights. Finally he killed eleven yearlings for my boss on one night. Eleven! Think of that. An' then I said to my boss, 'I reckon you'd better let me go kill that gray butcher.' An' my boss laughed at me. But he let me go. He'd have tried anythin'. I took a hunk of meat, a blanket, my gun, an' a pair of snow-shoes, an' I set out on old Lobo's tracks. . . . An', Miss Columbine, I *walked* old Lobo to death in the snow!"

"Why, how wonderful!" exclaimed the girl, breathless and glowing with interest. "Oh, it seems a pity such a splendid brute should be killed. Wild animals are cruel. I wish it were different."

"Life is cruel, miss, an' I echo your wish," replied Wade, sadly.

"You have had great experiences. Dad said to me, 'Collie, here at last is a man who can tell you enough stories!' . . . But I don't believe you ever could."

"You like stories?" asked Wade, curiously.

"Love them. All kinds, but I like adventure best. *I* should have been a boy. Isn't it strange, I can't hurt anything myself or bear to see even a steer slaughtered? But you can't tell too bloody and terrible stories for me. Except I hate Indian stories. The very thought of Indians makes me shudder. . . . Some day I'll tell you a story."

Wade could not find his tongue readily.

"I must go now," she continued, and moved off the porch. Then she hesitated, and turned with a smile that was wistful and impulsive. "I—I believe we'll be good friends."

"Miss Columbine, we sure will, if I can live up to my part," replied Wade.

Her smile deepened, even while her gaze grew unconsciously pene- trating. Wade felt how subtly they were drawn to each other. But she had no inkling of that.

"It takes two to make a bargain," she replied, seriously. "I've my part. Good-by."

Wade watched her lithe stride, and as she drew away the restraint he had put upon himself loosened. When she disappeared his feeling burst all bounds. Dragging the dogs inside, he closed the door. Then, like one broken and spent, he fell face against the wall, with the hoarsely whis- pered words, "I'm thankin' God!"

CHAPTER 6

September's glory of gold and red and purple began to fade with the autumnal equinox. It rained enough to soak the frost-bitten leaves, and then the mountain winds sent them flying and fluttering and scurrying to carpet the dells and spot the pools in the brooks and color the trails. When the weather cleared and the sun rose bright again many of the aspen thickets were leafless and bare, and the willows showed stark against the gray sage hills, and the vines had lost their fire. Hills and valleys had sobered with subtle change that left them none the less beautiful.

A mile or more down the road from White Slides, in a protected nook, nestled two cabins belonging to a cattleman named Andrews, who had formerly worked for Belllounds and had recently gone into the stock business for himself. He had a rather young wife, and several children, and a brother who rode for him. These people were the only neighbors of Belllounds for some ten miles on the road toward Kremmling.

Columbine liked Mrs. Andrews and often rode or walked down there for a little visit and a chat with her friend and a romp with the children.

Toward the end of September Columbine found herself combating a strong desire to go down to the Andrews ranch and try to learn some news about Wilson Moore. If anything had been heard at White Slides it certainly had not been told her. Jack Belllounds had ridden to Kremmling and back in one day, but Columbine would have endured much before asking him for information.

She did, however, inquire of the freighter who hauled Belllounds's supplies, and the answer she got was awkwardly evasive. That nettled Columbine. Also it raised a suspicion which she strove to subdue. Finally it seemed apparent that Wilson Moore's name was not to be mentioned to her.

First, in her growing resentment, she had an impulse to go to her new friend, the hunter Wade, and confide in him not only her longing to learn about Wilson, but also other matters that were growing daily more burdensome. How strange for her to feel that in some way Jack Belllounds had come between her and the old man she loved and called father! Columbine had not divined that until lately. She felt it now in the fact that she no longer sought the rancher as she used to, and he had apparently avoided her. But then, Columbine reflected, she might be entirely wrong, for when Belllounds did meet her at meal-times, or anywhere, he seemed just as affectionate as of old. Still he was not the same man. A chill, an atmosphere of shadow, had pervaded the once wholesome ranch. And so, feeling not yet well enough acquainted with Wade to confide so intimately in him, she stifled her impulses and resolved to make some effort herself to find out what she wanted to know.

As luck would have it, when she started out to walk down to the Andrews ranch she encountered Jack Belllounds.

"Where are you going?" he inquired, inquisitively.

"I'm going to see Mrs. Andrews," she replied.

"No, you're not!" he declared, quickly, with a flash.

Columbine felt a queer sensation deep within her, a hot little gathering that seemed foreign to her physical being, and ready to burst out. Of late it had stirred in her at words or acts of Jack Belllounds. She gazed steadily at him, and he returned her look with interest. What he was thinking she had no idea of, but for herself it was a recurrence and an emphasis of the fact that she seemed growing farther away from this young man she had to marry. The weeks since his arrival had been the most worrisome she could remember.

"I *am* going," she replied, slowly.

"No!" he replied, violently. "I won't have you running off down there to—to gossip with that Andrews woman."

"Oh, *you* won't?" inquired Columbine, very quietly. How little he understood her!

"That's what I said."

"You're not my boss yet, Mister Jack Belllounds," she flashed, her spirit rising. He could irritate her as no one else.

"I soon will be. And what's a matter of a week or a month?" he went on, calming down a little.

"I've promised, yes," she said, feeling her face blanch, "and I keep my promises. . . . But I didn't say when. If you talk like that to me it might be a good many weeks—or—or months before I name the day."

"*Columbine!*" he cried, as she turned away. There was genuine distress in his voice. Columbine felt again an assurance that had troubled her. No matter how she was reacting to this new relation, it seemed a fearful truth that Jack was really falling in love with her. This time she did not soften.

"I'll call dad to *make* you stay home," he burst out again, his temper rising.

Columbine wheeled as on a pivot.

"If you do you've got less sense than I thought."

Passion claimed him then.

Columbine turned her back upon Belllounds and swung away, every pulse in her throbbing and smarting. She hurried on into the road. She wanted to run, not to get out of sight or hearing, but to fly from something, she knew not what.

"Oh! it's more than his temper!" she cried, hot tears in her eyes. "He's mean—*mean*—MEAN! What's the use of me denying that—any more—just because I love dad? . . . My life will be wretched. . . . It *is* wretched!"

Her anger did not last long, nor did her resentment. She reproached herself for the tart replies that had inflamed Jack. Never again would she forget herself!

"But he—he makes me furious," she cried, in sudden excuse for herself. "What did he say? 'That club-footed cowboy Moore'! . . . Oh, that was vile. He's heard, then, that poor Wilson has a bad foot, perhaps permanently crippled. . . . If it's true . . . But why should he yell that he knew I wanted to see Wilson? . . . I did *not*! I *do* not. . . . Oh, but I do, I do!"

And then Columbine was to learn straightway that she would forget herself again, that she had forgotten, and that a sadder, stranger truth was dawning upon her—she was discovering another Columbine within herself, a wilful, passionate, different creature who would no longer be denied.

Almost before Columbine realized that she had started upon the visit she was within sight of the Andrews ranch. So swiftly had she walked! It behooved her to hide such excitement as had dominated her. And to that end she slowed her pace, trying to put her mind on other matters.

The children saw her first and rushed upon her, so that when she reached the cabin door she could not well have been otherwise than rosy and smiling. Mrs. Andrews, ruddy and strong, looked the pioneer rancher's hardworking wife. Her face brightened at the advent of Columbine, and showed a little surprise and curiosity as well.

"Laws, but it's good to see you, Columbine," was her greeting. "You ain't been here for a long spell."

"I've been coming, but just put it off," replied Columbine.

And so, after the manner of women neighbors, they began to talk of the fall round-up, and the near approach of winter with its loneliness, and the children, all of which naturally led to more personal and interesting topics.

"An' is it so, Columbine, that you're to marry Jack Belllounds?" asked Mrs. Andrews, presently.

"Yes, I guess it is," replied Columbine, smiling.

"Humph! I'm no relative of yours or even a particular, close friend, but I'd like to say—"

"Please don't," interposed Columbine.

"All right, my girl. I guess it's better I don't say anythin'. It's a pity, though, onless you love this Buster Jack. An' you never used to do that, I'll swan."

"No, I don't love Jack—yet—as I ought to love a husband. But I'll try, and if—if I—I never do—still, it's my duty to marry him."

"Some woman ought to talk to Bill Belllounds," declared Mrs. Andrews with a grimness that boded ill for the old rancher.

"Did you know we had a new man up at the ranch?" asked Columbine, changing the subject.

"You mean the hunter, Hell-Bent Wade?"

"Yes. But I hate that ridiculous name," said Columbine.

"It's queer, like lots of names men get in these parts. An' it'll stick. Wade's been here twice; once as he was passin' with the hounds, an' the other night. I like him, Columbine. He's true-blue, for all his strange name. My men-folks took to him like ducks to water."

"I'm glad. I took to him almost like that," rejoined Columbine. "He has the saddest face I ever saw."

"Sad? Wal, yes. That man has seen a good deal of what they tacked on to his name. I laughed when I seen him first. Little lame fellar, crooked-legged an' ragged, with thet awful homely face! But I forgot how he looked next time he came."

"That's just it. He's not much to look at, but you forget his homeliness right off," replied Columbine, warmly. "You feel something behind all his—his looks."

"Wal, you an' me are women, an' we feel different," replied Mrs. Andrews. "Now my men-folks take much store on what Wade can *do*. He fixed up Tom's gun, that's been out of whack for a year. He made our clock run ag'in, an' run better than ever. Then he saved our cow from that poison-weed. An' Tom gave her up to die."

"The boys up home were telling me Mr. Wade had saved some of our cattle. Dad was delighted. You know he's lost a good many head of stock from this poison-weed. I saw so many dead steers on my last ride up the mountain. It's too bad our new man didn't get here sooner to save them. I asked him how he did it, and he said he was a doctor."

"A cow-doctor," laughed Mrs. Andrews. "Wal, that's a new one on me. Accordin' to Tom, this here Wade, when he seen our sick cow, said she'd eat poison-weed—larkspur, I think he called it—an' then when she drank water it formed a gas in her stomach an' she swelled up terrible. Wade jest stuck his knife in her side a little an' let the gas out, and she got well."

"Ughh! . . . What cruel doctoring! But if it saves the cattle, then it's good."

"It'll save them if they can be got to right off," replied Mrs. Andrews.

"Speaking of doctors," went on Columbine, striving to make her query casual, "do you know whether or not Wilson Moore had his foot treated by a doctor at Kremmling?"

"He did not," answered Mrs. Andrews. "Wasn't no doctor there. They'd had to send to Denver, an', as Wils couldn't take that trip or wait so long, why, Mrs. Plummer fixed up his foot. She made a good job of it, too, as I can testify."

"Oh, I'm—very thankful!" murmured Columbine. "He'll not be crippled or—or club-footed, then?"

"I reckon not. You can see for yourself. For Wils's here. He was drove up night before last an' is stayin' with my brother-in-law—in the other cabin there."

Mrs. Andrews launched all this swiftly, with evident pleasure, but with more of woman's subtle motive. Her eyes were bent with shrewd kindness upon the younger woman.

"Here!" exclaimed Columbine, with a start, and for an instant she was at the mercy of conflicting surprise and joy and alarm. Alternately she flushed and paled.

"Sure he's here," replied Mrs. Andrews, now looking out of the door. "He ought to be in sight somewheres. He's walkin' with a crutch."

"Crutch!" cried Columbine, in dismay.

"Yes, crutch, an' he made it himself. . . . I don't see him nowheres. Mebbe he went in when he see you comin'. For he's powerful sensitive about that crutch."

"Then—if he's so—so sensitive, perhaps I'd better go," said Columbine, struggling with embarrassment and discomfiture. What if she happened to meet him! Would he imagine her purpose in coming there? Her heart began to beat unwontedly.

"Suit yourself, lass," replied Mrs. Andrews, kindly. "I know you and Wils quarreled, for he told me. An' it's a pity. . . . Wal, if you must go, I hope you'll come again before the snow flies. Good-by."

Columbine bade her a hurried good-by and ventured forth with misgivings. And almost around the corner of the second cabin, which she had to pass, and before she had time to recover her composure, she saw Wilson Moore, hobbling along on a crutch, holding a bandaged foot off the ground. He had seen her; he was hurrying to avoid a meeting, or to get behind the corrals there before she observed him.

"Wilson!" she called, involuntarily. The instant the name left her lips she regretted it. But too late! The cowboy halted, slowly turned.

Then Columbine walked swiftly up to him, suddenly as brave as she had been fearful. Sight of him had changed her.

"Wilson Moore, you meant to avoid me," she said, with reproach.

"Howdy, Columbine!" he drawled, ignoring her words.

"Oh, I was so sorry you were hurt!" she burst out. "And now I'm so glad—you're—you're . . . Wilson, you're thin and pale—you've suffered!"

"It pulled me down a bit," he replied.

Columbine had never before seen his face anything except bronzed and lean and healthy, but now it bore testimony to pain and strain and patient endurance. He looked older. Something in the fine, dark, hazel eyes hurt her deeply.

"You never sent me word," she went on, reproachfully. "No one would tell me anything. The boys said they didn't know. Dad was angry when I asked him. I'd never have asked Jack. And the freighter who drove up—he lied to me. So I came down here to-day purposely to ask news of you, but I never dreamed you were here, . . . Now I'm glad I came."

What a singular, darkly kind, yet strange glance he gave her!

"That was like you, Columbine," he said. "I knew you'd feel badly about my accident. But how could I send word to you?"

"You saved—Pronto," she returned, with a strong tremor in her voice. "I can't thank you enough."

"That was a funny thing. Pronto went out of his head. I hope he's all right."

"He's almost well. It took some time to pick all the splinters out of him. He'll be all right soon—none the worse for that—that cowboy trick of Mister Jack Belllounds."

Columbine finished bitterly. Moore turned his thoughtful gaze away from her.

"I hope Old Bill is well," he remarked, lamely.

"Have you told your folks of your accident?" asked Columbine, ignoring his remark.

"No."

"Oh, Wilson, you ought to have sent for them, or have written at least."

"Me? To go crying for them when I got in trouble? I couldn't see it that way."

"Wilson, you'll be going—home—soon—to Denver—won't you?" she faltered.

"No," he replied, shortly.

"But what will you do? Surely you can't work—not so soon?"

"Columbine, I'll never—be able to ride again—like I used to," he said, tragically. "I'll ride, yes, but never the old way."

"Oh!" Columbine's tone, and the exquisite softness and tenderness with which she placed a hand on the rude crutch would have been enlightening to any one but these two absorbed in themselves. "I can't bear to believe that."

"I'm afraid it's true. Bad smash, Columbine! I just missed being club-footed."

"You should have care. You should have . . . Wilson, do you intend to stay here with the Andrewses?"

"Not much. They have troubles of their own. Columbine, I'm going to homestead one hundred and sixty acres."

"Homestead!" she exclaimed, in amaze. "Where?"

"Up there under Old White Slides. I've long intended to. You know that pretty little valley under the red bluff. There's a fine spring. You've been there with me. There by the old cabin built by prospectors?"

"Yes, I know. It's a pretty place—fine valley, but Wils, you can't *live* there," she expostulated.

"Why not, I'd like to know?"

"That little cubby-hole! It's only a tiny one-room cabin, roof all gone, chinks open, chimney crumbling. . . . Wilson, you don't mean to tell me you want to live there alone?"

"Sure. What'd you think?" he replied, with sarcasm. "Expect me to *marry* some girl? Well, I wouldn't, even if any one would have a cripple."

"Who—who will take care of you?" she asked, blushing furiously.

"I'll take care of myself," he declared. "Good Lord! Columbine, I'm not an invalid yet. I've got a few friends who'll help me fix up the cabin. And that reminds me. There's a lot of my stuff up in the bunk-house at White Slides. I'm going to drive up soon to haul it away."

"Wilson Moore, do you mean it?" she asked, with grave wonder. "Are you going to homestead near White Slides Ranch—and *live* there—when—"

She could not finish. An overwhelming disaster, for which she had no name, seemed to be impending.

"Yes, I am," he replied. "Funny how things turn out, isn't it?"

"It's very—very funny," she said, dazedly, and she turned slowly away without another word.

"Good-by, Columbine," he called out after her, with farewell, indeed, in his voice.

All the way home Columbine was occupied with feelings that swayed her to the exclusion of rational consideration of the increasing perplexity of her situation. And to make matters worse, when she arrived at the ranch it was to meet Jack Belllounds with a face as black as a thunder-cloud.

"The old man wants to see you," he announced, with an accent that recalled his threat of a few hours back.

"Does he?" queried Columbine, loftily. "From the courteous way you speak I imagine it's important."

Belllounds did not deign to reply to this. He sat on the porch, where evidently he had awaited her return, and he looked anything but happy.

"Where is dad?" continued Columbine.

Jack motioned toward the second door, beyond which he sat, the one that opened into the room the rancher used as a kind of office and store-room. As Columbine walked by Jack he grasped her skirt.

"Columbine! You're angry?" he said, appealingly.

"I reckon I am," replied Columbine.

"Don't go in to dad when you're that way," implored Jack. "He's angry, too—and—and—it'll only make matters worse."

From long experience Columbine could divine when Jack had done something in the interest of self and then had awakened to possible consequences. She pulled away from him without replying, and knocked on the office door.

"Come in," called the rancher.

Columbine went in. "Hello, dad! Do you want me?"

Belllounds sat at an old table, bending over a soiled ledger, with a stubby pencil in his huge hand. When he looked up Columbine gave a little start.

"Where've you been?" he asked, gruffly.

"I've been calling on Mrs. Andrews," replied Columbine.

"Did you go thar to see her?"

"Why—certainly!" answered Columbine, with a slow break in her speech.

"You didn't go to meet Wilson Moore?"

"No."

"An' I reckon you'll say you hadn't heerd he was there?"

"I had not," flashed Columbine.

"Wal, *did* you see him?"

"Yes, sir, I did, but quite by accident."

"Ahuh! Columbine, are you lyin' to me?"

The hot blood flooded to Columbine's cheeks, as if she had been struck a blow.

"*Dad!*" she cried, in hurt amaze.

Belllounds seemed thick, imponderable, as if something had forced a crisis in him and his brain was deeply involved. The habitual, cool, easy, bold, and frank attitude in the meeting of all situations seemed to have been encroached upon by a break, a bewilderment, a lessening of confidence.

"Wal, are you lyin'?" he repeated, either blind to or unaware of her distress.

"I could not—lie to you," she faltered, "even—if—I wanted to."

The heavy, shadowed gaze of his big eyes was bent upon her as if she had become a new and perplexing problem.

"But you seen Moore?"

"Yes—sir." Columbine's spirit rose.

"An' talked with him?"

"Of course."

"Lass, I ain't likin' thet, an' I ain't likin' the way you look an' speak."

"I am sorry. I can't help either."

"What'd this cowboy say to you?"

"We talked mostly about his injured foot."

"An' what else?" went on Belllounds, his voice rising.

"About—what he meant to do now."

"Ahuh! An' thet's homesteadin' the Sage Creek Valley?"

"Yes, sir."

"Did you want him to do thet?"

"I! Indeed I didn't."

"Columbine, not so long ago you told me this fellar wasn't sweet on you. An' do you still say that to me—are you still insistin' he ain't in love with you?"

"He never said so—I never believed it . . . and now I'm sure—he isn't!"

"Ahuh! Wal, thet same day you was jest as sure you didn't care anythin' particular fer him. Are you thet sure now?"

"No!" whispered Columbine, very low. She trembled with a suggestion of unknown forces. Not to save a new and growing pride would she evade any question from this man upon whom she had no claim, to whom she owed her life and her bringing up. But something cold formed in her.

Belllounds, self-centered and serious as he strangely was, seemed to check his probing, either from fear of hearing more from her or from an awakening of former kindness. But her reply was a shock to him, and, throwing down his pencil with the gesture of a man upon whom decision was forced, he rose to tower over her.

"You've been like a daughter to me. I've done all I knowed how fer you. I've lived up to the best of my lights. An' I've loved you," he said, sonorously and pathetically. "You know what my hopes are—fer the boy—an' fer you. . . . We needn't waste any more talk. From this minnit you're free to do as you like. Whatever you do won't make any change in my carin' fer you. . . . But you gotta decide. Will you marry Jack or not?"

"I promised you—I would. I'll keep my word," replied Columbine, steadily.

"So far so good," went on the rancher. "I'm respectin' you fer what you say. . . . An' now, *when* will you marry him?"

The little room drifted around in Columbine's vague, blank sight. All seemed to be drifting. She had no solid anchor.

"Any—day you say—the sooner the—better," she whispered.

"Wal, lass, I'm thankin' you," he replied, with voice that sounded afar to her. "An' I swear, if I didn't believe it's best fer Jack an' you, why I'd never let you marry. . . . So we'll set the day. October first! Thet's the day you was fetched to me a baby—more 'n seventeen years ago."

"October—first—then, dad," she said, brokenly, and she kissed him as if in token of what she knew she owed him. Then she went out, closing the door behind her.

Jack, upon seeing her, hastily got up, with more than concern in his pale face.

"Columbine!" he cried, hoarsely. "How you look! . . . Tell me. What happened? Girl, don't tell me you've—you've—"

"Jack Belllounds," interrupted Columbine, in tragic amaze at this truth about to issue from her lips, "I've promised to marry you—on October first."

He let out a shout of boyish exultation and suddenly clasped her in his arms. But there was nothing boyish in the way he handled her, in the almost savage evidence of possession. "Collie, I'm mad about you," he began, ardently. "You never let me tell you. And I've grown worse and worse. To-day I—when I saw you going down there—where that Wilson Moore is—I got terribly jealous. I was sick. I'd been glad to kill him! . . . It made me see how I loved you. Oh, I didn't know. But now . . . Oh, I'm mad for you!" He crushed her to him, unmindful of her struggles; his face and neck were red; his eyes on fire. And he began trying to kiss her mouth, but failed, as she struggled desperately. His kisses fell upon cheek and ear and hair.

"Let me—go!" panted Columbine. "You've no—no—Oh, you might have waited." Breaking from him, she fled, and got inside her room with the door almost closed, when his foot intercepted it.

Belllounds was half laughing his exultation, half furious at her escape, and altogether beside himself.

"No," she replied, so violently that it appeared to awake him to the fact that there was some one besides himself to consider.

"Aw!" He heaved a deep sigh. "All right. I won't try to get in. Only listen. . . . Collie, don't mind my—my way of showing you how I felt. Fact is, I went plumb off my head. Is that any wonder, you—you darling—when I've been so scared you'd never have me? Collie, I've felt that you were the one thing in the world I wanted most and would never get. But now . . . October first! Listen. I promise you I'll not drink any more—nor gamble—nor nag dad for money. I don't like his way of running the ranch, but I'll do it, as long as he lives. I'll even try to tolerate that club-footed cowboy's brass in homesteading a ranch right under my nose. I'll—I'll do anything you ask of me."

"Then—please—go away!" cried Columbine, with a sob.

When he was gone Columbine barred the door and threw herself upon her bed to shut out the light and to give vent to her surcharged emotions. She wept like a girl whose youth was ending; and after the paroxysm had passed, leaving her weak and strangely changed, she tried to reason out what had happened to her. Over and over again she named the appeal of the rancher, the sense of her duty, the decision she had reached, and the disgust and terror inspired in her by Jack Belllounds's reception of her promise. These were facts of the day and they had made of her a palpitating, unhappy creature, who nevertheless had been brave to face the rancher and confess that which she had scarce confessed to herself. But now she trembled and cringed on the verge of a catastrophe that withheld its whole truth.

"I begin to see now," she whispered, after the thought had come and gone and returned to change again. "If Wilson had cared for me I—I might have—cared, too. . . . But I do—care—something. I couldn't lie to dad. Only I'm not sure—how much. I never dreamed of—of *loving* him, or any one. It's so strange. All at once I feel old. And I can't understand these—these feelings that shake me."

So Columbine brooded over the trouble that had come to her, never regretting her promise to the old rancher, but growing keener in the realization of a complexity in her nature that sooner or later would separate the life of her duty from the life of her desire. She seemed all alone, and when this feeling possessed her a strange reminder of the hunter Wade flashed up. She stifled another impulse to confide in him. Wade had the softness of a woman, and his face was a record of the trials and travails through which he had come unhardened, unembittered. Yet how could she tell her troubles to him? A stranger, a rough man of the wilds, whose name had preceded him, notorious and deadly, with that vital tang of the West in its meaning! Nevertheless, Wade drew her, and she thought of

him until the recurring memory of Jack Belllounds's rude clasp again
crept over her with an augmenting disgust and fear. Must she submit to
that? Had she promised that? And then Columbine felt the dawning of
realities.

CHAPTER 7

Columbine was awakened in the gray dawn by the barking of coyotes. She dreaded the daylight thus heralded. Never before in her life had she hated the rising of the sun. Resolutely she put the past behind her and faced the future, believing now that with the great decision made she needed only to keep her mind off what might have been, and to attend to her duty.

At breakfast she found the rancher in better spirits than he had been for weeks. He informed her that Jack had ridden off early for Kremmling, there to make arrangements for the wedding on October first.

"Jack's out of his head," said Belllounds. "Wal, thet comes only onct in a man's life. I remember . . . Jack's goin' to drive you to Kremmlin' an' ther take stage fer Denver. I allow you'd better put in your best licks on fixin' up an' packin' the clothes you'll need. Women-folk naturally want to look smart on weddin'-trips."

"Dad!" exclaimed Columbine, in dismay. "I never thought of clothes. And I don't want to leave White Slides."

"But, lass, you're goin' to be married!" expostulated Belllounds.

"Didn't it occur to Jack to take me to Kremmling? I can't make new dresses out of old ones."

"Wal, I reckon neither of us thought of thet. But you can buy what you like in Denver."

Columbine resigned herself. After all, what did it matter to her? The vague, haunting dreams of girlhood would never come true. So she went to her wardrobe and laid out all her wearing apparel. Taking stock of it this way caused her further dismay, for she had nothing fit to wear in which either to be married or to take a trip to Denver. There appeared to be nothing to do but take the rancher's advice, and Columbine set about refurbishing her meager wardrobe. She sewed all day.

What with self-control and work and the passing of hours, Columbine began to make some approach to tranquillity. In her simplicity she even began to hope that being good and steadfast and dutiful would earn her a little meed of happiness. Some haunting doubt of this flashed over her mind like a swift shadow of a black wing, but she dispelled that as she had dispelled the fear and disgust which often rose up in her mind.

To Columbine's surprise and to the rancher's concern the prospective bridegroom did not return from Kremmling on the second day. When night came Belllounds reluctantly gave up looking for him.

Jack's non-appearance suited Columbine, and she would have been glad to be let alone until October first, which date now seemed appallingly close. On the afternoon of Jack's third day of absence from the ranch Columbine rode out for some needed exercise. Pronto not being available, she rode another mustang and one that kept her busy. On the way back to the ranch she avoided the customary trail which led by the cabins of Wade and the cowboys. Columbine had not seen one of her friends since the unfortunate visit to the Andrews ranch. She particularly shrank from meeting Wade, which feeling was in strange contrast to her former impulses.

As she rode around the house she encountered Wilson Moore seated in a light wagon. Her mustang reared, almost unseating her. But she handled him roughly, being suddenly surprised and angry at this unexpected meeting with the cowboy.

"Howdy, Columbine!" greeted Wilson, as she brought the mustang to his feet. "You're sure learning to handle a horse—since I left this here ranch. Wonder who's teaching you! I never could get you to rake even a bronc!"

The cowboy had drawled out his admiring speech, half amused and half satiric.

"I'm—mad!" declared Columbine. "That's why."

"What're you mad at?" queried Wilson.

She did not reply, but kept on gazing steadily at him. Moore still looked pale and drawn, but he had improved since last she saw him.

"Aren't you going to speak to a fellow?" he went on.

"How are you, Wils?" she asked.

"Pretty good for a club-footed has-been cowpuncher."

"I wish you wouldn't call yourself such names," rejoined Columbine, peevishly. "You're not a club-foot. I hate that word!"

"Me, too. Well, joking aside, I'm better. My foot is fine. Now, if I don't hurt it again I'll sure never be a club-foot."

"You must be careful," she said, earnestly.

"Sure. But it's hard for me to be idle. Think of me lying still all day with nothing to do but read! That's what knocked me out. I wouldn't have minded the pain if I could have gotten about. . . . Columbine, I've moved in!"

"What! Moved in?" she queried, blankly.

"Sure. I'm in my cabin on the hill. It's plumb great. Tom Andrews and Bert and your hunter Wade fixed up the cabin for me. That Wade is sure a good fellow. And say! what he can do with his hands! He's been kind to me. Took an interest in me, and between you and me he sort of cheered me up."

"Cheered you up! Wils, were you unhappy?" she asked, directly.

"Well, rather. What'd you expect of a cowboy who'd crippled himself—and lost his girl?"

Columbine felt the smart of tingling blood in her face, and she looked from Wilson to the wagon. It contained saddles, blankets, and other cowboy accoutrements for which he had evidently come.

"That's a double misfortune," she replied, evenly. "It's too bad both came at once. It seems to me if I were a cowboy and—and felt so toward a girl, I'd have let her know."

"This girl I mean knew, all right," he said, nodding his head.

"She didn't—she didn't!" cried Columbine.

"How do *you* know?" he queried, with feigned surprise. He was bent upon torturing her.

"You meant me. I'm the girl you lost!"

"Yes, you are—God help me!" replied Moore, with genuine emotion.

"But you—you never told me—you never told me," faltered Columbine, in distress.

"Never told you what? That you were my girl?"

"No—no. But that you—you cared—"

"Columbine Belllounds, I told you—let you see—in every way under the sun," he flashed at her.

"Let me see—*what?*" faltered Columbine, feeling as if the world were about to end.

"That I loved you."

"Oh! . . . Wilson!" whispered Columbine, wildly.

"Yes—loved you. Could you have been so innocent—so blind you never knew? I can't believe it."

"But I never dreamed you—you—" She broke off dazedly, overwhelmed by a tragic, glorious truth.

"Collie! . . . Would it have made any difference?"

"Oh, all the difference in the world!" she wailed.

"What difference?" he asked, passionately.

Columbine gazed wide-eyed and helpless at the young man. She did not know how to tell him what all the difference in the world really was.

Suddenly Wilson turned away from her to listen. Then she heard rapid beating of hoofs on the road.

"That's Buster Jack," said the cowboy. "Just my luck! There wasn't any one here when I arrived. Reckon I oughtn't have stayed. Columbine, you look pretty much upset."

"What do I care how I look!" she exclaimed, with a sharp resentment attending this abrupt and painful break in her agitation.

Next moment Jack Belllounds galloped a foam-lashed horse into the courtyard and hauled up short with a recklessness he was noted for. He swung down hard and violently cast the reins from him.

"Ahuh! I gambled on just this," he declared, harshly.

Columbine's heart sank. His gaze was fixed on her face, with its telltale evidences of agitation.

"What've you been crying about?" he demanded.

"I haven't been," she retorted.

His bold and glaring eyes, hot with sudden temper, passed slowly from her to the cowboy. Columbine became aware then that Jack was under the influence of liquor. His heated red face grew darker with a sneering contempt.

"Where's dad?" he asked, wheeling toward her.

"I don't know. He's not here," replied Columbine, dismounting. The leap of thought and blood to Jack's face gave her a further sinking of the heart. The situation unnerved her.

Wilson Moore had grown a shade paler. He gathered up his reins, ready to drive off.

"Belllounds, I came up after my things I'd left in the bunk," he said, coolly. "Happened to meet Columbine and stopped to chat a minute."

"That's what *you* say," sneered Belllounds. "You were making love to Columbine. I saw that in her face. You know it—and she knows it—and I know it. . . . You're a liar!"

"Belllounds, I reckon I am," replied Moore, turning white. "I did tell Columbine what I thought she knew—what I ought to have told long ago."

"Ahuh! Well, I don't want to hear it. But I'm going to search that wagon."

"What!" ejaculated the cowboy, dropping his reins as if they stung him.

"You just hold on till I see what you've got in there," went on Belllounds, and he reached over into the wagon and pulled at a saddle.

"Say, do you mean anything? . . . This stuff's mine, every strap of it. Take your hands off."

Belllounds leaned on the wagon and looked up with insolent, dark intent.

"Moore, I wouldn't trust you. I think you'd steal anything you got your hands on."

Columbine uttered a passionate little cry of shame and protest.

"Jack, how dare you!"

"You shut up! Go in the house!" he ordered.

"You insult me," she replied, in bitter humiliation.

"Will you go in?" he shouted.

"No, I won't."

"All right, look on, then. I'd just as lief have you." Then he turned to the cowboy. "Moore, show up that wagon-load of stuff unless you want me to throw it out in the road."

"Belllounds, you know I can't do that," replied Moore, coldly. "And I'll give you a hunch. You'd better shut up yourself and let me drive on. . . . If not for her sake, then for your own."

Belllounds grasped the reins, and with a sudden jerk pulled them out of the cowboy's hands.

"You damn club-foot! Your gift of gab doesn't go with me," yelled Belllounds, as he swung up on the hub of the wheel. But it was manifest that his desire to search the wagon was only a pretense, for while he pulled at this and that his evil gaze was on the cowboy, keen to meet any move that might give excuse for violence. Moore evidently read this, for, gazing at Columbine, he shook his head, as if to acquaint her with a situation impossible to help.

"Columbine, please hand me up the reins," he said. "I'm lame, you know. Then I'll be going."

Columbine stepped forward to comply, when Belllounds, leaping down from the wheel, pushed her back with masterful hand. Opposition to him was like waving a red flag in the face of a bull. Columbine recoiled from his look as well as touch.

"You keep out of this or I'll teach you who's boss here," he said, stridently.

"You're going too far!" burst out Columbine.

Meanwhile Wilson had laboriously climbed down out of the wagon, and, utilizing his crutch, he hobbled to where Belllounds had thrown the reins, and stooped to pick them up. Belllounds shoved Columbine farther back, and then he leaped to confront the cowboy.

"I've got you now, Moore," he said, hoarse and low. Stripped of all pretense, he showed the ungovernable nature of his temper. His face grew corded and black. The hand he thrust out shook like a leaf. "You smooth-tongued liar! I'm on to your game. I know you'd put her against me. I know you'd try to win her—less than a week before her wedding-day. . . . But it's not for that I'm going to beat hell out of you! It's because I hate you! Ever since I can remember my father held *you* up to me! And he sent me to—to—he sent me away because of you. By God! that's why I hate you!"

All that was primitive and violent and base came out with strange frankness in Belllounds's tirade. Only when calm could his mind be capable of hidden calculation. The devil that was in him now seemed rampant.

"Belllounds, you're mighty brave to stack up this way against a one-legged man," declared the cowboy, with biting sarcasm.

"If you had two club-feet I'd only be the gladder," yelled Belllounds, and, swinging his arm, he slapped Moore so that it nearly toppled him over. Only the injured foot, coming down hard, saved him.

When Columbine saw that, and then how Wilson winced and grew deathly pale, she uttered a low cry, and she seemed suddenly rooted to the spot, weak, terrified at what was now inevitable, and growing sick and cold and faint.

"It's a damn lucky thing for you I'm not packing a gun," said Moore, grimly. "But you knew—or you'd never hit me—you coward."

"I'll make you swallow that," snarled Belllounds, and this time he swung his fist, aiming a heavy blow at Moore.

Then the cowboy whirled aloft the heavy crutch. "If you hit at me again I'll let out what little brains you've got. God knows that's little enough! . . . Belllounds, I'm going to call you to your face—before this girl your bat-eyed old man means to give you. You're not drunk. You're only ugly—mean. You've got a chance now to lick me because I'm crippled. And you're going to make the most of it. Why, you cur, I could come near licking you with only one leg. But if you touch me again I'll brain you! . . . You never were any good. You're no good now. You never will be anything but Buster Jack—half dotty, selfish as hell, bull-headed and mean! . . . And that's the last word I'll ever waste on you."

"I'll kill you!" bawled Belllounds, black with fury.

Moore wielded the crutch menacingly, but as he was not steady on his feet he was at the disadvantage his adversary had calculated upon. Belllounds ran around the cowboy, and suddenly plunged in to grapple with him. The crutch descended, but to little purpose. Belllounds's heavy onslaught threw Moore to the ground. Before he could rise Belllounds pounced upon him.

Columbine saw all this dazedly. As Wilson fell she closed her eyes, fighting a faintness that almost overcame her. She heard wrestling, threshing sounds, and sodden thumps, and a scattering of gravel. These noises seemed at first distant, then grew closer. As she gazed again with keener perception, Moore's horse plunged away from the fiercely struggling forms that had rolled almost under his feet. During the ensuing moments it was an equal battle so far as Columbine could tell. Repelled, yet fascinated, she watched. They beat each other, grappled and rolled over, first one on top, then the other. But the advantage of being uppermost presently was Belllounds's. Moore was weakening. That became noticeable more and more after each time he had wrestled and rolled about. Then Belllounds, getting this position, lay with his weight upon Moore, holding him down, and at the same time kicking with all his might. He was aiming to disable the cowboy by kicking the injured foot. And he was succeeding. Moore let out a strangled cry, and struggled desperately. But he was held and weighted down. Belllounds raised up now and, looking backward, he deliberately and furiously kicked Moore's bandaged foot; once, twice, again and again, until the straining form under him grew limp. Columbine, slowly freezing with horror, saw all this. She could not move. She could not scream. She wanted to rush in and drag Jack off of Wilson, to hurt him, to kill him, but her muscles were paralyzed. In her agony she could not even look away. Belllounds got up astride his prostrate adversary and began to beat him brutally, swinging heavy, sodden blows. His face then was terrible to see. He meant murder.

Columbine heard approaching voices and the thumping of hasty feet. That unclamped her cloven tongue. Wildly she screamed. Old Bill Belllounds appeared, striding off the porch. And the hunter Wade came running down the path.

"Dad! he's killing Wilson!" cried Columbine.

"Hyar, you devil!" roared the rancher.

Jack Belllounds got up. Panting, disheveled, with hair ruffled and face distorted, he was not a pleasant sight for even the father. Moore lay unconscious, with ghastly, bloody features, and his bandaged foot showed great splotches of red.

"My Gawd, son!" gasped Old Bill. "You didn't pick on this hyar crippled boy?"

The evidence was plain, in Moore's quiet, pathetic form, in the panting, purple-faced son. Jack Belllounds did not answer. He was in the grip of a passion that had at last been wholly unleashed and was still unsatisfied. Yet a malignant and exultant gratification showed in his face.

"That—evens us—up, Moore," he panted, and stalked away.

By this time Wade reached the cowboy and knelt beside him. Columbine came running to fall on her knees. The old rancher seemed stricken.

"Oh—Oh! it was terrible—" cried Columbine. "Oh—he's so white—and the blood—"

"Now, lass, that's no way for a woman," said Wade, and there was something in his kind tone, in his look, in his presence, that calmed Columbine. "I'll look after Moore. You go get some water an' a towel."

Columbine rose to totter into the house. She saw a red stain on the hand she had laid upon the cowboy's face and with a strange, hot, bursting sensation, strong and thrilling, she put that red place to her lips. Running out with the things required by Wade, she was in time to hear the rancher say, "Looks hurt bad, to me."

"Yes, I reckon," replied Wade.

While Columbine held Moore's head upon her lap the hunter bathed the bloody face. It was battered and bruised and cut, and in some places, as fast as Wade washed away the red, it welled out again.

Columbine watched that quiet face, while her heart throbbed and swelled with emotions wholly beyond her control and understanding. When at last Wilson opened his eyes, fluttering at first, and then wide, she felt a surge that shook her whole body. He smiled wanly at her, and at Wade, and then his gaze lifted to Belllounds.

"I guess—he licked me," he said, in weak voice. "He kept kicking my sore foot—till I fainted. But he licked me—all right."

"Wils, mebbe he did lick you," replied the old rancher, brokenly, "but I reckon he's damn little to be proud of—lickin' a crippled man—thet way."

"Boss, Jack'd been drinking," said Moore, weakly. "And he sure had—some excuse for going off his head. He caught me—talking sweet to Columbine . . . and then—I called him all the names—I could lay my tongue to."

"Ahuh!" The old man seemed at a loss for words, and presently he turned away, sagging in the shoulders, and plodded into the house.

The cowboy, supported by Wade on one side, with Columbine on the other, was helped to an upright position, and with considerable difficulty was gotten into the wagon. He tried to sit up, but made a sorry showing of it.

"I'll drive him home an' look after him," said Wade. "Now, Miss Collie, you're upset, which ain't no wonder. But now you brace. It might have been worse. Just you go to your room till you're sure of yourself again."

Moore smiled another wan smile at her. "I'm sorry," he said.

"What for? Me?" she asked.

"I mean I'm sorry I was so infernal unlucky—running into you—and bringing all this distress—to you. It was my fault. If I'd only kept—my mouth shut!"

"You need not be sorry you met me," she said, with her eyes straight upon his. "I'm glad. . . . But oh! if your foot is badly hurt I'll never—never—"

"Don't say it," interrupted Wilson.

"Lass, you're bent on doin' somethin'," said Wade, in his gentle voice.

"Bent?" she echoed, with something deep and rich in her voice. "Yes, I'm bent—*bent* like your name—to speak my mind!"

Then she ran toward the house and up on the porch, to enter the living-room with heaving breast and flashing eyes. Manifestly the rancher was berating his son. The former gaped at sight of her and the latter shrank.

"Jack Belllounds," she cried, "you're not half a man. . . . You're a coward and a brute!"

One tense moment she stood there, lightning scorn and passion in her gaze, and then she rushed out, impetuously, as she had come.

CHAPTER 8

Columbine did not leave her room any more that day. What she suffered there she did not want any one to know. What it cost her to
conquer herself again she had only a faint conception of. She did conquer, however, and that night made up the sleep she had lost the night
before.

Strangely enough, she did not feel afraid to face the rancher and his
son. Recent happenings had not only changed her, but had seemed to
give her strength. When she presented herself at the breakfast-table Jack
was absent. The old rancher greeted her with more than usual solicitude.

"Jack's sick," he remarked, presently.

"Indeed," replied Columbine.

"Yes. He said it was the drinkin' he's not accustomed to. Wal, I
reckon it was what you called him. He didn't take much store on what I
called him, which was wuss. . . . I tell you, lass, Jack's set his heart so hard
on you thet it's turrible."

"Queer way he has of showing the—the affections of his heart,"
replied Columbine, shortly.

"Thet was the drink," remonstrated the old man, pathetic and
earnest in his motive to smooth over the quarrel.

"But he promised me he would not drink any more."

Belllounds shook his gray old head sadly.

"Ahuh! Jack fires up an' promises anythin'. He means it at the time.

But the next hankerin' thet comes over him wipes out the promise. I know. . . . But he's had good excuse fer this break. The boys in town began celebratin' fer October first. Great wonder Jack didn't come home clean drunk."

"Dad, you're as good as gold," said Columbine, softening. How could she feel hard toward him?

"Collie, then you're not agoin' back on the ole man?"

"No."

"I was afeared you'd change your mind about marryin' Jack."

"When I promised I meant it. I didn't make it on conditions."

"But, lass, promises can be broke," he said, with the sonorous roll in his voice.

"I never yet broke one of mine."

"Wal, I hev. Not often, mebbe, but I hev. . . . An', lass, it's reasonable. Thar's times when a man jest can't live up to what he swore by. An' fer a girl—why, I can see how easy she'd change an' grow overnight. It's only fair fer me to say that no matter what you think you owe me you couldn't be blamed now fer dislikin' Jack."

"Dad, if by marrying Jack I can help him to be a better son to you, and more of a man, I'll be glad," she replied.

"Lass, I'm beginnin' to see how big an' fine you are," replied Belllounds, with strong feeling. "An' it's worryin' me. . . . My neighbors hev always accused me of seein' only my son. Only Buster Jack! I was blind an' deaf as to him! . . . Wal, I'm not so damn blind as I used to be. The scales are droppin' off my ole eyes. . . . But I've got one hope left as far as Jack's concerned. Thet's marryin' him to you. An' I'm stickin' to it."

"So will I stick to it, dad," she replied. "I'll go through with October first!"

Columbine broke off, vouchsafing no more, and soon left the breakfast-table, to take up the work she had laid out to do. And she accomplished it, though many times her hands dropped idle and her eyes peered out of her window at the drab slides of the old mountain.

Later, when she went out to ride, she saw the cowboy Lem working in the blacksmith shop.

"Wal, Miss Collie, air you-all still hangin' round this hyar ranch?" he asked, with welcoming smile.

"Lem, I'm almost ashamed now to face my good friends, I've neglected them so long," she replied.

"Aw, now, what're friends fer but to go to? . . . You're lookin' pale, I reckon. More like thet thar flower I see so much on the hills."

"Lem, I want to ride Pronto. Do you think he's all right, now?"

"I reckon some movin' round will do Pronto good. He's eatin' his haid off."

The cowboy went with her to the pasture gate and whistled Pronto up. The mustang came trotting, evidently none the worse for his injuries, and eager to resume the old climbs with his mistress. Lem saddled him, paying particular attention to the cinch.

"Reckon we'd better not cinch him tight," said Lem. "You jest be careful an' remember your saddle's loose."

"All right, Lem," replied Columbine, as she mounted. "Where are the boys this morning?"

"Blud an' Jim air repairin' fence up the crick."

"And where's Ben?"

"Ben? Oh, you mean Wade. Wal, I ain't seen him since yestidday. He was skinnin' a lion then, over hyar on the ridge. Thet was in the mawnin'. I reckon he's around, fer I seen some of the hounds."

"Then, Lem—you haven't heard about the fight yesterday between Jack and Wilson Moore?"

Lem straightened up quickly. "Nope, I ain't heerd a word."

"Well, they fought, all right," said Columbine, hurriedly. "I saw it. I was the only one there. Wilson was badly used up before dad and Ben got there. Ben drove off with him."

"But, Miss Collie, how'd it come off? I seen Wils the other day. Was up to his homestead. An' the boy jest manages to rustle round on a crutch. He couldn't fight."

"That was just it. Jack saw his opportunity, and he forced Wilson to fight—accused him of stealing. Wils tried to avoid trouble. Then Jack jumped him. Wilson fought and held his own until Jack began to kick his injured foot. Then Wilson fainted and—and Jack beat him."

Lem dropped his head, evidently to hide his expression. "Wal, dog-gone me!" he ejaculated. "Thet's too bad."

Columbine left the cowboy and rode up the lane toward Wade's cabin. She did not analyze her deliberate desire to tell the truth about that fight, but she would have liked to proclaim it to the whole range and to the world. Once clear of the house she felt free, unburdened, and to talk seemed to relieve some congestion of her thoughts.

The hounds heralded Columbine's approach with a deep and booming chorus. Sampson and Jim lay upon the porch, unleashed. The other hounds were chained separately in the aspen grove a few rods distant. Sampson thumped the boards with his big tail, but he did not get up, which laziness attested to the fact that there had been a lion chase the day before and he was weary and stiff. If Wade had been at home he would have come out to see what had occasioned the clamor. As Columbine rode by she saw another fresh lion-pelt pegged upon the wall of the cabin.

She followed the brook. It had cleared since the rains and was shining and sparkling in the rough, swift places, and limpid and green in the eddies. She passed the dam made by the solitary beaver that inhabited the valley. Freshly cut willows showed how the beaver was preparing for the long winter ahead. Columbine remembered then how greatly pleased Wade had been to learn about this old beaver; and more than once Wade had talked about trapping some younger beavers and bringing them there to make company for the old fellow.

The trail led across the brook at a wide, shallow place, where the splashing made by Pronto sent the trout scurrying for deeper water. Columbine kept to that trail, knowing that it led up into Sage Valley, where Wilson Moore had taken up the homestead property. Fresh horse tracks told her that Wade had ridden along there some time earlier. Pronto shied at the whirring of sage-hens. Presently Columbine ascertained they were flushed by the hound Kane, that had broken loose and followed her. He had done so before, and the fact had not displeased her.

"Kane! Kane! come here!" she called. He came readily, but halted a rod or so away, and made an attempt at wagging his tail, a function evidently somewhat difficult for him. When she resumed trotting he followed her.

Old White Slides had lost all but the drabs and dull yellows and greens, and of course those pale, light slopes that had given the mountain its name. Sage Valley was only one of the valleys at its base. It opened out half a mile wide, dominated by the looming peak, and bordered on the far side by an aspen-thicketed slope. The brook babbled along under the edge of this thicket. Cattle and horses grazed here and there on the rich, grassy levels. Columbine was surprised to see so many cattle and wondered to whom they belonged. All of Belllounds's stock had been driven lower down for the winter. There among the several horses that whistled at her approach she espied the white mustang Belllounds had given to Moore. It thrilled her to see him. And next, she suffered a pang to think that perhaps his owner might never ride him again. But Columbine held her emotions in abeyance.

The cabin stood high upon a level terrace, with clusters of aspens behind it, and was sheltered from winter blasts by a gray cliff, picturesque and crumbling, with its face overgrown by creeping vines and colorful shrubs. Wilson Moore could not have chosen a more secluded and beautiful valley for his homesteading adventure. The little gray cabin, with smoke curling from the stone chimney, had lost its look of dilapidation and disuse, yet there was nothing new that Columbine could see. The last quarter of the ascent of the slope, and the few rods across the level terrace, seemed extraordinarily long to Columbine. As she dismounted and tied Pronto her heart was beating and her breath was coming fast.

The door of the cabin was open. Kane trotted past the hesitating Columbine and went in.

"You son-of-a-hound-dog!" came to Columbine's listening ears in Wade's well-known voice. "I'll have to beat you—sure as you're born."

"I heard a horse," came in a lower voice, that was Wilson's.

"Darn me if I'm not gettin' deafer every day," was the reply.

Then Wade appeared in the doorway.

"It's nobody but Miss Collie," he announced, as he made way for her to enter.

"Good morning!" said Columbine, in a voice that had more than cheerfulness in it.

"*Collie!* . . . Did you come to see me?"

She heard this incredulous query just an instant before she saw Wilson at the far end of the room, lying under the light of a window. The inside of the cabin seemed vague and unfamiliar.

"I surely did," she replied, advancing. "How are you?"

"Oh, I'm all right. Tickled to death, right now. . . . Only, I hate to have you see this battered mug of mine."

"You needn't—care," said Columbine, unsteadily. And indeed, in that first glance she did not see him clearly. A mist blurred her sight and there was a lump in her throat. Then, to recover herself, she looked around the cabin.

"Well—Wils Moore—if this isn't fine!" she ejaculated, in amaze and delight. Columbine sustained an absolute surprise. A magic hand had transformed the interior of that rude old prospector's abode. A carpenter and a mason and a decorator had been wonderfully at work. From one end to the other Columbine gazed; from the big window under which Wilson lay on a blanketed couch to the open fireplace where Wade grinned she looked and looked, and then up to the clean, aspen-poled roof and down to the floor, carpeted with deer hides. The chinks between the logs of the walls were plastered with red clay; the dust and dirt were gone; the place smelled like sage and wood-smoke and fragrant, frying meat. Indeed, there were a glowing bed of embers and a steaming kettle and a smoking pot; and the way the smoke and steam curled up into the gray old chimney attested to its splendid draught. In each corner hung a deer-head, from the antlers of which depended accoutrements of a cowboy— spurs, ropes, belts, scarfs, guns. One corner contained a cupboard, ceiling high, with new, clean doors of wood, neatly made; and next to it stood a table, just as new. On the blank wall beyond that were pegs holding saddles, bridles, blankets, clothes.

"He did it—all this inside," burst out Moore, delighted with her delight. "Quicker than a flash! Collie, isn't this great? I don't mind being down on my back. . . . And he says they call him Hell-Bent Wade. I call him Heaven-Sent Wade!"

When Columbine turned to the hunter, bursting with her pleasure and gratitude, he suddenly dropped the forked stick he used as a lift, and she saw his hand shake when he stooped to recover it. How strangely that struck her!

"Ben, it's perfectly possible that you've been sent by Heaven," she remarked, with a humor which still held gravity in it.

"Me! A good angel? That'd be a new job for Bent Wade," he replied, with a queer laugh. "But I reckon I'd try to live up to it."

There were small sprigs of golden aspen leaves and crimson oak leaves on the wall above the foot of Wilson's bed. Beneath them, on pegs, hung a rifle. And on the window-sill stood a glass jar containing columbines. They were fresh. They had just been picked. They waved gently in the breeze, sweetly white and blue, strangely significant to the girl.

Moore laughed defiantly.

"Wade thought to fetch these flowers in," he explained. "They're his favorites as well as mine. It won't be long now till the frost kills them . . . and I want to be happy while I may!"

Again Columbine felt that deep surge within her, beyond her control, beyond her understanding, but now gathering and swelling, soon to be reckoned with. She did not look at Wilson's face then. Her downcast gaze saw that his right hand was bandaged, and she touched it with an unconscious tenderness.

"Your hand! Why is it all wrapped up?"

The cowboy laughed with grim humor.

"Have you seen Jack this morning?"

"No," she replied, shortly.

"Well, if you had, you'd know what happened to my fist."

"Did you hurt it on him?" she asked, with a queer little shudder that was not unpleasant.

"Collie, I busted that fist on his handsome face."

"Oh, it was dreadful!" she murmured. "Wilson, he meant to kill you."

"Sure. And I'd cheerfully have killed him."

"You two must never meet again," she went on.

"I hope to Heaven we never do," replied Moore, with a dark earnestness that meant more than his actual words.

"Wilson, will you avoid him—for my sake?" implored Columbine, unconsciously clasping the bandaged hand.

"I will. I'll take the back trails. I'll sneak like a coyote. I'll hide and I'll watch. . . . But, Columbine Belllounds, if he ever corners me again—"

"Why, you'll leave him to Hell-Bent Wade," interrupted the hunter, and he looked up from where he knelt, fixing those great, inscrutable eyes upon the cowboy. Columbine saw something beyond his face, deeper than the gloom, a passion and a spirit that drew her like a magnet. "An' now, Miss Collie," he went on, "I reckon you'll want to wait on our invalid. He's got to be fed."

"I surely will," replied Columbine, gladly, and she sat down on the edge of the bed. "Ben, you fetch that box and put his dinner on it."

While Wade complied, Columbine, shyly aware of her nearness to the cowboy, sought to keep up conversation.

"Couldn't you help yourself with your left hand?" she inquired.

"That one's worse," he answered, taking it from under the blanket, where it had been concealed.

"Oh!" cried Columbine, in dismay.

"Broke two bones in this one," said Wilson, with animation. "Say, Collie, our friend Wade is a doctor, too. Never saw his beat!"

"And a cook, too, for here's your dinner. You must sit up," ordered Columbine.

"Fold that blanket and help me up on it," replied Moore.

How strange and disturbing for Columbine to bend over him, to slip her arms under him and lift him! It recalled a long-forgotten motherliness of her doll-playing days. And her face flushed hot.

"Can't you move?" she asked, suddenly becoming aware of how dead a weight the cowboy appeared.

"Not—very much," he replied. Drops of sweat appeared on his bruised brow. It must have hurt him to move.

"You said your foot was all right."

"It is," he returned. "It's still on my leg, as I know darned well."

"Oh!" exclaimed Columbine, dubiously. Without further comment she began to feed him.

"It's worth getting licked to have this treat," he said.

"Nonsense!" she rejoined.

"I'd stand it again—to have you come here and feed me. . . . But not from *him*."

"Wilson, I never knew you to be facetious before. Here, take this."

Apparently he did not see her outstretched hand.

"Collie, you've changed. You're older. You're a woman, now—and the prettiest—"

"Are you going to eat?" demanded Columbine.

"Huh!" exclaimed the cowboy, blankly. "Eat? Oh yes, sure. I'm powerful hungry. And maybe Heaven-Sent Wade can't cook!"

But Columbine had trouble in feeding him. What with his helplessness, and his propensity to watch her face instead of her hands, and her own mounting sensations of a sweet, natural joy and fitness in her proximity to him, she was hard put to it to show some dexterity as a nurse. And all the time she was aware of Wade, with his quiet, forceful presence, hovering near. Could he not see her hands trembling? And would he not think that weakness strange? Then driftingly came the thought that she would not shrink from Wade's reading her mind. Perhaps even now he understood her better than she understood herself.

"I can't—eat any more," declared Moore, at last.

"You've done very well for an invalid," observed Columbine. Then, changing the subject, she asked, "Wilson, you're going to stay here—winter here, dad would call it?"

"Yes."

"Are those your cattle down in the valley?"

"Sure. I've got near a hundred head. I saved my money and bought cattle."

"That's a good start for you. I'm glad. But who's going to take care of you and your stock until you can work again?"

"Why, my friend there, Heaven-Sent Wade," replied Moore, indicating the little man busy with the utensils on the table, and apparently hearing nothing.

"Can I fetch you anything to eat—or read?" she inquired.

"Fetch yourself," he replied, softly.

"But, boy, how could I fetch you anything without fetching myself?"

"Sure, that's right. Then fetch me some jam and a book—to-morrow. Will you?"

"I surely will."

"That's a promise. I know your promises of old."

"Then good-by till to-morrow. I must go. I hope you'll be better."

"I'll stay sick in bed till you stop coming."

Columbine left rather precipitously, and when she got outdoors it seemed that the hills had never been so softly, dreamily gray, nor their loneliness so sweet, nor the sky so richly and deeply blue. As she untied Pronto the hunter came out with Kane at his heels.

"Miss Collie, if you'll go easy I'll ketch my horse an' ride down with you," he said.

She mounted, and walked Pronto out to the trail, and slowly faced the gradual descent. It was really higher up there than she had surmised. And the view was beautiful. The gray, rolling foothills, so exquisitely colored at that hour, and the black-fringed ranges, one above the other, and the distant peaks, sunset-flushed across the purple, all rose open and clear to her sight, so wildly and splendidly expressive of the Colorado she loved.

At the foot of the slope Wade joined her.

"Lass, I'm askin' you not to tell Belllounds that I'm carin' for Wils," he said, in his gentle, persuasive way.

"I won't. But why not tell dad? He wouldn't mind. He'd do that sort of thing himself."

"Reckon he would. But this deal's out of the ordinary. An' Wils's not in as good shape as he thinks. I'm not takin' any chances. I don't want to lose my job, an' I don't want to be hindered from attendin' to this boy."

They had ridden as far as the first aspen grove when Wade concluded this remark. Columbine halted her horse, causing her companion to do likewise. Her former misgivings were augmented by the intelligence of Wade's sad, lined face.

"Ben, tell me," she whispered, with a hand going to his arm.

"Miss Collie, I'm a sort of doctor in my way. I studied some medicine an' surgery. An' I know. I wouldn't tell you this if it wasn't that I've got to rely on you to help me."

"I will—but go on—tell me," interposed Columbine trying to fortify herself.

"Wils's foot is all messed up. Buster Jack kicked it all out of shape. An' it's a hundred times worse than ever. I'm afraid of blood-poisonin' an' gangrene. You know gangrene is a dyin' an' rottin' of the flesh. . . . I told the boy straight out that he'd better let me cut his foot off. An' he swore he'd keep his foot or die! . . . Well, if gangrene does set in we can't save his leg, an' maybe not his life."

"Oh, it can't be as bad as all that!" cried Columbine. "Oh, I knew—I knew there was something. . . . Ben, you mean even at best now—he'll be a—" She broke off, unable to finish.

"Miss Collie, in any case Wils'll never ride again—not like a cowboy."

That for Columbine seemed the worst and the last straw. Hot tears blinded her, hot blood gushed over her, hot heartbeats throbbed in her throat.

"Poor boy! That'll—ruin him," she cried. "He loved—a horse. He loved to ride. He was the—best rider of them all. And now he's ruined! He'll be lame—a cripple—club-footed! . . . All because of that Jack Bell-lounds! The brute—the coward! I hate him! Oh, I *hate* him! . . . And I've got to marry him—on October first! Oh, God pity me!"

Blindly Columbine reeled out of her saddle and slowly dropped to the grass, where she burst into a violent storm of sobs and tears. It shook her every fiber. It was hopeless, terrible grief. The dry grass received her flood of tears and her incoherent words.

Wade dismounted and, kneeling beside her, placed a gentle hand upon her heaving shoulder, but he spoke no word. By and by, when the storm had begun to subside, he raised her head.

"Lass, nothin' is ever so bad as it seems," he said softly. "Come, sit up. Let me talk to you."

"Oh, Ben, something terrible *has* happened," she cried. "It's in *me!* I don't know what it is. But it'll kill me."

"I know," he replied, as her head fell upon his shoulder. "Miss Collie, I'm an old fellow that's had everythin' happen to him, an' I'm livin' yet, tryin' to help people along. No one dies so easy. Why, you're a fine, strong girl—an' somethin' tells me you was made for happiness. I know how things turn out. Listen—"

"But, Ben—you don't know—about me," she sobbed. "I've told you—I—hate Jack Belllounds. But I've—got to marry him! . . . His father raised me—from a baby. He brought me up. I owe him—my life. . . . I've no relation—no mother—no father! No one loves me—for myself!"

"Nobody loves you!" echoed Wade, with an exquisite tone of repudiation. "Strange how people fool themselves! Lass, you're huggin' your troubles too hard. An' you're wrong. Why, everybody loves you! Lem an' Jim—why you just brighten the hard world they live in. An' that poor, hot-headed Jack—he loves you as well as he can love anythin'. An' the old man—no daughter could be loved more. . . . An' I—I love you, lass, just like—as if you—might have been my own. I'm goin' to be the friend—the brother you need. An' I reckon I can come somewheres near bein' a mother, if you'll let me."

Something, some subtle power or charm, stole over Columbine, assuaging her terrible sense of loss, of grief. There was tenderness in this man's hands, in his voice, and through them throbbed strong and passionate life and spirit.

"Do you really love me—*love* me?" she whispered, somehow comforted, somehow feeling that what he offered was what she had missed as a child. "And you want to be all that for me?"

"Yes, lass, an' I reckon you'd better try me."

"Oh, how good you are! I felt that—the very first time I was with you. I've wanted to come to you—to tell you my troubles. I love dad and he loves me, but he doesn't understand. Dad is wrapped up in his son. I've had no one. I never had any one."

"You have some one now," returned Wade, with a rich deep mellowness in his voice that soothed Columbine and made her wonder. "An' because I've been through so much I can tell you what'll help you. . . . Lass, if a woman isn't big an' brave, how will a man ever be. There's more in women than in men. Life has given you a hard knock, placin' you here— no real parents—an makin' you responsible to a man whose only fault is blinded love for his son. Well, you've got to meet it, face it, with what a woman has more of than any man. Courage! Suppose you do hate this Buster Jack. Suppose you do love this poor, crippled Wilson Moore. . . . Lass, don't look like that! Don't deny. You do love that boy. . . . Well, it's hell. But you can never tell what'll happen when you're honest and square. If you feel it your duty to pay your debt to the old man you call dad—to pay it by marryin' his son, why do it, an' be a woman. There's nothin' as great as a woman can be. There's happiness that comes in strange, unheard-of ways. There's more in this life than what you want most. *You* didn't place yourself in this fix. So if you meet it with courage an' faithfulness to yourself, why, it'll not turn out as you dread. . . . Some day, if you ever think you're broken-hearted, I'll tell you my story. An' then you'll not think your lot so hard. For I've had a broken heart an' ruined life, an' yet I've lived on an' on, findin' happiness I never dreamed would come, fightin' or workin'. An' how I found the world beautiful, an' how I love the flowers an' hills an' wild things so well—that, just that would be enough to live for! . . . An' think, lass, of what a wonderful happiness will come to me in showin' all this to you. That'll be the crownin' glory. An' if it's that much to me, then you be sure there's nothin' on earth I won't do for you."

Columbine lifted her tear-stained face with a light of inspiration.

"Oh, Wilson was right!" she murmured. "You are Heaven-sent! And I'm going to love you!"

CHAPTER 9

Anew spirit, or a liberation of her own, had fired Columbine, and was now burning within her, unquenchable and unutterable. Some divine spark had penetrated into that mysterious depth of her, to inflame and to illumine, so that when she arose from this hour of calamity she felt that to the tenderness and sorrow and fidelity in her soul had been added the lightning flash of passion.

"Oh, Ben—shall I be able to hold on to this?" she cried, flinging wide her arms, as if to embrace the winds of heaven.

"This what, lass?" he asked.

"This—this *woman!*" she answered, passionately, with her hands sweeping back to press her breast.

"No woman who wakes ever goes back to a girl again," he said, sadly.

"I wanted to die—and now I want to live—to fight. . . . Ben, you've uplifted me. I was little, weak, miserable . . . But in my dreams, or in some state I can't remember or understand, I've waited for your very words. I was ready. It's as if I knew you in some other world, before I was born on this earth; and when you spoke to me here, so wonderfully—as my mother might have spoken—my heart leaped up in recognition of you and your call to my womanhood! . . . Oh, how strange and beautiful!"

"Miss Collie," he replied, slowly, as he bent to his saddle-straps, "you're young, an' you've no understandin' of what's strange an' terrible in life. An' beautiful, too, as you say. . . . Who knows? Maybe in some former state I was somethin' to you. I believe in that. Reckon I can't say how or what. Maybe we were flowers or birds. I've a weakness for that idea."

"Birds! I like the thought, too," replied Columbine. "I love most birds. But there are hawks, crows, buzzards!"

"I reckon. Lass, there's got to be balance in nature. If it weren't for the ugly an' the evil, we wouldn't know the beautiful an' good. . . . An' now let's ride home. It's gettin' late."

"Ben, ought I not go back to Wilson right now?" she asked, slowly.

"What for?"

"To tell him—something—and why I can't come tomorrow, or ever afterward," she replied, low and tremulously.

Wade pondered over her words. It seemed to Columbine that her sharpened faculties sensed something of hostility, of opposition in him.

"Reckon to-morrow would be better," he said, presently. "Wilson's had enough excitement for one day."

"Then I'll go to-morrow," she returned.

In the gathering, cold twilight they rode down the trail in silence.

"Good night, lass," said Wade, as he reached his cabin. "An' remember you're not alone any more."

"Good night, my friend," she replied, and rode on.

Columbine encountered Jim Montana at the corrals, and it was not too dark for her to see his foam-lashed horse. Jim appeared non-committal, almost surly. But Columbine guessed that he had ridden to Kremmling and back in one day, on some order of Jack's.

"Miss Collie, I'll tend to Pronto," he offered. "An' yore supper'll be waitin'."

A bright fire blazed on the living-room hearth. The rancher was reading by its light.

"Hello, rosy-cheeks!" greeted the rancher, with unusual amiability. "Been ridin' ag'in' the wind, hey? Wal, if you ain't pretty, then my eyes are pore!"

"It's cold, dad," she replied, "and the wind stings. But I didn't ride fast nor far. . . . I've been up to see Wilson Moore."

"Ahuh! Wal, how's the boy?" asked Belllounds, gruffly.

"He said he was all right, but—but I guess that's not so," responded Columbine.

"Any friends lookin' after him?"

"Oh yes—he must have friends—the Andrewses and others. I'm glad to say his cabin is comfortable. He'll be looked after."

"Wal, I'm glad to hear thet. I'll send Lem or Wade up thar an' see if we can do anythin' fer the boy."

"Dad—that's just like you," replied Columbine, with her hand seeking his broad shoulder.

"Ahuh! Say, Collie, hyar's letters from 'most everybody in Kremmlin' wantin' to be invited up fer October first. How about askin' 'em?"

"The more the merrier," replied Columbine.

"Wal, I reckon I'll not ask anybody."

"Why not, dad?"

"No one can gamble on thet son of mine, even on his weddin'-day," replied Belllounds, gloomily.

"Dad, what'd Jack do to-day?"

"I'm not sayin' he did anythin'," answered the rancher.

"Dad, you can gamble on me."

"Wal, I should smile," he said, putting his big arm around her. "I wish you was Jack an' Jack was you."

At that moment the young man spoken of slouched into the room, with his head bandaged, and took a seat at the supper-table.

"Wal, Collie, let's go an' get it," said the rancher, cheerily. "I can always eat, anyhow."

"I'm hungry as a bear," rejoined Columbine, as she took her seat, which was opposite Jack.

"Where've you been?" he asked, curiously.

"Why, good evening, Jack! Did you finally notice me? . . . I've been riding Pronto, the first time since he was hurt. Had a lovely ride—up through Sage Valley."

Jack glowered at her with the one unbandaged eye, and growled something under his breath, and then began to stab meat and potatoes with his fork.

"What's the matter, Jack? Aren't you well?" asked Columbine, with a solicitude just a little too sweet to be genuine.

"Yes, I'm well," snapped Jack.

"But you look sick. That is, what I can see of your face looks sick. Your mouth droops at the corners. You're very pale—and red in spots. And your one eye glows with unearthly woe, as if you were not long for this world!"

The amazing nature of this speech, coming from the girl who had always been so sweet and quiet and backward, was attested to by the consternation of Jack and the mirth of his father.

"Are you making fun of me?" demanded Jack.

"Why, Jack! Do you think I would make fun of you? I only wanted to say how queer you look. . . . Are you going to be married with one eye?"

Jack collapsed at that, and the old man, after a long stare of openmouthed wonder, broke out: "Haw! Haw! Haw! . . . By Golly! lass—I'd never believed thet was in you. . . . Jack, be game an' take your medicine. . . . An' both of you forgive an' forget. Thar'll be quarrels enough, mebbe, without rakin' over the past."

When alone again Columbine reverted to a mood vastly removed from her apparent levity with the rancher and his son. A grave and inward-searching thought possessed her, and it had to do with the uplift, the spiritual advance, the rise above mere personal welfare, that had strangely come to her through Bent Wade. From their first meeting he had possessed a singular attraction for her that now, in the light of the meaning of his life, seemed to Columbine to be the man's nobility and wisdom, arising out of his travail, out of the terrible years that had left their record upon his face.

And so Columbine strove to bind forever in her soul the spirit which had arisen in her, interpreting from Wade's rude words of philosophy that which she needed for her own light and strength.

She appreciated her duty toward the man who had been a father to her. Whatever he asked that would she do. And as for the son she must live with the rest of her life, her duty there was to be a good wife, to bear with his faults, to strive always to help him by kindness, patience, loyalty, and such affection as was possible to her. Hate had to be reckoned with, and hate, she knew, had no place in a good woman's heart. It must be expelled, if that were humanly possible. All this was hard, would grow harder, but she accepted it, and knew her mind.

Her soul was her own, unchangeable through any adversity. She could be with that alone always, aloof from the petty cares and troubles common to people. Wade's words had thrilled her with their secret, with their limitless hope of an unknown world of thought and feeling. Happiness, in the ordinary sense, might never be hers. Alas for her dreams! But there had been given her a glimpse of something higher than pleasure and contentment. Dreams were but dreams. But she could still dream of what had been, of what might have been, of the beauty and mystery of life, of something in nature that called sweetly and irresistibly to her. Who could rob her of the rolling, gray, velvety hills, and the purple peaks and the black ranges, among which she had been found a waif, a little lost creature, born like a columbine under the spruces?

Love, sudden-dawning, inexplicable love, was her secret, still tremulously new, and perilous in its sweetness. That only did she fear to realize and to face, because it was an unknown factor, a threatening flame. Her sudden knowledge of it seemed inextricably merged with the mounting, strong, and steadfast stream of her spirit.

"I'll go to him. I'll tell him," she murmured. "He shall have *that!* . . . Then I must bid him—good-by—forever!"

To tell Wilson would be sweet; to leave him would be bitter. Vague possibilities haunted her. What might come of the telling? How dark loomed the bitterness! She could not know what hid in either of these acts until they were fulfilled. And the hours became long, and sleep far off, and the quietness of the house a torment, and the melancholy wail of coyotes a reminder of happy girlhood, never to return.

When next day the long-deferred hour came Columbine selected a horse that she could run, and she rode up the winding valley swift as the wind. But at the aspen grove, where Wade's keen, gentle voice had given her secret life, she suffered a reaction that made her halt and ascend the slope very slowly and with many stops.

Sight of Wade's horse haltered near the cabin relieved Columbine somewhat of a gathering might of emotion. The hunter would be inside and so she would not be compelled at once to confess her secret. This expectancy gave impetus to her lagging steps. Before she reached the open door she called out.

"Collie, you're late," answered Wilson, with both joy and reproach, as she entered. The cowboy lay upon his bed, and he was alone in the room.

"Oh! . . . Where is Ben?" exclaimed Columbine.

"He was here. He cooked my dinner. We waited, but you never came. The dinner got cold. I made sure you'd backed out—weren't coming at all—and I couldn't eat. . . . Wade said he knew you'd come. He went off with the hounds, somewhere . . . and oh, Collie, it's all right now!"

Columbine walked to his bedside and looked down upon him with a feeling as if some giant hand was tugging at her heart. He looked better. The swelling and redness of his face were less marked. And at that moment no pain shadowed his eyes. They were soft, dark, eloquent. If Columbine had not come with her avowed resolution and desire to unburden her heart she would have found that look in his eyes a desperately hard one to resist. Had it ever shone there before? Blind she had been.

"You're better," she said, happily.

"Sure—*now*. But I had a bad night. Didn't sleep till near daylight. Wade found me asleep. . . . Collie, it's good of you to come. You look so—so wonderful! I never saw your face glow like that. And your eyes—oh!"

"You think I'm pretty, then?" she asked, dreamily, not occupied at all with that thought.

He uttered a contemptuous laugh.

"Come closer," he said, reaching for her with a clumsy bandaged hand.

Down upon her knees Columbine fell. Both hands flew to cover her face. And as she swayed forward she shook violently, and there escaped her lips a little, muffled sound.

"Why—Collie!" cried Moore, astounded. "Good Heavens! Don't cry! I—I didn't mean anything. I only wanted to feel you—touch your hand."

"Here," she answered, blindly holding out her hand, groping for his till she found it. Her other was still pressed to her eyes. One moment longer would Columbine keep her secret—hide her eyes—revel in the unutterable joy and sadness of this crisis that could come to a woman only once.

"What in the world?" ejaculated the cowboy, now bewildered. But he possessed himself of the trembling hand offered. "Collie, you act so strange. . . . You're *not* crying! . . . Am I only locoed, or flighty, or what? Dear, look at me."

Columbine swept her hand from her eyes with a gesture of utter surrender.

"Wilson, I'm ashamed—and sad—and gloriously happy," she said, with swift breathlessness.

"Why?" he asked.

"Because of—of something I have to tell you," she whispered.

"What is that?"

She bent over him.

"Can't you guess?"

He turned pale, and his eyes burned with intense fire.

"I won't guess . . . I daren't guess."

"It's something that's been true for years—forever, it seems—something I never dreamed of till last night," she went on, softly.

"Collie!" he cried. "Don't torture me!"

"Do you remember long ago—when we quarreled so dreadfully—because you kissed me?" she asked.

"Do you think I could kiss *you*—and live to forget?"

"I love you!" she whispered, shyly, feeling the hot blood burn her.

That whisper transformed Wilson Moore. His arm flashed round her neck and pulled her face down to his, and, holding her in a close embrace, he kissed her lips and cheeks and wet eyes, and then again her lips, passionately and tenderly.

Then he pressed her head down upon his breast.

"My God! I can't believe! Say it again!" he cried, hoarsely.

Columbine buried her flaming face in the blanket covering him, and her hands clutched it tightly. The wildness of his joy, the strange strength and power of his kisses, utterly changed her. Upon his breast she lay, with out desire to lift her face. All seemed different, wilder, as she responded to his appeal: "Yes, I love you! Oh, I love—love—love you!"

"Dearest! . . . Lift your face. . . . It's true now. I know. It's proved. But let me look at you."

Columbine lifted herself as best she could. But she was blinded by tears and choked with utterance that would not come, and in the grip of a shuddering emotion that was realization of loss in a moment when she learned the supreme and imperious sweetness of love.

"Kiss me, Columbine," he demanded.

Through blurred eyes she saw his face, white and rapt, and she bent to it, meeting his lips with her first kiss, which was her last.

"Again, Collie—again!" he begged.

"No—no more," she whispered, very low, and encircling his neck with her arms she hid her face and held him convulsively, and stifled the sobs that shook her.

Then Moore was silent, holding her with his free hand, breathing hard, and slowly quieting down. Columbine felt then that he knew that there was something terribly wrong, and that perhaps he dared not voice his fear. At any rate, he silently held her, waiting. That silent wait grew unendurable for Columbine. She wanted to prolong this moment that was to be all she could ever surrender. But she dared not do so, for she knew if he ever kissed her again her duty to Belllounds would vanish like mist in the sun.

To release her hold upon him seemed like a tearing of her heart-strings. She sat up, she wiped the tears from her eyes, she rose to her feet, all the time striving for strength to face him again.

A loud voice, ringing from the cliffs outside, startled Columbine. It came from Wade calling the hounds. He had returned, and the fact stirred her.

"I'm to marry Jack Belllounds on October first."

The cowboy raised himself up as far as he was able. It was agonizing for Columbine to watch the changing and whitening of his face!

"No—no!" he gasped.

"Yes, it's true," she replied, hopelessly.

"*No!*" he exclaimed, hoarsely.

"But, Wilson, I tell you yes. I came to tell you. It's true—oh, it's true!"

"But, girl, you said you love me," he declared, transfixing her with dark, accusing eyes.

"That's just as terribly true."

He softened a little, and something of terror and horror took the place of anger.

Just then Wade entered the cabin with his soft tread, hesitated, and then came to Columbine's side. She could not unrivet her gaze from Moore to look at her friend, but she reached out with trembling hand to him. Wade clasped it in a horny palm.

Wilson fought for self-control in vain.

"Collie, if you love me, how can you marry Jack Belllounds?" he demanded.

"I must."

"Why must you?"

"I owe my life and my bringing up to his father. He wants me to do it. His heart is set upon my helping Jack to become a man. . . . Dad loves me, and I love him. I must stand by him. I must repay him. It is my duty."

"You've a duty to yourself—as a woman!" he rejoined, passionately. "Belllounds is wrapped up in his son. He's blind to the shame of such a marriage. But you're not."

"Shame?" faltered Columbine.

"Yes. The shame of marrying one man when you love another. You can't love two men. . . . You'll give yourself. You'll be his *wife!* Do you understand what that means?"

"I—I think—I do," replied Columbine, faintly. Where had vanished all her wonderful spirit? This fire-eyed boy was breaking her heart with his reproach.

"But you'll bear his children," cried Wilson. "Mother of—them—when you love me! . . . Didn't you think of that?"

"Oh no—I never did—I never did!" wailed Columbine.

"Then you'll think before it's too late?" he implored, wildly. "Dearest Collie, think. You won't ruin yourself! You won't? Say you won't!"

"But—Oh, Wilson, what *can* I say? I've got to marry him."

"Collie, I'll kill him before he gets you."

"You mustn't talk so. If you fought again—if anything terrible happened, it'd kill me."

"You'd be better off!" he flashed, white as a sheet.

Columbine leaned against Wade for support. She was fast weakening in strength, although her spirit held. She knew what was inevitable. But Wilson's agony was rending her.

"Listen," began the cowboy again. "It's your life—your happiness—your soul. . . . Belllounds is crazy over that spoiled boy. He thinks the sun rises and sets in him. . . . But Jack Belllounds is no good on this earth! . . . Collie dearest, don't think that's my jealousy. I am horribly jealous. But I know him. He's not worth *you!* No man is—and he the least. He'll break your heart, drag you down, ruin your health—kill you, as sure as you stand there. I want you to know I could prove to you what he is. But don't make me. Trust me, Collie. Believe me."

"Wilson, I do believe you," cried Columbine. "But it doesn't make any difference. It only makes my duty harder."

"He'll treat you like he treats a horse or a dog. He'll beat you—"

"He never will! If he ever lays a hand on me—"

"If not that, he'll tire of you. Jack Belllounds never stuck to anything in his life, and never will. It's not in him. He wants what he can't have. If he gets it, then right off he doesn't want it. Oh, I've known him since he was a kid. . . . Columbine, you've a mistaken sense of duty. No girl need sacrifice her all because some man found her a lost baby and gave her a home. A woman owes more to herself than to any one."

"Oh, that's true, Wilson. I've thought it all. . . . But you're unjust—hard. You make no allowance for—for some possible good in every one. Dad swears I can reform Jack. Maybe I can. I'll pray for it."

"Reform Jack Belllounds! How can you save a bad egg? That damned coward! Didn't he prove to you what he was when he jumped on me and kicked my broken foot till I fainted? . . . What do you want?"

"Don't say any more—please," cried Columbine. "Oh, I'm so sorry. . . . I oughtn't have come. . . . Ben, take me home."

"But, Collie, I love you," frantically urged Wilson. "And he—he may love you—but he's—Collie—he's been—"

Here Moore seemed to bite his tongue, to hold back speech, to fight something terrible and desperate and cowardly in himself.

Columbine heard only his impassioned declaration of love, and to that she vibrated.

"You speak as if this was one-sided," she burst out, as once more the gush of hot blood surged over her. "You don't love me any more than I love you. Not as much, for I'm a woman! . . . I love with all my heart and soul!"

Moore fell back upon the bed, spent and overcome.

"Wade, my friend, for God's sake do something," he whispered, appealing to the hunter as if in a last hope. "Tell Collie what it'll mean for her to marry Belllounds. If that doesn't change her, then tell her what it'll mean to me. I'll never go home. I'll never leave here. If she hadn't told me she loved me then, I might have stood anything. But now I can't. It'll kill me, Wade."

"Boy, you're talkin' flighty again," replied Wade. "This mornin' when I come you were dreamin' an' talkin'—clean out of your head. . . . Well, now, you an' Collie listen. You're right an' she's right. I reckon I never run across a deal with two people fixed just like you. But that doesn't hinder me from feelin' the same about it as I'd feel about somethin' I was used to."

He paused, and, gently releasing Columbine, he went to Moore, and retied his loosened bandage, and spread out the disarranged blankets. Then he sat down on the edge of the bed and bent over a little, running a roughened hand through the scant hair that had begun to silver upon his head. Presently he looked up, and from that sallow face, with its lines and furrows, and from the deep, inscrutable eyes, there fell a light which, however sad and wise in its infinite understanding of pain and strife, was still ruthless and unquenchable in its hope.

"Wade, for God's sake save Columbine!" importuned Wilson.

"Oh, if you only could!" cried Columbine, impelled beyond her power to resist by that prayer.

"Lass, you stand by your convictions," he said, impressively. "An' Moore, you be a man an' don't make it so hard for her. Neither of you can do anythin'. . . . Now there's Old Belllounds—he'll never change. He might r'ar up for this or that, but he'll never change his cherished hopes for his son. . . . But Jack might change! Lookin' back over all the years I remember many boys like this Buster Jack, an' I remember how in the nature of their doin's they just hanged themselves. I've a queer foresight about people whose trouble I've made my own. It's somethin' that never fails. When their trouble's goin' to turn out bad then I feel a terrible yearnin' to tell the story of Hell-Bent Wade. That foresight of trouble gave me my name. . . . But it's not operatin' here. . . . An' so, my young friends, you can believe me when I say somethin' will happen. As far as October first is concerned, or any time near, Collie isn't goin' to marry Jack Belllounds."

CHAPTER 10

O ne day Wade remarked to Belllounds: "You can never tell what a dog is until you know him. Dogs are like men. Some of 'em look good, but they're really bad. An' that works the other way round. If a dog's born to run wild an' be a sheep-killer, that's what he'll be. I've known dogs that loved men as no humans could have loved them. It doesn't make any dif-ference to a dog if his master is a worthless scamp."

"Wal, I reckon most of them hounds I bought had no good masters, judgin' from the way they act," replied the rancher.

"I'm developin' a first-rate pack," said Wade. "Jim hasn't any faults exceptin' he doesn't bay enough. Sampson's not as true-nosed as Jim, but he'll follow Jim, an' he has a deep, heavy bay you can hear for miles. So that makes up for Jim's one fault. These two hounds hang together, an' with them I'm developin' others. Denver will split off of bear or lion tracks when he jumps a deer. I reckon he's not young enough to be cured of that. Some of the younger hounds are comin' on fine. But there's two dogs in the bunch that beat me all hollow."

"Which ones?" asked Belllounds.

"There's that bloodhound, Kane," replied the hunter. "He's sure a queer dog. I can't win him. He minds me now because I licked him, an' once good an' hard when he bit me. . . . But he doesn't cotton to me worth a damn. He's gettin' fond of Miss Columbine, an' I believe might make a good watch-dog for her. Where'd he come from, Bellllounds?"

"Wal, if I don't disremember he was born in a prairie-schooner, comin' across the plains. His mother was a full-blood, an' come from Louisiana."

"That accounts for an instinct I see croppin' out in Kane," rejoined Wade. "He likes to trail a man. I've caught him doin' it. An' he doesn't take to huntin' lions or bear. Why, the other day, when the hounds treed a lion an' went howlin' wild, Kane came up, an' he looked disgusted an' went off by himself. He hunts by himself, anyhow. First off I thought he might be a sheep-killer. But I reckon not. He can trail men, an' that's about all the good he is. His mother must have been a slave-hunter, an' Kane inherits that trailin' instinct."

"Ahuh! Wal, train him on trailin' men, then. I've seen times when a dog like thet 'd come handy. An' if he takes to Collie an' you approve of him, let her have him. She's been coaxin' me fer a dog."

"That isn't a bad idea. Miss Collie walks an' rides alone a good deal, an' she never packs a gun."

"Funny about thet," said Belllounds. "Collie is game in most ways, but she'd never kill anythin'. . . . Wade, you ain't thinkin' she ought to stop them lonesome walks an' rides?"

"No, sure not, so long as she doesn't go too far away."

"Ahuh! Wal, supposin' she rode up out of the valley, west on the Black Range?"

"That won't do, Belllounds," replied Wade, seriously. "But Miss Collie's not goin' to, for I've cautioned her. Fact is I've run across some hard-lookin' men between here an' Buffalo Park. They're not hunters or prospectors or cattlemen or travelers."

"Wal, you don't say!" rejoined Belllounds. "Now, Wade, are you connectin' up them strangers with the stock I missed on this last round-up?"

"Reckon I can't go as far as that," returned Wade. "But I didn't like their looks."

"Thet comin' from you, Wade, is like the findin's of a jury. . . . It's gettin' along toward October. Snow'll be flyin' soon. You don't reckon them strangers will winter in the woods?"

"No, I don't. Neither does Lewis. You recollect him?"

"Yes, thet prospector who hangs out around Buffalo Park, lookin' fer gold. He's been hyar. Good fellar, but crazy on gold."

"I've met Lewis several times, one place and another. I lost the hounds day before yesterday. They treed a lion an' Lewis heard the racket, an' he stayed with them till I come up. Then he told me some interestin' news. You see he's been worryin' about this gang thet's rangin' around Buffalo Park, an' he's tried to get a line on them. Somebody took a shot at him in the woods. He couldn't swear it was one of that outfit, but he could swear he wasn't near shot by accident. Now Lewis says these men pack to an' fro from Elgeria, an' he has a hunch they're in cahoots with Smith, who runs a place there. You know Smith?"

"No, I don't, an' haven't any wish to," declared Belllounds, shortly. "He always looked shady to me. An' he's not been square with friends of mine in Elgeria. But no one ever proved him crooked, whatever was thought. Fer my part, I never missed a guess in my life. Men don't have scars on their face like his fer nothin'."

"Boss, I'm confidin' what I want kept under your hat," said Wade, quietly. "I knew Smith. He's as bad as the West makes them. I gave him that scar. . . . An' when he sees me he's goin' for his gun."

"Wal, I'll be darned! Doesn't surprise me. It's a small world. . . . Wade, I'll keep my mouth shut, sure. But what's your game?"

"Lewis an' I will find out if there is any connection between Smith an' this gang of strangers—an' the occasional loss of a few head of stock."

"Ahuh! Wal, you have my good will, you bet. . . . Sure thar's been some rustlin' of cattle. Not enough to make any rancher holler, an' I reckon there never will be any more of thet in Colorado. Still, if we get the drop on some outfit we sure ought to corral them."

"Boss, I'm tellin' you—"

"Wade, you ain't agoin' to start thet tellin' hell-bent happenin's to come hyar at White Slides?" interrupted Belllounds, plaintively.

"No, I reckon I've no hunch like that now," responded Wade, seriously. "But I was about to say that if Smith is in on any rustlin' of cattle he'll be hard to catch, an' if he's caught there'll be shootin' to pay. He's cunnin' an' has had long experience. It's not likely he'd work openly, as he did years ago. If he's stealin' stock or buyin' an' sellin' stock that some one steals for him, it's only on a small scale, an' it'll be hard to trace."

"Wal, he might be deep," said Belllounds, reflectively. "But men like thet, no matter how deep or cunnin' they are, always come to a bad end. Jest works out natural. . . . Had you any grudge ag'in' Smith?"

"What I give him was for somebody else, an' was sure little enough. He's got the grudge against me."

"Ahuh! Wal, then, don't you go huntin' fer trouble. Try an' make White Slides one place thet'll disprove your name. All the same, don't shy at sight of anythin' suspicious round the ranch."

The old man plodded thoughtfully away, leaving the hunter likewise in a brown study.

"He's gettin' a hunch that I'll tell him of some shadow hoverin' black over White Slides," soliloquized Wade. "Maybe—maybe so. But I don't see any yet. . . . Strange how a man will say what he didn't start out to say. Now, I started to tell him about that amazin' dog Fox."

Fox was the great dog of the whole pack, and he had been absolutely overlooked, which fact Wade regarded with contempt for himself. Discovery of this particular dog came about by accident. Somewhere in the big corral there was a hole where the smaller dogs could escape, but Wade had been unable to find it. For that matter the corral was full of holes, not any of which, however, it appeared to Wade, would permit anything except a squirrel to pass in and out.

One day when the hunter, very much exasperated, was prowling around and around inside the corral, searching for this mysterious vent, a rather small dog, with short gray and brown woolly hair, and shaggy brows half hiding big, bright eyes, came up wagging his stump of a tail.

"Well, what do you know about it?" demanded Wade. Of course he had noticed this particular dog, but to no purpose. On this occasion the dog repeated so unmistakably former overtures of friendship that Wade gave him close scrutiny. He was neither young nor comely nor thoroughbred, but there was something in his intelligent eyes that struck the hunter significantly. "Say, maybe I overlooked somethin'? But there's been a heap of dogs round here an' you're no great shucks for looks. Now, if you're talkin' to me come an' find that hole."

Whereupon Wade began another search around the corral. It covered nearly an acre of ground, and in some places the fence-poles had been sunk near rocks. More than once Wade got down upon his hands and knees to see if he could find the hole. The dog went with him, watching with knowing eyes that the hunter imagined actually laughed at him. But they were glad eyes, which began to make an appeal. Presently, when Wade came to a rough place, the dog slipped under a shelving rock, and thence through a half-concealed hole in the fence; and immediately came back through to wag his stump of a tail and look as if the finding of that hole was easy enough.

"You old fox," declared Wade, very much pleased, as he patted the dog. "You found it for me, didn't you? Good dog! Now I'll fix that hole, an' then you can come to the cabin with me. An' your name's Fox."

That was how Fox introduced himself to Wade, and found his opportunity. The fact that he was not a hound had operated against his being taken out hunting, and therefore little or no attention had been paid him. Very shortly Fox showed himself to be a dog of superior intelligence. The hunter had lived much with dogs and had come to learn that the longer he lived with them the more there was to marvel at and love.

Fox insisted so strongly on being taken out to hunt with the hounds that Wade, vowing not to be surprised at anything, let him go. It happened to be a particularly hard day on hounds because of old tracks and cross-tracks and difficult ground. Fox worked out a labyrinthine trail that Sampson gave up and Jim failed on. This delighted Wade, and that night he tried to find out from Andrews, who sold the dog to Belllounds, something about Fox. All the information obtainable was that Andrews suspected the fellow from whom he had gotten Fox had stolen him. Belllounds had never noticed him at all. Wade kept the possibilities of Fox to himself and reserved his judgment, and every day gave the dog another chance to show what he knew.

Long before the end of that week Wade loved Fox and decided that he was a wonderful animal. Fox liked to hunt, but it did not matter what he hunted. That depended upon the pleasure of his master. He would find hobbled horses that were hiding out and standing still to escape detection. He would trail cattle. He would tree squirrels and point grouse. Invariably he suited his mood to the kind of game he hunted. If put on an elk track, or that of deer, he would follow it, keeping well within sight of the hunter, and never uttering a single bark or yelp; and without any particular eagerness he would stick until he had found the game or until he was called off. Bear and cat tracks, however, roused the savage instinct in him, and transformed him. He yelped at every jump on a trail, and whenever his yelp became piercing and continuous Wade well knew the quarry was in sight. He fought bear like a wise old dog that knew when to rush in with a snap and when to keep away. When lions or wildcats were treed Fox lost much of his ferocity and interest. Then the matter of that particular quarry was ended. His most valuable characteristic, however, was his ability to stick on the track upon which he was put. Wade believed if he put Fox on the trail of a rabbit, and if a bear or lion were to cross that trail ahead of him, Fox would stick to the rabbit. Even more remarkable was it that Fox would not steal a piece of meat and that he would fight the other dogs for being thieves.

Fox and Kane, it seemed to the hunter in his reflective foreshadowing of events at White Slides, were destined to play most important parts.

Upon a certain morning, several days before October first—which date rankled in the mind of Wade—he left Moore's cabin, leading a pack-horse. The hounds he had left behind at the ranch, but Fox accompanied him.

"Wade, I want some elk steak," old Belllounds had said the day before. "Nothin' like a good rump steak! I was raised on elk meat. Now hyar, more 'n a week ago I told you I wanted some. There's elk all around. I heerd a bull whistle at sunup to-day. Made me wish I was young ag'in! . . . You go pack in an elk."

"I haven't run across any bulls lately," Wade had replied, but he did not mention that he had avoided such a circumstance. The fact was Wade admired and loved the elk above all horned wild animals. So strange was his attitude toward elk that he had gone meat-hungry many a time with these great stags bugling near his camp.

As he climbed the yellow, grassy mountain-side, working round above the valley, his mind was not centered on the task at hand, but on Wilson Moore, who had come to rely on him with the unconscious tenacity of a son whose faith in his father was unshakable. The crippled cowboy kept his hope, kept his cheerful, grateful spirit, obeyed and suffered with a patience that was fine. There had been no improvement in his injured foot. Wade worried about that much more than Moore. The thing that mostly occupied the cowboy was the near approach of October first, with its terrible possibility for him. He did not talk about it, except when fever made him irrational, but it was plain to Wade how he prayed and hoped and waited in silence. Strange how he trusted Wade to avert catastrophe of Columbine's marriage! Yet such trust seemed familiar to Wade, as he reflected over past years. Had he not wanted such trust—had he not invited it?

For twenty years no happiness had come to Wade in any sense comparable to that now secretly his, as he lived near Columbine Belllounds, divining more and more each day how truly she was his own flesh and the image of the girl he had loved and married and wronged. Columbine was his daughter. He saw himself in her. And Columbine, from being strongly attracted to him and trusting in him and relying upon him, had come to love him. That was the most beautiful and terrible fact of his life— beautiful because it brought back the past, her babyhood, and his barren years, and gave him this sudden change, where he lived transported with the sense and the joy of his possession. It was terrible because she was unhappy, because she was chained to duty and honor, because ruin faced her, and lastly because Wade began to have the vague, gloomy intimations of distant tragedy. Far off, like a cloud on the horizon, but there! Long ago he had learned the uselessness of fighting his morbid visitations. But he clung to hope, to faith in life, to the victory of the virtuous, to the defeat of evil. A thousand proofs had strengthened him in that clinging.

There were personal dread and poignant pain for Wade in Columbine Belllounds's situation. After all, he had only his subtle and intuitive assurance that matters would turn out well for her in the end. To trust that now, when the shadow began to creep over his own daughter, seemed unwise—a juggling with chance.

"I'm beginnin' to feel that I couldn't let her marry that Buster Jack," soliloquized Wade, as he rode along the grassy trail. "Fust off, seein' how strong was her sense of duty an' loyalty, I wasn't so set against it. But somethin's growin' in me. Her love for that crippled boy, now, an' his for her! Lord! they're so young an' life must be so hot an' love so sweet! I reckon that's why I couldn't let her marry Jack. . . . But, on the other hand, there's the old man's faith in his son, an' there's Collie's faith in herself an' in life. Now I believe in that. An' the years have proved to me there's hope for the worst of men. . . . I haven't even had a talk with this Buster Jack. I don't know him, except by hearsay. An' I'm sure prejudiced, which 's no wonder, considerin' where I saw him in Denver. . . . I reckon, before I go any farther, I'd better meet this Belllounds boy an' see what's in him."

It was characteristic of Wade that this soliloquy abruptly ended his thoughtful considerations for the time being. This was owing to the fact that he rested upon a decision, and also because it was time he began to attend to the object of his climb.

Bench after bench he had ascended, and the higher he got the denser and more numerous became the aspen thickets and the more luxuriant the grass. Presently the long black slope of spruce confronted him, with its edge like a dark wall. He entered the fragrant forest, where not a twig stirred nor a sound pervaded the silence. Upon the soft, matted earth the hoofs of the horses made no impression and scarcely a perceptible thud.

Wade headed to the left, avoiding rough, rocky defiles of weathered cliff and wind-fallen trees, and aimed to find easy going up to the summit of the mountain bluff far above. This was new forest to him, consisting of moderate-sized spruce-trees growing so closely together that he had to go carefully to keep from snapping dead twigs. Fox trotted on in the lead, now and then pausing to look up at his master, as if for instructions.

A brightening of the dark-green gloom ahead showed the hunter that he was approaching a large glade or open patch, where the sunlight fell strongly. It turned out to be a swale, or swampy place, some few acres in extent, and directly at the foot of a last steep, wooded slope. Here Fox put his nose into the air and halted.

"What're you scentin', Fox, old boy?" asked Wade, with low voice, as he peered ahead. The wind was in the wrong direction for him to approach close to game without being detected. Fox wagged his stumpy tail and looked up with knowing eyes. Wade proceeded cautiously. The swamp was a rank growth of long, weedy grasses and ferns, with here and there a green-mossed bog half hidden and a number of dwarf oak-trees. Wade's horse sank up to his knees in the mire. On the other side showed fresh tracks along the wet margin of the swale.

"It's elk, all right," said Wade, as he dismounted. "Heard us comin'. Now, Fox, stick your nose in that track. An' go slow."

With rifle ready Wade began the ascent of the slope on foot, leading his horse. An old elk trail showed a fresh track. Fox accommodated his pace to that of the toiling hunter. The ascent was steep and led up through dense forest. At intervals, when Wade halted to catch his breath and listen, he heard faint snapping of dead branches far above. At length he reached the top of the mountain, to find a wide, open space, with heavy forest in front, and a bare, ghastly, burned-over district to his right. Fox growled, and appeared about to dash forward. Then, in an opening through the forest, Wade espied a large bull elk, standing at gaze, evidently watching him. He was a gray old bull, with broken antlers. Wade made no move to shoot, and presently the elk walked out of sight.

"Too old an' tough, Fox," explained the hunter to the anxious dog. But perhaps that was not all Wade's motive in sparing him.

Once more mounted, Wade turned his attention to the burned district. It was a dreary, hideous splotch, a blackened slash in the green cover of the mountain. It sloped down into a wide hollow and up another bare slope. The ground was littered with bleached logs, trees that had been killed first by fire and then felled by wind. Here and there a lofty, spectral trunk still withstood the blasts. Across the hollow sloped a considerable area where all trees were dead and still standing—a melancholy sight. Beyond, and far round and down to the left, opened up a slope of spruce and bare ridge, where a few cedars showed dark, and then came black, spear-tipped forest again, leading the eye to the magnificent panorama of endless range on range, purple in the distance.

Wade found patches of grass where beds had been recently occupied.

"Mountain-sheep, by cracky!" exclaimed the hunter. "An' fresh tracks, too! . . . Now I wonder if it wouldn't do to kill a sheep an' tell Bell-lounds I couldn't find any elk."

The hunter had no qualms about killing mountain-sheep, but he loved the lordly stags and would have lied to spare them. He rode on, with keen gaze shifting everywhere to catch a movement of something in this wilderness before him. If there was any living animal in sight it did not move. Wade crossed the hollow, wended a circuitous route through the upstanding forest of dead timber, and entered a thick woods that skirted the rim of the mountain. Presently he came out upon the open rim, from which the depths of green and gray yawned mightily. Far across, Old White Slides loomed up, higher now, with a dignity and majesty unheralded from below.

Wade found fresh sheep tracks in the yellow clay of the rim, small as little deer tracks, showing that they had just been made by ewes and lambs. Not a ram track in the group!

"Well, that lets me out," said Wade, as he peered under the bluff for sight of the sheep. They had gone over the steep rim as if they had wings. "Beats hell how sheep can go down without fallin'! An' how they can hide!"

He knew they were near at hand and he wasted time peering to spy them out. Nevertheless, he could not locate them. Fox waited impatiently for the word to let him prove how easily he could rout them out, but this permission was not forthcoming.

"We're huntin' elk, you Jack-of-all-dogs," reprovingly spoke the hunter to Fox.

So they went on around the rim, and after a couple of miles of travel came to the forest, and then open heads of hollows that widened and deepened down. Here was excellent pasture and cover for elk. Wade left the rim to ride down these slow-descending half-open ridges, where cedars grew and jack-pines stood in clumps, and little grassy-bordered brooks babbled between. He saw tracks where a big buck deer had crossed ahead of him, and then he flushed a covey of grouse that scared the horses, and then he saw where a bear had pulled a rotten log to pieces. Fox did not show any interest in these things.

By and by Wade descended to the junction of these hollows, where three tiny brooklets united to form a stream of pure, swift, clear water, perhaps a foot deep and several yards wide.

"I reckon this's the head of the Troublesome," said Wade. "Whoever named this brook had no sense. . . . Yet here, at its source, it's gatherin' trouble for itself. That's the way of youth."

The grass grew thickly and luxuriantly and showed signs of recent grazing. Elk had been along the brook that morning. There were many tracks, like cow tracks, only smaller, deeper, and more oval; and there were beds where elk had lain, and torn-up places where bulls had plowed and stamped with heavy hoofs.

Fox trailed the herd to higher ground, where evidently they had entered the woods. Here Wade tied his horses, and, whispering to Fox, he proceeded stealthily through this strip of spruce. He came out to an open point, taking care, however, to keep well screened, from which he had a glimpse of a parklike hollow, grassy and watered. Working round to better vantage, he soon espied what had made Fox stand so stiff and bristling. A herd of elk were trooping up the opposite slope, scarcely a hundred yards distant. They had heard or scented him, but did not appear alarmed. They halted to look back. The hunter's quick estimate credited nearly two dozen to the herd, mostly cows. A magnificent bull, with wide-spreading antlers, and black head and shoulders and gray hind quarters, stalked out from the herd, and stood an instant, head aloft, splendidly significant of the wild. Then he trotted into the woods, his antlers noiselessly spreading the green. Others trotted off likewise. Wade raised his rifle and looked through the sight at the bull, and let him pass. Then he saw another over his rifle, and another. Reluctant and forced, he at last aimed and pulled trigger. The heavy Henry boomed out in the stillness. Fox dashed down with eager barks. When the smoke cleared away Wade saw the opposite slope bare except for one fallen elk.

Then he returned to his horses, and brought them back to where Fox perched beside the dead quarry.

"Well, Fox, that stag'll never bugle any more of a sunrise," said Wade. "Strange how we're made so we have to eat meat! I'd 'a liked it otherwise."

He cut up the elk, and packed all the meat the horse could carry, and hung the best of what was left out of the reach of coyotes. Mounting once more, he ascended to the rim and found a slope leading down to the west. Over the basin country below he had hunted several days. This way back to the ranch was longer, he calculated, but less arduous for man and beast. His pack-horse would have hard enough going in any event. From time to time Wade halted to rest the burdened pack-animal. At length he came to a trail he had himself made, which he now proceeded to follow. It led out of the basin, through burned and boggy ground and down upon the forest slope, thence to the grassy and aspened uplands. One aspen grove, where he had rested before, faced the west, and, for reasons hard to guess, had suffered little from frost. All the leaves were intact, some still green, but most of them a glorious gold against the blue. It was a large grove, sloping gently, carpeted with yellow grass and such a profusion of purple asters as Wade had never seen in his flower-loving life. Here he dismounted and sat against an aspen-tree. His horses ruthlessly cropped the purple blossoms.

Nature in her strong prodigality had outdone herself here. Pale white the aspen-trees shone, and above was the fluttering, quivering canopy of gold tinged with green, and below clustered the asters, thick as stars in the sky, waving, nodding, swaying gracefully to each little autumn breeze, lilac-hued and lavender and pale violet, and all the shades of exquisite purple.

Wade lingered, his senses predominating. This was one of those moments that colored his lonely wanderings. Only to see was enough. He would have shut out the encroaching thoughts of self, of others, of life, had that been wholly possible. But here, after the first few moments of exquisite riot of his senses, where fragrance of grass and blossom filled the air, and blaze of gold canopied the purple, he began to think how beautiful the earth was, how Nature hid her rarest gifts for those who loved her most, how good it was to live, if only for these blessings. And sadness crept into his meditations because all this beauty was ephemeral, all the gold would soon be gone, and the asters, so pale and pure and purple, would soon be like the glory of a dream that had passed.

Yet still followed the saving thought that frost and winter must again yield to sun, and spring, summer, autumn would return with the flowers of their season, in that perennial birth so gracious and promising. The aspen leaves would quiver and slowly gild, the grass would wave in the wind, the asters would bloom, lifting star-pale faces to the sky. Next autumn, and every year, and forever, as long as the sun warmed the earth!

It was only man who would not always return to the haunts he loved.

CHAPTER 11

When Bent Wade desired opportunities they seemed to gravitate to him.

Upon riding into the yard of White Slides Ranch he espied Jack Bell-lounds sitting in idle, moping posture on the porch. Something in his dejected appearance roused Wade's pity. No one else was in sight, so the hunter took advantage of the moment.

"Hey, Belllounds, will you give me a lift with this meat?" called Wade.

"Sure," replied Jack, readily enough, and he got up.

Wade led the pack-horse to the door of the store-cabin, which stood back of the kitchen and was joined to it by a roof. There, with Jack's assistance, he unloaded the meat and hung it up on pegs. This done, Wade set to work with knife in hand.

"I reckon a little trimmin' will improve the looks of this carcass," observed Wade.

"Wade, we never had any one round except dad who could cut up a steer or elk," said Jack. "But you've got him beat."

"I'm pretty handy at most things."

"Handy! . . . I wish I could do just one thing as well as you. I can ride, but that's all. No one ever taught me anything."

"You're a young fellow yet, an' you've time, if you only take kindly to learnin'. I was past your age when I learned most I know."

The hunter's voice and his look, and that fascination which subtly hid in his presence, for the first time seemed to find the response of interest in young Belllounds.

"I can't stick, dad says, and he swears at me," replied Belllounds. "But I'll bet I could learn from you."

"Reckon you could. Why can't you stick to anythin'?"

"I don't know. I've been as enthusiastic over work as over riding mustangs. To ride came natural, but in work, when I do it wrong, then I hate it."

"Ahuh! That's too bad. You oughtn't to hate work. Hard work makes for what I reckon you like in a man, but don't understand. As I look back over my life—an' let me say, young fellar, it's been a tough one—what I remember most an' feel best over are the hardest jobs I ever did, an' those that cost the most sweat an' blood."

As Wade warmed to his subject, hoping to sow a good seed in Belllounds's mind, he saw that he was wasting his earnestness. Belllounds did not keep to the train of thought. His mind wandered, and now he was examining Wade's rifle.

"Old Henry forty-four," he said. "Dad has one. Also an old needle-gun. Say, can I go hunting with you?"

"Glad to have you. How do you handle a rifle?"

"I used to shoot pretty well before I went to Denver," he replied. "Haven't tried since I've been home. . . . Suppose you let me take a shot at that post?" And from where he stood in the door he pointed to a big hitching-post near the corral gate.

The corral contained horses, and in the pasture beyond were cattle, any of which might be endangered by such a shot. Wade saw that the young man was in earnest, that he wanted to respond to the suggestion in his mind. Consequences of any kind did not awaken after the suggestion.

"Sure. Go ahead. Shoot low, now, a little below where you want to hit," said Wade.

Belllounds took aim and fired. A thundering report shook the cabin. Dust and splinters flew from the post.

"I hit it!" he exclaimed, in delight. "I was sure I wouldn't, because I aimed 'way under."

"Reckon you did. It was a good shot."

Then a door slammed and Old Bill Belllounds appeared, his hair up-standing, his look and gait proclaiming him on the rampage.

"Jack! What 'n hell are you doin'?" he roared, and he stamped up to the door to see his son standing there with the rifle in his hands. "By Heaven! If it ain't one thing it's another!"

"Boss, don't jump over the traces," said Wade. "I'll allow if I'd known the gun would let out a bellar like that I'd not have told Jack to shoot. Reckon it's because we're under the open roof that it made the racket. I'm wantin' to clean the gun while it's hot."

"Ahuh! Wal, I was scared fust, harkin' back to Indian days, an' then I was mad because I figgered Jack was up to mischief. . . . Did you fetch in the meat?"

"You bet. An' I'd like a piece for myself," replied Wade.

"Help yourself, man. An' say, come down an' eat with us fer supper."

"Much obliged, boss. I sure will."

Then the old rancher trudged back to the house.

"Wade, it was bully of you!" exclaimed Jack, gratefully. "You see how quick dad's ready to jump me? I'll bet he thought I'd picked a shooting-scrape with one of the cowboys."

"Well, he's gettin' old an' testy," replied Wade. "You ought to humor him. He'll not be here always."

Belllounds answered to that suggestion with a shadowing of eyes and look of realization, affection, remorse. Feelings seemed to have a quick rise and play in him, but were not lasting. Wade casually studied him, weighing his impressions, holding them in abeyance for a sum of judg-ment.

"Belllounds, has anybody told you about Wils Moore bein' bad hurt?" abruptly asked the hunter.

"He is, is he?" replied Jack, and to his voice and face came sudden change. "How bad?"

"I reckon he'll be a cripple for life," answered Wade, seriously, and now he stopped in his work to peer at Belllounds. The next moment might be critical for that young man.

"Club-footed! . . . He won't lord it over the cowboys any more—or ride that white mustang!" The softer, weaker expression of his face, that which gave him some title to good looks, changed to an ugliness hard for Wade to define, since it was neither glee, nor joy, nor gratification over his rival's misfortune. It was rush of blood to eyes and skin, a heated change that somehow to Wade suggested an anxious, selfish hunger. Belllounds lacked something, that seemed certain. But it remained to be proved how deserving he was of Wade's pity.

"Belllounds, it was a dirty trick—your jumpin' Moore," declared Wade, with deliberation.

"The hell you say!" Belllounds flared up, with scarlet in his face, with sneer of amaze, with promise of bursting rage. He slammed down the gun.

"Yes, the hell I say," returned the hunter. "They call me Hell-Bent Wade!"

"Are you friends with Moore?" asked Belllounds, beginning to shake.

"Yes, I'm that with every one. I'd like to be friends with you."

"I don't want you. And I'm giving you notice—you won't last long at White Slides."

"Neither will you!"

Belllounds turned dead white, not apparently from fury or fear, but from a shock that had its birth within the deep, mysterious, emotional reachings of his mind. He was utterly astounded, as if confronting a vague, terrible premonition of the future. Wade's swift words, like the ring of bells, had not been menacing, but prophetic.

"Young fellar, you need to be talked to, so if you've got any sense at all it'll get a wedge in your brain," went on Wade. "I'm a stranger here. But I happen to be a man who sees through things, an' I see how your dad handles you wrong. You don't know who I am an' you don't care. But if you'll listen you'll learn what might help you. . . . No boy can answer to all his wild impulses without ruinin' himself. It's not natural. There are other people—people who have wills an' desires, same as you have. You've got to live with people. Here's your dad an' Miss Columbine, an' the cowboys, an' me, an' all the ranchers, so down to Kremmlin' an' other places. These are the people you've got to live with. You can't go on as you've begun, without ruinin' yourself an' your dad an' the—the girl. . . . It's never too late to begin to be better. I know that. But it gets too late, sometimes, to save the happiness of others. Now I see where you're headin', as clear as if

I had pictures of the future. I've got a gift that way. . . . An', Belllounds, you'll not last. Unless you begin to control your temper, to forget yourself, to kill your wild impulses, to be kind, to learn what love is—you'll never last! . . . In the very nature of things, one comin' after another like your fights with Moore, an' your scarin' of Pronto, an' your drinkin' at Kremmlin', an' just now your r'arin' at me—it's in the very nature of life that goin' on so you'll sooner or later meet with hell! You've got to change, Belllounds. No half-way, spoiled-boy changin', but the straight right-about-face of a man! . . . It means you must see you're no good an' have a change of heart. Men have revolutions like that. I was no good. I did worse than you'll ever do, because you're not big enough to be really bad, an' yet I've turned out worth livin'. . . . There, I'm through, an' I'm offerin' to be your friend an' to help you."

Belllounds stood with arms spread outside the door, still astounded, still pale; but as the long admonition and appeal ended he exploded stridently. "Who the hell are *you?* . . . If I hadn't been so surprised—if I'd had a chance to get a word in—I'd shut your trap! Are you a preacher masquerading here as hunter? Let me tell you, I won't be talked to like that—not by any man. Keep your advice an' friendship to yourself."

"You don't want me, then?"

"No," Belllounds snapped.

"Reckon you don't need either advice or friend, hey?"

"No, you owl-eyed, soft-voiced fool!" yelled Belllounds.

It was then Wade felt a singular and familiar sensation, a cold, creeping thing, physical and elemental, that had not visited him since he had been at White Slides.

"I reckoned so," he said, with low and gloomy voice, and he knew, if Belllounds did not know, that he was not acquiescing with the other's harsh epithet, but only greeting the advent of something in himself.

Belllounds shrugged his burly shoulders and slouched away.

Wade finished his dressing of the meat. Then he rode up to spend an hour with Moore. When he returned to his cabin he proceeded to change his hunter garb for the best he owned. It was a proof of his unusual preoccupation that he did this before he fed the hounds. It was sunset when he left his cabin. Montana Jim and Lem hailed as he went by. Wade paused to listen to their good-natured raillery.

"See hyar, Bent, this ain't Sunday," said Lem.

"You're spruced up powerful fine. What's it fer?" added Montana.

"Boss asked me down to supper."

"Wal, you lucky son-of-a-gun! An' hyar we've no invite," returned Lem. "Say, Wade, I heerd Buster Jack roarin' at you. I was ridin' in by the storehouse. . . . 'Who the hell are you?' was what collared my attention, an' I had to laugh. An' I listened to all he said. So you was offerin' him advice an' friendship?"

"I reckon."

"Wal, all I say is thet you was wastin' yore breath," declared Lem. "You're a queer fellar, Wade."

"Queer? Aw, Lem, he ain't queer," said Montana. "He's jest white. Wade, I feel the same as you. I'd like to do somethin' fer thet locoed Buster Jack."

"Montana, you're the locoed one," rejoined Lem. "Buster Jack knows what he's doin'. He can play a slicker hand of poker than you."

"Wal, mebbe. Wade, do you play poker?"

"I'd hate to take your money," replied Wade.

"You needn't be so all-fired kind about thet. Come over to-night an' take some of it. Buster Jack invited himself up to our bunk. He's itchin' fer cards. So we says shore. Blud's goin' to sit in. Now you come an' make it five-handed."

"Wouldn't young Belllounds object to me?"

"What? Buster Jack shy at gamblin' with you? Not much. He's a born gambler. He'd bet with his grandmother an' he'd cheat the coppers off a dead nigger's eyes."

"Slick with cards, eh?" inquired Wade.

"Naw, Jack's not slick. But he tries to be. An' we jest go him one slicker."

"Wouldn't Old Bill object to this card-playin'?"

"He'd be ory-eyed. But, by Golly! we're not leadin' Jack astray. An' we ain't hankerin' to play with him. All the same a little game is welcome enough."

"I'll come over," replied Wade, and thoughtfully turned away.

When he presented himself at the ranch-house it was Columbine who let him in. She was prettily dressed, in a way he had never seen her before, and his heart throbbed. Her smile, her voice added to her name-less charm, that seemed to come from the past. Her look was eager and longing, as if his presence might bring something welcome to her.

Then the rancher stalked in. "Hullo, Wade! Supper's 'most ready. What's this trouble you had with Jack? He says he won't eat with you."

"I was offerin' him advice," replied Wade.

"What on?"

"Reckon on general principles."

"Humph! Wal, he told me you harangued him till you was black in the face, an'—"

"Jack had it wrong. He got black in the face," interrupted Wade.

"Did you say he was a spoiled boy an' thet he was no good an' was headin' plumb fer hell?"

"That was a little of what I said," returned Wade, gently.

"Ahuh! How'd thet come about?" queried Belllounds, gruffly. A slight stiffening and darkening overcast his face.

Wade then recalled and recounted the remarks that had passed between him and Jack; and he did not think he missed them very far. He had a great curiosity to see how Belllounds would take them, and especially the young man's scornful rejection of a sincerely offered friendship. All the time Wade was talking he was aware of Columbine watching him, and when he finished it was sweet to look at her.

"Wade, wasn't you takin' a lot on yourself?" queried the rancher, plainly displeased.

"Reckon I was. But my conscience is beholden to no man. If Jack had met me half-way that would have been better for him. An' for me, because I get good out of helpin' any one."

His reply silenced Belllounds. No more was said before supper was announced, and then the rancher seemed taciturn. Columbine did the serving, and most all of the talking. Wade felt strangely at ease. Some subtle difference was at work in him, transforming him, but the moment had not yet come for him to question himself. He enjoyed the supper. And when he ventured to look up at Columbine, to see her strong, capable hands and her warm, blue glance, glad for his presence, sweetly expressive of their common secret and darker with a shadow of meaning beyond her power to guess, then Wade felt havoc within him, the strife and pain and joy of the truth he never could reveal. For he could never reveal his identity to her without betraying his baseness to her mother. Otherwise, to hear her call him father would have been earning that happiness with a lie. Besides, she loved Belllounds as her father, and were this trouble of the present removed she would grow still closer to the old man in his declining days. Wade accepted the inevitable. She must never know. If she might love him it must be as the stranger who came to her gates, it must be through the mysterious affinity between them and through the service he meant to render.

Wade did not linger after the meal was ended despite the fact that Belllounds recovered his cordiality. It was dark when he went out. Columbine followed him, talking cheerfully. Once outside she squeezed his hand and whispered, "How's Wilson?"

The hunter nodded his reply, and, pausing at the porch step, he pressed her hand to make his assurance stronger. His reward was instant. In the bright starlight she stood white and eloquent, staring down at him with dark, wide eyes.

Presently she whispered: "Oh, my friend! It wants only three days till October first!"

"Lass, it might be a thousand years for all you need worry," he replied, his voice low and full. Then it seemed, as she flung up her arms, that she was about to embrace him. But her gesture was an appeal to the stars, to Heaven above, for something she did not speak.

Wade bade her good night and went his way.

The cowboys and the rancher's son were about to engage in a game of poker when Wade entered the dimly lighted, smoke-hazed room. Montana Jim was sticking tallow candles in the middle of a rude table; Lem was searching his clothes, manifestly for money; Bludsoe shuffled a greasy deck of cards; and Jack Belllounds was filling his pipe before a fire of blazing logs on the hearth.

"Dog-gone it! I hed more money 'n thet," complained Lem. "Jim, you rode to Kremmlin' last. Did you take my money?"

"Wal, come to think of it, I reckon I did," replied Jim, in surprise at the recollection.

"An' whar's it now?"

"Pard, I ain't no idee. I reckon it's still in Kremmlin'. But I'll pay you back."

"I should smile you will. Pony up now."

"Bent Wade, did you come over calkilated to git skinned?" queried Bludsoe.

"Boys, I was playin' poker tolerable well in Missouri when you all was nursin'," replied Wade, imperturbably.

"I heerd he was a card-sharp," said Jim. "Wal, grab a box or a chair to set on an' let's start. Come along, Jack; you don't look as keen to play as usual."

Belllounds stood with his back to the fire and his manner did not compare favorably with that of the genial cowboys.

"I prefer to play four-handed," he said.

This declaration caused a little check in the conversation and put an end to the amiability. The cowboys looked at one another, not embarrassed, but just a little taken aback, as if they had forgotten something that they should have remembered.

"You object to my playin'?" asked Wade, quietly.

"I certainly do," replied Belllounds.

"Why, may I ask?"

"For all I know, what Montana said about you may be true," returned Belllounds, insolently.

Such a remark flung in the face of a Westerner was an insult. The cowboys suddenly grew stiff, with steady eyes on Wade. He, however, did not change in the slightest.

"I might be a card-sharp at that," he replied, coolly. "You fellows play without me. I'm not carin' about poker any more. I'll look on."

Thus he carried over the moment that might have been dangerous. Lem gaped at him; Montana kicked a box forward to sit upon, and his action was expressive; Bludsoe slammed the cards down on the table and favored Wade with a comprehending look. Belllounds pulled a chair up to the table.

"What'll we make the limit?" asked Jim.

"Two bits," replied Lem, quickly.

Then began an argument. Belllounds was for a dollar limit. The cowboys objected.

"Why, Jack, if the ole man got on to us playin' a dollar limit he'd fire the outfit," protested Bludsoe.

This reasonable objection in no wise influenced the old man's son. He overruled the good arguments, and then hinted at the cowboys' lack of nerve. The fun faded out of their faces. Lem, in fact, grew red.

"Wal, if we're agoin' to *gamble*, thet's different," he said, with a cold ring in his voice, as he straddled a box and sat down. "Wade, lemme some money."

Wade slipped his hand into his pocket and drew forth a goodly handful of gold, which he handed to the cowboy. Not improbably, if this large amount had been shown earlier, before the change in the sentiment, Lem would have looked aghast and begged for mercy. As it was, he accepted it as if he were accustomed to borrowing that much every day. Belllounds had rendered futile the easygoing, friendly advances of the cowboys, as he had made it impossible to play a jolly little game for fun.

The game began, with Wade standing up, looking on. These boys did not know what a vast store of poker knowledge lay back of Wade's inscrutable eyes. As a boy he had learned the intricacies of poker in the country where it originated; and as a man he had played it with piles of yellow coins and guns on the table. His eagerness to look on here, as far as the cowboys were concerned, was mere pretense. In Belllounds's case, however, he had a profound interest. Rumors had drifted to him from time to time, since his advent at White Slides, regarding Belllounds's weakness for gambling. It might have been cowboy gossip. Wade held that there was nothing in the West as well calculated to test a boy, to prove his real character, as a game of poker.

Belllounds was a feverish better, an exultant winner, a poor loser. His understanding of the game was rudimentary. With him, the strong feeling beginning to be manifested to Wade was not the fun of matching wits and luck with his antagonists, nor a desire to accumulate money—for his recklessness disproved that—but the liberation of the gambling passion. Wade recognized that when he met it. And Jack Belllounds was not in any sense big. He was selfish and grasping in the numberless little ways common to the game, and positive about his own rights, while doubtful of the claims of others. His cheating was clumsy and crude. He held out cards, hiding them in his palm, he shuffled the deck so he left aces at the bottom, and these he would slip off to himself, and he was so blind that he could not detect his fellow-player in tricks as transparent as his own. Wade was amazed and disgusted. The pity he had felt for Belllounds shifted to the old father, who believed in his son with stubborn and unquenchable faith.

"Haven't you got something to drink?" Jack asked of his companions.

"Nope. Whar'd we git it?" replied Jim.

Belllounds evidently forgot, for presently he repeated the query. The cowboys shook their heads. Wade knew they were lying, for they did have liquor in the cabin. It occurred to him, then, to offer to go to his own cabin for some, just to see what this young man would say. But he refrained.

The luck went against Belllounds and so did the gambling. He was not a lamb among wolves, by any means, but the fleecing he got suggested that. According to Wade he was getting what he deserved. No cowboys, even such good-natured and fine fellows as these, could be expected to be subjects for Belllounds's cupidity. And they won all he had.

"I'll borrow," he said, with feverish impatience. His face was pale, clammy, yet heated, especially round the swollen bruises; his eyes stood out, bold, dark, rolling and glaring, full of sullen fire. But more than anything else his mouth betrayed the weakling, the born gambler, the self-centered, spoiled, intolerant youth. It was here his bad blood showed.

"Wal, I ain't lendin' money," replied Lem, as he assorted his winnings. "Wade, here's what you staked me, an' much obliged."

"I'm out, an' I can't lend you any," said Jim.

Bludsoe had a good share of the profits of that quick game, but he made no move to lend any of it. Belllounds glared impatiently at them.

"Hell! you took my money. I'll have satisfaction," he broke out, almost shouting.

"We won it, didn't we?" rejoined Lem, cool and easy. "An' you can have all the satisfaction you want, right now or any time."

Wade held out a handful of money to Belllounds.

"Here," he said, with his deep eyes gleaming in the dim room. Wade had made a gamble with himself, and it was that Belllounds would not even hesitate to take money.

"Come on, you stingy cowpunchers," he called out, snatching the money from Wade. His action then, violent and vivid as it was, did not reveal any more than his face.

But the cowboys showed amaze, and something more. They fell straightway to gambling, sharper and fiercer than before, actuated now by the flaming spirit of this son of Belllounds. Luck, misleading and alluring, favored Jack for a while, transforming him until he was radiant, boastful, exultant. Then it changed, as did his expression. His face grew dark.

"I tell you I want drink," he suddenly demanded. "I know damn well you cowpunchers have some here, for I smelled it when I came in."

"Jack, we drank the last drop," replied Jim, who seemed less stiff than his two bunk-mates.

"I've some very old rye," interposed Wade, looking at Jim but apparently addressing all. "Fine stuff, but awful strong an' hot! . . . Makes a fellow's blood dance."

"Go get it!" Belllounds's utterance was thick and full, as if he had something in his mouth.

Wade looked down into the heated face, into the burning eyes; and through the darkness of passion that brooked no interference with its fruition he saw this youth's stark and naked soul. Wade had seen into the depths of many such abysses.

"See hyar, Wade," broke in Jim, with his quiet force, "never mind fetchin' thet red-hot rye to-night. Some other time, mebbe, when Jack wants more satisfaction. Reckon we've got a drop or so left."

"All right, boys," replied Wade, "I'll be sayin' good night."

He left them playing and strode out to return to his cabin. The night was still, cold, starlit, and black in the shadows. A lonesome coyote barked, to be answered by a wakeful hound. Wade halted at his porch, and lingered there a moment, peering up at the gray old peak, bare and star-crowned.

"I'm sorry for the old man," muttered the hunter, "but I'd see Jack Belllounds in hell before I'd let Columbine marry him."

October first was a holiday at White Slides Ranch. It happened to be a glorious autumn day, with the sunlight streaming gold and amber over the grassy slopes. Far off the purple ranges loomed hauntingly.

Wade had come down from Wilson Moore's cabin, his ears ringing with the crippled boy's words of poignant fear.

Fox favored his master with unusually knowing gaze. There was not going to be any lion-chasing or elk-hunting this day. Something was in the wind. And Fox, as a privileged dog, manifested his interest and wonder.

Before noon a buckboard with team of sweating horses halted in the yard of the ranch-house. Besides the driver it contained two women whom Belllounds greeted as relatives, and a stranger, a pale man whose dark garb proclaimed him a minister.

"Come right in, folks," welcomed Belllounds, with hearty excitement.

It was Wade who showed the driver where to put the horses. Strangely, not a cowboy was in sight, an omission of duty the rancher had noted. Wade might have informed him where they were.

The door of the big living-room stood open, and from it came the sound of laughter and voices. Wade, who had returned to his seat on the end of the porch, listened to them, while his keen gaze seemed fixed down the lane toward the cabins. How intent must he have been not to hear Columbine's step behind him!

"Good morning, Ben," she said.

Wade wheeled as if internal violence had ordered his movement.

"Lass, good mornin'," he replied. "You sure look sweet this October first—like the flower for which you're named."

"My friend, it *is* October first—my marriage day!" murmured Columbine.

Wade felt her intensity, and he thrilled to the brave, sweet resignation of her face. Hope and faith were unquenchable in her, yet she had fortified herself to the wreck of dreams and love.

"I'd seen you before now, but I had some job with Wils, persuadin' him that we'd not have to offer you congratulations yet awhile," replied Wade, in his slow, gentle voice.

"*Oh!*" breathed Columbine.

Wade saw her full breast swell and the leaping blood wave over her pale face. She bent to him to see his eyes. And for Wade, when she peered with straining heart and soul, all at once to become transfigured, that instant was a sweet and all-fulfilling reward for his years of pain.

"You drive me mad!" she whispered.

The heavy tread of the rancher, like the last of successive steps of fate in Wade's tragic expectancy, sounded on the porch.

"Wal, lass, hyar you are," he said, with a gladness deep in his voice. "Now, whar's the boy?"

"Dad—I've not—seen Jack since breakfast," replied Columbine, tremulously.

"Sort of a laggard in love on his weddin'-day," rejoined the rancher. His gladness and forgetfulness were as big as his heart. "Wade, have you seen Jack?"

"No—I haven't," replied the hunter, with slow, long-drawn utterance. "But—I see—him now."

Wade pointed to the figure of Jack Bellounds approaching from the direction of the cabins. He was not walking straight.

Old man Bellounds shot out his gray head like a striking eagle.

"What the hell?" he muttered, as if bewildered at this strange, uneven gait of his son. "Wade, what's the matter with Jack?"

Wade did not reply. That moment had its sorrow for him as well as understanding of the wonder expressed by Columbine's cold little hand trembling in his.

The rancher suddenly recoiled.

"So help me Gawd—he's drunk!" he gasped, in a distress that unmanned him.

Then the parson and the invited relatives came out upon the porch, with gay voices and laughter that suddenly stilled when old Bellounds cried, brokenly: "Lass—go—in—the house."

But Columbine did not move, and Wade felt her shaking as she leaned against him.

The bridegroom approached. Drunk indeed he was; not hilariously, as one who celebrated his good fortune, but sullenly, tragically, hideously drunk.

Old Bellounds leaped off the porch. His gray hair stood up like the mane of a lion. Like a giant's were his strides. With a lunge he met his reeling son, swinging a huge fist into the sodden red face. Limply Jack fell to the ground.

"Lay there, you damned prodigal!" he roared, terrible in his rage. "You disgrace me—an' you disgrace the girl who's been a daughter to me! . . . If you ever have another weddin'-day it'll be me who sets it!"

CHAPTER 12

November was well advanced before there came indications that winter was near at hand.

One morning, when Wade rode up to Moore's cabin, the whole world seemed obscured in a dense gray fog, through which he could not see a rod ahead of him. Later, as he left, the fog had lifted shoulder-high to the mountains, and was breaking to let the blue sky show. Another morning it was worse, and apparently thicker and grayer. As Wade climbed the trail up toward the mountain-basin, where he hunted most these days, he expected the fog to lift. But it did not. The trail under the hoofs of the horse was scarcely perceptible to him, and he seemed lost in a dense, gray, soundless obscurity.

Suddenly Wade emerged from out the fog into brilliant sunshine. In amaze he halted. This phenomenon was new to him. He was high up on the mountain-side, the summit of which rose clear-cut and bold into the sky. Below him spread what resembled a white sea. It was an immense cloud-bank, filling all the valleys as if with creamy foam or snow, soft, thick, motionless, contrasting vividly with the blue sky above. Old White Slides stood out, gray and bleak and brilliant, as if it were an island rock in a rolling sea of fleece. Far across this strange, level cloud-floor rose the black line of the range. Wade watched the scene with a kind of rapture. He was alone on the heights. There was not a sound. The winds were stilled.

But there seemed a mighty being awake all around him, in the presence of which Wade felt how little were his sorrows and hopes.

Another day brought dull-gray scudding clouds, and gusts of wind and squalls of rain, and a wailing through the bare aspens. It grew colder and bleaker and darker. Rain changed to sleet and sleet to snow. That night brought winter.

Next morning, when Wade plodded up to Moore's cabin, it was through two feet of snow. A beautiful glistening white mantle covered valley and slope and mountain, transforming all into a world too dazzlingly brilliant for the unprotected gaze of man.

When Wade pushed open the door of the cabin and entered he awakened the cowboy.

"Mornin', Wils," drawled Wade, as he slapped the snow from boots and legs. "Summer has gone, winter has come, an' the flowers lay in their graves! How are you, boy?"

Moore had grown paler and thinner during his long confinement in bed. A weary shade shone in his face and a shadow of pain in his eyes. But the spirit of his smile was the same as always.

"Hello, Bent, old pard!" replied Moore. "I guess I'm fine. Nearly froze last night. Didn't sleep much."

"Well, I was worried about that," said the hunter. "We've got to arrange things somehow."

"I heard it snowing. Gee! how the wind howled! And I'm snowed in?"

"Sure are. Two feet on a level. It's good I snaked down a lot of firewood. Now I'll set to work an' cut it up an' stack it round the cabin. Reckon I'd better sleep up here with you, Wils."

"Won't Old Bill make a kick?"

"Let him kick. But I reckon he doesn't need to know anythin' about it. It is cold in here. Well, I'll soon warm it up. . . . Here's some letters Lem got at Kremmlin' the other day. You read while I rustle some grub for you."

Moore scanned the addresses on the several envelopes and sighed.

"From home! I hate to read them."

"Why?" queried Wade.

"Oh, because when I wrote I didn't tell them I was hurt. I feel like a liar."

"It's just as well, Wils, because you swear you'll not go home."

"Me? I should smile not. . . . Bent—I—I—hoped Collie might answer the note you took her from me."

"Not yet. Wils, give the lass time."

"Time? Heavens! it's three weeks and more."

"Go ahead an' read your letters or I'll knock you on the head with one of these chunks," ordered Wade, mildly.

The hunter soon had the room warm and cheerful, with steaming breakfast on the red-hot coals. Presently, when he made ready to serve Moore, he was surprised to find the boy crying over one of the letters.

"Wils, what's the trouble?" he asked.

"Oh, nothing. I—I—just feel bad, that's all," replied Moore.

"Ahuh! So it seems. Well, tell me about it?"

"Pard, my father—has forgiven me."

"The old son-of-a-gun! Good! What for? You never told me you'd done anythin'."

"I know—but I did—do a lot. I was sixteen then. We quarreled. And I ran off up here to punch cows. But after a while I wrote home to mother and my sister. Since then they've tried to coax me to come home. This letter's from the old man himself. Gee! . . . Well, he says he's had to knuckle. That he's ready to forgive me. But I must come home and take charge of his ranch. Isn't that great? . . . Only I can't go. And I couldn't— I couldn't ever ride a horse again—if I did go."

"Who says you couldn't?" queried Wade. "*I* never said so. I only said you'd never be a bronco-bustin' cowboy again. Well, suppose you're not? You'll be able to ride a little, if I can save that leg. . . . Boy, your letter is damn good news. I'm sure glad. That will make Collie happy."

The cowboy had a better appetite that morning, which fact mitigated somewhat the burden of Wade's worry. There was burden enough, however, and Wade had set this day to make important decisions about Moore's injured foot. He had dreaded to remove the last dressing because conditions at that time had been unimproved. He had done all he could to ward off the threatened gangrene.

"Wils, I'm goin' to look at your foot an' tell you things," declared Wade, when the dreaded time could be put off no longer.

"Go ahead. . . . And, pard, if you say my leg has to be cut off—why just pass me my gun!"

The cowboy's voice was gay and bantering, but his eyes were alight with a spirit that frightened the hunter.

"Ahuh! . . . I know how you feel. But, boy, I'd rather live with one leg an' be loved by Collie Belllounds than have nine legs for some other lass."

Wilson Moore groaned his helplessness.

"Damn you, Bent Wade! You always say what kills me! . . . Of course I would!"

"Well, lie quiet now, an' let me look at this poor, messed-up foot."

Wade's deft fingers did not work with the usual precision and speed natural to them. But at last Moore's injured member lay bare, discolored and misshapen. The first glance made the hunter quicker in his movements, closer in his scrutiny. Then he yelled his joy.

"Boy, it's better! No sign of gangrene! We'll save your leg!"

"Pard, I never feared I'd lose that. All I've feared was that I'd be club-footed. . . . Let me look," replied the cowboy, and he raised himself on his elbow. Wade lifted the unsightly foot.

"My God, it's crooked!" cried Moore, passionately. "Wade, it's healed. It'll stay that way always! I can't move it! . . . Oh, but Buster Jack's ruined me!"

The hunter pushed him back with gentle hands. "Wils, it might have been worse."

"But I never gave up hope," replied Moore, in poignant grief. "I couldn't. But *now!* . . . How can you look at that—that club-foot, and not swear?"

"Well, well, boy, cussin' won't do any good. Now lay still an' let me work. You've had lots of good news this mornin'. So I think you can stand to hear a little bad news."

"What! Bad news?" queried Moore, with a start.

"I reckon. Now listen. . . . The reason Collie hasn't answered your note is because she's been sick in bed for three weeks."

"Oh no!" exclaimed the cowboy, in amaze and distress.

"Yes, an' I'm her doctor," replied Wade, with pride. "First off they had Mrs. Andrews. An' Collie kept askin' for me. She was out of her head, you know. An' soon as I took charge she got better."

"Heavens! Collie ill and you never told me!" cried Moore. "I can't believe it. She's so healthy and strong. What ailed her, Bent?"

"Well, Mrs. Andrews said it was nervous breakdown. An' Old Bill was afraid of consumption. An' Jack Belllounds swore she was only sham-min'."

The cowboy cursed violently.

"Here—I won't tell you any more if you're goin' to cuss that way an' jerk around," protested Wade.

"I—I'll shut up," appealed Moore.

"Well, that puddin'-head Jack is more'n you called him, if you care to hear my opinion. . . . Now, Wils, the fact is that none of them know what ails Collie. But I know. She'd been under a high strain leadin' up to Octo-ber first. An' the way that weddin'-day turned out—with Old Bill layin' Jack cold, an' with no marriage at all—why, Collie had a shock. An' after that she seemed pale an' tired all the time an' she didn't eat right. Well, when Buster Jack got over that awful punch he'd got from the old man he made up to Collie harder than ever. She didn't tell me then, but I saw it. An' she couldn't avoid him, except by stayin' in her room, which she did a good deal. Then Jack showed a streak of bein' decent. He surprised every-body, even Collie. He delighted Old Bill. But he didn't pull the wool over my eyes. He was like a boy spoilin' for a new toy, an' he got crazy over Collie. He's sure terribly in love with her, an' for days he behaved himself in a way calculated to make up for his drinkin' too much. It shows he can behave himself when he wants to. I mean he can control his temper an' impulse. Anyway, he made himself so good that Old Bill changed his mind, after what he swore that day, an' set another day for the weddin'. Right off, then, Collie goes down on her back. . . . They didn't send for me very soon. But when I did get to see her, an' felt the way she grabbed me—as if she was drownin'—then I knew what ailed her. It was love."

"Love!" gasped Moore, breathlessly.

"Sure. Jest love for a dog-gone lucky cowboy named Wils Moore! . . . Her heart was breakin', an' she'd have died but for me! Don't imagine, Wils, that people can't die of broken hearts. They do. I know. Well, all Collie needed was me, an' I cured her ravin' and made her eat, an' now she's comin' along fine."

"Wade, I've believed in Heaven since you came down to White Slides," burst out Moore, with shining eyes. "But tell me—what did you tell her?"

"Well, my particular medicine first off was to whisper in her ear that she'd never have to marry Jack Belllounds. An' after that I gave her daily doses of talk about you."

"Pard! She loves me—still?" he whispered.

"Wils, hers is the kind that grows stronger with time. I know."

Moore strained in his intensity of emotion, and he clenched his fists and gritted his teeth.

"Oh God! this's hard on me!" he cried. "I'm a man. I love that girl more than life. And to know she's suffering for love of me—for fear of that marriage being forced upon her—to know that while I lie here a helpless cripple—it's almost unbearable."

"Boy, you've got to mend now. We've the best of hope now—for you—for her—for everythin'."

"Wade, I think I love you, too," said the cowboy. "You're saving me from madness. Somehow I have faith in you—to do whatever you want. But how could you tell Collie she'd never have to marry Buster Jack?"

"Because I know she never will," replied Wade, with his slow, gentle smile.

"You *know* that?"

"Sure."

"How on earth can you prevent it? Belllounds will never give up planning that marriage for his son. Jack will nag Collie till she can't call her soul her own. Between them they will wear her down. My friend, *how* can you prevent it?"

"Wils, fact is, I haven't reckoned out how I'm goin' to save Collie. But that's no matter. Sufficient unto the day is the evil thereof. I will do it. You can gamble on me, Wils. You must use that hope an' faith to help you get well. For we mustn't forget that you're in more danger than Collie."

"I *will* gamble on you—my life—my very soul," replied Moore, fervently. "By Heaven! I'll be the man I might have been. I'll rise out of despair. I'll even reconcile myself to being a cripple."

"An', Wils, will you rise above hate?" asked Wade, softly.

"Hate! Hate of whom?"

"Jack Belllounds."

The cowboy stared, and his lean, pale face contracted.

"Pard, you wouldn't—you couldn't expect me to—to forgive him?"

"No. I reckon not. But you needn't hate him. I don't. An' I reckon I've some reason, more than you could guess. . . . Wils, hate is a poison in the blood. It's worse for him who feels it than for him against whom it rages. I know. . . . Well, if you put thought of Jack out of your mind— quit broodin' over what he did to you—an' realize that he's not to blame, you'll overcome your hate. For the son of Old Bill is to be pitied. Yes, Jack Belllounds needs pity. He was ruined before he was born. He never should have been born. An' I want you to understand that, an' stop hatin' him. Will you try?"

"Wade, you're afraid I'll kill him?" whispered Moore.

"Sure. That's it. I'm afraid you might. An' consider how hard that would be for Columbine. She an' Jack were raised sister an' brother, almost. It would be hard on her. You see, Collie has a strange an' powerful sense of duty to Old Bill. If you killed Jack it would likely kill the old man, an' Collie would suffer all her life. You couldn't cure her of that. You want her to be happy."

"I do—I do. Wade, I swear I'll never kill Buster Jack. And for Collie's sake I'll try not to hate him."

"Well, that's fine. I'm sure glad to hear you promise that. Now I'll go out an' chop some wood. We mustn't let the fire go out any more."

"Pard, I'll write another note—a letter to Collie. Hand me the blank-book there. And my pencil. . . . And don't hurry with the wood."

Wade went outdoors with his two-bladed ax and shovel. The wood-pile was a great mound of snow. He cleaned a wide space and a path to the side of the cabin. Working in snow was not unpleasant for him. He liked the cleanness, the whiteness, the absolute purity of new-fallen snow. The air was crisp and nipping, the frost crackled under his feet, the smoke from his pipe seemed no thicker than the steam from his breath, the ax rang on the hard aspens. Wade swung this implement like a born woodsman. The chips flew and the dead wood smelled sweet. Some logs he chopped into three-foot pieces; others he chopped and split. When he tired a little of swinging the ax he carried the cut pieces to the cabin and stacked them near the door. Now and then he would halt a moment to gaze away across the whitened slopes and rolling hills. The sense of his physical power matched something within, and his heart warmed with more than the vigorous exercise.

When he had worked thus for about two hours and had stacked a pile of wood almost as large as the cabin he considered it sufficient for the day. So he went indoors. Moore was so busily and earnestly writing that he did not hear Wade come in. His face wore an eloquent glow.

"Say, Wils, are you writin' a book?" he inquired.

"Hello! Sure I am. But I'm 'most done now. . . . If Columbine doesn't answer *this* . . ."

"By the way, I'll have two letters to give her, then—for I never gave her the first one," replied Wade.

"You son-of-a-gun!"

"Well, hurry along, boy. I'll be goin' now. Here's a pole I've fetched in. You keep it there, where you can reach it, an' when the fire needs more wood you roll one of these logs on. I'll be up to-night before dark, an' if I don't fetch you a letter it'll be because I can't persuade Collie to write."

"Pard, if you bring me a letter I'll obey you—I'll lie still—I'll sleep—I'll stand—anything."

"Ahuh! Then I'll fetch one," replied Wade, as he took the little book and deposited it in his pocket. "Good-by, now, an' think of your good news that come with the snow."

"Good-by, Heaven-Sent Hell-Bent Wade!" called Moore. "It's no joke of a name any more. It's a fact."

Wade plodded down through the deep snow, stepping in his old tracks, and as he toiled on his thoughts were deep and comforting. He was thinking that if he had his life to live over again he would begin at once to find happiness in other people's happiness. Upon arriving at his cabin he set to work cleaning a path to the dog-corral. The snow had drifted there and he had no easy task. It was well that he had built an inclosed house for the hounds to winter in. Such a heavy snow as this one would put an end to hunting for the time being. The ranch had ample supply of deer, bear, and elk meat, all solidly frozen this morning, that would surely keep well until used. Wade reflected that his tasks round the ranch would be feeding hounds and stock, chopping wood, and doing such chores as came along in winter-time. The pack of hounds, which he had thinned out to a smaller number, would be a care on his hands. Kane

had become a much-prized possession of Columbine's and lived at the
house, where he had things his own way, and always greeted Wade with a
look of disdain and distrust. Kane would never forgive the hand that had
hurt him. Sampson and Jim and Fox, of course, shared Wade's cabin, and
vociferously announced his return.

Early in the afternoon Wade went down to the ranch-house. The
snow was not so deep there, having blown considerably in the open
places. Some one was pounding iron in the blacksmith shop; horses were
cavorting in the corrals; cattle were bawling round the hay-ricks in the
barn-yard.

The hunter knocked on Columbine's door.

"Come in," she called.

Wade entered, to find her alone. She was sitting up in bed, propped
up with pillows, and she wore a warm, woolly jacket or dressing-gown.
Her paleness was now marked, and the shadows under her eyes made
them appear large and mournful.

"Ben Wade, you don't care for me any more!" she exclaimed, reproachfully.

"Why not, lass?" he asked.

"You were so long in coming," she replied, now with petulance. "I
guess now I don't want you at all."

"Ahuh! That's the reward of people who worry an' work for others.
Well, then, I reckon I'll go back an' not give you what I brought."

He made a pretense of leaving, and he put a hand to his pocket as if
to insure the safety of some article. Columbine blushed. She held out her
hands. She was repentant of her words and curious as to his.

"Why, Ben Wade, I count the minutes before you come," she said.
"What'd you bring me?"

"Who's been in here?" he asked, going forward. "That's a poor fire.
I'll have to fix it."

"Mrs. Andrews just left. It was good of her to drive up. She came in
the sled, she said. Oh, Ben, it's winter. There was snow on my bed when I
woke up. I think I am better to-day. Jack hasn't been in here yet!"

At this Wade laughed, and Columbine followed suit.

"Well, you look a little sassy to-day, which I take is a good sign," said
Wade. "I've got some news that will come near to makin' you well."

"Oh, tell it quick!" she cried.

"Wils won't lose his leg. It's gettin' well. An' there was a letter from his father, forgivin' him for somethin' he never told me."

"My prayers were answered!" whispered Columbine, and she closed her eyes tight.

"An' his father wants him to come home to run the ranch," went on Wade.

"Oh!" Her eyes popped open with sudden fright. "But he can't—he won't go?"

"I reckon not. He wouldn't if he could. But some day he will, an' take you home with him."

Columbine covered her face with her hands, and was silent a moment.

"Such prophecies! They—they—" She could not conclude.

"Ahuh! I know. The strange fact is, lass, that they all come true. I wish I had all happy ones, instead of them black, croakin' ones that come like ravens. . . . Well, you're better to-day?"

"Yes. Oh yes. Ben, what have you got for me?"

"You're in an awful hurry. I want to talk to you, an' if I show what I've got then there will be no talkin'. You say Jack hasn't been in to-day?"

"Not yet, thank goodness."

"How about Old Bill?"

"Ben, you never call him my dad. I wish you would. When you *don't* it always reminds me that he's really *not* my dad."

"Ahuh! Well, well!" replied Wade, with his head bowed. "It is just queer I can never remember. . . . An' how was he to-day?"

"For a wonder he didn't mention poor me. He was full of talk about going to Kremmling. Means to take Jack along. Do you know, Ben, dad can't fool me. He's afraid to leave Jack here alone with me. So dad talked a lot about selling stock an' buying supplies, and how he needed Jack to go, and so forth. I'm mighty glad he means to take him. But my! won't Jack be sore."

"I reckon. It's time he broke out."

"And now, dear Ben—what have you got for me? I know it's from Wilson," she coaxed.

"Lass, would you give much for a little note from Wils?" asked Wade, teasingly.

"Would I? When I've been hoping and praying for just that!"

"Well, if you'd give so much for a note, how much would you give me for a whole bookful that took Wils two hours to write?"

"Ben! Oh, I'd—I'd give—" she cried, wild with delight. "I'd *kiss* you!"

"You mean it?" he queried, waving the book aloft.

"Mean it? Come here!"

There was fun in this for Wade, but also a deep and beautiful emotion that quivered through him. Bending over her, he placed the little book in her hand. He did not see clearly, then, as she pulled him lower and kissed him on the cheek, generously, with sweet, frank gratitude and affection.

Moments strong and all-satisfying had been multiplying for Bent Wade of late. But this one magnified all. As he sat back upon the chair he seemed a little husky of voice.

"Well, well, an' so you kissed ugly old Bent Wade?"

"Yes, and I've wanted to do it before," she retorted. The dark excitation in her eyes, the flush of her pale cheeks, made her beautiful then.

"Lass, now you read your letter an' answer it. You can tear out the pages. I'll sit here an' be makin' out to be readin' aloud out of this book here, if any one happens in sudden-like!"

"Oh, how you think of everything!"

The hunter sat beside her pretending to be occupied with the book he had taken from the table when really he was stealing glances at her face. Indeed, she was more than pretty then. Illness and pain had enhanced the sweetness of her expression. As she read on it was manifest that she had forgotten the hunter's presence. She grew pink, rosy, scarlet, radiant. And Wade thrilled with her as she thrilled, loved her more and more as she loved. Moore must have written words of enchantment. Wade's hungry heart suffered a pang of jealousy, but would not harbor it. He read in her perusal of that letter what no other dreamed of, not even the girl herself; and it was certitude of tragic and brief life for her if she could not live for Wilson Moore. Those moments of watching her were unutterably precious to Wade. He saw how some divine guidance had directed his footsteps to this home. How many years had it taken him to get there! Columbine read and read and reread—a girl with her first love-letter. And for Wade, with his keen eyes that seemed to see the senses and the soul, there shone something infinite through her rapture. Never until that unguarded moment had he divined her innocence, nor had any conception been given him of the exquisite torture of her maiden fears or the havoc of love fighting for itself. He learned then much of the mystery and meaning of a woman's heart.

CHAPTER 13

D EAR WILSON,—The note and letter from you have taken my breath away. I couldn't tell—I wouldn't dare tell, how they made me feel.

"Your good news fills me with joy. And when Ben told me you wouldn't lose your leg—that you would get well—then my eyes filled and my heart choked me, and I thanked God, who'd answered my prayers. After all the heartache and dread, it's so wonderful to find things not so terrible as they seemed. Oh, I am thankful! You have only to take care of yourself now, to lie patiently and wait, and obey Ben, and soon the time will have flown by and you will be well again. Maybe, after all, your foot will not be so bad. Maybe you can ride again, if not so wonderfully as before, then well enough to ride on your father's range and look after his stock. For, Wilson dear, you'll have to go home. It's your duty. Your father must be getting old now. He needs you. He has forgiven you—you bad boy! And you are very lucky. It almost kills me to think of your leaving White Slides. But that is selfish. I'm going to learn to be like Ben Wade. He never thinks of himself.

"Rest assured, Wilson, that I will never marry Jack Bell-lounds. It seems years since that awful October first. I gave my word then, and I would have lived up to it. But I've changed. I'm older. I see things differently. I love dad as well. I feel as sorry for

Jack Belllounds. I still think I might help him. I still believe in my duty to his father. But I can't marry him. It would be a sin. I have no right to marry a man whom I do not love. When it comes to thought of his touching me, then I hate him. Duty toward dad is one thing, and I hold it high, but that is not reason enough for a woman to give herself. Some duty to myself is higher than that. It's hard for me to tell you—for me to understand. Love of you has opened my eyes. Still I don't think it's love of you that makes me selfish. I'm true to something in me that I never knew before. I could marry Jack, loving you, and utterly sacrifice myself, if it were right. But it would be wrong. I never realized this until you kissed me. Since then the thought of anything that approaches personal relations—any hint of intimacy with Jack fills me with disgust.

"So I'm not engaged to Jack Belllounds, and I'm never going to be. There will be trouble here. I feel it. I see it coming. Dad keeps at me persistently. He grows older. I don't think he's failing, but then there's a loss of memory, and an almost childish obsession in regard to the marriage he has set his heart on. Then his passion for Jack seems greater as he learns little by little that Jack is not all he might be. Wilson, I give you my word; I believe if dad ever really sees Jack as I see him or you see him, then something dreadful will happen. In spite of everything dad still believes in Jack. It's beautiful and terrible. That's one reason why I've wanted to help Jack. Well, it's not to be. Every day, every hour, Jack Belllounds grows farther from me. He and his father will try to persuade me to consent to this marriage. They may even try to force me. But in that way I'll be as hard and as cold as Old White Slides. No! Never! For the rest, I'll do my duty to dad. I'll stick to him. I could not engage myself to you, no matter how much I love you. And that's more every minute! . . . So don't mention taking me to your home—don't ask me again. Please, Wilson; your asking shook my very soul! Oh, how sweet that would be—your wife I . . . But if dad turns me away—I don't think he would. Yet he's so strange and like iron for all concerning Jack. If ever he turned me out I'd have no home. I'm a waif, you know. Then—then, Wilson . . . Oh, it's horrible to be in the position I'm in. I won't say any more. You'll understand, dear.

"It's your love that awoke me, and it's Ben Wade who has saved me. Wilson, I love him almost as I do dad, only strangely. Do you know I believe he had something to do with Jack getting drunk that awful October first. I don't mean Ben would stoop to get Jack drunk. But he might have cunningly put that opportunity in Jack's way. Drink is Jack's weakness, as gambling is his passion. Well, I know that the liquor was some fine old stuff which Ben gave to the cowboys. And it's significant now how Jack avoids Ben. He hates him. He's afraid of him. He's jealous because Ben is so much with me. I've heard Jack rave to dad about this. But dad is just to others, if he can't be to his son.

"And so I want you to know that it's Ben Wade who has saved me. Since I've been sick I've learned more of Ben. He's like a woman. He understands. I never have to tell him anything. You, Wilson, were sometimes stupid or stubborn (forgive me) about little things that girls feel but can't explain. Ben knows. I tell you this because I want you to understand how and why I love him. I think I love him most for his goodness to you. Dear boy, if I hadn't loved you before Ben Wade came I'd have fallen in love with you since, just listening to his talk of you. But this will make you conceited. So I'll go on about Ben. He's our friend. Why, Wilson, that sweetness, softness, gentleness about him, the heart that makes him love us, that must be only the woman in him. I don't know what a mother would feel like, but I do know that I seem strangely happier since I've confessed my troubles to this man. It was Lem who told me how Ben offered to be a friend to Jack. And Jack flouted him. I've a queer notion that the moment Jack did this he turned his back on a better life.

"To repeat, then, Ben Wade is our friend, and to me something more that I've tried to explain. Maybe telling you this will make you think more of him and listen to his advice. I hope so. Did any boy and girl ever before so need a friend? I need that something he instils in me. If I lost it I'd be miserable. And,

Wilson, I'm such a coward. I'm so weak. I have such sinkings and burnings and tossings. Oh, I'm only a woman! But I'll die fighting. That is what Ben Wade instils into me. While there was life this strange little man would never give up hope. He makes me feel that he knows more than he tells. Through him I shall get the strength to live up to my convictions, to be true to myself, to be faithful to you.

"WITH LOVE,
"COLUMBINE."

"*December 3d.*
"DEAREST COLLIE,—Your last was only a note, and I told Wade if he didn't fetch more than a note next time there would be trouble round this bunk-house. And then he brought your letter!

"I'm feeling exuberant (I think it's that) to-day. First time I've been up. Collie, I'm able to get up! WHOOPEE! I walk with a crutch, and don't dare put my foot down. Not that it hurts, but that my boss would have a fit! I'm glad you've stopped heaping praise upon our friend Ben. Because now I can get over my jealousy and be half decent. He's the whitest man I ever knew.

"Now listen, Collie. I've had ideas lately. I've begun to eat and get stronger and to feel good. The pain is gone. And to think I swore to Wade I'd forgive Jack Belllounds and never hate him—or kill him! . . . There, that's letting the cat out of the bag, and it's done now. But no matter. The truth is, though, that I never could stop hating Jack while the pain lasted. Now I could shake hands with him and smile at him.

"Well, as I said, I've ideas. They're great. Grab hold of the pommel now so you won't get thrown! I'm going to pitch! . . . When I get well—able to ride and go about, which Ben says will be in the spring—I'll send for my father to come to White Slides. He'll come. Then I'll tell him everything, and if Ben and I can't win him to our side then *you* can. Father never could resist you. When he has fallen in love with you, which won't take long, then we'll go to old Bill Belllounds and lay the case before him. Are you still in the saddle, Collie?

"Well, if you are, be sure to get a better hold, for I'm going to run some next. Ben Wade approved of my plan. He says Bell-lounds can be brought to reason. He says he can *make* him see the ruin for everybody were you forced to marry Jack. Strange, Collie, how Wade included himself with you, me, Jack, and the old man, in the foreshadowed ruin! Wade is as deep as the cañon there. Sometimes when he's thoughtful he gives me a creepy feeling. At others, when he comes out with one of his easy, cool assurances that we are all right—that we will get each other— why, then something grim takes possession of me. I believe him, I'm happy, but there crosses my mind a fleeting realization—not of what our friend is now, but what he has been. And it disturbs me, chills me. I don't understand it. For, Collie, though I under-stand your feeling of what he is, I don't understand mine. You see, I'm a man. I've been a cowboy for ten years and more. I've seen some hard experiences and worked with a good many rough boys and men. Cowboys, Indians, Mexicans, miners, prospectors, ranchers, hunters—some of whom were bad medicine. So I've come to see men as you couldn't see them. And Bent Wade has been everything a man could be. He seems all men in one. And despite all his kindness and goodness and hopefulness, there is the sense I have of something deadly and terrible and inevitable in him.

"It makes my heart almost stop beating to know I have this man on my side. Because I sense in him the man element, the physical—oh, I can't put it in words, but I mean something great in him that can't be beaten. What he says *must* come true! . . . And so I've already begun to dream and to think of you as my wife. If you ever are—no! *when* you are, then I will owe it to Bent Wade. No man ever owed another for so precious a gift. But, Collie, I can't help a little vague dread—of what, I don't know, unless it's a sense of the possibilities of Hell-Bent Wade. . . . Dearest, I don't want to worry you or frighten you, and I can't follow out my own gloomy fancies. Don't you mind too much what I think. Only you must realize that Wade is the greatest fac-tor in our hopes of the future. My faith in him is so unshakable

that it's foolish. Next to you I love him best. He seems even dearer to me than my own people. He has made me look at life differently. Likewise he has inspired you. But you, dearest Columbine, are only a sensitive, delicate girl, a frail and tender thing like the columbine flowers of the hills. And for your own sake you must not be blind to what Wade is capable of. If you keep on loving him and idealizing him, blind to what has made him great, that is, blind to the tragic side of him, then if he did something terrible here for you and for me the shock would be bad for you. Lord knows I have no suspicions of Wade. I have no clear ideas at all. But I do know that for you he would not stop at anything. He loves you as much as I do, only differently. Such power a pale, sweet-faced girl has over the lives of men!
"Good-by for this time.

> "FAITHFULLY,
> "WILSON."

> *"January 10th.*
"DEAR WILSON,—In every letter I tell you I'm better! Why, pretty soon there'll be nothing left to say about my health. I've been up and around now for days, but only lately have I begun to gain. Since Jack has been away I'm getting fat. I eat, and that's one reason I suppose. Then I move around more.

"You ask me to tell you all I do. Goodness! I couldn't and I wouldn't. You are getting mighty bossy since you're able to hobble around, as you call it. But you can't boss *me!* However, I'll be nice and tell you a little. I don't work very much. I've helped dad with his accounts, all so hopelessly muddled since he let Jack keep the books. I read a good deal. Your letters are worn out! Then, when it snows, I sit by the window and watch. I love to see the snowflakes fall, so fleecy and white and soft! But I don't like the snowy world after the storm has passed. I shiver and hug the fire. I must have Indian in me. On moonlit nights to look out at Old White Slides, so cold and icy and grand, and over the white hills and ranges, makes me shudder. I don't know why. It's all beautiful. But it seems to me like death. . . . Well, I sit idly a lot and think of you and how terribly big my love has grown, and . . . but that's all about that!

"As you know, Jack has been gone since before New Year's Day. He said he was going to Kremmling. But dad heard he went to Elgeria. Well, I didn't tell you that dad and Jack quarreled over money. Jack kept up his good behavior for so long that I actually believed he'd changed for the better. He kept at me, not so much on the marriage question, but to love him. Wilson, he nearly drove me frantic with his lovemaking. Finally I got mad and I pitched into him. Oh, I convinced him! Then he came back to his own self again. Like a flash he was Buster Jack once more. 'You can go to hell!' he yelled at me. And such a look! . . . Well, he went out, and that's when he quarreled with dad. It was about money. I couldn't help but hear some of it. I don't know whether or not dad gave Jack money, but I think he didn't. Anyway, Jack went.

"Dad was all right for a few days. Really, he seemed nicer and kinder for Jack's absence. Then all at once he sank into the glooms. I couldn't cheer him up. When Ben Wade came in after supper dad always got him to tell some of those terrible stories. You know what perfectly terrible stories Ben can tell. Well, dad had to hear the worst ones. And poor me, I didn't want to listen, but I couldn't resist. Ben *can* tell stories. And oh, what he's lived through!

"I got the idea it wasn't Jack's absence so much that made dad sit by the hour before the fire, staring at the coals, sighing, and looking so God-forsaken. My heart just aches for dad. He broods and broods. He'll break out some day, and then I don't want to be here. There doesn't seem to be any idea when Jack will come home. He might never come. But Ben says he will. He says Jack hates work and that he couldn't be gambler enough or wicked enough to support himself without working. Can't you hear Ben Wade say that? 'I'll tell you,' he begins, and then comes a prophecy of trouble or evil. And, on the other hand, think how he used to say: 'Wait! Don't give up! Nothin' is ever so bad as it seems at first! Be true to what your heart says is right! It's never too late! Love is the only good in life! Love each other and wait and trust! It'll all come right in the end!' . . . And Wilson, I'm bound to confess that both his sense of calamity and his hope of good seem infallible. Ben Wade is supernatural. Sometimes, just for a moment, I dare to let myself believe in what he says—that our dream will come true and I'll be yours. Then oh! oh! oh! joy and stars and bells and heaven! I—I . . . But what *am* I writing? Wilson Moore, this is quite enough for to-day. Take care you don't believe I'm so—so *very* much in love.

"EVER,

"COLUMBINE."

"*February*—.

"DEAREST COLLIE,—I don't know the date, but spring's coming. To-day I kicked Bent Wade with my once sore foot. It didn't hurt me, but hurt Wade's feelings. He says there'll be no holding me soon. I should say not. I'll eat you up. I'm as hungry as the mountain-lion that's been prowling round my cabin of nights. He's sure starved. Wade tracked him to a hole in the cliff.

"Collie, I can get around first rate. Don't need my crutch any more. I can make a fire and cook a meal. Wade doesn't think so, but I do. He says if I want to hold your affection, not to let you eat anything I cook. I can rustle around, too. Haven't been far yet. My stock has wintered fairly well. This valley is sheltered, you know. Snow hasn't been too deep. Then I bought hay from Andrews. I'm hoping for spring now, and the good old sunshine on the gray sage hills. And summer, with its columbines! Wade has gone back to his own cabin to sleep. I miss him. But I'm glad to have the nights alone once more. I've got a future to plan! Read that over, Collie.

"To-day, when Wade came with your letter, he asked me, sort of queer, 'Say, Wils, do you know how many letters I've fetched you from Collie?' I said, 'Lord, no, I don't, but they're a lot.' Then he said there were just forty-seven letters. Forty-seven! I couldn't believe it, and told him he was crazy. I never had such good fortune. Well, he made me count them, and, dog-gone it, he was right. Forty-seven wonderful love-letters from the sweetest girl on earth! But think of Wade remembering every one! It beats me. He's beyond understanding.

"So Jack Belllounds still stays away from White Slides. Collie, I'm sure sorry for his father. What it would be to have a son like Buster Jack! My God! But for your sake I go around yelling and singing like a locoed Indian. Pretty soon spring will come. Then, you wild-flower of the hills, you girl with the sweet mouth and the sad eyes—then I'm coming after you! And all the king's horses and all the king's men can never take you away from me again!

"YOUR FAITHFUL

"WILSON."

"*March 19th.*

"DEAREST WILSON,—Your last letters have been read and reread, and kept under my pillow, and have been both my help and my weakness during these trying days since Jack's return.

"It has not been that I was afraid to write—though, Heaven knows, if this letter should fall into the hands of dad it would mean trouble for me, and if Jack read it—I *am* afraid to think of that! I just have not had the heart to write you. But all the time I knew I must write and that I would. Only, now, what to say tortures me. I am certain that confiding in you relieves me. That's why I've told you so much. But of late I find it harder to tell what I know about Jack Belllounds. I'm in a queer state of mind, Wilson dear. And you'll wonder, and you'll be sorry to know I haven't seen much of Ben lately—that is, not to talk to. It seems I can't *bear* his faith in me, his hope, his love—when lately matters have driven me into torturing doubt.

"But lest you might misunderstand, I'm going to try to tell you something of what is on my mind, and I want you to read it to Ben. He has been hurt by my strange reluctance to be with him.

"Jack came home on the night of March second. You'll remember that day, so gloomy and dark and dreary. It snowed and sleeted and rained. I remember how the rain roared on the roof. It roared so loud we didn't hear the horse. But we heard heavy boots on the porch outside the living-room, and the swish of a slicker thrown to the floor. There was a bright fire. Dad looked up with a wild joy. All of a sudden he changed. He blazed. He recognized the heavy tread of his son. If I ever pitied and loved him it was then. I thought of the return of the Prodigal Son! . . . There came a knock on the door. Then dad recovered. He threw it open wide. The streaming light fell upon Jack Belllounds, indeed, but not as I knew him. He entered. It was the first time I ever saw Jack look in the least like a man. He was pale, haggard, much older, sullen, and bold. He strode in with a 'Howdy, folks,' and threw his wet hat on the floor, and walked to the fire. His boots were soaked with water and mud. His clothes began to steam.

"When I looked at dad I was surprised. He seemed cool and bright, with the self-contained force usual for him when something critical is about to happen.

" 'Ahuh! So you come back,' he said.

" 'Yes, I'm home,' replied Jack.

" 'Wal, it took you quite a spell to get hyar.'

" 'Do you want me to stay?'

"This question from Jack seemed to stump dad. He stared. Jack had appeared suddenly, and his manner was different from that with which he used to face dad. He had something up his sleeve, as the cowboys say. He wore an air of defiance and indifference.

" 'I reckon I do,' replied dad, deliberately. 'What do you mean by askin' me thet?'

" 'I'm of age, long ago. You can't make me stay home. I can do as I like.'

" 'Ahuh! I reckon you think you can. But not hyar at White Slides. If you ever expect to get this property you'll not do as you like.'

" 'To hell with that. I don't care whether I ever get it or not.'

"Dad's face went as white as a sheet. He seemed shocked. After a moment he told me I'd better go to my room. I was about to go when Jack said: 'No, let her stay. She'd best hear now what I've got to say. It concerns her.'

" 'So ho! Then you've got a heap to say?' exclaimed dad, queerly. 'All right, you have your say first.'

"Jack then began to talk in a level and monotonous voice, so unlike him that I sat there amazed. He told how early in the winter, before he left the ranch, he had found out that he was honestly in love with me. That it had changed him—made him see he had never been any good—and inflamed him with the resolve to be better. He had tried. He had succeeded. For six weeks he had been all that could have been asked of any young man. I am bound to confess that he was! . . . Well, he went on to say how he had fought it out with himself until he absolutely *knew* he could control himself. The courage and inspiration had come from his love for me. That was the only good thing he'd ever felt. He wanted dad and he wanted me to understand absolutely, without any doubt, that he had found a way to hold on to his good intentions and good feelings. And that was for *me!* . . . I was struck all a-tremble at the truth. It was true! Well, then he forced me to a decision. Forced me, without ever hinting of this change, this possibility in him. I had told him I *couldn't* love him. Never! Then he said I could go to hell and he gave up. Failing to get money from dad he stole it, without compunction and without regret! He had gone to Kremmling, then to Elgeria.

" 'I let myself go,' he said, without shame, 'and I drank and gambled. When I was drunk I didn't remember Collie. But when I was sober I did. And she haunted me. That grew worse all the time. So I drank to forget her. . . . The money lasted a great deal longer than I expected. But that was because I won as much as I lost, until lately. Then I borrowed a good deal from those men I gambled with, but mostly from ranchers who knew my father would be responsible. . . . I had a shooting-scrape with a man named Elbert, in Smith's place at Elgeria. We quarreled over cards. He cheated. And when I hit him he drew on me. But he missed. Then I shot him. . . . He lived three days—and died. That sobered me. And once more there came to me truth of what I might have been. I went back to Kremmling. And I tried myself out again. I worked awhile for Judson, who was the rancher I had borrowed most from. At night I went into town and to the saloons, where I met my gambling cronies. I put myself in the atmosphere of drink and cards. And I resisted both. I could make myself indifferent to both. As soon as I was sure of myself I decided to come home. And here I am.'

"This long speech of Jack's had a terrible effect upon me. I was stunned and sick. But if it did that to me *what* did it do to dad? Heaven knows, I can't tell you. Dad gave a lurch, and a great heave, as if at the removal of a rope that had all but strangled him.

" 'Ahuh-huh!' he groaned. 'An' now you're hyar—what's thet mean?'

" 'It means that it's not yet too late,' replied Jack. 'Don't misunderstand me. I'm not repenting with that side of me which is bad. But I've sobered up. I've had a shock. I see my ruin. I still love you, dad, despite—the cruel thing you did to me. I'm your son and I'd like to make up to you for all my shortcomings. And so help me Heaven! I can do that, and will do it, if Collie will marry me. Not only marry me—that'd not be enough—but love me—I'm crazy for her love. It's terrible.'

" 'You spoiled weaklin'!' thundered dad. 'How 'n hell can I believe you?'

" 'Because I know it,' declared Jack, standing right up to his father, white and unflinching.

"Then dad broke out in such a rage that I sat there scared so stiff I could not move. My heart beat thick and heavy. Dad got livid of face, his hair stood up, his eyes rolled. He called Jack every name I ever heard any one call him, and then a thousand more. Then he cursed him. Such dreadful curses! Oh, how sad and terrible to hear dad!

" 'Right you are!' cried Jack, bitter and hard and ringing of voice. 'Right, by God! But am I all to blame? Did I bring myself here on this earth! . . . There's something wrong in me that's not all my fault. . . . You can't shame me or scare me or hurt me. I could fling in your face those damned three years of hell you sent me to! But what's the use for you to roar at me or for me to reproach you? I'm ruined unless you give me Collie—make her love me. That will save me. And I want it for your sake and hers—not for my own. Even if I do love her madly I'm not wanting her for that. I'm no good. I'm not fit to touch her. . . . I've just come to tell you the truth. I feel for Collie—I'd do for Collie—as you did for my mother! Can't you understand? I'm your son. I've some of you in me. And I've found out what it is. Do you and Collie want to take me at my word?'

"I think it took dad longer to read something strange and convincing in Jack than it took me. Anyway, dad got the stunning consciousness that Jack *knew* by some divine or intuitive power that his reformation was inevitable, if I loved him. Never have I had such a distressing and terrible moment as that revelation brought to me! I felt the truth. I could save Jack Belllounds. No woman is ever fooled at such critical moments of life. Ben Wade once said that I could have reformed Jack were it possible to love him. Now the truth of that came home to me, and somehow it was overwhelming.

"Dad received this truth—and it was beyond me to realize what it meant to him. He must have seen all his earlier hopes fulfilled, his pride vindicated, his shame forgotten, his love rewarded. Yet he must have seen all that, as would a man leaning with one foot over a bottomless abyss. He looked transfigured, yet conscious of terrible peril. His great heart seemed to leap to meet this last opportunity, with all forgiveness, with all gratitude; but his will yielded with a final and irrevocable resolve. A resolve dark and sinister!

"He raised his huge fists higher and higher, and all his body lifted and strained, towering and trembling, while his face was that of a righteous and angry god.

"'My son, I take your word!' he rolled out, his voice filling the room and reverberating through the house. 'I give you Collie! . . . She will be yours! . . . But, by the love I bore your mother—I swear—if you ever steal again—I'll kill you!'

"I can't say any more—

"Columbine."

CHAPTER 14

Spring came early that year at White Slides Ranch. The snow melted off the valleys, and the wild flowers peeped from the greening grass while yet the mountain domes were white. The long stone slides were glistening wet, and the brooks ran full-banked, noisy and turbulent and roily.

Soft and fresh of color the gray old sage slopes came out from under their winter mantle; the bleached tufts of grass waved in the wind and showed tiny blades of green at the roots; the aspens and oaks, and the vines on fences and cliffs, and the round-clumped, brook-bordering willows took on a hue of spring.

The mustangs and colts in the pastures snorted and ran and kicked and cavorted; and on the hillsides the cows began to climb higher, searching for the tender greens, bawling for the new-born calves. Eagles shrieked the release of the snowbound peaks, and the elks bugled their piercing calls. The grouse-cocks spread their gorgeous brown plumage in parade before their twittering mates, and the jays screeched in the woods, and the sage-hens sailed along the bosom of the gray slopes.

Black bears, and browns, and grizzlies came out of their winter's sleep, and left huge, muddy tracks on the trails; the timber wolves at dusk mourned their hungry calls for life, for meat, for the wildness that was passing; the coyotes yelped at sunset, joyous and sharp and impudent.

But winter yielded reluctantly its hold on the mountains. The black, scudding clouds, and the squalls of rain and sleet and snow, whitening and melting and vanishing, and the cold, clear nights, with crackling frost, all retarded the work of the warming sun. The day came, however, when the greens held their own with the grays; and this was the assurance of nature that spring could not be denied, and that summer would follow.

B ent Wade was hiding in the willows along the trail that followed one of the brooks. Of late, on several mornings, he had skulked like an Indian under cover, watching for some one. On this morning, when Columbine Belllounds came riding along, he stepped out into the trail in front of her.

"Oh, Ben! You startled me!" she exclaimed, as she held hard on the frightened horse.

"Good mornin', Collie," replied Wade. "I'm sorry to scare you, but I'm particular anxious to see you. An' considerin' how you avoid me these days, I had to waylay you in regular road-agent style."

Wade gazed up searchingly at her. It had been some time since he had been given the privilege and pleasure of seeing her close at hand. He needed only one look at her to confirm his fears. The pale, sweet, resolute face told him much.

"Well, now you've waylaid me, what do you want?" she queried, deliberately.

"I'm goin' to take you to see Wils Moore," replied Wade, watching her closely.

"No!" she cried, with the red staining her temples.

"Collie, see here. Did I ever oppose anythin' you wanted to do?"

"Not—yet," she said.

"I reckon you expect me to?"

She did not answer that. Her eyes drooped, and she nervously twisted the bridle reins.

"Do you doubt my—my good intentions toward you—my love for you?" he asked, in gentle and husky voice.

"Oh, Ben! No! No! It's that I'm afraid of your love for me! I can't bear—what I have to bear—if I see you, if I listen to you."

"Then you've weakened? You're no proud, high-strung, thoroughbred girl any more? You're showin' yellow?"

"Ben Wade, I deny that," she answered, spiritedly, with an uplift of her head. "It's not weakness, but strength I've found."

"Ahuh! Well, I reckon I understand. Collie, listen. Wils let me read your last letter to him."

"I expected that. I think I told him to. Anyway, I wanted you to know—what—what ailed me."

"Lass, it was a fine, brave letter—written by a girl facin' an upheaval of conscience an' soul. But in your own trouble you forget the effect that letter might have on Wils Moore."

"Ben! . . . I—I've lain awake at night—Oh, was he hurt?"

"Collie, I reckon if you don't see Wils he'll kill himself or kill Buster Jack," replied Wade, gravely.

"I'll see—him!" she faltered. "But oh, Ben—you don't mean that Wilson would be so base—so cowardly?"

"Collie, you're a child. You don't realize the depths to which a man can sink. Wils has had a long, hard pull this winter. My nursin' an' your letters have saved his life. He's well, now, but that long, dark spell of mind left its shadow on him. He's morbid."

"What does he—want to see me—for?" asked Columbine, tremulously. There were tears in her eyes. "It'll only cause more pain—make matters worse."

"Reckon I don't agree with you. Wils just wants an' needs to *see* you. Why, he appreciated your position. I've heard him cry like a woman over it an' our helplessness. What ails him is lovesickness, the awful feelin' which comes to a man who believes he has lost his sweetheart's love."

"Poor boy! So he imagines I don't love him any more? Good Heavens! How stupid men are! . . . I'll see him, Ben. Take me to him."

For answer, Wade grasped the bridle of her horse and, turning him, took a course leading away behind the hill that lay between them and the ranch-house. The trail was narrow and brushy, making it necessary for him to walk ahead of the horse. So the hunter did not speak to her or look at her for some time. He plodded on with his eyes downcast. Something tugged at Wade's mind, an old, familiar, beckoning thing, vague and mysterious and black, a presage of catastrophe. But it was only an opening wedge into his mind. It had not entered. Gravity and unhappiness occupied him. His senses, nevertheless, were alert. He heard the low roar of the flooded brook, the whir of rising grouse ahead, the hoofs of deer on stones, the song of spring birds. He had an eye also for the wan wild flowers in the shaded corners. Presently he led the horse out of the willows into the open and up a low-swelling, long slope of fragrant sage. Here he dropped back to Columbine's side and put his hand upon the pommel of her saddle. It was not long until her own hand softly fell upon his and clasped it. Wade thrilled under the warm touch. How well he knew her heart! When she ceased to love any one to whom she had given her love then she would have ceased to breathe.

"Lass, this isn't the first mornin' I've waited for you," he said, presently. "An' when I had to go back to Wils without you—well, it was hard."

"Then he wants to see me—so badly?" she asked.

"Reckon you've not thought much about him or me lately," said Wade.

"No. I've tried to put you out of my mind. I've had so much to think of—why, even the sleepless nights have flown!"

"Are you goin' to confide in me—as you used to?"

"Ben, there's nothing to confide. I'm just where I left off in that letter to Wilson. And the more I think the more muddled I get."

Wade greeted this reply with a long silence. It was enough to feel her hand upon his and to have the glad comfort and charm of her presence once more. He seemed to have grown older lately. The fragrant breath of the sage slopes came to him as something precious he must feel and love more. A haunting transience mocked him from these rolling gray hills. Old White Slides loomed gray and dark up into the blue, grim and stern reminder of age and of fleeting time. There was a cloud on Wade's horizon.

"Wils is waitin' down there," said Wade, pointing to a grove of aspens below. "Reckon it's pretty close to the house, an' a trail runs along there. But Wils can't ride very well yet, an' this appeared to be the best place."

"Ben, I don't care if dad or Jack know I've met Wilson. I'll tell them," said Columbine.

"Ahuh! Well, if I were you I wouldn't," he replied.

They went down the slope and entered the grove. It was an open, pretty spot, with grass and wild flowers, and old, bleached logs, half sunny and half shady under the new-born, fluttering aspen leaves. Wade saw Moore sitting on his horse. And it struck the hunter significantly that the cowboy should be mounted when an hour back he had left him sitting disconsolately on a log. Moore wanted Columbine to see him first, after all these months of fear and dread, mounted upon his horse. Wade heard Columbine's glad little cry, but he did not turn to look at her then. But when they reached the spot where Moore stood Wade could not resist the desire to see the meeting between the lovers.

Columbine, being a woman, and therefore capable of hiding agitation, except in moments of stress, met that trying situation with more apparent composure than the cowboy. Moore's long, piercing gaze took the rose out of Columbine's cheeks.

"Oh, Wilson! I'm so happy to see you on your horse again!" she exclaimed. "It's too good to be true. I've prayed for that more than anything else. Can you get up into your saddle like you used to? Can you ride well again? . . . Let me see your foot."

Moore held out a bulky foot. He wore a shoe, and it was slashed.

"I can't wear a boot," he explained.

"Oh, I see!" exclaimed Columbine, slowly, with her glad smile fading. "You can't put that—that foot in a stirrup, can you?"

"No."

"But—it—it will—you'll be able to wear a boot soon," she implored.

"Never again, Collie," he said, sadly.

And then Wade perceived that, like a flash, the old spirit leaped up in Columbine. It was all he wanted to see.

"Now, folks," he said, "I reckon two's company an' three's a crowd. I'll go off a little ways an' keep watch."

"Ben, you stay here," replied Columbine, hurriedly.

"Why, Collie? Are you afraid—or ashamed to be with me alone?" asked Moore, bitterly.

Columbine's eyes flashed. It was seldom they lost their sweet tranquillity. But now they had depth and fire.

"No, Wilson, I'm neither afraid nor ashamed to be with you alone," she declared. "But I can be as natural—as much myself with Ben here as I could be alone. Why can't you be? If dad and Jack heard of our meeting the fact of Ben's presence might make it look different to them. And why should I heap trouble upon my shoulders?"

"I beg pardon, Collie," said the cowboy. "I've just been afraid of—of things."

"My horse is restless," returned Columbine. "Let's get off and talk."

So they dismounted. It warmed Wade's gloomy heart to see the woman-look in Columbine's eyes as she watched the cowboy get off and walk. For a crippled man he did very well. But that moment was fraught with meaning for Wade. These unfortunate lovers, brave and fine in their suffering, did not realize the peril they invited by proximity. But Wade knew. He pitied them, he thrilled for them, he lived their torture with them.

"Tell me—everything," said Columbine, impulsively.

Moore, with dragging step, approached an aspen log that lay off the ground, propped by the stump, and here he leaned for support. Columbine laid her gloves on the log.

"There's nothing to tell that you don't know," replied Moore. "I wrote you all there was to write, except"—here he dropped his head— "except that the last three weeks have been hell."

"They've not been exactly heaven for me," replied Columbine, with a little laugh that gave Wade a twinge.

Then the lovers began to talk about spring coming, about horses and cattle, and feed, about commonplace ranch matters not interesting to them, but which seemed to make conversation and hide their true thoughts. Wade listened, and it seemed to him that he could read their hearts.

"Lass, an' you, Wils—you're wastin' time an' gettin' nowhere," interposed Wade. "Now let me go, so's you'll be alone."

"You stay right there," ordered Moore.

"Why, Ben, I'm ashamed to say that I actually forgot you were here," said Columbine.

"Then I'll remind you," rejoined the hunter. "Collie, tell us about Old Bill an' Jack."

"Tell you? What?"

"Well, I've seen changes in both. So has Wils, though Wils hasn't seen as much as he's heard from Lem an' Montana an' the Andrews boys."

"Oh! . . ." Columbine choked a little over her exclamation of understanding. "Dad has gotten a new lease on life, I guess. He's happy, like a boy sometimes, an' good as gold. . . . It's all because of the change in Jack. That is remarkable. I've not been able to believe my own eyes. Since that night Jack came home and had the—the understanding with dad he has been another person. He has left me alone. He treats me with deference, but not a familiar word or look. He's kind. He offers the little civilities that occur, you know. But he never intrudes upon me. Not one word of the past! It is as if he would earn my respect, and have that or nothing. . . . Then he works as he never worked before—on dad's books, in the shop, out on the range. He seems obsessed with some thought all the time. He talks little. All the old petulance, obstinacy, selfishness, and especially his sudden, queer impulses, and bull-headed tenacity—all gone! He has suffered physical distress, because he never was used to hard work. And more, he's suffered terribly for the want of liquor. I've heard him say to dad: 'It's hell—this burning thirst. I never knew I had it. I'll stand it, if it kills me. . . . But wouldn't it be easier on me to take a drink now and then, at these bad times?' . . . And dad said: 'No, son. Break off fer keeps! This taperin' off is no good way to stop drinkin'. Stand the burnin'. An' when it's gone you'll be all the gladder an' I'll be all the prouder.' . . . I have not forgotten all Jack's former failings, but I am forgetting them, little by little. For dad's sake I'm overjoyed. For Jack's I am glad. I'm convinced now that he's had his lesson—that he's sowed his wild oats—that he has become a man."

Moore listened eagerly, and when she had concluded he thoughtfully bent his head and began to cut little chips out of the log with his knife.

"Collie, I've heard a good deal of the change in Jack," he said, earnestly. "Honest Injun, I'm glad—glad for his father's sake, for his own, and for yours. The boys think Jack's locoed. But his reformation is not strange to me. If I were no good—just like he was—well, I could change as greatly for—for you."

Columbine hastily averted her face. Wade's keen eyes, apparently hidden under his old hat, saw how wet her lashes were, how her lips trembled.

"Wilson, you think then—you believe Jack will last—will stick to his new ways?" she queried, hurriedly.

"Yes, I do," he replied, nodding.

"How good of you! Oh! Wilson, it's like you to be noble—splendid. When you might have—when it'd have been so natural for you to doubt—to scorn him!"

"Collie, I'm honest about that. And now you be just as honest. Do you think Jack will stand to his colors? Never drink—never gamble—never fly off the handle again?"

"Yes, I honestly believe that—providing he gets—providing I—"

Her voice trailed off faintly.

Moore wheeled to address the hunter.

"Pard, what do you think? Tell me now. Tell us. It will help me, and Collie, too. I've asked you before, but you wouldn't—Tell us now, do you believe Buster Jack will live up to his new ideals?"

Wade had long parried that question, because the time to answer it had not come till this moment.

"No," he replied, gently.

Columbine uttered a little cry.

"Why not?" demanded Moore, his face darkening.

"Reckon there are reasons that you young folks wouldn't think of, an' couldn't know."

"Wade, it's not like you to be hopeless for any man," said Moore.

"Yes, I reckon it is, sometimes," replied Wade, wagging his head solemnly. "Young folks, I'm grantin' all you say as to Jack's reformation, except that it's permanent. I'm grantin' he's sincere—that he's not playin' a part—that his vicious instincts are smothered under a noble impulse to be what he ought to be. It's no trick. Buster Jack has all but done the impossible."

"Then why isn't his sincerity and good work to be permanent?" asked Moore, impatiently, and his gesture was violent.

"Wils, his change is not moral force. It's passion."

The cowboy paled. Columbine stood silent, with intent eyes upon the hunter. Neither of them seemed to understand him well enough to make reply.

"Love can work marvels in any man," went on Wade. "But love can't change the fiber of a man's heart. A man is born so an' so. He loves an' hates an' feels accordin' to the nature. It'd be accordin' to nature for Jack

Belllounds to stay reformed if his love for Collie lasted. An' that's the point. It can't last. Not in a man of his stripe."

"Why not?" demanded Moore.

"Because Jack's love will never be returned—satisfied. It takes a man of different caliber to love a woman who'll never love him. Jack's obsessed by passion now. He'd perform miracles. But that's not possible. The miracle necessary here would be for him to change his moral force, his blood, the habits of his mind. That's beyond his power."

Columbine flung out an appealing hand.

"Ben, I could pretend to love him—I might *make* myself love him, if that would give him the power."

"Lass, don't delude yourself. You can't do that," replied Wade.

"How do you know what I can do?" she queried, struggling with her helplessness.

"Why, child, I know you better than you know yourself."

"Wilson, he's right, he's right!" she cried. "That's why it's so terrible for me now. He knows my very heart. He reads my soul. . . . I can *never* love Jack Belllounds. Nor *ever* pretend love!"

"Collie, if Ben knows you so well, you ought to listen to him, as you used to," said Moore, touching her hand with infinite sympathy.

Wade watched them. His pity and affection did not obstruct the ruthless expression of his opinions or the direction of his intentions.

"Lass, an' you, Wils, listen," he said, with all his gentleness. "It's bad enough without you makin' it worse. Don't blind yourselves. That's the hell with so many people in trouble. It's hard to see clear when you're sufferin' and fightin'. But *I* see clear. . . . Now with just a word I could fetch this new Jack Belllounds back to his Buster Jack tricks!"

"Oh, Ben! No! No! No!" cried Columbine, in a distress that showed how his force dominated her.

Moore's face turned as white as ashes.

Wade divined then that Moore was aware of what he himself knew about Jack Belllounds. And to his love for Moore was added an infinite respect.

"I won't unless Collie forces me to," he said, significantly.

This was the critical moment, and suddenly Wade answered to it without restraint. He leaped up, startling Columbine.

"Wils, you call me pard, don't you? I reckon you never knew me. Why, the game's 'most played out, an' I haven't showed my hand! . . . I'd see Jack Belllounds in hell before I'd let him have Collie. An' if she carried out her strange an' lofty idea of duty—an' married him right this afternoon—I could an' I would part them before night!"

He ended that speech in a voice neither had ever heard him use before. And the look of him must have been in harmony with it. Columbine, wide-eyed and gasping, seemed struck to the heart. Moore's white face showed awe and fear and irresponsible primitive joy. Wade turned away from them, the better to control the passion that had mastered him. And it did not subside in an instant. He paced to and fro, his head bowed. Presently, when he faced around, it was to see what he had expected to see.

Columbine was clasped in Moore's arms.

"Collie, you didn't—you haven't—promised to marry him—again!"

"No, oh—no! I haven't! I was only—only trying to—to make up my mind. Wilson, don't look at me so terribly!"

"You'll not agree again? You'll not set another day?" demanded Moore, passionately. He strained her to him, yet held her so he could see her face, thus dominating her with both strength and will. His face was corded now, and darkly flushed. His jaw quivered. "You'll never marry Jack Belllounds! You'll not let sudden impulse—sudden persuasion or force change you? Promise! Swear you'll never marry him. Swear!"

"Oh, Wilson, I promise—I swear!" she cried. "Never! I'm yours. It would be a sin. I've been mad to—to blind myself."

"You love me! You love me!" he cried, in a sudden transport.

"Oh, yes, yes! I do."

"Say it then! Say it—so I'll never doubt—never suffer again!"

"I love you, Wilson! I—I love you—unutterably," she whispered. "I love you—so—I'm broken-hearted now. I'll never live without you. I'll die—I love you so!"

"You—you flower—you angel!" he whispered in return. "You woman! You precious creature! I've been crazed at loss of you!"

Wade paced out of earshot, and this time he remained way for a considerable time. He lived again moments of his own past, unforgettable and sad. When at length he returned toward the young couple they were sitting apart, composed once more, talking earnestly. As he neared them Columbine rose to greet him with wonderful eyes, in which reproach blended with affection.

"Ben, so this is what you've done!" she exclaimed.

"Lass, I'm only a humble instrument, an' I believe God guides me right," replied the hunter.

"I love you more, it seems, for what you make me suffer," she said, and she kissed him with a serious sweetness. "I'm only a leaf in the storm. But—let what will come. . . . Take me home."

They said good-by to Wilson, who sat with head bowed upon his hands. His voice trembled as he answered them. Wade found the trail while Columbine mounted. As they went slowly down the gentle slope, stepping over the numerous logs fallen across the way, Wade caught out the tail of his eye a moving object along the outer edge the aspen grove above them. It was the figure of a man, skulking behind the trees. He disappeared. Wade usually remarked to Columbine that now she could spur the pony and hurry on home. But Columbine refused. When they got a little farther on, out of sight of Moore and somewhat around to the left, Wade espied the man again. He carried a rifle. Wade grew somewhat perturbed.

"Collie, you run on home," he said, sharply.

"Why? You've complained of not seeing me. Now that I want to be with you . . . Ben, you see some one!"

Columbine's keen faculties evidently sensed the change in Wade, and the direction of his uneasy glance convinced her.

"Oh, there's a man! . . . Ben, it is—yes, it's Jack," she exclaimed, excitedly.

"Reckon you'd have it better if you say Buster Jack," replied Wade, with his tragic smile.

"Ah!" whispered Columbine, as she gazed up at the aspen slope, with eyes lighting to battle.

"Run home, Collie, an' leave him to me," said Wade.

"Ben, you mean he—he saw us up there in the grove? Saw me in Wilson's arms—saw me kissing him?"

"Sure as you're born, Collie. He watched us. He saw all your love-makin'. I can tell that by the way he walks. It's Buster Jack again! Alas for the new an' noble Jack! I told you, Collie. Now you run on an' leave him to me."

Wade became aware that she turned at his last words and regarded him attentively. But his gaze was riveted on the striding form of Belllounds.

"Leave him to you? For what reason, my friend?" she asked.

"Buster Jack's on the rampage. Can't you see that? He'll insult you. He'll—"

"I will not go," interrupted Columbine, and, halting her pony, she deliberately dismounted.

Wade grew concerned with the appearance of young Belllounds, and it was with a melancholy reminder of the infallibility of his presentiments. As he and Columbine halted in the trail, Belllounds's hurried stride lengthened until he almost ran. He carried the rifle forward in a most significant manner. Black as a thunder-cloud was his face. Alas for the dignity and pain and resolve that had only recently showed there!

Belllounds reached them. He was frothing at the mouth. He cocked the rifle and thrust it toward Wade, holding low down.

"You—meddling sneak! If you open your trap I'll bore you!" he shouted, almost incoherently.

Wade knew when danger of life loomed imminent. He fixed his glance upon the glaring eyes of Belllounds.

"Jack, seein' I'm not packin' a gun, it'd look sorta natural, along with your other tricks, if you bored me."

His gentle voice, his cool mien, his satire, were as giant's arms to drag Belllounds back from murder. The rifle was raised, the hammer reset, the butt lowered to the ground, while Belllounds, snarling and choking, fought for speech.

"I'll get even—with you," he said, huskily. "I'm on to your game now. I'll fix you later. But—I'll do you harm now if you mix in with this!"

Then he wheeled to Columbine, and as if he had just recognized her, a change that was pitiful and shocking convulsed his face. He leaned toward her, pointing with shaking, accusing hand.

"I saw you—up there. I watched—you," he panted.

Columbine faced him, white and mute.

"It was you—wasn't it?" he yelled.

"Yes, of course it was."

She might have struck him, for the way he flinched.

"What was that—a trick—a game—a play all fixed up for my benefit?"

"I don't understand you," she replied.

"Bah! You—you white-faced cat! . . . I saw you! Saw you in Moore's arms! Saw him hug you—kiss you! . . . Then—I saw—you put up your arms—round his neck—kiss him—kiss him—kiss him! . . . I saw all that— didn't I?"

"You must have, since you say so," she returned, with perfect composure.

"But *did* you?" he almost shrieked, the blood cording and bulging red, as if about to burst the veins of temples and neck.

"Yes, I did," she flashed. There was primitive woman uppermost in her now, and a spirit no man might provoke with impunity.

"*You love him?*" he asked, very low, incredulously, with almost insane eagerness for denial in his query.

Then Wade saw the glory of her—saw her mother again in that proud, fierce uplift of face, that flamed red and then blazed white—saw hate and passion and love in all their primal nakedness.

"Love him! Love Wilson Moore? Yes, you fool! I love him! Yes! *Yes! YES!*"

That voice would have pierced the heart of a wooden image, so Wade thought, as all his strung nerves quivered and thrilled.

Belllounds uttered a low cry of realization, and all his instinctive energy seemed on the verge of collapse. He grew limp, he sagged, he tottered. His sensorial perceptions seemed momentarily blunted.

Wade divined the tragedy, and a pang of great compassion overcame him. Whatever Jack Belllounds was in character, he had inherited his father's power to love, and he was human. Wade felt the death in that stricken soul, and it was the last flash of pity he ever had for Jack Belllounds.

"You—you—" muttered Belllounds, raising a hand that gathered speed and strength in the action. The moment of a great blow had passed, like a storm-blast through a leafless tree. Now the thousand devils of his nature leaped into ascendancy. "You!—" He could not articulate. Dark and terrible became his energy. It was like a resistless current forced through leaping thought and leaping muscle.

He struck her on the mouth, a cruel blow that would have felled her but for Wade; and then he lunged away, bowed and trembling, yet with fierce, instinctive motion, as if driven to run with the spirit of his rage.

CHAPTER 15

Wade noticed that after her trying experience with him and Wilson and Belllounds Columbine did not ride frequently.

He managed to get a word or two with her whenever he went to the ranch-house, and he needed only look at her to read her sensitive mind. All was well with Columbine, despite her trouble. She remained upheld in spirit, while yet she seemed to brood over an unsolvable problem. She had said, "But—let what will come!"—and she was waiting.

Wade hunted for more than lions and wolves these days. Like an Indian scout who scented peril or heard an unknown step upon his trail, Wade rode the hills, and spent long hours hidden on the lonely slopes, watching with somber, keen eyes. They were eyes that knew what they were looking for. They had marked the strange sight of the son of Bill Belllounds, gliding along that trail where Moore had met Columbine, sneaking and stooping, at last with many a covert glance about, to kneel in the trail and compare the horse tracks there with horseshoes he took from his pocket. That alone made Bent Wade eternally vigilant. He kept his counsel. He worked more swiftly, so that he might have leisure for his peculiar seeking. He spent an hour each night with the cowboys, listening to their recounting of the day and to their homely and shrewd opinions. He haunted the vicinity of the ranch-house at night, watching and listening for that moment which was to aid him in the crisis that was impending. Many a time he had been near when Columbine passed from the living-room to her corner of the house. He had heard her sigh and could almost have touched her.

Buster Jack had suffered a regurgitation of the old driving and insatiate temper, and there was gloom in the house of Belllounds. Trouble clouded the old man's eyes.

May came with the spring round-up. Wade was called to use a rope and brand calves under the order of Jack Belllounds, foreman of White Slides. That round-up showed a loss of one hundred head of stock, some branded steers, and yearlings, and many calves, in all a mixed herd. Belllounds received the amazing news with a roar. He had been ready for something to roar at. The cowboys gave as reasons winter-kill, and lions, and perhaps some head stolen since the thaw. Wade emphatically denied this. Very few cattle had fallen prey to the big cats, and none, so far as he could find, had been frozen or caught in drifts. It was the young foreman who stunned them all. "Rustled," he said, darkly. "There's too many loafers and homesteaders in these hills!" And he stalked out to leave his hearers food for reflection.

Jack Belllounds drank, but no one saw him drunk, and no one could tell where he got the liquor. He rode hard and fast; he drove the cowboys one way while he went another; he had grown shifty, cunning, more intolerant than ever. Some nights he rode to Kremmling, or said he had been there, when next day the cowboys found another spent and broken horse to turn out. On other nights he coaxed and bullied them into playing poker. They won more of his money than they cared to count.

Columbine confided to Wade, with mournful whisper, that Jack paid no attention to her whatever, and that the old rancher attributed this coldness, and Jack's backsliding, to her irresponsiveness and her tardiness in setting the wedding-day that must be set. To this Wade had whispered in reply, "Don't ever forget what I said to you an' Wils that day!"

So Wade upheld Columbine with his subtle dominance, and watched over her, as it were, from afar. No longer was he welcome in the big living-room. Belllounds reacted to his son's influence.

Twice in the early mornings Wade had surprised Jack Belllounds in the blacksmith shop. The meetings were accidental, yet Wade ever remembered how coincidence beckoned him thither and how circumstance magnified strange reflections. There was no reason why Jack should not be tinkering in the blacksmith shop early of a morning. But Wade followed an uncanny guidance. Like his dog Fox, he never split on trails. When opportunity afforded he went into the shop and looked it over with eyes as keen as the nose of his dog. And in the dust of the floor he had discovered little circles with dots in the middle, all uniform in size. Sight of them did not shock him until they recalled vividly the little circles with dots in the earthen floor of Wilson Moore's cabin. Little marks made by the end of Moore's crutch! Wade grinned then like a wolf showing his fangs. And the vitals of a wolf could no more strongly have felt the instinct to rend.

For Wade, the cloud on his horizon spread and darkened, gathered sinister shape of storm, harboring lightning and havoc. It was the cloud in his mind, the foreshadowing of his soul, the prophetic sense of like to like. Where he wandered there the blight fell!

Significant was the fact that Belllounds hired new men. Bludsoe had quit. Montana Jim grew surly these days and packed a gun. Lem Billings had threatened to leave. New and strange hands for Jack Belllounds to direct had a tendency to release a strain and tide things over.

Every time the old rancher saw Wade he rolled his eyes and wagged his head, as if combating superstition with an intelligent sense of justice. Wade knew what troubled Belllounds, and it strengthened the gloomy mood that, like a poison lichen, seemed finding root.

Every day Wade visited his friend Wilson Moore, and most of their conversation centered round that which had become a ruling passion for both. But the time came when Wade deviated from his gentleness of speech and leisure of action.

"Bent, you're not like you were," said Moore, once, in surprise at the discovery. "You're losing hope and confidence."

"No. I've only somethin' on my mind."

"What?"

"I reckon I'm not goin' to tell you now."

"You've got *hell* on your mind!" flashed the cowboy, in grim inspiration.

Wade ignored the insinuation and turned the conversation to another subject.

"Wils, you're buyin' stock right along?"

"Sure am. I saved some money, you know. And what's the use to hoard it? I'll buy cheap. In five years I'll have five hundred, maybe a thousand head. Wade, my old dad will be pleased to find out I've made the start I have."

"Well, it's a fine start, I'll allow. Have you picked up any unbranded stock?"

"Sure I have. Say, pard, are you worrying about this two-bit rustler work that's been going on?"

"Wils, it ain't two bits any more. I reckon it's gettin' into the four-bit class."

"I've been careful to have my business transactions all in writing," said Moore. "It makes these fellows sore, because some of them can't write. And they're not used to it. But I'm starting this game in my own way."

"Have you sold any stock?"

"Not yet. But the Andrews boys are driving some thirty-odd head to Kremmling for me to be sold."

"Ahuh! Well, I'll be goin'," Wade replied, and it was significant of his state of mind that he left his young friend sorely puzzled. Not that Wade did not see Moore's anxiety! But the drift of events at White Slides had passed beyond the stage where sympathetic and inspiring hope might serve Wade's purpose. Besides, his mood was gradually changing as these events, like many fibers of a web, gradually closed in toward a culminating knot.

That night Wade lounged with the cowboys and new hands in front of the little storehouse where Belllounds kept supplies for all. He had lounged there before in the expectation of seeing the rancher's son. And this time anticipation was verified. Jack Belllounds swaggered over from the ranch-house. He met civility and obedience now where formerly he had earned but ridicule and opposition. So long as he worked hard himself the cowboys endured. The subtle change in him seemed of sterner stuff. The talk, as usual, centered round the stock subjects and the banter and gossip of ranch-hands. Wade selected an interval when there was a lull in the conversation, and with eyes that burned under the shadow of his broad-brimmed sombrero he watched the son of Belllounds.

"Say, boys, Wils Moore has begun sellin' cattle," remarked Wade, casually. "The Andrews brothers are drivin' for him."

"Wal, so Wils's spread-eaglin' into a real rancher!" ejaculated Lem Billings. "Mighty glad to hear it. Thet boy shore will git rich."

Wade's remark incited no further expressions of interest. But it was Jack Belllounds's secret mind that Wade wished to pierce. He saw the leaping of a thought that was neither interest nor indifference nor contempt, but a creative thing which lent a fleeting flash to the face, a slight shock to the body. Then Jack Belllounds bent his head, lounged there for a little while longer, lost in absorption, and presently he strolled away.

Whatever that mounting thought of Jack Belllounds's was it brought instant decision to Wade. He went to the ranch-house and knocked upon the living-room door. There was a light within, sending rays out through the windows into the semi-darkness. Columbine opened the door and admitted Wade. A bright fire crackled in the hearth. Wade flashed a reassuring look at Columbine.

"Evenin', Miss Collie. Is your dad in?"

"Oh, it's you, Ben!" she replied, after her start. "Yes, dad's here."

The old rancher looked up from his reading. "Howdy, Wade! What can I do fer you?"

"Belllounds, I've cleaned out the cats an' most of the varmints on your range. An' my work, lately, has been all sorts, not leavin' me any time for little jobs of my own. An' I want to quit."

"Wade, you've clashed with Jack!" exclaimed the rancher, jerking erect.

"Nothin' of the kind. Jack an' me haven't had words for a good while. I'm not denyin' we might, an' probably would clash sooner or later. But that's not my reason for quittin'."

Manifestly this put an entirely different complexion upon the matter. Belllounds appeared immensely relieved.

"Wal, all right. I'll pay you at the end of the month. Let's see, thet's not long now. You can lay off tomorrow."

Wade thanked him and waited for further remarks. Columbine had fixed big, questioning eyes upon Wade, which he found hard to endure. Again he tried to flash her a message of reassurance. But Columbine did not lose her look of blank wonder and gravity.

"Ben! Oh, you're not going to leave White Slides?" she asked.

"Reckon I'll hang around yet awhile," he replied.

Belllounds was wagging his head regretfully and ponderingly.

"Wal, I remember the day when no man quit me. Wal, wal!—times change. I'm an old man now. Mebbe, mebbe I'm testy. An' then thar's thet boy!"

With a shrug of his broad shoulders he dismissed what seemed an encroachment of pessimistic thought.

"Wade, you're packin' off, then, on the trail? Always on the go, eh?"

"No, I'm not hurryin' off," replied Wade.

"Wal, might I ask what you're figgerin' on?"

"Sure. I'm considerin' a cattle deal with Moore. He's a pretty keen boy an' his father has big ranchin' interests. I've saved a little money an' I'm no spring chicken any more. Wils has begun to buy an' sell stock, so I reckon I'll go in with him."

"Ahuh!" Belllounds gave a grunt of comprehension. He frowned, and his big eyes set seriously upon the blazing fire. He grasped complications in this information.

"Wal, it's a free country," he said at length, and evidently his personal anxieties were subjected to his sense of justice. "Owin' to the peculiar circumstances hyar at my range, I'd prefer thet Moore an' you began somewhar else. Thet's natural. But you've my good will to start on an' I hope I've yours."

"Belllounds, you've every man's good will," replied Wade. "I hope you won't take offense at my leavin'. You see I'm on Wils Moore's side in—in what you called these peculiar circumstances. He's got nobody else. An' I reckon you can look back an' remember how you've taken sides with some poor devil an' stuck to him. Can't you?"

"Wal, I reckon I can. An' I'm not thinkin' less of you fer speakin' out like thet."

"All right. Now about the dogs. I turn the pack over to you, an' it's a good one. I'd like to buy Fox."

"Buy nothin', man. You can have Fox, an' welcome."

"Much obliged," returned the hunter, as he turned to go. "Fox will sure be help for me. Belllounds, I'm goin' to round up this outfit that's rustlin' your cattle. They're gettin' sort of bold."

"Wade, you'll do thet on your own hook?" asked the rancher, in surprise.

"Sure. I like huntin' men more than other varmints. Then I've a personal interest. You know the hint about homesteaders hereabouts reflects some on Wils Moore."

"Stuff!" exploded the rancher, heartily. "Do you think any cattleman in these hills would believe Wils Moore a rustler?"

"The hunch has been whispered," said Wade. "An' you know how all ranchers say they rustled a little on the start."

"Aw, hell! Thet's different. Every new rancher drives in a few unbranded calves an' keeps them. But stealin' stock—thet's different. An' I'd as soon suspect my own son of rustlin' as Wils Moore."

Belllounds spoke with a sincere and frank ardor of defense for a young man once employed by him and known to be honest. The significance of the comparison he used had not struck him. His was the epitome of a successful rancher, sure in his opinions, speaking proudly and unreflectingly of his own son, and being just to another man.

Wade bowed and backed out of the door. "Sure that's what I'd reckon you'd say, Belllounds. . . . I'll drop in on you if I find any sign in the woods. Good night."

Columbine went with him to the end of the porch, as she had used to go before the shadow had settled over the lives of the Belllounds.

"Ben, you're up to something," she whispered, seizing him with hands that shook.

"Sure. But don't you worry," he whispered back.

"Do they hint that Wilson is a rustler?" she asked, intensely.

"Somebody did, Collie."

"How vile! Who? Who?" she demanded, and her face gleamed white.

"Hush, lass! You're all a-tremble," he returned, warily, and he held her hands.

"Ben, they're pressing me hard to set another wedding-day. Dad is angry with me now. Jack has begun again to demand. Oh, I'm afraid of him! He has no respect for me. He catches at me with hands like claws. I have to jerk away. . . . Oh, Ben, Ben! dear friend, what on earth shall I do?"

"Don't give in. Fight Jack! Tell the old man you must have time.

Watch your chance when Jack is away an' ride up the Buffalo Park trail an' look for me."

Wade had to release his hands from her clasp and urge her gently back. How pale and tragic her face gleamed!

Wade took his horses, his outfit, and the dog Fox, and made his abode with Wilson Moore. The cowboy hailed Wade's coming with joy and pestered him with endless questions.

From that day Wade haunted the hills above White Slides, early and late, alone with his thoughts, his plans, more and more feeling the suspense of happenings to come. It was on a June day when Jack Belllounds rode to Kremmling that Wade met Columbine on the Buffalo Park trail. She needed to see him, to find comfort and strength. Wade far exceeded his own confidence in his effort to uphold her. Columbine was in a strange state, not of vacillation between two courses, but of a standstill, as if her will had become obstructed and waited for some force to upset the hindrance. She did not inquire as to the welfare of Wilson Moore, and Wade vouchsafed no word of him. But she importuned the hunter to see her every day or no more at all. And Wade answered her appeal and her need by assuring her that he would see her, come what might. So she was to risk more frequent rides.

During the second week of June Wade rode up to visit the prospector, Lewis, and learned that which complicated the matter of the rustlers. Lewis had been suspicious, and active on his own account. According to the best of his evidence and judgment there had been a gang of rough men come of late to Gore Peak, where they presumably were prospecting. This gang was composed of strangers to Lewis. They had ridden to his cabin, bought and borrowed of him, and, during his absence, had stolen from him. He believed they were in hiding, probably being guilty of some depredation in another locality. They gave both Kremmling and Elgeria a wide berth. On the other hand, the Smith gang from Elgeria rode to and fro, like ranchers searching for lost horses. There were only three in this gang, including Smith. Lewis had seen these men driving unbranded stock. And lastly, Lewis casually imparted the information, highly interesting to Wade, that he had seen Jack Belllounds riding through the forest. The prospector did not in the least, however, connect the appearance of the son of Belllounds with the other facts so peculiarly interesting to Wade. Cowboys and hunters rode trails across the range, and though they did so rather infrequently, there was nothing unusual about encountering them.

Wade remained all night with Lewis, and next morning rode six miles along the divide, and then down into a valley, where at length he found a cabin described by the prospector. It was well hidden in the edge of the forest, where a spring gushed from under a low cliff. But for water and horse tracks Wade would not have found it easily. Rifle in hand, and on foot, he slipped around in the woods, as a hunter might have, to stalk drinking deer. There were no smoke, no noise, no horses anywhere round the cabin, and after watching awhile Wade went forward to look at it. It was an old ramshackle hunter's or prospector's cabin, with dirt floor, a crumbling fireplace and chimney, and a bed platform made of boughs. Including the door, it had three apertures, and the two smaller ones, serving as windows, looked as if they had been intended for port-holes as well. The inside of the cabin was large and unusually well lighted, owing to the windows and to the open chinks between the logs. Wade saw a deck of cards lying bent and scattered in one corner, as if a violent hand had flung them against the wall. Strange that Wade's memory returned a vivid picture of Jack Belllounds in just that act of violence! The only other thing around the place which earned scrutiny from Wade was a number of horseshoe tracks outside, with the left front shoe track familiar to him. He examined the clearest imprints very carefully. If they had not been put there by Wilson Moore's white mustang, Spottie, then they had been made by a horse with a strangely similar hoof and shoe. Spottie had a hoof malformed, somewhat in the shape of a triangle, and the iron shoe to fit it always had to be bent, so that the curve was sharp and the ends closer together than those of his other shoes.

Wade rode down to White Slides that day, and at the evening meal he casually asked Moore if he had been riding Spottie of late.

"Sure. What other horse could I ride? Do you think I'm up to trying one of those broncs?" asked Moore, in derision.

"Reckon you haven't been leavin' any tracks up Buffalo Park way?"

The cowboy slammed down his knife. "Say, Wade, are you growing dotty? Good Lord! if I'd ridden that far—if I was able to do it—wouldn't you hear me yell?"

"Reckon so, come to think of it. I just saw a track like Spottie's, made two days ago."

"Well, it wasn't his, you can gamble on that," returned the cowboy.

Wade spent four days hiding in an aspen grove, on top of one of the highest foothills above White Slides Ranch. There he lay at ease, like an Indian, calm and somber, watching the trails below, waiting for what he knew was to come.

On the fifth morning he was at his post at sunrise. A casual remark of one of the new cowboys the night before accounted for the early hour of Wade's reconnoiter. The dawn was fresh and cool, with sweet odor of sage on the air; the jays were squalling their annoyance at this early disturber of their grove; the east was rosy above the black range and soon glowed with gold and then changed to fire. The sun had risen. All the mountain world of black range and gray hill and green valley, with its shining stream, was transformed as if by magic color. Wade sat down with his back to an aspen-tree, his gaze down upon the ranch-house and the corrals. A lazy column of blue smoke curled up toward the sky, to be lost there. The burros were braying, the calves were bawling, the colts were whistling. One of the hounds bayed full and clear.

The scene was pastoral and beautiful. Wade saw it clearly and whole. Peace and plenty, a happy rancher's home, the joy of the dawn and the birth of summer, the rewards of toil—all seemed significant there. But Wade pondered on how pregnant with life that scene was—nature in its simplicity and freedom and hidden cruelty, and the existence of people, blindly hating, loving, sacrificing, mostly serving some noble aim, and yet with baseness among them, the lees with the wine, evil intermixed with good.

By and by the cowboys appeared on their spring mustangs, and in twos and threes they rode off in different directions. But none rode Wade's way. The sun rose higher, and there was warmth in the air. Bees began to hum by Wade, and fluttering moths winged uncertain sight over him.

At the end of another hour Jack Belllounds came out of the house, gazed around him, and then stalked to the barn where he kept his horses. For a little while he was not in sight; then he reappeared, mounted on a white horse, and he rode into the pasture, and across that to the hay-field, and along the edge of this to the slope of the hill. Here he climbed to a small clump of aspens. This grove was not so far from Wilson Moore's cabin; in fact, it marked the boundary-line between the rancher's range and the acres that Moore had acquired. Jack vanished from sight here, but not before Wade had made sure he was dismounting.

"Reckon he kept to that grassy ground for a reason of his own—and plainer to me than any tracks," soliloquized Wade, as he strained his eyes. At length Belllounds came out of the grove, and led his horse round to where Wade knew there was a trail leading to and from Moore's cabin. At this point Jack mounted and rode west. Contrary to his usual custom, which was to ride hard and fast, he trotted the white horse as a cowboy might have done when going out on a day's work. Wade had to change his position to watch Belllounds, and his somber gaze followed him across the hill, down the slope, along the willow-bordered brook, and so on to the opposite side of the great valley, where Jack began to climb in the direction of Buffalo Park.

After Belllounds had disappeared and had been gone for an hour, Wade went down on the other side of the hill, found his horse where he had left him, in a thicket, and, mounting, he rode around to strike the trail upon which Belllounds had ridden. The imprint of fresh horse tracks showed clear in the soft dust. And the left front track had been made by a shoe crudely triangular in shape, identical with that peculiar to Wilson Moore's horse.

"Ahuh!" muttered Wade, in greeting to what he had expected to see. "Well, Buster Jack, it's a plain trail now—damn your crooked soul!"

The hunter took up that trail, and he followed it into the woods. There he hesitated. Men who left crooked trails frequently ambushed them, and Belllounds had made no effort to conceal his tracks. Indeed, he had chosen the soft, open ground, even after he had left the trail to take to the grassy, wooded benches. There were cattle here, but not as many as on the more open aspen slopes across the valley. After deliberating a moment, Wade decided that he must risk being caught trailing

Belllounds. But he would go slowly, trusting to eye and ear, to outwit this strangely acting foreman of White Slides Ranch.

To that end he dismounted and took the trail. Wade had not followed it far before he became convinced that Belllounds had been looking in the thickets for cattle; and he had not climbed another mile through the aspens and spruce before he discovered that Belllounds was driving cattle. Thereafter Wade proceeded more cautiously. If the long grass had not been wet he would have encountered great difficulty in trailing Belllounds. Evidence was clear now that he was hiding the tracks of the cattle by keeping to the grassy levels and slopes which, after the sun had dried them, would not leave a trace. There were stretches where even the keen-eyed hunter had to work to find the direction taken by Belllounds. But here and there, in other localities, there showed faint signs of cattle and horse tracks.

The morning passed, with Wade slowly climbing to the edge of the black timber. Then, in a hollow where a spring gushed forth, he saw the tracks of a few cattle that had halted to drink, and on top of these the tracks of a horse with a crooked left front shoe. The rider of this horse had dismounted. There was an imprint of a cowboy's boot, and near it little sharp circles with dots in the center.

"Well, I'll be damned!" ejaculated Wade. "I call that mighty cunnin'. Here they are—proofs as plain as writin'—that Wils Moore rustled Old Bill's cattle! . . . Buster Jack, you're not such a fool as I thought. . . . He's made somethin' like the end of Wils's crutch. An' knowin' how Wils uses that every time he gets off his horse, why, the dirty pup carried his instrument with him an' made these tracks!"

Wade left the trail then, and, leading his horse to a covert of spruce, he sat down to rest and think. Was there any reason for following Belllounds farther? It did not seem needful to take the risk of being discovered. The forest above was open. No doubt Belllounds would drive the cattle somewhere and turn them over to his accomplices.

"Buster Jack's outbusted himself this time, sure," soliloquized Wade. "He's double-crossin' his rustler friends, same as he is Moore. For he's goin' to blame this cattle-stealin' onto Wils. An' to do that he's layin' his tracks so he can follow them, or so any good trailer can. It doesn't concern me so much now who're his pards in this deal. Reckon it's Smith an' some of his gang."

Suddenly it dawned upon Wade that Jack Belllounds was stealing cattle from his father. "Whew!" he whistled softly. "Awful hard on the old man! Who's to tell him when all this comes out? Aw, I'd hate to do it. I wouldn't. There's some things even I'd not tell."

Straightway this strange aspect of the case confronted Wade and gripped his soul. He seemed to feel himself changing inwardly, as if a gray, gloomy, sodden hand, as intangible as a ghostly dream, had taken him bodily from himself and was now leading him into shadows, into drear, lonely, dark solitude, where all was cold and bleak; and on and on over naked shingles that marked the world of tragedy. Here he must tell his tale, and as he plodded on his relentless leader forced him to tell his tale anew.

Wade recognized this as his black mood. It was a morbid dominance of the mind. He fought it as he would have fought a devil. And mastery still was his. But his brow was clammy and his heart was leaden when he had wrested that somber, mystic control from his will.

"Reckon I'd do well to take up this trail to-morrow an' see where it leads," he said, and as a gloomy man, burdened with thought, he retraced his way down the long slope, and over the benches, to the grassy slopes and aspen groves, and thus to the sage hills.

It was dark when he reached the cabin, and Moore had supper almost ready.

"Well, old-timer, you look fagged out," called out the cowboy, cheerily. "Throw off your boots, wash up, and come and get it!"

"Pard Wils, I'm not reboundin' as natural as I'd like. I reckon I've lived some years before I got here, an' a lifetime since."

"Wade, you have a queer look, lately," observed Moore, shaking his head solemnly. "Why, I've seen a dying man look just like you—now—round the mouth—but most in the eyes!"

"Maybe the end of the long trail is White Slides Ranch," replied Wade, sadly and dreamily, as if to himself.

"If Collie heard you say that!" exclaimed Moore, in anxious concern.

"Collie an' you will hear me say a lot before long," returned Wade. "But, as it's calculated to make you happy—why, all's well. I'm tired an' hungry."

Wade did not choose to sit round the fire that night, fearing to invite interrogation from his anxious friend, and for that matter from his other inquisitively morbid self.

Next morning, though Wade felt rested, and the sky was blue and full of fleecy clouds, and the melody of birds charmed his ear, and over all the June air seemed thick and beating with the invisible spirit he loved, he sensed the oppression, the nameless something that presaged catastrophe.

Therefore, when he looked out of the door to see Columbine swiftly riding up the trail, her fair hair flying and shining in the sunlight, he merely ejaculated, "Ahuh!"

"What's that?" queried Moore, sharp to catch the inflection.

"Look out," replied Wade, as he began to fill his pipe.

"Heavens! It's Collie! Look at her riding! Uphill, too!"

Wade followed him outdoors. Columbine was not long in arriving at the cabin, and she threw the bridle and swung off in the same motion, landing with a light thud. Then she faced them, pale, resolute, stern, all the sweetness gone to bitter strength—another and a strange Columbine.

"I've not slept a wink!" she said. "And I came as soon as I could get away."

Moore had no word for her, not even a greeting. The look of her had stricken him. It could have only one meaning.

"Mornin', lass," said the hunter, and he took her hand. "I couldn't tell you looked sleepy, for all you said. Let's go into the cabin."

So he led Columbine in, and Moore followed. The girl manifestly was in a high state of agitation, but she was neither trembling nor frightened nor sorrowful. Nor did she betray any lack of an unflinching and indomitable spirit. Wade read the truth of what she imagined was her doom in the white glow of her, in the matured lines of womanhood that had come since yesternight, in the sustained passion of her look.

"Ben! Wilson! The worst has come!" she announced.

Moore could not speak. Wade held Columbine's hand in both of his.

"Worst! Now, Collie, that's a terrible word. I've heard it many times. An' all my life the worst's been comin'. An' it hasn't come yet. You—only twenty years old—talkin' wild—the worst has come! . . . Tell me your trouble now an' I'll tell you where you're wrong."

"Jack's a thief—a cattle-thief!" rang Columbine's voice, high and clear.

"Ahuh! Well, go on," said Wade.

"Jack has taken money from rustlers—*for cattle stolen from his father!*"

Wade felt the lift of her passion, and he vibrated to it.

"Reckon that's no news to me," he replied.

Then she quivered up to a strong and passionate delivery of the thing that had transformed her.

"I'M GOING TO MARRY JACK BELLLOUNDS!"

Wilson Moore leaped toward her with a cry, to be held back by Wade's hand.

"Now, Collie," he soothed, "tell us all about it."

Columbine, still upheld by the strength of her spirit, related how she had ridden out the day before, early in the afternoon, in the hope of meeting Wade. She rode over the sage hills, along the edges of the aspen benches, everywhere that she might expect to meet or see the hunter, but as he did not appear, and as she was greatly desirous of talking with him, she went on up into the woods, following the line of the Buffalo Park trail, though keeping aside from it. She rode very slowly and cautiously, remembering Wade's instructions. In this way she ascended the aspen benches, and the spruce-bordered ridges, and then the first rise of the black forest. Finally she had gone farther than ever before and farther than was wise.

When she was about to turn back she heard the thud of hoofs ahead of her. Pronto shot up his ears. Alarmed and anxious, Columbine swiftly gazed about her. It would not do for her to be seen. Yet, on the other hand, the chances were that the approaching horse carried Wade. It was lucky that she was on Pronto, for he could be trusted to stand still and not neigh. Columbine rode into a thick clump of spruces that had long, shelving branches, reaching down. Here she hid, holding Pronto motionless.

Presently the sound of hoofs denoted the approach of several horses. That augmented Columbine's anxiety. Peering out of her covert, she espied three horsemen trotting along the trail, and one of them was Jack Belllounds. They appeared to be in strong argument, judging from gestures and emphatic movements of their heads. As chance would have it they halted their horses not half a dozen rods from Columbine's place of concealment. The two men with Belllounds were rough-looking, one of them, evidently a leader, having a dark face disfigured by a horrible scar.

Naturally they did not talk loud, and Columbine had to strain her ears to catch anything. But a word distinguished here and there, and accompanying actions, made transparent the meaning of their presence and argument. The big man refused to ride any farther. Evidently he had come so far without realizing it. His importunities were for "more head of stock." His scorn was for a "measly little bunch not worth the risk." His anger was for Belllounds's foolhardiness in "leavin' a trail." Belllounds had little to say, and most of that was spoken in a tone too low to be heard. His manner seemed indifferent, even reckless. But he wanted "money." The scar-faced man's name was "Smith." Then Columbine gathered from Smith's dogged and forceful gestures, and his words, "no money" and "bigger bunch," that he was unwilling to pay what had been agreed upon unless Belllounds promised to bring a larger number of cattle. Here Belllounds roundly cursed the rustler, and apparently argued that course "next to impossible." Smith made a sweeping movement with his arm, pointing south, indicating some place afar, and part of his speech was "Gore Peak." The little man, companion of Smith, got into the argument, and, dismounting from his horse, he made marks upon the smooth earth of the trail. He was drawing a rude map showing direction and locality. At length, when Belllounds nodded as if convinced or now informed, this third member of the party remounted, and seemed to have no more to say. Belllounds pondered sullenly. He snatched a switch from off a bough overhead and flicked his boot and stirrup with it, an action that made his horse restive. Smith leered and spoke derisively, of which speech Columbine heard, "Aw hell!" and "yellow streak," and "no one'd ever," and "son of Bill Belllounds," and "rustlin' stock." Then this scar-faced man drew out a buckskin bag. Either the contempt or the gold, or both, overbalanced vacillation in the weak mind of Jack Belllounds, for he lifted his head, showing his face pale and malignant, and without trace of shame or compunction he snatched the bag of gold, shouted a hoarse, "All right, damn you!" and, wheeling the white mustang, he spurred away, quickly disappearing.

The rustlers sat their horses, gazing down the trail, and Smith wagged his dark head doubtfully. Then he spoke quite distinctly, "I ain't a-trustin' thet Belllounds pup!" and his comrade replied, "Boss, we ain't stealin' the stock, so what th' hell!" Then they turned their horses and trotted out of sight and hearing up the timbered slope.

Columbine was so stunned, and so frightened and horrified, that she remained hidden there for a long time before she ventured forth. Then, heading homeward, she skirted the trail and kept to the edge of the forest, making a wide detour over the hills, finally reaching the ranch at sunset. Jack did not appear at the evening meal. His father had one of his spells of depression and seemed not to have noticed her absence. She lay awake all night thinking and praying.

Columbine concluded her narrative there, and, panting from her agitation and hurry, she gazed at the bowed figure of Moore, and then at Wade.

"I *had* to tell you this shameful secret," she began again. "I'm forced. If you do not help me, if something is not done, there'll be a horrible— end to all!"

"We'll help you, but how?" asked Moore, raising a white face.

"I don't know yet. I only *feel*—I only *feel* what may happen, if I don't prevent it. . . . Wilson, you must go home—at least for a while."

"It'll not look right for Wils to leave White Slides now," interposed Wade, positively.

"But why? Oh, I fear—"

"Never mind now, lass. It's a good reason. An' you mustn't fear anythin'. I agree with you—we've got to prevent this—this that's goin' to happen."

"Oh, Ben, my dear friend, we must prevent it—you *must!*"

"Ahuh! . . . So I was figurin'."

"Ben, you must go to Jack an' tell him—show him the peril—frighten him terribly—so that he will not do—do this shameful thing again."

"Lass, I reckon I could scare Jack out of his skin. But what good would that do?"

"It'll stop this—this madness. . . . Then I'll marry him—and keep him safe—after that!"

"Collie, do you think marryin' Buster Jack will stop his bustin' out?"

"Oh, I *know* it will. He had conquered over the evil in him. I saw that.

I felt it. He conquered over his baser nature for love of me. Then—when he heard—from my own lips—that I loved Wilson—why, then he fell. He didn't care. He drank again. He let go. He sank. And now he'll ruin us all. Oh, it looks as if he meant it that way! . . . But I can change him. I will marry him. I will love him—or I will *live a lie!* I will make him think I love him!"

Wilson Moore, deadly pale, faced her with flaming eyes.

"Collie, *why?* For God's sake, explain why you will shame your womanhood and ruin me—all for that coward—that thief?"

Columbine broke from Wade and ran to Wilson, as if to clasp him, but something halted her and she stood before him.

"Because dad will kill him!" she cried.

"My God! what are you saying?" exclaimed Moore, incredulously. "Old Bill would roar and rage, but hurt that boy of his—never!"

"Wils, I reckon Collie is right. You haven't got Old Bill figured. I know," interposed Wade, with one of his forceful gestures.

"Wilson, listen, and don't set your heart against me. For I *must* do this thing," pleaded Columbine. "I heard dad swear he'd kill Jack. Oh, I'll never forget! He was terrible! If he ever finds out that Jack stole from his own father—stole cattle like a common rustler, and sold them for gold to gamble and drink with—he will kill him! . . . That's as true as fate. . . . Think how horrible that would be for me! Because I'm to blame here, mostly. I fell in love with *you*, Wilson Moore, otherwise I could have saved Jack already.

"But it's not that I think of myself. Dad has loved me. He has been as a father to me. You know he's not my real father. Oh, if I only had a real one! . . . And I owe him so much. But then it's not because I owe him or because I love him. It's because of his own soul! . . . That splendid, noble old man, who has been so good to every one—who had only one fault, and that love of his son—must he be let go in blinded and insane rage at the failure of his life, the ruin of his son—must he be allowed to kill his own flesh and blood? . . . It would be *murder!* It would damn dad's soul to everlasting torment. No! No! I'll not let that be!"

"Collie—how about—your own soul?" whispered Moore, lifting himself as if about to expend a tremendous breath.

"That doesn't matter," she replied.

"Collie—Collie—" he stammered, but could not go on.

Then it seemed to Wade that they both turned to him unconscious of the inevitableness of his relation to this catastrophe, yet looking to him for the spirit, the guidance that became habitual to them. It brought the warm blood back to Wade's cold heart. It was his great reward. How intensely and implacably did his soul mount to that crisis!

"Collie, I'll never fail you," he said, and his gentle voice was deep and full. "If Jack can be scared into haltin' in his mad ride to hell—then I'll do it. I'm not promisin' so much for him. But I'll swear to you that Old Bell-lounds's hands will never be stained with his son's blood!"

"Oh, Ben! Ben!" she cried, in passionate gratitude. "I'll love you—bless you all my life!"

"Hush, lass! I'm not one to bless. . . . An' now you must do as I say. Go home an' tell them you'll marry Jack in August. Say August thirteenth."

"So long! Oh, why put it off? Wouldn't it be better—safer, to settle it all—once and forever?"

"No man can tell everythin'. But that's my judgment."

"Why August thirteenth?" she queried, with strange curiosity. "An unlucky date!"

"Well, it just happened to come to my mind—that date," replied Wade, in his slow, soft voice of reminiscence. "I was married on August thirteenth—twenty-one years ago. . . . An', Collie, my wife looked somethin' like you. Isn't that strange, now? It's a little world. . . . An' she's been gone eighteen years!"

"Ben, I never dreamed you ever had a wife," said Columbine, softly, with her hands going to his shoulder. "You must tell me of her some day. . . . But now—if you want time—if you think it best—I'll not marry Jack till August thirteenth."

"That'll give me time," replied Wade. "I'm thinkin' Jack ought to be—reformed, let's call it—before you marry him. If all you say is true—why we can turn him round. Your promise will do most. . . . So, then, it's settled?"

"Yes—dear—friends," faltered the girl, tremulously, on the verge of a breakdown, now that the ordeal was past.

Wilson Moore stood gazing out of the door, his eyes far away on the gray slopes.

"Queer how things turn out," he said, dreamily. "August thirteenth! . . . That's about the time the columbines blow on the hills. . . . And I always meant columbine-time—"

Here he sharply interrupted himself, and the dreamy musing gave way to passion. "But I mean it yet! I'll—I'll die before I give up hope of you!"

CHAPTER 16

Wade, watching Columbine ride down the slope on her homeward way, did some of the hardest thinking he had yet been called upon to do. It was not necessary to acquaint Wilson Moore with the deeper and more subtle motives that had begun to actuate him. It would not utterly break the cowboy's spirit to live in suspense. Columbine was safe for the present. He had insured her against fatality. Time was all he needed. Possibility of an actual consummation of her marriage to Jack Belllounds did not lodge for an instant in Wade's consciousness. In Moore's case, however, the present moment seemed critical. What should he tell Moore—what should he conceal from him?

"Son, come in here," he called to the cowboy.

"Pard, it looks—bad!" said Moore, brokenly.

Wade looked at the tragic face and cursed under his breath.

"Buck up! It's never as bad as it looks. Anyway, we *know* now what to expect, an' that's well."

Moore shook his head. "Couldn't you see how like steel Collie was? . . . But I'm on to you, Wade. You think by persuading Collie to put that marriage off that we'll gain time. You're gambling with time. You swear Buster Jack will hang himself. You won't quit fighting this deal."

"Buster Jack has slung the noose over a tree, an' he's about ready to slip his head into it," replied Wade.

"Bah! . . . You drive me wild," cried Moore, passionately. "How can you? Where's all that feeling you seemed to have for me? You nursed me—you saved my leg—and my life. You must have cared about me. But now—you talk about that dolt—that spoiled old man's pet—that damned cur, as if you believed he'd ruin himself. No such luck! no such hope! . . . Every day things grow worse. Yet the worse they grow the stronger you seem! It's all out of proportion. It's dreams. Wade, I hate to say it, but I'm sure you're not always—just right in your mind."

"Wils, now ain't that queer?" replied Wade, sadly. "I'm agreein' with you."

"Aw!" Moore shook himself savagely and laid an affectionate and appealing arm on his friend's shoulder. "Forgive me, pard! . . . It's me who's out of his head. . . . But my heart's broken."

"That's what you think," rejoined Wade, stoutly. "But a man's heart can't break in a day. I know. . . . An' the God's truth is Buster Jack will hang himself!"

Moore raised his head sharply, flinging himself back from his friend so as to scrutinize his face. Wade felt the piercing power of that gaze.

"Wade, what do you mean?"

"Collie told us some interestin' news about Jack, didn't she? Well, she didn't know what I know. Jack Belllounds had laid a cunnin' an' devilish trap to prove you guilty of rustlin' his father's cattle."

"Absurd!" ejaculated Moore, with white lips.

"I'd never given him credit for brains to hatch such a plot," went on Wade. "Now listen. Not long ago Buster Jack made a remark in front of the whole outfit, includin' his father, that the homesteaders on the range were rustlin' cattle. It fell sort of flat, that remark. But no one could calculate on his infernal cunnin'. I quit workin' for Belllounds that night, an' I've put my time in spyin' on the boy. In my day I've done a good deal of spyin', but I've never run across any one slicker than Buster Jack. To cut it short—he got himself a white-speckled mustang that's a dead ringer for Spottie. He measured the tracks of your horse's left front foot—the bad hoof, you know, an' he made a shoe exactly the same as Spottie wears. Also, he made some kind of a contraption that's like the end of your crutch. These he packs with him. I saw him ride across the pasture to hide his tracks, climb up the sage for the same reason, an' then hide in that grove of aspens over there near the trail you use. Here, you can bet, he changed shoes on the left front foot of his horse. Then he took to the trail, an' he left tracks for a while, an' then he was careful to hide them again. He stole his father's stock an' drove it up over the grassy benches where even you or I couldn't track him next day. But up on top, when it suited him, he left some horse tracks, an' in the mud near a spring-hole he gets off his horse, steppin' with one foot—an' makin' little circles with dots like those made by the end of your crutch. Then 'way over in the woods there's a cabin where he meets his accomplices. Here he leaves the same horse tracks an' crutch tracks. . . . Simple as a b c, Wils, when you see how he did it. But I'll tell you straight—if I hadn't been suspicious of Buster Jack—that trick of his would have made you a rustler!"

"Damn him!" hissed the cowboy, in utter consternation and fury.

"Ahuh! That's my sentiment exactly."

"I swore to Collie I'd never kill him!"

"Sure you did, son. An' you've got to keep that oath. I pin you down to it. You can't break faith with Collie. . . . An' you don't want his bad blood on your hands."

"No! No!" he replied, violently. "Of course I don't. I won't. But God! how sweet it would be to tear out his lying tongue—to—"

"I reckon it would. Only don't talk about that," interrupted Wade, bluntly. "You see, now, don't you, how he's about hanged himself."

"No, pard, I don't. We can't squeal that on him, any more than we can squeal what Collie told us."

"Son, you're young in dealin' with crooked men. You don't get the drift of motives. Buster Jack is not only robbin' his father an' hatchin' a dirty trap for you, but he's double-crossin' the rustlers he's sellin' the cattle to. He's riskin' their necks. He's goin' to find *your* tracks, showin' you dealt with them. Sure, he won't give them away, an' he's figurin' on their gettin' out of it, maybe by leavin' the range, or a shootin'-fray, or some way. The big thing with Jack is that he's goin' to accuse you of rustlin' an' show your tracks to his father. Well, that's a risk he's given the rustlers. It happens that I know this scar-face Smith. We've met before. Now it's easy to see from what Collie heard that Smith is not trustin' Buster Jack. So, all underneath this Jack Belllounds's game, there's forces workin' unbeknown to him, beyond his control, an' sure to ruin him."

"I see. I see. By Heaven! Wade, nothing else but ruin seems possible! . . . But suppose it works out his way! . . . What then? What of Collie?"

"Son, I've not got that far along in my reckonin'," replied Wade.

"But for my sake—think. If Buster Jack gets away with his trick—if he doesn't hang himself by some blunder or fit of temper or spree—what then of Collie?"

Wade could not answer this natural and inevitable query for the reason that he had found it impossible of consideration.

"Sufficient unto the day is the evil thereof," he replied.

"Wade, you've said that before. It helped me. But now I need more than a few words from the Bible. My faith is low. I . . . oh, I tried to pray because Collie told me she had prayed! But what are prayers? We're dealing with a stubborn, iron-willed old man who idolizes his son; we're dealing with a crazy boy, absolutely self-centered, crafty, and vicious, who'll stop at nothing. And, lastly, we're dealing with a girl who's so noble and high-souled that she'll sacrifice her all—her life to pay her debt. If she were really Bill Belllounds's daughter she'd *never* marry Jack, saying, of course, that he was not her brother. . . . Do you know that it will *kill* her, if she marries him?"

"Ahuh! I reckon it would," replied Wade, with his head bowed. Moore roused his gloomy forebodings. He did not care to show this feeling or the effect the cowboy's pleading had upon him.

"Ah! so you admit it? Well, then, what of Collie?"

"*If* she marries him—she'll have to die, I suppose," replied Wade.

Then Wilson Moore leaped at his friend and with ungentle hands lifted him, pushed him erect.

"Damn you, Wade! You're not square with me! You don't tell me all!" he cried, hoarsely.

"Now, Wils, you're set up. I've told you all I know. I swear that."

"But you couldn't stand the thought of Collie dying for that brute! You couldn't! Oh, I know. I can feel some things that are hard to tell. So, you're either out of your head or you've something up your sleeve. It's hard to explain how you affect me. One minute I'm ready to choke you for that damned strangeness—whatever it is. The next minute I feel it—I trust it, myself. . . . Wade, you're not—you *can't* be infallible!"

"I'm only a man, Wils, an' your friend. I reckon you do find me queer. But that's no matter. Now let's look at this deal—each from his own side of the fence. An' each actin' up to his own lights! You do what your conscience dictates, always thinkin' of Collie—not of yourself! An' I'll live up to my principles. Can we do more?"

"No, indeed, Wade, we can't," replied Moore, eloquently.

"Well, then, here's my hand. I've talked too much, I reckon. An' the time for talkin' is past."

In silence Moore gripped the hand held out to him, trying to read Wade's mind, apparently once more uplifted and strengthened by that which he could not divine.

Wade's observations during the following week brought forth the fact that Jack Belllounds was not letting any grass grow under his feet. He endeavored to fulfil his agreement with Smith, and drove a number of cattle by moonlight. These were part of the stock that the rancher had sold to buyers at Kremmling, and which had been collected and held in the big, fenced pasture down the valley next to the Andrews ranch. The loss was not discovered until the cattle had been counted at Kremmling. Then they were credited to loss by straying. In driving a considerable herd of half-wild steers, with an inadequate force of cowboys, it was no unusual thing to lose a number.

Wade, however, was in possession of the facts not later than the day after this midnight steal in the moonlight. He was forced to acknowledge that no one would have believed it possible for Jack Belllounds to perform a feat which might well have been difficult for the best of cowboys. But Jack accomplished it and got back home before daylight. And Wade was bound to admit that circumstantial evidence against Wilson Moore, which, of course, Jack Belllounds would soon present, would be damning and apparently irrefutable.

Waiting for further developments, Wade closely watched the ranch-house, which duty interfered with his attention to the outlying trails. What he did not want to miss was being present when Jack Belllounds accused Wilson Moore of rustling cattle.

So it chanced that Wade was chatting with the cowboys one Sunday afternoon when Jack, accompanied by three strangers, all mounted on dusty, tired horses, rode up to the porch and dismounted.

Lem Billings manifested unusual excitement.

"Montana, ain't thet Sheriff Burley from Kremmlin'?" he queried.

"Shore looks like him. . . . Yep, thet's him. Now, what's doin'?"

The cowboys exchanged curious glances, and then turned to Wade.

"Bent, what do you make of thet?" asked Lem, as he waved his hand toward the house. "Buster Jack ridin' up with Sheriff Burley."

The rancher, Belllounds, who was on the porch, greeted the visitors, and then they all went into the house.

"Boys, it's what I've been lookin' for," replied Wade.

"Shore. Reckon we all have idees. An' if my idee is correct I'm agoin' to git pretty damn sore pronto," declared Lem.

They were all silent for a few moments, meditating over this singular occurrence, and watching the house. Presently Old Bill Belllounds strode out upon the porch, and, walking out into the court, he peered around as if looking for some one. Then he espied the little group of cowboys.

"Hey!" he yelled. "One of you boys ride up an' fetch Wils Moore down hyar!"

"All right, boss," called Lem, in reply, as he got up and gave a hitch to his belt.

The rancher hurried back, head down, as if burdened.

"Wade, I reckon you want to go fetch Wils?" queried Lem.

"If it's all the same to you, I'd rather not," replied Wade.

"By Golly! I don't blame you. Boys, shore 'n hell, Burley's after Wils."

"Wal, suppos'n' he is," said Montana. "You can gamble Wils ain't agoin' to run. I'd jest like to see him face thet outfit. Burley's a pretty square fellar. An' he's no fool."

"It's as plain as your nose, Montana, an' thet's shore big enough," returned Lem, with a hard light in his eyes. "Buster Jack's busted out, an' he's figgered Wils in some deal thet's rung in the sheriff. Wal, I'll fetch Wils." And, growling to himself, the cowboy slouched off after his horse.

Wade got up, deliberate and thoughtful, and started away.

"Say, Bent, you're shore goin' to see what's up?" asked Montana, in surprise.

"I'll be around, Jim," replied Wade, and he strolled off to be alone. He wanted to think over this startling procedure of Jack Belllounds's. Wade was astonished. He had expected that an accusation would be made against Moore by Jack, and an exploitation of such proofs as had been craftily prepared, but he had never imagined Jack would be bold enough to carry matters so far. Sheriff Burley was a man of wide experience, keen, practical, shrewd. He was also one of the countless men Wade had rubbed elbows with in the eventful past. It had been Wade's idea that Jack would be satisfied to face his father with the accusation of Moore, and thus cover his tracks. Whatever Old Belllounds might have felt over the loss of a few cattle, he would never have hounded and arrested a cowboy who had done well by him. Burley, however, was a sheriff, and a conscientious one, and he happened to be particularly set against rustlers.

Here was a complication of circumstances. What would Jack Belllounds insist upon? How would Columbine take this plot against the honor and liberty of Wilson Moore? How would Moore himself react to it? Wade confessed that he was helpless to solve these queries, and there seemed to be a further one, insistent and gathering—what was to be his own attitude here? That could not be answered, either, because only a future moment, over which he had no control, and which must decide events, held that secret. Worry beset Wade, but he still found himself proof against the insidious gloom ever hovering near, like his shadow.

He waited near the trail to intercept Billings and Moore on their way to the ranch-house; and to his surprise they appeared sooner than it would have been reasonable to expect them. Wade stepped out of the willows and held up his hand. He did not see anything unusual in Moore's appearance.

"Wils, I reckon we'd do well to talk this over," said Wade.

"Talk what over?" queried the cowboy, sharply.

"Why, Old Bill's sendin' for you, an' the fact of Sheriff Burley bein' here."

"Talk nothing. Let's see what they want, and then talk. Pard, you remember the agreement we made not long ago?"

"Sure. But I'm sort of worried, an' maybe—"

"You needn't worry about me. Come on," interrupted Moore. "I'd like you to be there. And, Lem, fetch the boys."

"I shore will, an' if you need any backin' you'll git it."

When they reached the open Lem turned off toward the corrals, and Wade walked beside Moore's horse up to the house.

Belllounds appeared at the door, evidently having heard the sound of hoofs.

"Hello, Moore! Get down an' come in," he said, gruffly.

"Belllounds, if it's all the same to you I'll take mine in the open," replied the cowboy, coolly.

The rancher looked troubled. He did not have the ease and force habitual to him in big moments.

"Come out hyar, you men," he called in the door.

Voices, heavy footsteps, the clinking of spurs, preceded the appearance of the three strangers, followed by Jack Belllounds. The foremost was a tall man in black, sandy-haired and freckled, with clear gray eyes, and a drooping mustache that did not hide stern lips and rugged chin. He wore a silver star on his vest, packed a gun in a greasy holster worn low down on his right side, and under his left arm he carried a package.

It suited Wade, then, to step forward; and if he expected surprise and pleasure to break across the sheriff's stern face he certainly had not reckoned in vain.

"Wal, I'm a son-of-a-gun!" ejaculated Burley, bending low, with quick movement, to peer at Wade.

"Howdy, Jim. How's tricks?" said Wade, extending his hand, and the smile that came so seldom illumined his sallow face.

"Hell-Bent Wade, as I'm a born sinner!" shouted the sheriff, and his hand leaped out to grasp Wade's and grip it and wring it. His face worked. "My Gawd! I'm glad to see you, old-timer! Wal, you haven't changed at all! . . . Ten years! How time flies! An' it's shore you?"

"Same, Jim, an' powerful glad to meet you," replied Wade.

"Shake hands with Bridges an' Lindsay," said Burley, indicating his two comrades. "Stockmen from Grand Lake. . . . Boys, you've heerd me talk about him. Wade an' I was both in the old fight at Blair's ranch on the Gunnison. An' I've shore reason to recollect him! . . . Wade, what're you doin' up in these diggin's?"

"Drifted over last fall, Jim, an' have been huntin' varmints for Belllounds," replied Wade. "Cleaned the range up fair to middlin'. An' since I quit Belllounds I've been hangin' round with my young pard here, Wils Moore, an' interestin' myself in lookin' up cattle tracks."

Burley's back was toward Belllounds and his son, so it was impossible for them to see the sudden little curious light that gleamed in his eyes as he looked hard at Wade, and then at Moore.

"Wils Moore. How d'ye do? I reckon I remember you, though I don't ride up this way much of late years."

The cowboy returned the greeting civilly enough, but with brevity.

Belllounds cleared his throat and stepped forward. His manner showed he had a distasteful business at hand.

"Moore, I sent for you on a serious matter, I'm sorry to say."

"Well, here I am. What is it?" returned the cowboy, with clear, hazel eyes, full of fire, steady on the old rancher's.

"Jack, you know, is foreman of White Slides now. An' he's made a charge against you."

"Then let him face me with it," snapped Moore.

Jack Belllounds came forward, hands in his pockets, self-possessed, even a little swaggering, and his pale face and bold eyes showed the gravity of the situation and his mastery over it.

Wade watched this meeting of the rivals and enemies with an attention powerfully stimulated by the penetrating scrutiny Burley laid upon them. Jack did not speak quickly. He looked hard into the tense face of Moore. Wade detected a vibration of Jack's frame and a gleam of eye that showed him not wholly in control of exultation and revenge. Fear had not struck him yet.

"Well, Buster Jack, what's the charge?" demanded Moore, impatiently.

The old name, sharply flung at Jack by this cowboy, seemed to sting and reveal and inflame. But he restrained himself as with roving glance he searched Moore's person for sight of a weapon. The cowboy was unarmed.

"I accuse you of stealing my father's cattle," declared Jack, in low, husky accents. After he got the speech out he swallowed hard.

Moore's face turned a dead white. For a fleeting instant a red and savage gleam flamed in his steady glance. Then it vanished.

The cowboys, who had come up, moved restlessly. Lem Billings dropped his head, muttering. Montana Jim froze in his tracks.

Moore's dark eyes, scornful and piercing, never moved from Jack's face. It seemed as if the cowboy would never speak again.

"You call me thief! *You?*" at length he exclaimed.

"Yes, I do," replied Belllounds, loudly.

"Before this sheriff and your father you accuse me of stealing cattle?"

"Yes."

"And you accuse me before this man who saved my life, who *knows* me—before Hell-Bent Wade?" demanded Moore, as he pointed to the hunter.

Mention of Wade in that significant tone of passion and wonder was not without effect upon Jack Belllounds.

"What in hell do I care for Wade?" he burst out, with the old intolerance. "Yes, I accuse you. Thief, rustler! . . . And for all I know your precious Hell-Bent Wade may be—"

He was interrupted by Burley's quick and authoritative interference.

"Hyar, young man, I'm allowin' for your natural feelin's," he said, dryly, "but I advise you to bite your tongue. I ain't acquainted with Mister Moore, but I happen to know Wade. Do you savvy? . . . Wal, then, if you've any more to say to Moore get it over."

"I've had my say," replied Belllounds, sullenly.

"On what grounds do you accuse me?" demanded Moore.

"I trailed you. I've got my proofs."

Burley stepped off the porch and carefully laid down his package.

"Moore, will you get off your hoss?" he asked. And when the cowboy had dismounted and limped aside the sheriff continued, "Is this the hoss you ride most?"

"He's the only one I have."

Burley sat down upon the edge of the porch and, carefully unwrapping the package, he disclosed some pieces of hard-baked yellow mud. The smaller ones bore the imprint of a circle with a dot in the center, very clearly defined. The larger piece bore the imperfect but reasonably clear track of a curiously shaped horseshoe, somewhat triangular. The sheriff placed these pieces upon the ground. Then he laid hold of Moore's crutch, which was carried like a rifle in a sheath hanging from the saddle, and, drawing it forth, he carefully studied the round cap on the end. Next he inserted this end into both the little circles on the pieces of mud. They fitted perfectly. The cowboys bent over to get a closer view, and Billings was wagging his head. Old Belllounds had an earnest eye for them, also.

Burley's next move was to lift the left front foot of Moore's horse and expose the bottom to view. Evidently the white mustang did not like these proceedings, but he behaved himself. The iron shoe on this hoof was somewhat triangular in shape. When Burley held the larger piece of mud, with its imprint, close to the hoof, it was not possible to believe that this iron shoe had not made the triangular-shaped track.

Burley let go of the hoof and laid the pieces of mud down. Slowly the other men straightened up. Some one breathed hard.

"Moore, what do them tracks look like to you?" asked the sheriff.

"They look like mine," replied the cowboy.

"They are yours."

"I'm not denying that."

"I cut them pieces of mud from beside a water-hole over hyar under Gore Peak. We'd trailed the cattle Belllounds lost, an' then we kept on trailin' them, clear to the road that goes over the ridge to Elgeria. . . . Now Bridges an' Lindsay hyar bought stock lately from strange cattlemen who didn't give no clear idee of their range. Jest buyin' an' sellin', they claimed. . . . I reckon the extra hoss tracks we run across at Gore Peak connects up them buyers an' sellers with whoever drove Belllounds's cattle up thar. . . . Have you anythin' more to say?"

"No. Not here," replied Moore, quietly.

"Then I'll have to arrest you an' take you to Kremmlin' fer trial."

"All right. I'll go."

The old rancher seemed genuinely shocked. Red tinged his cheek and a flame flared in his eyes.

"Wils, you done me dirt," he said, wrathfully. "An' I always swore by you. . . . Make a clean breast of the whole damn bizness, if you want me to treat you white. You must have been locoed or drunk, to double-cross me thet way. Come on, out with it."

"I've nothing to say," replied Moore.

"You act amazin' strange fer a cowboy I've knowed to lean toward fightin' at the drop of a hat. I tell you, speak out an' I'll do right by you. . . . I ain't forgettin' thet White Slides gave you a hard knock. An' I was young once an' had hot blood."

The old rancher's wrathful pathos stirred the cowboy to a straining-point of his unnatural, almost haughty composure. He seemed about to break into violent utterance. Grief and horror and anger seemed at the back of his trembling lips. The look he gave Belllounds was assuredly a strange one, to come from a cowboy who was supposed to have stolen his former employer's cattle. Whatever he might have replied was cut off by the sudden appearance of Columbine.

"Dad, I heard you!" she cried, as she swept upon them, fearful and wide-eyed. "What has Wilson Moore done—that you'll do right by him?"

"Collie, go back in the house," he ordered.

"No. There's something wrong here," she said, with mounting dread in the swift glance she shot from man to man. "Oh! You're—Sheriff Burley!" she gasped.

"I reckon I am, miss, an' if young Moore's a friend of yours I'm sorry I came," replied Burley.

Wade himself reacted subtly and thrillingly to the presence of the girl. She was alive, keen, strung, growing white, with darkening eyes of blue fire, beginning to grasp intuitively the meaning here.

"My friend! He *was* more than that—not long ago. . . . What has he done? Why are you here?"

"Miss, I'm arrestin' him."

"Oh! . . . For what?"

"Rustlin' your father's cattle."

For a moment Columbine was speechless. Then she burst out, "Oh, there's a terrible mistake!"

"Miss Columbine, I shore hope so," replied Burley, much embarrassed and distressed. Like most men of his kind, he could not bear to hurt a woman. "But it looks bad fer Moore. . . . See hyar! There! Look at the tracks of his hoss—left front foot—shoe all crooked. Thet's his hoss's. He acknowledges thet. An', see hyar. Look at the little circles an' dots. . . . I found these 'way over at Gore Peak, with the tracks of the stolen cattle. An' no *other* tracks, Miss Columbine!"

"Who put you on that trail?" she asked, piercingly.

"Jack, hyar. He found it fust, an' rode to Kremmlin' fer me."

"Jack! Jack Belllounds!" she cried, bursting into wild and furious laughter. Like a tigress she leaped at Jack as if to tear him to pieces. "You put the sheriff on that trail! You accuse Wilson Moore of stealing dad's cattle!"

"Yes, and I proved it," replied Jack, hoarsely.

"You! *You* proved it? So that's your revenge? . . . But you're to reckon with me, Jack Belllounds! You villain! You devil! You—" Suddenly she shrank back with a strong shudder. She gasped. Her face grew ghastly white. "*Oh, my God!* . . . horrible—unspeakable!" . . . She covered her face with her hands, and every muscle of her seemed to contract until she was stiff. Then her hands shot out to Moore.

"Wilson Moore, what have *you* to say—to this sheriff—to Jack Belllounds—to *me?*"

Moore bent upon her a gaze that must have pierced her soul, so like it was to a lightning flash of love and meaning and eloquence.

"Collie, they've got the proof. I'll take my medicine. . . . Your dad is good. He'll be easy on me!'

"*You lie!*" she whispered. "And I will tell why you lie!"

Moore did not show the shame and guilt that should have been natural with his confession. But he showed an agony of distress. His hand sought Wade and dragged at him.

It did not need this mute appeal to tell Wade that in another moment Columbine would have flung the shameful truth into the face of Jack Belllounds. She was rising to that. She was terrible and beautiful to see.

"Collie," said Wade, with that voice he knew had strange power over her, with a clasp of her outflung hand, "no more! This is a man's game. It's not for a woman to judge. Not here! It's Wils's game—an' it's *mine*. I'm his friend. Whatever his trouble or guilt, I take it on my shoulders. An' it will be as if it were not!"

Moaning and wringing her hands, Columbine staggered with the burden of the struggle in her.

"I'm quite—quite mad—or dreaming. Oh, Ben!" she cried.

"Brace up, Collie. It's sure hard. Wils, your friend and playmate so many years—it's hard to believe! We all understand, Collie. Now you go in, an' don't listen to any more or look any more."

He led her down the porch to the door of her room, and as he pushed it open he whispered, "I will save you, Collie, an' Wils, an' the old man you call dad!"

Then he returned to the silent group in the yard.

"Jim, if I answer fer Wils Moore bein' in Kremmlin' the day you say, will you leave him with me?"

"Wal, I shore will, Wade," replied Burley, heartily.

"I object to that," interposed Jack Belllounds, stridently. "He confessed. He's got to go to jail."

"Wal, my hot-tempered young fellar, thar ain't any jail nearer 'n Denver. Did you know that?" returned Burley, with his dry, grim humor. "Moore's under arrest. An' he'll be as well off hyar with Wade as with me in Kremmlin', an' a damn sight happier."

The cowboy had mounted, and Wade walked beside him as he started homeward. They had not progressed far when Wade's keen ears caught the words, "Say, Belllounds, I got it figgered thet you an' your son don't savvy this fellar Wade."

"Wal, I reckon not," replied the old rancher.

And his son let out a peal of laughter, bitter and scornful and unsatisfied.

CHAPTER 17

Gore Peak was the highest point of the black range that extended for miles westward from Buffalo Park. It was a rounded dome, covered with timber and visible as a landmark from the surrounding country. All along the eastern slope of that range an unbroken forest of spruce and pine spread down to the edge of the valley. This valley narrowed toward its source, which was Buffalo Park. A few well-beaten trails crossed that country, one following Red Brook down to Kremmling; another crossing from the Park to White Slides; and another going over the divide down to Elgeria. The only well-known trail leading to Gore Peak was a branch-off from the valley, and it went round to the south and more accessible side of the mountain.

All that immense slope of timbered ridges, benches, ravines, and swales west of Buffalo Park was exceedingly wild and rough country. Here the buffalo took to cover from hunters, and were safe until they ventured forth into the parks again. Elk and deer and bear made this forest their home.

Bent Wade, hunter now for bigger game than wild beasts of the range, left his horse at Lewis's cabin and penetrated the dense forest alone, like a deer-stalker or an Indian in his movements. Lewis had acted as scout for Wade, and had ridden furiously down to Sage Valley with news of the rustlers. Wade had accompanied him back to Buffalo Park that night, riding in the dark. There were urgent reasons for speed. Jack

Belllounds had ridden to Kremmling, and the hunter did not believe he would return by the road he had taken.

Fox, Wade's favorite dog, much to his disgust, was left behind with Lewis. The bloodhound, Kane, accompanied Wade. Kane had been ill-treated and then beaten by Jack Belllounds, and he had left White Slides to take up his home at Moore's cabin. And at last he had seemed to reconcile himself to the hunter, not with love, but without distrust. Kane never forgave; but he recognized his friend and master. Wade carried his rifle and a buckskin pouch containing meat and bread. His belt, heavily studded with shells, contained two guns, both now worn in plain sight, with the one on the right side hanging low. Wade's character seemed to have undergone some remarkable change, yet what he represented then was not unfamiliar.

He headed for the concealed cabin on the edge of the high valley, under the black brow of Gore Peak. It was early morning of a July day, with summer fresh and new to the forest. Along the park edges the birds and squirrels were holding carnival. The grass was crisp and bediamonded with sparkling frost. Tracks of game showed sharp in the white patches. Wade paused once, listening. Ah! That most beautiful of forest melodies for him—the bugle of an elk. Clear, resonant, penetrating, with these qualities held and blended by a note of wildness, it rang thrillingly through all Wade's being. The hound listened, but was not interested. He kept close beside the hunter or at his heels, a stealthily stepping, warily glancing hound, not scenting the four-footed denizens of the forest. He expected his master to put him on the trail of men.

The distance from the Park to Gore Peak, as a crow would have flown, was not great. But Wade progressed slowly; he kept to the dense parts of the forest; he avoided the open aisles, the swales, the glades, the high ridges, the rocky ground. When he came to the Elgeria trail he was not disappointed to find it smooth, untrodden by any recent travel. Half a mile farther on through the forest, however, he encountered tracks of three horses, made early the day before. Still farther on he found cattle and horse tracks, now growing old and dim. These tracks, pointed toward Elgeria, were like words of a printed page to Wade.

About noon he climbed a rocky eminence that jutted out from a slow-descending ridge, and from this vantage-point he saw down the wavering black and green bosom of the mountain slope. A narrow valley, almost hidden, gleamed yellow in the sunlight. At the edge of this valley a faint column of blue smoke curled upward.

"Ahuh!" muttered the hunter, as he looked. The hound whined and pushed a cool nose into Wade's hand.

Then Wade resumed his noiseless and stealthy course through the woods. He began a descent, leading off somewhat to the right of the point where the smoke had arisen. The presence of the rustlers in the cabin was of importance, yet not so paramount as another possibility. He expected Jack Belllounds to be with them or meet them there, and that was the thing he wanted to ascertain. When he got down below the little valley he swung around to the left to cross the trail that came up from the main valley, some miles still farther down. He found it, and was not surprised to see fresh horse tracks, made that morning. He recognized those tracks. Jack Belllounds was with the rustlers, come, no doubt, to receive his pay.

Then the change in Wade, and the actions of a trailer of men, became more singularly manifest. He reverted to some former habit of mind and body. He was as slow as a shadow, absolutely silent, and the gaze that roved ahead and all around must have taken note of every living thing, of every moving leaf or fern or bough. The hound, with hair curling up stiff on his back, stayed close to Wade, watching, listening, and stepping with him. Certainly Wade expected the rustlers to have someone of their number doing duty as a lookout. So he kept uphill, above the cabin, and made his careful way through the thicket coverts, which at that place were dense and matted clumps of jack-pine and spruce. At last he could see the cabin and the narrow, grassy valley just beyond. To his relief the horses were unsaddled and grazing. No man was in sight. But there might be a dog. The hunter, in his slow advance, used keen and unrelaxing vigilance, and at length he decided that if there had been a dog he would have been tied outside to give an alarm.

Wade had now reached his objective point. He was some eighty paces from the cabin, in line with an open aisle down which he could see into the cleared space before the door. On his left were thick, small spruces, with low-spreading branches, and they extended all the way to the cabin on that side, and in fact screened two walls of it. Wade knew exactly what he was going to do. No longer did he hesitate. Laying down his rifle, he tied the hound to a little spruce, patting him and whispering for him to stay there and be still.

Then Wade's action in looking to his belt-guns was that of a man who expected to have recourse to them speedily and by whom the necessity was neither regretted nor feared. Stooping low, he entered the thicket of spruces. The soft, spruce-matted ground, devoid of brush or twig, did not give forth the slightest sound of step, nor did the brushing of the branches against his body. In some cases he had to bend the boughs. Thus, swiftly and silently, with the gliding steps of an Indian, he approached the cabin till the brown-barked logs loomed before him, shutting off the clearer light.

He smelled a mingling of wood and tobacco smoke; he heard low, deep voices of men; the shuffling and patting of cards; the musical click of gold. Resting on his knees a moment the hunter deliberated. All was exactly as he had expected. Luck favored him. These gamblers would be absorbed in their game. The door of the cabin was just around the corner, and he could glide noiselessly to it or gain it in a few leaps. Either method would serve. But which he must try depended upon the position of the men inside and that of their weapons.

Rising silently, Wade stepped up to the wall and peeped through a chink between the logs. The sunshine streamed through windows and door. Jack Belllounds sat on the ground, full in its light, back to the wall. He was in his shirt-sleeves. The gambling fever and the grievous soreness of a loser shone upon his pale face. Smith sat with back to Wade, opposite Belllounds. The other men completed the square. All were close enough together to reach comfortably for the cards and gold before them. Wade's keen eyes took this in at a single glance, and then steadied searchingly for smaller features of the scene. Belllounds had no weapon. Smith's belt and gun lay in the sunlight on the hard, clay floor, out of reach except by violent effort. The other two rustlers both wore their weapons. Wade gave a long scrutiny to the faces of these comrades of Smith, and evidently satisfied himself as to what he had to expect from them.

Wade hesitated; then stooping low, he softly swept aside the intervening boughs of spruce, glided out of the thicket into the open. Two noiseless bounds! Another, and he was inside the door!

"Howdy, rustlers! Don't move!" he called.

The surprise of his appearance, or his voice, or both, stunned the four men. Belllounds dropped his cards, and his jaw dropped at the same instant. These were absolutely the only visible movements.

"I'm in talkin' humor, an' the longer you listen the longer you'll have to live," said Wade. "But don't move!"

"We ain't movin'," burst out Smith. "Who're you, an' what d'ye want?"

It was singular that the rustler leader had not had a look at Wade, whose movements had been swift and who now stood directly behind him. Also it was obvious that Smith was sitting very stiff-necked and straight. Not improbably he had encountered such situations before.

"Who're you?" he shouted, hoarsely.

"You ought to know me." The voice was Wade's, gentle, cold, with depth and ring in it.

"I've heerd your voice somewhars—I'll gamble on thet."

"Sure. You ought to recognize my voice, Cap," returned Wade.

The rustler gave a violent start—a start that he controlled instantly.

"Cap! You callin' me thet?"

"Sure. We're old friends—*Cap Folsom!*"

In the silence, then, the rustler's hard breathing could be heard; his neck bulged red; only the eyes of his two comrades moved; Belllounds began to recover somewhat from his consternation. Fear had clamped him also, but not fear of personal harm or peril. His mind had not yet awakened to that.

"You've got me pat! But who're you?" said Folsom, huskily.

Wade kept silent.

"Who 'n hell is thet man?" yelled the rustler. It was not a query to his comrades any more than to the four winds. It was a furious questioning of a memory that stirred and haunted, and as well a passionate and fearful denial.

"His name's Wade," put in Belllounds, harshly. "He's the friend of Wils Moore. He's the hunter I told you about—worked for my father last winter."

"Wade? . . . What? *Wade!* You never told me his name. It ain't—it ain't—"

"Yes, it is, Cap," interrupted Wade. "It's the old boy that spoiled your handsome mug—long ago."

"*Hell-Bent Wade!*" gasped Folsom, in terrible accents. He shook all over. An ashen paleness crept into his face. Instinctively his right hand jerked toward his gun; then, as in his former motion, froze in the very act.

"Careful, Cap!" warned Wade. "It'd be a shame not to hear me talk a little. . . . Turn around now an' greet an old pard of the Gunnison days."

Folsom turned as if a resistless, heavy force was revolving his head.

"By Gawd! . . . Wade!" he ejaculated. The tone of his voice, the light in his eyes, must have been a spiritual acceptance of a dreadful and ir-refutable fact—perhaps the proximity of death. But he was no coward. Despite the hunter's order, given as he stood there, gun drawn and ready, Folsom wheeled back again, savagely to throw the deck of cards in Bell-lounds's face. He cursed horribly. . . . "You spoiled brat of a rich rancher! Why 'n hell didn't you tell me thet varmint-hunter was Wade."

"I did tell you," shouted Belllounds, flaming of face.

"You're a liar! You never said Wade—W-a-d-e, right out, so I'd hear it. An' I'd never passed by Hell-Bent Wade."

"Aw, that name made me tired," replied Belllounds, contemptuously.

"Haw! Haw! Haw!" bawled the rustler. "Made you tired, hey? Think you're funny? Wal, if you knowed how many men thet name's made tired—an' tired fer keeps—you'd not think it so damn funny."

"Say, what're you giving me? That Sheriff Burley tried to tell me and dad a lot of rot about this Wade. Why, he's only a little, bow-legged, big-nosed meddler—a man with a woman's voice—a sneaking cook and camp-doctor and cow-milker, and God only knows what else."

"Boy, you're correct. God only knows what else! . . . It's the *else* you've got to learn. An' I'll gamble you'll learn it. . . . Wade, have you changed or grown old thet you let a pup like this yap such talk?"

"Well, Cap, he's very amusin' just now, an' I want you-all to enjoy him. Because, if you don't force my hand I'm goin' to tell you some in-terestin' stuff about this Buster Jack. . . . Now, will you be quiet an' listen—an' answer for your pards?"

"Wade, I answer fer no man. But, so far as I've noticed, my pards ain't hankerin' to make any loud noise," Folsom replied, indicating his comrades, with sarcasm.

The red-bearded one, a man of large frame and gaunt face, wicked and wild-looking, spoke out, "Say, Smith, or whatever the hell's yore right handle—is this hyar a game we're playin'?"

"I reckon. An' if you turn a trick you'll be damn lucky," growled Folsom.

The other rustler did not speak. He was small, swarthy-faced, with sloe-black eyes and matted hair, evidently a white man with Mexican blood. Keen, strung, furtive, he kept motionless, awaiting events.

"Buster Jack, these new pards of yours are low-down rustlers, an' one of them's worse, as I could prove," said Wade, "but compared with you they're all gentlemen."

Belllounds leered. But he was losing his bravado. Something began to dawn upon his obtuse consciousness.

"What do I care for you or your gabby talk?" he flashed, sullenly.

"You'll care when I tell these rustlers how you double-crossed them."

Belllounds made a spring, like that of a wolf in a trap; but when halfway up he slipped. The rustler on his right kicked him, and he sprawled down again, back to the wall.

"Buster, look into this!" called Wade, and he leveled the gun that quivered momentarily, like a compass needle, and then crashed fire and smoke. The bullet spat into a log. But it had cut the lobe of Belllounds's ear, bringing blood. His face turned a ghastly, livid hue. All in a second terror possessed him—shuddering, primitive terror of death.

Folsom haw-hawed derisively and in crude delight. "Say, Buster Jack, don't get any idee thet my ole pard Wade was shootin' at your head. Aw, no!"

The other rustlers understood then, if Belllounds had not, that the situation was in control of a man not in any sense ordinary.

"Cap, did you know Buster Jack accused my friend, Wils Moore, of stealin' these cattle you're sellin'?" asked Wade, deliberately.

"What cattle did you say?" asked the rustler, as if he had not heard aright.

"The cattle Buster Jack stole from his father an' sold to you."

"Wal, now! Bent Wade at his old tricks! I might have knowed it, once I seen you. . . . Naw, I'd no idee Belllounds blamed thet stealin' on to any one."

"He did."

"Ahuh! Wal, who's this Wils Moore?"

"He's a cowboy, as fine a youngster as ever straddled a horse. Buster Jack hates him. He licked Jack a couple of times an' won the love of a girl that Jack wants."

"Ho! Ho! Quite romantic, I declare. . . . Say, thar's some damn queer notions I'm gettin' about you, Buster Jack."

Belllounds lay propped against the wall, sagging there, laboring of chest, sweating of face. The boldness of brow held, because it was fixed, but that of his eyes had gone; and his mouth and chin showed craven weakness. He stared in dread suspense at Wade.

"Listen. An' all of you sit tight," went on Wade, swiftly. "Jack stole the cattle from his father. He's a thief at heart. But he had a double motive. He left a trail—he left tracks behind. He made a crooked horseshoe, like that Wils Moore's horse wears, an' he put that on his own horse. An' he made a contraption—a little iron ring with a dot in it, an' he left the crooked shoe tracks, an' he left the little ring tracks—"

"By Gawd! I seen them funny tracks!" ejaculated Folsom. "At the water-hole an' right hyar in front of the cabin. I seen them. I knowed Jack made them, somehow, but I didn't think. His white hoss has a crooked left front shoe."

"Yes, he has, when Jack takes off the regular shoe an' nails on the crooked one. . . . Men, I followed those tracks. They lead up here to your cabin. Belllounds made them with a purpose. . . . An' he went to Kremmlin' to get Sheriff Burley. An' he put him wise to the rustlin' of cattle to Elgeria. An' he fetched him up to White Slides to accuse Wils Moore. An' he trailed his own tracks up here, showin' Burley the crooked horse track an' the little circle—that was supposed to be made by the end of Moore's crutch—an' he led Burley with his men right to this cabin an' to the trail where you drove the cattle over the divide. . . . An' then he had Burley dig out some cakes of mud holdin' these tracks, an' they fetched them down to White Slides. Buster Jack blamed the stealin' on to Moore. An' Burley arrested Moore. The trial comes off next week at Kremmlin'."

"Damn me!" exclaimed Folsom, wonderingly. "A man's never too old to learn! I knowed this pup was stealin' from his own father, but I reckoned he was jest a natural-born, honest rustler, with a hunch fer drink an' cards."

"Well, he's double-crossed you, Cap. An' if I hadn't rounded you up your chances would have been good for swingin'."

"Ahuh! Wade, I'd sure preferred them chances of swingin' to your over-kind interferin' in my bizness. Allus interferin', Wade, thet's your weakness! . . . But gimme a gun!"

"I reckon not, Cap."

"Gimme a gun!" roared the rustler. "Lemme sit hyar an' shoot the eyes outen this—lyin' pup of a Belllounds! . . . Wade, put a gun in my hand—a gun with two shells—or only one. You can stand with your gun at my head. . . . Let me kill this skunk!"

For all Belllounds could tell, death was indeed close. No trace of a Belllounds was apparent about him then, and his face was a horrid spectacle for a man to be forced to see. A froth foamed over his hanging lower lip.

"Cap, I ain't trustin' you with a gun just this particular minute," said Wade.

Folsom then bawled his curses to his comrades.

"———! Kill him! Throw your guns an' bore him—right in them bulgin' eyes! . . . I'm tellin' you—we've gotta fight, anyhow. We're agoin' to cash right hyar. But kill him first!"

Neither of Folsom's lieutenants yielded to the fierce exhortation of their leader or to their own evilly expressed passions. It was Wade who dominated them. Then ensued a silence fraught with suspense, growing more charged every long instant. The balance here seemed about to be struck.

"Wade, I've been a gambler all my life, an' a damn smart one, if I do say it myself," declared the rustler leader, his voice inharmonious with the facetiousness of his words. "An' I'll make a last bet."

"Go ahead, Cap. What'll you bet?" answered the cold voice, still gentle, but different now in its inflection.

"By Gawd! I'll bet all the gold hyar that Hell-Bent Wade wouldn't shoot any man in the back!"

"You win!"

Slowly and stiffly the rustler rose to his feet. When he reached his height he deliberately swung his leg to kick Belllounds in the face.

"Thar! I'd like to have a reckonin' with you, Buster Jack," he said. "I ain't dealin' the cards hyar. But somethin' tells me thet, shaky as I am in my boots, I'd liefer be in mine than yours."

With that, and expelling a heavy breath, he wrestled around to confront the hunter.

"Wade, I've no hunch to your game, but it's slower 'n I recollect you."

"Why, Cap, I was in a talkin' humor," replied Wade.

"Hell! You're up to some dodge. What'd you care fer my learnin' thet pup had double-crossed me? You won't let me kill him."

"I reckon I wanted him to learn what real men thought of him."

"Ahuh! Wal, an' now I've onlightened him, what's the next deal?"

"You'll all go to Kremmlin' with me an' I'll turn you over to Sheriff Burley."

That was the gauntlet thrown down by Wade. It was not unexpected, and acceptance seemed a relief. Folsom's eyeballs became living fire with the desperate gleam of the reckless chances of life. Cutthroat he might have been, but he was brave, and he proved the significance of Wade's attitude.

"Pards, hyar's to luck!" he rang out, hoarsely, and with pantherish quickness he leaped for his gun.

A tense, surcharged instant—then all four men, as if released by some galvanized current of rapidity, flashed into action. Guns boomed in unison. Spurts of red, clouds of smoke, ringing reports, and hoarse cries filled the cabin. Wade had fired as he leaped. There was a thudding patter of lead upon the walls. The hunter flung himself prostrate behind the bough framework that had served as bedstead. It was made of spruce boughs, thick and substantial. Wade had not calculated falsely in estimating it as a bulwark of defense. Pulling his second gun, he peeped from behind the covert.

Smoke was lifting, and drifting out of door and windows. The atmosphere cleared. Belllounds sagged against the wall, pallid, with protruding eyes of horror on the scene before him. The dark-skinned little man lay writhing. All at once a tremor stilled his convulsions. His body relaxed limply. As if by magic his hand loosened on the smoking gun. Folsom was on his knees, reeling and swaying, waving his gun, peering like a drunken man for some lost object. His temple appeared half shot away, a bloody and horrible sight.

"Pards, I got him!" he said, in strange, half-strangled whisper. "I got him! . . . Hell-Bent Wade! My respects! I'll meet you—thar!"

His reeling motion brought his gaze in line with Belllounds. The violence of his start sent drops of blood flying from his gory temple.

"Ahuh! The cards run—my way. Belllounds, hyar's to your—lyin' eyes!"

The gun wavered and trembled and circled. Folsom strained in last terrible effort of will to aim it straight. He fired. The bullet tore hair from Belllounds's head, but missed him. Again the rustler aimed, and the gun wavered and shook. He pulled trigger. The hammer clicked upon an empty chamber. With low and gurgling cry of baffled rage Folsom dropped the gun and sank face forward, slowly stretching out.

The red-bearded rustler had leaped behind the stone chimney that all but hid his body. The position made it difficult for him to shoot because his gun-hand was on the inside, and he had to press his body tight to squeeze it behind the corner of ragged stone. Wade had the advantage. He was lying prone with his right hand round the corner of the framework. An overhang of the bough-ends above protected his head when he peeped out. While he watched for a chance to shoot he loaded his empty gun with his left hand. The rustler strained and writhed his body, twisting his neck, and suddenly darting out his head and arm, he shot. His bullet tore the overhang of boughs above Wade's face. And Wade's answering shot, just a second too late, chipped the stone corner where the rustler's face had flashed out. The bullet, glancing, hummed out of the window. It was a close shave. The rustler let out a hissing, inarticulate cry. He was trapped. In his effort to press in closer he projected his left elbow beyond the corner of the chimney. Wade's quick shot shattered his arm.

There was no asking or offering of quarter here. This was the old feud of the West—of the vicious and the righteous in strife—both reared in the same stern school. The rustler gave his body such contortion that he was twisted almost clear around, with his right hand over his left shoulder. He punched the muzzle of his gun into a crack between two stones, and he pried to open them. The dry clay cement crumbled, the crack widened. Sighting along the barrel he alined it with the narrow strip of Wade's shoulder that was visible above the framework. Then he shot and hit. Wade shrank flatter and closer, hiding himself to better advantage. The rustler made his great blunder then, for in that moment he might have rushed out and killed his adversary. But, instead, he shot again—another time—a third. And his heavy bullets tore and splintered the boughs dangerously close to the hunter's head. Then came an awkward, almost hopeless task for the rustler, in maintaining his position while reloading his gun. He did it, and his panting attested to the labor and pain it cost him.

So much, in fact, that he let his knee protrude. Wade fired, breaking that knee. The rustler sagged in his tracks, his hip stuck out to afford a target for the remorseless Wade. Still the doomed man did not cry out, though it was evident that he could not now keep his body from sagging into sight of the hunter. Then with a desperate courage worthy of a better cause, and with a spirit great in its defeat, the rustler plunged out from his hiding-place, gun extended. His red beard, his gaunt face, fierce and baleful, his wabbling plunge that was really a fall, made a sight which was terrible. He hopped out of that fall. His gun began to blaze. But it only matched the blazes of Wade's. And the rustler pitched headlong over the framework, falling heavily against the wall beyond.

Then there was silence for a long moment. Wade stirred, as if to look around. Belllounds also stirred, and gulped, as if to breathe. The three prostrate rustlers lay inert, their positions singularly tragic and settled. The smoke again began to lift, to float out of the door and windows. In another moment the big room seemed less hazy.

Wade rose, not without effort, and he had a gun in each hand. Those hands were bloody; there was blood on his face, and his left shoulder was red. He approached Belllounds.

Wade was terrible then—terrible with a ruthlessness that was no pretense. To Belllounds it must have represented death—a bloody death which he was not prepared to meet.

"Come out of your trance, you pup rustler!" yelled Wade.

"For God's sake, don't kill me!" implored Belllounds, stricken with terror.

"Why not? Look around! My busy day, Buster! . . . An' for that Cap Folsom it's been ten years comin' . . . I'm goin' to shoot you in the belly an' watch you get sick to your stomach!"

Belllounds, with whisper, and hands, and face, begged for his life in an abjectness of sheer panic.

"What!" roared the hunter. "Didn't you know I come to kill you?"

"Yes—yes! I've seen—that. It's awful! . . . I never harmed you. . . . Don't kill me! Let me live, Wade. I swear to God I'll—I'll never do it again. . . . For dad's sake—for Collie's sake—don't kill me!"

"I'm Hell-Bent Wade! . . . You wouldn't listen to them—when they wanted to tell you who I am!"

Every word of Wade's drove home to this boy the primal meaning of sudden death. It inspired him with an unutterable fear. That was what clamped his brow in a sweaty band and upreared his hair and rolled his eyeballs. His magnified intelligence, almost ghastly, grasped a hope in Wade's apparent vacillation and in the utterance of the name of Columbine. Intuition, a subtle sense, inspired him to beg in that name.

"Swear you'll give up Collie!" demanded Wade, brandishing his guns with bloody hands.

"Yes—yes! My God, I'll do anything!" moaned Belllounds.

"Swear you'll tell your father you'd had a change of heart. You'll give Collie up! . . . Let Moore have her!"

"I swear! . . . But if you tell dad—I stole his cattle—he'll do for me!"

"We won't squeal that. I'll save you if you give up the girl. Once more, Buster Jack—try an' make me believe you'll square the deal."

Belllounds had lost his voice. But his mute, fluttering lips were infinite proof of the vow he could not speak. The boyishness, the stunted moral force, replaced the manhood in him then. He was only a factor in the lives of others, protected even from this Nemesis by the greatness of his father's love.

"Get up, an' take my scarf," said Wade, "an' bandage these bullet-holes I got."

CHAPTER 18

Wade's wounds were not in any way serious, and with Belllounds's assistance he got to the cabin of Lewis, where weakness from loss of blood made it necessary that he remain. Belllounds went home.

The next day Wade sent Lewis with pack-horse down to the rustlers' cabin, to bury the dead men and fetch back their effects. Lewis returned that night, accompanied by Sheriff Burley and two deputies, who had been busy on their own account. They had followed horse tracks from the water-hole under Gore Peak to the scene of the fight, and had arrived to find Lewis there. Burley had appropriated the considerable amount of gold, which he said could be identified by cattlemen who had bought the stolen cattle.

When opportunity afforded Burley took advantage of it to speak to Wade when the others were out of earshot.

"Thar was another man in thet cabin when the fight come off," announced the sheriff. "An' he come up hyar with you."

"Jim, you're locoed," replied Wade.

The sheriff laughed, and his shrewd eyes had a kindly, curious gleam.

"Next you'll be givin' me a hunch thet you're in a fever an' out of your head."

"Jim, I'm not as clear-headed as I might be."

"Wal, tell me or not, jest as you like. I seen his tracks—follered them.

An' Wade, old pard, I've reckoned long ago thar's a nigger in the wood-pile."

"Sure. An' you know me. I'd take it friendly of you to put Moore's trial off fer a while—till I'm able to ride to Kremmlin'. Maybe then I can tell you a story."

Burley threw up his hands in genuine apprehension. "Not much! You ain't agoin' to tell *me* no story! . . . But I'll wait on you, an' welcome. Reckon I owe you a good deal on this rustler round-up. Wade, thet must have been a man-sized fight, even fer you. I picked up twenty-six empty shells. An' the little half-breed had one empty shell an' five loaded ones in his gun. You must have got him quick. Hey?"

"Jim, I'm observin' you're a heap more curious than ever, an' you always was an inquisitive cuss," complained Wade. "I don't recollect what happened."

"Wal, wal, have it your own way," replied Burley, with good nature. "Now, Wade, I'll pitch camp hyar in the park to-night, an' to-morrer I'll ride down to White Slides on my way to Kremmlin'. What're you wantin' me to tell Belllounds?"

The hunter pondered a moment.

"Reckon it's just as well that you tell him somethin'. . . . You can say the rustlers are done for an' that he'll get his stock back. I'd like you to tell him that the rustlers were more to blame than Wils Moore. Just say that an' nothin' else about Wils. Don't mention about your suspectin' there was another man around when the fight come off. . . . Tell the cowboys that I'll be down in a few days. An' if you happen to get a chance for a word alone with Miss Collie, just say I'm not bad hurt an' that all will be well."

"Ahuh!" Burley grunted out the familiar exclamation. He did not say any more then, but he gazed thoughtfully down upon the pale hunter, as if that strange individual was one infinitely to respect, but never to comprehend.

Wade's wounds healed quickly; nevertheless, it was more than several days before he felt spirit enough to undertake the ride. He had to return to White Slides, but he was reluctant to do so. Memory of Jack Belllounds dragged at him, and when he drove it away it continually returned. This feeling was almost equivalent to an augmentation of his gloomy foreboding, which ever hovered on the fringe of his consciousness. But one morning he started early, and, riding very slowly, with many rests, he reached the Sage Valley cabin before sunset. Moore saw him coming, yelled his delight and concern, and almost lifted him off the horse. Wade was too tired to talk much, but he allowed himself to be fed and put to bed and worked over.

"Boot's on the other foot now, pard," said Moore, with delight at the prospect of returning service. "Say, you're all shot up! And it's I who'll be nurse!"

"Wils, I'll be around to-morrow," replied the hunter. "Have you heard any news from down below?"

"Sure. I've met Lem every night."

Then he related Burley's version of Wade's fight with the rustlers in the cabin. From the sheriff's lips the story gained much. Old Bill Belllounds had received the news in a singular mood; he offered no encomiums to the victor; contrary to his usual custom of lauding every achievement of labor or endurance, he now seemed almost to regret the affray. Jack Belllounds had returned from Kremmling and he was present when Burley brought news of the rustlers. What he thought none of the cowboys vouchsafed to say, but he was drunk the next day, and he lost a handful of gold to them. Never had he gambled so recklessly. Indeed, it was as if he hated the gold he lost. Little had been seen of Columbine, but little was sufficient to make the cowboys feel concern.

Wade made scarcely any comment upon this news from the ranch; next day, however, he was up, and caring for himself, and he told Moore about the fight and how he had terrorized Belllounds and exhorted the promises from him.

"Never in God's world will Buster Jack live up to those promises!" cried Moore, with absolute conviction. "I know him, Ben. He meant them when he made them. He'd swear his soul away—then next day he'd lie or forget or betray."

"I'm not believin' that till I know," replied the hunter, gloomily. "But I'm afraid of him. . . . I've known bad men to change. There's a grain of good in all men—somethin' divine. An' it comes out now an' then. Men rise on steppin'-stones of their dead selves to higher things! . . . This is

Belllounds's chance for the good in him. If it's not there he will do as you say. If it is—that scare he had will be the turnin'-point in his life. I'm hopin', but I'm afraid."

"Ben, you wait and see," said Moore, earnestly. "Heaven knows I'm not one to lose hope for my fellowmen—hope for the higher things you've taught me. . . . But human nature is human nature. Jack *can't* give Collie up, just the same as I *can't*. That's self-preservation as well as love."

The day came when Wade walked down to White Slides. There seemed to be a fever in his blood, which he tried to convince himself was a result of his wounds instead of the condition of his mind. It was Sunday, a day of sunshine and squall, of azure-blue sky, and great, sailing, purple clouds. The sage of the hills glistened and there was a sweetness in the air.

The cowboys made much of Wade. But the old rancher, seeing him from the porch, abruptly went into the house. No one but Wade noticed this omission of courtesy. Directly, Columbine appeared, waving her hand, and running to meet him.

"Dad saw you. He told me to come out and excuse him. . . . Oh, Ben, I'm so happy to see you! You don't look hurt at all. What a fight you had! . . . Oh, I was sick! But let me forget that. . . . How are you? And how's Wils?"

Thus she babbled until out of breath.

"Collie, it's sure good to see you," said Wade, feeling the old, rich thrill at her presence. "I'm comin' on tolerable well. I wasn't bad hurt, but I bled a lot. An' I reckon I'm older 'n I was when packin' gun-shot holes was nothin'. Every year tells. Only a man doesn't know till after. . . . An' how are you, Collie?"

Her blue eyes clouded, and a tremor changed the expression of her sweet lips.

"I am unhappy, Ben," she said. "But what could we expect? It might be worse. For instance, you might have been killed. I've much to be thankful for."

"I reckon so. We all have. . . . I fetched a message from Wils, but I oughtn't tell it."

"Please do," she begged, wistfully.

"Well, Wils says, tell Collie I love her every day more an' more, an' that my love keeps up my courage an' my belief in God, an' if she ever marries Jack Belllounds she can come up to visit my grave among the columbines on the hill."

Strange how Wade experienced comfort in thus torturing her! She was rosy at the beginning of his speech and white at its close. "Oh, it's true!" she whispered. "It'll kill him, as it will me!"

"Cheer up, Columbine," said Wade. "It's a long time till August thirteenth. . . . An' now tell me, why did Old Bill run when he saw me comin'?"

"Ben, I suspect dad has the queerest notion you want to tell him some awful bloody story about the rustlers."

"Ahuh! Well, not yet. . . . An' how's Jack Belllounds actin' these days?"

Wade felt the momentousness of that query, but it seemed her face had been telltale enough, without confirmation of words.

"My friend, somehow I hate to tell you. You're always so hopeful, so ready to think good instead of evil. . . . But Jack has been rough with me, almost brutal. He was drunk once. Every day he drinks, sometimes a little, sometimes more. But drink changes him. And it's dragging dad down. Dad doesn't say so, yet I feel he's afraid of what will come next. . . . Jack has nagged me to marry him right off. He wanted to the day he came back from Kremmling. He's eager to leave White Slides. Dad knows that, also, and it worries him. But of course I refused."

The presence of Columbine, so vivid and sweet and stirring, and all about her the sunlight, the golden gleams on the sage hills, and Wade's heart and brain and spirit sustained a subtle transformation. It was as if what had been beautiful with light had suddenly, strangely darkened. Then Wade imagined he stood alone in a gloomy house, which was his own heart, and he was listening to the arrival of a tragic messenger whose foot sounded heavy on the stairs, whose hand turned slowly upon the knob, whose gray presence opened the door and crossed the threshold.

"Buster Jack didn't break off with you, Collie?" asked the hunter.

"Break off with me! . . . No, indeed! Whatever possessed you to say that?"

"An' he didn't offer to give you up to Wils Moore?"

"Ben, are you crazy?" cried Columbine.

"Collie, listen. I'll tell you." The old urge knocked at Wade's mind. "Buster Jack was in the cabin, gamblin' with the rustlers, when I cornered them. You remember I meant to scare Buster Jack within an inch of his life? Well, I made use of my opportunity. I worked up the rustlers. Then I told Jack I'd give away his secret. He made to jump an' run, I reckon. But he hadn't the nerve. I shot a piece out of his ear, just to begin the fun. An' then I told the rustlers how Jack had double-crossed them. Folsom, the boss rustler, roared like a mad steer. He was wild to kill Jack. He begged for a gun to shoot out Jack's eyes. An' so were the other rustlers burnin' to kill him. Bad outfit. There was a fight, which, I'm bound to confess, was not short an' sweet. There was a lot of shootin'. An' in a cabin gunshots almost lift the roof. Folsom was on his knees, dyin', wavin' his gun, whisperin' in fiendish glee that he had done for me. When he saw Jack an' remembered he shook so with fury that he scattered blood all over. An' he took long aim at Jack, tryin' to steady his gun. He couldn't, an' he missed, an' then fell over dead with his head on Jack's knees. That left the red-bearded rustler, who had hid behind the chimney. Jack watched the rest of that fight, an' for a youngster it must have been nerve-rackin'. I broke the rustler's arm, an' then his knee, an' then I got him in the hip two more times before he hobbled out to his finish. He'd shot me up considerable, so that when I braced Jack I must have been a hair-raisin' sight. I made Jack believe I meant to murder him. He begged an' cried, an' he got to prayin' for his life for your sake. It was sickenin', but it was what I wanted. So then I made him swear he'd free you an' give you up to Moore."

"Oh! Oh, Ben, how awful!" whispered Columbine, shuddering. "How *could* you tell me such a horrible story?"

"Reckon I wanted you to know how Jack come to make the promises an' what they were."

"Promises! What are promises or oaths to Jack Belllounds?" she cried, in passionate contempt. "You wasted your breath. Coward—liar that he is!"

"Ahuh!" Wade looked straight ahead of him as if he saw some expected and unpleasant thing far in the distance. Then with irresistible steps, neither swift nor slow, but ponderous, he strode to the porch and mounted the steps.

"Why, Ben, where are you going?" called Columbine, in surprise, as she followed him.

He did not answer. He approached the closed door of the living-room.

"Ben!" cried Columbine, in alarm.

But he had no reply for her—indeed, no thought of her. Without knocking, he opened the door with rude and powerful hand, and, striding in, closed it after him.

Bill Belllounds was standing, back against the great stone chimney, arms folded, a stolid and grim figure, apparently fortified against an intrusion he had expected.

"Wal, what do you want?" he asked, gruffly. He had sensed catastrophe in the first sight of the hunter.

"Belllounds, I reckon I want a hell of a lot," replied Wade. "An' I'm askin' you to see we're not disturbed."

"Bar the door."

Wade dropped the bar in place, and then, removing his sombrero, he wiped his moist brow.

"Do you see an enemy in me?" he asked, curiously.

"Speakin' out fair, Wade, there ain't any reason I can see that you're an enemy to me," replied Belllounds. "But I feel somethin'. It ain't because I'm takin' my son's side. It's more than that. A queer feelin', an' one I never had before. I got it first when you told the story of the Gunnison feud."

"Belllounds, we can't escape our fates. An' it was written long ago I was to tell you a worse an' harder story than that."

"Wal, mebbe I'll listen an' mebbe I won't. I ain't promisin', these days."

"Are you goin' to make Collie marry Jack?" demanded the hunter.

"She's willin'."

"You know that's not true. Collie's willin' to sacrifice love, honor, an' life itself, to square her debt to you."

The old rancher flushed a burning red, and in his eyes flared a spirit of earlier years.

"Wade, you can go too far," he warned. "I'm appreciatin' your good-heartedness. It sort of warms me toward you. . . . But this is my business.

You've no call to interfere. You've done that too much already. An' I'm reckonin' Collie would be married to Jack now if it hadn't been for you."

"Ahuh! . . . That's why I'm thankin' God I happened along to White Slides. Belllounds, your big mistake is thinkin' your son is good enough for this girl. An' you're makin' mistakes about me. I've interfered here, an' you may take my word for it I had the right."

"Strange talk, Wade, but I'll make allowances."

"You needn't. I'll back my talk . . . But, first, I'm askin' you—an' if this talk hurts, I'm sorry—why don't you give some of your love for your no-good Buster Jack to Collie?"

Belllounds clenched his huge fists and glared. Anger leaped within him. He recognized in Wade an outspoken, bitter adversary to his cherished hopes for his son and his stubborn, precious pride.

"By Heaven! Wade, I'll—"

"Belllounds, I can make you swallow that kind of talk," interrupted Wade. "It's man to man now. An' I'm a match for you any day. Savvy? . . . Do you think I'm damn fool enough to come here an' brace you unless I knew that. Talk to me as you'd talk about some other man's son."

"It ain't possible," rejoined the rancher, stridently.

"Then listen to me first. . . . Your son Jack, to say the least, will ruin Collie. Do you see that?"

"By Gawd! I'm afraid so," groaned Belllounds, big in his humiliation. "But it's my one last bet, an' I'm goin' to play it."

"Do you know marryin' him will *kill* her?"

"What! . . . You're overdoin' your fears, Wade. Women don't die so easy."

"Some of them die, an' Collie's one that will, *if* she ever marries Jack."

"*If*! . . . Wal, she's goin' to."

"We don't agree," said Wade, curtly.

"Are you runnin' my family?"

"No. But I'm runnin' a large-sized *if* in this game. You'll admit that presently. . . . Belllounds, you make me mad. You don't meet me man to man. You're not the Bill Belllounds of old. Why, all over this state of Colorado you're known as the whitest of the white. Your name's a byword for all that's square an' big an' splendid. But you're so blinded by your worship of that wild boy that you're another man in all pertainin' to him. I don't want to harp on his shortcomin's. I'm for the girl. She doesn't love him. She can't. She will only drag herself down an' die of a broken heart. . . . Now, I'm askin' you, before it's too late—give up this marriage."

"Wade! I've shot men for less than you've said!" thundered the rancher, beside himself with rage and shame.

"Ahuh! I reckon you have. But not men like me. . . . I tell you, straight to your face, it's a fool deal you're workin'—a damn selfish one—a dirty job, to put on an innocent, sweet girl—an' as sure as you stand there, if you do it, you'll ruin four lives!"

"Four!" exclaimed Belllounds. But any word would have expressed his humiliation.

"I should have said three, leavin' Jack out. I meant Collie's an' yours an' Wils Moore's."

"Moore's is about ruined already, I've a hunch."

"You can get hunches you never dreamed of, Belllounds, old as you are. An' I'll give you one presently. . . . But we drift off. Can't you keep cool?"

"Cool! With you rantin' hell-bent for election? Haw! Haw! . . . Wade, you're locoed. You always struck me queer. . . . An' if you'll excuse me, I'm gettin' tired of this talk. We're as far apart as the poles. An' to save what good feelin's we both have, let's quit."

"You don't love Collie, then?" queried Wade, imperturbably.

"Yes, I do. That's a fool idee of yours. It puts me out of patience."

"Belllounds, you're not her real father."

The rancher gave a start, and he stared as he had stared before, fixedly and perplexedly at Wade.

"No, I'm not."

"If she *were* your real daughter—your own flesh an' blood—an' Jack Belllounds was *my* son, would you let her marry him?"

"Wal, Wade, I reckon I wouldn't."

"Then how can you expect my consent to her marriage with your son?"

"WHAT!" Belllounds lunged over to Wade, leaned down, shaken by overwhelming amaze.

"Collie is my daughter!"

A loud expulsion of breath escaped Belllounds. Lower he leaned, and looked with piercing gaze into the face and eyes that in this moment bore strange resemblance to Columbine.

"So help me Gawd! . . . That's the secret? . . . Hell-Bent Wade! An' you've been on my trail!"

He staggered to his big chair and fell into it. No trace of doubt showed in his face. The revelation had struck home because of its very greatness.

Wade took the chair opposite. His likeness to Columbine had faded now. It had been love, a spirit, a radiance, a glory. It was gone. And Wade's face became the emblem of tragedy.

"Listen, Belllounds. I'll tell you! . . . The ways of God are inscrutable. I've been twenty years tryin' to atone for the wrong I did Collie's mother. I've been a prospector for the trouble of others. I've been a bearer of their burdens. An' if I can save Collie's happiness an' her soul, I reckon I won't be denied the peace of meetin' her mother in the other world. . . . I recognized Collie the moment I laid eyes on her. She favors her mother in looks, an' she has her mother's sensitiveness, her fire an' pride, an' she even has her voice. It's low an' sweet—alto, they used to call it. . . . But I'd recognized Collie as my own if I'd been blind an' deaf. . . . It's over eighteen years ago that we had the trouble. I was no boy, but I was terribly in love with Lucy. An' she loved me with a passion I never learned till too late. We came West from Missouri. She was born in Texas. I had a rovin' disposition an' didn't stick long at any kind of work. But I was lookin' for a ranch. My wife had some money an' I had high hopes. We spent our first year of married life travelin' through Kansas. At Dodge I got tied up for a while. You know, in them days Dodge was about the wildest camp on the plains. My wife's brother run a place there. He wasn't much good. But she thought he was perfect. Strange how blood-relations can't see the truth about their own people! Anyway, her brother Spencer had no use for me, because I could tell how slick he was with the cards an' beat him at his own game. Spencer had a gamblin' pard, a cowboy run out of Texas, one Cap Fol—But no matter about his name. One night they were fleecin' a stranger an' I broke into the game, winnin' all they had. The game ended in a fight, with bloodshed, but nobody killed. That set Spencer an' his pard Cap against me. The stranger was a planter from Louisiana. He'd been an officer in the rebel army. A high-strung, handsome Southerner, fond of wine an' cards an' women. Well, he got to payin' my wife a good deal of attention when I was away, which happened to be often. She never told me. I was jealous those days.

"My little girl you call Columbine was born there durin' a long absence of mine. When I got home Lucy an' the baby were gone. Also the Southerner! . . . Spencer an' his pard Cap, an' others they had in the deal, proved to me, so it seemed, that the little girl was not really mine! . . . An' so I set out on a hunt for my wife an' her lover. I found them. An' I killed him before her eyes. But she was innocent, an' so was he, as came out too late. He'd been, indeed, her friend. She scorned me. She told me how her brother Spencer an' his friends had established guilt of mine that had driven her from me.

"I went back to Dodge to have a little quiet smoke with these men who had ruined me. They were gone. The trail led to Colorado. Nearly a year later I rounded them all up in a big wagon-train post north of Denver. Another brother of my wife's, an' her father, had come West, an' by accident or fate we all met there. We had a family quarrel. My wife would not forgive me—would not speak to me, an' her people backed her up. I made the great mistake to take her father an' other brothers to belong to the same brand as Spencer. In this I wronged them an' her.

"What I did to them, Belllounds, is one story I'll never tell to any man who might live to repeat it. But it drove my wife near crazy. An' it made me Hell-Bent Wade! . . . She ran off from me there, an' I trailed her all over Colorado. An' the end of that trail was not a hundred miles from where we stand now. The last trace I had was of the burnin' of a prairie-schooner by Arapahoes as they were goin' home from a foray on the Utes. . . . The little girl might have toddled off the trail. But I reckon she was hidden or dropped by her mother, or some one fleein' for life. Your men found her in the columbines."

Belllounds drew a long, deep breath.

"What a man never expects always comes true. . . . Wade, the lass is yours. I can see it in the way you look at me. I can feel it. . . . She's been like my own. I've done my best, accordin' to my conscience. An' I've loved her, for all they say I couldn't see aught but Jack. . . . You'll take her away from me?"

"No. Never," was the melancholy reply.

"What! Why not?"

"Because she loves you. . . . I could never reveal myself to Collie. I couldn't win her love with a lie. An' I'd have to lie, to be false as hell. . . . False to her mother an' to Collie an' to all I hold high! I'd have to tell Collie the truth—the wrong I did her mother—the *hell* I visited upon her mother's people. . . . She'd fear me."

"Ahuh! . . . An' you'll never change—I reckon that!" exclaimed Belllounds.

"No. I changed once, eighteen years ago. I can't go back. . . . I can't undo all I hoped was good."

"You think Collie'd fear you?"

"She'd never *love* me as she does you, or as she loves me even now. That is my rock of refuge."

"She'd hate you, Wade."

"I reckon. An' so she must never know."

"Ahuh! . . . Wal, wal, life is a hell of a deal! Wade, if you could live yours over again, knowin' what you know now, an' that you'd love an' suffer the same—would you want to do it?"

"Yes. I love life, with all it brings. I wouldn't have the joy without the pain. But I reckon only men who've come to our years would want it over again."

"Wal, I'm with you thar. I'd take what came. Rain an' sun! . . . But all this you tell, an' the hell you hint at, ain't changin' this hyar deal of Jack's an' Collie's. Not one jot! . . . If she remains my adopted daughter she marries my son. . . . Wade, I'm haltered like the north star in that."

"Belllounds, will you take a day to think it over?" appealed Wade.

"Ahuh! But that won't change me."

"Won't it change you to know that if you force this marriage you'll lose all?"

"All! Ain't that more queer talk?"

"I mean lose all—your son, your adopted daughter—his chance of reformin', her hope of happiness. These ought to be all in life left to you."

"Wal, they are. But I can't see your argument. You're beyond me, Wade. You're holdin' back, like you did with your hell-bent story."

Ponderously, as if the burden and the doom of the world weighed him down, the hunter got up and fronted Belllounds.

"When I'm driven to tell I'll come. . . . But, once more, old man, choose between generosity an' selfishness. Between blood tie an' noble loyalty to your good deed in its beginnin'. . . . Will you give up this marriage for your son—so that Collie can have the man she loves?"

"You mean your young pard an' two-bit of a rustler—Wils Moore?"

"Wils Moore, yes. My friend, an' a man, Belllounds, such as you or I never was."

"No!" thundered the rancher, purple in the face.

With bowed head and dragging step Wade left the room.

By slow degrees of plodding steps, and periods of abstracted lagging, the hunter made his way back to Moore's cabin. At his entrance the cowboy leaped up with a startled cry.

"Oh, Wade! . . . Is Collie dead?" he cried.

Such was the extent of calamity he imagined from the somber face of Wade.

"No. Collie's well."

"Then, man, what on earth's happened?"

"Nothin' yet. . . . But somethin' is goin' on in my mind. . . . Moore, I'd like you to let me alone."

At sunset Wade was pacing the aspen grove on the hill. There was sunlight and shade under the trees, a rosy gold on the sage slopes, a purple-and-violet veil between the black ranges and the sinking sun.

Twilight fell. The stars came out white and clear. Night cloaked the valley with dark shadows and the hills with its obscurity. The blue vault overhead deepened and darkened. The hunter patrolled his beat, and hours were moments to him. He heard the low hum of the insects, the murmur of running water, the rustle of the wind. A coyote cut the keen air with high-keyed, staccato cry. The owls hooted, with dismal and weird plaint, one to the other. Then a wolf mourned. But these sounds only accentuated the loneliness and wildness of the silent night.

Wade listened to them, to the silence. He felt the wildness and loneliness of the place, the breathing of nature; he peered aloft at the velvet blue of the mysterious sky with its deceiving stars. All that had been of help to him through days of trial was now as if it had never been. When he lifted his eyes to the great, dark peak, so bold and clear-cut against the sky, it was not to receive strength again. Nature in its cruelty mocked him. His struggle had to do with the most perfect of nature's works—man.

Wade was now in passionate strife with the encroaching mood that was a mocker of his idealism. Many times during the strange, long martyrdom of his penance had he faced this crisis, only to go down to defeat before elemental instincts. His soul was steeped in gloom, but his intelligence had not yet succumbed to passion. The beauty of Columbine's character and the nobility of Moore's were not illusions to Wade. They were true. These two were of the finest fiber of human nature. They loved. They represented youth and hope—a progress through the ages toward a better race. Wade believed in the good to be, in the future of men. Nevertheless, all that was fine and worthy in Columbine and Moore was to go unrewarded, unfulfilled, because of the selfish pride of an old man and the evil passion of the son. It was a conflict as old as life. Of what avail were Columbine's high sense of duty, Moore's fine manhood, the many victories they had won over the headlong and imperious desires of love? What avail were Wade's good offices, his spiritual teaching, his eternal hope in the order of circumstances working out to good? These beautiful characteristics of virtue were not so strong as the unchangeable passion of old Belllounds and the vicious depravity of his son. Wade could not imagine himself a god, proving that the wages of sin was death. Yet in his life he had often been an impassive destiny, meting out terrible consequences. Here he was incalculably involved. This was the cumulative end of years of mounting plots, tangled and woven into the web of his pain and his remorse and his ideal. But hope was dying. That was his strife—realization against the morbid clairvoyance of his mind. He could not help Jack Belllounds to be a better man. He could not inspire the old rancher to a forgetfulness of selfish and blinded aims. He could not prove to Moore the truth of the reward that came from unflagging hope and unassailable virtue. He could not save Columbine with his ideals.

The night wore on, and Wade plodded under the rustling aspens. The insects ceased to hum, the owls to hoot, the wolves to mourn. The shadows of the long spruces gradually merged into the darkness of night. Above, infinitely high, burned the pale stars, wise and cold, aloof and indifferent, eyes of other worlds of mystery.

In those night hours something in Wade died, but his idealism, unquenchable and inexplicable, the very soul of the man, saw its justification and fulfilment in the distant future.

The gray of the dawn stole over the eastern range, and before its opaque gloom the blackness of night retreated, until valley and slope and grove were shrouded in spectral light, where all seemed unreal.

And with it the gray-gloomed giant of Wade's mind, the morbid and brooding spell, had gained its long-encroaching ascendancy. He had again found the man to whom he must tell his story. Tragic and irrevocable decree! It was his life that forced him, his crime, his remorse, his agony, his endless striving. How true had been his steps! They had led, by devious and tortuous paths, to the home of his daughter.

Wade crouched under the aspens, accepting this burden as a man being physically loaded with tremendous weights. His shoulders bent to them. His breast was sunken and labored. All his muscles were cramped. His blood flowed sluggishly. His heart beat with slow, muffled throbs in his ears. There was a creeping cold in his veins, ice in his marrow, and death in his soul. The giant that had been shrouded in gray threw off his cloak, to stand revealed, black and terrible. And it was he who spoke to Wade, in dreadful tones, like knells. Bent Wade—man of misery—who could find no peace on earth—whose presence unknit the tranquil lives of people and poisoned their blood and marked them for doom! Wherever he wandered there followed the curse! Always this had been so. He was the harbinger of catastrophe. He who preached wisdom and claimed to be taught by the flowers, who loved life and hated injustice, who mingled with his kind, ever searching for that one who needed him, he must become the woe and the bane and curse of those he would only serve! Insupportable and pitiful fate! The fiends of the past mocked him, like wicked ghouls, voiceless and dim. The faces of the men he had killed were around him in the gray gloom, pale, drifting visages of distortion, accusing him, claiming him. Likewise, these gleams of faces were specters of his mind, a procession eternal, mournful, and silent, wending their way on and on through the regions of his thought. All were united, all drove him, all put him on the trail of catastrophe. They fore-shadowed the future, they inclosed events, they lured him with his endless illusions. He was in the vortex of a vast whirlpool, not of water or of wind, but of life. Alas! he seemed indeed the very current of that whirlpool, a monstrous force, around which evil circled and lurked and conquered. Wade—who had the ill-omened croak of the raven—Wade—who bent his driven steps toward hell!

In the brilliant sunlight of the summer morning Wade bent his resistless steps down toward White Slides Ranch. The pendulum had swung. The hours were propitious. Seemingly, events that already cast their shadows waited for him. He saw Jack Belllounds going out on the fast and furious ride which had become his morning habit.

Columbine intercepted Wade. The shade of woe and tragedy in her face were the same as he had pictured there in his gloomy vigil of the night.

"My friend, I was coming to you. . . . Oh, I can bear no more!"

Her hair was disheveled, her dress disordered, the hands she tremblingly held out bore discolored marks. Wade led her into the seclusion of the willow trail.

"Oh, Ben! . . . He fought me—like—a beast!" she panted.

"Collie, you needn't tell me more," said Wade, gently. "Go up to Wils. Tell him."

"But I must tell you. I can bear—no more. . . . He fought me—hurt me—and when dad heard us—and came—Jack lied. . . . Oh, the dog! . . . Ben, his father believed—when Jack swore he was only mad—only trying to shake me—for my indifference and scorn. . . . But, my God!—Jack meant . . ."

"Collie, go up to Wils," interposed the hunter.

"I want to see Wils. I need to—I must. But I'm afraid. . . . Oh, it will make things worse!"

"Go!"

She turned away, actuated by more than her will.

"*Collie!*" came the call, piercingly and strangely after her. Bewildered, startled by the wildness of that cry, she wheeled. But Wade was gone. The shaking of the willows attested to his hurry.

Old Belllounds braced his huge shoulders against the wall in the attitude of a man driven to his last stand.

"Ahuh!" he rolled, sonorously. "So hyar you are again? . . . Wal, tell your worst, Hell-Bent Wade, an' let's have an end to your croakin'."

Belllounds had fortified himself, not with convictions or with illusions, but with the last desperate courage of a man true to himself.

"I'll tell you . . ." began the hunter.

And the rancher threw up his hands in a mockery that was furious, yet with outward shrinking.

"Just now, when Buster Jack fought with Collie, he meant bad by her!"

"Aw, no! . . . He was jest rude—tryin' to be masterful. . . . An' the lass's like a wild filly. She needs a tamin' down."

Wade stretched forth a lean and quivering hand that seemed the symbol of presaged and tragic truth.

"Listen, Belllounds, an' I'll tell you. . . . No use tryin' to hatch a rotten egg! There's no good in your son. His good intentions he paraded for virtues, believin' himself that he'd changed. But a flip of the wind made him Buster Jack again. . . . Collie would sacrifice her life for duty to you—whom she loves as her father. Wils Moore sacrificed his honor for Collie—rather than let you learn the truth. . . . But they call me Hell-Bent Wade, an' I will tell you!"

The straining hulk of Belllounds crouched lower, as if to gather impetus for a leap. Both huge hands were outspread as if to ward off attack from an unseen but long-dreaded foe. The great eyes rolled. And underneath the terror and certainty and tragedy of his appearance seemed to surge the resistless and rising swell of a dammed-up, terrible rage.

"I'll tell you . . ." went on the remorseless voice. "I watched your Buster Jack. I watched him gamble an' drink. I trailed him. I found the little circles an' the crooked horse tracks—made to trap Wils Moore. . . . A damned cunnin' trick! . . . Burley suspects a nigger in the wood-pile. Wils Moore knows the truth. He lied for Collie's sake an' yours. He'd have stood the trial—an' gone to jail to save Collie from what she dreaded. . . . Belllounds, your son was in the cabin gamblin' with the rustlers when I cornered them. . . . I offered to keep Jack's secret if he'd swear to give Collie up. He swore on his knees, beggin' in her name! . . . An' he comes back to bully her, an' worse. . . . Buster Jack! . . . He's the thorn in your heart, Belllounds. He's the rustler who stole your cattle! . . . Your pet son—a sneakin' thief!"

CHAPTER 19

Jack Belllounds came riding down the valley trail. His horse was in a lather of sweat. Both hair and blood showed on the long spurs this son of a great pioneer used in his pleasure rides. He had never loved a horse.

At a point where the trail met the brook there were thick willow patches, with open, grassy spots between. As Belllounds reached this place a man stepped out of the willows and laid hold of the bridle. The horse shied and tried to plunge, but an iron arm held him.

"Get down, Buster," ordered the man.

It was Wade.

Belllounds had given as sharp a start as his horse. He was sober, though the heated red tinge of his face gave indication of a recent use of the bottle. That color quickly receded. Events of the last month had left traces of the hardening and lowering of Jack Belllounds's nature.

"Wha-at? . . . Let go that bridle!" he ejaculated.

Wade held it fast, while he gazed up into the prominent eyes, where fear shone and struggled with intolerance and arrogance and quickening gleams of thought.

"You an' I have somethin' to talk over," said the hunter.

Belllounds shrank from the low, cold, even voice, that evidently reminded him of the last time he had heard it.

"No, we haven't," he declared, quickly. He seemed to gather assurance with his spoken thought, and conscious fear left him. "Wade, you took advantage of me that day—when you made me swear things. I've changed my mind. . . . And as for that deal with the rustlers, I've got my story. It's as good as yours. I've been waiting for you to tell my father. You've got some reason for not telling him. I've a hunch it's Collie. I'm on to you, and I've got my nerve back. You can gamble I—"

He had grown excited when Wade interrupted him.

"Will you get off that horse?"

"No, I won't," replied Belllounds, bluntly.

With swift and powerful lunge Wade pulled Belllounds down, sliding him shoulders first into the grass. The released horse shied again and moved away. Buster Jack raised himself upon his elbow, pale with rage and alarm. Wade kicked him, not with any particular violence.

"Get up!" he ordered.

The kick had brought out the rage in Belllounds at the expense of the amaze and alarm.

"Did you kick *me?*" he shouted.

"Buster, I was only handin' you a bunch of flowers—some columbines, as your taste runs," replied Wade, contemptuously.

"I'll—I'll—" returned Buster Jack, wildly, bursting for expression. His hand went to his gun.

"Go ahead, Buster. Throw your gun on me. That'll save maybe a hell of a lot of talk."

It was then Jack Belllounds's face turned livid. Comprehension had dawned upon him.

"You—you want me to fight you?" he queried, in hoarse accents.

"I reckon that's what I meant."

No affront, no insult, no blow could have affected Buster Jack as that sudden knowledge.

"Why—why—you're crazy! Me fight you—a gunman," he stammered. "No—no. It wouldn't be fair. Not an even break! . . . No, I'd have no chance on earth!"

"I'll give you first shot," went on Wade, in his strange, monotonous voice.

"Bah! You're lying to me," replied Belllounds, with pale grimace.

"You just want me to get a gun in my hand—then you'll drop me, and claim an even break."

"No. I'm square. You saw me play square with your rustler pard. He was a lifelong enemy of mine. An' a gun-fighter to boot! . . . Pull your gun an' let drive. I'll take my chances."

Buster Jack's eyes dilated. He gasped huskily. He pulled his gun, but actually did not have strength or courage enough to raise it. His arm shook so that the gun rattled against his chaps.

"No nerve, hey? Not half a man! . . . Buster Jack, why don't you finish game? Make up for your low-down tricks. At the last try to be worthy of your dad. In his day he was a real man. . . . Let him have the consolation that you faced Hell-Bent Wade an' died in your boots!"

"I—can't—fight you!" panted Belllounds. "I know now! . . . I saw you throw a gun! It wouldn't be fair!"

"But I'll make you fight me," returned Wade, in steely tones. "I'm givin' you a chance to dig up a little manhood. Askin' you to meet me man to man! Handin' you a little the best of it to make the odds even! . . . Once more, will you be game?"

"Wade, I'll not fight—I'm going—" replied Belllounds, and he moved as if to turn.

"Halt! . . ." Wade leaped at the white Belllounds. "If you run I'll break a leg for you—an' then I'll beat your miserable brains out! . . . Have you no sense? Can't you recognize what's comin'? . . . *I'm goin' to kill you, Buster Jack!*"

"My God!" whispered the other, understanding fully at last.

"Here's where you pay for your dirty work. The time comes to every man. You've a choice, not to live—for you'll never get away from Hell-Bent Wade—but to rise above yourself at last."

"But what for? Why do you want to kill me? I never harmed you."

"Columbine is my daughter!" replied the hunter.

"Ah!" breathed Belllounds.

"She loves Wils Moore, who's as white a man as you are black."

Across the pallid, convulsed face of Belllounds spread a slow, dull crimson.

"Aha, Buster Jack! I struck home there," flashed Wade, his voice rising.

"That gives your eyes the ugly look. . . . I hate them lyin', bulgin' eyes of yours. An' when my time comes to shoot I'm goin' to put them both out."

"By Heaven! Wade, you'll have to kill me if you ever expect that club-foot Moore to get Collie!"

"He'll get her," replied Wade, triumphantly. "Collie's with him now. I sent her. I told her to tell Wils how you tried to force her—"

Belllounds began to shake all over. A torture of jealous hate and deadly terror convulsed him.

"Buster, did you ever think you'd get her kisses—as Wils's gettin' right now?" queried the hunter. "Good Lord! the conceit of some men! . . . Why, you poor, weak-minded, cowardly pet of a blinded old man—you conceited ass—you selfish an' spoiled boy! . . . Collie never had any use for you. An' now she hates you."

"It was you who made her!" yelled Belllounds, foaming at the mouth.

"Sure," went on the deliberate voice, ringing with scorn. "An' only a little while ago she called you a dog. . . . I reckon she meant a different kind of a dog than the hounds over there. For to say they were like you would be an insult to them. . . . Sure she hates you, an' I'll gamble right now she's got her arms around Wils's neck!"

"_____!" hissed Belllounds.

"Well, you've got a gun in your hand," went on the taunting voice. "Ahuh! . . . Have it your way. I'm warmin' up now, an' I'd like to tell you . . ."

"Shut up!" interrupted the other, frantically. The blood in him was rising to a fever heat. But fear still clamped him. He could not raise the gun and he seemed in agony.

"Your father knows you're a thief," declared Wade, with remorseless, deliberate intent. "I told him how I watched you—trailed you—an' learned the plot you hatched against Wils Moore. . . . Buster Jack busted himself at last, stealin' his own father's cattle. . . . I've seen some ragin' men in my day, but Old Bill had them beaten. You've disgraced him—broken his heart—embittered the end of his life. . . . An' he'd mean for you what I mean now!"

"He'd never—harm me!" gasped Buster Jack, shuddering.

"He'd kill you—you white-livered pup!" cried Wade, with terrible force. "Kill you before he'd let you go to worse dishonor! . . . An' I'm goin' to save him stainin' his hands."

"I'll kill *you!*" burst out Belllounds, ending in a shriek. But this was not the temper that always produced heedless action in him. It was hate. He could not raise the gun. His intelligence still dominated his will. Yet fury had mitigated his terror.

"You'll be doin' me a service, Buster. . . . But you're mighty slow at startin'. I reckon I'll have to play my last trump to make you fight. Oh, by God! I can tell you! . . . Belllounds, there're dead men callin' me now. Callin' me not to murder you in cold blood! I killed one man once—a man who wouldn't fight—an innocent man! I killed him with my bare hands, an' if I tell you my story—an' how I killed him—an' that I'll do the same for you. . . . You'll save me that, Buster. No man with a gun in his hands could face what he knew. . . . But save me more. Save me the tellin'!"

"No! No! I won't listen!"

"Maybe I won't have to," replied Wade, mournfully. He paused, breathing heavily. The sober calm was gone.

Belllounds lowered the half-raised gun, instantly answering to the strange break in Wade's strained dominance.

"Don't tell me—any more! I'll not listen! . . . I won't fight! Wade, you're crazy! Let me off an' I swear—"

"Buster, I told Collie you were three years in jail!" suddenly interrupted Wade.

A mortal blow dealt Belllounds would not have caused such a shock of amaze, of torture. The secret of the punishment meted out to him by his father! The hideous thing which, instead of reforming, had ruined him! All of hell was expressed in his burning eyes.

"Ahuh! . . . I've known it long!" cried Wade, tragically. "Buster Jack, you're the man who must hear my story. . . . *I'll tell you.* . . ."

In the aspen grove up the slope of Sage Valley Columbine and Wilson were sitting on a log. Whatever had been their discourse, it had left Moore with head bowed in his hands, and with Columbine staring with sad eyes that did not see what they looked at. Columbine's mind then seemed a dull blank. Suddenly she started.

"Wils!" she cried. "Did you hear—anything?"

"No," he replied, wearily raising his head.

"I thought I heard a shot," said Columbine. "It—it sort of made me jump. I'm nervous."

Scarcely had she finished speaking when two clear, deep detonations rang out. Gunshots!

"There! . . . Oh, Wils! Did you hear?"

"Hear!" whispered Moore. He grew singularly white. "Yes—yes! . . . Collie—"

"Wils," she interrupted, wildly, as she began to shake. "Just a little bit ago—I saw Jack riding down the trail!"

"Collie! . . . Those two shots came from Wade's gun! I'd know it among a thousand! . . . Are you sure you heard a shot before?"

"Oh, something dreadful has happened! Yes, I'm sure. Perfectly sure. A shot not so loud or heavy."

"My God!" exclaimed Moore, staring aghast at Columbine. "Maybe that's what Wade meant. I never saw through him."

"Tell me. Oh, I don't understand!" wailed Columbine, wringing her hands.

Moore did not explain what he meant. For a crippled man, he made quick time in getting to his horse and mounting.

"Collie, I'll ride down there. I'm afraid something has happened. . . . I never understood him! . . . I forgot he was Hell-Bent Wade! If there's been a—a fight or any trouble—I'll ride back and meet you."

Then he rode down the trail.

Columbine had come without her horse, and she started homeward on foot. Her steps dragged. She knew something dreadful had happened. Her heart beat slowly and painfully; there was an oppression upon her breast; her brain whirled with contending tides of thought. She remembered Wade's face. How blind she had been! It exhausted her to walk, though she went so slowly. There seemed to be a chill and a darkening in the atmosphere, an unreality in the familiar slopes and groves, a strangeness and shadow upon White Slides Valley.

Moore did not return to meet her. His white horse grazed in the pasture opposite the first clump of willows, where Sage Valley merged into the larger valley. Then she saw other horses, among them Lem Billings's bay mustang. Columbine faltered on, when suddenly she recognized the horse Jack had ridden—a sorrel, spent and foam-covered, standing saddled, with bridle down and riderless—then certainty of something awful clamped her with horror. Men's husky voices reached her throbbing ears. Some one was running. Footsteps thudded and died away. Then she saw Lem Billings come out of the willows, look her way, and hurry toward her. His awkward, cowboy gait seemed too slow for his earnestness. Columbine felt the piercing gaze of his eyes as her own became dim.

"Miss Collie, thar's been—turrible fight!" he panted.

"Oh, Lem! . . . I know. It was Ben—and Jack," she cried.

"Shore. Your hunch's correct. An' it couldn't be no 'wuss!'"

Columbine tried to see his face, the meaning that must have accompanied his hoarse voice; but she seemed going blind.

"Then—then—" she whispered, reaching out for Lem.

"Hyar, Miss Collie," he said, in great concern, as he took kind and gentle hold of her. "Reckon you'd better wait. Let me take you home."

"Yes. But tell—tell me first," she cried, fanatically. She could not bear suspense, and she felt her senses slipping away from her.

"My Gawd! who'd ever have thought such hell would come to White Slides!" exclaimed Lem, with strong emotion. "Miss Collie, I'm powerful sorry fer you. But mebbe it's best so. . . . They're both dead! . . . Wade just died with his head on Wils's lap. But Jack never knowed what hit him. He was shot plumb center—both his eyes shot out! . . . Wade was shot low down. . . . Montana an' me agreed thet Jack throwed his gun first an' Wade killed him after bein' mortal shot himself."

Late that afternoon, as Columbine lay upon her bed, the strange stillness of the house was disturbed by a heavy tread. It passed out of the living-room and came down the porch toward her door. Then followed a knock.

"Dad!" she called, swiftly rising.

Belllounds entered, leaving the door ajar. The sunlight streamed in.

"Wal, Collie, I see you're bracin' up," he said.

"Oh yes, dad, I'm—I'm all right," she replied, eager to help or comfort him.

The old rancher seemed different from the man of the past months.

The pallor of a great shock, the havoc of spent passion, the agony of terrible hours, showed in his face. But Old Bill Belllounds had come into his own again—back to the calm, iron pioneer who had lived all events, over whom storm of years had broken, whose great spirit had accepted this crowning catastrophe as it had all the others, who saw his own life clearly, now that its bitterest lesson was told.

"Are you strong enough to bear another shock, my lass, an' bear it now—so to make an end—so to-morrer we can begin anew?" he asked, with the voice she had not heard for many a day. It was the voice that told of consideration for her.

"Yes, dad," she replied, going to him.

"Wal, come with me. I want you to see Wade."

He led her out upon the porch, and thence into the living-room, and from there into the room where lay the two dead men, one on each side. Blankets covered the prone, quiet forms.

Columbine had meant to beg to see Wade once before he was laid away forever. She dreaded the ordeal, yet strangely longed for it. And here she was self-contained, ready for some nameless shock and uplift, which she divined was coming as she had divined the change in Belllounds.

Then he stripped back the blanket, disclosing Wade's face. Columbine thrilled to the core of her heart. Death was there, white and cold and merciless, but as it had released the tragic soul, the instant of deliverance had been stamped on the rugged, cadaverous visage, by a beautiful light; not of peace, nor of joy, nor of grief, but of hope! Hope had been the last emotion of Hell-Bent Wade.

"Collie, listen," said the old rancher, in deep and trembling tones. "When a man's dead, what he's been comes to us with startlin' truth. Wade was the whitest man I ever knew. He had a queer idee—a twist in his mind—an' it was thet his steps were bent toward hell. He imagined thet everywhere he traveled there he fetched hell. But he was wrong. His own trouble led him to the trouble of others. He saw through life. An' he was as big in his hope fer the good as he was terrible in his dealin' with the bad. I never saw his like. . . . He loved you, Collie, better than you ever knew. Better than Jack, or Wils, or me! You know what the Bible says about him who gives his life fer his friend. Wal, Wade was my friend, an' Jack's, only we never could see! . . . An' he was Wils's friend. An' to you he must have been more than words can tell. . . . We all know what child's play it would have been fer Wade to kill Jack without bein' hurt himself. But he wouldn't do it. So he spared me an' Jack, an' I reckon himself. Somehow he made Jack fight an' die like a man. God only knows how he did that. But it saved me from—from hell—an' you an' Wils from misery. . . . Wade could have taken you from me an' Jack. He had only to tell you his secret, an' he wouldn't. He saw how you loved me, as if you were my real child. . . . But, Collie, lass, it was *he* who was your father!"

With bursting heart Columbine fell upon her knees beside that cold, still form.

Belllounds softly left the room and closed the door behind him.

CHAPTER 20

Nature was prodigal with her colors that autumn. The frosts came late, so that the leaves did not gradually change their green. One day, as if by magic, there was gold among the green, and in another there was purple and red. Then the hilltops blazed with their crowns of aspen groves; and the slopes of sage shone mellow gray in the sunlight; and the vines on the stone fences straggled away in lines of bronze; and the patches of ferns under the cliffs faded fast; and the great rock slides and black-timbered reaches stood out in their somber shades.

Columbines bloomed in all the dells among the spruces, beautiful stalks with heavy blossoms, the sweetest and palest of blue-white flowers. Motionless they lifted their faces to the light. Out in the aspen groves, where the grass was turning gold, the columbines blew gracefully in the wind, nodding and swaying. The most exquisite and finest of these columbines hid in the shaded nooks, star-sweet in the silent gloom of the woods.

Wade's last few whispered words to Moore had been interpreted that the hunter desired to be buried among the columbines in the aspen grove on the slope above Sage Valley. Here, then, had been made his grave.

One day Belllounds sent Columbine to fetch Moore down to White Slides. It was a warm, Indian-summer afternoon, and the old rancher sat out on the porch in his shirt-sleeves. His hair was white now, but no other change was visible in him. No restraint attended his greeting to the cowboy.

"Wils, I reckon I'd be glad if you'd take your old job as foreman of White Slides," he said.

"Are you asking me?" queried Moore, eagerly.

"Wal, I reckon so."

"Yes, I'll come," replied the cowboy.

"What'll your dad say?"

"I don't know. That worries me. He's coming to visit me. I heard from him again lately, and he means to take stage for Kremmling soon."

"Wal, that's fine. I'll be glad to see him. . . . Wils, you're goin' to be a big cattleman before you know it. Hey, Collie?"

"If you say so, dad, it'll come true," replied Columbine, with her hand on his shoulder.

"Wils, you'll be runnin' White Slides Ranch before long, unless Collie runs you. Haw! Haw!"

Collie could not reply to this startling announcement from the old rancher, and Moore appeared distressed with embarrassment.

"Wal, I reckon you young folks had better ride down to Kremmlin' an' get married."

This kindly, matter-of-fact suggestion completely stunned the cowboy, and all Columbine could do was to gaze at the rancher.

"Say, I hope I ain't intrudin' my wishes on a young couple that's got over dyin' fer each other," dryly continued Belllounds, with his huge smile.

"Dad!" cried Columbine, and then she threw her arms around him and buried her head on his shoulder.

"Wal, wal, I reckon that answers that," he said, holding her close. "Moore, she's yours, with my blessin' an' all I have. . . . An' you must understand I'm glad things have worked out to your good an' to Collie's happiness. . . . Life's not over fer me yet. But I reckon the storms are past, thank God! . . . We learn as we live. I'd hold it onworthy not to look forward an' to hope. I'm wantin' peace an' quiet now, with grandchildren around me in my old age. . . . So ride along to Kremmlin' an' hurry home."

The evening of the day Columbine came home to White Slides the bride of Wilson Moore she slipped away from the simple festivities in her honor and climbed to the aspen grove on the hill to spend a little while beside the grave of her father.

The afterglow of sunset burned dull gold and rose in the western sky, rendering glorious the veil of purple over the ranges. Down in the lowlands twilight had come, softly gray. The owls were hooting; a coyote barked; from far away floated the mourn of a wolf.

Under the aspens it was silent and lonely and sad. The leaves quivered without any sound of rustling. Columbine's heart was full of a happiness that she longed to express somehow, there beside this lonely grave. It was what she owed the strange man who slept here in the shadows. Grief abided with her, and always there would be an eternal remorse and regret. Yet she had loved him. She had been his, all unconsciously. His life had been terrible, but it had been great. As the hours of quiet thinking had multiplied, Columbine had grown in her divination of Wade's meaning. His had been the spirit of man lighting the dark places; his had been the ruthless hand against all evil, terrible to destroy.

Her father! After all, how closely was she linked to the past! How closely protected, even in the hours of most helpless despair! Thus she understood him. Love was the food of life, and hope was its spirituality, and beauty was its reward to the seeing eye. Wade had lived these great virtues, even while he had earned a tragic name.

"I will live them. I will have faith and hope and love, for I am his daughter," she said. A faint, cool breeze strayed through the aspens, rustling the leaves whisperingly, and the slender columbines, gleaming pale in the twilight, lifted their sweet faces.

THE LONE
STAR RANGER

INTRODUCTION

It may seem strange to you that out of all the stories I heard on the Rio Grande I should choose as first that of Buck Duane—outlaw and gunman.

But, indeed, Ranger Coffee's story of the last of the Duanes has haunted me, and I have given full rein to imagination and have retold it in my own way. It deals with the old law—the old border days—therefore it is better first. Soon, perchance, I shall have the pleasure of writing of the border of to-day, which in Joe Sitter's laconic speech, "Shore is 'most as bad an' wild as ever!"

In the North and East there is a popular idea that the frontier of the West is a thing long past, and remembered now only in stories. As I think of this I remember Ranger Sitter when he made that remark, while he grimly stroked an unhealed bullet wound. And I remember the giant Vaughn, that typical son of stalwart Texas, sitting there quietly with bandaged head, his thoughtful eye boding ill to the outlaw who had ambushed him. Only a few months have passed since then—when I had my memorable sojourn with you—and yet, in that short time, Russell and Moore have crossed the Divide, like Rangers.

Gentlemen,—I have the honor to dedicate this book to you, and the hope that it shall fall to my lot to tell the world the truth about a strange, unique, and misunderstood body of men—the Texas Rangers—who made the great Lone Star State habitable, who never know peaceful rest and sleep, who are passing, who surely will not be forgotten and will some day come into their own.

Zane Grey.

BOOK I

THE OUTLAW

CHAPTER 1

So it was in him, then—an inherited fighting instinct, a driving intensity to kill. He was the last of the Duanes, that old fighting stock of
Texas. But not the memory of his dead father, nor the pleading of his
soft-voiced mother, nor the warning of this uncle who stood before him
now, had brought to Buck Duane so much realization of the dark passionate strain in his blood. It was the recurrence, a hundredfold increased
in power, of a strange emotion that for the last three years had arisen in
him.

"Yes, Cal Bain's in town, full of bad whisky an' huntin' for you," repeated the elder man, gravely.

"It's the second time," muttered Duane, as if to himself.

"Son, you can't avoid a meetin'. Leave town till Cal sobers up. He
ain't got it in for you when he's not drinkin'."

"But what's he want me for?" demanded Duane. "To insult me again?
I won't stand that twice."

"He's got a fever that's rampant in Texas these days, my boy. He
wants gun-play. If he meets you he'll try to kill you."

Here it stirred in Duane again, that bursting gush of blood, like a
wind of flame shaking all his inner being, and subsiding to leave him
strangely chilled.

"Kill me! What for?" he asked.

"Lord knows there ain't any reason. But what's that to do with most

of the shootin' these days? Didn't five cowboys over to Everall's kill one
another dead all because they got to jerkin' at a quirt among themselves?
An' Cal has no reason to love you. His girl was sweet on you."

"I quit when I found out she was his girl."

"I reckon she ain't quit. But never mind her or reasons. Cal's here,
just drunk enough to be ugly. He's achin' to kill somebody. He's one of
them four-flush gun-fighters. He'd like to be thought bad. There's a lot
of wild cowboys who 're ambitious for a reputation. They talk about how
quick they are on the draw. They ape Bland, an' King Fisher, an' Hardin,
an' all the big outlaws. They make threats about joinin' the gangs along
the Rio Grande. They laugh at the sheriffs an' brag about how they'd fix
the rangers. Cal's sure not much for you to bother with, if you only keep
out of his way."

"You mean for me to run?" asked Duane, in scorn.

"I reckon I wouldn't put it that way. Just avoid him. Buck, I'm not
afraid Cal would get you if you met down there in town. You've your father's eye an' his slick hand with a gun. What I'm most afraid of is that
you'll kill Bain."

Duane was silent, letting his uncle's earnest words sink in, trying to
realize their significance.

"If Texas ever recovers from that fool war an' kills off these outlaws,
why, a young man will have a lookout," went on the uncle. "You're
twenty-three now, an' a powerful sight of a fine fellow, barrin' your temper. You've a chance in life. But if you go gun-fightin', if you kill a man,
you're ruined. Then you'll kill another. It'll be the same old story. An' the
rangers would make you an outlaw. The rangers mean law an' order for
Texas. This even-break business doesn't work with them. If you resist arrest they'll kill you. If you submit to arrest, then you go to jail, an' mebbe
you hang."

"I'd never hang," muttered Duane, darkly.

"I reckon you wouldn't," replied the old man. "You'd be like your father. He was ever ready to draw—too ready. In times like these, with the
Texas Rangers enforcin' the law, your Dad would have been driven to the
river. An', son, I'm afraid you're a chip off the old block. Can't you hold
in—keep your temper—run away from trouble? Because it'll only result
in you gettin' the worst of it in the end. Your father was killed in a street-

fight. An' it was told of him that he shot twice after a bullet had passed through his heart. Think of the terrible nature of a man to be able to do that. If you have any such blood in you, never give it a chance."

"What you say is all very well, uncle," returned Duane, "but the only way out for me is to run, and I won't do it. Cal Bain and his outfit have already made me look like a coward. He says I'm afraid to come out and face him. A man simply can't stand that in this country. Besides, Cal would shoot me in the back some day if I didn't face him."

"Well, then, what 're you goin' to do?" inquired the elder man.

"I haven't decided—yet."

"No, but you're comin' to it mighty fast. That damned spell is workin' in you. You're different to-day. I remember how you used to be moody an' lose your temper an' talk wild. Never was much afraid of you then. But now you're gettin' cool an' quiet, an' you think deep, an' I don't like the light in your eye. It reminds me of your father."

"I wonder what dad would say to me to-day if he were alive and here," said Duane.

"What do you think? What could you expect of a man who never wore a glove on his right hand for twenty years?"

"Well, he'd hardly have said much. Dad never talked. But he would have done a lot. And I guess I'll go down-town and let Cal Bain find me."

Then followed a long silence, during which Duane sat with downcast eyes, and the uncle appeared lost in sad thought of the future. Presently he turned to Duane with an expression that denoted resignation, and yet a spirit which showed wherein they were of the same blood.

"You've got a fast horse—the fastest I know of in this country. After you meet Bain hurry back home. I'll have a saddle-bag packed for you and the horse ready."

With that he turned on his heel and went into the house, leaving Duane to revolve in his mind his singular speech. Buck wondered presently if he shared his uncle's opinion of the result of a meeting between himself and Bain. His thoughts were vague. But on the instant of final decision, when he had settled with himself that he would meet Bain, such a storm of passion assailed him that he felt as if he was being shaken with ague. Yet it was all internal, inside his breast, for his hand was like a rock and, for all he could see, not a muscle about him quivered. He had no fear of Bain or of any other man; but a vague fear of himself, of this strange force in him, made him ponder and shake his head. It was as if he had not all to say in this matter. There appeared to have been in him a reluctance to let himself go, and some voice, some spirit from a distance, something he was not accountable for, had compelled him. That hour of Duane's life was like years of actual living, and in it he became a thoughtful man.

He went into the house and buckled on his belt and gun. The gun was a Colt .45, six-shot, and heavy, with an ivory handle. He had packed it, on and off, for five years. Before that it had been used by his father. There were a number of notches filed in the bulge of the ivory handle. This gun was the one his father had fired twice after being shot through the heart, and his hand had stiffened so tightly upon it in the death-grip that his fingers had to be pried open. It had never been drawn upon any man since it had come into Duane's possession. But the cold, bright polish of the weapon showed how it had been used. Duane could draw it with inconceivable rapidity, and at twenty feet he could split a card pointing edgewise toward him.

Duane wished to avoid meeting his mother. Fortunately, as he thought, she was away from home. He went out and down the path toward the gate. The air was full of the fragrance of blossoms and the melody of birds. Outside in the road a neighbor woman stood talking to a countryman in a wagon; they spoke to him; and he heard, but did not reply. Then he began to stride down the road toward the town.

Wellston was a small town, but important in that unsettled part of the great state because it was the trading-center of several hundred miles of territory. On the main street there were perhaps fifty buildings, some brick, some frame, mostly adobe, and one-third of the lot, and by far the most prosperous, were saloons. From the road Duane turned into this street. It was a wide thoroughfare lined by hitching-rails and saddled horses and vehicles of various kinds. Duane's eye ranged down the street, taking in all at a glance, particularly persons moving leisurely up and down. Not a cowboy was in sight. Duane slackened his stride, and by the time he reached Sol White's place, which was the first saloon, he was walking slowly. Several people spoke to him and turned to look back after they had passed. He paused at the door of White's saloon, took a sharp survey of the interior, then stepped inside.

The saloon was large and cool, full of men and noise and smoke. The noise ceased upon his entrance, and the silence ensuing presently broke to the clink of Mexican silver dollars at a *monte* table. Sol White, who was behind the bar, straightened up when he saw Duane; then, without speaking, he bent over to rinse a glass. All eyes except those of the Mexican gamblers were turned upon Duane; and these glances were keen, speculative, questioning. These men knew Bain was looking for trouble; they probably had heard his boasts. But what did Duane intend to do? Several of the cowboys and ranchers present exchanged glances. Duane had been weighed by unerring Texas instinct, by men who all packed guns. The boy was the son of his father. Whereupon they greeted him and returned to their drinks and cards. Sol White stood with his big red hands out upon the bar; he was a tall, raw-boned Texan with a long mustache waxed to sharp points.

"Howdy, Buck," was his greeting to Duane. He spoke carelessly and averted his dark gaze for an instant.

"Howdy, Sol," replied Duane, slowly. "Say, Sol, I hear there's a gent in town looking for me bad."

"Reckon there is, Buck," replied White. "He came in heah aboot an hour ago. Shore he was some riled an' a-roarin' for gore. Told me confidential a certain party had given you a white silk scarf, an' he was hell-bent on wearin' it home spotted red."

"Anybody with him?" queried Duane.

"Burt an' Sam Outcalt an' a little cowpuncher I never seen before. They-all was coaxin' him to leave town. But he's looked on the flowin' glass, Buck, an' he's heah for keeps."

"Why doesn't Sheriff Oaks lock him up if he's that bad?"

"Oaks went away with the rangers. There's been another raid at Flesher's ranch. The King Fisher gang, likely. An' so the town's shore wide open."

Duane stalked outdoors and faced down the street. He walked the whole length of the long block, meeting many people—farmers, ranchers, clerks, merchants, Mexicans, cowboys, and women. It was a singular fact that when he turned to retrace his steps the street was almost empty. He had not returned a hundred yards on his way when the street was wholly deserted. A few heads protruded from doors and around corners.

That main street of Wellston saw some such situation every few days. If it was an instinct for Texans to fight, it was also instinctive for them to sense with remarkable quickness the signs of a coming gun-play. Rumor could not fly so swiftly. In less than ten minutes everybody who had been on the street or in the shops knew that Buck Duane had come forth to meet his enemy.

Duane walked on. When he came to within fifty paces of a saloon he swerved out into the middle of the street, stood there for a moment, then went ahead and back to the sidewalk. He passed on in this way the length of the block. Sol White was standing in the door of his saloon.

"Buck, I'm a-tippin' you off," he said, quick and low-voiced. "Cal Bain's over at Everall's. If he's a-huntin' you bad, as he brags, he'll show there."

Duane crossed the street and started down. Notwithstanding White's statement Duane was wary and slow at every door. Nothing happened, and he traversed almost the whole length of the block without seeing a person. Everall's place was on the corner.

Duane knew himself to be cold, steady. He was conscious of a strange fury that made him want to leap ahead. He seemed to long for this encounter more than anything he had ever wanted. But, vivid as were his sensations, he felt as if in a dream.

Before he reached Everall's he heard loud voices, one of which was raised high. Then the short door swung outward as if impelled by a vigorous hand. A bow-legged cowboy wearing woolly chaps burst out upon the sidewalk. At sight of Duane he seemed to bound into the air, and he uttered a savage roar.

Duane stopped in his tracks at the outer edge of the sidewalk, perhaps a dozen rods from Everall's door.

If Bain was drunk he did not show it in his movement. He swaggered forward, rapidly closing up the gap. Red, sweaty, disheveled, and hatless, his face distorted and expressive of the most malignant intent, he was a wild and sinister figure. He had already killed a man, and this showed in his demeanor. His hands were extended before him, the right hand a little lower than the left. At every step he bellowed his rancor in speech mostly curses. Gradually he slowed his walk, then halted. A good twenty-five paces separated the men.

"Won't nothin' make you draw, you—!" he shouted, fiercely.

"I'm waitin' on you, Cal," replied Duane.

Bain's right hand stiffened—moved. Duane threw his gun as a boy throws a ball underhand—a draw his father had taught him. He pulled twice, his shots almost as one. Bain's big Colt boomed while it was pointed downward and he was falling. His bullet scattered dust and gravel at Duane's feet. He fell loosely, without contortion.

In a flash all was reality for Duane. He went forward and held his gun ready for the slightest movement on the part of Bain. But Bain lay upon his back, and all that moved were his breast and his eyes. How strangely the red had left his face—and also the distortion! The devil that had showed in Bain was gone. He was sober and conscious. He tried to speak, but failed. His eyes expressed something pitifully human. They changed—rolled—set blankly.

Duane drew a deep breath and sheathed his gun. He felt calm and cool, glad the fray was over. One violent expression burst from him. "The fool!"

When he looked up there were men around him.

"Plumb center," said one.

Another, a cowboy who evidently had just left the gaming-table, leaned down and pulled open Bain's shirt. He had the ace of spades in his hand. He laid it on Bain's breast, and the black figure on the card covered the two bullet-holes just over Bain's heart.

Duane wheeled and hurried away. He heard another man say:

"Reckon Cal got what he deserved. Buck Duane's first gun-play. Like father like son!"

CHAPTER 2

A thought kept repeating itself to Duane, and it was that he might have spared himself concern through his imagining how awful it would be to kill a man. He had no such feeling now. He had rid the community of a drunken, bragging, quarrelsome cowboy.

When he came to the gate of his home and saw his uncle there with a mettlesome horse, saddled, with canteen, rope, and bags all in place, a subtle shock pervaded his spirit. It had slipped his mind—the consequence of his act. But sight of the horse and the look of his uncle recalled the fact that he must now become a fugitive. An unreasonable anger took hold of him.

"The damned fool!" he exclaimed, hotly. "Meeting Bain wasn't much, Uncle Jim. He dusted my boots, that's all. And for that I've got to go on the dodge."

"Son, you killed him—then?" asked the uncle, huskily.

"Yes. I stood over him—watched him die. I did as I would have been done by."

"I knew it. Long ago I saw it comin'. But now we can't stop to cry over spilt blood. You've got to leave town an' this part of the country."

"Mother!" exclaimed Duane.

"She's away from home. You can't wait. I'll break it to her—what she always feared."

Suddenly Duane sat down and covered his face with his hands.

"My God! Uncle, what have I done?" His broad shoulders shook.

"Listen, son, an' remember what I say," replied the elder man, earnestly. "Don't ever forget. You're not to blame. I'm glad to see you take it this way, because maybe you'll never grow hard an' callous. You're not to blame. This is Texas. You're your father's son. These are wild times. The law as the rangers are laying it down now can't change life all in a minute. Even your mother, who's a good, true woman, has had her share in making you what you are this moment. For she was one of the pioneers—the fightin' pioneers of this state. Those years of wild times, before you was born, developed in her instinct to fight, to save her life, her children, an' that instinct has cropped out in you. It will be many years before it dies out of the boys born in Texas."

"I'm a murderer," said Duane, shuddering.

"No, son, you're not. An' you never will be. But you've got to be an outlaw till time makes it safe for you to come home."

"An outlaw?"

"I said it. If we had money an' influence we'd risk a trial. But we've neither. An' I reckon the scaffold or jail is no place for Buckley Duane. Strike for the wild country, an' wherever you go an' whatever you do—be a man. Live honestly, if that's possible. If it isn't, be as honest as you can. If you have to herd with outlaws try not to become bad. There are outlaws who 're not all bad—many who have been driven to the river by such a deal as this you had. When you get among these men avoid brawls. Don't drink; don't gamble. I needn't tell you what to do if it comes to gun-play, as likely it will. You can't come home. When this thing is lived down, if that time ever comes, I'll get word into the unsettled country. It'll reach you some day. That's all. Remember, be a man. Good-by."

Duane, with blurred sight and contracting throat, gripped his uncle's hand and bade him a wordless farewell. Then he leaped astride the black and rode out of town.

As swiftly as was consistent with a care for his steed, Duane put a distance of fifteen or eighteen miles behind him. With that he slowed up, and the matter of riding did not require all his faculties. He passed several ranches and was seen by men. This did not suit him, and he took an old trail across country. It was a flat region with a poor growth of mesquite and prickly-pear cactus. Occasionally he caught a glimpse of low hills in the distance. He had hunted often in that section, and knew where to find grass and water. When he reached this higher ground he did not, however, halt at the first favorable camping-spot, but went on and on. Once he came out upon the brow of a hill and saw a considerable stretch of country beneath him. It had the gray sameness characterizing all that he had traversed. He seemed to want to see wide spaces—to get a glimpse of the great wilderness lying somewhere beyond to the southwest. It was sunset when he decided to camp at a likely spot he came across. He led the horse to water, and then began searching through the shallow valley for a suitable place to camp. He passed by old camp-sites that he well remembered. These, however, did not strike his fancy this time, and the significance of the change in him did not occur at the moment. At last he found a secluded spot, under cover of thick mesquites and oaks, at a goodly distance from the old trail. He took saddle and pack off the horse. He looked among his effects for a hobble, and, finding that his uncle had failed to put one in, he suddenly remembered that he seldom used a hobble, and never on this horse. He cut a few feet off the end of his lasso and used that. The horse, unused to such hampering of his free movements, had to be driven out upon the grass.

Duane made a small fire, prepared and ate his supper. This done, ending the work of that day, he sat down and filled his pipe. Twilight had waned into dusk. A few wan stars had just begun to show and brighten. Above the low continuous hum of insects sounded the evening carol of robins. Presently the birds ceased their singing, and then the quiet was more noticeable. When night set in and the place seemed all the more isolated and lonely for that, Duane had a sense of relief.

It dawned upon him all at once that he was nervous, watchful, sleepless. The fact caused him surprise, and he began to think back, to take note of his late actions and their motives. The change one day had wrought amazed him. He who had always been free, easy, happy, especially when out alone in the open, had become in a few short hours bound, serious, preoccupied. The silence that had once been sweet now meant nothing to him except a medium whereby he might the better hear the sounds of pursuit. The loneliness, the night, the wild, that had always been beautiful to him, now only conveyed a sense of safety for the present. He watched, he listened, he thought. He felt tired, yet had no inclination to rest. He intended to be off by dawn, heading toward the southwest. Had he a destination? It was vague as his knowledge of that great waste of mesquite and rock bordering the Rio Grande. Somewhere out there was a refuge. For he was a fugitive from justice, an outlaw.

This being an outlaw then meant eternal vigilance. No home, no rest, no sleep, no content, no life worth the living! He must be a lone wolf or he must herd among men obnoxious to him. If he worked for an honest living he still must hide his identity and take risks of detection. If he did not work on some distant outlying ranch, how was he to live? The idea of stealing was repugnant to him. The future seemed gray and somber enough. And he was twenty-three years old.

Why had this hard life been imposed upon him?

The bitter question seemed to start a strange iciness that stole along his veins. What was wrong with him? He stirred the few sticks of mesquite into a last flickering blaze. He was cold, and for some reason he wanted some light. The black circle of darkness weighed down upon him, closed in around him. Suddenly he sat bolt upright and then froze in that position. He had heard a step. It was behind him—no—on the side. Some one was there. He forced his hand down to his gun, and the touch of cold steel was another icy shock. Then he waited. But all was silent—silent as only a wilderness arroyo can be, with its low murmuring of wind in the mesquite. Had he heard a step? He began to breathe again.

But what was the matter with the light of his camp-fire? It had taken on a strange green luster and seemed to be waving off into the outer shadows. Duane heard no step, saw no movement; nevertheless, there was another present at that camp-fire vigil. Duane saw him. He lay there in the middle of the green brightness, prostrate, motionless, dying. Cal Bain! His features were wonderfully distinct, clearer than any cameo, more sharply outlined than those of any picture. It was a hard face softening at the threshold of eternity. The red tan of sun, the coarse signs of drunkenness, the ferocity and hate so characteristic of Bain were no longer there. This face represented a different Bain, showed all that was human in him fading, fading as swiftly as it blanched white. The lips wanted to speak, but had not the power. The eyes held an agony of thought. They revealed what might have been possible for this man if he lived—that he saw his mistake too late. Then they rolled, set blankly, and closed in death.

That haunting visitation left Duane sitting there in a cold sweat, a remorse gnawing at his vitals, realizing the curse that was on him. He divined that never would he be able to keep off that phantom. He remembered how his father had been eternally pursued by the furies of accusing guilt, how he had never been able to forget in work or in sleep those men he had killed.

The hour was late when Duane's mind let him sleep, and then dreams troubled him. In the morning he bestirred himself so early that in the gray gloom he had difficulty in finding his horse. Day had just broken when he struck the old trail again.

He rode hard all morning and halted in a shady spot to rest and graze his horse. In the afternoon he took to the trail at an easy trot. The country grew wilder. Bald, rugged mountains broke the level of the monotonous horizon. About three in the afternoon he came to a little river which marked the boundary line of his hunting territory.

The decision he made to travel upstream for a while was owing to two facts: the river was high with quicksand bars on each side, and he felt reluctant to cross into that region where his presence alone meant that he was a marked man. The bottom-lands through which the river wound to the southwest were more inviting than the barrens he had traversed. The rest of that day he rode leisurely upstream. At sunset he penetrated the brakes of willow and cottonwood to spend the night. It seemed to him that in this lonely cover he would feel easy and content. But he did not. Every feeling, every imagining he had experienced the previous night returned somewhat more vividly and accentuated by newer ones of the same intensity and color.

In this kind of travel and camping he spent three more days, during which he crossed a number of trails, and one road where cattle—stolen cattle, probably—had recently passed. This time exhausted his supply of food, except salt, pepper, coffee, and sugar, of which he had a quantity. There were deer in the brakes; but, as he could not get close enough to kill them with a revolver, he had to satisfy himself with a rabbit. He knew he might as well content himself with the hard fare that assuredly would be his lot.

Somewhere up this river there was a village called Huntsville. It was distant about a hundred miles from Wellston, and had a reputation throughout southwestern Texas. He had never been there. The fact was this reputation was such that honest travelers gave the town a wide berth. Duane had considerable money for him in his possession, and he concluded to visit Huntsville, if he could find it, and buy a stock of provisions.

The following day, toward evening, he happened upon a road which he believed might lead to the village. There were a good many fresh horse-tracks in the sand, and these made him thoughtful. Nevertheless, he followed the road, proceeding cautiously. He had not gone very far when the sound of rapid hoof-beats caught his ears. They came from his rear. In the darkening twilight he could not see any great distance back along the road. Voices, however, warned him that these riders, whoever they were, had approached closer than he liked. To go farther down the road was not to be thought of, so he turned a little way in among the mesquites and halted, hoping to escape being seen or heard. As he was now a fugitive, it seemed every man was his enemy and pursuer.

The horsemen were fast approaching. Presently they were abreast of Duane's position, so near that he could hear the creak of saddles, the clink of spurs.

"Shore he crossed the river below," said one man.

"I reckon you're right, Bill. He's slipped us," replied another.

Rangers or a posse of ranchers in pursuit of a fugitive! The knowledge gave Duane a strange thrill. Certainly they could not have been hunting him. But the feeling their proximity gave him was identical to what it would have been had he been this particular hunted man. He held his breath; he clenched his teeth; he pressed a quieting hand upon his horse. Suddenly he became aware that these horsemen had halted. They were whispering. He could just make out a dark group closely massed. What had made them halt so suspiciously?

"You're wrong, Bill," said a man, in a low but distinct voice. "This idee of hearin' a hoss heave! You're wuss'n a ranger. An' you're hell-bent on killin' that rustler. Now I say let's go home an' eat."

"Wal, I'll just take a look at the sand," replied the man called Bill.

Duane heard the clink of spurs on steel stirrup and the thud of boots on the ground. There followed a short silence which was broken by a sharply breathed exclamation.

Duane waited for no more. They had found his trail. He spurred his horse straight into the brush. At the second crashing bound there came yells from the road, and then shots. Duane heard the hiss of a bullet close by his ear, and as it struck a branch it made a peculiar singing sound. These shots and the proximity of that lead missile roused in Duane a quick, hot resentment which mounted into a passion almost ungovernable. He must escape, yet it seemed that he did not care whether he did or not. Something grim kept urging him to halt and return the fire of these men. After running a couple of hundred yards he raised himself from over the pommel, where he had bent to avoid the stinging branches, and tried to guide his horse. In the dark shadows under mesquites and cottonwoods he was hard put to it to find open passage; however, he succeeded so well and made such little noise that gradually he drew away from his pursuers. The sound of their horses crashing through the thickets died away. Duane reined in and listened. He had distanced them. Probably they would go into camp till daylight, then follow his tracks. He started on again, walking his horse, and peered sharply at the ground, so that he might take advantage of the first trail he crossed. It seemed a long while until he came upon one. He followed it until a late hour, when, striking the willow brakes again and hence the neighborhood of the river, he picketed his horse and lay down to rest. But he did not sleep. His mind bitterly revolved the fate that had come upon him. He made efforts to think of other things, but in vain. Every moment he expected the chill, the sense of loneliness that yet was ominous of a strange visitation, the peculiarly imagined lights and shades of the night—these things that presaged the coming of Cal Bain. Doggedly Duane fought against the insidious phantom. He kept telling himself that it was just imagination, that it would wear off in time. Still in his heart he did not believe what he hoped. But he would not give up; he would not accept the ghost of his victim as a reality.

Gray dawn found him in the saddle again headed for the river. Half an hour of riding brought him to the dense chaparral and willow thickets. These he threaded to come at length to the ford. It was a gravel bottom, and therefore an easy crossing. Once upon the opposite shore he reined in his horse and looked darkly back. This action marked his ac-knowledgment of his situation: he had voluntarily sought the refuge of the outlaws; he was beyond the pale. A bitter and passionate curse passed his lips as he spurred his horse into the brakes on that alien shore.

He rode perhaps twenty miles, not sparing his horse nor caring whether or not he left a plain trail.

"Let them hunt me!" he muttered.

When the heat of the day began to be oppressive, and hunger and thirst made themselves manifest, Duane began to look about him for a place to halt for the noon-hours. The trail led into a road which was hard packed and smooth from the tracks of cattle. He doubted not that he had come across one of the roads used by border raiders. He headed into it, and had scarcely traveled a mile when, turning a curve, he came point-blank upon a single horseman riding toward him. Both riders wheeled their mounts sharply and were ready to run and shoot back. Not more than a hundred paces separated them. They stood then for a moment watching each other.

"Mawnin', stranger," called the man, dropping his hand from his hip.

"Howdy," replied Duane, shortly.

They rode toward each other, closing half the gap, then they halted again.

"I seen you ain't no ranger," called the rider, "an' shore I ain't none."

He laughed loudly, as if he had made a joke.

"How'd you know I wasn't a ranger?" asked Duane, curiously. Some-how he had instantly divined that this horseman was no officer, or even a rancher trailing stolen stock.

"Wal," said the fellow, starting his horse forward at a walk, "a ranger'd never git ready to run the other way from one man."

He laughed again. He was small and wiry, slouchy of attire, and armed to the teeth, and he bestrode a fine bay horse. He had quick, danc-ing brown eyes, at once frank and bold, and a coarse, bronzed face. Evi-dently he was a good-natured ruffian.

Duane acknowledged the truth of the assertion, and turned over in his mind how shrewdly the fellow had guessed him to be a hunted man.

"My name's Luke Stevens, an' I hail from the river. Who 're you?" said the stranger.

Duane was silent.

"I reckon you're Buck Duane," went on Stevens. "I heerd you was a damn bad man with a gun."

This time Duane laughed, not at the doubtful compliment, but at the idea that the first outlaw he met should know him. Here was proof of how swiftly facts about gun-play traveled on the Texas border.

"Wal, Buck," said Stevens, in a friendly manner, "I ain't presumin' on your time or company. I see you're headin' fer the river. But will you stop long enough to stake a feller to a bite of grub?"

"I'm out of grub, and pretty hungry myself," admitted Duane.

"Been pushin' your hoss, I see. Wal, I reckon you'd better stock up before you hit thet stretch of country."

He made a wide sweep of his right arm, indicating the southwest, and there was that in his action which seemed significant of a vast and barren region.

"Stock up?" queried Duane, thoughtfully.

"Shore. A feller has jest got to eat. I can rustle along without whisky, but not without grub. Thet's what makes it so embarrassin' travelin' these parts dodgin' your shadow. Now, I'm on my way to Mercer. It's a little two-bit town up the river a ways. I'm goin' to pack out some grub."

Stevens's tone was inviting. Evidently he would welcome Duane's companionship, but he did not openly say so. Duane kept silence, however, and then Stevens went on.

"Stranger, in this here country two's a crowd. It's safer. I never was much of this lone-wolf dodgin', though I've done it of necessity. It takes a damn good man to travel alone any length of time. Why, I've been thet sick I was jest achin' fer some ranger to come along an' plug me. Give me a pardner any day. Now, mebbe you're not thet kind of a feller, an' I'm shore not presumin' to ask. But I jest declares myself sufficient."

"You mean you'd like me to go with you?" asked Duane.

Stevens grinned. "Wal, I should smile. I'd be particular proud to be braced with a man of your reputation."

"See here, my good fellow, that's all nonsense," declared Duane, in some haste.

"Shore I think modesty becomin' to a youngster," replied Stevens. "I hate a brag. An' I've no use fer these four-flush cowboys thet 're always lookin' fer trouble an' talkin' gun-play. Buck, I don't know much about you. But every man who's lived along the Texas border remembers a lot about your dad. It was expected of you, I reckon, an' much of your rep was established before you throwed your gun. I jest heerd that you was lightnin' on the draw, an' when you cut loose with a gun, why the figger on the ace of spades would cover your cluster of bullet-holes. Thet's the word thet's gone down the border. It's the kind of reputation most sure to fly far an' swift ahead of a man in this country. An' the safest, too; I'll gamble on thet. It's the land of the draw. I see now you're only a boy, though you're shore a strappin' husky one. Now, Buck, I'm not a spring chicken, an' I've been long on the dodge. Mebbe a little of my society won't hurt you none. You'll need to learn the country."

There was something sincere and likable about this outlaw.

"I dare say you're right," replied Duane, quietly. "And I'll go to Mercer with you."

Next moment he was riding down the road with Stevens. Duane had never been much of a talker, and now he found speech difficult. But his companion did not seem to mind that. He was a jocose, voluble fellow, probably glad now to hear the sound of his own voice. Duane listened, and sometimes he thought with a pang of the distinction of name and heritage of blood his father had left to him.

CHAPTER 3

Late that day, a couple of hours before sunset, Duane and Stevens, having rested their horses in the shade of some mesquites near the town of Mercer, saddled up and prepared to move.

"Buck, as we're lookin' fer grub, an' not trouble, I reckon you'd better hang up out here," Stevens was saying, as he mounted. "You see, towns an' sheriffs an' rangers are always lookin' fer new fellers gone bad. They sort of forget most of the old boys, except those as are plumb bad. "Now nobody in Mercer will take notice of me. Reckon there's been a thousand men run into the river country to become outlaws since yours truly. You jest wait here an' be ready to ride hard. Mebbe my besettin' sin will go operatin' in spite of my good intentions. In which case there'll be—"

His pause was significant. He grinned, and his brown eyes danced with a kind of wild humor.

"Stevens, have you got any money?" asked Duane.

"Money!" exclaimed Luke, blankly. "Say, I haven't owned a two-bit piece since—wal, fer some time."

"I'll furnish money for grub," returned Duane. "And for whisky, too, providing you hurry back here—without making trouble."

"Shore you're a downright good pard," declared Stevens, in admiration, as he took the money. "I give my word, Buck, an' I'm here to say I never broke it yet. Lay low, an' look fer me back quick."

With that he spurred his horse and rode out of the mesquites toward the town. At that distance, about a quarter of a mile, Mercer appeared to be a cluster of low adobe houses set in a grove of cottonwoods. Pastures of alfalfa were dotted by horses and cattle. Duane saw a sheep-herder driving in a meager flock.

Presently Stevens rode out of sight into the town. Duane waited, hoping the outlaw would make good his word. Probably not a quarter of an hour had elapsed when Duane heard the clear reports of a Winchester rifle, the clatter of rapid hoof-beats, and yells unmistakably the kind to mean danger for a man like Stevens. Duane mounted and rode to the edge of the mesquites.

He saw a cloud of dust down the road and a bay horse running fast. Stevens apparently had not been wounded by any of the shots, for he had a steady seat in his saddle and his riding, even at that moment, struck Duane as admirable. He carried a large pack over the pommel, and he kept looking back. The shots had ceased, but the yells increased. Duane saw several men running and waving their arms. Then he spurred his horse and got into a swift stride, so Stevens would not pass him. Presently the outlaw caught up with him. Stevens was grinning, but there was now no fun in the dancing eyes. It was a devil that danced in them. His face seemed a shade paler.

"Was jest comin' out of the store," yelled Stevens. "Run plumb into a rancher—who knowed me. He opened up with a rifle. Think they'll chase us."

They covered several miles before there were any signs of pursuit, and when horsemen did move into sight out of the cottonwoods Duane and his companion steadily drew farther away.

"No hosses in thet bunch to worry us," called out Stevens.

Duane had the same conviction, and he did not look back again. He rode somewhat to the fore, and was constantly aware of the rapid thudding of hoofs behind, as Stevens kept close to him. At sunset they reached the willow brakes and the river. Duane's horse was winded and lashed with sweat and lather. It was not until the crossing had been accomplished that Duane halted to rest his animal. Stevens was riding up the low, sandy bank. He reeled in the saddle. With an exclamation of surprise Duane leaped off and ran to the outlaw's side.

Stevens was pale, and his face bore beads of sweat. The whole front of his shirt was soaked with blood.

"You're shot!" cried Duane.

"Wal, who 'n hell said I wasn't? Would you mind givin' me a lift—on this here pack?"

Duane lifted the heavy pack down and then helped Stevens to dismount. The outlaw had a bloody foam on his lips, and he was spitting blood.

"Oh, why didn't you *say* so!" cried Duane. "I never thought. You seemed all right."

"Wal, Luke Stevens may be as gabby as an old woman, but sometimes he doesn't say anythin'. It wouldn't have done no good."

Duane bade him sit down, removed his shirt, and washed the blood from his breast and back. Stevens had been shot in the breast, fairly low down, and the bullet had gone clear through him. His ride, holding himself and that heavy pack in the saddle, had been a feat little short of marvelous. Duane did not see how it had been possible, and he felt no hope for the outlaw. But he plugged the wounds and bound them tightly.

"Feller's name was Brown," Stevens said. "Me an' him fell out over a hoss I stole from him over in Huntsville. We had a shootin'-scrape then. Wal, as I was saddlin' my hoss back there in Mercer I seen this Brown, an' seen him before he seen me. Could have killed him, too. But I wasn't breakin' my word to you. I kind of hoped he wouldn't spot me. But he did—an' fust shot he got me here. What do you think of this hole?"

"It's pretty bad," replied Duane; and he could not look the cheerful outlaw in the eyes.

"I reckon it is. Wal, I've had some bad wounds I lived over. Guess mebbe I can stand this one. Now, Buck, get me some place in the brakes, leave me some grub an' water at my hand, an' then you clear out."

"Leave you here alone?" asked Duane, sharply.

"Shore. You see, I can't keep up with you. Brown an' his friends will foller us acrost the river a ways. You've got to think of number one in this game."

"What would you do in my case?" asked Duane, curiously.

"Wal, I reckon I'd clear out an' save my hide," replied Stevens.

Duane felt inclined to doubt the outlaw's assertion. For his own part he decided his conduct without further speech. First he watered the horses, filled canteens and water-bag, and then tied the pack upon his own horse. That done, he lifted Stevens upon his horse, and, holding him in the saddle, turned into the brakes, being careful to pick out hard or grassy ground that left little signs of tracks. Just about dark he ran across a trail that Stevens said was a good one to take into the wild country.

"Reckon we'd better keep right on in the dark—till I drop," concluded Stevens, with a laugh.

All that night Duane, gloomy and thoughtful, attentive to the wounded outlaw, walked the trail and never halted till daybreak. He was tired then and very hungry. Stevens seemed in bad shape, although he was still spirited and cheerful. Duane made camp. The outlaw refused food, but asked for both whisky and water. Then he stretched out.

"Buck, will you take off my boots?" he asked, with a faint smile on his pallid face.

Duane removed them, wondering if the outlaw had the thought that he did not want to die with his boots on. Stevens seemed to read his mind.

"Buck, my old daddy used to say thet I was born to be hanged. But I wasn't—an' dyin' with your boots on is the next wust way to croak."

"You've a chance to—to get over this," said Duane.

"Shore. But I want to be correct about the boots—an' say, pard, if I do go over, jest you remember thet I was appreciatin' of your kindness."

Then he closed his eyes and seemed to sleep.

Duane could not find water for the horses, but there was an abundance of dew–wet grass upon which he hobbled them. After that was done he prepared himself a much-needed meal. The sun was getting warm when he lay down to sleep, and when he awoke it was sinking in the west. Stevens was still alive, for he breathed heavily. The horses were in sight. All was quiet except the hum of insects in the brush. Duane listened awhile, then rose and went for the horses.

When he returned with them he found Stevens awake, bright-eyed, cheerful as usual, and apparently stronger.

"Wal, Buck, I'm still with you an' good fer another night's ride," he said. "Guess about all I need now is a big pull on thet bottle. Help me, will you? There! thet was bully. I ain't swallowin' my blood this evenin'. Mebbe I've bled all there was in me."

While Duane got a hurried meal for himself, packed up the little outfit, and saddled the horses Stevens kept on talking. He seemed to be in a hurry to tell Duane all about the country. Another night ride would put them beyond fear of pursuit, within striking distance of the Rio Grande and the hiding-places of the outlaws.

When it came time for mounting the horses Stevens said, "Reckon you can pull on my boots once more." In spite of the laugh accompanying the words Duane detected a subtle change in the outlaw's spirit.

On this night travel was facilitated by the fact that the trail was broad enough for two horses abreast, enabling Duane to ride while upholding Stevens in the saddle.

The difficulty most persistent was in keeping the horses in a walk. They were used to a trot, and that kind of gait would not do for Stevens. The red died out of the west; a pale afterglow prevailed for a while; darkness set in; then the broad expanse of blue darkened and the stars brightened. After a while Stevens ceased talking and drooped in his saddle. Duane kept the horses going, however, and the slow hours wore away. Duane thought the quiet night would never break to dawn, that there was no end to the melancholy, brooding plain. But at length a grayness blotted out the stars and mantled the level of mesquite and cactus.

Dawn caught the fugitives at a green camping-site on the bank of a rocky little stream. Stevens fell a dead weight into Duane's arms, and one look at the haggard face showed Duane that the outlaw had taken his last ride. He knew it, too. Yet that cheerfulness prevailed.

"Buck, my feet are orful tired packin' them heavy boots," he said, and seemed immensely relieved when Duane had removed them.

This matter of the outlaw's boots was strange, Duane thought. He made Stevens as comfortable as possible, then attended to his own needs. And the outlaw took up the thread of his conversation where he had left off the night before.

"This trail splits up a ways from here, an' every branch of it leads to a hole where you'll find men—a few, mebbe, like yourself—some like me—an' gangs of no-good hoss-thieves, rustlers, an' such. It's easy livin', Buck. I reckon, though, that you'll not find it easy. You'll never mix in. You'll be a lone wolf. I seen that right off. Wal, if a man can stand the loneliness, an' if he's quick on the draw, mebbe lone-wolfin' it is the best. Shore I don't know. But these fellas in here will be suspicious of a man who goes it alone. If they get a chance they'll kill you."

Stevens asked for water several times. He had forgotten or he did not want the whisky. His voice grew perceptibly weaker.

"Be quiet," said Duane. "Talking uses up your strength."

"Aw, I'll talk till—I'm done," he replied, doggedly. "See here, pard, you can gamble on what I'm tellin' you. An' it 'll be useful. From this camp we'll—you'll meet men right along. An' none of them will be honest men. All the same, some are better 'n others. I've lived along the river fer twelve years. There's three big gangs of outlaws. King Fisher—you know him, I reckon, fer he's half the time livin' among respectable folks. King is a pretty good feller. It 'll do to tie up with him an' his gang. Now, there's Cheseldine, who hangs out in the Rim Rock way up the river. He's an outlaw chief. I never seen him, though I stayed once right in his camp. Late years he's got rich an' keeps back pretty well hid. But Bland—I knowed Bland fer years. An' I haven't any use fer him. Bland has the biggest gang. You ain't likely to miss strikin' his place sometime or other. He's got a regular town, I might say. Shore there's some gamblin' an' gun-fightin' goin' on at Bland's camp all the time. Bland has killed some twenty men, an' thet's not countin' Mexicans."

Here Stevens took another drink and then rested for a while.

"You ain't likely to get on with Bland," he resumed, presently. "You're too strappin' big an' good-lookin' to please the chief. Fer he's got women in his camp. Then he'd be jealous of your possibilities with a gun. Shore I reckon he'd be careful, though. Bland's no fool, an' he loves his hide. I reckon any of the other gangs would be better fer you when you ain't goin' it alone."

Apparently that exhausted the fund of information and advice Stevens had been eager to impart. He lapsed into silence and lay with closed eyes. Meanwhile the sun rose warm; the breeze waved the mesquites; the birds came down to splash in the shallow stream; Duane dozed in a comfortable seat. By and by something roused him. Stevens was once more talking, but with a changed tone.

"Feller's name—was Brown," he rambled. "We fell out—over a hoss I stole from him—in Huntsville. He stole it fust. Brown's one of them sneaks—afraid of the open—he steals an' pretends to be honest. Say, Buck, mebbe you'll meet Brown some day— You an' me are pards now."

"I'll remember, if I ever meet him," said Duane.

That seemed to satisfy the outlaw. Presently he tried to lift his head, but had not the strength. A strange shade was creeping across the bronzed rough face.

"My feet are pretty heavy. Shore you got my boots off?"

Duane held them up, but was not certain that Stevens could see them. The outlaw closed his eyes again and muttered incoherently. Then he fell asleep. Duane believed that sleep was final. The day passed, with Duane watching and waiting. Toward sundown Stevens awoke, and his eyes seemed clearer. Duane went to get some fresh water, thinking his comrade would surely want some. When he returned Stevens made no sign that he wanted anything. There was something bright about him, and suddenly Duane realized what it meant.

"Pard, you—stuck—to me!" the outlaw whispered.

Duane caught a hint of gladness in the voice; he traced a faint surprise in the haggard face. Stevens seemed like a little child.

To Duane the moment was sad, elemental, big, with a burden of mystery he could not understand.

Duane buried him in a shallow arroyo and heaped up a pile of stones to mark the grave. That done, he saddled his comrade's horse, hung the weapons over the pommel; and, mounting his own steed, he rode down the trail in the gathering twilight.

CHAPTER 4

Two days later, about the middle of the forenoon, Duane dragged the two horses up the last ascent of an exceedingly rough trail and found himself on top of the Rim Rock, with a beautiful green valley at his feet, the yellow, sluggish Rio Grande shining in the sun, and the great, wild, mountainous barren of Mexico stretching to the south.

Duane had not fallen in with any travelers. He had taken the likeliest-looking trail he had come across. Where it had led him he had not the slightest idea, except that here was the river, and probably the in-closed valley was the retreat of some famous outlaw.

No wonder outlaws were safe in that wild refuge! Duane had spent the last two days climbing the roughest and most difficult trail he had ever seen. From the looks of the descent he imagined the worst part of his travel was yet to come. Not improbably it was two thousand feet down to the river. The wedge-shaped valley, green with alfalfa and cottonwood, and nestling down amid the bare walls of yellow rock, was a delight and a relief to his tired eyes. Eager to get down to a level and to find a place to rest, Duane began the descent.

The trail proved to be the kind that could not be descended slowly. He kept dodging rocks which his horses loosed behind him. And in a short time he reached the valley, entering at the apex of the wedge. A stream of clear water tumbled out of the rocks here, and most of it ran into irrigation-ditches. His horses drank thirstily. And he drank with that fullness and gratefulness common to the desert traveler finding sweet water. Then he mounted and rode down the valley wondering what would be his reception.

The valley was much larger than it had appeared from the high elevation. Well watered, green with grass and tree, and farmed evidently by good hands, it gave Duane a considerable surprise. Horses and cattle were everywhere. Every clump of cottonwoods surrounded a small adobe house. Duane saw Mexicans working in the fields and horsemen going to and fro. Presently he passed a house bigger than the others with a porch attached. A woman, young and pretty he thought, watched him from a door. No one else appeared to notice him.

Presently the trail widened into a road, and that into a kind of square lined by a number of adobe and log buildings of rudest structure. Within sight were horses, dogs, a couple of steers, Mexican women with children, and white men, all of whom appeared to be doing nothing. His advent created no interest until he rode up to the white men, who were lolling in the shade of a house. This place evidently was a store and saloon, and from the inside came a lazy hum of voices.

As Duane reined to a halt one of the loungers in the shade rose with a loud exclamation:

"Bust me if thet ain't Luke's hoss!"

The others accorded their interest, if not assent, by rising to advance toward Duane.

"How about it, Euchre? Ain't thet Luke's baby?" queried the first man.

"Plain as your nose," replied the fellow called Euchre.

"There ain't no doubt about thet, then," laughed another, "fer Bosomer's nose is shore plain on the landscape."

These men lined up before Duane, and as he coolly regarded them he thought they could have been recognized anywhere as desperadoes. The man called Bosomer, who had stepped forward, had a forbidding face which showed yellow eyes, an enormous nose, and a skin the color of dust, with a thatch of sandy hair.

"Stranger, who are you an' where in the hell did you git thet bay hoss?" he demanded. His yellow eyes took in Stevens's horse, then the weapons hung on the saddle, and finally turned their glinting, hard light upward to Duane.

Duane did not like the tone in which he had been addressed, and he remained silent. At least half his mind seemed busy with curious interest in regard to something that leaped inside him and made his breast feel tight. He recognized it as that strange emotion which had shot through him often of late, and which had decided him to go out to the meeting with Bain. Only now it was different, more powerful.

"Stranger, who are you?" asked another man, somewhat more civilly.

"My name's Duane," replied Duane, curtly.

"An' how'd you come by the hoss?"

Duane answered briefly, and his words were followed by a short silence, during which the men looked at him. Bosomer began to twist the ends of his beard.

"Reckon he's dead, all right, or nobody'd hev his hoss an' guns," presently said Euchre.

"Mister Duane," began Bosomer, in low, stinging tones, "I happen to be Luke Stevens's side-pardner."

Duane looked him over, from dusty, worn-out boots to his slouchy sombrero. That look seemed to inflame Bosomer.

"An' I want the hoss an' them guns," he shouted.

"You or anybody else can have them, for all I care. I just fetched them in. But the pack is mine," replied Duane. "And say, I befriended your pard. If you can't use a civil tongue you'd better cinch it."

"Civil? Haw, haw!" rejoined the outlaw. "I don't know you. How do we know you didn't plug Stevens, an' stole his hoss, an' jest happened to stumble down here?"

"You'll have to take my word, that's all," replied Duane sharply.

"God damn! I ain't takin' your word! Savvy thet? An' I was Luke's pard!"

With that Bosomer wheeled and, pushing his companions aside, he stamped into the saloon, where his voice broke out in a roar.

Duane dismounted and threw his bridle.

"Stranger, Bosomer is shore hot-headed," said the man Euchre. He did not appear unfriendly, nor were the others hostile.

At this juncture several more outlaws crowded out of the door, and the one in the lead was a tall man of stalwart physique. His manner proclaimed him a leader. He had a long face, a flaming red beard, and clear, cold blue eyes that fixed in close scrutiny upon Duane. He was not a Texan; in truth, Duane did not recognize one of these outlaws as native to his state.

"I'm Bland," said the tall man, authoritatively. "Who 're you and what 're you doing here?"

Duane looked at Bland as he had at the others. This outlaw chief appeared to be reasonable, if he was not courteous. Duane told his story again, this time a little more in detail.

"I believe you," replied Bland, at once. "Think I know when a fellow is lying."

"I reckon you're on the right trail," put in Euchre. "Thet about Luke wantin' his boots took off—thet satisfies me. Luke hed a mortal dread of dyin' with his boots on."

At this sally the chief and his men laughed.

"You said Duane—Buck Duane?" queried Bland. "Are you a son of that Duane who was a gun-fighter some years back?"

"Yes," replied Duane.

"Never met him, and glad I didn't," said Bland, with a grim humor. "So you got in trouble and had to go on the dodge? What kind of trouble?"

"Had a fight."

"Fight? Do you mean gun-play?" questioned Bland. He seemed eager, curious, speculative.

"Yes. It ended in gun-play, I'm sorry to say," answered Duane.

"Guess I needn't ask the son of Duane if he killed his man," went on Bland, ironically. "Well, I'm sorry you bucked against trouble in my camp. But as it is, I guess you'd be wise to make yourself scarce."

"Do you mean I'm politely told to move on?" asked Duane, quietly.

"Not exactly that," said Bland, as if irritated. "If this isn't a free place there isn't one on earth. Every man is equal here. Do you want to join my band?"

"No, I don't."

"Well, even if you did I imagine that wouldn't stop Bosomer. He's an ugly fellow. He's one of the few gunmen I've met who wants to kill somebody all the time. Most men like that are four-flushes. But Bosomer is all one color, and that's red. Merely for your own sake I advise you to hit the trail."

"Thanks. But if that's all I'll stay," returned Duane. Even as he spoke he felt that he did not know himself.

Bosomer appeared at the door, pushing men who tried to detain him, and as he jumped clear of a last reaching hand he uttered a snarl like an angry dog. Manifestly the short while he had spent inside the saloon had been devoted to drinking and talking himself into a frenzy. Bland and the other outlaws quickly moved aside, letting Duane stand alone. When Bosomer saw Duane standing motionless and watchful a strange change passed quickly in him. He halted in his tracks, and as he did that the men who had followed him out piled over one another in their hurry to get to one side.

Duane saw all the swift action, felt intuitively the meaning of it, and in Bosomer's sudden change of front. The outlaw was keen, and he had expected a shrinking, or at least a frightened antagonist. Duane knew he was neither. He felt like iron, and yet thrill after thrill ran through him. It was almost as if this situation had been one long familiar to him. Somehow he understood this yellow-eyed Bosomer. The outlaw had come out to kill him. And now, though somewhat checked by the stand of a stranger, he still meant to kill. Like so many desperadoes of his ilk, he was victim of a passion to kill for the sake of killing. Duane divined that no sudden animosity was driving Bosomer. It was just his chance. In that moment murder would have been joy to him. Very likely he had forgotten his pretext for a quarrel. Very probably his faculties were absorbed in conjecture as to Duane's possibilities.

But he did not speak a word. He remained motionless for a long moment, his eyes pale and steady, his right hand like a claw.

That instant gave Duane a power to read in his enemy's eyes the thought that preceded action. But Duane did not want to kill another man. Still he would have to fight, and he decided to cripple Bosomer. When Bosomer's hand moved Duane's gun was spouting fire. Two shots only—both from Duane's gun—and the outlaw fell with his right arm shattered. Bosomer cursed harshly and floundered in the dust, trying to reach the gun with his left hand. His comrades, however, seeing that Duane would not kill unless forced, closed in upon Bosomer and prevented any further madness on his part.

CHAPTER 5

Of the outlaws present Euchre appeared to be the one most inclined to lend friendliness to curiosity; and he led Duane and the horses away to a small adobe shack. He tied the horses in an open shed and removed their saddles. Then, gathering up Stevens's weapons, he invited his visitor to enter the house.

It had two rooms—windows without coverings—bare floors. One room contained blankets, weapons, saddles, and bridles; the other a stone fireplace, rude table and bench, two bunks, a box cupboard, and various blackened utensils.

"Make yourself to home as long as you want to stay," said Euchre. "I ain't rich in this world's goods, but I own what's here, an' you're welcome."

"Thanks. I'll stay awhile and rest. I'm pretty well played out," replied Duane.

Euchre gave him a keen glance.

"Go ahead an' rest. I'll take your horses to grass."

Euchre left Duane alone in the house. Duane relaxed then, and mechanically he wiped the sweat from his face. He was laboring under some kind of a spell or shock which did not pass off quickly. When it had worn away he took off his coat and belt and made himself comfortable on the blankets. And he had a thought that if he rested or slept what difference would it make on the morrow? No rest, no sleep could change the gray outlook of the future. He felt glad when Euchre came bustling in, and for the first time he took notice of the outlaw.

Euchre was old in years. What little hair he had was gray, his face clean-shaven and full of wrinkles; his eyes were half shut from long gazing through the sun and dust. He stooped. But his thin frame denoted strength and endurance still unimpaired.

"Hev a drink or a smoke?" he asked.

Duane shook his head. He had not been unfamiliar with whisky, and he had used tobacco moderately since he was sixteen. But now, strangely, he felt a disgust at the idea of stimulants. He did not understand clearly what he felt. There was that vague idea of something wild in his blood, something that made him fear himself.

Euchre wagged his old head sympathetically. "Reckon you feel a little sick. When it comes to shootin' I run. What's your age?"

"I'm twenty-three," replied Duane.

Euchre showed surprise. "You're only a boy! I thought you thirty anyways. Buck, I heard what you told Bland, an' puttin' thet with my own figgerin', I reckon you're no criminal yet. Throwin' a gun in self-defense—thet ain't no crime!"

Duane, finding relief in talking, told more about himself.

"Huh," replied the old man. "I've been on this river fer years, an' I've seen hundreds of boys come in on the dodge. Most of them, though, was no good. An' thet kind don't last long. This river country has been an' is the refuge fer criminals from all over the states. I've bunked with bank cashiers, forgers, plain thieves, an' out-an'-out murderers, all of which had no bizness on the Texas border. Fellers like Bland are exceptions. He's no Texan—you seen thet. The gang he rules here come from all over, an' they're tough cusses, you can bet on thet. They live fat an' easy. If it wasn't fer the fightin' among themselves they'd shore grow populous. The Rim Rock is no place for a peaceable, decent feller. I heard you tell Bland you wouldn't join his gang. Thet 'll not make him take a likin' to you. Have you any money?"

"Not much," replied Duane.

"Could you live by gamblin'? Are you any good at cards?"

"No."

"You wouldn't steal hosses or rustle cattle?"

"No."

"When your money's gone how 'n hell will you live? There ain't any work a decent feller could do. You can't herd with Mexicans. Why, Bland's men would shoot at you in the fields. What 'll you do, son?"

"God knows," replied Duane, hopelessly. "I'll make my money last as long as possible—then starve."

"Wal, I'm pretty pore, but you'll never starve while I got anythin'."

Here it struck Duane again—that something human and kind and eager which he had seen in Stevens. Duane's estimate of outlaws had lacked this quality. He had not accorded them any virtues. To him, as to the outside world, they had been merely vicious men without one redeeming feature.

"I'm much obliged to you, Euchre," replied Duane. "But of course I won't live with any one unless I can pay my share."

"Have it any way you like, my son," said Euchre, good-humoredly. "You make a fire, an' I'll set about gettin' grub. I'm a sour-dough, Buck. Thet man doesn't live who can beat my bread."

"How do you ever pack supplies in here?" asked Duane, thinking of the almost inaccessible nature of the valley.

"Some comes across from Mexico, an' the rest down the river. Thet river trip is a bird. It's more'n five hundred miles to any supply point. Bland has *mozos*, Mexican boatmen. Sometimes, too, he gets supplies in from down-river. You see Bland sells thousands of cattle in Cuba. An' all this stock has to go down by boat to meet the ships."

"Where on earth are the cattle driven down to the river?" asked Duane.

"Thet's not my secret," replied Euchre, shortly. "Fact is, I don't know. I've rustled cattle for Bland, but he never sent me through the Rim Rock with them."

Duane experienced a sort of pleasure in the realization that interest had been stirred in him. He was curious about Bland and his gang, and glad to have something to think about. For every once in a while he had a sensation that was almost like a pang. He wanted to forget. In the next hour he did forget, and enjoyed helping in the preparation and eating of the meal. Euchre, after washing and hanging up the several utensils, put on his hat and turned to go out.

"Come along or stay here, as you want," he said to Duane.

"I'll stay," rejoined Duane, slowly.

The old outlaw left the room and trudged away, whistling cheerfully.

Duane looked around him for a book or paper, anything to read; but all the printed matter he could find consisted of a few words on cartridge-boxes and an advertisement on the back of a tobacco-pouch. There seemed to be nothing for him to do. He had rested; he did not want to lie down any more. He began to walk to and fro, from one end of the room to the other. And as he walked he fell into the lately acquired habit of brooding over his misfortune.

Suddenly he straightened up with a jerk. Unconsciously he had drawn his gun. Standing there with the bright cold weapon in his hand, he looked at it in consternation. How had he come to draw it? With difficulty he traced his thoughts backward, but could not find any that was accountable for his act. He discovered, however, that he had a remarkable tendency to drop his hand to his gun. That might have come from the habit long practice in drawing had given him. Likewise, it might have come from a subtle sense, scarcely thought of at all, of the late, close, and inevitable relation between that weapon and himself. He was amazed to find that, bitter as he had grown at fate, the desire to live burned strong in him. If he had been as unfortunately situated, but with the difference that no man wanted to put him in jail or take his life, he felt that this burning passion to be free, to save himself, might not have been so powerful. Life certainly held no bright prospects for him. Already he had begun to despair of ever getting back to his home. But to give up like a white-hearted coward, to let himself be handcuffed and jailed, to run from a drunken, bragging cowboy, or be shot in cold blood by some border brute who merely wanted to add another notch to his gun—these things were impossible for Duane because there was in him the temper to fight. In that hour he yielded only to fate and the spirit inborn in him. Hereafter this gun must be a living part of him. Right then and there he returned to a practice he had long discontinued—the draw. It was now a stern, bitter, deadly business with him. He did not need to fire the gun, for accuracy was a gift and had become assured. Swiftness on the draw, however, could be improved, and he set himself to acquire the limit of speed possible to any man. He stood still in his tracks; he paced the room;

he sat down, lay down, put himself in awkward positions; and from every position he practiced throwing his gun—practiced it till he was hot and tired and his arm ached and his hand burned. That practice he determined to keep up every day. It was one thing, at least, that would help pass the weary hours.

Later he went outdoors to the cooler shade of the cottonwoods. From this point he could see a good deal of the valley. Under different circumstances Duane felt that he would have enjoyed such a beautiful spot. Euchre's shack sat against the first rise of the slope of the wall, and Duane, by climbing a few rods, got a view of the whole valley. Assuredly it was an outlaw settlement. He saw a good many Mexicans, who, of course, were hand and glove with Bland. Also he saw enormous flatboats, crude of structure, moored along the banks of the river. The Rio Grande rolled away between high bluffs. A cable, sagging deep in the middle, was stretched over the wide yellow stream, and an old scow, evidently used as a ferry, lay anchored on the far shore.

The valley was an ideal retreat for an outlaw band operating on a big scale. Pursuit scarcely need be feared over the broken trails of the Rim Rock. And the open end of the valley could be defended against almost any number of men coming down the river. Access to Mexico was easy and quick. What puzzled Duane was how Bland got cattle down to the river, and he wondered if the rustler really did get rid of his stolen stock by use of boats.

Duane must have idled considerable time up on the hill, for when he returned to the shack Euchre was busily engaged around the camp-fire.

"Wal, glad to see you ain't so pale about the gills as you was," he said, by way of greeting. "Pitch in an' we'll soon have grub ready. There's shore one consolin' fact round this here camp."

"What's that?" asked Duane.

"Plenty of good juicy beef to eat. An' it doesn't cost a short bit."

"But it costs hard rides and trouble, bad conscience, and life, too, doesn't it?"

"I ain't shore about the bad conscience. Mine never bothered me none. An' as for life, why, thet's cheap in Texas."

"Who is Bland?" asked Duane, quickly changing the subject. "What do you know about him?"

"We don't know who he is or where he hails from," replied Euchre. "Thet's always been somethin' to interest the gang. He must have been a young man when he struck Texas. Now he's middle-aged. I remember how years ago he was softspoken an' not rough in talk or act like he is now. Bland ain't likely his right name. He knows a lot. He can doctor you, an' he's shore a knowin' feller with tools. He's the kind thet rules men. Outlaws are always ridin' in here to join his gang, an' if it hadn't been fer the gamblin' an' gun-play he'd have a thousand men around him."

"How many in his gang now?"

"I reckon there's short of a hundred now. The number varies. Then Bland has several small camps up an' down the river. Also he has men back on the cattle-ranges."

"How does he control such a big force?" asked Duane. "Especially when his band's composed of bad men. Luke Stevens said he had no use for Bland. And I heard once somewhere that Bland was a devil."

"Thet's it. He is a devil. He's as hard as flint, violent in temper, never made any friends except his right-hand men, Dave Rugg an' Chess Alloway. Bland 'll shoot at a wink. He's killed a lot of fellers, an' some fer nothin'. The reason thet outlaws gather round him an' stick is because he's a safe refuge, an' then he's well heeled. Bland is rich. They say he has a hundred thousand *pesos* hid somewhere, an' lots of gold. But he's free with money. He gambles when he's not off with a shipment of cattle. He throws money around. An' the fact is there's always plenty of money where he is. Thet's what holds the gang. Dirty, bloody money!"

"It's a wonder he hasn't been killed. All these years on the border!" exclaimed Duane.

"Wal," replied Euchre, dryly, "he's been quicker on the draw than the other fellers who hankered to kill him, thet's all."

Euchre's reply rather chilled Duane's interest for the moment. Such remarks always made his mind revolve round facts pertaining to himself.

"Speakin' of this here swift wrist game," went on Euchre, "there's been considerable talk in camp about your throwin' of a gun. You know, Buck, thet among us fellers—us hunted men—there ain't anythin' calculated to rouse respect like a slick hand with a gun. I heard Bland say this afternoon—an' he said it serious-like an' speculative—thet he'd never seen your equal. He was watchin' of you close, he said, an' just couldn't follow your hand when you drawed. All the fellers who seen you meet Bosomer had somethin' to say. Bo was about as handy with a gun as any man in this camp, barrin' Chess Alloway an' mebbe Bland himself. Chess is the captain with a Colt—or he was. An' he shore didn't like the references made about your speed. Bland was honest in acknowledgin' it, but he didn't like it, neither. Some of the fellers allowed your draw might have been just accident. But most of them figgered different. An' they all shut up when Bland told who an' what your Dad was. 'Pears to me I once seen your Dad in a gunscrape over at Santone, years ago. Wal, I put my oar in to-day among the fellers, an' I says: 'What ails you locoed gents? Did young Duane budge an inch when Bo came roarin' out, blood in his eye? Wasn't he cool an' quiet, steady of lips, an' weren't his eyes readin' Bo's mind? An' thet lightnin' draw—can't you-all see thet's a family gift?'"

Euchre's narrow eyes twinkled, and he gave the dough he was rolling a slap with his flour-whitened hand. Manifestly he had proclaimed himself a champion and partner of Duane's, with all the pride an old man could feel in a young one whom he admired.

"Wal," he resumed, presently, "thet's your introduction to the border, Buck. An' your card was a high trump. You'll be let severely alone by real gun-fighters an' men like Bland, Alloway, Rugg, an' the bosses of the other gangs. After all, these real men *are* men, you know, an' onless you cross them they're no more likely to interfere with you than you are with them. But there's a sight of fellers like Bosomer in the river country. They'll all want your game. An' every town you ride into will scare up some cowpuncher full of booze or a long-haired four-flush gunman or a sheriff—an' these men will be playin' to the crowd an' yellin' for your blood. Thet's the Texas of it. You'll have to hide fer ever in the brakes or you'll have to *kill* such men. Buck, I reckon this ain't cheerful news to a decent chap like you. I'm only tellin' you because I've taken a likin' to you, an' I seen right off thet you ain't border-wise. Let's eat now, an' afterward we'll go out so the gang can see you're not hidin'."

When Duane went out with Euchre the sun was setting behind a blue range of mountains across the river in Mexico. The valley appeared to open to the southwest. It was a tranquil, beautiful scene. Somewhere in a house near at hand a woman was singing. And in the road Duane saw a little Mexican boy driving home some cows, one of which wore a bell. The sweet, happy voice of a woman and a whistling barefoot boy—these seemed utterly out of place here.

Euchre presently led to the square and the row of rough houses Duane remembered. He almost stepped on a wide imprint in the dust where Bosomer had confronted him. And a sudden fury beset him that he should be affected strangely by the sight of it.

"Let's have a look in here," said Euchre.

Duane had to bend his head to enter the door. He found himself in a very large room inclosed by adobe walls and roofed with brush. It was full of rude benches, tables, seats. At one corner a number of kegs and barrels lay side by side in a rack. A Mexican boy was lighting lamps hung on posts that sustained the log rafters of the roof.

"The only feller who's goin' to put a close eye on you is Benson," said Euchre. "He runs the place an' sells drinks. The gang calls him Jackrabbit Benson, because he's always got his eye peeled an' his ear cocked. Don't notice him if he looks you over, Buck. Benson is scared to death of every newcomer who rustles into Bland's camp. An' the reason, I take it, is because he's done somebody dirt. He's hidin'. Not from a sheriff or ranger! Men who hide from them don't act like Jackrabbit Benson. He's hidin' from some guy who's huntin' him to kill him. Wal, I'm always expectin' to see some feller ride in here an' throw a gun on Benson. Can't say I'd be grieved."

Duane casually glanced in the direction indicated, and he saw a spare, gaunt man with a face strikingly white beside the red and bronze and dark skins of the men around him. It was a cadaverous face. The black mustache hung down; a heavy lock of black hair dropped down over the brow; deep-set, hollow, staring eyes looked out piercingly. The man had a restless, alert, nervous manner. He put his hands on the board that served as a bar and stared at Duane. But when he met Duane's glance he turned hurriedly to go on serving out liquor.

"What have you got against him?" inquired Duane, as he sat down beside Euchre. He asked more for something to say than from real interest. What did he care about a mean, haunted, craven-faced criminal?

"Wal, mebbe I'm cross-grained," replied Euchre, apologetically. "Shore an outlaw an' rustler such as me can't be touchy. But I never stole nothin' but cattle from some rancher who never missed 'em anyway. Thet sneak Benson—he was the means of puttin' a little girl in Bland's way."

"Girl?" queried Duane, now with real attention.

"Shore. Bland's great on women. I'll tell you about this girl when we get out of here. Some of the gang are goin' to be sociable, an' I can't talk about the chief."

During the ensuing half-hour a number of outlaws passed by Duane and Euchre, halted for a greeting or sat down for a moment. They were all gruff, loud-voiced, merry, and good-natured. Duane replied civilly and agreeably when he was personally addressed; but he refused all invitations to drink and gamble. Evidently he had been accepted, in a way, as one of their clan. No one made any hint of an allusion to his affair with Bosomer. Duane saw readily that Euchre was well liked. One outlaw borrowed money from him; another asked for tobacco.

By the time it was dark the big room was full of outlaws and Mexicans, most of whom were engaged at *monte*. These gamblers, especially the Mexicans, were intense and quiet. The noise in the place came from the drinkers, the loungers. Duane had seen gambling-resorts—some of the famous ones in San Antonio and El Paso, a few in border towns where license went unchecked. But this place of Jackrabbit Benson's impressed him as one where guns and knives were accessories to the game. To his perhaps rather distinguishing eye the most prominent thing about the gamesters appeared to be their weapons. On several of the tables were piles of silver—Mexican *pesos*—as large and high as the crown of his hat. There were also piles of gold and silver in United States coin. Duane needed no experienced eyes to see that betting was heavy and that heavy sums exchanged hands. The Mexicans showed a sterner obsession, an intenser passion. Some of the Americans staked freely, nonchalantly, as befitted men to whom money was nothing. These latter were manifestly winning, for there were brother outlaws there who wagered coin with grudging, sullen, greedy eyes. Boisterous talk and laughter among the drinking men drowned, except at intervals, the low, brief talk of the gamblers. The clink of coin sounded incessantly; sometimes just low, steady musical rings; and again, when a pile was tumbled quickly, there was a silvery crash. Here an outlaw pounded on a table with the butt of his gun; there another noisily palmed a roll of dollars while he studied his opponent's face. The noises, however, in Benson's den did not contribute to any extent to the sinister aspect of the place. That seemed to come from the grim and reckless faces, from the bent, intent heads, from the dark lights and shades. There were bright lights, but these served only to make the shadows. And in the shadows lurked unrestrained lust of gain, a spirit ruthless and reckless, a something at once suggesting lawlessness, theft, murder, and hell.

"Bland's not here to-night," Euchre was saying. "He left to-day on one of his trips, takin' Alloway an' some others. But his other man, Rugg, he's here. See him standin' with them three fellers, all close to Benson. Rugg's the little bow-legged man with the half of his face shot off. He's one-eyed. But he can shore see out of the one he's got. An,' darn me! there's Hardin. You know him? He's got an outlaw gang as big as Bland's. Hardin is standin' next to Benson. See how quiet an' unassumin' he looks. Yes, thet's Hardin. He comes here once in a while to see Bland. They're friends, which's shore strange. Do you see thet Mexican there— the one with gold an' lace on his sombrero? Thet's Manuel, a Mexican bandit. He's a great gambler. Comes here often to drop his coin. Next to him is Bill Marr—the feller with the bandana round his head. Bill rode in the other day with some fresh bullet-holes. He's been shot more'n any feller I ever heard of. He's full of lead. Funny, because Bill's no trouble-hunter, an', like me, he'd rather run than shoot. But he's the best rustler Bland's got—a grand rider, an' a wonder with cattle. An' see the tow-headed youngster. Thet's Kid Fuller, the kid of Bland's gang. Fuller has hit the pace hard, an' he won't last the year out on the border. He killed his sweetheart's father, got run out of Staceytown, took to stealin' hosses. An' next he's here with Bland. Another boy gone wrong, an' now shore a hard nut."

Euchre went on calling Duane's attention to other men, just as he happened to glance over them. Any one of them would have been a marked man in a respectable crowd. Here each took his place with more or less distinction, according to the record of his past wild prowess and his present possibilities. Duane, realizing that he was tolerated there, received in careless friendly spirit by this terrible class of outcasts, experienced a feeling of revulsion that amounted almost to horror. Was his being there not an ugly dream? What had he in common with such ruffians? Then in a flash of memory came the painful proof—he was a criminal in sight of Texas law; he, too, was an outcast.

For the moment Duane was wrapped up in painful reflections; but Euchre's heavy hand, clapping with a warning hold on his arm, brought him back to outside things.

The hum of voices, the clink of coin, the loud laughter had ceased. There was a silence that manifestly had followed some unusual word or action sufficient to still the room. It was broken by a harsh curse and the scrape of a bench on the floor. Some man had risen.

"You stacked the cards, you ——!"

"Say that twice," another voice replied, so different in its cool, ominous tone from the other.

"I'll say it twice," returned the first gamester, in hot haste. "I'll say it three times. I'll whistle it. Are you deaf? You light-fingered gent! You stacked the cards!"

Silence ensued, deeper than before, pregnant with meaning. For all that Duane saw, not an outlaw moved for a full moment. Then suddenly the room was full of disorder as men rose and ran and dived everywhere.

"Run or duck!" yelled Euchre, close to Duane's ear. With that he dashed for the door. Duane leaped after him. They ran into a jostling mob. Heavy gun-shots and hoarse yells hurried the crowd Duane was with pell-mell out into the darkness. There they all halted, and several peeped in at the door.

"Who was the Kid callin'?" asked one outlaw.

"Bud Marsh," replied another.

"I reckon them fust shots was Bud's. *Adios* Kid. It was comin' to him," went on yet another.

"How many shots?"

"Three or four, I counted."

"Three heavy an' one light. Thet light one was the Kid's .38. Listen! There's the Kid hollerin' now. He ain't cashed, anyway."

At this juncture most of the outlaws began to file back into the room. Duane thought he had seen and heard enough in Benson's den for one night and he started slowly down the walk. Presently Euchre caught up with him.

"Nobody hurt much, which's shore some strange," he said. "The Kid—young Fuller thet I was tellin' you about—he was drinkin' an' losin'. Lost his nut, too, callin' Bud Marsh thet way. Bud's as straight at cards as any of 'em. Somebody grabbed Bud, who shot into the roof. An' Fuller's arm was knocked up. He only hit a Mexican."

CHAPTER 6

Next morning Duane found that a moody and despondent spell had fastened on him. Wishing to be alone, he went out and walked a trail leading round the river bluff. He thought and thought. After a while he made out that the trouble with him probably was that he could not resign himself to his fate. He abhorred the possibility chance seemed to hold in store for him. He could not believe there was no hope. But what to do appeared beyond his power to tell.

Duane had intelligence and keenness enough to see his peril—the danger threatening his character as a man, just as much as that which threatened his life. He cared vastly more, he discovered, for what he considered honor and integrity than he did for life. He saw that it was bad for him to be alone. But, it appeared, lonely months and perhaps years inevitably must be his. Another thing puzzled him. In the bright light of day he could not recall the state of mind that was his at twilight or dusk or in the dark night. By day these visitations became to him what they really were—phantoms of his conscience. He could dismiss the thought of them then. He could scarcely remember or believe that this strange feat of fancy or imagination had troubled him, pained him, made him sleepless and sick.

That morning Duane spent an unhappy hour wrestling decision out of the unstable condition of his mind. But at length he determined to create interest in all that he came across and so forget himself as much as possible. He had an opportunity now to see just what the outlaw's life really was. He meant to force himself to be curious, sympathetic, clear-sighted. And he would stay there in the valley until its possibilities had been exhausted or until circumstances sent him out upon his uncertain way.

When he returned to the shack Euchre was cooking dinner.

"Say, Buck, I've news for you," he said; and his tone conveyed either pride in his possession of such news or pride in Duane. "Feller named Bradley rode in this mornin'. He's heard some about you. Told about the ace of spades they put over the bullet-holes in thet cowpuncher Bain you plugged. Then there was a rancher shot at a water-hole twenty miles south of Wellston. Reckon you didn't do it?"

"No, I certainly did not," replied Duane.

"Wal, you get the blame. It ain't nothin' for a feller to be saddled with gun-plays he never made. An', Buck, if you ever get famous, as seems likely, you'll be blamed for many a crime. The border 'll make an outlaw an' murderer out of you. Wal, thet's enough of thet. I've more news. You're goin' to be popular."

"Popular? What do you mean?"

"I met Bland's wife this mornin'. She seen you the other day when you rode in. She shore wants to meet you, an' so do some of the other women in camp. They always want to meet the new fellers who've just come in. It's lonesome for women here, an' they like to hear news from the towns."

"Well, Euchre, I don't want to be impolite, but I'd rather not meet any women," rejoined Duane.

"I was afraid you wouldn't. Don't blame you much. Women are hell. I was hopin', though, you might talk a little to thet poor lonesome kid."

"What kid?" inquired Duane, in surprise.

"Didn't I tell you about Jennie—the girl Bland's holdin' here—the one Jackrabbit Benson had a hand in stealin'?"

"You mentioned a girl. That's all. Tell me now," replied Duane, abruptly.

"Wal, I got it this way. Mebbe it's straight, an mebbe it ain't. Some years ago Benson made a trip over the river to buy mescal an' other drinks. He'll sneak over there once in a while. An' as I get it he run across a gang of Mexicans with some gringo prisoners. I don't know, but I reckon there was some barterin', perhaps murderin'. Anyway, Benson fetched the girl back. She was more dead than alive. But it turned out she was only starved an' scared half to death. She hadn't been harmed. I reckon she was then about fourteen years old. Benson's idee, he said, was to use her in his den sellin' drinks an' the like. But I never went much on Jackrabbit's word. Bland seen the kid right off and took her—bought her from Benson. You can gamble Bland didn't do thet from notions of chivalry. I ain't gainsayin', however, but thet Jennie was better off with Kate Bland. She's been hard on Jennie, but she's kept Bland an' the other men from treatin' the kid shameful. Late Jennie has growed into an all-fired pretty girl, an' Kate is powerful jealous of her. I can see hell brewin' over there in Bland's cabin. Thet's why I wish you'd come over with me. Bland's hardly ever home. His wife's invited you. Shore, if she gets sweet on you, as she has on— Wal, thet 'd complicate matters. But you'd get to see Jennie, an' mebbe you could help her. Mind, I ain't hintin' nothing'. I'm just wantin' to put her in your way. You're a man an' can think fer yourself. I had a baby girl once, an' if she'd lived she be as big as Jennie now, an', by Gawd, I wouldn't want her here in Bland's camp."

"I'll go, Euchre. Take me over," replied Duane. He felt Euchre's eyes upon him. The old outlaw, however, had no more to say.

In the afternoon Euchre set off with Duane, and soon they reached Bland's cabin. Duane remembered it as the one where he had seen the pretty woman watching him ride by. He could not recall what she looked like. The cabin was the same as the other adobe structures in the valley, but it was larger and pleasantly located rather high up in a grove of cottonwoods. In the windows and upon the porch were evidences of a woman's hand. Through the open door Duane caught a glimpse of bright Mexican blankets and rugs.

Euchre knocked upon the side of the door.

"Is that you, Euchre?" asked a girl's voice, low, hesitatingly. The tone of it, rather deep and with a note of fear, struck Duane. He wondered what she would be like.

"Yes, it's me, Jennie. Where's Mrs. Bland?" answered Euchre.

"She went over to Deger's. There's somebody sick," replied the girl.

Euchre turned and whispered something about luck. The snap of the outlaw's eyes was adding significance to Duane.

"Jennie, come out or let us come in. Here's the young man I was tellin' you about," Euchre said.

"Oh, I can't! I look so—so—"

"Never mind how you look," interrupted the outlaw, in a whisper. "It ain't no time to care fer thet. Here's young Duane. Jennie, he's no rustler, no thief. He's different. Come out, Jennie, an' mebbe he'll—"

Euchre did not complete his sentence. He had spoken low, with his glance shifting from side to side.

But what he said was sufficient to bring the girl quickly. She appeared in the doorway with downcast eyes and a stain of red in her white cheek. She had a pretty, sad face and bright hair.

"Don't be bashful, Jennie," said Euchre. "You an' Duane have a chance to talk a little. Now I'll go fetch Mrs. Bland, but I won't be hurryin'."

With that Euchre went away through the cottonwoods.

"I'm glad to meet you, Miss—Miss Jennie," said Duane. "Euchre didn't mention your last name. He asked me to come over to—"

Duane's attempt at pleasantry halted short when Jennie lifted her lashes to look at him. Some kind of a shock went through Duane. Her gray eyes were beautiful, but it had not been beauty that cut short his speech. He seemed to see a tragic struggle between hope and doubt that shone in her piercing gaze. She kept looking, and Duane could not break the silence. It was no ordinary moment.

"What did you come here for?" she asked, at last.

"To see you," replied Duane, glad to speak.

"Why?"

"Well—Euchre thought—he wanted me to talk to you, cheer you up a bit," replied Duane, somewhat lamely. The earnest eyes embarrassed him.

"Euchre's good. He's the only person in this awful place who's been good to me. But he's afraid of Bland. He said you were different. Who are you?"

Duane told her.

"You're not a robber or rustler or murderer or some bad man come here to hide?"

"No, I'm not," replied Duane, trying to smile.

"Then why are you here?"

"I'm on the dodge. You know what that means. I got in a shooting-scrape at home and had to run off. When it blows over I hope to go back."

"But you can't be honest here?"

"Yes, I can."

"Oh, I know what these outlaws are. Yes, you're different." She kept the strained gaze upon him, but hope was kindling, and the hard lines of her youthful face were softening.

Something sweet and warm stirred deep in Duane as he realized the unfortunate girl was experiencing a birth of trust in him.

"O God! Maybe you're the man to save me—to take me away before it's too late!"

Duane's spirit leaped.

"Maybe I am," he replied, instantly.

She seemed to check a blind impulse to run into his arms. Her cheek flamed, her lips quivered, her bosom swelled under her ragged dress. Then the glow began to fade; doubt once more assailed her.

"It can't be. You're only—after me, too, like Bland—like all of them."

Duane's long arms were out and his hands clasped her shoulders. He shook her.

"Look at me—straight in the eye. There are decent men. Haven't you a father—a brother?"

"They're dead—killed by raiders. We lived in Dimmit County. I was carried away," Jennie replied, hurriedly. She put up an appealing hand to him. "Forgive me. I believe—I know you're good. It was only—I live so much in fear—I'm half crazy—I've almost forgotten what good men are like. Mister Duane, you'll help me?"

"Yes, Jennie, I will. Tell me how. What must I do? Have you any plan?"

"Oh no. But take me away."

"I'll try," said Duane, simply. "That won't be easy, though. I must have time to think. You must help me. There are many things to consider. Horses, food, trails, and then the best time to make the attempt. Are you watched—kept prisoner?"

"No. I could have run off lots of times. But I was afraid. I'd only have fallen into worse hands. Euchre has told me that. Mrs. Bland beats me, half starves me, but she has kept me from her husband and these other dogs. She's been as good as that, and I'm grateful. She hasn't done it for love of me, though. She always hated me. And lately she's growing jealous. There was a man came here by the name of Spence—so he called himself. He tried to be kind to me. But she wouldn't let him. She was in love with him. She's a bad woman. Bland finally shot Spence, and that ended that. She's been jealous ever since. I hear her fighting with Bland about me. She swears she'll kill me before he gets me. And Bland laughs in her face. Then I've heard Chess Alloway try to persuade Bland to give me to him. But Bland doesn't laugh then. Just lately before Bland went away things almost came to a head. I couldn't sleep. I wished Mrs. Bland would kill me. I'll certainly kill myself if they ruin me. Duane, you must be quick if you'd save me."

"I realize that," replied he, thoughtfully. "I think my difficulty will be to fool Mrs. Bland. If she suspected me she'd have the whole gang of outlaws on me at once."

"She would that. You've got to be careful—and quick."

"What kind of woman is she?" inquired Duane.

"She's—she's brazen. I've heard her with her lovers. They get drunk sometimes when Bland's away. She's got a terrible temper. She's vain. She likes flattery. Oh, you could fool her easy enough if you'd lower yourself to—to—"

"To make love to her?" interrupted Duane.

Jennie bravely turned shamed eyes to meet his.

"My girl, I'd do worse than that to get you away from here," he said, bluntly.

"But—Duane," she faltered, and again she put out the appealing hand. "Bland will kill you."

Duane made no reply to this. He was trying to still a rising strange tumult in his breast. The old emotion—the rush of an instinct to kill! He turned cold all over.

"Chess Alloway will kill you if Bland doesn't," went on Jennie, with her tragic eyes on Duane's.

"Maybe he will," replied Duane. It was difficult for him to force a smile. But he achieved one.

"Oh, better take me off at once," she said. "Save me without risking so much—without making love to Mrs. Bland!"

"Surely, if I can. There! I see Euchre coming with a woman."

"That's her. Oh, she mustn't see me with you."

"Wait—a moment," whispered Duane, as Jennie slipped indoors. "We've settled it. Don't forget. I'll find some way to get word to you, perhaps through Euchre. Meanwhile keep up your courage. Remember I'll save you somehow. We'll try strategy first. Whatever you see or hear me do, don't think less of me—"

Jennie checked him with a gesture and a wonderful gray flash of eyes.

"I'll bless you with every drop of blood in my heart," she whispered, passionately.

It was only as she turned away into the room that Duane saw she was lame and that she wore Mexican sandals over bare feet.

He sat down upon a bench on the porch and directed his attention to the approaching couple. The trees of the grove were thick enough for him to make reasonably sure that Mrs. Bland had not seen him talking to Jennie. When the outlaw's wife drew near Duane saw that she was a tall, strong, full-bodied woman, rather good-looking with a full-blown, bold attractiveness. Duane was more concerned with her expression than with her good looks; and as she appeared unsuspicious he felt relieved. The situation then took on a singular zest.

Euchre came up on the porch and awkwardly introduced Duane to Mrs. Bland. She was young, probably not over twenty-five, and not quite so prepossessing at close range. Her eyes were large, rather prominent, and brown in color. Her mouth, too, was large, with the lips full, and she had white teeth.

Duane took her proffered hand and remarked frankly that he was glad to meet her.

Mrs. Bland appeared pleased; and her laugh, which followed, was loud and rather musical.

"Mr. Duane—Buck Duane, Euchre said, didn't he?" she asked.

"Buckley," corrected Duane. "The nickname's not of my choosing."

"I'm certainly glad to meet you, Buckley Duane," she said, as she took the seat Duane offered her. "Sorry to have been out. Kid Fuller's lying over at Deger's. You know he was shot last night. He's got fever to-day. When Bland's away I have to nurse all these shot-up boys, and it sure takes my time. Have you been waiting here alone? Didn't see that slattern girl of mine?"

She gave him a sharp glance. The woman had an extraordinary play of feature, Duane thought, and unless she was smiling was not pretty at all.

"I've been alone," replied Duane. "Haven't seen anybody but a sick-looking girl with a bucket. And she ran when she saw me."

"That was Jen," said Mrs. Bland. "She's the kid we keep here, and she sure hardly pays her keep. Did Euchre tell you about her?"

"Now that I think of it, he did say something or other."

"What did he tell you about me?" bluntly asked Mrs. Bland.

"Wal, Kate," replied Euchre, speaking for himself, "you needn't worry none, for I told Buck nothin' but compliments."

Evidently the outlaw's wife liked Euchre, for her keen glance rested with amusement upon him.

"As for Jen, I'll tell you her story some day," went on the woman. "It's a common enough story along this river. Euchre here is a tender-hearted old fool, and Jen has taken him in."

"Wal, seein' as you've got me figgered correct," replied Euchre, dryly, "I'll go in an' talk to Jennie, if I may."

"Certainly. Go ahead. Jen calls you her best friend," said Mrs. Bland, amiably. "You're always fetching some Mexican stuff, and that's why, I guess."

When Euchre had shuffled into the house Mrs. Bland turned to Duane with curiosity and interest in her gaze.

"Bland told me about you."

"What did he say?" queried Duane, in pretended alarm.

"Oh, you needn't think he's done you dirt. Bland's not that kind of a man. He said: 'Kate, there's a young fellow in camp—rode in here on the dodge. He's no criminal, and he refused to join my band. Wish he would. Slickest hand with a gun I've seen for many a day! I'd like to see him and Chess meet out there in the road.' Then Bland went on to tell how you and Bosomer came together."

"What did you say?" inquired Duane, as she paused.

"Me? Why, I asked him what you looked like," she replied, gayly.

"Well?" went on Duane.

"Magnificent chap, Bland said. Bigger than any man in the valley. Just a great blue-eyed, sunburned boy!"

"Humph!" exclaimed Duane. "I'm sorry he led you to expect somebody worth seeing."

"But I'm not disappointed," she returned, archly. "Duane, are you going to stay long here in camp?"

"Yes, till I run out of money and have to move. Why?"

Mrs. Bland's face underwent one of the singular changes. The smiles and flushes and glances, all that had been coquettish about her, had lent her a certain attractiveness, almost beauty and youth. But with some powerful emotion she changed and instantly became a woman of discontent, Duane imagined, of deep, violent nature.

"I'll tell you, Duane," she said, earnestly, "I'm sure glad if you mean to bide here awhile. I'm a miserable woman, Duane. I'm an outlaw's wife, and I hate him and the life I have to lead. I come of a good family in Brownsville. I never knew Bland was an outlaw till long after he married me. We were separated at times, and I imagined he was away on business. But the truth came out. Bland shot my own cousin, who told me. My family cast me off, and I had to flee with Bland. I was only eighteen then. I've lived here since. I never see a decent woman or man. I never hear anything about my old home or folks or friends. I'm buried here—buried alive with a lot of thieves and murderers. Can you blame me for being glad to see a young fellow—a gentleman—like the boys I used to go with? I tell you it makes me feel full—I want to cry. I'm sick for somebody to talk to. I have no children, thank God! If I had I'd not stay here. I'm sick of this hole. I'm lonely—"

There appeared to be no doubt about the truth of all this. Genuine emotion checked, then halted the hurried speech. She broke down and cried. It seemed strange to Duane that an outlaw's wife—and a woman who fitted her consort and the wild nature of their surroundings—should have weakness enough to weep. Duane believed and pitied her.

"I'm sorry for you," he said.

"Don't be *sorry* for me," she said. "That only makes me see the—the difference between you and me. And don't pay any attention to what these outlaws say about me. They're ignorant. They couldn't understand me. You'll hear that Bland killed men who ran after me. But that's a lie. Bland, like all the other outlaws along this river, is always looking for somebody to kill. He *swears* not, but I don't believe him. He explains that gun-play gravitates to men who are the real thing—that it is provoked by the four-flushes, the bad men. I don't know. All I know is that somebody is being killed every other day. He hated Spence before Spence ever saw me."

"Would Bland object if I called on you occasionally?" inquired Duane.

"No, he wouldn't. He likes me to have friends. Ask him yourself when he comes back. The trouble has been that two or three of his men fell in love with me, and when half drunk got to fighting. You're not going to do that."

"I'm not going to get half drunk, that's certain," replied Duane.

He was surprised to see her eyes dilate, then glow with fire. Before she could reply Euchre returned to the porch, and that put an end to the conversation.

Duane was content to let the matter rest there, and had little more to say. Euchre and Mrs. Bland talked and joked, while Duane listened. He tried to form some estimate of her character. Manifestly she had suffered a wrong, if not worse, at Bland's hands. She was bitter, morbid, overemotional. If she was a liar, which seemed likely enough, she was a frank one, and believed herself. She had no cunning. The thing which struck Duane so forcibly was that she thirsted for respect. In that, better than in her weakness of vanity, he thought he had discovered a trait through which he could manage her.

Once, while he was revolving these thoughts, he happened to glance into the house, and deep in the shadow of a corner he caught a pale gleam of Jennie's face with great, staring eyes on him. She had been watching him, listening to what he said. He saw from her expression that she had realized what had been so hard for her to believe. Watching his chance, he flashed a look at her; and then it seemed to him the change in her face was wonderful.

Later, after he had left Mrs. Bland with a meaning *"Adios—mañana,"* and was walking along beside the old outlaw, he found himself thinking of the girl instead of the woman, and of how he had seen her face blaze with hope and gratitude.

CHAPTER 7

That night Duane was not troubled by ghosts haunting his waking and sleeping hours. He awoke feeling bright and eager, and grateful to Euchre for having put something worth while into his mind. During breakfast, however, he was unusually thoughtful, working over the idea of how much or how little he would confide in the outlaw. He was aware of Euchre's scrutiny.

"Wal," began the old man, at last, "how'd you make out with the kid?"

"Kid?" inquired Duane, tentatively.

"Jennie, I mean. What 'd you an' she talk about?"

"We had a little chat. You know you wanted me to cheer her up."

Euchre sat with coffee-cup poised and narrow eyes studying Duane.

"Reckon you cheered her, all right. What I'm afeared of is mebbe you done the job too well."

"How so?"

"Wal, when I went in to Jen last night I thought she was half crazy. She was burstin' with excitement, an' the look in her eyes hurt me. She wouldn't tell me a darn word you said. But she hung onto my hands, an' showed every way without speakin' how she wanted to thank me fer bringin' you over. Buck, it was plain to me thet you'd either gone the limit or else you'd been kinder prodigal of cheer an' hope. I'd hate to think you'd led Jennie to hope more'n ever would come true."

Euchre paused, and, as there seemed no reply forthcoming, he went on:

"Buck, I've seen some outlaws whose word was good. Mine is. You can trust me. I trusted you, didn't I, takin' you over there an' puttin' you wise to my tryin' to help thet poor kid?"

Thus enjoined by Euchre, Duane began to tell the conversations with Jennie and Mrs. Bland word for word. Long before he had reached an end Euchre set down the coffee-cup and began to stare, and at the conclusion of the story his face lost some of its red color and beads of sweat stood out thickly on his brow.

"Wal, if thet doesn't floor me!" he exclaimed, blinking at Duane. "Young man, I figgered you was some swift, an' sure to make your mark on this river; but I reckon I missed your real caliber. So thet's what it means to be a man! I guess I'd forgot. Wal, I'm old, an' even if my heart was in the right place I never was built fer big stunts. Do you know what it'll take to do all you promised Jen?"

"I haven't any idea," replied Duane, gravely.

"You'll have to pull the wool over Kate Bland's eyes, an' even if she falls in love with you, which 's shore likely, thet won't be easy. An' she'd kill you in a minnit, Buck, if she ever got wise. You ain't mistaken her none, are you?"

"Not me, Euchre. She's a woman. I'd fear her more than any man."

"Wal, you'll have to kill Bland an' Chess Alloway an' Rugg, an' mebbe some others, before you can ride off into the hills with thet girl."

"Why? Can't we plan to be nice to Mrs. Bland and then at an opportune time sneak off without any gun-play?"

"Don't see how on earth," returned Euchre, earnestly. "When Bland's away he leaves all kinds of spies an' scouts watchin' the valley trails. They've all got rifles. You couldn't git by them. But when the boss is home there's a difference. Only, of course, him an' Chess keep their eyes peeled. They both stay to home pretty much, except when they're playin' *monte* or poker over at Benson's. So I say the best bet is to pick out a good time in the afternoon, drift over careless-like with a couple of hosses, choke Mrs. Bland or knock her on the head, take Jennie with you, an' make a rush to git out of the valley. If you had luck you might pull thet stunt without throwin' a gun. But I reckon the best figgerin' would include dodgin' some lead an' leavin' at least Bland or Alloway dead behind you. I'm fig-gerin', of course, thet when they come home an' find out you're visitin' Kate frequent they'll jest naturally look fer results. Chess don't like you, fer no reason except you're swift on the draw—mebbe swifter'n him. Thet's the hell of this gun-play business. No one can ever tell who's the swifter of two gunmen till they meet. Thet fact holds a fascination mebbe you'll learn some day. Bland would treat you civil onless there was reason not to, an' then I don't believe he'd invite himself to a meetin' with you. He'd set Chess or Rugg to put you out of the way. Still Bland's no coward, an' if you came across him at a bad moment you'd have to be quicker 'n you was with Bosomer."

"All right. I'll meet what comes," said Duane, quietly. "The great point is to have horses ready and pick the right moment, then rush the trick through."

"Thet's the *only* chance fer success. An' you can't do it alone."

"I'll have to. I wouldn't ask you to help me. Leave you behind!"

"Wal, I'll take my chances," replied Euchre, gruffly. "I'm goin' to help Jennie, you can gamble your last peso on thet. There's only four men in this camp who would shoot me—Bland, an' his right-hand pards, an' thet rabbit-faced Benson. If you happened to put out Bland and Chess, I'd stand a good show with the other two. Anyway, I'm old an' tired—what's the difference if I do git plugged? I can risk as much as you, Buck, even if I am afraid of gun-play. You said correct, 'Hosses ready, the right minnit, then rush the trick.' Thet much 's settled. Now let's figger all the little details."

They talked and planned, though in truth it was Euchre who planned, Duane who listened and agreed. While awaiting the return of Bland and his lieutenants it would be well for Duane to grow friendly with the other outlaws, to sit in a few games of *monte*, or show a willingness to spend a little money. The two schemers were to call upon Mrs. Bland every day—Euchre to carry messages of cheer and warning to Jennie, Duane to blind the elder woman at any cost. These preliminaries decided upon, they proceeded to put them into action.

No hard task was it to win the friendship of the most of those good-natured outlaws. They were used to men of a better order than theirs coming to the hidden camps and sooner or later sinking to their lower level. Besides, with them everything was easy come, easy go. That was why life itself went on so carelessly and usually ended so cheaply. There were men among them, however, that made Duane feel that terrible inexplicable wrath rise in his breast. He could not bear to be near them. He could not trust himself. He felt that any instant a word, a deed, something might call too deeply to that instinct he could no longer control. Jackrabbit Benson was one of these men. Because of him and other outlaws of his ilk Duane could scarcely ever forget the reality of things. This was a hidden valley, a robbers' den, a rendezvous for murderers, a wild place stained red by deeds of wild men. And because of that there was always a charged atmosphere. The merriest, idlest, most careless moment might in the flash of an eye end in ruthless and tragic action. In an assemblage of desperate characters it could not be otherwise. The terrible thing that Duane sensed was this. The valley was beautiful, sunny, fragrant, a place to dream in; the mountain-tops were always blue or gold rimmed, the yellow river slid slowly and majestically by, the birds sang in the cottonwoods, the horses grazed and pranced, children played and women longed for love, freedom, happiness; the outlaws rode in and out, free with money and speech; they lived comfortably in their adobe homes, smoked, gambled, talked, laughed, whiled away the idle hours— and all the time life there was wrong, and the simplest moment might be precipitated by that evil into the most awful of contrasts. Duane felt rather than saw a dark, brooding shadow over the valley.

Then, without any solicitation or encouragement from Duane, the Bland woman fell passionately in love with him. His conscience was never troubled about the beginning of that affair. She launched herself. It took no great perspicuity on his part to see that. And the thing which evidently held her in check was the newness, the strangeness, and for the moment the all-satisfying fact of his respect for her. Duane exerted himself to please, to amuse, to interest, to fascinate her, and always with deference. That was his strong point, and it had made his part easy so far. He believed he could carry the whole scheme through without involving himself any deeper.

He was playing at a game of love—playing with life and death! Sometimes he trembled, not that he feared Bland or Alloway or any other man, but at the deeps of life he had come to see into. He was carried out of his old mood. Not once since this daring motive had stirred him had he been haunted by the phantom of Bain beside his bed. Rather had he been haunted by Jennie's sad face, her wistful smile, her eyes. He never was able to speak a word to her. What little communication he had with her was through Euchre, who carried short messages. But he caught glimpses of her every time he went to the Bland house. She contrived somehow to pass door or window, to give him a look when chance afforded. And Duane discovered with surprise that these moments were more thrilling to him than any with Mrs. Bland. Often Duane knew Jennie was sitting just inside the window, and then he felt inspired in his talk, and it was all made for her. So at least she came to know him while as yet she was almost a stranger. Jennie had been instructed by Euchre to listen, to understand that this was Duane's only chance to help keep her mind from constant worry, to gather the import of every word which had a double meaning.

Euchre said that the girl had begun to wither under the strain, to burn up with intense hope which had flamed within her. But all the difference Duane could see was a paler face and darker, more wonderful eyes. The eyes seemed to be entreating him to hurry, that time was flying, that soon it might be too late. Then there was another meaning in them, a light, a strange fire wholly inexplicable to Duane. It was only a flash gone in an instant. But he remembered it because he had never seen it in any other woman's eyes. And all through those waiting days he knew that Jennie's face, and especially the warm, fleeting glance she gave him, was responsible for a subtle and gradual change in him. This change, he fancied, was only that through remembrance of her he got rid of his pale, sickening ghosts.

One day a careless Mexican threw a lighted cigarette up into the brush matting that served as a ceiling for Benson's den, and there was a fire which left little more than the adobe walls standing. The result was that while repairs were being made there was no gambling and drinking. Time hung very heavily on the hands of some twoscore outlaws. Days passed by without a brawl, and Bland's valley saw more successive hours of peace than ever before. Duane, however, found the hours anything but empty. He spent more time at Mrs. Bland's; he walked miles on all the trails leading out of the valley; he had a care for the condition of his two horses.

Upon his return from the latest of these tramps Euchre suggested that they go down to the river to the boat-landing.

"Ferry couldn't run ashore this mornin'," said Euchre. "River gettin' low an' sand-bars makin' it hard fer hosses. There's a Mexican freight-wagon stuck in the mud. I reckon we might hear news from the freighters. Bland's supposed to be in Mexico."

Nearly all the outlaws in camp were assembled on the river-bank, lolling in the shade of the cottonwoods. The heat was oppressive. Not an outlaw offered to help the freighters, who were trying to dig a heavily freighted wagon out of the quicksand. Few outlaws would work for themselves, let alone for the despised Mexicans.

Duane and Euchre joined the lazy group and sat down with them. Euchre lighted a black pipe, and, drawing his hat over his eyes, lay back in comfort after the manner of the majority of the outlaws. But Duane was alert, observing, thoughtful. He never missed anything. It was his belief that any moment an idle word might be of benefit to him. Moreover, these rough men were always interesting.

"Bland's been chased acrost the river," said one.

"Naw, he's deliverin' cattle to thet Cuban ship," replied another.

"Big deal on, hey?"

"Some big. Rugg says the boss hed an order fer fifteen thousand."

"Say, that order 'll take a year to fill."

"Naw. Hardin is in cahoots with Bland. Between 'em they'll fill orders bigger 'n thet."

"Wondered what Hardin was rustlin' in here fer."

Duane could not possibly attend to all the conversation among the outlaws. He endeavored to get the drift of talk nearest to him.

"Kid Fuller's goin' to cash," said a sandy-whiskered little outlaw.

"So Jim was tellin' me. Blood-poison, ain't it? Thet hole wasn't bad. But he took the fever," rejoined a comrade.

"Deger says the Kid might pull through if he hed nursin'."

"Wal, Kate Bland ain't nursin' any shot-up boys these days. She hasn't got time."

A laugh followed this sally; then came a penetrating silence. Some of the outlaws glanced good-naturedly at Duane. They bore him no ill will. Manifestly they were aware of Mrs. Bland's infatuation.

"Pete, 'pears to me you've said thet before."

"Shore. Wal, it's happened before."

This remark drew louder laughter and more significant glances at Duane. He did not choose to ignore them any longer.

"Boys, poke all the fun you like at me, but don't mention any lady's name again. My hand is nervous and itchy these days."

He smiled as he spoke, and his speech was drawled; but the good humor in no wise weakened it. Then his latter remark was significant to a class of men who from inclination and necessity practiced at gun-drawing until they wore callous and sore places on their thumbs and inculcated in the very deeps of their nervous organization a habit that made even the simplest and most innocent motion of the hand end at or near the hip. There was something remarkable about a gun-fighter's hand. It never seemed to be gloved, never to be injured, never out of sight or in an awkward position.

There were grizzled outlaws in that group, some of whom had many notches on their gun-handles, and they, with their comrades, accorded Duane silence that carried conviction of the regard in which he was held.

Duane could not recall any other instance where he had let fall a familiar speech to these men, and certainly he had never before hinted of his possibilities. He saw instantly that he could not have done better.

"Orful hot, ain't it?" remarked Bill Black, presently. Bill could not keep quiet for long. He was a typical Texas desperado, had never been anything else. He was stoop-shouldered and bow-legged from much riding; a wiry little man, all muscle, with a square head, a hard face partly black from scrubby beard and red from sun, and a bright, roving, cruel eye. His shirt was open at the neck, showing a grizzled breast.

"Is there any guy in this heah outfit sport enough to go swimmin'?" he asked.

"My Gawd, Bill, you ain't agoin' to wash!" exclaimed a comrade.

This raised a laugh in which Black joined. But no one seemed eager to join him in a bath.

"Laziest outfit I ever rustled with," went on Bill, discontentedly. "Nuthin' to do! Say, if nobody wants to swim maybe some of you'll gamble?"

He produced a dirty pack of cards and waved them at the motionless crowd.

"Bill, you're too good at cards," replied a lanky outlaw.

"Now, Jasper, you say thet powerful sweet, an' you look sweet, er I might take it to heart," replied Black, with a sudden change of tone.

Here it was again—that upflashing passion. What Jasper saw fit to reply would mollify the outlaw or it would not. There was an even balance.

"No offense, Bill," said Jasper, placidly, without moving.

Bill grunted and forgot Jasper. But he seemed restless and dissatisfied. Duane knew him to be an inveterate gambler. And as Benson's place was out of running-order, Black was like a fish on dry land.

"Wal, if you-all are afraid of the cairds, what will you bet on?" he asked, in disgust.

"Bill, I'll play you a game of mumbly peg fer two bits," replied one.

Black eagerly accepted. Betting to him was a serious matter. The game obsessed him, not the stakes. He entered into the mumbly-peg contest with a thoughtful mien and a corded brow. He won. Other comrades tried their luck with him and lost. Finally, when Bill had exhausted their supply of two-bit pieces or their desire for that particular game, he offered to bet on anything.

"See thet turtle-dove there?" he said, pointing. "I'll bet he'll scare at one stone or he won't. Five pesos he'll fly or he won't fly when some one chucks a stone. Who'll take me up?"

That appeared to be more than the gambling spirit of several outlaws could withstand.

"Take thet. Easy money," said one.

"Who's goin' to chuck the stone?" asked another.

"Anybody," replied Bill.

"Wal, I'll bet you I can scare him with one stone," said the first outlaw.

"We're in on thet, Jim to fire the darnick," chimed in the others.

The money was put up, the stone thrown. The turtle-dove took flight, to the great joy of all the outlaws except Bill.

"I'll bet you-all he'll come back to thet tree inside of five minnits," he offered, imperturbably.

Hereupon the outlaws did not show any laziness in their alacrity to cover Bill's money as it lay on the grass. Somebody had a watch, and they all sat down, dividing attention between the timepiece and the tree. The minutes dragged by to the accompaniment of various jocular remarks anent a fool and his money. When four and three-quarter minutes had passed a turtle-dove alighted in the cottonwood. Then ensued an impressive silence while Bill calmly pocketed the fifty dollars.

"But it hain't the same dove!" exclaimed one outlaw, excitedly. "This 'n' is smaller, dustier, not so purple."

Bill eyed the speaker loftily.

"Wal, you'll have to ketch the other one to prove thet. *Sabe*, pard? Now I'll bet any gent heah the fifty I won thet I can scare thet dove with one stone."

No one offered to take his wager.

"Wal, then, I'll bet any of you even money thet you *can't* scare him with one stone."

Not proof against this chance, the outlaws made up a purse, in no wise disconcerted by Bill's contemptuous allusions to their banding together. The stone was thrown. The dove did not fly. Thereafter, in regard to that bird, Bill was unable to coax or scorn his comrades into any kind of wager.

He tried them with a multiplicity of offers, and in vain. Then he appeared at a loss for some unusual and seductive wager. Presently a little ragged Mexican boy came along the river trail, a particularly starved and poor-looking little fellow. Bill called to him and gave him a handful of silver coins. Speechless, dazed, he went his way hugging the money.

"I'll bet he drops some before he gits to the road," declared Bill. "I'll bet he runs. Hurry, you four-flush gamblers."

Bill failed to interest any of his companions, and forthwith became sullen and silent. Strangely his good humor departed in spite of the fact that he had won considerable.

Duane, watching the disgruntled outlaw, marveled at him and wondered what was in his mind. These men were more variable than children, as unstable as water, as dangerous as dynamite.

"Bill, I'll bet you ten you can't spill whatever's in the bucket thet peon's packin'," said the outlaw called Jim.

Black's head came up with the action of a hawk about to swoop.

Duane glanced from Black to the road, where he saw a crippled peon carrying a tin bucket toward the river. This peon was a half-witted Indian who lived in a shack and did odd jobs for the Mexicans. Duane had met him often.

"Jim, I'll take you up," replied Black.

Something, perhaps a harshness in his voice, caused Duane to whirl. He caught a leaping gleam in the outlaw's eye.

"Aw, Bill, thet's too fur a shot," said Jasper, as Black rested an elbow on his knee and sighted over the long, heavy Colt. The distance to the peon was about fifty paces, too far for even the most expert shot to hit a moving object so small as a bucket.

Duane, marvelously keen in the alignment of sights, was positive that Black held too high. Another look at the hard face, now tense and dark with blood, confirmed Duane's suspicion that the outlaw was not aiming at the bucket at all. Duane leaped and struck the leveled gun out of his hand. Another outlaw picked it up.

Black fell back astounded. Deprived of his weapon, he did not seem the same man, or else he was cowed by Duane's significant and formidable front. Sullenly he turned away without even asking for his gun.

CHAPTER 8

What a contrast, Duane thought, the evening of that day presented to the state of his soul!

The sunset lingered in golden glory over the distant Mexican mountains; twilight came slowly; a faint breeze blew from the river cool and sweet; the late cooing of a dove and the tinkle of a cowbell were the only sounds; a serene and tranquil peace lay over the valley.

Inside Duane's body there was strife. This third facing of a desperate man had thrown him off his balance. It had not been fatal, but it threatened so much. The better side of his nature seemed to urge him to die rather than to go on fighting or opposing ignorant, unfortunate, savage men. But the perversity of him was so great that it dwarfed reason, conscience. He could not resist it. He felt something dying in him. He suffered. Hope seemed far away. Despair had seized upon him and was driving him into a reckless mood when he thought of Jennie.

He had forgotten her. He had forgotten that he had promised to save her. He had forgotten that he meant to snuff out as many lives as might stand between her and freedom. The very remembrance sheered off his morbid introspection. She made a difference. How strange for him to realize that! He felt grateful to her. He had been forced into outlawry; she had been stolen from her people and carried into captivity. They had met in the river fastness, he to instill hope into her despairing life, she to be the means, perhaps, of keeping him from sinking to the level of her captors. He became conscious of a strong and beating desire to see her, talk with her.

These thoughts had run through his mind while on his way to Mrs. Bland's house. He had let Euchre go on ahead because he wanted more time to compose himself. Darkness had about set in when he reached his destination. There was no light in the house. Mrs. Bland was waiting for him on the porch.

She embraced him, and the sudden, violent, unfamiliar contact sent such a shock through him that he all but forgot the deep game he was playing. She, however, in her agitation did not notice his shrinking. From her embrace and the tender, incoherent words that flowed with it he gathered that Euchre had acquainted her of his action with Black.

"He might have killed you!" she whispered, more clearly; and if Duane had ever heard love in a voice he heard it then. It softened him. After all, she was a woman, weak, fated through her nature, unfortunate in her experience of life, doomed to unhappiness and tragedy. He met her advance so far that he returned the embrace and kissed her. Emotion such as she showed would have made any woman sweet, and she had a certain charm. It was easy, even pleasant, to kiss her; but Duane resolved that, whatever her abandonment might become, he would not go further than the lie she made him act.

"Buck, you love me?" she whispered.

"Yes—yes," he burst out, eager to get it over, and even as he spoke he caught the pale gleam of Jennie's face through the window. He felt a shame he was glad she could not see. Did she remember that she had promised not to misunderstand any action of his? What did she think of him, seeing him out there in the dusk with this bold woman in his arms? Somehow that dim sight of Jennie's pale face, the big dark eyes, thrilled him, inspired him to his hard task of the present.

"Listen, dear," he said to the woman, and he meant his words for the girl. "I'm going to take you away from this outlaw den if I have to kill Bland, Alloway, Rugg—anybody who stands in my path. You were dragged here. You are good—I know it. There's happiness for you somewhere—a home among good people who will care for you. Just wait till—"

His voice trailed off and failed from excess of emotion. Kate Bland closed her eyes and leaned her head on his breast. Duane felt her heart beat against his, and conscience smote him a keen blow. If she loved him so much! But memory and understanding of her character hardened him again, and he gave her such commiseration as was due her sex, and no more.

"Boy, that's good of you," she whispered, "but it's too late. I'm done for. I can't leave Bland. All I ask is that you love me a little and stop your gun-throwing."

The moon had risen over the eastern bulge of dark mountain, and now the valley was flooded with mellow light, and shadows of cotton-woods wavered against the silver.

Suddenly the clip-clop, clip-clop of hoofs caused Duane to raise his head and listen. Horses were coming down the road from the head of the valley. The hour was unusual for riders to come in. Presently the narrow, moonlit lane was crossed at its far end by black moving objects. Two horses Duane discerned.

"It's Bland!" whispered the woman, grasping Duane with shaking hands. "You must run! No, he'd see you. That 'd be worse. It's Bland! I know his horse's trot."

"But you said he wouldn't mind my calling here," protested Duane. "Euchre's with me. It 'll be all right."

"Maybe so," she replied, with visible effort at self-control. Manifestly she had a great fear of Bland. "If I could only think!"

Then she dragged Duane to the door, pushed him in.

"Euchre, come out with me! Duane, you stay with the girl! I'll tell Bland you're in love with her. Jen, if you give us away I'll wring your neck."

The swift action and fierce whisper told Duane that Mrs. Bland was herself again. Duane stepped close to Jennie, who stood near the window. Neither spoke, but her hands were outstretched to meet his own. They were small, trembling hands, cold as ice. He held them close, trying to convey what he felt—that he would protect her. She leaned against him, and they looked out of the window. Duane felt calm and sure of himself. His most pronounced feeling besides that for the frightened girl was a curiosity as to how Mrs. Bland would rise to the occasion. He saw the riders dismount down the lane and wearily come forward. A boy led away the horses. Euchre, the old fox, was talking loud and with remarkable ease, considering what he claimed was his natural cowardice.

"—that was way back in the sixties, about the time of the war," he was saying. "Rustlin' cattle wasn't nuthin' then to what it is now. An' times is rougher these days. This gun-throwin' has come to be a disease. Men have an itch for the draw same as they used to have fer poker. The only real gambler outside of Mexicans we ever had here was Bill, an' I presume Bill is burnin' now."

The approaching outlaws, hearing voices, halted a rod or so from the porch. Then Mrs. Bland uttered an exclamation, ostensibly meant to express surprise, and hurried out to meet them. She greeted her husband warmly and gave welcome to the other man. Duane could not see well enough in the shadow to recognize Bland's companion, but he believed it was Alloway.

"Dog-tired we are and starved," said Bland, heavily. "Who's here with you?"

"That's Euchre on the porch. Duane is inside at the window with Jen," replied Mrs. Bland.

"Duane!" he exclaimed. Then he whispered low—something Duane could not catch.

"Why, I asked him to come," said the chief's wife. She spoke easily and naturally and made no change in tone. "Jen has been ailing. She gets thinner and whiter every day. Duane came here one day with Euchre, saw Jen, and went loony over her pretty face, same as all you men. So I let him come."

Bland cursed low and deep under his breath. The other man made a violent action of some kind and apparently was quieted by a restraining hand.

"Kate, you let Duane make love to Jennie?" queried Bland, incredulously.

"Yes, I did," replied the wife, stubbornly. "Why not? Jen's in love with him. If he takes her away and marries her she can be a decent woman."

Bland kept silent a moment, then his laugh pealed out loud and harsh.

"Chess, did you get that? Well, by God! what do you think of my wife?"

"She's lyin' or she's crazy," replied Alloway, and his voice carried an unpleasant ring.

Mrs. Bland promptly and indignantly told her husband's lieutenant to keep his mouth shut.

"Ho, ho, ho!" rolled out Bland's laugh.

Then he led the way to the porch, his spurs clinking, the weapons he was carrying rattling, and he flopped down on a bench.

"How are you, boss?" asked Euchre.

"Hello, old man. I'm well, but all in."

Alloway slowly walked on to the porch and leaned against the rail. He answered Euchre's greeting with a nod. Then he stood there a dark, silent figure.

Mrs. Bland's full voice in eager questioning had a tendency to ease the situation. Bland replied briefly to her, reporting a remarkably successful trip.

Duane thought it time to show himself. He had a feeling that Bland and Alloway would let him go for the moment. They were plainly nonplussed, and Alloway seemed sullen, brooding.

"Jennie," whispered Duane, "that was clever of Mrs. Bland. We'll keep up the deception. Any day now be ready!"

She pressed close to him, and a barely audible "Hurry!" came breathing into his ear.

"Good night, Jennie," he said, aloud. "Hope you feel better to-morrow."

Then he stepped out into the moonlight and spoke. Bland returned the greeting, and, though he was not amiable, he did not show resentment.

"Met Jasper as I rode in," said Bland, presently. "He told me you made Bill Black mad, and there's liable to be a fight. What did you go off the handle about?"

Duane explained the incident. "I'm sorry I happened to be there," he went on. "It wasn't my business."

"Scurvy trick that 'd been," muttered Bland. "You did right. All the same, Duane, I want you to stop quarreling with my men. If you were one of us—that 'd be different. I can't keep my men from fighting. But I'm not called on to let an outsider hang around my camp and plug my rustlers."

"I guess I'll have to be hitting the trail for somewhere," said Duane.

"Why not join my band? You've got a bad start already, Duane, and if I know this border you'll never be a respectable citizen again. You're a born killer. I know every bad man on this frontier. More than one of them have told me that something exploded in their brain, and when sense came back there lay another dead man. It's not so with me. I've done a little shooting, too, but I never wanted to kill another man just to rid myself of the last one. My dead men don't sit on my chest at night. That's the gun-fighter's trouble. He's crazy. He has to kill a new man—he's driven to it to forget the last one."

"But I'm no gun-fighter," protested Duane. "Circumstances made me—"

"No doubt," interrupted Bland, with a laugh. "Circumstances made me a rustler. You don't know yourself. You're young; you've got a temper; your father was one of the most dangerous men Texas ever had. I don't see any other career for you. Instead of going it alone—a lone wolf, as the Texans say—why not make friends with other outlaws? You'll live longer."

Euchre squirmed in his seat.

"Boss, I've been givin' the boy egzactly thet same line of talk. Thet's why I took him in to bunk with me. If he makes pards among us there won't be any more trouble. An' he'd be a grand feller fer the gang. I've seen Wild Bill Hickok throw a gun, an' Billy the Kid, an' Hardin, an' Chess here—all the fastest men on the border. An' with apologies to present company, I'm here to say Duane has them all skinned. His draw is different. You can't see how he does it."

Euchre's admiring praise served to create an effective little silence. Alloway shifted uneasily on his feet, his spurs jangling faintly, and did not lift his head. Bland seemed thoughtful.

"That's about the only qualification I have to make me eligible for your band," said Duane, easily.

"It's good enough," replied Bland, shortly. "Will you consider the idea?"

"I'll think it over. Good night."

He left the group, followed by Euchre. When they reached the end of the lane, and before they had exchanged a word, Bland called Euchre back. Duane proceeded slowly along the moonlit road to the cabin and sat down under the cottonwoods to wait for Euchre. The night was intense and quiet, a low hum of insects giving the effect of a congestion of life. The beauty of the soaring moon, the ebony cañons of shadow under the mountain, the melancholy serenity of the perfect night, made Duane shudder in the realization of how far aloof he now was from enjoyment of these things. Never again so long as he lived could he be natural. His mind was clouded. His eye and ear henceforth must register impressions of nature, but the joy of them had fled.

Still, as he sat there with a foreboding of more and darker work ahead of him there was yet a strange sweetness left to him, and it lay in thought of Jennie. The pressure of her cold little hands lingered in his. He did not think of her as a woman, and he did not analyze his feelings. He just had vague, dreamy thoughts and imaginations that were interspersed in the constant and stern revolving of plans to save her.

A shuffling step roused him. Euchre's dark figure came crossing the moonlit grass under the cottonwoods. The moment the outlaw reached him Duane saw that he was laboring under great excitement. It scarcely affected Duane. He seemed to be acquiring patience, calmness, strength.

"Bland kept you pretty long," he said.

"Wait till I git my breath," replied Euchre. He sat silent a little while, fanning himself with a sombrero, though the night was cool, and then he went into the cabin to return presently with a lighted pipe.

"Fine night," he said; and his tone further acquainted Duane with Euchre's quaint humor. "Fine night for love-affairs, by gum!"

"I'd noticed that," rejoined Duane, dryly.

"Wal, I'm a son of a gun if I didn't stand an' watch Bland choke his wife till her tongue stuck out an' she got black in the face."

"No!" exclaimed Duane.

"Hope to die if I didn't. Buck, listen to this here yarn. When I got back to the porch I seen Bland was wakin' up. He'd been too fagged out to figger much. Alloway an' Kate had gone in the house, where they lit up the lamps. I heard Kate's high voice, but Alloway never chirped. He's not the talkin' kind, an' he's damn dangerous when he's thet way. Bland asked me some questions right from the shoulder. I was ready for them, an' I swore the moon was green cheese. He was satisfied. Bland always trusted me, an' liked me, too, I reckon. I hated to lie black thet way. But he's a hard man with bad intentions toward Jennie, an' I'd double-cross him any day.

"Then we went into the house. Jennie had gone to her little room, an' Bland called her to come out. She said she was undressin'. An' he ordered her to put her clothes back on. Then, Buck, his next move was some surprisin'. He deliberately throwed a gun on Kate. Yes sir, he pointed his big blue Colt right at her, an' he says:

"'I've a mind to blow out your brains.'

"'Go ahead,' says Kate, cool as could be.

"'You lied to me,' he roars.

"Kate laughed in his face. Bland slammed the gun down an' made a grab fer her. She fought him, but wasn't a match fer him, an' he got her by the throat. He choked her till I thought she was strangled. Alloway made him stop. She flopped down on the bed an' gasped fer a while. When she come to them hard-shelled cusses went after her, trying to make her give herself away. I think Bland was jealous. He suspected she'd got thick with you an' was foolin' him. I reckon thet's a sore feelin' fer a man to have—to guess pretty nice, but not to *be* sure. Bland gave it up after a while. An' then he cussed an' raved at her. One sayin' of his is worth pinnin' in your sombrero: 'It ain't nuthin' to kill a man. I don't need much fer thet. But I want to *know*, you hussy!'

"Then he went in an' dragged poor Jen out. She'd had time to dress. He was so mad he hurt her sore leg. You know Jen got thet injury fightin' off one of them devils in the dark. An' when I seen Bland twist her—hurt her—I had a odd hot feelin' deep down in me, an' fer the only time in my life I wished I was a gun-fighter.

"Wal, Jen amazed me. She was whiter 'n a sheet, an' her eyes were big and stary, but she had nerve. Fust time I ever seen her show any.

"'Jennie,' he said, 'my wife said Duane came here to see you. I believe she's lyin'. I think she's been carryin' on with him, an' I want to *know*. If she's been an' you tell me the truth I'll let you go. I'll send you out to Huntsville, where you can communicate with your friends. I'll give you money.'

"Thet must hev been a hell of a minnit fer Kate Bland. If ever I seen death in a man's eye I seen it in Bland's. He loves her. Thet's the strange part of it.

" 'Has Duane been comin' here to see my wife?' Bland asked, fierce-like.

" 'No,' said Jennie.

" 'He's been after you?'

" 'Yes.'

" 'He has fallen in love with you? Kate said thet.'

" 'I—I'm not—I don't know—he hasn't told me.'

" 'But you're in love with him?'

" 'Yes,' she said; an', Buck, if you only could have seen her! She throwed up her head, an' her eyes were full of fire. Bland seemed dazed at sight of her. An' Alloway, why, thet little skunk of an outlaw cried right out. He was hit plumb center. He's in love with Jen. An' the look of her then was enough to make any feller quit. He jest slunk out of the room. I told you, mebbe, thet he'd been tryin' to git Bland to marry Jen to him. So even a tough like Alloway can love a woman!

"Bland stamped up an' down the room. He sure was dyin' hard.

" 'Jennie,' he said, once more turnin' to her. 'You swear in fear of your life thet you're tellin' truth. Kate's not in love with Duane? She's let him come to see *you*? There's been nuthin' between them?'

" 'No. I swear,' answered Jennie; an' Bland sat down like a man licked.

" 'Go to bed, you white-faced—' Bland choked on some word or other—a bad one, I reckon—an' he positively shook in his chair.

"Jennie went then, an' Kate began to have hysterics. An' your uncle Euchre ducked his nut out of the door an' come home."

Duane did not have a word to say at the end of Euchre's long harangue. He experienced relief. As a matter of fact, he had expected a good deal worse. He thrilled at the thought of Jennie perjuring herself to save that abandoned woman. What mysteries these feminine creatures were!

"Wal, there's where our little deal stands now," resumed Euchre, meditatively. "You know, Buck, as well as me thet if you'd been some feller who hadn't shown he was a wonder with a gun you'd now be full of lead. If you'd happen to kill Bland an' Alloway, I reckon you'd be as safe on this here border as you would in Santone. Such is gun fame in this land of the draw."

CHAPTER 9

Both men were awake early, silent with the premonition of trouble
ahead, thoughtful of the fact that the time for the long-planned action was at hand. It was remarkable that a man as loquacious as Euchre
could hold his tongue so long; and this was significant of the deadly nature of the intended deed. During breakfast he said a few words customary in the service of food. At the conclusion of the meal he seemed to
come to an end of deliberation.

"Buck, the sooner the better now," he declared, with a glint in his
eye. "The more time we use up now the less surprised Bland 'll be."

"I'm ready when you are," replied Duane, quietly, and he rose from
the table.

"Wal, saddle up, then," went on Euchre, gruffly. "Tie on them two
packs I made, one fer each saddle. You can't tell—mebbe either hoss will
be carryin' double. It's good they're both big, strong hosses. Guess thet
wasn't a wise move of your uncle Euchre's—bringin' in your hosses an'
havin' them ready?"

"Euchre, I hope you're not going to get in bad here. I'm afraid you
are. Let me do the rest now," said Duane.

The old outlaw eyed him sarcastically.

"Thet 'd be turrible now, wouldn't it? If you want to know, why, I'm
in bad already. I didn't tell you thet Alloway called me last night. He's
gettin' wise pretty quick."

"Euchre, you're going with me?" queried Duane, suddenly divining the truth.

"Wal, I reckon. Either to hell or safe over the mountain! I wisht I was a gun-fighter. I hate to leave here without takin' a peg at Jackrabbit Benson. Now, Buck, you do some hard figgerin' while I go nosin' round. It's pretty early, which 's all the better."

Euchre put on his sombrero, and as he went out Duane saw that he wore a gun-and-cartridge belt. It was the first time Duane had ever seen the outlaw armed.

Duane packed his few belongings into his saddle-bags, and then carried the saddles out to the corral. An abundance of alfalfa in the corral showed that the horses had fared well. They had gotten almost fat during his stay in the valley. He watered them, put on the saddles loosely cinched, and then the bridles. His next move was to fill the two canvas water-bottles. That done, he returned to the cabin to wait.

At the moment he felt no excitement or agitation of any kind. There was no more thinking and planning to do. The hour had arrived, and he was ready. He understood perfectly the desperate chances he must take. His thoughts became confined to Euchre and the surprising loyalty and goodness in the hardened old outlaw. Time passed slowly. Duane kept glancing at his watch. He hoped to start the thing and get away before the outlaws were out of their beds. Finally he heard the shuffle of Euchre's boots on the hard path. The sound was quicker than usual.

When Euchre came around the corner of the cabin Duane was not so astounded as he was concerned to see the outlaw white and shaking. Sweat dripped from him. He had a wild look.

"Luck ours—so—fur, Buck!" he panted.

"You don't look it," replied Duane.

"I'm turrible sick. Jest killed a man. Fust one I ever killed!"

"Who?" asked Duane, startled.

"Jackrabbit Benson. An' sick as I am, I'm gloryin' in it. I went nosin' round up the road. Saw Alloway goin' into Deger's. He's thick with the Degers. Reckon he's askin' questions. Anyway, I was sure glad to see him away from Bland's. An' he didn't see me. When I dropped into Benson's there wasn't nobody there but Jackrabbit an' some Mexicans he was startin' to work. Benson never had no use fer me. An' he up an' said he wouldn't give a two-bit piece fer my life. I asked him why.

"'You're double-crossin' the boss an' Chess,' he said.

"'Jack, what 'd you give fer your own life?' I asked him.

"He straightened up surprised an' mean-lookin'. An' I let him have it, plumb center! He wilted, an' the Mexicans run. I reckon I'll never sleep again. But I had to do it."

Duane asked if the shot had attracted any attention outside.

"I didn't see anybody but the Mexicans, an' I sure looked sharp. Comin' back I cut across through the cottonwoods past Bland's cabin. I meant to keep out of sight, but somehow I had an idee I might find out if Bland was awake yet. Sure enough I run plumb into Beppo, the boy who tends Bland's hosses. Beppo likes me. An' when I inquired of his boss he said Bland had been up all night fightin' with the señora. An', Buck, here's how I figger. Bland couldn't let up last night. He was sore, an' he went after Kate again, tryin' to wear her down. Jest as likely he might have went after Jennie, with wuss intentions. Anyway, he an' Kate must have had it hot an' heavy. We're pretty lucky."

"It seems so. Well, I'm going," said Duane, tersely.

"Lucky! I should smile! Bland's been up all night after a most draggin' ride home. He'll be fagged out this mornin', sleepy, sore, an' he won't be expectin' hell before breakfast. Now, you walk over to his house. Meet him how you like. Thet's your game. But I'm suggestin', if he comes out an' you want to parley, you can jest say you'd thought over his proposition an' was ready to join his band, or you ain't. You'll have to kill him, an' it 'd save time to go fer your gun on sight. Might be wise, too, fer it's likely he'll do thet same."

"How about the horses?"

"I'll fetch them an' come along about two minnits behind you. 'Pears to me you ought to have the job done an' Jennie outside by the time I git there. Once on them hosses, we can ride out of camp before Alloway or anybody else gits into action. Jennie ain't much heavier 'n a rabbit. Thet big black will carry you both."

"All right. But once more let me persuade you to stay—not to mix any more in this," said Duane, earnestly.

"Nope. I'm goin'. You heard what Benson told me. Alloway wouldn't give me the benefit of any doubts. Buck, a last word—look out fer thet Bland woman!"

Duane merely nodded, and then, saying that the horses were ready, he strode away through the grove. Accounting for the short cut across grove and field, it was about five minutes' walk up to Bland's house. To Duane it seemed long in time and distance, and he had difficulty in restraining his pace. As he walked there came a gradual and subtle change in his feelings. Again he was going out to meet a man in conflict. He could have avoided this meeting. But despite the fact of his courting the encounter he had not as yet felt that hot, inexplicable rush of blood. The motive of this deadly action was not personal, and somehow that made a difference.

No outlaws were in sight. He saw several Mexican herders with cattle. Blue columns of smoke curled up over some of the cabins. The fragrant smell of it reminded Duane of his home and cutting wood for the stove. He noted a cloud of creamy mist rising above the river, dissolving in the sunlight.

Then he entered Bland's lane.

While yet some distance from the cabin he heard loud, angry voices of man and woman. Bland and Kate still quarreling! He took a quick survey of the surroundings. There was now not even a Mexican in sight. Then he hurried a little. Half-way down the lane he turned his head to peer through the cottonwoods. This time he saw Euchre coming with the horses. There was no indication that the old outlaw might lose his nerve at the end. Duane had feared this.

Duane now changed his walk to a leisurely saunter. He reached the porch and then distinguished what was said inside the cabin.

"If you do, Bland, by Heaven I'll fix you and her!" That was panted out in Kate Bland's full voice.

"Let me loose! I'm going in there, I tell you!" replied Bland, hoarsely. "What for?"

"I want to make a little love to her. Ha! ha! It 'll be fun to have the laugh on her new lover."

"You lie!" cried Kate Bland.

"I'm not saying what I'll do to her *afterward*!" His voice grew hoarser with passion. "Let me go now!"

"No! no! I won't let you go. You'll choke the—the truth out of her—you'll kill her."

"The *truth*!" hissed Bland.

"Yes. I lied. Jen lied. But she lied to save me. You needn't—murder her—for that."

Bland cursed horribly. Then followed a wrestling sound of bodies in violent straining contact—the scrape of feet—the jangle of spurs—a crash of sliding table or chair, and then the cry of a woman in pain.

Duane stepped into the open door, inside the room. Kate Bland lay half across a table where she had been flung, and she was trying to get to her feet. Bland's back was turned. He had opened the door into Jennie's room and had one foot across the threshold. Duane caught the girl's low, shuddering cry. Then he called out loud and clear.

With cat-like swiftness Bland wheeled, then froze on the threshold. His sight, quick as his action, caught Duane's menacing, unmistakable position.

Bland's big frame filled the door. He was in a bad place to reach for his gun. But he would not have time for a step. Duane read in his eyes the desperate calculation of chances. For a fleeting instant Bland shifted his glance to his wife. Then his whole body seemed to vibrate with the swing of his arm.

Duane shot him. He fell forward, his gun exploding as it hit into the floor, and dropped loose from stretching fingers. Duane stood over him, stooped to turn him on his back. Bland looked up with clouded gaze, then gasped his last.

"Duane, you've killed him!" cried Kate Bland, huskily. "I knew you'd have to!"

She staggered against the wall, her eyes dilating, her strong hands clenching, her face slowly whitening. She appeared shocked, half stunned, but showed no grief.

"Jennie!" called Duane, sharply.

"Oh—Duane!" came a halting reply.

"Yes. Come out. Hurry!"

She came out with uneven steps, seeing only him, and she stumbled over Bland's body. Duane caught her arm, swung her behind him. He feared the woman when she realized how she had been duped. His action was protective, and his movement toward the door equally as significant.

"Duane!" cried Mrs. Bland.

It was no time for talk. Duane edged on, keeping Jennie behind him. At that moment there was a pounding of iron-shod hoofs out in the lane. Kate Bland bounded to the door. When she turned back her amazement was changing to realization.

"Where 're you taking Jen?" she cried, her voice like a man's.

"Get out of my way," replied Duane. His look perhaps, without speech, was enough for her. In an instant she was transformed into a fury.

"You hound! All the time you were fooling me! You made love to me! You let me believe—you swore you loved me! Now I see what was odd about you. All for that girl! But you can't have her. You'll never leave here alive. Give me that girl! Let me—get at her! She'll never win any more men in this camp."

She was a powerful woman, and it took all Duane's strength to ward off her onslaughts. She clawed at Jennie over his upheld arm. Every second her fury increased.

"*Help! help! help!*" she shrieked, in a voice that must have penetrated to the remotest cabin in the valley.

"Let go! Let go!" cried Duane, low and sharp. He still held his gun in his right hand, and it began to be hard for him to ward the woman off. His coolness had gone with her shriek for help. "Let go!" he repeated, and he shoved her fiercely.

Suddenly she snatched a rifle off the wall and backed away, her strong hands fumbling at the lever. As she jerked it down, throwing a shell into the chamber and cocking the weapon, Duane leaped upon her. He struck up the rifle as it went off, the powder burning his face.

"Jennie, run out! Get on a horse!" he said.

Jennie flashed out of the door.

With an iron grasp Duane held to the rifle-barrel. He had grasped it with his left hand, and he gave such a pull that he swung the crazed woman off the floor. But he could not loose her grip. She was as strong as he.

"Kate! Let go!"

He tried to intimidate her. She did not see his gun thrust in her face, or reason had given way to such an extent to passion that she did not care.

She cursed. Her husband had used the same curses, and from her lips they seemed strange, unsexed, more deadly. Like a tigress she fought him; her face no longer resembled a woman's. The evil of that outlaw life, the wildness and rage, the meaning to kill, was even in such a moment terribly impressed upon Duane.

He heard a cry from outside—a man's cry, hoarse and alarming.

It made him think of loss of time. This demon of a woman might yet block his plan.

"Let go!" he whispered, and felt his lips stiff. In the grimness of that instant he relaxed his hold on the rifle-barrel.

With sudden, redoubled, irresistible strength she wrenched the rifle down and discharged it. Duane felt a blow—a shock—a burning agony tearing through his breast. Then in a frenzy he jerked so powerfully upon the rifle that he threw the woman against the wall. She fell and seemed stunned.

Duane leaped back, whirled, flew out of the door to the porch. The sharp cracking of a gun halted him. He saw Jennie holding to the bridle of his bay horse. Euchre was astride the other, and he had a Colt leveled, and he was firing down the lane. Then came a single shot, heavier, and Euchre's ceased. He fell from the horse.

A swift glance back showed to Duane a man coming down the lane. Chess Alloway! His gun was smoking. He broke into a run. Then in an instant he saw Duane, and tried to check his pace as he swung up his arm. But that slight pause was fatal. Duane shot, and Alloway was falling when his gun went off. His bullet whistled close to Duane and thudded into the cabin.

Duane bounded down to the horses. Jennie was trying to hold the plunging bay. Euchre lay flat on his back, dead, a bullet-hole in his shirt, his face set hard, and his hands twisted round gun and bridle.

"Jennie, you've nerve, all right!" cried Duane, as he dragged down the horse she was holding. "Up with you now! There! Never mind—long stirrups! Hang on somehow!"

He caught his bridle out of Euchre's clutching grip and leaped astride. The frightened horses jumped into a run and thundered down the lane into the road. Duane saw men running from cabins. He heard shouts. But there were no shots fired. Jennie seemed able to stay on her horse, but without stirrups she was thrown about so much that Duane rode closer and reached out to grasp her arm.

Thus they rode through the valley to the trail that led up over the steep and broken Rim Rock. As they began to climb Duane looked back. No pursuers were in sight.

"Jennie, we're going to get away!" he cried, exultation for her in his voice.

She was gazing horror-stricken at his breast, as in turning to look back he faced her.

"Oh, Duane, your shirt's all bloody!" she faltered, pointing with trembling fingers.

With her words Duane became aware of two things—the hand he instinctively placed to his breast still held his gun, and he had sustained a terrible wound.

Duane had been shot through the breast far enough down to give him grave apprehension of his life. The clean-cut hole made by the bullet bled freely both at its entrance and where it had come out, but with no signs of hemorrhage. He did not bleed at the mouth; however, he began to cough up a reddish-tinged foam.

As they rode on Jennie, with pale face and mute lips, looked at him.

"I'm badly hurt, Jennie," he said, "but I guess I'll stick it out."

"The woman—did she shoot you?"

"Yes. She was a devil. Euchre told me to look out for her. I wasn't quick enough."

"You didn't have to—to—" shivered the girl.

"No! no!" he replied.

They did not stop climbing while Duane tore a scarf and made compresses, which he bound tightly over his wounds. The fresh horses made fast time up the rough trail. From open places Duane looked down. When they surmounted the steep ascent and stood on top of the Rim Rock, with no signs of pursuit down in the valley, and with the wild, broken fastnesses before them, Duane turned to the girl and assured her that they now had every chance of escape.

"But—your—wound!" she faltered, with dark, troubled eyes. "I see—the blood—dripping from your back!"

"Jennie, I'll take a lot of killing," he said.

Then he became silent and attended to the uneven trail. He was aware presently that he had not come into Bland's camp by this route. But that did not matter; any trail leading out beyond the Rim Rock was safe enough. What he wanted was to get far away into some wild retreat where he could hide till he recovered from his wound. He seemed to feel a fire inside his breast, and his throat burned so that it was necessary for him to take a swallow of water every little while. He began to suffer considerable pain, which increased as the hours went by and then gave way to a numbness. From that time on he had need of his great strength and endurance. Gradually he lost his steadiness and his keen sight; and he realized that if he were to meet foes, or if pursuing outlaws should come up with him, he could make only a poor stand. So he turned off on a trail that appeared seldom traveled.

Soon after this move he became conscious of a further thickening of his senses. He felt able to hold on to his saddle for a while longer, but he was failing. Then he thought he ought to advise Jennie, so in case she was left alone she would have some idea of what to do.

"Jennie, I'll give out soon," he said. "No—I don't mean—what you think. But I'll drop soon. My strength's going. If I die—you ride back to the main trail. Hide and rest by day. Ride at night. That trail goes to water. I believe you could get across the Nueces, where some rancher will take you in."

Duane could not get the meaning of her incoherent reply. He rode on, and soon he could not see the trail or hear his horse. He did not know whether they traveled a mile or many times that far. But he was conscious when the horse stopped, and had a vague sense of falling and feeling Jennie's arms before all became dark to him.

When consciousness returned he found himself lying in a little hut of mesquite branches. It was well built and evidently some years old. There were two doors or openings, one in front and the other at the back. Duane imagined it had been built by a fugitive—one who meant to keep an eye both ways and not to be surprised. Duane felt weak and had no desire to move. Where was he, anyway? A strange, intangible sense of time, distance, of something far behind weighed upon him. Sight of the two packs Euchre had made brought his thought to Jennie. What had become of her? There was evidence of her work in a smoldering fire and a little blackened coffee-pot. Probably she was outside looking after the horses or getting water. He thought he heard a step and listened, but he felt tired, and presently his eyes closed and he fell into a doze.

Awakening from this, he saw Jennie sitting beside him. In some way she seemed to have changed. When he spoke she gave a start and turned eagerly to him.

"Duane!" she cried.

"Hello. How 're you, Jennie, and how am I?" he said, finding it a little difficult to talk.

"Oh, I'm all right," she replied. "And you've come to—your wound's healed; but you've been sick. Fever, I guess. I did all I could."

Duane saw now that the difference in her was a whiteness and tightness of skin, a hollowness of eye, a look of strain.

"Fever? How long have we been here?" he asked.

She took some pebbles from the crown of his sombrero and counted them.

"Nine. Nine days," she answered.

"Nine days!" he exclaimed, incredulously. But another look at her assured him that she meant what she said. "I've been sick all the time? You nursed me?"

"Yes."

"Bland's men didn't come along here?"

"No."

"Where are the horses?"

"I keep them grazing down in a gorge back of here. There's good grass and water."

"Have you slept any?"

"A little. Lately I couldn't keep awake."

"Good Lord! I should think not. You've had a time of it sitting here day and night nursing me, watching for the outlaws. Come, tell me all about it."

"There's nothing much to tell."

"I want to know, anyway, just what you did—how you felt."

"I can't remember very well," she replied, simply. "We must have ridden forty miles that day we got away. You bled all the time. Toward evening you lay on your horse's neck. When we came to this place you fell out of the saddle. I dragged you in here and stopped your bleeding. I thought you'd die that night. But in the morning I had a little hope. I had forgotten the horses. But luckily they didn't stray far. I caught them and kept them down in the gorge. When your wounds closed and you began to breathe stronger I thought you'd get well quick. It was fever that put you back. You raved a lot, and that worried me, because I couldn't stop you. Anybody trailing us could have heard you a good ways. I don't know whether I was scared most then or when you were quiet, and it was so dark and lonely and still all around. Every day I put a stone in your hat."

"Jennie, you saved my life," said Duane.

"I don't know. Maybe. I did all I knew how to do," she replied. "You saved mine—more than my life."

Their eyes met in a long gaze, and then their hands in a close clasp.

"Jennie, we're going to get away," he said, with gladness. "I'll be well in a few days. You don't know how strong I am. We'll hide by day and travel by night. I can get you across the river."

"And then?" she asked.

"We'll find some honest rancher."

"And then?" she persisted.

"Why," he began, slowly, "that's as far as my thoughts ever got. It was pretty hard, I tell you, to assure myself of so much. It means your safety. You'll tell your story. You'll be sent to some village or town and taken care of until a relative or friend is notified."

"And you?" she inquired, in a strange voice.

Duane kept silence.

"What will you do?" she went on.

"Jennie, I'll go back to the brakes. I daren't show my face among respectable people. I'm an outlaw."

"You're no criminal!" she declared, with deep passion.

"Jennie, on this border the little difference between an outlaw and a criminal doesn't count for much."

"You won't go back among those terrible men? You, with your gentleness and sweetness—all that's good about you? Oh, Duane, don't—don't go!"

"I can't go back to the outlaws, at least not Bland's band. No, I'll go alone. I'll lone-wolf it, as they say on the border. What else can I do, Jennie?"

"Oh, I don't know. Couldn't you hide? Couldn't you slip out of Texas—go far away?"

"I could never get out of Texas without being arrested. I could hide, but a man must live. Never mind about me, Jennie."

In three days Duane was able with great difficulty to mount his horse. During daylight, by short relays, he and Jennie rode back to the main trail, where they hid again till he had rested. Then in the dark they rode out of the cañons and gullies of the Rim Rock, and early in the morning halted at the first water to camp.

From that point they traveled after nightfall and went into hiding during the day. Once across the Nueces River, Duane was assured of safety for her and great danger for himself. They had crossed into a country he did not know. Somewhere east of the river there were scattered ranches. But he was as liable to find the rancher in touch with the outlaws as he was likely to find him honest. Duane hoped his good fortune would not desert him in this last service to Jennie. Next to the worry of that was realization of his condition. He had gotten up too soon; he had ridden too far and hard, and now he felt that any moment he might fall from his saddle. At last, far ahead over a barren mesquite-dotted stretch of dusty ground, he espied a patch of green and a little flat, red ranch-house. He headed his horse for it and turned a face he tried to make cheerful for Jennie's sake. She seemed both happy and sorry.

When near at hand he saw that the rancher was a thrifty farmer. And thrift spoke for honesty. There were fields of alfalfa, fruit-trees, corrals, windmill pumps, irrigation-ditches, all surrounding a neat little adobe house. Some children were playing in the yard. The way they ran at sight of Duane hinted of both the loneliness and the fear of their isolated lives. Duane saw a woman come to the door, then a man. The latter looked keenly, then stepped outside. He was a sandy-haired, freckled Texan.

"Howdy, stranger," he called, as Duane halted. "Get down, you an' your woman. Say, now, air you sick or shot or what? Let me—"

Duane, reeling in his saddle, bent searching eyes upon the rancher. He thought he saw good will, kindness, honesty. He risked all on that one sharp glance. Then he almost plunged from the saddle.

The rancher caught him, helped him to a bench.

"Martha, come out here!" he called. "This man's sick. No; he's shot, or I don't know blood-stains."

Jennie had slipped off her horse and to Duane's side. Duane appeared about to faint.

"Air you his wife?" asked the rancher.

"No. I'm only a girl he saved from outlaws. Oh, he's so pale! Duane, Duane!"

"Buck Duane!" exclaimed the rancher, excitedly. "The man who killed Bland an' Alloway? Say, I owe him a good turn, an' I'll pay it, young woman."

The rancher's wife came out, and with a manner at once kind and practical essayed to make Duane drink from a flask. He was not so far gone that he could not recognize its contents, which he refused, and weakly asked for water. When that was given him he found his voice.

"Yes, I'm Duane. I've only overdone myself—just all in. The wounds I got at Bland's are healing. Will you take this girl in—hide her awhile till the excitement's over among the outlaws?"

"I shore will," replied the Texan.

"Thanks. I'll remember you—I'll square it."

"What 're you goin' to do?"

"I'll rest a bit—then go back to the brakes."

"Young man, you ain't in any shape to travel. See here—any rustlers on your trail?"

"I think we gave Bland's gang the slip."

"Good. I'll tell you what. I'll take you in along with the girl, an' hide both of you till you get well. It 'll be safe. My nearest neighbor is five miles off. We don't have much company."

"You risk a great deal. Both outlaws and rangers are hunting me," said Duane.

"Never seen a ranger yet in these parts. An' have always got along with outlaws, mebbe exceptin' Bland. I tell you I owe you a good turn."

"My horses might betray you," added Duane.

"I'll hide them in a place where there's water an' grass. Nobody goes to it. Come now, let me help you indoors."

Duane's last fading sensations of that hard day were the strange feel of a bed, a relief at the removal of his heavy boots, and of Jennie's soft, cool hands on his hot face.

He lay ill for three weeks before he began to mend, and it was another week then before he could walk out a little in the dusk of the evenings. After that his strength returned rapidly. And it was only at the end of this long siege that he recovered his spirits. During most of his illness he had been silent, moody.

"Jennie, I'll be riding off soon," he said, one evening. "I can't impose on this good man Andrews much longer. I'll never forget his kindness. His wife, too—she's been so good to us. Yes, Jennie, you and I will have to say good-by very soon."

"Don't hurry away," she replied.

Lately Jennie had appeared strange to him. She had changed from the girl he used to see at Mrs. Bland's house. He took her reluctance to say good-by as another indication of her regret that he must go back to the brakes. Yet somehow it made him observe her more closely. She wore a plain, white dress made from material Mrs. Andrews had given her. Sleep and good food had improved her. If she had been pretty out there in the outlaw den, now she was more than that. But she had the same paleness, the same strained look, the same dark eyes full of haunting shadows. After Duane's realization of the change in her he watched her more, with a growing certainty that he would be sorry not to see her again.

"It's likely we won't ever see each other again," he said. "That's strange to think of. We've been through some hard days, and I seem to have known you a long time."

Jennie appeared shy, almost sad, so Duane changed the subject to something less personal.

Andrews returned one evening from a several days' trip to Huntsville. "Duane, everybody's talkin' about how you cleaned up the Bland outfit," he said, important and full of news. "It's some exaggerated, accordin' to what you told me; but you've shore made friends on this side of the Nueces. I reckon there ain't a town where you wouldn't find people to welcome you. Huntsville, you know, is some divided in its ideas. Half the people are crooked. Likely enough, all them who was so loud in praise of you are the crookedest. For instance, I met King Fisher, the boss outlaw of these parts. Well, King thinks he's a decent citizen. He was tellin' me what a grand job yours was for the border an' honest cattlemen. Now that Bland and Alloway are done for, King Fisher will find rustlin' easier. There's talk of Hardin movin' his camp over to Bland's. But I don't know how true it is. I reckon there ain't much to it. In the past when a big outlaw chief went under, his band almost always broke up an' scattered. There's no one left who could run thet outfit."

"Did you hear of any outlaws hunting me?" asked Duane.

"Nobody from Bland's outfit is huntin' you, thet's shore," replied Andrews. "Fisher said there never was a hoss straddled to go on your trail. Nobody had any use for Bland. Anyhow, his men would be afraid to trail you. An' you could go right in to Huntsville, where you'd be some popular. Reckon you'd be safe, too, except when some of them fool saloon loafers or bad cowpunchers would try to shoot you for the glory in it. Them kind of men will bob up everywhere you go, Duane."

"I'll be able to ride and take care of myself in a day or two," went on Duane. "Then I'll go—I'd like to talk to you about Jennie."

"She's welcome to a home here with us."

"Thank you, Andrews. You're a kind man. But I want Jennie to get farther away from the Rio Grande. She'd never be safe here. Besides, she may be able to find relatives. She has some, though she doesn't know where they are."

"All right, Duane. Whatever you think best. I reckon now you'd better take her to some town. Go north an' strike for Shelbyville or Crockett. Them's both good towns. I'll tell Jennie the names of men who'll help her. You needn't ride into town at all."

"Which place is nearer, and how far is it?"

"Shelbyville. I reckon about two days' ride. Poor stock country, so you ain't liable to meet rustlers. All the same, better hit the trail at night an' go careful."

At sunset two days later Duane and Jennie mounted their horses and said good-by to the rancher and his wife. Andrews would not listen to Duane's thanks.

"I tell you I'm beholden to you yet," he declared.

"Well, what can I do for you?" asked Duane. "I may come along here again some day."

"Get down an' come in, then, or you're no friend of mine. I reckon there ain't nothin' I can think of— I just happen to remember—" Here he led Duane out of earshot of the women and went on in a whisper. "Buck, I used to be well-to-do. Got skinned by a man named Brown— Rodney Brown. He lives in Huntsville, an' he's my enemy. I never was much on fightin', or I'd fixed him. Brown ruined me—stole all I had. He's a hoss an' cattle thief, an' he has pull enough at home to protect him. I reckon I needn't say any more."

"Is this Brown a man who shot an outlaw named Stevens?" queried Duane, curiously.

"Shore, he's the same. I heard thet story. Brown swears he plugged Stevens through the middle. But the outlaw rode off, an' nobody ever knew for shore."

"Luke Stevens died of that shot. I buried him," said Duane.

Andrews made no further comment, and the two men returned to the women.

"The main road for about three miles, then where it forks take the left-hand road and keep on straight. That what you said, Andrews?"

"Shore. An' good luck to you both!"

Duane and Jennie trotted away into the gathering twilight. At the moment an insistent thought bothered Duane. Both Luke Stevens and the rancher Andrews had hinted to Duane to kill a man named Brown. Duane wished with all his heart that they had not mentioned it, let alone taken for granted the execution of the deed. What a bloody place Texas was! Men who robbed and men who were robbed both wanted murder. It was in the spirit of the country. Duane certainly meant to avoid ever meeting this Rodney Brown. And that very determination showed Duane how dangerous he really was—to men and to himself. Sometimes he had a feeling of how little stood between his sane and better self and a self utterly wild and terrible. He reasoned that only intelligence could save him—only a thoughtful understanding of his danger and a hold upon some ideal.

Then he fell into low conversation with Jennie, holding out hopeful views of her future, and presently darkness set in. The sky was overcast with heavy clouds; there was no air moving; the heat and oppression threatened storm. By and by Duane could not see a rod in front of him, though his horse had no difficulty in keeping to the road. Duane was bothered by the blackness of the night. Traveling fast was impossible, and any moment he might miss the road that led off to the left. So he was compelled to give all his attention to peering into the thick shadows ahead. As good luck would have it, he came to higher ground where there was less mesquite, and therefore not such impenetrable darkness; and at this point he came to where the road split.

Once headed in the right direction, he felt easier in mind. To his annoyance, however, a fine, misty rain set in. Jennie was not well dressed for wet weather; and, for that matter, neither was he. His coat, which in that dry warm climate he seldom needed, was tied behind his saddle, and he put it on Jennie.

They traveled on. The rain fell steadily; if anything, growing thicker. Duane grew uncomfortably wet and chilly. Jennie, however, fared somewhat better by reason of the heavy coat. The night passed quickly despite the discomfort, and soon a gray, dismal, rainy dawn greeted the travelers.

Jennie insisted that he find some shelter where a fire could be built to dry his clothes. He was not in a fit condition to risk catching cold. In fact, Duane's teeth were chattering. To find a shelter in that barren waste seemed a futile task. Quite unexpectedly, however, they happened upon a deserted adobe cabin situated a little off the road. Not only did it prove to have a dry interior, but also there was firewood. Water was available in pools everywhere; however, there was no grass for the horses.

A good fire and hot food and drink changed the aspect of their condition as far as comfort went. And Jennie lay down to sleep. For Duane, however, there must be vigilance. This cabin was no hiding-place. The rain fell harder all the time, and the wind changed to the north. "It's a norther, all right," muttered Duane. "Two or three days." And he felt that his extraordinary luck had not held out. Still one point favored him, and it was that travelers were not likely to come along during the storm.

Jennie slept while Duane watched. The saving of this girl meant more to him than any task he had ever assumed. First it had been partly from a human feeling to succor an unfortunate woman, and partly a motive to establish clearly to himself that he was no outlaw. Lately, however, had come a different sense, a strange one, with something personal and warm and protective in it.

As he looked down upon her, a slight, slender girl with bedraggled dress and disheveled hair, her face, pale and quiet, a little stern in sleep, and her long, dark lashes lying on her cheek, he seemed to see her fragility, her prettiness, her femininity as never before. But for him she might at that very moment have been a broken, ruined girl lying back in that cabin of the Blands'. The fact gave him a feeling of his importance in this shifting of her destiny. She was unharmed, still young; she would forget and be happy; she would live to be a good wife and mother. Somehow the thought swelled his heart. His act, death-dealing as it had been, was a noble one, and helped him to hold on to his drifting hopes. Hardly once since Jennie had entered into his thought had those ghosts returned to torment him.

To-morrow she would be gone among good, kind people with a possibility of finding her relatives. He thanked God for that; nevertheless, he felt a pang.

She slept more than half the day. Duane kept guard, always alert, whether he was sitting, standing, or walking. The rain pattered steadily on the roof and sometimes came in gusty flurries through the door. The horses were outside in a shed that afforded poor shelter, and they stamped restlessly. Duane kept them saddled and bridled.

About the middle of the afternoon Jennie awoke. They cooked a meal and afterward sat beside the little fire. She had never been, in his observation of her, anything but a tragic figure, an unhappy girl, the farthest removed from serenity and poise. That characteristic capacity for agitation struck him as stronger in her this day. He attributed it, however, to the long strain, the suspense nearing an end. Yet sometimes when her eyes were on him she did not seem to be thinking of her freedom, of her future.

"This time to-morrow you'll be in Shelbyville," he said.

"Where will you be?" she asked, quickly.

"Me? Oh, I'll be making tracks for some lonesome place," he replied.

The girl shuddered.

"I've been brought up in Texas. I remember what a hard lot the men of my family had. But poor as they were, they had a roof over their heads, a hearth with a fire, a warm bed—somebody to love them. And you, Duane—oh, my God! What must your life be? You must ride and hide and watch eternally. No decent food, no pillow, no friendly word, no clean clothes, no woman's hand! Horses, guns, trails, rocks, holes—these must be the important things in your life. You must go on riding, hiding, killing until you meet—"

She ended with a sob and dropped her head on her knees. Duane was amazed, deeply touched.

"My girl, thank you for that thought of me," he said, with a tremor in his voice. "You don't know how much that means to me."

She raised her face, and it was tear-stained, eloquent, beautiful.

"I've heard tell—the best of men go to the bad out there. You won't. Promise me you won't. I never—knew any man—like you. I—I—we may never see each other again—after to-day. I'll never forget you. I'll pray for you, and I'll never give up trying to—to do something. Don't despair. It's never too late. It was my hope that kept me alive—out there at Bland's—before you came. I was only a poor weak girl. But if I could hope—so can you. Stay away from men. Be a lone wolf. Fight for your life. Stick out your exile—and maybe—some day—"

Then she lost her voice. Duane clasped her hand and with feeling as deep as hers promised to remember her words. In her despair for him she had spoken wisdom—pointed out the only course.

Duane's vigilance, momentarily broken by emotion, had no sooner reasserted itself than he discovered the bay horse, the one Jennie rode, had broken his halter and gone off. The soft wet earth had deadened the sound of his hoofs. His tracks were plain in the mud. There were clumps of mesquite in sight, among which the horse might have strayed. It turned out, however, that he had not done so.

Duane did not want to leave Jennie alone in the cabin so near the road. So he put her up on his horse and bade her follow. The rain had ceased for the time being, though evidently the storm was not yet over. The tracks led up a wash to a wide flat where mesquite, prickly pear, and thorn-bush grew so thickly that Jennie could not ride into it. Duane was thoroughly concerned. He must have her horse. Time was flying. It would soon be night. He could not expect her to scramble quickly through that brake on foot. Therefore he decided to risk leaving her at the edge of the thicket and go in alone.

As he went in a sound startled him. Was it the breaking of a branch he had stepped on or thrust aside? He heard the impatient pound of his horse's hoofs. Then all was quiet. Still he listened, not wholly satisfied. He was never satisfied in regard to safety; he knew too well that there never could be safety for him in this country.

The bay horse had threaded the aisles of the thicket. Duane wondered what had drawn him there. Certainly it had not been grass, for there was none. Presently he heard the horse tramping along, and then he ran. The mud was deep, and the sharp thorns made going difficult. He came up with the horse, and at the same moment crossed a multitude of fresh horse-tracks.

He bent lower to examine them, and was alarmed to find that they had been made very recently, even since it had ceased raining. They were tracks of well-shod horses. Duane straightened up with a cautious glance all around. His instant decision was to hurry back to Jennie. But he had come a goodly way through the thicket, and it was impossible to rush back. Once or twice he imagined he heard crashings in the brush, but did not halt to make sure. Certain he was now that some kind of danger threatened.

Suddenly there came an unmistakable thump of horses' hoofs off somewhere to the fore. Then a scream rent the air. It ended abruptly. Duane leaped forward, tore his way through the thorny brake. He heard Jennie cry again—an appealing call quickly hushed. It seemed more to his right, and he plunged that way. He burst into a glade where a smoldering fire and ground covered with footprints and tracks showed that campers had lately been. Rushing across this, he broke his passage out to the open. But he was too late. His horse had disappeared. Jennie was gone. There were no riders in sight. There was no sound. There was a heavy trail of horses going north. Jennie had been carried off—probably by outlaws. Duane realized that pursuit was out of the question—that Jennie was lost.

CHAPTER 10

A hundred miles from the haunts most familiar with Duane's deeds, far up where the Nueces ran a trickling clear stream between yellow cliffs, stood a small deserted shack of covered mesquite poles. It had been made long ago, but was well preserved. A door faced the overgrown trail, and another faced down into a gorge of dense thickets. On the border fugitives from law and men who hid in fear of some one they had wronged never lived in houses with only one door.

It was a wild spot, lonely, not fit for human habitation except for the outcast. He, perhaps, might have found it hard to leave for most of the other wild nooks in that barren country. Down in the gorge there was never-failing sweet water, grass all the year round, cool, shady retreats, deer, rabbits, turkeys, fruit, and miles and miles of narrow-twisting, deep cañon full of broken rocks and impenetrable thickets. The scream of the panther was heard there, the squall of the wildcat, the cough of the jaguar. Innumerable bees buzzed in the spring blossoms, and, it seemed, scattered honey to the winds. All day there was continuous song of birds, that of the mocking-bird loud and sweet and mocking above the rest.

On clear days—and rare indeed were cloudy days—with the subsiding of the wind at sunset a hush seemed to fall around the little hut. Far-distant dim-blue mountains stood gold-rimmed gradually to fade with the shading of light.

At this quiet hour a man climbed up out of the gorge and sat in the westward door of the hut. This lonely watcher of the west and listener to the silence was Duane. And this hut was the one where, three years before, Jennie had nursed him back to life.

The killing of a man named Sellers, and the combination of circumstances that had made the tragedy a memorable regret, had marked, if not a change, at least a cessation in Duane's activities. He had trailed Sellers to kill him for the supposed abducting of Jennie. He had trailed him long after he had learned Sellers traveled alone. Duane wanted absolute assurance of Jennie's death. Vague rumors, a few words here and there, unauthenticated stories, were all Duane had gathered in years to substantiate his belief—that Jennie died shortly after the beginning of her second captivity. But Duane did not know surely. Sellers might have told him. Duane expected, if not to force it from him at the end, to read it in his eyes. But the bullet went too unerringly; it locked his lips and fixed his eyes.

After that meeting Duane lay long at the ranch-house of a friend, and when he recovered from the wound Sellers had given him he started with two horses and a pack for the lonely gorge on the Nueces. There he had been hidden for months, a prey to remorse, a dreamer, a victim of phantoms.

It took work for him to find subsistence in that rocky fastness. And work, action, helped to pass the hours. But he could not work all the time, even if he had found it to do. Then in his idle moments and at night his task was to live with the hell in his mind.

The sunset and the twilight hour made all the rest bearable. The little hut on the rim of the gorge seemed to hold Jennie's presence. It was not as if he felt her spirit. If it had been he would have been sure of her death. He hoped Jennie had not survived her second misfortune; and that intense hope had burned into belief, if not surety. Upon his return to that locality, on the occasion of his first visit to the hut, he had found things just as they had left them, and a poor, faded piece of ribbon Jennie had used to tie around her bright hair. No wandering outlaw or traveler had happened upon the lonely spot, which further endeared it to Duane.

A strange feature of this memory of Jennie was the freshness of it— the failure of years, toil, strife, death-dealing to dim it—to deaden the thought of what might have been. He had a marvelous gift of visualization. He could shut his eyes and see Jennie before him just as clearly as if she had stood there in the flesh. For hours he did that, dreaming, dreaming of life he had never tasted and now never would taste. He saw Jennie's slender, graceful figure, the old brown ragged dress in which he had seen her first at Bland's, her little feet in Mexican sandals, her fine hands coarsened by work, her round arms and swelling throat, and her pale, sad, beautiful face with its staring dark eyes. He remembered every look she had given him, every word she had spoken to him, every time she had touched him. He thought of her beauty and sweetness, of the few things which had come to mean to him that she must have loved him; and he trained himself to think of these in preference to her life at Bland's, the escape with him, and then her recapture, because such memories led to bitter, fruitless pain. He had to fight suffering because it was eating out his heart.

Sitting there, eyes wide open, he dreamed of the old homestead and his white-haired mother. He saw the old home life, sweetened and filled by dear new faces and added joys, go on before his eyes with him a part of it.

Then in the inevitable reaction, in the reflux of bitter reality, he would send out a voiceless cry no less poignant because it was silent: "Poor fool! No, I shall never see mother again—never go home—never have a home. I am Duane, the Lone Wolf! Oh, God! I wish it were over! These dreams torture me! What have I to do with a mother, a home, a wife? No bright-haired boy, no dark-eyed girl will ever love me. I am an outlaw, an outcast, dead to the good and decent world. I am alone— alone. Better be a callous brute or better dead! I shall go mad thinking! Man, what is left to you? A hiding-place like a wolf's—lonely silent days, lonely nights with phantoms! Or the trail and the road with their bloody tracks, and then the hard ride, the sleepless, hungry ride to some hole in rocks or brakes. What hellish thing drives me? Why can't I end it all? What is left? Only that damned unquenchable spirit of the gun-fighter to live—to hang on to miserable life—to have no fear of death, yet to cling like a leach—to die as gun-fighters seldom die, with boots off! Bain, you were first, and you're long avenged. I'd change with you. And Sellers, you were last, and you're avenged. And you others—you're avenged. Lie quiet in your graves and give me peace!"

But they did not lie quiet in their graves and give him peace.

A group of specters trooped out of the shadows of dusk and, gathering round him, escorted him to his bed.

When Duane had been riding the trails passion-bent to escape pursuers, or passion-bent in his search, the constant action and toil and exhaustion made him sleep. But when in hiding, as time passed, gradually he required less rest and sleep, and his mind became more active. Little by little his phantoms gained hold on him, and at length, but for the saving power of his dreams, they would have claimed him utterly.

How many times he had said to himself: "I am an intelligent man. I'm not crazy. I'm in full possession of my faculties. All this is fancy— imagination—conscience. I've no work, no duty, no ideal, no hope— and my mind is obsessed, thronged with images. And these images naturally are of the men with whom I have dealt. I can't forget them. They come back to me, hour after hour; and when my tortured mind grows weak, then maybe I'm not just right till the mood wears out and lets me sleep."

So he reasoned as he lay down in his comfortable camp. The night was star-bright above the cañon-walls, darkly shadowing down between them. The insects hummed and chirped and thrummed a continuous thick song, low and monotonous. Slow-running water splashed softly over stones in the stream-bed. From far down the cañon came the mournful hoot of an owl. The moment he lay down, thereby giving up action for the day, all these things weighed upon him like a great heavy mantle of loneliness. In truth, they did not constitute loneliness.

And he could no more have dispelled thought than he could have reached out to touch a cold, bright star.

He wondered how many outcasts like him lay under this star-studded, velvety sky across the fifteen hundred miles of wild country between El Paso and the mouth of the river. A vast wild territory—a refuge for outlaws! Somewhere he had heard or read that the Texas Rangers kept a book with names and records of outlaws—three thousand known outlaws! Yet these could scarcely be half of that unfortunate horde which had been recruited from all over the states. Duane had traveled from camp to camp, den to den, hiding-place to hiding-place, and he knew these men. Most of them were hopeless criminals; some were avengers; a few were wronged wanderers; and among them occasionally was a man, human in his way, honest as he could be, not yet lost to good.

But all of them were akin in one sense—their outlawry; and that starry night they lay with their dark faces up, some in packs like wolves, others alone like the gray wolf who knew no mate. It did not make much difference in Duane's thought of them that the majority were steeped in crime and brutality, more often than not stupid from rum, incapable of a fine feeling, just lost wild dogs.

Duane doubted that there was a man among them who did not realize his moral wreck and ruin. He had met poor, half-witted wretches who knew it. He believed he could enter into their minds and feel the truth of all their lives—the hardened outlaw, coarse, ignorant, bestial, who murdered as Bill Black had murdered, who stole for the sake of stealing, who craved money to gamble and drink, defiantly ready for death, and, like that terrible outlaw, Helm, who cried out on the scaffold, "Let her rip!"

The wild youngsters seeking notoriety and reckless adventure; the cowboys with a notch on their guns, with boastful pride in the knowledge that they were marked by rangers; the crooked men from the North, defaulters, forgers, murderers, all pale-faced, flat-chested men not fit for that wilderness and not surviving; the dishonest cattlemen, hand and glove with outlaws, driven from their homes; the old grizzled, bow-legged genuine rustlers—all these Duane had come in contact with, had watched and known, and as he felt with them he seemed to see that as their lives were bad, sooner or later to end dismally or tragically, so they must pay some kind of earthly penalty—if not of conscience, then of fear; if not of fear, then of that most terrible of all things to restless, active men—pain, the pang of flesh and bone.

Duane knew, for he had seen them pay. Best of all, moreover, he knew the internal life of the gun-fighter of that select but by no means small class of which he was representative. The world that judged him and his kind judged him as a machine, a killing-machine, with only mind enough to hunt, to meet, to slay another man. It had taken three endless years for Duane to understand his own father. Duane knew beyond all doubt that the gun-fighters like Bland, like Alloway, like Sellers, men who were evil and had no remorse, no spiritual accusing Nemesis, had something far more torturing to mind, more haunting, more murderous of rest and sleep and peace; and that something was abnormal fear of death. Duane knew this, for he had shot these men; he had seen the quick, dark shadow in eyes, the presentiment that the will could not control, and then the horrible certainty. These men must have been in agony at every meeting with a possible or certain foe—more agony than the hot rend of a bullet. They were haunted, too, haunted by this fear, by every victim calling from the grave that nothing was so inevitable as death, which lurked behind every corner, hid in every shadow, lay deep in the dark tube of every gun. These men could not have a friend; they could not love or trust a woman. They knew their one chance of holding on to life lay in their own distrust, watchfulness, dexterity, and that hope, by the very nature of their lives, could not be lasting. They had doomed themselves. What, then, could possibly have dwelt in the depths of their minds as they went to their beds on a starry night like this, with mystery in silence and shadow, with time passing surely, and the dark future and its secret approaching every hour—what, then, but hell?

The hell in Duane's mind was not fear of man or fear of death. He would have been glad to lay down the burden of life, providing death came naturally. Many times he had prayed for it. But that overdeveloped, superhuman spirit of defense in him precluded suicide or the inviting of an enemy's bullet. Sometimes he had a vague, scarcely analyzed idea that this spirit was what had made the Southwest habitable for the white man.

Every one of his victims, singly and collectively, returned to him for ever, it seemed, in cold, passionless, accusing domination of these haunted hours. They did not accuse him of dishonor or cowardice or brutality or murder; they only accused him of Death. It was as if they knew more than when they were alive, had learned that life was a divine mysterious gift not to be taken. They thronged about him with their voiceless clamoring, drifted around him with their fading eyes.

CHAPTER 11

After nearly six months in the Nueces gorge the loneliness and inaction of his life drove Duane out upon the trails seeking anything rather than to hide longer alone, a prey to the scourge of his thoughts. The moment he rode into sight of men a remarkable transformation occurred in him. A strange warmth stirred in him—a longing to see the faces of people, to hear their voices—a pleasurable emotion sad and strange. But it was only a precursor of his old bitter, sleepless, and eternal vigilance. When he hid alone in the brakes he was safe from all except his deeper, better self; when he escaped from this into the haunts of men his force and will went to the preservation of his life.

Mercer was the first village he rode into. He had many friends there. Mercer claimed to owe Duane a debt. On the outskirts of the village there was a grave overgrown by brush so that the rude-lettered post which marked it was scarcely visible to Duane as he rode by. He had never read the inscription. But he thought now of Hardin, no other than the erstwhile ally of Bland. For many years Hardin had harassed the stockmen and ranchers in and around Mercer. On an evil day for him he or his outlaws had beaten and robbed a man who once succored Duane when sore in need. Duane met Hardin in the little plaza of the village, called him every name known to border men, taunted him to draw, and killed him in the act.

Duane went to the house of one Jones, a Texan who had known his father, and there he was warmly received. The feel of an honest hand, the voice of a friend, the prattle of children who were not afraid of him or his gun, good wholesome food, and change of clothes—these things for the time being made a changed man of Duane. To be sure, he did not often speak. The price on his head and the weight of his burden made him silent. But eagerly he drank in all the news that was told him. In the years of his absence from home he had never heard a word about his mother or uncle. Those who were his real friends on the border would have been the last to make inquiries, to write or receive letters that might give a clue to Duane's whereabouts.

Duane remained all day with this hospitable Jones, and as twilight fell was loath to go and yielded to a pressing invitation to remain overnight. It was seldom indeed that Duane slept under a roof. Early in the evening, while Duane sat on the porch with two awed and hero-worshiping sons of the house, Jones returned from a quick visit down to the post-office. Summarily he sent the boys off. He labored under intense excitement.

"Duane, there's rangers in town," he whispered. "It's all over town, too, that you're here. You rode in long after sunup. Lots of people saw you. I don't believe there's a man or boy that'd squeal on you. But the women might. They gossip, and these rangers are handsome fellows—devils with the women."

"What company of rangers?" asked Duane quietly.

"Company A, under Captain MacNelly, that new ranger. He made a big name in the war. And since he's been in the ranger service he's done wonders. He's cleaned up some bad places south, and he's working north."

"MacNelly. I've heard of him. Describe him to me."

"Slight-built chap, but wiry and tough. Clean face, black mustache and hair. Sharp black eyes. He's got a look of authority. MacNelly's a fine man, Duane. Belongs to a good Southern family. I'd hate to have him look you up."

Duane did not speak.

"MacNelly's got nerve, and his rangers are all experienced men. If they find out you're here they'll come after you. MacNelly's no gun-fighter, but he wouldn't hesitate to do his duty, even if he faced sure death. Which he would in this case. Duane, you mustn't meet Captain MacNelly. Your record is clean, if it is terrible. You never met a ranger or any officer except a rotten sheriff now and then, like Rod Brown."

Still Duane kept silence. He was not thinking of danger, but of the fact of how fleeting must be his stay among friends.

"I've already fixed up a pack of grub," went on Jones. "I'll slip out to saddle your horse. You watch here."

He had scarcely uttered the last words when soft, swift footsteps sounded on the hard path. A man turned in at the gate. The light was dim, yet clean enough to disclose an unusually tall figure. When it appeared nearer he was seen to be walking with both arms raised, hands high. He slowed his stride.

"Does Burt Jones live here?" he asked, in a low, hurried voice.

"I reckon. I'm Burt. What can I do for you?" replied Jones.

The stranger peered around, stealthily came closer, still with his hands up.

"It is known that Buck Duane is here. Captain MacNelly's camping on the river just out of town. He sends word to Duane to come out there after dark."

The stranger wheeled and departed as swiftly and strangely as he had come.

"Bust me! Duane, whatever do you make of that?" exclaimed Jones.

"A new one on me," replied Duane, thoughtfully.

"First fool thing I ever heard of MacNelly doing. Can't make head nor tails of it. I'd have said off-hand that MacNelly wouldn't double-cross anybody. He struck me as a square man, sand all through. But, hell! he must mean treachery. I can't see anything else in that deal."

"Maybe the Captain wants to give me a fair chance to surrender without bloodshed," observed Duane. "Pretty decent of him, if he meant that."

"He *invites* you out to his camp *after dark*. Something strange about this, Duane. But MacNelly's a new man out here. He does some strange things. Perhaps he's getting a swelled head. Well, whatever his intentions, his presence around Mercer is enough for us. Duane, you hit the road and put some miles between you and the amiable Captain before daylight. Tomorrow I'll go out there and ask him what in the devil he meant."

"That messenger he sent—he was a ranger," said Duane.

"Sure he was, and a nervy one! It must have taken sand to come bracing you that way. Duane, that fellow didn't pack a gun. I'll swear to that. Pretty odd, this trick. But you can't trust it. Hit the road, Duane."

A little later a black horse with muffled hoofs, bearing a tall, dark rider who peered keenly into every shadow, trotted down a pasture lane back of Jones's house, turned into the road, and then, breaking into a swifter gait, rapidly left Mercer behind.

Fifteen or twenty miles out Duane drew rein in a forest of mesquite, dismounted, and searched about for a glade with a little grass. Here he staked his horse on a long lariat; and, using his saddle for a pillow, his saddle-blanket for covering, he went to sleep.

Next morning he was off again, working south. During the next few days he paid brief visits to several villages that lay in his path. And in each some one particular friend had a piece of news to impart that made Duane profoundly thoughtful. A ranger had made a quiet, unobtrusive call upon these friends and left this message. "Tell Buck Duane to ride into Captain MacNelly's camp some time after night."

Duane concluded, and his friends all agreed with him, that the new ranger's main purpose in the Nueces country was to capture or kill Buck Duane, and that this message was simply an original and striking ruse, the daring of which might appeal to certain outlaws.

But it did not appeal to Duane. His curiosity was aroused; it did not, however, tempt him to any foolhardy act. He turned southwest and rode a hundred miles until he again reached the sparsely settled country. Here he heard no more of rangers. It was a barren region he had never but once ridden through and that ride had cost him dear. He had been compelled to shoot his way out. Outlaws were not in accord with the few ranchers and their cowboys who ranged there. He learned that both outlaws and Mexican raiders had long been at bitter enmity with these ranchers. Being unfamiliar with roads and trails, Duane had pushed on into the heart of this district, when all the time he really believed he was traveling around it. A rifle-shot from a ranch-house, a deliberate attempt to kill him because he was an unknown rider in those parts, discovered to Duane his mistake; and a hard ride to get away persuaded him to return to his old methods of hiding by day and traveling by night.

He got into rough country, rode for three days without covering much ground, but believed that he was getting on safer territory. Twice he came to a wide bottom-land green with willow and cottonwood and thick as chaparral, somewhere through the middle of which ran a river he decided must be the lower Nueces.

One evening, as he stole out from a covert where he had camped, he saw the lights of a village. He tried to pass it on the left, but was unable to because the brakes of this bottom-land extended in almost to the outskirts of the village, and he had to retrace his steps and go round to the right. Wire fences and horses in pastures made this a task, so it was well after midnight before he accomplished it. He made ten miles or more than by daylight, and after that proceeded cautiously along a road which appeared to be well worn from travel. He passed several thickets where he would have halted to hide during the day but for the fact that he had to find water.

He was a long while in coming to it, and then there was no thicket or clump of mesquite near the water-hole that would afford him covert. So he kept on.

The country before him was ridgy and began to show cottonwoods here and there in hollows and yucca and mesquite on the higher ground. As he mounted a ridge he noted that the road made a sharp turn, and he could not see what was beyond it. He slowed up and was making the turn, which was downhill between high banks of yellow clay, when his mettlesome horse heard something to frighten him or shied at something and bolted.

The few bounds he took before Duane's iron arm checked him were enough to reach the curve. One flashing glance showed Duane the open once more, a little valley below with a wide, shallow, rocky stream, a clump of cottonwoods beyond, a somber group of men facing him, and two dark, limp, strangely grotesque figures hanging from branches.

The sight was common enough in southwest Texas, but Duane had never before found himself so unpleasantly close.

A hoarse voice pealed out: "By hell! there's another one!"

"Stranger, ride down an' account fer yourself!" yelled another.

"Hands up!"

"Thet's right, Jack; don't take no chances. Plug him!"

These remarks were so swiftly uttered as almost to be continuous. Duane was wheeling his horse when a rifle cracked. The bullet struck his left forearm and he thought broke it, for he dropped the rein. The frightened horse leaped. Another bullet whistled past Duane. Then the bend in the road saved him probably from certain death. Like the wind his fleet steed went down the long hill.

Duane was in no hurry to look back. He knew what to expect. His chief concern of the moment was for his injured arm. He found that the bones were still intact; but the wound, having been made by a soft bullet, was an exceedingly bad one. Blood poured from it. Giving the horse his head, Duane wound his scarf tightly round the holes, and with teeth and hand tied it tightly. That done, he looked back over his shoulder.

Riders were making the dust fly on the hillside road. There were more coming round the cut where the road curved. The leader was perhaps a quarter of a mile back, and the others strung out behind him. Duane needed only one glance to tell him that they were fast and hard-riding cowboys in a land where all riders were good. They would not have owned any but strong, swift horses. Moreover, it was a district where ranchers had suffered beyond all endurance the greed and brutality of outlaws. Duane had simply been so unfortunate as to run right into a lynching party at a time of all times when any stranger would be in danger and any outlaw put to his limit to escape with his life.

Duane did not look back again till he had crossed the ridgy piece of ground and had gotten to the level road. He had gained upon his pursuers. When he ascertained this he tried to save his horse, to check a little that killing gait. This horse was a magnificent animal, big, strong, fast; but his endurance had never been put to a grueling test. And that worried Duane. His life had made it impossible to keep one horse very long at a time, and this one was an unknown quantity.

Duane had only one plan—the only plan possible in this case—and that was to make the river-bottoms, where he might elude his pursuers in the willow brakes. Fifteen miles or so would bring him to the river, and this was not a hopeless distance for any good horse if not too closely pressed. Duane concluded presently that the cowboys behind were losing a little in the chase because they were not extending their horses. It was decidedly unusual for such riders to save their mounts. Duane pondered over this, looking backward several times to see if their horses were stretched out. They were not, and the fact was disturbing. Only one reason presented itself to Duane's conjecturing, and it was that with him headed straight on the road his pursuers were satisfied not to force the running. He began to hope and look for a trail or a road turning off to right or left. There was none. A rough, mesquite-dotted and yucca-spired country extended away on either side. Duane believed that he would be compelled to take to this hard going. One thing was certain— he had to go round the village. The river, however, was on the outskirts of the village; and once in the willows, he would be safe.

Dust-clouds far ahead caused his alarm to grow. He watched with his eyes strained; he hoped to see a wagon, a few stray cattle. But no, he soon descried several horsemen. Shots and yells behind him attested to the fact that his pursuers likewise had seen these newcomers on the scene. More than a mile separated these two parties, yet that distance did not keep them from soon understanding each other. Duane waited only to see this new factor show signs of sudden quick action, and then, with a muttered curse, he spurred his horse off the road into the brush.

He chose the right side, because the river lay nearer that way. There were patches of open sandy ground between clumps of cactus and mesquite, and he found that despite a zigzag course he made better time. It was impossible for him to locate his pursuers. They would come together, he decided, and take to his tracks.

What, then, was his surprise and dismay to run out of a thicket right into a low ridge of rough, broken rock, impossible to get a horse over. He wheeled to the left along its base. The sandy ground gave place to a harder soil, where his horse did not labor so. Here the growths of mesquite and cactus became scanter, affording better travel but poor cover. He kept sharp eyes ahead, and, as he had expected, soon saw moving dust-clouds and the dark figures of horses. They were half a mile away, and swinging obliquely across the flat, which fact proved that they had entertained a fair idea of the country and the fugitive's difficulty.

Without an instant's hesitation Duane put his horse to his best efforts, straight ahead. He had to pass those men. When this was seemingly made impossible by a deep wash from which he had to turn, Duane began to feel cold and sick. Was this the end? Always there had to be an end to an outlaw's career. He wanted then to ride straight at these pursuers. But reason outweighed instinct. He was fleeing for his life; nevertheless, the strongest instinct at the time was his desire to fight.

He knew when these three horsemen saw him, and a moment afterward he lost sight of them as he got into the mesquite again. He meant now to try to reach the road, and pushed his mount severely, though still saving him for a final burst. Rocks, thickets, bunches of cactus, washes—all operated against his following a straight line. Almost he lost his bearings, and finally would have ridden toward his enemies had not good fortune favored him in the matter of an open burned-over stretch of ground.

Here he saw both groups of pursuers, one on each side and almost within gunshot. Their sharp yells, as much as his cruel spurs, drove his horse into that pace which now meant life or death for him. And never had Duane bestrode a gamer, swifter, stancher beast. He seemed about to accomplish the impossible. In the dragging sand he was far superior to any horse in pursuit, and on this sandy open stretch he gained enough to spare a little in the brush beyond. Heated now and thoroughly terrorized, he kept the pace through thickets that almost tore Duane from his saddle. He was going to get out in front! The horse had speed, fire, stamina.

Duane dashed out into another open place dotted by few trees, and here, right in his path, within pistol-range, stood horsemen waiting. They yelled, they spurred toward him, but did not fire at him. He turned his horse—faced to the right. Only one thing kept him from standing his ground to fight it out. He remembered those dangling limp figures hanging from the cottonwoods. These ranchers would rather hang an outlaw than do anything. They might draw all his fire and then capture him. His horror of hanging was so great as to be all out of proportion compared to his gun-fighter's instinct of self-preservation.

A race began then, a dusty, crashing drive through gray mesquite. Duane could scarcely see, he was so blinded by stinging branches across his eyes. The hollow wind roared in his ears. He lost his sense of the nearness of his pursuers. But they must have been close. Did they shoot at him? He imagined he heard shots. But that might have been the cracking of dead snags. His left arm hung limp, almost useless; he handled the reins with his right; and most of the time he hung low over the pommel. The gray walls flashing by him, the whip of twigs, the rush of wind, the heavy, rapid pound of hoofs, the violent motion of his horse—these vied in sensation with the smart of sweat in his eyes, the rack of his wound, the cold, sick cramp in his stomach. With these also was dull, raging fury. He had to run when he wanted to fight. It took all his mind to force back that bitter hate of himself, of his pursuers, of this race for his useless life.

Suddenly he burst out of a line of mesquite into the road. A long stretch of lonely road! How fiercely, with hot, strange joy, he wheeled his horse upon it! Then he was sweeping along, sure now that he was out in front. His horse still had strength and speed, but showed signs of breaking. Presently Duane looked back. Pursuers—he could not count how many—were loping along in his rear. He paid no more attention to them, and with teeth set he faced ahead, grimmer now in his determination to foil them.

He passed a few scattered ranch-houses where horses whistled from corrals, and men curiously watched him fly past. He saw one rancher running, and he felt intuitively that this fellow was going to join in the chase. Duane's steed pounded on, not noticeably slower, but with a lack of former smoothness, with a strained, convulsive, jerking stride which showed he was almost done.

Sight of the village ahead surprised Duane. He had reached it sooner than he expected. Then he made a discovery—he had entered the zone of wire fences. As he dared not turn back now, he kept on, intending to ride through the village. Looking backward, he saw that his pursuers were half a mile distant, too far to alarm any villagers in time to intercept him in his flight. As he rode by the first houses his horse broke and began to labor. Duane did not believe he would last long enough to go through the village.

Saddled horses in front of a store gave Duane an idea, not by any means new, and one he had carried out successfully before. As he pulled in his heaving mount and leaped off, a couple of ranchers came out of the place, and one of them stepped to a clean-limbed, fiery bay. He was about to get into his saddle when he saw Duane, and then he halted, a foot in the stirrup.

Duane strode forward, grasped the bridle of this man's horse.

"Mine's done—but not killed," he panted. "Trade with me."

"Wal, stranger, I'm shore always ready to trade," drawled the man. "But ain't you a little swift?"

Duane glanced back up the road. His pursuers were entering the village.

"I'm Duane—Buck Duane," he cried, menacingly. "Will you trade? Hurry!"

The rancher, turning white, dropped his foot from the stirrup and fell back.

"I reckon I'll trade," he said.

Bounding up, Duane dug spurs into the bay's flanks. The horse snorted in fright, plunged into a run. He was fresh, swift, half wild. Duane flashed by the remaining houses on the street out into the open. But the road ended at that village or else led out from some other quarter, for he had ridden straight into the fields and from them into rough desert. When he reached the cover of mesquite once more he looked back to find six horsemen within rifle-shot of him, and more coming behind them.

His new horse had not had time to get warm before Duane reached a high sandy bluff below which lay the willow brakes. As far as he could see extended an immense flat strip of red-tinged willow. How welcome it was to his eye! He felt like a hunted wolf that, weary and lame, had reached his hole in the rocks. Zigzagging down the soft slope, he put the bay to the dense wall of leaf and branch. But the horse balked.

There was little time to lose. Dismounting, he dragged the stubborn beast into the thicket. This was harder and slower work than Duane cared to risk. If he had not been rushed he might have had better success. So he had to abandon the horse—a circumstance that only such sore straits could have driven him to. Then he went slipping swiftly through the narrow aisles.

He had not gotten under cover any too soon. For he heard his pursuers piling over the bluff, loud-voiced, confident, brutal. They crashed into the willows.

"Hi, Sid! Heah's your hoss!" called one, evidently to the man Duane had forced into a trade.

"Say, if you locoed gents 'll hold up a little I'll tell you somethin'!" replied a voice from the bluff.

"Come on, Sid! We got him corralled," said the first speaker.

"Wal, mebbe, an' if you hev it's liable to be damn hot. *Thet feller was Buck Duane!*"

Absolute silence followed that statement. Presently it was broken by a rattling of loose gravel and then low voices.

"He can't git acrost the river, I tell you," came to Duane's ears. "He's corralled in the brake. I know thet hole."

Then Duane, gliding silently and swiftly through the willows, heard no more from his pursuers. He headed straight for the river. Threading a passage through a willow brake was an old task for him. Many days and nights had gone to the acquiring of a skill that might have been envied by an Indian.

The Rio Grande and its tributaries for the most of their length in Texas ran between wide, low, flat lands covered by a dense growth of willow. Cottonwood, mesquite, prickly pear, and other growths mingled with the willow, and altogether they made a matted, tangled copse, a thicket that an inexperienced man would have considered impenetrable. From above, these wild brakes looked green and red; from the inside they were gray and yellow—a striped wall. Trails and glades were scarce. There were a few deer-runways and sometimes little paths made by peccaries—the *jabali*, or wild pigs, of Mexico. The ground was clay and unusually dry, sometimes baked so hard that it left no imprint of a track. Where a growth of cottonwood had held back the encroachment of willows there usually was thick grass and underbrush. The willows were short, slender poles with stems so close together that they almost touched, and with the leafy foliage forming a thick covering.

The depths of this brake Duane had penetrated was a silent, dreamy, strange place. In the middle of the day the light was weird and dim. When a breeze fluttered the foliage, then slender shafts and spears of sunshine pierced the green mantle and danced like gold on the ground.

Duane had always felt the strangeness of this kind of place, and likewise he had felt a protecting, harboring something which always seemed to him to be the sympathy of the brake for a hunted creature. Any unwounded creature, strong and resourceful, was safe when he had glided under the low, rustling green roof of this wild covert. It was not hard to conceal tracks; the springy soil gave forth no sound; and men could hunt each other for weeks, pass within a few yards of each other and never know it. The problem of sustaining life was difficult; but, then, hunted men and animals survived on very little.

Duane wanted to cross the river if that was possible, and, keeping in the brake, work his way upstream till he had reached country more hospitable. Remembering what the man had said in regard to the river, Duane had his doubts about crossing. But he would take any chance to put the river between him and his hunters. He pushed on. His left arm had to be favored, as he could scarcely move it. Using his right to spread the willows, he slipped sideways between them and made fast time. There were narrow aisles and washes and holes low down and paths brushed by animals, all of which he took advantage of, running, walking, crawling, stooping any way to get along. To keep in a straight line was not easy—he did it by marking some bright sunlit stem or tree ahead, and when he reached it looked straight on to mark another. His progress necessarily grew slower, for as he advanced the brake became wilder, denser, darker. Mosquitoes began to whine about his head. He kept on without pause. Deepening shadows under the willows told him that the afternoon was far advanced. He began to fear he had wandered in a wrong direction. Finally a strip of light ahead relieved his anxiety, and after a toilsome penetration of still denser brush he broke through to the bank of the river.

He faced a wide, shallow, muddy stream with brakes on the opposite bank extending like a green and yellow wall. Duane perceived at a glance the futility of his trying to cross at this point. Everywhere the sluggish water laved quicksand bars. In fact, the bed of the river was all quicksand, and very likely there was not a foot of water anywhere. He could not swim; he could not crawl; he could not push a log across. Any solid thing touching that smooth yellow sand would be grasped and sucked down. To prove this he seized a long pole and, reaching down from the high bank, thrust it into the stream. Right there near shore there apparently was no bottom to the treacherous quicksand. He abandoned any hope of crossing the river. Probably for miles up and down it would be just the same as here. Before leaving the bank he tied his hat upon the pole and lifted enough water to quench his thirst. Then he worked his way back to where thinner growth made advancement easier, and kept on upstream till the shadows were so deep he could not see. Feeling around for a place big enough to stretch out on, he lay down. For the time being he was as safe there as he would have been beyond in the Rim Rock. He was tired, though not exhausted, and in spite of the throbbing pain in his arm he dropped at once into sleep.

CHAPTER 12

Some time during the night Duane awoke. A stillness seemingly so thick and heavy as to have substance blanketed the black willow brake. He could not see a star or a branch or tree-trunk or even his hand before his eyes. He lay there waiting, listening, sure that he had been awakened by an unusual sound. Ordinary noises of the night in the wilderness never disturbed his rest. His facilities, like those of old fugitives and hunted creatures, had become trained to a marvelous keenness. A long low breath of slow wind moaned through the willows, passed away; some stealthy, soft-footed beast trotted by him in the darkness; there was a rustling among dry leaves; a fox barked lonesomely in the distance. But none of these sounds had broken his slumber.

Suddenly, piercing the stillness, came a bay of a bloodhound. Quickly Duane sat up, chilled to his marrow. The action made him aware of his crippled arm. Then came other bays, lower, more distant. Silence enfolded him again, all the more oppressive and menacing in his suspense. Bloodhounds had been put on his trail, and the leader was not far away. All his life Duane had been familiar with bloodhounds; and he knew that if the pack surrounded him in this impenetrable darkness he would be held at bay or dragged down as wolves dragged a stag. Rising to his feet, prepared to flee as best he could, he waited to be sure of the direction he should take.

The leader of the hounds broke into cry again, a deep, full-toned, ringing bay, strange, ominous, terribly significant in its power. It caused a cold sweat to ooze out all over Duane's body. He turned from it, and with his uninjured arm outstretched to feel for the willows he groped his way along. As it was impossible to pick out the narrow passages, he had to slip and squeeze and plunge between the yielding stems. He made such a crashing that he no longer heard the baying of the hounds. He had no hope to elude them. He meant to climb the first cottonwood that he stumbled upon in his blind flight. But it appeared he never was going to be lucky enough to run against one. Often he fell, sometimes flat, at others upheld by the willows. What made the work so hard was the fact that he had only one arm to open a clump of close-growing stems and his feet would catch or tangle in the narrow crotches, holding him fast. He had to struggle desperately. It was as if the willows were clutching hands, his enemies, fiendishly impeding his progress. He tore his clothes on sharp branches and his flesh suffered many a prick. But in a terrible earnestness he kept on until he brought up hard against a cottonwood tree.

There he leaned and rested. He found himself as nearly exhausted as he had ever been, wet with sweat, his hands torn and burning, his breast laboring, his legs stinging from innumerable bruises. While he leaned there to catch his breath he listened for the pursuing hounds. For a long time there was no sound from them. This, however, did not deceive him into any hopefulness. There were bloodhounds that bayed often on a trail, and others that ran mostly silent. The former were more valuable to their owner and the latter more dangerous to the fugitive. Presently Duane's ears were filled by a chorus of short ringing yelps. The pack had found where he had slept, and now the trail was hot. Satisfied that they would soon overtake him, Duane set about climbing the cottonwood, which in his condition was difficult of ascent.

It happened to be a fairly large tree with a fork about fifteen feet up, and branches thereafter in succession. Duane climbed until he got above the enshrouding belt of blackness. A pale gray mist hung above the brake, and through it shone a line of dim lights. Duane decided these were bonfires made along the bluff to render his escape more difficult on that side. Away round in the direction he thought was north he imagined he saw more fires, but, as the mist was thick, he could not be sure. While he sat there pondering the matter, listening for the hounds, the mist and the gloom of one side lightened; and this side he concluded was east and meant that dawn was near. Satisfying himself on this score, he descended to the first branch of the tree.

His situation now, though still critical, did not appear to be so hopeless as it had been. The hounds would soon close in on him, and he would kill them or drive them away. It was beyond the bounds of possibility that any men could have followed running hounds through that brake in the night. The thing that worried Duane was the fact of the bonfires. He had gathered from the words of one of his pursuers that the brake was a kind of trap, and he began to believe there was only one way out of it, and that was along the bank where he had entered, and where obviously all night long his pursuers had kept fires burning. Further conjecture on this point, however, was interrupted by a crashing in the willows and the rapid patter of feet.

Underneath Duane lay a gray, foggy obscurity. He could not see the ground, nor any object but the black trunk of the tree. Sight would not be needed to tell him when the pack arrived. With a pattering rush through the willows the hounds reached the tree; and then high above crash of brush and thud of heavy paws rose a hideous clamor. Duane's pursuers far off to the south would hear that and know what it meant. And at daybreak, perhaps before, they would take a short cut across the brake, guided by the baying of hounds that had treed their quarry.

It wanted only a few moments, however, till Duane could distinguish the vague forms of the hounds in the gray shadow below. Still he waited. He had no shots to spare. And he knew how to treat bloodhounds. Gradually the obscurity lightened, and at length Duane had good enough sight of the hounds for his purpose. His first shot killed the huge brute leader of the pack. Then, with unerring shots, he crippled several others. That stopped the baying. Piercing howls arose. The pack took fright and fled, its course easily marked by the howls of the crippled members. Duane reloaded his gun, and, making certain all the hounds had gone, he descended to the ground and set off at a rapid pace to the northward.

The mist had dissolved under a rising sun when Duane made his first halt some miles north of the scene where he had waited for the hounds. A barrier to further progress, in shape of a precipitous rocky bluff, rose sheer from the willow brake. He skirted the base of the cliff, where walking was comparatively easy, around in the direction of the river. He reached the end finally to see there was absolutely no chance to escape from the brake at that corner. It took extreme labor, attended by some hazard and considerable pain to his arm, to get down where he could fill his sombrero with water. After quenching his thirst he had a look at his wound. It was caked over with blood and dirt. When washed off the arm was seen to be inflamed and swollen around the bullet-hole. He bathed it, experiencing a soothing relief in the cool water. Then he bandaged it as best he could and arranged a sling round his neck. This mitigated the pain of the injured member and held it in a quiet and restful position, where it had a chance to begin mending.

As Duane turned away from the river he felt refreshed. His great strength and endurance had always made fatigue something almost unknown to him. However, tramping on foot day and night was as unusual to him as to any other riders of the Southwest, and it had begun to tell on him. Retracing his steps, he reached the point where he had abruptly come upon the bluff, and here he determined to follow along its base in the other direction until he found a way out or discovered the futility of such effort.

Duane covered ground rapidly. From time to time he paused to listen. But he was always listening, and his eyes were ever roving. This alertness had become second nature with him, so that except in extreme cases of caution he performed it while he pondered his gloomy and fateful situation. Such habit of alertness and thought made time fly swiftly.

By noon he had rounded the wide curve of the brake and was facing south. The bluff had petered out from a high, mountainous wall to a low abutment of rock, but it still held to its steep, rough nature and afforded no crack or slope where quick ascent could have been possible. He pushed on, growing warier as he approached the danger-zone, finding that as he neared the river on this side it was imperative to go deeper into the willows. In the afternoon he reached a point where he could see men pacing to and fro on the bluff. This assured him that whatever place was guarded was one by which he might escape. He headed toward these men and approached to within a hundred paces of the bluff where they were. There were several men and several boys, all armed and, after the manner of Texans, taking their task leisurely. Farther down Duane made out black dots on the horizon of the bluff-line, and there he concluded were more guards stationed at another outlet. Probably all the available men in the district were on duty. Texans took a grim pleasure in such work. Duane remembered that upon several occasions he had served such duty himself.

Duane peered through the branches and studied the lay of the land. For several hundred yards the bluff could be climbed. He took stock of those careless guards. They had rifles, and that made vain any attempt to pass them in daylight. He believed an attempt by night might be successful; and he was swiftly coming to a determination to hide there till dark and then try it, when the sudden yelping of a dog betrayed him to the guards on the bluff.

The dog had likely been placed there to give an alarm, and he was lustily true to his trust. Duane saw the men run together and begin to talk excitedly and peer into the brake, which was a signal for him to slip away under the willows. He made no noise, and he assured himself he must be invisible. Nevertheless, he heard shouts, then the cracking of rifles, and bullets began to zip and swish through the leafy covert. The day was hot and windless, and Duane concluded that whenever he touched a willow stem, even ever so slightly, it vibrated to the top and sent a quiver among the leaves. Through this the guards had located his position. Once a bullet hissed by him; another thudded into the ground before him. This shooting loosed a rage in Duane. He had to fly from these men, and he hated them and himself because of it. Always in the fury of such moments he wanted to give back shot for shot. But he slipped on through the willows, and at length the rifles ceased to crack.

He sheered to the left again, in line with the rocky barrier, and kept on, wondering what the next mile would bring.

It brought worse, for he was seen by sharp-eyed scouts, and a hot fusillade drove him to run for his life, luckily to escape with no more than a bullet-creased shoulder.

Later that day, still undaunted, he sheered again toward the trap-wall, and found that the nearer he approached to the place where he had come down into the brake the greater his danger. To attempt to run the blockade of that trail by day would be fatal. He waited for night, and after the brightness of the fires had somewhat lessened he assayed to creep out of the brake. He succeeded in reaching the foot of the bluff, here only a bank, and had begun to crawl stealthily up under cover of a shadow when a hound again betrayed his position. Retreating to the willows was as perilous a task as had ever confronted Duane; and when he had accomplished it, right under what seemed a hundred blazing rifles, he felt that he had indeed been favored by Providence. This time men followed him a goodly ways into the brake, and the ripping of lead through the willows sounded on all sides of him.

When the noise of pursuit ceased Duane sat down in the darkness, his mind clamped between two things—whether to try again to escape or wait for possible opportunity. He seemed incapable of decision. His intelligence told him that every hour lessened his chances for escape. He had little enough chance in any case, and that was what made another attempt so desperately hard. Still it was not love of life that bound him. There would come an hour, sooner or later, when he would wrench decision out of this chaos of emotion and thought. But that time was not yet.

When he had remained quiet long enough to cool off and recover from his run he found that he was tired. He stretched out to rest. But the swarms of vicious mosquitoes prevented sleep. This corner of the brake was low and near the river, a breeding-ground for the blood-suckers. They sang and hummed and whined around him in the ever-increasing horde. He covered his head and hands with his coat and lay there patiently. That was a long and wretched night. Morning found him still strong physically, but in a dreadful state of mind.

First he hurried for the river. He could withstand the pangs of hunger, but it was imperative to quench thirst. His wound made him feverish, and therefore more than usually hot and thirsty. Again he was refreshed. That morning he was hard put to it to hold himself back from attempting to cross the river. If he could find a light log it was within the bounds of possibility that he might ford the shallow water and bars of quicksand. But not yet! Wearily, doggedly he faced about toward the bluff.

All that day and all that night, all the next day and all the next night, he stole like a hunted savage from river to bluff; and every hour forced upon him the bitter certainty that he was trapped.

Duane lost track of days, of events. He had come to an evil pass. There arrived an hour when, closely pressed by pursuers at the extreme southern corner of the brake, he took to a dense thicket of willows, driven to what he believed was his last stand.

If only these human bloodhounds would swiftly close in on him! Let him fight to the last bitter gasp and have it over! But these hunters, eager as they were to get him, had care of their own skins. They took few risks. They had him cornered.

It was the middle of the day, hot, dusty, oppressive, threatening storm. Like a snake Duane crawled into a little space in the darkest part of the thicket and lay still. Men had cut him off from the bluff, from the river, seemingly from all sides. But he heard voices only from in front and toward his left. Even if his passage to the river had not been blocked, it might just as well have been.

"Come on fellers—down hyar," called one man from the bluff.

"Got him corralled at last," shouted another.

"Reckon ye needn't be too shore. We thought thet more'n once," taunted another.

"I seen him, I tell you."

"Aw, thet was a deer."

"But Bill found fresh tracks an' blood on the willows."

"If he's winged we needn't hurry."

"Hold on thar, boys," came a shout in authoritative tones from farther up the bluff. "Go slow. You–all air gittin' foolish at the end of a long chase."

"Thet's right, Colonel. Hold 'em back. There's nothin' shorer than somebody'll be stoppin' lead pretty quick. He'll be huntin' us soon!"

"Let's surround this corner an' starve him out."

"Fire the brake."

How clearly all this talk pierced Duane's ears! In it he seemed to hear his doom. This, then, was the end he had always expected, which had been close to him before, yet never like now.

"By God!" whispered Duane, "the thing for me to do now—is go out—meet them!"

That was prompted by the fighting, the killing instinct in him. In that moment it had almost superhuman power. If he must die, that was the way for him to die. What else could be expected of Buck Duane? He got to his knees and drew his gun. With his swollen and almost useless hand he held what spare ammunition he had left. He ought to creep out noiselessly to the edge of the willows, suddenly face his pursuers, then, while there was a beat left in his heart, kill, kill, kill. These men all had rifles. The fight would be short. But the marksmen did not live on earth who could make such a fight go wholly against him. Confronting them suddenly he could kill a man for every shot in his gun.

Thus Duane reasoned. So he hoped to accept his fate—to meet this end. But when he tried to step forward something checked him. He forced himself; yet he could not go. The obstruction that opposed his will was as insurmountable as it had been physically impossible for him to climb the bluff.

Slowly he fell back, crouched low, and then lay flat. The grim and ghastly dignity that had been his a moment before fell away from him. He lay there stripped of his last shred of self-respect. He wondered was he afraid; had he, the last of the Duanes—had he come to feel fear? No! Never in all his wild life had he so longed to go out and meet men face to face. It was not fear that held him back. He hated this hiding, this eternal vigilance, this hopeless life. The damnable paradox of the situation was that if he went out to meet these men there was absolutely no doubt of his doom. If he clung to his covert there was a chance, a merest chance, for his life. These pursuers, dogged and unflagging as they had been, were mortally afraid of him. It was his fame that made them cowards. Duane's keenness told him that at the very darkest and most perilous moment there was still a chance for him. And the blood in him, the temper of his father, the years of his outlawry, the pride of his unsought and hated career, the nameless, inexplicable something in him made him accept that slim chance.

Waiting then became a physical and mental agony. He lay under the burning sun, parched by thirst, laboring to breathe, sweating and bleeding. His uncared-for wound was like a red-hot prong in his flesh. Blotched and swollen from the never-ending attack of flies and mosquitoes his face seemed twice its natural size, and it ached and stung.

On one side, then, was this physical torture; on the other the old hell, terribly augmented at this crisis, in his mind. It seemed that thought and imagination had never been so swift. If death found him presently, how would it come? Would he get decent burial or be left for the peccaries and the coyotes? Would his people ever know where he had fallen? How wretched, how miserable his state! It was cowardly, it was monstrous for him to cling longer to this doomed life. Then the hate in his heart, the hellish hate of these men on his trail—that was like a scourge. He felt no longer human. He had degenerated into an animal that could think. His heart pounded, his pulse beat, his breast heaved; and this internal strife seemed to thunder into his ears. He was now enacting the tragedy of all crippled, starved, hunted wolves at bay in their dens. Only his tragedy was infinitely more terrible because he had mind enough to see his plight, his resemblance to a lonely wolf, bloody-fanged, dripping, snarling, fire-eyed in a last instinctive defiance.

Mounted upon the horror of Duane's thought was a watching, listening intensity so supreme that it registered impressions which were creations of his imagination. He heard stealthy steps that were not there; he saw shadowy moving figures that were only leaves. A hundred times when he was about to pull trigger he discovered his error. Yet voices came from a distance, and steps and crackings in the willows, and other sounds real enough. But Duane could not distinguish the real from the false. There were times when the wind which had arisen sent a hot, pattering breath down the willow aisles, and Duane heard it as an approaching army.

This straining of Duane's faculties brought on a reaction which in itself was a respite. He saw the sun darkened by thick slow spreading clouds. A storm appeared to be coming. How slowly it moved! The air was like steam. If there broke one of those dark, violent storms common though rare to the country, Duane believed he might slip away in the fury of wind and rain. Hope, that seemed unquenchable in him, resurged again. He hailed it with a bitterness that was sickening.

Then at a rustling step he froze into the old strained attention. He heard a slow patter of soft feet. A tawny shape crossed a little opening in the thicket. It was that of a dog. The moment while that beast came into full view was an age. The dog was not a bloodhound, and if he had a trail or a scent he seemed to be at fault on it. Duane waited for the inevitable discovery. Any kind of a hunting-dog could have found him in that thicket. Voices from outside could be heard urging on the dog. Rover they called him. Duane sat up at the moment the dog entered the little shaded covert. Duane expected a yelping, a baying, or at least a bark that would tell of his hiding-place. A strange relief swiftly swayed over Duane. The end was near now. He had no further choice. Let them come— a quick fierce exchange of shots—and then this torture past! He waited for the dog to give the alarm.

But the dog looked at him and trotted by into the thicket without a yelp. Duane could not believe the evidence of his senses. He thought he had suddenly gone deaf. He saw the dog disappear, heard him running to and fro among the willows, getting farther and farther away, till all sound from him ceased.

"Thar's Rover," called a voice from the bluff-side. "He's been through thet black patch."

"Nary a rabbit in there," replied another.

"Bah! Thet pup's no good," scornfully growled another man. "Put a hound at thet clump of willows."

"Fire's the game. Burn the brake before the rain comes."

The voices droned off as their owners evidently walked up the ridge.

Then upon Duane fell the crushing burden of the old waiting, watching, listening spell. After all, it was not to end just now. His chance still persisted—looked a little brighter—led him on, perhaps, to forlorn hopes.

All at once twilight settled quickly down upon the willow brake, or else Duane noted it suddenly. He imagined it to be caused by the approaching storm. But there was little movement of air or cloud, and thunder still muttered and rumbled at a distance. The fact was the sun had set, and at this time of overcast sky night was at hand.

Duane realized it with the awakening of all his old force. He would yet elude his pursuers. That was the moment when he seized the significance of all these fortunate circumstances which had aided him. Without haste and without sound he began to crawl in the direction of the river. It was not far, and he reached the bank before darkness set in. There were men up on the bluff carrying wood to build a bonfire. For a moment he half yielded to a temptation to try to slip along the river-shore, close in under the willows. But when he raised himself to peer out he saw that an attempt of this kind would be liable to failure. At the same moment he saw a rough-hewn plank lying beneath him, lodged against some willows. The end of the plank extended in almost to a point beneath him. Quick as a flash he saw where a desperate chance invited him. Then he tied his gun in an oilskin bag and put it in his pocket.

The bank was steep and crumbly. He must not break off any earth to splash into the water. There was a willow growing back some few feet from the edge of the bank. Cautiously he pulled it down, bent it over the water so that when he released it there would be no springing back. Then he trusted his weight to it, with his feet sliding carefully down the bank. He went into the water almost up to his knees, felt the quicksand grip his feet; then, leaning forward till he reached the plank, he pulled it toward him and lay upon it.

Without a sound one end went slowly under water and the farther end appeared lightly braced against the overhanging willows. Very carefully then Duane began to extricate his right foot from the sucking sand. It seemed as if his foot was incased in solid rock. But there was a movement upward, and he pulled with all the power he dared use. It came slowly and at length was free. The left one he released with less difficulty. The next few moments he put all his attention on the plank to ascertain if his weight would sink it into the sand. The far end slipped off the willows with a little splash and gradually settled to rest upon the bottom. But it sank no farther, and Duane's greatest concern was relieved. However, as it was manifestly impossible for him to keep his head up for long he carefully crawled out upon the plank until he could rest an arm and shoulder upon the willows.

When he looked up it was to find the night strangely luminous with fires. There was a bonfire on the extreme end of the bluff, another a hundred paces beyond. A great flare extended over the brake in that direction. Duane heard a roaring on the wind, and he knew his pursuers had fired the willows. He did not believe that would help them much. The brake was dry enough, but too green to burn readily. And as for the bonfires he discovered that the men, probably having run out of wood, were keeping up the light with oil and stuff from the village. A dozen men kept watch on the bluff scarcely fifty paces from where Duane lay concealed by the willows. They talked, cracked jokes, sang songs, and manifestly considered this outlaw-hunting a great lark. As long as the bright light lasted Duane dared not move. He had the patience and the endurance to wait for the breaking of the storm, and if that did not come, then the early hour before dawn when the gray fog and gloom were over the river.

Escape was now in his grasp. He felt it. And with that in his mind he waited, strong as steel in his conviction, capable of withstanding any strain endurable by the human frame.

The wind blew in puffs, grew wilder, and roared through the willows, carrying bright sparks upward. Thunder rolled down over the river, and lightning began to flash. The flashes of lightning and the broad flares played so incessantly that Duane could not trust himself out on the open river. Certainly the storm rather increased the watchfulness of the men on the bluff. He knew how to wait, and he waited, grimly standing pain and cramp and chill. The storm wore away as desultorily as it had come, and the long night set in. There were times when Duane thought he was paralyzed, others when he grew sick, giddy, weak from the strained posture. The first paling of the stars quickened him with a kind of wild joy. He watched them grow paler, dimmer, disappear one by one. A shadow hovered down, rested upon the river, and gradually thickened. The bonfire on the bluff showed as through a foggy veil. The watchers were mere groping dark figures.

Duane, aware of how cramped he had become from long inaction, began to move his legs and uninjured arm and body, and at length overcame a paralyzing stiffness. Then, digging his hand in the sand and holding the plank with his knees, he edged it out into the river. Inch by inch he advanced until clear of the willows. Looking upward, he saw the shadowy figures of the men on the bluff. He realized they ought to see him, feared that they would. But he kept on, cautiously, noiselessly, with a heart-numbing slowness. From time to time his elbow made a little gurgle and splash in the water. Try as he might, he could not prevent this. It got to be like the hollow roar of a rapid filling his ears with mocking sound. There was a perceptible current out in the river, and it hindered straight advancement. Inch by inch he crept on, expecting to hear the bang of rifles, the spattering of bullets. He tried not to look backward, but failed. The fire appeared a little dimmer, the moving shadows a little darker.

Once the plank stuck in the sand and felt as if it were settling. Bringing feet to aid his hand, he shoved it over the treacherous place. This way he made faster progress. The obscurity of the river seemed to be enveloping him. When he looked back again the figures of the men were coalescing with the surrounding gloom, the fires were streaky, blurred patches of light. But the sky above was brighter. Dawn was not far off.

To the west all was dark. With infinite care and implacable spirit and waning strength Duane shoved the plank along, and when at last he discerned the black border of bank it came in time, he thought, to save him. He crawled out, rested till the gray dawn broke, and then headed north through the willows.

CHAPTER 13

How long Duane was traveling out of that region he never knew. But he reached familiar country and found a rancher who had before befriended him. Here his arm was attended to; he had food and sleep; and in a couple of weeks he was himself again.

When the time came for Duane to ride away on his endless trail his friend reluctantly imparted the information that some thirty miles south, near the village of Shirley, there was posted at a certain crossroad a reward for Buck Duane dead or alive. Duane had heard of such notices, but he had never seen one. His friend's reluctance and refusal to state for what particular deed this reward was offered roused Duane's curiosity. He had never been any closer to Shirley than this rancher's home. Doubtless some post-office burglary, some gun-shooting scrape had been attributed to him. And he had been accused of worse deeds. Abruptly Duane decided to ride over there and find out who wanted him dead or alive, and why.

As he started south on the road he reflected that this was the first time he had ever deliberately hunted trouble. Introspection awarded him this knowledge; during that last terrible flight on the lower Nueces and while he lay abed recuperating he had changed. A fixed, immutable, hopeless bitterness abided with him. He had reached the end of his rope. All the power of his mind and soul were unavailable to turn him back from his fate. That fate was to become an outlaw in every sense of the term, to be what he was credited with being—that is to say, to embrace evil. He had never committed a crime. He wondered now was crime close to him? He reasoned finally that the desperation of crime had been forced upon him, if not its motive; and that if driven, there was no limit to his possibilities. He understood now many of the hitherto inexplicable actions of certain noted outlaws—why they had returned to the scene of the crime that had outlawed them; why they took such strangely fatal chances; why life was no more to them than a breath of wind; why they rode straight into the jaws of death to confront wronged men or hunting rangers, vigilantes, to laugh in their very faces. It was such bitterness as his that drove these men.

Toward afternoon, from the top of a long hill, Duane saw the green fields and trees and shining roofs of a town he considered must be Shirley. And at the bottom of the hill he came upon an intersecting road. There was a placard nailed on the crossroad sign-post. Duane drew rein near it and leaned close to read the faded print. $1000 REWARD FOR BUCK DUANE DEAD OR ALIVE. Peering closer to read the finer, more faded print, Duane learned that he was wanted for the murder of Mrs. Jeff Aiken at her ranch near Shirley. The month September was named, but the date was illegible. The reward was offered by the woman's husband, whose name appeared with that of a sheriff's at the bottom of the placard.

Duane read the thing twice. When he straightened he was sick with the horror of his fate, wild with passion at those misguided fools who could believe that he had harmed a woman. Then he remembered Kate Bland, and, as always when she returned to him, he quaked inwardly. Years before word had gone abroad that he had killed her, and so it was easy for men wanting to fix a crime to name him. Perhaps it had been done often. Probably he bore on his shoulders a burden of numberless crimes.

A dark, passionate fury possessed him. It shook him like a storm shakes the oak. When it passed, leaving him cold, with clouded brow and piercing eye, his mind was set. Spurring his horse, he rode straight toward the village.

Shirley appeared to be a large, pretentious country town. A branch of some railroad terminated there. The main street was wide, bordered by trees and commodious houses, and many of the stores were of brick. A large plaza shaded by giant cottonwood trees occupied a central location.

Duane pulled his running horse and halted him, plunging and snorting, before a group of idle men who lounged on benches in the shade of a spreading cottonwood. How many times had Duane seen just that kind of lazy shirt-sleeved Texas group! Not often, however, had he seen such placid, lolling, good-natured men change their expression, their attitude so swiftly. His advent apparently was momentous. They evidently took him for an unusual visitor. So far as Duane could tell, not one of them recognized him, had a hint of his identity.

"I'm Buck Duane," he said. "I saw that placard—out there on a signpost. It's a damn lie! Somebody find this man Jeff Aiken. I want to see him."

His announcement was taken in absolute silence. That was the only effect he noted, for he avoided looking at these villagers. The reason was simple enough; Duane felt himself overcome with emotion. There were tears in his eyes. He sat down on a bench, put his elbows on his knees and his hands to his face. For once he had absolutely no concern for his fate. This ignominy was the last straw.

Presently, however, he became aware of some kind of commotion among these villagers. He heard whisperings, low, hoarse voices, then the shuffle of rapid feet moving away. All at once a violent hand jerked his gun from its holster. When Duane rose a gaunt man, livid of face, shaking like a leaf, confronted him with his own gun.

"Hands up, thar, you Buck Duane!" he roared, waving the gun.

That appeared to be the cue for pandemonium to break loose. Duane opened his lips to speak but if he had yelled at the top of his lungs he could not have made himself heard. In weary disgust he looked at the gaunt man, and then at the others, who were working themselves into a frenzy. He made no move, however, to hold up his hands. The villagers surrounded him, emboldened by finding him now unarmed. Then several men lay hold of his arms and pinioned them behind his back. Resistance was useless even if Duane had had the spirit. Some of them fetched his halter from his saddle, and with this they bound him helpless.

People were running now from the street, the stores, the houses. Old men, cowboys, clerks, boys, ranchers came on the trot. The crowd grew. The increasing clamor began to attract women as well as men. A group of girls ran up, then hung back in fright and pity.

The presence of cowboys made a difference. They split up the crowd, got to Duane, and lay hold of him with rough, business-like hands. One of them lifted his fists and roared at the frenzied mob to fall back, to stop the racket. He beat them back into a circle; but it was some little time before the hubbub quieted down so a voice could be heard.

"—shut up, will you-all?" he was yelling. "Give us a chance to hear somethin'. Easy now—soho. There ain't nobody goin' to be hurt. Thet's right; everybody quiet now. Let's see what's come off."

This cowboy, evidently one of authority, or at least one of strong personality, turned to the gaunt man, who still waved Duane's gun.

"Abe, put the gun down," he said. "It might go off. Here, give it to me. Now, what's wrong? Who's this roped gent, an' what's he done?"

The gaunt fellow, who appeared now about to collapse, lifted a shaking hand and pointed.

"Thet thar feller—he's Buck Duane!" he panted.

An angry murmur ran through the surrounding crowd.

"The rope! The rope! Throw it over a branch! String him up!" cried an excited villager.

"Buck Duane! Buck Duane!"

"Hang him!"

The cowboy silenced these cries.

"Abe, how do you know this fellow is Buck Duane?" he asked, sharply.

"Why—he said so," replied the man called Abe.

"What!" came the exclamation, incredulously.

"It's a tarnal fact," panted Abe, waving his hands importantly. He was an old man and appeared to be carried away with the significance of his deed. "He like to rid' his hoss right over us-all. Then he jumped off, says he was Buck Duane, an' he wanted to see Jeff Aiken bad."

This speech caused a second commotion as noisy though not so enduring as the first. When the cowboy, assisted by a couple of his mates, had restored order again, some one had slipped the noose-end of Duane's rope over his head.

"Up with him!" screeched a wild-eyed youth.

The mob surged closer and was shoved back by the cowboys.

"Abe, if you ain't drunk or crazy tell thet over," ordered Abe's interlocutor.

With some show of resentment and more of dignity Abe reiterated his former statement.

"If he's Buck Duane how'n hell did you get hold of his gun!" bluntly queried the cowboy.

"Why—he set down thar—an' he kind of hid his face on his hand. An' I grabbed his gun an' got the drop on him."

What the cowboy thought of this was expressed in a laugh. His mates likewise grinned broadly. Then the leader turned to Duane.

"Stranger, I reckon you'd better speak up for yourself," he said.

That stilled the crowd as no command had done.

"I'm Buck Duane, all right," said Duane, quietly. "It was this way—"

The big cowboy seemed to vibrate with a shock. All the ruddy warmth left his face; his jaw began to bulge; the corded veins in his neck stood out in knots. In an instant he had a hard, stern, strange look. He shot out a powerful hand that fastened in the front of Duane's blouse.

"Somethin' odd here. But if you're Duane you're sure in bad. Any fool ought to know that. You mean it, then?"

"Yes."

"Rode in to shoot up the town, eh? Some old stunt of you gunfighters? Meant to kill the man who offered a reward? Wanted to see Jeff Aiken bad, huh?"

"No," replied Duane. "Your citizen here misrepresented things. He seems a little off his head."

"Reckon he is. Somebody is, that's sure. You claim Buck Duane, then, an' all his doings?"

"I'm Duane; yes. But I won't stand for the blame of things I never did. That's why I'm here. I saw that placard out there offering the reward. Until now I never was within half a day's ride of this town. I'm blamed for what I never did. I rode in here, told who I was, asked somebody to send for Jeff Aiken."

"An' then you set down an' let this old guy throw your own gun on you?" queried the cowboy in amazement.

"I guess that's it," replied Duane.

"Well, it's powerful strange, if you're really Buck Duane."

A man elbowed his way into the circle.

"It's Duane. I recognize him. I seen him in more'n one place," he said. "Sibert, you can rely on what I tell you. I don't know if he's locoed or what. But I do know he's the genuine Buck Duane. Any one who'd ever seen him once would never forget him."

"What do you want to see Aiken for?" asked the cowboy Sibert.

"I want to face him, to tell him I never harmed his wife."

"Why?"

"Because I'm innocent, that's all."

"Suppose we send for Aiken an' he hears you an' doesn't believe you; what then?"

"If he won't believe me—why, then my case's so bad—I'd be better off dead."

A momentary silence was broken by Sibert.

"If this isn't a strange deal! Boys, reckon we'd better send for Jeff."

"Somebody went for him. He'll be comin' soon," replied a man.

Duane stood a head taller than that circle of curious faces. He gazed out above and beyond them. It was in this way that he chanced to see a number of women on the outskirts of the crowd. Some were old, with hard faces, like the men. Some were young and comely, and most of these seemed agitated by excitement or distress. They cast fearful, pitying glances upon Duane as he stood there with that noose round his neck. Women were more human than men, Duane thought. He met eyes that dilated, seemed fascinated at his gaze, but were not averted. It was the old women who were voluble, loud in expression of their feelings.

Near the trunk of the cottonwood stood a slender woman in white. Duane's wandering glance rested upon her. Her eyes were riveted upon him. A softhearted woman, probably, who did not want to see him hanged!

"Thar comes Jeff Aiken now," called a man, loudly.

The crowd shifted and trampled in eagerness.

Duane saw two men coming fast, one of whom, in the lead, was of stalwart build. He had a gun in his hand, and his manner was that of fierce energy.

The cowboy Sibert thrust open the jostling circle of men.

"Hold on, Jeff," he called, and he blocked the man with the gun. He spoke so low Duane could not hear what he said, and his form hid Aiken's face. At the juncture the crowd spread out, closed in, and Aiken and Sibert were caught in the circle. There was a pushing forward, a pressing of many bodies, hoarse cries and flinging hands—again the insane tumult was about to break out—the demand for an outlaw's blood, the call for a wild justice executed a thousand times before on Texas's bloody soil.

Sibert bellowed at the dark encroaching mass. The cowboys with him beat and cuffed in vain.

"Jeff, will you listen?" broke in Sibert, hurriedly, his hand on the other man's arm.

Aiken nodded coolly. Duane, who had seen many men in perfect control of themselves under circumstances like these, recognized the spirit that dominated Aiken. He was white, cold, passionless. There were lines of bitter grief deep round his lips. If Duane ever felt the meaning of death he felt it then.

"Sure this 's your game, Aiken," said Sibert. "But hear me a minute. Reckon there's no doubt about this man bein' Buck Duane. He seen the placard out at the crossroads. He rides in to Shirley. He says he's Buck Duane an' he's lookin' for Jeff Aiken. That's all clear enough. You know how these gun-fighters go lookin' for trouble. But here's what stumps me. Duane sits down there on the bench and lets old Abe Strickland grab his gun an' get the drop on him. More'n that, he gives me some strange talk about how, if he couldn't make you believe he's innocent, he'd better be dead. You see for yourself Duane ain't drunk or crazy or locoed. He doesn't strike me as a man who rode in here huntin' blood. So I reckon you'd better hold on till you hear what he has to say."

Then for the first time the drawn-faced, hungry-eyed giant turned his gaze upon Duane. He had intelligence which was not yet subservient to passion. Moreover, he seemed the kind of man Duane would care to have judge him in a critical moment like this.

"Listen," said Duane, gravely, with his eyes steady on Aiken's, "I'm Buck Duane. I never lied to any man in my life. I was forced into outlawry. I've never had a chance to leave the country. I've killed men to save my own life. I never intentionally harmed any woman. I rode thirty miles today—deliberately to see what this reward was, who made it, what for. When I read the placard I went sick to the bottom of my soul. So I rode in here to find you—to tell you this: I never saw Shirley before to-day. It was impossible for me to have—killed your wife. Last September I was two hundred miles north of here on the upper Nueces. I can prove that. Men who know me will tell you I couldn't murder a woman. I haven't any idea why such a deed should be laid at my hands. It's just that wild border gossip. I have no idea what reasons you have for holding me responsible. I only know—you're wrong. You've been deceived. And see here, Aiken. You understand I'm a miserable man. I'm about broken, I guess. I don't care any more for life, for anything. If you can't look me in the eyes, man to man, and believe what I say—why, by God! you can kill me!"

Aiken heaved a great breath.

"Buck Duane, whether I'm impressed or not by what you say needn't matter. You've had accusers, justly or unjustly, as will soon appear. The thing is we can prove you innocent or guilty. My girl Lucy saw my wife's assailant."

He motioned for the crowd of men to open up.

"Somebody—you, Sibert—go for Lucy. That'll settle this thing."

Duane heard as a man in an ugly dream. The faces around him, the hum of voices, all seemed far off. His life hung by the merest thread. Yet he did not think of that so much as of the brand of a woman-murderer which be soon sealed upon him by a frightened, imaginative child.

The crowd trooped apart and closed again. Duane caught a blurred image of a slight girl clinging to Sibert's hand. He could not see distinctly. Aiken lifted the child, whispered soothingly to her not to be afraid. Then he fetched her closer to Duane.

"Lucy, tell me. Did you ever see this man before?" asked Aiken, huskily and low. "Is he the one—who came in the house that day—struck you down—and dragged mam—?"

Aiken's voice failed.

A lightning flash seemed to clear Duane's blurred sight. He saw a pale, sad face and violet eyes fixed in gloom and horror upon his. No terrible moment in Duane's life equaled this one of silence—of suspense.

"It ain't him!" cried the child.

Then Sibert was flinging the noose off Duane's neck and unwinding the bonds round his arms. The spellbound crowd awoke to hoarse exclamations.

"See there, my locoed gents, how easy you'd hang the wrong man," burst out the cowboy, as he made the rope-end hiss. "You-all are a lot of wise rangers. Haw! haw!"

He freed Duane and thrust the bone-handled gun back in Duane's holster.

"You Abe, there. Reckon you pulled a stunt! But don't try the like again. And, men, I'll gamble there's a hell of a lot of bad work Buck Duane's named for—which all he never done. Clear away there. Where's his hoss? Duane, the road's open out of Shirley."

Sibert swept the gaping watchers aside and pressed Duane toward the horse, which another cowboy held. Mechanically Duane mounted, felt a lift as he went up. Then the cowboy's hard face softened in a smile.

"I reckon it ain't uncivil of me to say—hit that road quick!" he said, frankly.

He led the horse out of the crowd. Aiken joined him, and between them they escorted Duane across the plaza. The crowd appeared irresistibly drawn to follow.

Aiken paused with his big hand on Duane's knee. In it, unconsciously probably, he still held the gun.

"Duane, a word with you," he said. "I believe you're not so black as you've been painted. I wish there was time to say more. Tell me this, anyway. Do you know the Ranger Captain MacNelly?"

"I do not," replied Duane, in surprise.

"I met him only a week ago over in Fairfield," went on Aiken, hurriedly. "He declared you never killed my wife. I didn't believe him—argued with him. We almost had hard words over it. Now—I'm sorry. The last thing he said was: 'If you ever see Duane don't kill him. Send him into my camp after dark!' He meant something strange. What—I can't say. But he was right, and I was wrong. If Lucy had batted an eye I'd have killed you. Still, I wouldn't advise you to hunt up MacNelly's camp. He's clever. Maybe he believes there's no treachery in his new ideas of ranger tactics. I tell you for all it's worth. Good-by. May God help you further as he did this day!"

Duane said good-by and touched the horse with his spurs.

"So long, Buck!" called Sibert, with that frank smile breaking warm over his brown face; and he held his sombrero high.

CHAPTER 14

When Duane reached the crossing of the roads the name Fairfield on the sign-post seemed to be the thing that tipped the oscillating balance of decision in favor of that direction.

He answered here to unfathomable impulse. If he had been driven to hunt up Jeff Aiken, now he was called to find this unknown ranger captain. In Duane's state of mind clear reasoning, common sense, or keenness were out of the question. He went because he felt he was compelled.

Dusk had fallen when he rode into a town which inquiry discovered to be Fairfield. Captain MacNelly's camp was stationed just out of the village limits on the other side.

No one except the boy Duane questioned appeared to notice his arrival. Like Shirley, the town of Fairfield was large and prosperous, compared to the innumerable hamlets dotting the vast extent of southwestern Texas. As Duane rode through, being careful to get off the main street, he heard the tolling of a church-bell that was a melancholy reminder of his old home.

There did not appear to be any camp on the outskirts of the town. But as Duane sat his horse, peering around and undecided what further move to make, he caught the glint of flickering lights through the darkness. Heading toward them, he rode perhaps a quarter of a mile to come upon a grove of mesquite. The brightness of several fires made the surrounding darkness all the blacker. Duane saw the moving forms of men and heard horses. He advanced naturally, expecting any moment to be halted.

"Who goes there?" came the sharp call out of the gloom.

Duane pulled his horse. The gloom was impenetrable.

"One man—alone," replied Duane.

"A stranger?"

"Yes."

"What do you want?"

"I'm trying to find the ranger camp."

"You've struck it. What's your errand?"

"I want to see Captain MacNelly."

"Get down and advance. Slow. Don't move your hands. It's dark, but I can see."

Duane dismounted, and, leading his horse, slowly advanced a few paces. He saw a dully bright object—a gun—before he discovered the man who held it. A few more steps showed a dark figure blocking the trail. Here Duane halted.

"Come closer, stranger. Let's have a look at you," the guard ordered, curtly.

Duane advanced again until he stood before the man. Here the rays of light from the fires flickered upon Duane's face.

"Reckon you're a stranger, all right. What's your name and your business with the Captain?"

Duane hesitated, pondering what best to say.

"Tell Captain MacNelly I'm the man he's been asking to ride into his camp—after dark," finally said Duane.

The ranger bent forward to peer hard at this night visitor. His manner had been alert, and now it became tense.

"Come here, one of you men, quick," he called, without turning in the least toward the camp-fire.

"Hello! What's up, Pickens?" came the swift reply. It was followed by a rapid thud of boots on soft ground. A dark form crossed the gleams from the fire-light. Then a ranger loomed up to reach the side of the guard. Duane heard whispering, the purport of which he could not catch. The second ranger swore under his breath. Then he turned away and started back.

"Here, ranger, before you go, understand this. My visit is peaceful—friendly if you'll let it be. Mind, I was asked to come here—after dark."

Duane's clear, penetrating voice carried far. The listening rangers at the camp-fire heard what he said.

"Ho, Pickens! Tell that fellow to wait," replied an authoritative voice. Then a slim figure detached itself from the dark, moving group at the camp-fire and hurried out.

"Better be foxy, Cap," shouted a ranger, in warning.

"Shut up—all of you," was the reply.

This officer, obviously Captain MacNelly, soon joined the two rangers who were confronting Duane. He had no fear. He strode straight up to Duane.

"I'm MacNelly," he said. "If you're my man, don't mention your name—yet."

All this seemed so strange to Duane, in keeping with much that had happened lately.

"I met Jeff Aiken to-day," said Duane. "He sent me—"

"You've met Aiken!" exclaimed MacNelly, sharp, eager, low. "By all that's bully!" Then he appeared to catch himself, to grow restrained.

"Men, fall back, leave us alone a moment."

The rangers slowly withdrew.

"Buck Duane! It's you?" he whispered, eagerly.

"Yes."

"If I give my word you'll not be arrested—you'll be treated fairly—will you come into camp and consult with me?"

"Certainly."

"Duane, I'm sure glad to meet you," went on MacNelly; and he extended his hand.

Amazed and touched, scarcely realizing this actuality, Duane gave his hand and felt no unmistakable grip of warmth.

"It doesn't seem natural, Captain MacNelly, but I believe I'm glad to meet you," said Duane, soberly.

"You will be. Now we'll go back to camp. Keep your identity mum for the present."

He led Duane in the direction of the camp-fire.

"Pickens, go back on duty," he ordered, "and, Beeson, you look after this horse."

When Duane got beyond the line of mesquite, which had hid a good view of the camp-site, he saw a group of perhaps fifteen rangers sitting around the fires, near a long low shed where horses were feeding, and a small adobe house at one side.

"We've just had grub, but I'll see you get some. Then we'll talk," said MacNelly. "I've taken up temporary quarters here. Have a rustler job on hand. Now, when you've eaten, come right into the house."

Duane was hungry, but he hurried through the ample supper that was set before him, urged on by curiosity and astonishment. The only way he could account for his presence there in a ranger's camp was that MacNelly hoped to get useful information out of him. Still that would hardly have made this captain so eager. There was a mystery here, and Duane could scarcely wait for it to be solved. While eating he bent keen eyes around him. After a first quiet scrutiny the rangers apparently paid no more attention to him. They were all veterans in service—Duane saw that—and rugged, powerful men of iron constitution. Despite the occasional joke and sally of the more youthful members, and a general conversation of camp-fire nature, Duane was not deceived about the fact that his advent had been an unusual and striking one, which had caused an undercurrent of conjecture and even consternation among them. These rangers were too well trained to appear openly curious about their captain's guest. If they had not deliberately attempted to be oblivious of his presence Duane would have concluded they thought him an ordinary visitor, somehow of use to MacNelly. As it was, Duane felt a suspense that must have been due to a hint of his identity.

He was not long in presenting himself at the door of the house.

"Come in and have a chair," said MacNelly motioning for the one other occupant of the room to rise. "Leave us, Russell, and close the door. I'll be through these reports right off."

MacNelly sat at a table upon which was a lamp and various papers. Seen in the light he was a fine-looking, soldierly man of about forty years, dark-haired and dark-eyed, with a bronzed face, shrewd, stern, strong, yet not wanting in kindliness. He scanned hastily over some papers, fussed with them, and finally put them in envelopes. Without looking up he pushed a cigar-case toward Duane, and upon Duane's re-fusal to smoke he took a cigar, rose to light it at the lamp-chimney, and then, settling back in his chair, he faced Duane, making a vain attempt to hide what must have been the fulfilment of a long-nourished curiosity.

"Duane, I've been hoping for this for two years," he began.

Duane smiled a little—a smile that felt strange on his face. He had never been much of a talker. And speech here seemed more than ordi-narily difficult.

MacNelly must have felt that.

He looked long and earnestly at Duane, and his quick, nervous man-ner changed to grave thoughtfulness.

"I've lots to say, but where to begin," he mused. "Duane, you've had a hard life since you went on the dodge. I never met you before, don't know what you looked like as a boy. But I can see what—well, even ranger life isn't all roses."

He rolled his cigar between his lips and puffed clouds of smoke.

"Ever hear from home since you left Wellston?" he asked, abruptly.

"No."

"Never a word?"

"Not one," replied Duane, sadly.

"That's tough. I'm glad to be able to tell you that up to just lately your mother, sister, uncle—all your folks, I believe—were well. I've kept posted. But haven't heard lately."

Duane averted his face a moment, hesitated till the swelling left his throat, and then said, "It's worth what I went through to-day to hear that."

"I can imagine how you feel about it. When I was in the war—but let's get down to the business of this meeting."

He pulled his chair close to Duane's.

"You've had word more than once in the last two years that I wanted to see you?"

"Three times, I remember," replied Duane.

"Why didn't you hunt me up?"

"I supposed you imagined me one of those gun-fighters who couldn't take a dare and expected me to ride up to your camp and be arrested."

"That was natural, I suppose," went on MacNelly. "You didn't know me, otherwise you would have come. I've been a long time getting to you. But the nature of my job, as far as you're concerned, made me cautious. Duane, you're aware of the hard name you bear all over the Southwest?"

"Once in a while I'm jarred into realizing," replied Duane.

"It's the hardest, barring Murrell and Cheseldine, on the Texas border. But there's this difference. Murrell in his day was known to deserve his infamous name. Cheseldine in his day also. But I've found hundreds of men in southwest Texas who're your friends, who swear you never committed a crime. The farther south I get the clearer this becomes. What I want to know is the truth. Have you ever done anything criminal? Tell me the truth, Duane. It won't make any difference in my plan. And when I say crime I mean what *I* would call crime, or any reasonable Texan."

"That way my hands are clean," replied Duane.

"You never held up a man, robbed a store for grub, stole a horse when you needed him bad—never anything like that?"

"Somehow I always kept out of that, just when pressed the hardest."

"Duane, I'm damn glad!" MacNelly exclaimed, gripping Duane's hand. "Glad for your mother's sake! But, all the same, in spite of this, you are a Texas outlaw accountable to the state. You're perfectly aware that under existing circumstances, if you fell into the hands of the law, you'd probably hang, at least go to jail for a long term."

"That's what kept me on the dodge all these years," replied Duane.

"Certainly." MacNelly removed his cigar. His eyes narrowed and glittered. The muscles along his brown cheeks set hard and tense. He leaned close to Duane, laid sinewy, pressing fingers upon Duane's knee.

"Listen to this," he whispered, hoarsely. "If I place a pardon in your hand—make you a free, honest citizen once more, clear your name of infamy, make your mother, your sister proud of you—will you swear yourself to a service, *any* service I demand of you?"

Duane sat stock still, stunned.

Slowly, more persuasively, with show of earnest agitation, Captain MacNelly reiterated his startling query.

"My God!" burst from Duane. "What's this? MacNelly, you *can't* be in earnest!"

"Never more so in my life. I've a deep game. I'm playing it square. What do you say?"

He rose to his feet. Duane, as if impelled, rose with him. Ranger and outlaw then locked eyes that searched each other's soul. In MacNelly's Duane read truth, strong, fiery purpose, hope, even gladness, and a fugitive mounting assurance of victory.

Twice Duane endeavored to speak, failed of all save a hoarse, incoherent sound, until, forcing back a flood of speech, he found a voice.

"Any service? Every service! MacNelly, I give my word," said Duane.

A light played over MacNelly's face, warming out all the grim darkness. He held out his hand. Duane met it with his in a clasp that men unconsciously give in moments of stress.

When they unclasped and Duane stepped back to drop into a chair MacNelly fumbled for another cigar—he had bitten the other into shreds—and lighting it as before, he turned to his visitor, now calm and cool. He had the look of a man who had justly won something at considerable cost. His next move was to take a long leather case from his pocket and extract from it several folded papers.

"Here's your pardon from the Governor," he said, quietly. "You'll see, when you look it over, that it's conditional. When you sign the paper I have here the condition will be met."

He smoothed out the paper, handed Duane a pen, ran his forefinger along a dotted line.

Duane's hand was shaky. Years had passed since he had held a pen. It was with difficulty that he achieved his signature. Buckley Duane—how strange the name looked!

"Right here ends the career of Buck Duane, outlaw and gun-fighter," said MacNelly; and, seating himself, he took the pen from Duane's fingers and wrote several lines in several places upon the paper. Then with a smile he handed it to Duane.

"That makes you a member of Company A, Texas Rangers."

"So that's it!" burst out Duane, a light breaking in upon his bewilderment. "You want me for ranger service?"

"Sure. That's it," replied the Captain, dryly. "Now to hear what that service is to be. I've been a busy man since I took this job, and, as you may have heard, I've done a few things. I don't mind telling you that political influence put me in here and that up Austin way there's a good deal of friction in the Department of State in regard to whether or not the ranger service is any good—whether it should be discontinued or not. I'm on the party side who's defending the ranger service. I contend that it's made Texas habitable. Well, it's been up to me to produce results. So far I have been successful. My great ambition is to break up the outlaw gangs along the river. I have never ventured in there yet because I've been waiting to get the lieutenant I needed. You, of course, are the man I had in mind. It's my idea to start way up the Rio Grande and begin with Cheseldine. He's the strongest, the worst outlaw of the times. He's more than rustler. It's Cheseldine and his gang who are operating on the banks. They're doing bank-robbing. That's my private opinion, but it's not been backed up by any evidence. Cheseldine doesn't leave evidence. He's intelligent, cunning. No one seems to have seen him—to know what he looks like. I assume, of course, that you are a stranger to the country he dominates. It's five hundred miles west of your ground. There's a little town over there called Fairdale. It's the nest of a rustler gang. They rustle and murder at will. Nobody knows who the leader is. I want you to find out. Well, whatever way you decide is best you will proceed to act upon. You are your own boss. You know such men and how they can be approached. You will take all the time needed, if it's months. It will be necessary for you to communicate with me, and that will be a difficult matter. For Cheseldine dominates several whole counties. You must find some way to let me know when I and my rangers are needed. The plan is to break up Cheseldine's gang. It's the toughest job on the border. Arresting him alone isn't to be heard of. He couldn't be brought out. Killing him isn't much better, for his select men, the ones he operates with, are as dangerous to the community as he is. We want to kill or jail this choice selection of robbers and break up the rest of the gang. To find them, to get among them somehow, to learn their movements, to lay your trap for us rangers to spring—that, Duane, is your service to me, and God knows it's a great one!"

"I have accepted it," replied Duane.

"Your work will be secret. You are now a ranger in my service. But no one except the few I choose to tell will know of it until we pull off the job. You will simply be Buck Duane till it suits our purpose to acquaint Texas with the fact that you're a ranger. You'll see there's no date on that paper. No one will ever know when you entered the service. Perhaps we can make it appear that all or most of your outlawry has really been good service to the state. At that, I'll believe it'll turn out so."

MacNelly paused a moment in his rapid talk, chewed his cigar, drew his brows together in a dark frown, and went on. "No man on the border knows so well as you the deadly nature of this service. It's a thousand to one that you'll be killed. I'd say there was no chance at all for any other man beside you. Your reputation will go far among the outlaws. Maybe that and your nerve and your gun-play will pull you through. I'm hoping so. But it's a long, long chance against your ever coming back."

"That's not the point," said Duane. "But in case I get killed out there—what—"

"Leave that to me," interrupted Captain MacNelly. "You folks will know at once of your pardon and your ranger duty. If you lose your life out there I'll see your name cleared—the service you render known. You can rest assured of that."

"I am satisfied," replied Duane. "That's so much more than I've dared to hope."

"Well, it's settled, then. I'll give you money for expenses. You'll start as soon as you like—the sooner the better. I hope to think of other suggestions, especially about communicating with me."

Long after the lights were out and the low hum of voices had ceased round the camp-fire Duane lay wide awake, eyes staring into the blackness, marveling over the strange events of the day. He was humble, grateful to the depths of his soul. A huge and crushing burden had been lifted from his heart. He welcomed this hazardous service to the man who had saved him. Thought of his mother and sister and Uncle Jim, of his home, of old friends came rushing over him, the first time in years that he had happiness in the memory. The disgrace he had put upon them would now be removed; and in the light of that, his wasted life of the past, and its probably tragic end in future service as atonement changed their aspects. And as he lay there, with the approach of sleep finally dimming the vividness of his thought, so full of mystery, shadowy faces floated in the blackness around him, haunting him as he had always been haunted.

It was broad daylight when he awakened. MacNelly was calling him to breakfast. Outside sounded voices of men, crackling of fires, snorting and stamping of horses, the barking of dogs. Duane rolled out of his blankets and made good use of the soap and towel and razor and brush near by on a bench—things of rare luxury to an outlaw on the ride. The face he saw in the mirror was as strange as the past he had tried so hard to recall. Then he stepped to the door and went out.

The rangers were eating in a circle round a tarpaulin spread upon the ground.

"Fellows," said MacNelly, "shake hands with Buck Duane. He's on secret ranger service for me. Service that'll likely make you all hump soon! Mind you, keep mum about it."

The rangers surprised Duane with a roaring greeting, the warmth of which he soon divined was divided between pride of his acquisition to their ranks and eagerness to meet that violent service of which their captain hinted. They were jolly wild fellows, with just enough gravity in their welcome to show Duane their respect and appreciation, while not forgetting his lone-wolf record. When he had seated himself in that circle, now one of them, a feeling subtle and uplifting pervaded him.

After the meal Captain MacNelly drew Duane aside.

"Here's the money. Make it go as far as you can. Better strike straight for El Paso, snook around there and hear things. Then go to Valentine. That's near the river and within fifty miles or so of the edge of the Rim Rock. Somewhere up there Cheseldine holds fort. Somewhere to the north is the town Fairdale. But he doesn't hide all the time in the rocks. Only after some daring raid or holdup. Cheseldine's got border towns on his staff, or scared of him, and these places we want to know about, especially Fairdale. Write me care of the adjutant at Austin. I don't have to warn you to be careful where you mail letters. Ride a hundred, two hundred miles, if necessary, or go clear to El Paso."

MacNelly stopped with an air of finality, and then Duane slowly rose.

"I'll start at once," he said, extending his hand to the Captain. "I wish—I'd like to thank you!"

"Hell, man! Don't thank me!" replied MacNelly, crushing the proffered hand. "I've sent a lot of good men to their deaths, and maybe you're another. But, as I've said, you've one chance in a thousand. And, by Heaven! I'd hate to be Cheseldine or any other man you were trailing. No, not good-by—*Adios*, Duane! May we meet again!"

BOOK II

THE RANGER

CHAPTER 15

West of the Pecos River Texas extended a vast wild region, barren in the north where the Llano Estacado spread its shifting sands, fertile in the south along the Rio Grande. A railroad marked an undeviating course across five hundred miles of this country, and the only villages and towns lay on or near this line of steel. Unsettled as was this western Texas, and despite the acknowledged dominance of the outlaw bands, the pioneers pushed steadily into it. First had come the lone rancher; then his neighbors in near and far valleys; then the hamlets; at last the railroad and the towns. And still the pioneers came, spreading deeper into the valleys, farther and wider over the plains. It was mesquite-dotted, cactus-covered desert, but rich soil upon which water acted like magic. There was little grass to an acre, but there were millions of acres. The climate was wonderful. Cattle flourished and ranchers prospered.

The Rio Grande flowed almost due south along the western boundary for a thousand miles, and then, weary of its course, turned abruptly north, to make what was called the Big Bend. The railroad, running west, cut across this bend, and all that country bounded on the north by the railroad and on the south by the river was as wild as the Staked Plains. It contained not one settlement. Across the face of this Big Bend, as if to isolate it, stretched the Ord mountain range, of which Mount Ord, Cathedral Mount, and Elephant Mount raised bleak peaks above their fellows. In the valleys of the foothills and out across the plains were ranches, and farther north villages, and the towns of Alpine and Marfa.

Like other parts of the great Lone Star State, this section of Texas was a world in itself—a world where the riches of the rancher were ever enriching the outlaw. The village closest to the gateway of this outlaw-infested region was a little place called Ord, named after the dark peak that loomed some miles to the south. It had been settled originally by Mexicans—there were still the ruins of adobe missions—but with the advent of the rustler and outlaw many inhabitants were shot or driven away, so that at the height of Ord's prosperity and evil sway there were but few Mexicans living there, and these had their choice between holding hand-and-glove with the outlaws or furnishing target practice for that wild element.

Toward the close of a day in September a stranger rode into Ord, and in a community where all men were remarkable for one reason or another he excited interest. His horse, perhaps, received the first and most engaging attention—horses in that region being apparently more important than men. This particular horse did not attract with beauty. At first glance he seemed ugly. But he was a giant, black as coal, rough despite the care manifestly bestowed upon him, long of body, ponderous of limb, huge in every way. A bystander remarked that he had a grand head. True, if only his head had been seen he would have been a beautiful horse. Like men, horses show what they are in the shape, the size, the line, the character of the head. This one denoted fire, speed, blood, loyalty, and his eyes were as soft and dark as a woman's. His face was solid black, except in the middle of his forehead, where there was a round spot of white.

"Say mister, mind tellin' me his name?" asked a ragged urchin, with born love of a horse in his eyes.

"Bullet," replied the rider.

"Thet there's fer the white mark, ain't it?" whispered the youngster to another. "Say, ain't he a whopper? Biggest hoss I ever seen."

Bullet carried a huge black silver-ornamented saddle of Mexican make, a lariat and canteen, and a small pack rolled into a tarpaulin.

This rider apparently put all care of appearances upon his horse. His apparel was the ordinary jeans of the cowboy without vanity, and it was corn and travel-stained. His boots showed evidence of an intimate acquaintance with cactus. Like his horse, this man was a giant in stature, but rangier, not so heavily built. Otherwise the only striking thing about him was his somber face with its piercing eyes, and hair white over the temples. He packed two guns, both low down—but that was too common a thing to attract notice in the Big Bend. A close observer, however, would have noted a singular fact—this rider's right hand was more bronzed, more weather-beaten than his left. He never wore a glove on that right hand!

He had dismounted before a ramshackle structure that bore upon its wide, high-boarded front the sign, "Hotel." There were horsemen coming and going down the wide street between its rows of old stores, saloons, and houses. Ord certainly did not look enterprising. Americans had manifestly assimilated much of the leisure of the Mexicans. The hotel had a wide platform in front, and this did duty as porch and sidewalk. Upon it, and leaning against a hitching-rail, were men of varying ages, most of them slovenly in old jeans and slouched sombreros. Some were booted, belted, and spurred. No man there wore a coat, but all wore vests. The guns in that group would have outnumbered the men.

It was a crowd seemingly too lazy to be curious. Good nature did not appear to be wanting, but it was not the frank and boisterous kind natural to the cowboy or rancher in town for a day. These men were idlers; what else, perhaps, was easy to conjecture. Certainly to this arriving stranger, who flashed a keen eye over them, they wore an atmosphere never associated with work.

Presently a tall man, with a drooping, sandy mustache, leisurely detached himself from the crowd.

"Howdy, stranger," he said.

The stranger had bent over to loosen the cinches; he straightened up and nodded. Then: "I'm thirsty!"

That brought a broad smile to faces. It was characteristic greeting. One and all trooped after the stranger into the hotel. It was a dark, ill-smelling barn of a place, with a bar as high as a short man's head. A bartender with a scarred face was serving drinks.

"Line up, gents," said the stranger.

They piled over one another to get to the bar, with coarse jests and oaths and laughter. None of them noted that the stranger did not appear so thirsty as he had claimed to be. In fact, though he went through the motions, he did not drink at all.

"My name's Jim Fletcher," said the tall man with the drooping, sandy mustache. He spoke laconically, nevertheless there was a tone that showed he expected to be known. Something went with that name. The stranger did not appear to be impressed.

"My name might be Blazes, but it ain't," he replied. "What do you call this burg?"

"Stranger, this heah me-tropoles bears the handle Ord. Is thet new to you?"

He leaned back against the bar, and now his little yellow eyes, clear as crystal, flawless as a hawk's, fixed on the stranger. Other men crowded close, forming a circle, curious, ready to be friendly or otherwise, according to how the tall interrogator marked the newcomer.

"Sure, Ord's a little strange to me. Off the railroad some, ain't it? Funny trails hereabouts."

"How fur was you goin'?"

"I reckon I was goin' as far as I could," replied the stranger, with a hard laugh.

His reply had subtle reaction on that listening circle. Some of the men exchanged glances. Fletcher stroked his drooping mustache, seemed thoughtful, but lost something of that piercing scrutiny.

"Wal, Ord's the jumpin'-off place," he said, presently. "Sure you've heerd of the Big Bend country?"

"I sure have, an' was makin' tracks fer it," replied the stranger.

Fletcher turned toward a man in the outer edge of the group. "Knell, come in heah."

This individual elbowed his way in and was seen to be scarcely more than a boy, almost pale beside those bronzed men, with a long, expressionless face, thin and sharp.

"Knell, this heah's—" Fletcher wheeled to the stranger. "What'd you call yourself?"

"I'd hate to mention what I've been callin' myself lately."

This sally fetched another laugh. The stranger appeared cool, careless, indifferent. Perhaps he knew, as the others present knew, that this show of Fletcher's, this pretense of introduction, was merely talk while he was looked over.

Knell stepped up, and it was easy to see, from the way Fletcher relinquished his part in the situation, that a man greater than he had appeared upon the scene.

"Any business here?" he queried, curtly. When he spoke his expressionless face was in strange contrast with the ring, the quality, the cruelty of his voice. This voice betrayed an absence of humor, of friendliness, of heart.

"Nope," replied the stranger.

"Know anybody hereabouts?"

"Nary one."

"Jest ridin' through?"

"Yep."

"Slopin' fer back country, eh?"

There came a pause. The stranger appeared to grow a little resentful and drew himself up disdainfully.

"Wal, considerin' you-all seem so damn friendly an' oncurious down here in this Big Bend country, I don't mind sayin' yes—I am in on the dodge," he replied, with deliberate sarcasm.

"From west of Ord—out El Paso way, mebbe?"

"Sure."

"A-huh! Thet so?" Knell's words cut the air, stilled the room. "You're from way down the river. Thet's what they say down there—'on the dodge.' . . . Stranger, you're a liar!"

With swift clink of spur and thump of boot the crowd split, leaving Knell and the stranger in the center.

Wild breed of that ilk never made a mistake in judging a man's nerve. Knell had cut out with the trenchant call, and stood ready. The stranger suddenly lost his every semblance to the rough and easy character before manifest in him. He became bronze. That situation seemed familiar to him. His eyes held a singular piercing light that danced like a compass-needle.

"Sure I lied," he said; "so I ain't takin' offense at the way you called me. I'm lookin' to make friends, not enemies. You don't strike me as one of them four-flushes, achin' to kill somebody. But if you are—go ahead an' open the ball. . . . You see, I never throw a gun on them fellers till they go fer theirs."

Knell coolly eyed his antagonist, his strange face not changing in the least. Yet somehow it was evident in his look that here was metal which rang differently from what he had expected. Invited to start a fight or withdraw, as he chose, Knell proved himself big in the manner characteristic of only the genuine gunman.

"Stranger, I pass," he said, and, turning to the bar, he ordered liquor.

The tension relaxed, the silence broke, the men filled up the gap; the incident seemed closed. Jim Fletcher attached himself to the stranger, and now both respect and friendliness tempered his asperity.

"Wal, fer want of a better handle I'll call you Dodge," he said.

"Dodge's as good as any. . . . Gents, line up again—an' if you can't be friendly, be careful!"

Such was Buck Duane's debut in the little outlaw hamlet of Ord.

Duane had been three months out of the Nueces country. At El Paso he bought the finest horse he could find, and, armed and otherwise outfitted to suit him, he had taken to unknown trails. Leisurely he rode from town to town, village to village, ranch to ranch, fitting his talk and his occupation to the impression he wanted to make upon different people whom he met. He was in turn a cowboy, a rancher, a cattleman, a stock-buyer, a boomer, a land-hunter; and long before he reached the wild and inhospitable Ord he had acted the part of an outlaw, drifting into new territory. He passed on leisurely because he wanted to learn the lay of the country, the location of villages and ranches, the work, habit, gossip, pleasures, and fears of the people with whom he came in contact. The one subject most impelling to him—outlaws—he never mentioned; but by talking all around it, sifting the old ranch and cattle story, he acquired a knowledge calculated to aid his plot. In this game time was of no moment; if necessary he would take years to accomplish his task. The stupendous and perilous nature of it showed in the slow, wary preparation. When he heard Fletcher's name and faced Knell he knew he had reached the place he sought. Ord was a hamlet on the fringe of the grazing country, of doubtful honesty, from which, surely, winding trails led down into that free and never-disturbed paradise of outlaws—the Big Bend.

Duane made himself agreeable, yet not too much so, to Fletcher and several other men disposed to talk and drink and eat; and then, after having a care for his horse, he rode out of town a couple of miles to a grove he had marked, and there, well hidden, he prepared to spend the night. This proceeding served a double purpose—he was safer, and the habit would look well in the eyes of outlaws, who would be more inclined to see in him the lone-wolf fugitive.

Long since Duane had fought out a battle with himself, won a hard-earned victory. His outer life, the action, was much the same as it had been; but the inner life had tremendously changed. He could never become a happy man, he could never shake utterly those haunting phantoms that had once been his despair and madness; but he had assumed a task impossible for any man save one like him, he had felt the meaning of it grow strangely and wonderfully, and through that flourished up consciousness of how passionately he now clung to this thing which would blot out his former infamy. The iron fetters no more threatened his hands; the iron door no more haunted his dreams. He never forgot that he was free. Strangely, too, along with this feeling of new manhood there gathered the force of imperious desire to run these chief outlaws to their dooms. He never called them outlaws—but rustlers, thieves, robbers, murderers, criminals. He sensed the growth of a relentless driving passion, and sometimes he feared that, more than the newly acquired zeal and pride in this ranger service, it was the old, terrible inherited killing instinct lifting its hydra-head in new guise. But of that he could not be sure. He dreaded the thought. He could only wait.

Another aspect of the change in Duane, neither passionate nor driving, yet not improbably even more potent of new significance to life, was the imperceptible return of an old love of nature dead during his outlaw days.

For years a horse had been only a machine of locomotion, to carry him from place to place, to beat and spur and goad mercilessly in flight; now this giant black, with his splendid head, was a companion, a friend, a brother, a loved thing, guarded jealously, fed and trained and ridden with an intense appreciation of his great speed and endurance. For years the daytime, with its birth of sunrise on through long hours to the ruddy close, had been used for sleep or rest in some rocky hole or willow brake or deserted hut, had been hated because it augmented danger of pursuit, because it drove the fugitive to lonely, wretched hiding; now the dawn was a greeting, a promise of another day to ride, to plan, to remember, and sun, wind, cloud, rain, sky—all were joys to him, somehow speaking his freedom. For years the night had been a black space, during which he had to ride unseen along the endless trails, to peer with cat-eyes through gloom for the moving shape that ever pursued him; now the twilight and the dusk and the shadows of grove and cañon darkened into night with its train of stars, and brought him calm reflection of the day's happenings, of the morrow's possibilities, perhaps a sad, brief procession of the old phantoms, then sleep. For years cañons and valleys and mountains had been looked at as retreats that might be dark and wild enough to hide even an outlaw; now he saw these features of the great desert with something of the eyes of the boy who had once burned for adventure and life among them.

This night a wonderful afterglow lingered long in the west, and against the golden-red of clear sky the bold, black head of Mount Ord reared itself aloft, beautiful but aloof, sinister yet calling. Small wonder that Duane gazed in fascination upon the peak! Somewhere deep in its corrugated sides or lost in a rugged cañon was hidden the secret stronghold of the master outlaw Cheseldine. All down along the ride from El Paso Duane had heard of Cheseldine, of his band, his fearful deeds, his cunning, his widely separated raids, of his flitting here and there like a Jack-o'-lantern; but never a word of his den, never a word of his appearance.

Next morning Duane did not return to Ord. He struck off to the north, riding down a rough, slow-descending road that appeared to have been used occasionally for cattle-driving. As he had ridden in from the west, this northern direction led him into totally unfamiliar country. While he passed on, however, he exercised such keen observation that in the future he would know whatever might be of service to him if he chanced that way again.

The rough, wild, brush-covered slope down from the foothills gradually leveled out into plain, a magnificent grazing country, upon which till noon of that day Duane did not see a herd of cattle or a ranch. About that time he made out smoke from the railroad, and after a couple of hours' riding he entered a town which inquiry discovered to be Bradford. It was the largest town he had visited since Marfa, and he calculated must have a thousand or fifteen hundred inhabitants, not including Mexicans. He decided this would be a good place for him to hold up for a while, being the nearest town to Ord, only forty miles away. So he hitched his horse in front of a store and leisurely set about studying Bradford.

It was after dark, however, that Duane verified his suspicions concerning Bradford. The town was awake after dark, and there was one long row of saloons, dance-halls, gambling-resorts in full blast. Duane visited them all, and was surprised to see wildness and license equal to that of the old river camp of Bland's in its palmiest days. Here it was forced upon him that the farther west one traveled along the river the sparser the respectable settlements, the more numerous the hard characters, and in consequence the greater the element of lawlessness. Duane returned to his lodging-house with the conviction that MacNelly's task of cleaning up the Big Bend country was a stupendous one. Yet, he reflected, a company of intrepid and quick-shooting rangers could have soon cleaned up this Bradford.

The innkeeper had one other guest that night, a long black-coated and wide-sombreroed Texan who reminded Duane of his grandfather. This man had penetrating eyes, a courtly manner, and an unmistakable leaning toward companionship and mint-juleps. The gentleman introduced himself as Colonel Webb, of Marfa, and took it as a matter of course that Duane made no comment about himself.

"Sir, it's all one to me," he said, blandly, waving his hand. "I have traveled. Texas is free, and this frontier is one where it's healthier and just as friendly for a man to have no curiosity about his companion. You might be Cheseldine, of the Big Bend, or you might be Judge Little, of El Paso—it's all one to me. I enjoy drinking with you anyway."

Duane thanked him, conscious of a reserve and dignity that he could not have felt or pretended three months before. And then, as always, he was a good listener. Colonel Webb told, among other things, that he had come out to the Big Bend to look over the affairs of a deceased brother who had been a rancher and a sheriff of one of the towns, Fairdale by name.

"Found no affairs, no ranch, not even his grave," said Colonel Webb.

"And I tell you sir, if hell's any tougher than this Fairdale I don't want to expiate my sins there."

"Fairdale. . . . I imagine sheriffs have a hard row to hoe out here," replied Duane, trying not to appear curious.

The Colonel swore lustily.

"My brother was the only honest sheriff Fairdale ever had. It was wonderful how long he lasted. But he had nerve, he could throw a gun, and he was on the square. Then he was wise enough to confine his work to offenders of his own town and neighborhood. He let the riding out-laws alone, else he wouldn't have lasted at all. . . . What this frontier needs, sir, is about six companies of Texas Rangers."

Duane was aware of the Colonel's close scrutiny.

"Do you know anything about the service?" he asked.

"I used to. Ten years ago when I lived in San Antonio. A fine body of men, sir, and the salvation of Texas."

"Governor Stone doesn't entertain that opinion," said Duane.

Here Colonel Webb exploded. Manifestly the Governor was not his choice for a chief executive of the great state. He talked politics for a while, and of the vast territory west of the Pecos that seemed never to get a benefit from Austin. He talked enough for Duane to realize that here was just the kind of intelligent, well-informed, honest citizen that he had been trying to meet. He exerted himself thereafter to be agreeable and interesting; and he saw presently that here was an opportunity to make a valuable acquaintance, if not a friend.

"I'm a stranger in these parts," said Duane, finally. "What is this out-law situation you speak of?"

"It's damnable, sir, and unbelievable. Not rustling any more, but just wholesale herd-stealing, in which some big cattlemen, supposed to be honest, are equally guilty with the outlaws. On this border, you know, the rustler has always been able to steal cattle in any numbers. But to get rid of big bunches—that's the hard job. The gang operating between here and Valentine evidently have not this trouble. Nobody knows where the stolen stock goes. But I'm not alone in my opinion that most of it goes to several big stockmen. They ship to San Antonio, Austin, New Orleans, also to El Paso. If you travel the stock-road between here and Marfa and Valentine you'll see dead cattle all along the line and stray cattle out in the scrub. The herds have been driven fast and far, and stragglers are not rounded up."

"Wholesale business, eh?" remarked Duane. "Who are these—er—big stock-buyers?"

Colonel Webb seemed a little startled at the abrupt query. He bent his penetrating gaze upon Duane and thoughtfully stroked his pointed beard.

"Names, of course, I'll not mention. Opinions are one thing, direct accusation another. This is not a healthy country for the informer."

When it came to the outlaws themselves Colonel Webb was disposed to talk freely. Duane could not judge whether the Colonel had a hobby of that subject or the outlaws were so striking in personality and deed that any man would know all about them. The great name along the river was Cheseldine, but it seemed to be a name detached from an individual. No person of veracity known to Colonel Webb had ever seen Cheseldine, and those who claimed that doubtful honor varied so diversely in descriptions of the chief that they confused the reality and lent to the outlaw only further mystery. Strange to say of an outlaw leader, as there was no one who could identify him, so there was no one who could prove he had actually killed a man. Blood flowed like water over the Big Bend country, and it was Cheseldine who spilled it. Yet the fact remained there were no eye-witnesses to connect any individual called Cheseldine with these deeds of violence. But in striking contrast to this mystery was the person, character, and cold-blooded action of Poggin and Knell, the chief's lieutenants. They were familiar figures in all the towns within two hundred miles of Bradford. Knell had a record, but as gunman with an incredible list of victims Poggin was supreme. If Poggin had a friend no one ever heard of him. There were a hundred stories of his nerve, his wonderful speed with a gun, his passion for gambling, his love of a horse—his cold, implacable, inhuman wiping out of his path any man that crossed it.

"Cheseldine is a name, a terrible name," said Colonel Webb. "Sometimes I wonder if he's not only a name. In that case where does the brains of this gang come from? No; there must be a master craftsman behind this border pillage; a master capable of handling those terrors Poggin and Knell. Of all the thousands of outlaws developed by western Texas in the last twenty years these three are the greatest. In southern Texas, down between the Pecos and the Nueces, there have been and are still many bad men. But I doubt if any outlaw there, possibly excepting Buck Duane, ever equaled Poggin. You've heard of this Duane?"

"Yes, a little," replied Duane, quietly. "I'm from southern Texas. Buck Duane, then, is known out here?"

"Why, man, where isn't his name known?" returned Colonel Webb. "I've kept track of his record as I have all the others. Of course, Duane, being a lone outlaw, is somewhat of a mystery also, but not like Cheseldine. Out here there have drifted many stories of Duane, horrible some of them. But despite them a sort of romance clings to that Nueces outlaw. He's killed three great outlaw leaders, I believe—Bland, Hardin, and the other I forgot. Hardin was known in the Big Bend, had friends there. Bland had a hard name at Del Rio."

"Then this man Duane enjoys rather an unusual repute west of the Pecos?" inquired Duane.

"He's considered more of an enemy to his kind than to honest men. I understand Duane had many friends, that whole counties swear by him—secretly, of course, for he's a hunted outlaw with rewards on his head. His fame in this country appears to hang on his matchless gun-play and his enmity toward outlaw chiefs. I've heard many a rancher say: 'I wish to God that Buck Duane would drift out here! I'd give a hundred pesos to see him and Poggin meet.' It's a singular thing, stranger, how jealous these great outlaws are of each other."

"Yes, indeed, all about them is singular," replied Duane. "Has Cheseldine's gang been busy lately?"

"No. This section has been free of rustling for months, though there's unexplained movements of stock. Probably all the stock that's being shipped now was rustled long ago. Cheseldine works over a wide section, too wide for news to travel inside of weeks. Then sometimes he's not heard of at all for a spell. These lulls are pretty surely indicative of a big storm sooner or later. And Cheseldine's deals, as they grow fewer and farther between, certainly get bigger, more daring. There are some people who think Cheseldine had nothing to do with the bank-robberies and train-holdups during the last few years in this country. But that's poor reasoning. The jobs have been too well done, too surely covered, to be the works of Mexicans or ordinary outlaws."

"What's your view of the outlook? How's all this going to wind up? Will the outlaw ever be driven out?" asked Duane.

"Never. There will always be outlaws along the Rio Grande. All the armies in the world couldn't comb the wild brakes of that fifteen hundred miles of river. But the sway of the outlaw, such as is enjoyed by these great leaders, will sooner or later be past. The criminal element flock to the Southwest. But not so thick and fast as the pioneers. Besides, the outlaws kill themselves, and the ranchers are slowly rising in wrath, if not in action. That will come soon. If they only had a leader to start the fight! But that will come. There's talk of vigilantes, the same that were organized in California and are now in force in Idaho. So far it's only talk. But the time will come. And the days of Cheseldine and Poggin are numbered."

Duane went to bed that night exceedingly thoughtful. The long trail was growing hot. This voluble colonel had given him new ideas. It came to Duane in surprise that he was famous along the upper Rio Grande. Assuredly he would not long be able to conceal his identity. He had no doubt that he would soon meet the chiefs of this clever and bold rustling gang. He could not decide whether he would be safer unknown or known. In the latter case his one chance lay in the fatality connected with his name, in his power to look it and act it. Duane had never dreamed of any sleuth-hound tendency in his nature, but now he felt something like one. Above all others his mind fixed on Poggin—Poggin the brute, the executor of Cheseldine's will, but mostly upon Poggin the gunman. This in itself was a warning to Duane. He felt terrible forces at work within him. There was the stern and indomitable resolve to make MacNelly's boast good to the Governor of the state—to break up Cheseldine's gang. Yet this was not in Duane's mind before a strange grim and deadly instinct—which he had to drive away for fear he would find in it a passion to kill Poggin, not for the state, nor for his word to MacNelly, but for himself. Had his father's blood and the hard years made Duane the kind of man who instinctively wanted to meet Poggin? He was sworn to MacNelly's service, and he fought himself to keep that, and that only, in his mind.

Duane ascertained that Fairdale was situated two days' ride from

Bradford toward the north. There was a stage which made the journey twice a week.

Next morning Duane mounted his horse and headed for Fairdale. He rode leisurely, as he wanted to learn all he could about the country. There were few ranches. The farther he traveled the better grazing he encountered, and, strange to note, the fewer herds of cattle.

It was just sunset when he made out a cluster of adobe houses that marked the half-way point between Bradford and Fairdale. Here, Duane had learned, was stationed a comfortable inn for wayfarers.

When he drew up before the inn the landlord and his family and a number of loungers greeted him laconically.

"Beat the stage in, hey?" remarked one.

"There she comes now," said another. "Joel shore is drivin' to-night."

Far down the road Duane saw a cloud of dust and horses and a lumbering coach. When he had looked after the needs of his horse he returned to the group before the inn. They awaited the stage with that interest common to isolated people. Presently it rolled up, a large mud-bespattered and dusty vehicle, littered with baggage on top and tied on behind. A number of passengers alighted, three of whom excited Duane's interest. One was a tall, dark, striking-looking man, and the other two were ladies, wearing long gray ulsters and veils. Duane heard the proprietor of the inn address the man as Colonel Longstreth, and as the party entered the inn Duane's quick ears caught a few words which acquainted him with the fact that Longstreth was the Mayor of Fairdale.

Duane passed inside himself to learn that supper would soon be ready. At table he found himself opposite the three who had attracted his attention.

"Ruth, I envy the lucky cowboys," Longstreth was saying.

Ruth was a curly-headed girl with gray or hazel eyes.

"I'm crazy to ride bronchos," she said.

Duane gathered she was on a visit to western Texas. The other girl's deep voice, sweet like a bell, made Duane regard her closer. She had beauty as he had never seen it in another woman. She was slender, but the development of her figure gave Duane the impression she was twenty years old or more. She had the most exquisite hands Duane had ever seen. She did not resemble the Colonel, who was evidently her father.

She looked tired, quiet, even melancholy. A finely chiseled oval face; clear, olive-tinted skin, long eyes set wide apart and black as coal, beautiful to look into; a slender, straight nose that had something nervous and delicate about it which made Duane think of a thoroughbred; and a mouth by no means small, but perfectly curved; and hair like jet—all these features proclaimed her beauty to Duane. Duane believed her a descendant of one of the old French families of eastern Texas. He was sure of it when she looked at him, drawn by his rather persistent gaze. There were pride, fire, and passion in her eyes. Duane felt himself blushing in confusion. His stare at her had been rude, perhaps, but unconscious. How many years had passed since he had seen a girl like her! Thereafter he kept his eyes upon his plate, yet he seemed to be aware that he had aroused the interest of both girls.

After supper the guests assembled in a big sitting-room where an open fireplace with blazing mesquite sticks gave out warmth and cheery glow. Duane took a seat by a table in the corner, and, finding a paper, began to read. Presently when he glanced up he saw two dark-faced men, strangers who had not appeared before, and were peering in from a doorway. When they saw Duane had observed them they stepped back out of sight.

It flashed over Duane that the strangers acted suspiciously. In Texas in the seventies it was always bad policy to let strangers go unheeded. Duane pondered a moment. Then he went out to look over these two men. The doorway opened into a patio, and across that was a little dingy, dim-lighted barroom. Here Duane found the innkeeper dispensing drinks to the two strangers. They glanced up when he entered, and one of them whispered. He imagined he had seen one of them before. In Texas, where outdoor men were so rough, bronzed, bold, and sometimes grim of aspect, it was no easy task to pick out the crooked ones. But Duane's years on the border had augmented a natural instinct or gift to read character, or at least to sense the evil in men; and he knew at once that these strangers were dishonest.

"Hev somethin'?" one of them asked, leering. Both looked Duane up and down.

"No thanks, I don't drink," Duane replied, and returned their scrutiny with interest. "How's tricks in the Big Bend?"

Both men stared. It had taken only a close glance for Duane to recognize a type of ruffian most frequently met along the river. These strangers had that stamp, and their surprise proved he was right. Here the innkeeper showed signs of uneasiness, and seconded the surprise of his customers. No more was said at the instant, and the two rather hurriedly went out.

"Say, boss, do you know those fellows?" Duane asked the innkeeper.

"Nope."

"Which way did they come?"

"Now I think of it, them fellers rid in from both corners to-day," he replied, and he put both hands on the bar and looked at Duane. "They nooned heah, comin' from Bradford, they said, an' trailed in after the stage."

When Duane returned to the sitting-room Colonel Longstreth was absent, also several of the other passengers. Miss Ruth sat in the chair he had vacated, and across the table from her sat Miss Longstreth. Duane went directly to them.

"Excuse me," said Duane, addressing them. "I want to tell you there are a couple of rough-looking men here. I've just seen them. They mean evil. Tell your father to be careful. Lock your doors—bar your windows to-night."

"Oh!" cried Ruth, very low. "Ray, do you hear?"

"Thank you; we'll be careful," said Miss Longstreth, gracefully. The rich color had faded in her cheek. "I saw those men watching you from that door. They had such bright black eyes. Is there really danger—here?"

"I think so," was Duane's reply.

Soft swift steps behind him preceded a harsh voice: "Hands up!"

No man quicker than Duane to recognize the intent in those words! His hands shot up. Miss Ruth uttered a little frightened cry and sank into her chair. Miss Longstreth turned white, her eyes dilated. Both girls were staring at some one behind Duane.

"Turn around!" ordered the harsh voice.

The big, dark stranger, the bearded one who had whispered to his comrade in the barroom and asked Duane to drink, had him covered with a cocked gun. He strode forward, his eyes gleaming, pressed the gun against him, and with his other hand dove into his inside coat pocket and tore out his roll of bills. Then he reached low at Duane's hip, felt his gun, and took it. Then he slapped the other hip, evidently in search of another weapon. That done, he backed away, wearing an expression of fiendish satisfaction that made Duane think he was only a common thief, a novice at this kind of game.

His comrade stood in the door with a gun leveled at two other men, who stood there frightened, speechless.

"Git a move on, Bill," called this fellow; and he took a hasty glance backward. A stamp of hoofs came from outside. Of course the robbers had horses waiting. The one called Bill strode across the room, and with brutal, careless haste began to prod the two men with his weapon and to search them. The robber in the doorway called "Rustle!" and disappeared.

Duane wondered where the innkeeper was, and Colonel Longstreth and the other two passengers. The bearded robber quickly got through with his searching, and from his growls Duane gathered he had not been well remunerated. Then he wheeled once more. Duane had not moved a muscle, stood perfectly calm with his arms high. The robber strode back with his bloodshot eyes fastened upon the girls. Miss Longstreth never flinched, but the little girl appeared about to faint.

"Don't yap, there!" he said, low and hard. He thrust the gun close to Ruth. Then Duane knew for sure that he was no knight of the road, but a plain cutthroat robber. Danger always made Duane exult in a kind of cold glow. But now something hot worked within him. He had a little gun in his pocket. The robber had missed it. And he began to calculate chances.

"Any money, jewelry, diamonds!" ordered the ruffian, fiercely.

Miss Ruth collapsed. Then he made at Miss Longstreth. She stood with her hands at her breast. Evidently the robber took this position to mean that she had valuables concealed there. But Duane fancied she had instinctively pressed her hands against a throbbing heart.

"Come out with it!" he said, harshly, reaching for her.

"Don't dare touch me!" she cried, her eyes ablaze. She did not move. She had nerve.

It made Duane thrill. He saw he was going to get a chance. Waiting had been a science with him. But here it was hard. Miss Ruth had fainted, and that was well. Miss Longstreth had fight in her, which fact helped Duane, yet made injury possible to her. She eluded two lunges the man made at her. Then his rough hand caught her waist, and with one pull ripped it asunder, exposing her beautiful shoulder, white as snow.

She cried out. The prospect of being robbed or even killed had not shaken Miss Longstreth's nerve as had this brutal tearing off of half her waist.

The ruffian was only turned partially away from Duane. For himself he could have waited no longer. But for her! That gun was still held dangerously upward close to her. Duane watched only that. Then a bellow made him jerk his head. Colonel Longstreth stood in the doorway in a magnificent rage. He had no weapon. Strange how he showed no fear! He bellowed something again.

Duane's shifting glance caught the robber's sudden movement. It was a kind of start. He seemed stricken. Duane expected him to shoot Longstreth. Instead the hand that clutched Miss Longstreth's torn waist loosened its hold. The other hand with its cocked weapon slowly dropped till it pointed to the floor. That was Duane's chance.

Swift as a flash he drew his gun and fired. Thud! went his bullet, and he could not tell on the instant whether it hit the robber or went into the ceiling. Then the robber's gun boomed harmlessly. He fell with blood spurting over his face. Duane realized he had hit him, but the small bullet had glanced.

Miss Longstreth reeled and might have fallen had Duane not supported her. It was only a few steps to a couch, to which he half led, half carried her. Then he rushed out of the room, across the patio, through the bar to the yard. Nevertheless, he was cautious. In the gloom stood a saddled horse, probably the one belonging to the fellow he had shot. His comrade had escaped. Returning to the sitting-room, Duane found a condition approaching pandemonium.

The innkeeper rushed in, pitchfork in hands. Evidently he had been out at the barn. He was now shouting to find out what had happened. Joel, the stage-driver, was trying to quiet the men who had been robbed. The woman, wife of one of the men, had come in, and she had hysterics. The girls were still and white. The robber Bill lay where he had fallen, and

Duane guessed he had made a fair shot, after all. And, lastly, the thing that struck Duane most of all was Longstreth's rage. He never saw such passion. Like a caged lion Longstreth stalked and roared. There came a quieter moment in which the innkeeper shrilly protested:

"Man, what're you ravin' aboot? Nobody's hurt, an' thet's lucky. I swear to God I hadn't nothin' to do with them fellers!"

"I ought to kill you anyhow!" replied Longstreth. And his voice now astounded Duane, it was so full of power.

Upon examination Duane found that his bullet had furrowed the robber's temple, torn a great piece out of his scalp, and, as Duane had guessed, had glanced. He was not seriously injured, and already showed signs of returning consciousness.

"Drag him out of here!" ordered Longstreth; and he turned to his daughter.

Before the innkeeper reached the robber Duane had secured the money and gun taken from him; and presently recovered the property of the other men. Joel helped the innkeeper carry the injured man somewhere outside.

Miss Longstreth was sitting white but composed upon the couch, where lay Miss Ruth, who evidently had been carried there by the Colonel. Duane did not think she had wholly lost consciousness, and now she lay very still, with eyes dark and shadowy, her face pallid and wet. The Colonel, now that he finally remembered his women-folk, seemed to be gentle and kind. He talked soothingly to Miss Ruth, made light of the adventure, said she must learn to have nerve out here where things happened.

"Can I be of any service?" asked Duane, solicitously.

"Thanks; I guess there's nothing you can do. Talk to these frightened girls while I go see what's to be done with that thick-skulled robber," he replied, and, telling the girls that there was no more danger, he went out.

Miss Longstreth sat with one hand holding her torn waist in place; the other she extended to Duane. He took it awkwardly, and he felt a strange thrill.

"You saved my life," she said, in grave, sweet seriousness.

"No, no!" Duane exclaimed. "He might have struck you, hurt you, but no more."

"I saw murder in his eyes. He thought I had jewels under my dress. I couldn't bear his touch. The beast! I'd have fought. Surely my life was in peril."

"Did you kill him?" asked Miss Ruth, who lay listening.

"Oh no. He's not badly hurt."

"I'm very glad he's alive," said Miss Longstreth, shuddering.

"My intention was bad enough," Duane went on. "It was a ticklish place for me. You see, he was half drunk, and I was afraid his gun might go off. Fool careless he was!"

"Yet you say you didn't save me," Miss Longstreth returned, quickly.

"Well, let it go at that," Duane responded. "I saved you something."

"Tell me all about it?" asked Miss Ruth, who was fast recovering.

Rather embarrassed, Duane briefly told the incident from his point of view.

"Then you stood there all the time with your hands up thinking of nothing—watching for nothing except a little moment when you might draw your gun?" asked Miss Ruth.

"I guess that's about it," he replied.

"Cousin," said Miss Longstreth, thoughtfully, "it was fortunate for us that this gentleman happened to be here. Papa scouts—laughs at danger. He seemed to think there was no danger. Yet he raved after it came."

"Go with us all the way to Fairdale—please?" asked Miss Ruth, sweetly offering her hand. "I am Ruth Herbert. And this is my cousin, Ray Longstreth."

"I'm traveling that way," replied Duane, in great confusion. He did not know how to meet the situation.

Colonel Longstreth returned then, and after bidding Duane a good night, which seemed rather curt by contrast to the graciousness of the girls, he led them away.

Before going to bed Duane went outside to take a look at the injured robber and perhaps to ask him a few questions. To Duane's surprise, he was gone, and so was his horse. The innkeeper was dumfounded. He said that he left the fellow on the floor in the barroom.

"Had he come to?" inquired Duane.

"Sure. He asked for whisky."

"Did he say anything else?"

"Not to me. I heard him talkin' to the father of them girls."

"You mean Colonel Longstreth?"

"I reckon. He sure was some riled, wasn't he? Jest as if I was to blame fer that two-bit of a holdup!"

"What did you make of the old gent's rage?" asked Duane, watching the innkeeper. He scratched his head dubiously. He was sincere, and Duane believed in his honesty.

"Wal, I'm doggoned if I know what to make of it. But I reckon he's either crazy or got more nerve than most Texans."

"More nerve, maybe," Duane replied. "Show me a bed now, innkeeper."

Once in bed in the dark, Duane composed himself to think over the several events of the evening. He called up the details of the holdup and carefully revolved them in mind. The Colonel's wrath, under circumstances where almost any Texan would have been cool, non-plussed Duane, and he put it down to a choleric temperament. He pondered long on the action of the robber when Longstreth's bellow of rage burst in upon him. This ruffian, as bold and mean a type as Duane had ever encountered, had, from some cause or other, been startled. From whatever point Duane viewed the man's strange indecision he could come to only one conclusion—his start, his check, his fear had been that of recognition. Duane compared this effect with the suddenly acquired sense he had gotten of Colonel Longstreth's powerful personality. Why had that desperate robber lowered his gun and stood paralyzed at sight and sound of the Mayor of Fairdale? This was not answerable. There might have been a number of reasons, all to Colonel Longstreth's credit, but Duane could not understand. Longstreth had not appeared to see danger for his daughter, even though she had been roughly handled, and had advanced in front of a cocked gun. Duane probed deep into this singular fact, and he brought to bear on the thing all his knowledge and experience of violent Texas life. And he found that the instant Colonel Longstreth had appeared on the scene there *was* no further danger threatening his daughter. Why? That likewise Duane could not answer. Then his rage, Duane concluded, had been solely at the idea of *his* daughter being assaulted by a robber. This deduction was indeed a thought-disturber, but Duane put it aside to crystallize and for more careful consideration.

Next morning Duane found that the little town was called Sanderson. It was larger than he had at first supposed. He walked up the main street and back again. Just as he arrived some horsemen rode up to the inn and dismounted. And at this juncture the Longstreth party came out. Duane heard Colonel Longstreth utter an exclamation. Then he saw him shake hands with a tall man. Longstreth looked surprised and angry, and he spoke with force; but Duane could not hear what it was he said. The fellow laughed, yet somehow he struck Duane as sullen, until suddenly he espied Miss Longstreth. Then his face changed, and he removed his sombrero. Duane went closer.

"Floyd, did you come with the teams?" asked Longstreth, sharply.

"Not me. I rode a horse, good and hard," was the reply.

"Humph! I'll have a word to say to you later." Then Longstreth turned to his daughter. "Ray, here's the cousin I've told you about. You used to play with him ten years ago—Floyd Lawson. Floyd, my daughter—and my niece, Ruth Herbert."

Duane always scrutinized every one he met, and now with a dangerous game to play, with a consciousness of Longstreth's unusual and significant personality, he bent a keen and searching glance upon this Floyd Lawson.

He was under thirty, yet gray at his temples—dark, smooth-shaven, with lines left by wildness, dissipation, shadows under dark eyes, a mouth strong and bitter, and a square chin—a reckless, careless, handsome, sinister face strangely losing the hardness when he smiled. The grace of a gentleman clung round him, seemed like an echo in his mellow voice. Duane doubted not that he, like many a young man, had drifted out to the frontier, where rough and wild life had wrought sternly but had not quite effaced the mark of good family.

Colonel Longstreth apparently did not share the pleasure of his daughter and his niece in the advent of this cousin. Something hinged on this meeting. Duane grew intensely curious, but, as the stage appeared ready for the journey, he had no further opportunity to gratify it.

CHAPTER 16

Duane followed the stage through the town, out into the open, on to a wide, hard-packed road showing years of travel. It headed northwest. To the left rose a range of low, bleak mountains he had noted yesterday, and to the right sloped the mesquite-patched sweep of ridge and flat. The driver pushed his team to a fast trot, which gait surely covered ground rapidly.

The stage made three stops in the forenoon, one at a place where the horses could be watered, the second at a chuck-wagon belonging to cowboys who were riding after stock, and the third at a small cluster of adobe and stone houses constituting a hamlet the driver called Longstreth, named after the Colonel. From that point on to Fairdale there were only a few ranches, each one controlling great acreage.

Early in the afternoon from a ridge-top Duane sighted Fairdale, a green patch in the mass of gray. For the barrens of Texas it was indeed a fair sight. But he was more concerned with its remoteness from civilization than its beauty. At that time, in the early seventies, when the vast western third of Texas was a wilderness, the pioneer had done wonders to settle there and establish places like Fairdale.

It needed only a glance for Duane to pick out Colonel Longstreth's ranch. The house was situated on the only elevation around Fairdale, and it was not high, nor more than a few minutes' walk from the edge of the town. It was a low, flat-roofed structure made of red adobe bricks, and covered what appeared to be fully an acre of ground. All was green about it, except where the fenced corrals and numerous barns or sheds showed gray and red.

Duane soon reached the shady outskirts of Fairdale, and entered the town with mingled feelings of curiosity, eagerness, and expectation. The street he rode down was a main one, and on both sides of the street was a solid row of saloons, resorts, hotels. Saddled horses stood hitched all along the sidewalk in two long lines, with a buckboard and team here and there breaking the continuity. This block was busy and noisy.

From all outside appearances Fairdale was no different from other frontier towns, and Duane's expectations were scarcely realized. As the afternoon was waning he halted at a little inn. A boy took charge of his horse. Duane questioned the lad about Fairdale and gradually drew to the subject most in mind.

"Colonel Longstreth has a big outfit, eh?"

"Reckon he has," replied the lad. "Doan know how many cowboys. They're always comin' and goin'. I ain't acquainted with half of them."

"Much movement of stock these days?"

"Stock's always movin'," he replied, with a sly look.

"Rustlers?"

But he did not follow up that look with the affirmative Duane expected.

"Lively place, I hear—Fairdale is?"

"Ain't so lively as Sanderson, but it's bigger."

"Yes, I heard it was. Fellow down there was talking about two cowboys who were arrested."

"Sure. I heered all about that. Joe Bean an' Brick Higgins—they belong heah, but they ain't heah much. Longstreth's boys."

Duane did not want to appear over-inquisitive, so he turned the talk into other channels.

After getting supper Duane strolled up and down the main street. When darkness set in he went into a hotel, bought cigars, sat around, and watched. Then he passed out and went into the next place. This was of rough crude exterior, but the inside was comparatively pretentious and ablaze with lights. It was full of men coming and going—a dusty-booted crowd that smelled of horses and smoke. Duane sat down for a while, with wide eyes and open ears. Then he hunted up the bar, where most of the guests had been or were going. He found a great square room lighted by six huge lamps, a bar at one side, and all the floor-space taken up by tables and chairs. This was the only gambling-place of any size in southern Texas in which he had noted the absence of Mexicans. There was some card-playing going on at this moment. Duane stayed in there for a while, and knew that strangers were too common in Fairdale to be conspicuous. Then he returned to the inn where he had engaged a room.

Duane sat down on the steps of the dingy little restaurant. Two men were conversing inside, and they had not noticed Duane.

"Laramie, what's the stranger's name?" asked one.

"He didn't say," replied the other.

"Sure was a strappin' big man. Struck me a little odd, he did. No cattleman, him. How'd you size him?"

"Well, like one of them cool, easy, quiet Texans who's been lookin' for a man for years—to kill him when he found him."

"Right you are, Laramie; and, between you an' me, I hope he's lookin' for Long—"

" 'S-sh!" interrupted Laramie. "You must be half drunk, to go talkin' that way."

Thereafter they conversed in too low a tone for Duane to hear, and presently Laramie's visitor left. Duane went inside, and, making himself agreeable, began to ask casual questions about Fairdale. Laramie was not communicative.

Duane went to his room in a thoughtful frame of mind. Had Laramie's visitor meant he hoped some one had come to kill Longstreth? Duane inferred just that from the interrupted remark. There was something wrong about the Mayor of Fairdale. Duane felt it. And he felt also, if there was a crooked and dangerous man, it was this Floyd Lawson. The innkeeper Laramie would be worth cultivating. And last in Duane's thoughts that night was Miss Longstreth. He could not help thinking of her—how strangely the meeting with her had affected him. It made him remember that long-past time when girls had been a part of his life. What a sad and dark and endless void lay between that past and the present! He had no right even to dream of a beautiful woman like Ray Longstreth. That conviction, however, did not dispel her; indeed, it seemed perversely to make her grow more fascinating. Duane grew conscious of a strange, unaccountable hunger, a something that was like a pang in his breast.

Next day he lounged about the inn. He did not make any overtures to the taciturn proprietor. Duane had no need of hurry now. He contented himself with watching and listening. And at the close of that day he decided Fairdale was what MacNelly had claimed it to be, and that he was on the track of an unusual adventure. The following day he spent in much the same way, though on one occasion he told Laramie he was looking for a man. The innkeeper grew a little less furtive and reticent after that. He would answer casual queries, and it did not take Duane long to learn that Laramie had seen better days—that he was now broken, bitter, and hard. Some one had wronged him.

Several days passed. Duane did not succeed in getting any closer to Laramie, but he found the idlers on the corners and in front of the stores unsuspicious and willing to talk. It did not take him long to find out that Fairdale stood parallel with Huntsville for gambling, drinking, and fighting. The street was always lined with dusty, saddled horses, the town full of strangers. Money appeared more abundant than in any place Duane had ever visited; and it was spent with the abandon that spoke forcibly of easy and crooked acquirement. Duane decided that Sanderson, Bradford, and Ord were but notorious outposts to this Fairdale, which was a secret center of rustlers and outlaws. And what struck Duane strangest of all was the fact that Longstreth was mayor here and held court daily. Duane knew intuitively, before a chance remark gave him proof, that this court was a sham, a farce. And he wondered if it were not a blind. This wonder of his was equivalent to suspicion of Colonel Longstreth, and Duane reproached himself. Then he realized that the reproach was because of the daughter. Inquiry had brought him the fact that Ray Longstreth had just come to live with her father. Longstreth had originally been a planter in Louisiana, where his family had remained after his advent in the West. He was a rich rancher; he owned half of Fairdale; he was a cattle-buyer on a large scale. Floyd Lawson was his lieutenant and associate in deals.

On the afternoon of the fifth day of Duane's stay in Fairdale he returned to the inn from his usual stroll, and upon entering was amazed to have a rough-looking young fellow rush by him out of the door. Inside

Laramie was lying on the floor, with a bloody bruise on his face. He did not appear to be dangerously hurt.

"Bo Snecker! He hit me and went after the cash-drawer," said Laramie, laboring to his feet.

"Are you hurt much?" queried Duane.

"I guess not. But Bo needn't to have soaked me. I've been robbed before without that."

"Well, I'll take a look after Bo," replied Duane.

He went out and glanced down the street toward the center of the town. He did not see any one he could take for the innkeeper's assailant. Then he looked up the street, and he saw the young fellow about a block away, hurrying along and gazing back.

Duane yelled for him to stop and started to go after him. Snecker broke into a run. Then Duane set out to overhaul him. There were two motives in Duane's action—one of anger, and the other a desire to make a friend of this man Laramie, whom Duane believed could tell him much.

Duane was light on his feet, and he had a giant stride. He gained rapidly upon Snecker, who, turning this way and that, could not get out of sight. Then he took to the open country and ran straight for the green hill where Longstreth's house stood. Duane had almost caught Snecker when he reached the shrubbery and trees and there eluded him. But Duane kept him in sight, in the shade, on the paths, and up the road into the courtyard, and he saw Snecker go straight for Longstreth's house.

Duane was not to be turned back by that, singular as it was. He did not stop to consider. It seemed enough to know that fate had directed him to the path of this rancher Longstreth. Duane entered the first open door on that side of the court. It opened into a corridor which led into a plaza. It had wide, smooth stone porches, and flowers and shrubbery in the center. Duane hurried through to burst into the presence of Miss Longstreth and a number of young people. Evidently she was giving a little party.

Lawson stood leaning against one of the pillars that supported the porch roof; at sight of Duane his face changed remarkably, expressing amazement, consternation, then fear.

In the quick ensuing silence Miss Longstreth rose white as her dress.

The young women present stared in astonishment, if they were not equally perturbed. There were cowboys present who suddenly grew intent and still. By these things Duane gathered that his appearance must be disconcerting. He was panting. He wore no hat or coat. His big gun-sheath showed plainly at his hip.

Sight of Miss Longstreth had an unaccountable effect upon Duane. He was plunged into confusion. For the moment he saw no one but her.

"Miss Longstreth—I came—to search—your house," panted Duane.

He hardly knew what he was saying, yet the instant he spoke he realized that that should have been the last thing for him to say. He had blundered. But he was not used to women, and this dark-eyed girl made him thrill and his heart beat thickly and his wits go scattering.

"Search my house!" exclaimed Miss Longstreth; and red succeeded the white in her cheeks. She appeared astonished and angry. "What for? Why, how dare you! This is unwarrantable!"

"A man—Bo Snecker—assaulted and robbed Jim Laramie," replied Duane, hurriedly. "I chased Snecker here—saw him run into the house."

"Here? Oh, sir, you must be mistaken. We have seen no one. In the absence of my father I'm mistress here. I'll not permit you to search."

Lawson appeared to come out of his astonishment. He stepped forward.

"Ray, don't be bothered now," he said, to his cousin. "This fellow's making a bluff. I'll settle him. See here, Mister, you clear out!"

"I want Snecker. He's here, and I'm going to get him," replied Duane, quietly.

"Bah! That's all a bluff," sneered Lawson. "I'm on to your game. You just wanted an excuse to break in here—to see my cousin again. When you saw the company you invented that excuse. Now, be off, or it'll be the worse for you."

Duane felt his face burn with a tide of hot blood. Almost he felt that he was guilty of such motive. Had he not been unable to put this Ray Longstreth out of his mind? There seemed to be scorn in her eyes now. And somehow that checked his embarrassment.

"Miss Longstreth, will you let me search the house?" he asked.

"No."

"Then—I regret to say—I'll do so without your permission."

"You'll not dare!" she flashed. She stood erect, her bosom swelling.

"Pardon me—yes, I will."

"Who are you?" she demanded, suddenly.

"I'm a Texas Ranger," replied Duane.

"*A Texas Ranger!*" she echoed.

Floyd Lawson's dark face turned pale.

"Miss Longstreth, I don't need warrants to search houses," said Duane. "I'm sorry to annoy you. I'd prefer to have your permission. A ruffian has taken refuge here—in your father's house. He's hidden somewhere. May I look for him?"

"If you are indeed a ranger."

Duane produced his papers. Miss Longstreth haughtily refused to look at them.

"Miss Longstreth, I've come to make Fairdale a safer, cleaner, better place for women and children. I don't wonder at your resentment. But to doubt me—insult me. Some day you may be sorry."

Floyd Lawson made a violent motion with his hands.

"All stuff! Cousin, go on with your party. I'll take a couple of cowboys and go with this—this Texas Ranger."

"Thanks," said Duane, coolly, as he eyed Lawson. "Perhaps you'll be able to find Snecker quicker than I could."

"What do you mean?" demanded Lawson, and now he grew livid. Evidently he was a man of fierce quick passions.

"Don't quarrel," said Miss Longstreth. "Floyd, you go with him. Please hurry. I'll be nervous till—the man's found or you're sure there's not one."

They started with several cowboys to search the house. They went through the rooms searching, calling out, peering into dark places. It struck Duane more than forcibly that Lawson did all the calling. He was hurried, too, tried to keep in the lead. Duane wondered if he knew his voice would be recognized by the hiding man. Be that as it might, it was Duane who peered into a dark corner and then, with a gun leveled, said, "Come out!"

He came forth into the flare—a tall, slim, dark-faced youth, wearing sombrero, blouse, and trousers. Duane collared him before any of the others could move and held the gun close enough to make him shrink.

But he did not impress Duane as being frightened just then; nevertheless, he had a clammy face, the pallid look of a man who had just gotten over a shock. He peered into Duane's face, then into that of the cowboy next to him, then into Lawson's, and if ever in Duane's life he beheld relief it was then. That was all Duane needed to know, but he meant to find out more if he could.

"Who're you?" asked Duane, quietly.

"Bo Snecker," he said.

"What'd you hide here for?"

He appeared to grow sullen.

"Reckoned I'd be as safe in Longstreth's as anywheres."

"Ranger, what 'll you do with him?" Lawson queried, as if uncertain, now the capture was made.

"I'll see to that," replied Duane, and he pushed Snecker in front of him out into the court.

Duane had suddenly conceived the idea of taking Snecker before Mayor Longstreth in the court.

When Duane arrived at the hall where court was held there were other men there, a dozen or more, and all seemed excited; evidently, news of Duane had preceded him. Longstreth sat at a table up on a platform. Near him sat a thick-set grizzled man, with deep eyes, and this was Hanford Owens, county judge. To the right stood a tall, angular, yellow-faced fellow with a drooping sandy mustache. Conspicuous on his vest was a huge silver shield. This was Gorsech, one of Longstreth's sheriffs. There were four other men whom Duane knew by sight, several whose faces were familiar, and half a dozen strangers, all dusty horsemen.

Longstreth pounded hard on the table to be heard. Mayor or not, he was unable at once to quell the excitement. Gradually, however, it subsided, and from the last few utterances before quiet was restored Duane gathered that he had intruded upon some kind of a meeting in the hall.

"What'd you break in here for," demanded Longstreth.

"Isn't this the court? Aren't you the Mayor of Fairdale?" interrogated Duane. His voice was clear and loud, almost piercing.

"Yes," replied Longstreth. Like flint he seemed, yet Duane felt his intense interest.

"I've arrested a criminal," said Duane.

"Arrested a criminal!" exclaimed Longstreth. "*You?* Who 're you?"

"I'm a ranger," replied Duane.

A significant silence ensued.

"I charge Snecker with assault on Laramie and attempted robbery—if not murder. He's had a shady past here, as this court will know if it keeps a record."

"What's this I hear about you, Bo? Get up and speak for yourself," said Longstreth, gruffly.

Snecker got up, not without a furtive glance at Duane, and he had shuffled forward a few steps toward the Mayor. He had an evil front, but not the boldness even of a rustler.

"It ain't so, Longstreth," he began, loudly. "I went in Laramie's place fer grub. Some feller I never seen before come in from the hall an' hit Laramie an' wrastled him on the floor. I went out. Then this big ranger chased me an' fetched me here. I didn't do nothin'. This ranger's hankerin' to arrest somebody. Thet's my hunch, Longstreth."

Longstreth said something in an undertone to Judge Owens, and that worthy nodded his great bushy head.

"Bo, you're discharged," said Longstreth, bluntly. "Now the rest of you clear out of here."

He absolutely ignored the ranger. That was his rebuff to Duane—his slap in the face to an interfering ranger service. If Longstreth was crooked he certainly had magnificent nerve. Duane almost decided he was above suspicion. But his nonchalance, his air of finality, his authoritative assurance—these to Duane's keen and practiced eyes were in significant contrast to a certain tenseness of line about his mouth and a slow paling of his olive skin. In that momentary lull Duane's scrutiny of Longstreth gathered an impression of the man's intense curiosity.

Then the prisoner, Snecker, with a cough that broke the spell of silence, shuffled a couple of steps toward the door.

"Hold on!" called Duane. The call halted Snecker, as if it had been a bullet.

"Longstreth, I saw Snecker attack Laramie," said Duane, his voice still ringing. "What has the court to say to that?"

"The court has this to say. West of the Pecos we'll not aid any ranger service. We don't want you out here. Fairdale doesn't need you."

"That's a lie, Longstreth," retorted Duane. "I've letters from Fairdale citizens all begging for ranger service."

Longstreth turned white. The veins corded at his temples. He appeared about to burst into rage. He was at a loss for quick reply.

Floyd Lawson rushed in and up to the table. The blood showed black and thick in his face; his utterance was incoherent, his uncontrollable outbreak of temper seemed out of all proportion to any cause he should reasonably have had for anger. Longstreth shoved him back with a curse and a warning glare.

"Where's your warrant to arrest Snecker?" shouted Longstreth.

"I don't need warrants to make arrests. Longstreth, you're ignorant of the power of Texas Rangers."

"You'll come none of your damned ranger stunts out here. I'll block you."

That passionate reply of Longstreth's was the signal Duane had been waiting for. He had helped on the crisis. He wanted to force Longstreth's hand and show the town his stand.

Duane backed clear of everybody.

"Men! I call on you all!" cried Duane, piercingly. "I call on you to witness the arrest of a criminal prevented by Longstreth, Mayor of Fairdale. It will be recorded in the report to the Adjutant-General at Austin. Longstreth, you'll never prevent another arrest."

Longstreth sat white with working jaw.

"Longstreth, you've shown your hand," said Duane, in a voice that carried far and held those who heard. "Any honest citizen of Fairdale can now see what's plain—yours is a damn poor hand! You're going to hear me call a spade a spade. In the two years you've been Mayor you've never arrested one rustler. Strange, when Fairdale's a nest for rustlers! You've never sent a prisoner to Del Rio, let alone to Austin. You have no jail. There have been nine murders during your office—innumerable street-fights and holdups. Not one arrest! But you have ordered arrests for trivial offenses, and have punished these out of all proportion. There have been lawsuits in your court—suits over water-rights, cattle deals, property lines. Strange how in these lawsuits you or Lawson or other men close to you were always involved! Strange how it seems the law was stretched to favor your interest!"

Duane paused in his cold, ringing speech. In the silence, both outside and inside the hall, could be heard the deep breathing of agitated men. Longstreth was indeed a study. Yet did he betray anything but rage at this interloper?

"Longstreth, here's plain talk for you and Fairdale," went on Duane. "I don't accuse you and your court of dishonesty. I say *strange*! Law here has been a farce. The motive behind all this laxity isn't plain to me—yet. But I call your hand!"

CHAPTER 17

D uane left the hall, elbowed his way through the crowd, and went down the street. He was certain that on the faces of some men he had seen ill-concealed wonder and satisfaction. He had struck some kind of a hot trail, and he meant to see where it led. It was by no means unlikely that Cheseldine might be at the other end. Duane controlled a mounting eagerness. But ever and anon it was shot through with a remembrance of Ray Longstreth. He suspected her father of being not what he pretended. He might, very probably would, bring sorrow and shame to this young woman. The thought made him smart with pain. She began to haunt him, and then he was thinking more of her beauty and sweetness than of the disgrace he might bring upon her. Some strange emotion, long locked inside Duane's heart, knocked to be heard, to be let out. He was troubled.

Upon returning to the inn he found Laramie there, apparently none the worse for his injury.

"How are you, Laramie?" he asked.

"Reckon I'm feelin' as well as could be expected," replied Laramie. His head was circled by a bandage that did not conceal the lump where he had been struck. He looked pale, but was bright enough.

"That was a good crack Snecker gave you," remarked Duane.

"I ain't accusin' Bo," remonstrated Laramie, with eyes that made Duane thoughtful.

"Well, I accuse him. I caught him—took him to Longstreth's court. But they let him go."

Laramie appeared to be agitated by this intimation of friendship.

"See here, Laramie," went on Duane, "in some parts of Texas it's policy to be close-mouthed. Policy and health-preserving! Between ourselves, I want you to know I lean on your side of the fence."

Laramie gave a quick start. Presently Duane turned and frankly met his gaze. He had startled Laramie out of his habitual set taciturnity; but even as he looked the light that might have been amaze and joy faded out of his face, leaving it the same old mask. Still Duane had seen enough. Like a bloodhound he had a scent.

"Talking about work, Laramie, who'd you say Snecker worked for?"

"I didn't say."

"Well, say so now, can't you? Laramie, you're powerful peevish today. It's that bump on your head. Who does Snecker work for?"

"When he works at all, which sure ain't often, he rides for Longstreth."

"Humph! Seems to me that Longstreth's the whole circus round Fairdale. I was some sore the other day to find I was losing good money at Longstreth's faro game. Sure if I'd won I wouldn't have been sore—ha, ha! But I was surprised to hear some one say Longstreth owned the Hope So joint."

"He owns considerable property hereabouts." replied Laramie, constrainedly.

"Humph again! Laramie, like every other fellow I meet in this town, you're afraid to open your trap about Longstreth. Get me straight, Laramie. I don't care a damn for Colonel Mayor Longstreth. And for cause I'd throw a gun on him just as quick as on any rustler in Pecos."

"Talk's cheap," replied Laramie, making light of his bluster, but the red was deeper in his face.

"Sure. I know that," Duane said. "And usually I don't talk. Then it's not well known that Longstreth owns the Hope So?"

"Reckon it's known in Pecos, all right. But Longstreth's name isn't connected with the Hope So. Blandy runs the place."

"That Blandy. His faro game's crooked, or I'm a locoed bronch. Not that we don't have lots of crooked faro-dealers. A fellow can stand for them. But Blandy's mean, back-handed, never looks you in the eyes. That Hope So place ought to be run by a good fellow like you, Laramie."

"Thanks," replied he; and Duane imagined his voice a little husky. "Didn't you hear I used to—run it?"

"No. Did you?" Duane said, quickly.

"I reckon. I built the place, made additions twice, owned it for eleven years."

"Well, I'll be doggoned." It was indeed Duane's turn to be surprised, and with the surprise came a glimmering. "I'm sorry you're not there now. Did you sell out?"

"No. Just lost the place."

Laramie was bursting for relief now—to talk, to tell. Sympathy had made him soft.

"It was two years ago—two years last March," he went on. "I was in a big cattle deal with Longstreth. We got the stock—an' my share, eighteen hundred head, was rustled off. I owed Longstreth. He pressed me. It come to a lawsuit—an' I—was ruined."

It hurt Duane to look at Laramie. He was white, and tears rolled down his cheeks. Duane saw the bitterness, the defeat, the agony of the man. He had failed to meet his obligations; nevertheless, he had been swindled. All that he suppressed, all that would have been passion had the man's spirit not been broken, lay bare for Duane to see. He had now the secret of his bitterness. But the reason he did not openly accuse Longstreth, the secret of his reticence and fear—these Duane thought best to try to learn at some later time.

"Hard luck! It certainly was tough," Duane said. "But you're a good loser. And the wheel turns! Now, Laramie, here's what. I need your advice. I've got a little money. But before I lose it I want to invest some. Buy some stock, or buy an interest in some rancher's herd. What I want you to steer me on is a good square rancher. Or maybe a couple of ranchers, if there happen to be two honest ones. Ha, ha! No deals with ranchers who ride in the dark with rustlers! I've a hunch Fairdale is full of them. Now, Laramie, you've been here for years. Sure you must know a couple of men above suspicion."

"Thank God I do," he replied, feelingly. "Frank Morton an' Si Zimmer, my friends an' neighbors all my prosperous days, an' friends still.

You can gamble on Frank an' Si. But if you want advice from me—don't invest money in stock now."

"Why?"

"Because any new feller buyin' stock these days will be rustled quicker 'n he can say Jack Robinson. The pioneers, the new cattlemen—these are easy pickin' for the rustlers. Lord knows all the ranchers are easy enough pickin'. But the new fellers have to learn the ropes. They don't know anythin' or anybody. An' the old ranchers are wise an' sore. They'd fight if they—"

"What?" Duane put in, as he paused. "If they knew who was rustling the stock?"

"Nope."

"If they had the nerve?"

"Not thet so much."

"What then? What'd make them fight?"

"A leader!"

"Howdy thar, Jim," boomed a big voice.

A man of great bulk, with a ruddy, merry face, entered the room.

"Hello, Morton," replied Laramie. "I'd introduce you to my guest here, but I don't know his name."

"Haw! Haw! Thet's all right. Few men out hyar go by their right names."

"Say, Morton," put in Duane, "Laramie gave me a hunch you'd be a good man to tie to. Now, I've a little money and before I lose it I'd like to invest it in stock."

Morton smiled broadly.

"I'm on the square," Duane said, bluntly. "If you fellows never size up your neighbors any better than you have sized me—well, you won't get any richer."

It was enjoyment for Duane to make his remarks to these men pregnant with meaning. Morton showed his pleasure, his interest, but his faith held aloof.

"I've got some money. Will you let me in on some kind of deal? Will you start me up as a stockman with a little herd all my own?"

"Wal, stranger, to come out flat-footed, you'd be foolish to buy cattle now. I don't want to take your money an' see you lose out. Better go back across the Pecos where the rustlers ain't so strong. I haven't had more'n twenty-five hundred herd of stock for ten years. The rustlers let me hang on to a breedin' herd. Kind of them, ain't it?"

"Sort of kind. All I hear is rustlers, Morton," replied Duane, with impatience. "You see, I haven't ever lived long in a rustler-run county. Who heads the gang, anyway?"

Morton looked at Duane with a curiously amused smile, then snapped his big jaw as if to shut in impulsive words.

"Look here, Morton. It stands to reason, no matter how strong these rustlers are, how hidden their work, however involved with supposedly honest men—they *can't* last."

"They come with the pioneers, an' they'll last till thar's a single steer left," he declared.

"Well, if you take that view of circumstances I just figure you as one of the rustlers!"

Morton looked as if he were about to brain Duane with the butt of his whip. His anger flashed by then, evidently as unworthy of him; and, something striking him as funny, he boomed out a laugh.

"It's not so funny," Duane went on. "If you're going to pretend a yellow streak, what else will I think?"

"Pretend?" he repeated.

"Sure. I know men of nerve. And here they're not any different from those in other places. I say if you show anything like a lack of sand it's all bluff. By nature you've got nerve. There are a lot of men around Fairdale who're afraid of their shadows—afraid to be out after dark—afraid to open their mouths. But you're not one. So I say if you claim these rustlers will last you're pretending lack of nerve just to help the popular idea along. For they *can't* last. What you need out here is some new blood. Savvy what I mean?"

"Wal, I reckon I do," he replied, looking as if a storm had blown over him. "Stranger, I'll look you up the next time I come to town."

Then he went out.

Laramie had eyes like flint striking fire.

He breathed a deep breath and looked around the room before his gaze fixed again on Duane.

"Wal," he replied, speaking low. "You've picked the right men. Now, who in the hell are you?"

Reaching into the inside pocket of his buckskin vest Duane turned the lining out. A star-shaped bright silver object flashed as he shoved it, pocket and all, under Jim's hard eyes.

"*Ranger!*" he whispered, cracking the table with his fist. "You sure rung true to me."

"Laramie, do you know who's boss of this secret gang of rustlers hereabouts?" asked Duane, bluntly. It was characteristic of him to come sharp to the point. His voice—something deep, easy, cool about him— seemed to steady Laramie.

"No," replied Laramie.

"Does anybody know?" went on Duane.

"Wal, I reckon there's not one honest native who *knows.*"

"But you have your suspicions?"

"We have."

"Give me your idea about this crowd that hangs round the saloons— the regulars."

"Jest a bad lot," replied Laramie, with the quick assurance of knowledge. "Most of them have been here years. Others have drifted in. Some of them work, odd times. They rustle a few steers, steal, rob, anythin' for a little money to drink an' gamble. Jest a bad lot!"

"Have you any idea whether Cheseldine and his gang are associated with this gang here?"

"Lord knows. I've always suspected them the same gang. None of us ever seen Cheseldine—an' thet's strange, when Knell, Poggin, Panhandle Smith, Blossom Kane, and Fletcher, they all ride here often. No, Poggin doesn't come often. But the others do. For thet matter, they're around all over west of the Pecos."

"Now I'm puzzled over this," said Duane. "Why do men—apparently honest men—seem to be so close-mouthed here? Is that a fact, or only my impression?"

"It's a sure fact," replied Laramie, darkly. "Men have lost cattle an' property in Fairdale—lost them honestly or otherwise, as hasn't been proved. An' in some cases when they talked—hinted a little—they was found dead. Apparently held up an' robbed. But dead. Dead men don't talk! Thet's why we're close-mouthed."

Duane felt a dark, somber sternness. Rustling cattle was not intolerable. Western Texas had gone on prospering, growing in spite of the hordes of rustlers ranging its vast stretches; but a cold, secret, murderous hold on a little struggling community was something too strange, too terrible for men to stand long.

The ranger was about to speak again when the clatter of hoofs interrupted him. Horses halted out in front, and one rider got down. Floyd Lawson entered. He called for tobacco.

If his visit surprised Laramie he did not show any evidence. But Lawson showed rage as he saw the ranger, and then a dark glint flitted from the eyes that shifted from Duane to Laramie and back again. Duane leaned easily against the counter.

"Say, that was a bad break of yours," Lawson said. "If you come fooling round the ranch again there'll be hell."

It seemed strange that a man who had lived west of the Pecos for ten years could not see in Duane something which forbade that kind of talk. It certainly was not nerve Lawson showed; men of courage were seldom intolerant. With the matchless nerve that characterized the great gunmen of the day there was a cool, unobtrusive manner, a speech brief, almost gentle, certainly courteous. Lawson was a hot-headed Louisianian of French extraction; a man, evidently, who had never been crossed in anything, and who was strong, brutal, passionate, which qualities in the face of a situation like this made him simply a fool.

"I'm saying again, you used your ranger bluff just to get near Ray Longstreth," Lawson sneered. "Mind you, if you come up there again there'll be hell."

"You're right. But not the kind you think," Duane retorted, his voice sharp and cold.

"Ray Longstreth wouldn't stoop to know a dirty blood-tracker like you," said Lawson, hotly. He did not seem to have a deliberate intention to rouse Duane; the man was simply rancorous, jealous. "I'll call you right. You cheap bluffer! You four-flush! You damned interfering, conceited ranger!"

"Lawson, I'll not take offense, because you seem to be championing your beautiful cousin," replied Duane, in slow speech. "But let me return your compliment. You're a fine Southerner! Why, you're only a cheap four-flush—damned, bull-headed *rustler*!"

Duane hissed the last word. Then for him there was the truth in Lawson's working passion-blackened face.

Lawson jerked, moved, meant to draw. But how slow! Duane lunged forward. His long arm swept up. And Lawson staggered backward knocking table and chairs, to fall hard, in a half-sitting posture against the wall.

"Don't draw!" warned Duane.

"Lawson, git away from your gun!" yelled Laramie.

But Lawson was crazed with fury. He tugged at his hip, his face corded with purple welts, malignant, murderous. Duane kicked the gun out of his hand. Lawson got up, raging, and rushed out.

Laramie lifted his shaking hands.

"What'd you wing him for?" he wailed. "He was drawin' on you. Kickin' men like him won't do out here."

"That bull-headed fool will roar and butt himself with all his gang right into our hands. He's just the man I've needed to meet. Besides, shooting him would have been murder."

"Murder!" exclaimed Laramie.

"Yes, for me," replied Duane.

"That may be true—whoever you are—but if Lawson's the man you think he is he'll begin thet secret underground bizness. Why, Lawson won't sleep of nights now. He an' Longstreth have always been after me."

"Laramie, what are your eyes for?" demanded Duane. "Watch out. And now here. See your friend Morton. Tell him this game grows hot. Together you approach four or five men you know well and can absolutely trust. I may need your help."

Then Duane went from place to place, corner to corner, bar to bar, watching, listening, recording. The excitement had preceded him, and speculation was rife. He thought best to keep out of it. After dark he stole up to Longstreth's ranch. The evening was warm; the doors were open; and in the twilight the only lamps that had been lit were in Longstreth's big sitting-room, at the far end of the house. When a buckboard drove up and Longstreth and Lawson alighted, Duane was well hidden in the bushes, so well screened that he could get but a fleeting glimpse of Longstreth as he went in. For all Duane could see, he appeared to be a calm and quiet man, intense beneath the surface, with an air of dignity under insult. Duane's chance to observe Lawson was lost. They went into the house without speaking and closed the door.

At the other end of the porch, close under a window, was an offset between step and wall, and there in the shadow Duane hid. So Duane waited there in the darkness with patience born of many hours of hiding.

Presently a lamp was lit; and Duane heard the swish of skirts.

"Something's happened surely, Ruth," he heard Miss Longstreth say, anxiously. "Papa just met me in the hall and didn't speak. He seemed pale, worried."

"Cousin Floyd looked like a thunder-cloud," said Ruth. "For once he didn't try to kiss me. Something's happened. Well, Ray, this has been a bad day."

"Oh, dear! Ruth, what can we do? These are wild men. Floyd makes life miserable for me. And he teases you unmer—"

"I don't call it teasing. Floyd wants to spoon," declared Ruth, emphatically. "He'd run after any woman."

"A fine compliment to me, Cousin Ruth," laughed Ray.

"I don't care," replied Ruth, stubbornly. "It's so. He's mushy. And when he's been drinking and tries to kiss me—I hate him!"

There were steps on the hall floor.

"Hello, girls!" sounded out Lawson's voice, minus its usual gaiety.

"Floyd, what's the matter?" asked Ray, presently. "I never saw papa as he is to-night, nor you so—so worried. Tell me, what has happened?"

"Well, Ray, we had a jar to-day," replied Lawson, with a blunt, expressive laugh.

"Jar?" echoed both the girls, curiously.

"We had to submit to a damnable outrage," added Lawson, passionately, as if the sound of his voice augmented his feeling. "Listen, girls; I'll tell you all about it." He coughed, cleared his throat in a way that betrayed he had been drinking.

Duane sunk deeper into the shadow of his covert, and, stiffening his muscles for a protracted spell of rigidity, prepared to listen with all acuteness and intensity. Just one word from this Lawson, inadvertently uttered in a moment of passion, might be the word Duane needed for his clue.

"It happened at the town hall," began Lawson, rapidly. "Your father and Judge Owens and I were there in consultation with three ranchers from out of town. Then that damned ranger stalked in dragging Snecker, the fellow who hid here in the house. He had arrested Snecker for alleged assault on a restaurant-keeper named Laramie. Snecker being obviously innocent, he was discharged. Then this ranger began shouting his insults. Law was a farce in Fairdale. The court was a farce. There was no law. Your father's office as mayor should be impeached. He made arrests only for petty offenses. He was afraid of the rustlers, highwaymen, murderers. He was afraid or—he just let them alone. He used his office to cheat ranchers and cattlemen in lawsuits. All this the ranger yelled for every one to hear. A damnable outrage. Your father, Ray, insulted in his own court by a rowdy ranger!"

"Oh!" cried Ray Longstreth, in mingled distress and anger.

"The ranger service wants to rule western Texas," went on Lawson. "These rangers are all a low set, many of them worse than the outlaws they hunt. Some of them were outlaws and gun-fighters before they became rangers. This is one of the worst of the lot. He's keen, intelligent, smooth, and that makes him more to be feared. For he is to be feared. He wanted to kill. He would kill. If your father had made the least move he would have shot him. He's a cold-nerved devil—the born gunman. My God, any instant I expected to see your father fall dead at my feet!"

"Oh, Floyd! The unspeakable ruffian!" cried Ray Longstreth, passionately.

"You see, Ray, this fellow, like all rangers, seeks notoriety. He made that play with Snecker just for a chance to rant against your father. He tried to inflame all Fairdale against him. That about the lawsuits was the worst! Damn him! He'll make us enemies."

"What do you care for the insinuations of such a man?" said Ray Longstreth, her voice now deep and rich with feeling. "After a moment's thought no one will be influenced by them. Do not worry, Floyd. Tell papa not to worry. Surely after all these years he can't be injured in reputation by—by an adventurer."

"Yes, he can be injured," replied Floyd, quickly. "The frontier is a strange place. There are many bitter men here—men who have failed at ranching. And your father has been wonderfully successful. The ranger has dropped poison, and it'll spread."

CHAPTER 18

Strangers rode into Fairdale; and other hard-looking customers, new to Duane if not to Fairdale, helped to create a charged and waiting atmosphere. The saloons did unusual business and were never closed. Respectable citizens of the town were awakened in the early dawn by rowdies carousing in the streets.

Duane kept pretty close under cover during the day. He did not entertain the opinion that the first time he walked down-street he would be a target for guns. Things seldom happened that way; and when they did happen so, it was more accident than design. But at night he was not idle. He met Laramie, Morton, Zimmer, and others of like character; a secret club had been formed; and all the members were ready for action. Duane spent hours at night watching the house where Floyd Lawson stayed when he was not up at Longstreth's. At night he was visited, or at least the house was, by strange men who were swift, stealthy, mysterious—all that kindly disposed friends or neighbors would not have been. Duane had not been able to recognize any of these night visitors; and he did not think the time was ripe for a bold holding-up of one of them. Nevertheless, he was sure such an event would discover Lawson, or some one in that house, to be in touch with crooked men.

Laramie was right. Not twenty-fours hours after his last talk with Duane, in which he advised quick action, he was found behind the little bar of his restaurant with a bullet-hole in his breast, dead. No one could be found who had heard a shot. It had been deliberate murder, for upon the bar had been left a piece of paper rudely scrawled with a pencil: "All friends of rangers look for the same."

This roused Duane. His first move, however, was to bury Laramie. None of Laramie's neighbors evinced any interest in the dead man or the unfortunate family he had left. Duane saw that these neighbors were held in check by fear. Mrs. Laramie was ill; the shock of her husband's death was hard on her; and she had been left almost destitute with five children. Duane rented a small adobe house on the outskirts of town and moved the family into it. Then he played the part of provider and nurse and friend.

After several days Duane went boldly into town and showed that he meant business. It was his opinion that there were men in Fairdale secretly glad of a ranger's presence. What he intended to do was food for great speculation. A company of militia could not have had the effect upon the wild element of Fairdale that Duane's presence had. It got out that he was a gunman lightning swift on the draw. It was death to face him. He had killed thirty men—wildest rumor of all. It was actually said of him he had the gun-skill of Buck Duane or of Poggin.

At first there had not only been great conjecture among the vicious element, but also a very decided checking of all kinds of action calculated to be conspicuous to a keen-eyed ranger. At the tables, at the bars and lounging-places Duane heard the remarks: "Who's thet ranger after? What 'll he do fust off? Is he waitin' fer somebody? Who's goin' to draw on him fust—an' go to hell? Jest about how soon will he be found somewheres full of lead?"

When it came out somewhere that Duane was openly cultivating the honest stay-at-home citizens to array them in time against the other element, then Fairdale showed its wolf teeth. Several times Duane was shot at in the dark and once slightly injured. Rumor had it that Poggin, the gunman, was coming to meet him. But the lawless element did not rise up in a mass to slay Duane on sight. It was not so much that the enemies of the law awaited his next move, but just a slowness peculiar to the frontier. The ranger was in their midst. He was interesting, if formidable. He would have been welcomed at card-tables, at the bars, to play and drink with the men who knew they were under suspicion. There was a rude kind of good humor even in their open hostility.

Besides, one ranger or a company of rangers could not have held the undivided attention of these men from their games and drinks and quarrels except by some decided move. Excitement, greed, appetite were rife in them. Duane marked, however, a striking exception to the usual run of strangers he had been in the habit of seeing. Snecker had gone or was under cover. Again Duane caught a vague rumor of the coming of Poggin, yet he never seemed to arrive. Moreover, the goings-on among the habitués of the resorts and the cowboys who came in to drink and gamble were unusually mild in comparison with former conduct. This lull, however, did not deceive Duane. It could not last. The wonder was that it had lasted so long.

Duane went often to see Mrs. Laramie and her children. One afternoon while he was there he saw Miss Longstreth and Ruth ride up to the door. They carried a basket. Evidently they had heard of Mrs. Laramie's trouble. Duane felt strangely glad, but he went into an adjoining room rather than meet them.

"Mrs. Laramie, I've come to see you," said Miss Longstreth, cheerfully.

The little room was not very light, there being only one window and the doors, but Duane could see plainly enough. Mrs. Laramie lay, hollow-cheeked and haggard, on a bed. Once she had evidently been a woman of some comeliness. The ravages of trouble and grief were there to read in her worn face; it had not, however, any of the hard and bitter lines that had characterized her husband's.

Duane wondered, considering that Longstreth had ruined Laramie, how Mrs. Laramie was going to regard the daughter of an enemy.

"So you're Granger Longstreth's girl?" queried the woman, with her bright, black eyes fixed on her visitor.

"Yes," replied Miss Longstreth, simply. "This is my cousin, Ruth Herbert. We've come to nurse you, take care of the children, help you in any way you'll let us."

There was a long silence.

"Well, you look a little like Longstreth," finally said Mrs. Laramie, "but you're not *at all* like him. You must take after your mother. Miss Longstreth, I don't know if I can—if I ought accept anything from you. Your father ruined my husband."

"Yes, I know," replied the girl, sadly. "That's all the more reason you should let me help you. Pray don't refuse. It will—mean so much to me."

If this poor, stricken woman had any resentment it speedily melted in the warmth and sweetness of Miss Longstreth's manner. Duane's idea was that the impression of Ray Longstreth's beauty was always swiftly succeeded by that of her generosity and nobility. At any rate, she had started well with Mrs. Laramie, and no sooner had she begun to talk to the children than both they and the mother were won. The opening of that big basket was an event. Poor, starved little beggars! Duane's feelings seemed too easily roused. Hard indeed would it have gone with Jim Laramie's slayer if he could have laid eyes on him then. However, Miss Longstreth and Ruth, after the nature of tender and practical girls, did not appear to take the sad situation to heart. The havoc was wrought in that household. The needs now were cheerfulness, kindness, help, action—and these the girls furnished with a spirit that did Duane good.

"Mrs. Laramie, who dressed this baby?" presently asked Miss Longstreth. Duane peeped in to see a dilapidated youngster on her knee. That sight if any other was needed, completed his full and splendid estimate of Ray Longstreth and wrought strangely upon his heart.

"The ranger," replied Mrs. Laramie.

"The ranger!" exclaimed Miss Longstreth.

"Yes, he's taken care of us all since—since—" Mrs. Laramie choked.

"Oh! So you've had no help but his," replied Miss Longstreth, hastily. "No women. Too bad! I'll send some one, Mrs. Laramie, and I'll come myself."

"It'll be good of you," went on the older woman. "You see, Jim had few friends—that is, right in town. And they've been afraid to help us—afraid they'd get what poor Jim—"

"That's awful!" burst out Miss Longstreth, passionately. "A brave lot of friends! Mrs. Laramie, don't you worry any more. We'll take care of you. Here, Ruth, help me. Whatever is the matter with baby's dress?"

Manifestly Miss Longstreth had some difficulty in subduing her emotion.

"Why, it's on hind side before," declared Ruth. "I guess Mr. Ranger hasn't dressed many babies."

"He did the best he could," said Mrs. Laramie. "Lord only knows what would have become of us!"

"Then he is—is something more than a ranger?" queried Miss Longstreth, with a little break in her voice.

"He's more than I can tell," replied Mrs. Laramie. "He buried Jim. He paid our debts. He fetched us here. He bought food for us. He cooked for us and fed us. He washed and dressed the baby. He sat with me the first two nights after Jim's death, when I thought I'd die myself. He's so kind, so gentle, so patient. He has kept me up just by being near. Sometimes I'd wake from a doze, an', seeing him there, I'd know how false were all these tales Jim heard about him and believed at first. Why, he plays with the children just—just like any good man might. When he has the baby up I just can't believe he's a bloody gunman, as they say. He's good, but he isn't happy. He has such sad eyes. He looks far off sometimes when the children climb round him. They love him. His life is sad. Nobody need tell me—he sees the good in things. Once he said somebody had to be a ranger. Well, I say, 'Thank God for a ranger like him!'"

Duane did not want to hear more, so he walked into the room.

"It was thoughtful of you," Duane said. "Womankind are needed here. I could do so little. Mrs. Laramie, you look better already. I'm glad. And here's baby, all clean and white. Baby, what a time I had trying to puzzle out the way your clothes went on! Well, Mrs. Laramie, didn't I tell you—friends would come? So will the brighter side."

"Yes, I've more faith than I had," replied Mrs. Laramie. "Granger Longstreth's daughter has come to me. There for a while after Jim's death I thought I'd sink. We have nothing. How could I ever take care of my little ones? But I'm gaining courage to—"

"Mrs. Laramie, do not distress yourself any more," said Miss Longstreth. "I shall see you are well cared for. I promise you."

"Miss Longstreth, that's fine!" exclaimed Duane. "It's what I'd have—expected of you."

It must have been sweet praise to her, for the whiteness of her face burned out in a beautiful blush.

"And it's good of you, too, Miss Herbert, to come," added Duane. "Let me thank you both. I'm glad I have you girls as allies in part of my lonely task here. More than glad for the sake of this good woman and the little ones. But both of you be careful about coming here alone. There's risk. And now I'll be going. Good-by, Mrs. Laramie. I'll drop in again to-night. Good-by."

"Mr. Ranger, wait!" called Miss Longstreth, as he went out. She was white and wonderful. She stepped out of the door close to him.

"I have wronged you!" she said, impulsively.

"Miss Longstreth! How can you say that?" he returned.

"I believed what my father and Floyd Lawson said about you. Now I see—I wronged you."

"You make me very glad. But, Miss Longstreth, please don't speak of wronging me. I have been a—a gunman, I *am* a ranger—and much said of me is true. My duty is hard on others—sometimes on those who are innocent, alas! But God knows that duty is hard, too, on me."

"I did wrong you. If you entered my home again I would think it an honor. I—"

"Please—please don't, Miss Longstreth," interrupted Duane.

"But, sir, my conscience flays me," she went on. There was no other sound like her voice. "Will you take my hand? Will you forgive me?"

She gave it royally, while the other was there pressing at her breast. Duane took the proffered hand. He did not know what else to do.

Then it seemed to dawn upon him that there was more behind this white, sweet, noble intensity of her than just the making amends for a fancied or real wrong. Duane thought the man did not live on earth who could have resisted her then.

"I honor you for your goodness to this unfortunate woman," she said, and now her speech came swiftly. "When she was all alone and help-less you were her friend. It was the deed of a man. But Mrs. Laramie isn't the only unfortunate woman in the world. I, too, am unfortunate. Ah, how *I* may soon need a friend! Will *you* be my friend? I'm so alone. I'm terribly worried. I fear—I fear— Oh, surely I'll need a friend soon—soon. Oh, I'm afraid of what you'll find out sooner or later. I want to help you. Let us save life if not honor. Must I stand alone—all alone? Will you—will you be—" Her voice failed.

It seemed to Duane that she must have discovered what he had begun to suspect—that her father and Lawson were not the honest ranchers they pretended to be. Perhaps she knew more! Her appeal to Duane shook him deeply. He wanted to help her more than he had ever wanted anything. And with the meaning of the tumultuous sweetness she stirred in him there came realization of a dangerous situation.

"I must be true to my duty," he said, hoarsely.

"If you knew me you'd know I could never ask you to be false to it."

"Well, then—I'll do anything for you."

"Oh, thank you! I'm ashamed that I believed my cousin Floyd! He lied—he lied. I'm all in the dark, strangely distressed. My father wants me to go back home. Floyd is trying to keep me here. They've quarreled. Oh, I know something dreadful will happen. I know I'll need you if— if— Will you help me?"

"Yes," replied Duane, and his look brought the blood to her face.

CHAPTER 19

After supper Duane stole out for his usual evening's spying. The night was dark, without starlight, and a stiff wind rustled the leaves. Duane bent his steps toward Longstreth's ranch-house. He had so much to think about that he never knew where the time went. This night when he reached the edge of the shrubbery he heard Lawson's well-known footsteps and saw Longstreth's door open, flashing a broad bar of light in the darkness. Lawson crossed the threshold, the door closed, and all was dark again outside. Not a ray of light escaped from the window.

Little doubt there was that his talk with Longstreth would be interesting to Duane. He tiptoed to the door and listened, but could hear only a murmur of voices. Besides, that position was too risky. He went round the corner of the house.

This side of the big adobe house was of much older construction than the back and larger part. There was a narrow passage between the houses, leading from the outside through to the patio.

This passage now afforded Duane an opportunity, and he decided to avail himself of it in spite of the very great danger. Crawling on very stealthily, he got under the shrubbery to the entrance of the passage. In the blackness a faint streak of light showed the location of a crack in the wall. He had to slip in sidewise. It was a tight squeeze, but he entered without the slightest noise. As he progressed the passage grew a very little wider in that direction, and that fact gave rise to the thought that in case of a necessary and hurried exit he would do best by working toward the patio. It seemed a good deal of time was consumed in reaching a vantage-point. When he did get there the crack he had marked was a foot over his head. There was nothing to do but find toe-holes in the crumbling walls, and by bracing knees on one side, back against the other, hold himself up. Once with his eye there he did not care what risk he ran. Longstreth appeared disturbed; he sat stroking his mustache; his brow was clouded. Lawson's face seemed darker, more sullen, yet lighted by some indomitable resolve.

"We'll settle both deals to-night," Lawson was saying. "That's what I came for."

"But suppose I don't choose to talk here?" protested Longstreth, impatiently. "I never before made my house a place to—"

"We've waited long enough. This place 's as good as any. You've lost your nerve since that ranger hit the town. First now, will you give Ray to me?"

"Floyd, you talk like a spoiled boy. Give Ray to you! Why, she's a woman, and I'm finding out that she's got a mind of her own. I told you I was willing for her to marry you. I tried to persuade her. But Ray hasn't any use for you now. She liked you at first. But now she doesn't. So what can I do?"

"You can make her marry me," replied Lawson.

"Make that girl do what she doesn't want to? It couldn't be done even if I tried. And I don't believe I'll try. I haven't the highest opinion of you as a prospective son-in-law, Floyd. But if Ray loved you I would consent. We'd all go away together before this damned miserable business is out. Then she'd never know. And maybe you might be more like you used to be before the West ruined you. But as matters stand, you fight your own game with her. And I'll tell you now you'll lose."

"What 'd you want to let her come out here for?" demanded Lawson, hotly. "It was a dead mistake. I've lost my head over her. I'll have her or die. Don't you think if she was my wife I'd soon pull myself together? Since she came nothing has been right. And the gang has put up a holler. No, Longstreth, we've got to settle things to-night."

"Well, we can settle what Ray's concerned in, right now," replied Longstreth, rising. "Come on; we'll ask her. See where you stand."

They went out, leaving the door open. Duane dropped down to rest himself and to wait. He would have liked to hear Miss Longstreth's answer. But he could guess what it would be. Lawson appeared to be all Duane had thought him, and he believed he was going to find out presently that he was worse.

The men seemed to be absent a good while, though that feeling might have been occasioned by Duane's thrilling interest and anxiety. Finally he heard heavy steps. Lawson came in alone. He was leaden-faced, humiliated. Then something abject in him gave place to rage. He strode the room; he cursed. Then Longstreth returned, now appreciably calmer. Duane could not but decide that he felt relief at the evident rejection of Lawson's proposal.

"Don't fuss about it, Floyd," he said. "You see I can't help it. We're pretty wild out here, but I can't rope my daughter and give her to you as I would an unruly steer."

"Longstreth, I can *make* her marry me," declared Lawson, thickly.

"How?"

"You know the hold I got on you—the deal that made you boss of this rustler gang?"

"It isn't likely I'd forget," replied Longstreth, grimly.

"I can go to Ray, tell her that, make her believe I'd tell it broadcast—tell this ranger—unless she'd marry me."

Lawson spoke breathlessly, with haggard face and shadowed eyes. He had no shame. He was simply in the grip of passion.

Longstreth gazed with dark, controlled fury at this relative. In that look Duane saw a strong, unscrupulous man fallen into evil ways, but still a man. It betrayed Lawson to be the wild and passionate weakling. Duane seemed to see also how during all the years of association this strong man had upheld the weak one. But that time had gone for ever, both in intent on Longstreth's part and in possibility. Lawson, like the great majority of evil and unrestrained men on the border, had reached a point where influence was futile. Reason had degenerated. He saw only himself.

"But, Floyd, Ray's the one person on earth who must never know I'm a rustler, a thief, a red-handed ruler of the worst gang on the border," replied Longstreth, impressively.

Floyd bowed his head at that, as if the significance had just occurred to him. But he was not long at a loss.

"She's going to find it out sooner or later. I tell you she knows now there's something wrong out here. She's got eyes. Mark what I say."

"Ray has changed, I know. But she hasn't any idea yet that her daddy's a boss rustler. Ray's concerned about what she calls my duty as mayor. Also I think she's not satisfied with my explanations in regard to certain property."

Lawson halted in his restless walk and leaned against the stone mantelpiece. He had his hands in his pockets. He squared himself as if this was his last stand. He looked desperate, but on the moment showed an absence of his usual nervous excitement.

"Longstreth, that may well be true," he said. "No doubt all you say is true. But it doesn't help me. I want the girl. If I don't get her—I reckon we'll all go to hell!"

He might have meant anything, probably meant the worst. He certainly had something more in mind. Longstreth gave a slight start, barely perceptible, like the switch of an awakening tiger. He sat there, head down, stroking his mustache. Almost Duane saw his thought. He had long experience in reading men under stress of such emotion. He had no means to vindicate his judgment, but his conviction was that Longstreth right then and there decided that the thing to do was to kill Lawson. For Duane's part he wondered that Longstreth had not come to such a conclusion before. Not improbably the advent of his daughter had put Longstreth in conflict with himself.

Suddenly he threw off a somber cast of countenance, and he began to talk. He talked swiftly, persuasively, yet Duane imagined he was talking to smooth Lawson's passion for the moment. Lawson no more caught the fateful significance of a line crossed, a limit reached, a decree decided than if he had not been present. He was obsessed with himself. How, Duane wondered, had a man of his mind ever lived so long and gone so far among the exacting conditions of the Southwest? The answer was, perhaps, that Longstreth had guided him, upheld him, protected him. The coming of Ray Longstreth had been the entering-wedge of dissension.

"You're too impatient," concluded Longstreth. "You'll ruin any chance of happiness if you rush Ray. She might be won. If you told her who I am she'd hate you for ever. She might marry you to save me, but she'd hate you. That isn't the way. Wait. Play for time. Be different with her. Cut out your drinking. She despises that. Let's plan to sell out here—stock, ranch, property—and leave the country. Then you'd have a show with her."

"I told you we've got to stick," growled Lawson. "The gang won't stand for our going. It can't be done unless you want to sacrifice everything."

"You mean double-cross the men? Go without their knowing? Leave them here to face whatever comes?"

"I mean just that."

"I'm bad enough, but not that bad," returned Longstreth. "If I can't get the gang to let me off, I'll stay and face the music. All the same, Lawson, did it ever strike you that most of the deals the last few years have been *yours*?"

"Yes. If I hadn't rung them in there wouldn't have been any. You've had cold feet, and especially since this ranger has been here."

"Well, call it cold feet if you like. But I call it sense. We reached our limit long ago. We began by rustling a few cattle—at a time when rustling was laughed at. But as our greed grew so did our boldness. Then came the gang, the regular trips, the one thing and another till, before we knew it—before *I* knew it—we had shady deals, holdups, and *murders* on our record. Then we *had* to go on. Too late to turn back!"

"I reckon we've all said that. None of the gang wants to quit. They all think, and I think, we can't be touched. We may be blamed, but nothing can be proved. We're too strong."

"There's where you're dead wrong," rejoined Longstreth, emphatically. "I imagined that once, not long ago. I was bull-headed. Who would ever connect Granger Longstreth with a rustler gang? I've changed my mind. I've begun to think. I've reasoned out things. We're crooked, and we can't last. It's the nature of life, even here, for conditions to grow better. The wise deal for us would be to divide equally and leave the country, all of us."

"But you and I have all the stock—all the gain," protested Lawson.

"I'll split mine."

"I won't—that settles that," added Lawson, instantly.

Longstreth spread wide his hands as if it was useless to try to convince this man. Talking had not increased his calmness, and he now showed more than impatience. A dull glint gleamed deep in his eyes.

"Your stock and property will last a long time—do you lots of good when this ranger—"

"Bah!" hoarsely croaked Lawson. The ranger's name was a match applied to powder. "Haven't I told you he'd be dead soon—any time—same as Laramie is?"

"Yes, you mentioned the—the supposition," replied Longstreth, sarcastically. "I inquired, too, just how that very desired event was to be brought about."

"The gang will lay him out."

"Bah!" retorted Longstreth, in turn. He laughed contemptuously.

"Floyd, don't be a fool. You've been on the border for ten years. You've packed a gun and you've used it. You've been with rustlers when they killed their men. You've been present at many fights. But you never in all that time saw a man like this ranger. You haven't got sense enough to see him right if you had a chance. Neither have any of you. The only way to get rid of him is for the gang to draw on him, all at once. Then he's going to drop some of them."

"Longstreth, you say that like a man who wouldn't care much if he did drop some of them," declared Lawson; and now he was sarcastic.

"To tell you the truth, I wouldn't," returned the other, bluntly. "I'm pretty sick of this mess."

Lawson cursed in amazement. His emotions were all out of proportion to his intelligence. He was not at all quick-witted. Duane had never seen a vainer or more arrogant man.

"Longstreth, I don't like your talk," he said.

"If you don't like the way I talk you know what you can do," replied Longstreth, quickly. He stood up then, cool and quiet, with flash of eyes and set of lips that told Duane he was dangerous.

"Well, after all, that's neither here nor there," went on Lawson, unconsciously cowed by the other. "The thing is, do I get the girl?"

"Not by any means except her consent."

"You'll not make her marry me?"

"No. No," replied Longstreth, his voice still cold, low-pitched.

"All right. Then I'll make her."

Evidently Longstreth understood the man before him so well that he wasted no more words. Duane knew what Lawson never dreamed of, and that was that Longstreth had a gun somewhere within reach and meant to use it. Then heavy footsteps sounded outside tramping upon the porch. Duane might have been mistaken, but he believed those footsteps saved Lawson's life.

"There they are," said Lawson, and he opened the door.

Five masked men entered. They all wore coats hiding any weapons. A big man with burly shoulders shook hands with Longstreth, and the others stood back.

The atmosphere of that room had changed. Lawson might have been a nonentity for all he counted. Longstreth was another man—a stranger to Duane. If he had entertained a hope of freeing himself from this band, of getting away to a safer country, he abandoned it at the very sight of these men. There was power here, and he was bound.

The big man spoke in low, hoarse whispers, and at this all the others gathered around him close to the table. There were evidently some signs of membership not plain to Duane. Then all the heads were bent over the table. Low voices spoke, queried, answered, argued. By straining his ears Duane caught a word here and there. They were planning, and they were brief. Duane gathered they were to have a rendezvous at or near Ord.

Then the big man, who evidently was the leader of the present convention, got up to depart. He went as swiftly as he had come, and was followed by his comrades. Longstreth prepared for a quiet smoke. Lawson seemed uncommunicative and unsociable. He smoked fiercely and drank continually. All at once he straightened up as if listening.

"What's that?" he called, suddenly.

Duane's strained ears were pervaded by a slight rustling sound.

"Must be a rat," replied Longstreth.

The rustle became a rattle.

"Sounds like a rattlesnake to me," said Lawson.

Longstreth got up from the table and peered round the room.

Just at that instant Duane felt an almost inappreciable movement of the adobe wall which supported him. He could scarcely credit his senses. But the rattle inside Longstreth's room was mingling with little dull thuds of falling dirt. The adobe wall, merely dried mud, was crumbling. Duane distinctly felt a tremor pass through it. Then the blood gushed back to his heart.

"What in the hell!" exclaimed Longstreth.

"I smell dust," said Lawson, sharply.

That was the signal for Duane to drop down from his perch, yet despite his care he made a noise.

"Did you hear a step?" queried Longstreth.

No one answered. But a heavy piece of the adobe wall fell with a thud. Duane heard it crack, felt it shake.

"There's somebody between the walls!" thundered Longstreth.

Then a section of the wall fell inward with a crash. Duane began to squeeze his body through the narrow passage toward the patio.

"Hear him!" yelled Lawson. "This side!"

"No, he's going that way," yelled Longstreth.

The tramp of heavy boots lent Duane the strength of desperation. He was not shirking a fight, but to be cornered like a trapped coyote was another matter. He almost tore his clothes off in that passage. The dust nearly stifled him. When he burst into the patio it was not a single instant too soon. But one deep gasp of breath revived him and he was up, gun in hand, running for the outlet into the court. Thumping footsteps turned him back. While there was a chance to get away he did not want to fight. He thought he heard some one running into the patio from the other end. He stole along, and coming to a door, without any idea of where it might lead, he softly pushed it open a little way and slipped in.

CHAPTER 20

A low cry greeted Duane. The room was light. He saw Ray Longstreth sitting on her bed in her dressing-gown. With a warning gesture to her to be silent he turned to close the door. It was a heavy door without bolt or bar, and when Duane had shut it he felt safe only for the moment. Then he gazed around the room. There was one window with blind closely drawn. He listened and seemed to hear footsteps retreating, dying away.

Then Duane turned to Miss Longstreth. She had slipped off the bed, half to her knees, and was holding out trembling hands. She was as white as the pillow on her bed. She was terribly frightened. Again with warning hand commanding silence, Duane stepped softly forward, meaning to reassure her.

"Oh!" she whispered, wildly; and Duane thought she was going to faint. When he got close and looked into her eyes he understood the strange, dark expression in them. She was terrified because she believed he meant to kill her, or do worse, probably worse. Duane realized he must have looked pretty hard and fierce bursting into her room with that big gun in hand.

The way she searched Duane's face with doubtful fearful eyes hurt him.

"Listen. I didn't know this was your room. I came here to get away— to save my life. I was pursued. I was spying on—on your father and his men. They heard me, but did not see me. They don't know who was listening. They're after me now."

Her eyes changed from blank gulfs to dilating, shadowing, quickening windows of thought.

Then she stood up and faced Duane with the fire and intelligence of a woman in her eyes.

"Tell me now. You were spying on my father?"

Briefly Duane told her what had happened before he entered her room, not omitting a terse word as to the character of the men he had watched.

"My God! So it's that? I knew something was terribly wrong here—with him—with the place—the people. And right off I hated Floyd Lawson. Oh, it'll kill me if—if— It's so much worse than I dreamed. What shall I do?"

The sound of soft steps somewhere near distracted Duane's attention, reminded him of her peril, and now, what counted more with him, made clear the probability of being discovered in her room.

"I'll have to get out of here," whispered Duane.

"Wait," she replied. "Didn't you say they were hunting for you?"

"They sure are," he returned, grimly.

"Oh, then you mustn't go. They might shoot you before you got away. Stay. If we hear them you can hide. I'll turn out the light. I'll meet them at the door. You can trust me. Wait till all quiets down, if we have to wait till morning. Then you can slip out."

"I oughtn't to stay. I don't want to—I won't," Duane replied, perplexed and stubborn.

"But you must. It's the only safe way. They won't come here."

"Suppose they should? It's an even chance Longstreth 'll search every room and corner in this old house. If they found me here I couldn't start a fight. You might be hurt. Then—the fact of my being here—"

Duane did not finish what he meant, but instead made a step toward the door. White of face and dark of eye, she took hold of him to detain him. She was as strong and supple as a panther. But she need not have been either resolute or strong, for the clasp of her hand was enough to make Duane weak.

"Up yet, Ray?" came Longstreth's clear voice, too strained, too eager to be natural.

"No. I'm in bed reading. Good night," instantly replied Miss Longstreth, so calmly and naturally that Duane marveled at the difference between man and woman. Then she motioned for Duane to hide in the closet. He slipped in, but the door would not close altogether.

"Are you alone?" went on Longstreth's penetrating voice.

"Yes," she replied. "Ruth went to bed."

The door swung inward with a swift scrape and jar. Longstreth half entered, haggard, flaming-eyed. Behind him Duane saw Lawson, and indistinctly another man.

Longstreth barred Lawson from entering, which action showed control as well as distrust. He wanted to see into the room. When he had glanced around he went out and closed the door.

Then what seemed a long interval ensued. The house grew silent once more. Duane could not see Miss Longstreth, but he heard her quick breathing. How long did she mean to let him stay hidden there? Hard and perilous as his life had been, this was a new kind of adventure. He had divined the strange softness of his feeling as something due to the magnetism of this beautiful woman. It hardly seemed possible that he, who had been outside the pale for so many years, could have fallen in love. Yet that must be the secret of his agitation.

Presently he pushed open the closet door and stepped forth. Miss Longstreth had her head lowered upon her arms and appeared to be in distress. At his touch she raised a quivering face.

"I think I can go now—safely," he whispered.

"Go then, if you must, but you may stay till you're safe," she replied.

"I—I couldn't thank you enough. It's been hard on me—this finding out—and you his daughter. I feel strange. I don't understand myself well. But I want you to know—if I were not an outlaw—a ranger—I'd lay my life at your feet."

"Oh! You have seen so—so little of me," she faltered.

"All the same it's true. And that makes me feel more the trouble my coming caused you."

"You will not fight my father?"

"Not if I can help it. I'm trying to get out of his way."

"But you spied upon him."

"I am a ranger, Miss Longstreth."

"And oh! I am a rustler's daughter," she cried. "That's so much more terrible than I'd suspected. It was tricky cattle deals I imagined he was engaged in. But only to-night I had strong suspicions aroused."

"How? Tell me."

"I overheard Floyd say that men were coming to-night to arrange a meeting for my father at a rendezvous near Ord. Father did not want to go. Floyd taunted him with a name."

"What name?" queried Duane.

"It was Cheseldine."

"*Cheseldine*! My God! Miss Longstreth, why did *you* tell me that?"

"What difference does that make?"

"Your father and Cheseldine are one and the same," whispered Duane, hoarsely.

"I gathered so much myself," she replied, miserably. "But Longstreth is father's real name."

Duane felt so stunned he could not speak at once. It was the girl's part in this tragedy that weakened him. The instant she betrayed the secret Duane realized perfectly that he did love her. The emotion was like a great flood.

"Miss Longstreth, all this seems so unbelievable," he whispered. "Cheseldine is the rustler chief I've come out here to get. He's only a name. Your father is the real man. I've sworn to get him. I'm bound by more than laws or oaths. I can't break what binds me. And I must disgrace you—wreck your life! Why, Miss Longstreth, I believe I—I love you. It's all come in a rush. I'd die for you if I could. How fatal—terrible—this is! How things work out!"

She slipped to her knees, with her hands on his.

"You won't kill him?" she implored. "If you care for me—you won't kill him?"

"No. That I promise you."

With a low moan she dropped her head upon the bed.

Duane opened the door and stealthily stole out through the corridor to the court.

When Duane got out into the dark, where his hot face cooled in the wind, his relief equaled his other feelings.

The night was dark, windy, stormy, yet there was no rain. Duane hoped as soon as he got clear of the ranch to lose something of the pain he felt. But long after he had tramped out into the open there was a lump in his throat and an ache in his breast. All his thought centered around Ray Longstreth. What a woman she had turned out to be! He seemed to have a vague, hopeless hope that there might be, there must be, some way he could save her.

CHAPTER 21

Before going to sleep that night Duane had decided to go to Ord and try to find the rendezvous where Longstreth was to meet his men. These men Duane wanted even more than their leader. If Longstreth, or Cheseldine, was the brains of that gang, Poggin was the executor. It was Poggin who needed to be found and stopped. Poggin and his right-hand men! Duane experienced a strange, tigerish thrill. It was thought of Poggin more than thought of success for MacNelly's plan. Duane felt dubious over this emotion.

Next day he set out for Bradford. He was glad to get away from Fairdale for a while. But the hours and the miles in no wise changed the new pain in his heart. The only way he could forget Miss Longstreth was to let his mind dwell upon Poggin, and even this was not always effective.

He avoided Sanderson, and at the end of a day and a half he arrived at Bradford.

The night of the day before he reached Bradford, No. 6, the mail and express train going east, was held up by train-robbers, the Wells-Fargo messenger killed over his safe, the mail-clerk wounded, the bags carried away. The engine of No. 6 came into town minus even a tender, and engineer and fireman told conflicting stories. A posse of railroad men and citizens, led by a sheriff Duane suspected was crooked, was made up before the engine steamed back to pick up the rest of the train. Duane had the sudden inspiration that he had been cudgeling his mind to find; and, acting upon it, he mounted his horse again and left Bradford unobserved. As he rode out into the night, over a dark trail in the direction of Ord, he uttered a short, grim, sardonic laugh at the hope that he might be taken for a train-robber.

He rode at an easy trot most of the night, and when the black peak of Ord Mountain loomed up against the stars he halted, tied his horse, and slept until dawn. He had brought a small pack, and now he took his time cooking breakfast. When the sun was well up he saddled Bullet, and, leaving the trail where his tracks showed plain in the ground, he put his horse to the rocks and brush. He selected an exceedingly rough, round-about, and difficult course to Ord, hid his tracks with the skill of a long-hunted fugitive, and arrived there with his horse winded and covered with lather. It added considerable to his arrival that the man Duane remembered as Fletcher and several others saw him come in the back way through the lots and jump a fence into the road.

Duane led Bullet up to the porch where Fletcher stood wiping his beard. He was hatless, vestless, and evidently had just enjoyed a morning drink.

"Howdy, Dodge," said Fletcher, laconically.

Duane replied, and the other man returned the greeting with interest.

"Jim, my hoss's done up. I want to hide him from any chance tourists as might happen to ride up curious-like."

"Haw! haw! haw!"

Duane gathered encouragement from that chorus of coarse laughter.

"Wal, if them tourists ain't too durned snooky the hoss'll be safe in the 'dobe shack back of Bill's here. Feed thar, too, but you'll hev to rustle water."

Duane led Bullet to the place indicated, had care of his welfare, and left him there. Upon returning to the tavern porch Duane saw the group of men had been added to by others, some of whom he had seen before. Without comment Duane walked along the edge of the road, and wherever one of the tracks of his horse showed he carefully obliterated it. This procedure was attentively watched by Fletcher and his companions.

"Wal, Dodge," remarked Fletcher, as Duane returned, "thet's safer 'n prayin' fer rain."

Duane's reply was a remark as loquacious as Fletcher's, to the effect that a long, slow, monotonous ride was conducive to thirst. They all joined him, unmistakably friendly. But Knell was not there, and most assuredly not Poggin. Fletcher was no common outlaw, but, whatever his ability, it probably lay in execution of orders. Apparently at that time these men had nothing to do but drink and lounge around the tavern. Evidently they were poorly supplied with money, though Duane observed they could borrow a peso occasionally from the bartender. Duane set out to make himself agreeable and succeeded. There was card-playing for small stakes, idle jests of coarse nature, much bantering among the younger fellows, and occasionally a mild quarrel. All morning men came and went, until, all told, Duane calculated he had seen at least fifty. Toward the middle of the afternoon a young fellow burst into the saloon and yelled one word:

"Posse!"

From the scramble to get outdoors Duane judged that word and the ensuing action was rare in Ord.

"What the hell!" muttered Fletcher, as he gazed down the road at a dark, compact bunch of horses and riders. "Fust time I ever seen thet in Ord! We're gettin' popular like them camps out in Valentine. Wish Phil was here or Poggy. Now all you gents keep quiet. I'll do the talkin'."

The posse entered the town, trotted up on dusty horses, and halted in a bunch before the tavern. The party consisted of about twenty men, all heavily armed, and evidently in charge of a clean-cut, lean-limbed cowboy. Duane experienced considerable satisfaction at the absence of the sheriff who he had understood was to lead the posse. Perhaps he was out in another direction with a different force.

"Hello, Jim Fletcher," called the cowboy.

"Howdy," replied Fletcher.

At his short, dry response and the way he strode leisurely out before the posse Duane found himself modifying his contempt for Fletcher. The outlaw was different now.

"Fletcher, we've tracked a man to all but three miles of this place. Tracks as plain as the nose on your face. Found his camp. Then he hit into the brush, an' we lost the trail. Didn't have no tracker with us. Think he went into the mountains. But we took a chance an' rid over the rest of the way, seein' Ord was so close. Anybody come in here late last night or early this mornin'?"

"Nope," replied Fletcher.

His response was what Duane had expected from his manner, and evidently the cowboy took it as a matter of course. He turned to the others of the posse, entering into a low consultation. Evidently there was difference of opinion, if not real dissension, in that posse.

"Didn't I tell ye this was a wild-goose chase, comin' way out here?" protested an old hawk-faced rancher. "Them hoss tracks we follored ain't like any of them we seen at the water-tank where the train was held up."

"I'm not so sure of that," replied the leader.

"Wal, Guthrie, I've follored tracks all my life—"

"But you couldn't keep to the trail this feller made in the brush."

"Gimme time, an' I could. Thet takes time. An' heah you go hellbent fer election! But it's a wrong lead out this way. If you're right this road-agent, after he killed his pals, would hev rid back right through town. An' with them mail-bags! Supposin' they was Mexicans? Some Mexicans has sense, an' when it comes to thievin' they're shore cute."

"But we ain't got any reason to believe this robber who murdered the Mexicans is a Mexican himself. I tell you it was a slick job done by no ordinary sneak. Didn't you hear the facts? One Mexican hopped the engine an' covered the engineeer an' fireman. Another Mexican kept flashin' his gun outside the train. The big man who shoved back the car-door an' did the killin' he was the real gent, an' don't you forget it."

Some of the posse sided with the cowboy leader and some with the old cattleman. Finally the young leader disgustedly gathered up his bridle.

"Aw, hell! Thet sheriff shoved you off this trail. Mebbe he hed reason! Savvy thet? If I hed a bunch of cowboys with me—I tell you what—I'd take a chance an' clean up this hole!"

All the while Jim Fletcher stood quietly with his hands in his pockets.

"Guthrie, I'm shore treasurin' up your friendly talk," he said. The menace was in the tone, not the content of his speech.

"You can—an' be damned to you, Fletcher!" called Guthrie, as the horses started.

Fletcher, standing out alone before the others of his clan, watched the posse out of sight.

"Luck fer you-all thet Poggy wasn't here," he said, as they disappeared. Then with a thoughtful mien he strode up on the porch and led Duane away from the others into the barroom. When he looked into Duane's face it was somehow an entirely changed scrutiny.

"Dodge, where'd you hide the stuff? I reckon I git in on this deal, seein' I staved off Guthrie."

Duane played his part. Here was his opportunity, and like a tiger after prey he seized it. First he coolly eyed the outlaw and then disclaimed any knowledge whatever of the train-robbery other than Fletcher had heard himself. Then at Fletcher's persistence and admiration and increasing show of friendliness he laughed occasionally and allowed himself to swell with pride, though still denying. Next he feigned a lack of consistent will-power and seemed to be wavering under Fletcher's persuasion and grew silent, then surly. Fletcher, evidently sure of ultimate victory, desisted for the time being; however, in his solicitous regard and close companionship for the rest of that day he betrayed the bent of his mind.

Later, when Duane started up announcing his intention to get his horse and make for camp out in the brush, Fletcher seemed grievously offended.

"Why don't you stay with me? I've got a comfortable 'dobe over here. Didn't I stick by you when Guthrie an' his bunch come up? Supposin' I hedn't showed down a cold hand to him? You'd be swingin' somewheres now. I tell you, Dodge, it ain't square."

"I'll square it. I pay my debts," replied Duane. "But I can't put up here all night. If I belonged to the gang it 'd be different."

"What gang?" asked Fletcher, bluntly.

"Why, Cheseldine's."

Fletcher's beard nodded as his jaw dropped.

Duane laughed. "I run into him the other day. Knowed him on sight. Sure, he's the king-pin rustler. When he seen me an' asked me what reason I had for bein' on earth or some such like—why, I up an' told him."

Fletcher appeared staggered.

"Who in all-fired hell air you talkin' about?"

"Didn't I tell you once? Cheseldine. He calls himself Longstreth over there."

All of Fletcher's face not covered by hair turned a dirty white.

"Cheseldine—Longstreth!" he whispered, hoarsely. "Gord Almighty! You braced the—" Then a remarkable transformation came over the outlaw. He gulped; he straightened his face; he controlled his agitation. But he could not send the healthy brown back to his face. Duane, watching this rude man, marveled at the change in him, the sudden checking movement, the proof of a wonderful fear and loyalty. It all meant Cheseldine, a master of men!

"*Who air you?*" queried Fletcher, in a strained voice.

"You gave me a handle, didn't you? Dodge. Thet's as good as any. Shore it hits me hard. Jim, I've been pretty lonely for years, an' I'm gettin' in need of pals. Think it over, will you? See you *mañana*."

The outlaw watched Duane go off after his horse, watched him as he returned to the tavern, watched him ride out into the darkness—all without a word.

Duane left the town, threaded a quiet passage through cactus and mesquite to a spot he had marked before, and made ready for the night. His mind was so full that he found sleep aloof. Luck at last was playing his game. He sensed the first slow heave of a mighty crisis. The end, always haunting, had to be sternly blotted from thought. It was the approach that needed all his mind.

He passed the night there, and late in the morning, after watching trail and road from a ridge, he returned to Ord. If Jim Fletcher tried to disguise his surprise the effort was a failure. Certainly he had not expected to see Duane again. Duane allowed himself a little freedom with Fletcher, an attitude hitherto lacking.

That afternoon a horseman rode in from Bradford, an outlaw evidently well known and liked by his fellows, and Duane heard him say, before he could possibly have been told the train-robber was in Ord, that the loss of money in the holdup was slight. Like a flash Duane saw the luck of this report. He pretended not to have heard.

In the early twilight at an opportune moment he called Fletcher to him, and, linking his arm within the outlaw's, he drew him off in a stroll to a log bridge spanning a little gully. Here after gazing around, he took out a roll of bills, spread it out, split it equally, and without a word handed one half to Fletcher. With clumsy fingers Fletcher ran through the roll.

"Five hundred!" he exclaimed. "Dodge, thet's damn handsome of you, considerin' the job wasn't—

"Considerin' nothin'," interrupted Duane. "I'm makin' no reference to a job here or there. You did me a good turn. I split my pile. If thet doesn't make us pards, good turns an' money ain't no use in this country."

Fletcher was won.

The two men spent much time together. Duane made up a short fictitious history about himself that satisfied the outlaw, only it drew forth a laughing jest upon Duane's modesty. For Fletcher did not hide his belief that this new partner was a man of achievements. Knell and Poggin, and then Cheseldine himself, would be persuaded of this fact, so Fletcher boasted. He had influence. He would use it. He thought he pulled a stroke with Knell. But nobody on earth, not even the boss, had any influence on Poggin. Poggin was concentrated ice part of the time; all the rest he was bursting hell. But Poggin loved a horse. He never loved anything else. He could be won with that black horse Bullet. Cheseldine was already won by Duane's monumental nerve; otherwise he would have killed Duane.

Little by little the next few days Duane learned the points he longed to know; and how indelibly they etched themselves in his memory! Cheseldine's hiding-place was on the far slope of Mount Ord, in a deep, high-walled valley. He always went there just before a contemplated job, where he met and planned with his lieutenants. Then while they executed he basked in the sunshine before one or another of the public places he owned. He was there in the Ord den now, getting ready to plan the biggest job yet. It was a bank-robbery; but where, Fletcher had not as yet been advised.

Then when Duane had pumped the now amenable outlaw of all details pertaining to the present he gathered data and facts and places covering a period of ten years Fletcher had been with Cheseldine. And herewith was unfolded a history so dark in its bloody régime, so incredible in its brazen daring, so appalling in its proof of the outlaw's sweep and grasp of the country from Pecos to Rio Grande, that Duane was stunned. Compared to this Cheseldine of the Big Bend, to this rancher, stock-buyer, cattle-speculator, property-holder, all the outlaws Duane had ever known sank into insignificance. The power of the man stunned

Duane; the strange fidelity given him stunned Duane; the intricate inside working of his great system was equally stunning. But when Duane recovered from that the old terrible passion to kill consumed him, and it raged fiercely and it could not be checked. If that red-handed Poggin, if that cold-eyed, dead-faced Knell had only been at Ord! But they were not, and Duane with help of time got what he hoped was the upper hand of himself.

CHAPTER 22

Again inaction and suspense dragged at Duane's spirit. Like a leashed hound with a keen scent in his face Duane wanted to leap forth when he was bound. He almost fretted. Something called to him over the bold, wild brow of Mount Ord. But while Fletcher stayed in Ord waiting for Knell and Poggin, or for orders, Duane knew his game was again a waiting one.

But one day there were signs of the long quiet of Ord being broken. A messenger strange to Duane rode in on a secret mission that had to do with Fletcher. When he went away Fletcher became addicted to thoughtful moods and lonely walks. He seldom drank, and this in itself was a striking contrast to former behavior. The messenger came again. Whatever communication he brought, it had a remarkable effect upon the outlaw. Duane was present in the tavern when the fellow arrived, saw the few words whispered, but did not hear them. Fletcher turned white with anger or fear, perhaps both, and he cursed like a madman. The messenger, a lean, dark-faced, hard-riding fellow reminding Duane of the cowboy Guthrie, left the tavern without even a drink and rode away off to the west. This west mystified and fascinated Duane as much as the south beyond Mount Ord. Where were Knell and Poggin? Apparently they were not at present with the leader on the mountain. After the messenger left Fletcher grew silent and surly. He had presented a variety of moods to Duane's observation, and this latest one was provocative of thought.

Fletcher was dangerous. It became clear now that the other outlaws of the camp feared him, kept out of his way. Duane let him alone, yet closely watched him.

Perhaps an hour after the messenger had left, not longer, Fletcher manifestly arrived at some decision, and he called for his horse. Then he went to his shack and returned. To Duane the outlaw looked in shape both to ride and to fight. He gave orders for the men in camp to keep close until he returned. Then he mounted.

"Come here, Dodge," he called.

Duane went up and laid a hand on the pommel of the saddle. Fletcher walked his horse, with Duane beside him, till they reached the log bridge, when he halted.

"Dodge, I'm in bad with Knell," he said. "An' it 'pears I'm the cause of friction between Knell an' Poggy. Knell never had any use fer me, but Poggy's been square, if not friendly. The boss has a big deal on, an' here it's been held up because of this scrap. He's waitin' over there on the mountain to give orders to Knell or Poggy, an' neither one's showin' up. I've got to stand in the breach, an' I ain't enjoyin' the prospects."

"What's the trouble about, Jim?" asked Duane.

"Reckon it's a little about you, Dodge," said Fletcher, dryly. "Knell hadn't any use fer you thet day. He ain't got no use fer a man onless he can rule him. Some of the boys here hev blabbed before I edged in with my say, an' there's hell to pay. Knell claims to know somethin' about you that'll make both the boss an' Poggy sick when he springs it. But he's keepin' quiet. Hard man to figger, thet Knell. Reckon you'd better go back to Bradford fer a day or so, then camp out near here till I come back."

"Why?"

"Wal, because there ain't any use fer you to git in bad, too. The gang will ride over here any day. If they're friendly I'll light a fire on the hill there, say three nights from to-night. If you don't see it thet night you hit the trail. I'll do what I can. Jim Fletcher sticks to his pals. So long, Dodge."

Then he rode away.

He left Duane in a quandary. This news was black. Things had been working out so well. Here was a setback. At the moment Duane did not know which way to turn, but certainly he had no idea of going back to Bradford. Friction between the two great lieutenants of Cheseldine! Open hostility between one of them and another of the chief's right-hand men! Among outlaws that sort of thing was deadly serious. Generally such matters were settled with guns. Duane gathered encouragement even from disaster. Perhaps the disintegration of Cheseldine's great band had already begun. But what did Knell know? Duane did not circle around the idea with doubts and hopes; if Knell knew anything it was that this stranger in Ord, this new partner of Fletcher's, was no less than Buck Duane. Well, it was about time, thought Duane, that he made use of his name if it were to help him at all. That name had been MacNelly's hope. He had anchored all his scheme to Duane's fame. Duane was tempted to ride off after Fletcher and stay with him. This, however, would hardly be fair to an outlaw who had been fair to him. Duane concluded to await developments and when the gang rode in to Ord, probably from their various hiding-places, he would be there ready to be denounced by Knell. Duane could not see any other culmination of this series of events than a meeting between Knell and himself. If that terminated fatally for Knell there was all probability of Duane's being in no worse situation that he was now. If Poggin took up the quarrel! Here Duane accused himself again—tried in vain to revolt from a judgment that he was only reasoning out excuses to meet these outlaws.

Meanwhile, instead of waiting, why not hunt up Cheseldine in his mountain retreat? The thought no sooner struck Duane than he was hurrying for his horse.

He left Ord, ostensibly toward Bradford, but, once out of sight, he turned off the road, circled through the brush, and several miles south of town he struck a narrow grass-grown trail that Fletcher had told him led to Cheseldine's camp. The horse tracks along this trail were not less than a week old, and very likely much more. It wound between low, brush-covered foothills, through arroyos and gullies lined with mesquite, cottonwood, and scrub-oak.

In an hour Duane struck the slope of Mount Ord, and as he climbed he got a view of the rolling, black-spotted country, partly desert, partly fertile, with long, bright lines of dry stream-beds winding away to grow dim in the distance. He got among broken rocks and cliffs, and here the open, downward-rolling land disappeared, and he was hard put to it to find the trail. He lost it repeatedly and made slow progress. Finally he climbed into a region of all rock benches, rough here, smooth there, with only an occasional scratch of iron horseshoe to guide him. Many times he had to go ahead and then work to right or left till he found his way again. It was slow work; it took all day; and night found him half-way up the mountain. He halted at a little side-cañon with grass and water, and here he made camp. The night was clear and cool at that height, with a dark-blue sky and a streak of stars blinking across. With this day of action behind him he felt better satisfied than he had been for some time. Here, on this venture, he was answering to a call that had so often directed his movements, perhaps his life, and it was one that logic or intelligence could take little stock of. And on this night, lonely like the ones he used to spend in the Nueces gorge, and memorable of them because of a likeness to that old hiding-place, he felt the pressing return of old haunting things—the past so long ago, wild flights, dead faces—and the places of these were taken by one quiveringly alive, white, tragic, with its dark, intent, speaking eyes—Ray Longstreth's.

That last memory he yielded to until he slept.

In the morning, satisfied that he had left still fewer tracks than he had followed up this trail, he led his horse up to the head of the cañon, there a narrow crack in low cliffs, and with branches of cedar fenced him in. Then he went back and took up the trail on foot.

Without the horse he made better time and climbed through deep clefts, wide cañons, over ridges, up shelving slopes, along precipices—a long, hard climb—till he reached what he concluded was a divide. Going down was easier, though the farther he followed this dim and winding trail the wider the broken battlements of rock. Above him he saw the black fringe of piñon and pine, and above that the bold peak, bare, yellow, like a desert butte. Once, through a wide gateway between great escarpments, he saw the lower country beyond the range, and beyond this, vast and clear as it lay in his sight, was the great river that made the Big Bend. He went down and down, wondering how a horse could follow that broken trail, believing there must be another better one somewhere into Cheseldine's hiding-place.

He rounded a jutting corner, where view had been shut off, and presently came out upon the rim of a high wall. Beneath, like a green gulf seen through blue haze, lay an amphitheater walled in on the two sides he could see. It lay perhaps a thousand feet below him; and, plain as all the other features of that wild environment, there shone out a big red stone or adobe cabin, white water shining away between great borders, and horses and cattle dotting the levels. It was a peaceful, beautiful scene. Duane could not help grinding his teeth at the thought of rustlers living there in quiet and ease.

Duane worked half-way down to the level, and, well hidden in a niche, he settled himself to watch both trail and valley. He made note of the position of the sun and saw that if anything developed or if he decided to descend any farther there was small likelihood of his getting back to his camp before dark. To try that after nightfall he imagined would be vain effort.

Then he bent his keen eyes downward. The cabin appeared to be a crude structure. Though large in size, it had, of course, been built by outlaws.

There was no garden, no cultivated field, no corral. Excepting for the rude pile of stones and logs plastered together with mud, the valley was as wild, probably, as on the day of discovery. Duane seemed to have been watching for a long time before he saw any sign of man, and this one apparently went to the stream for water and returned to the cabin.

The sun went down behind the wall, and shadows were born in the darker places of the valley. Duane began to want to get closer to that cabin. What had he taken this arduous climb for? He held back, however, trying to evolve further plans.

While he was pondering the shadows quickly gathered and darkened. If he was to go back to camp he must set out at once. Still he lingered. And suddenly his wide-roving eye caught sight of two horsemen riding up the valley. They must have entered at a point below, round the huge abutment of rock, beyond Duane's range of sight. Their horses were tired and stopped at the stream for a long drink.

Duane left his perch, took to the steep trail, and descended as fast as he could without making noise. It did not take him long to reach the valley floor. It was almost level, with deep grass, and here and there clumps of bushes. Twilight was already thick down there. Duane marked the location of the trail, and then began to slip like a shadow through the grass and from bush to bush. He saw a bright light before he made out the dark outline of the cabin. Then he heard voices, a merry whistle, a coarse song, and the clink of iron cooking-utensils. He smelled fragrant wood-smoke. He saw moving dark figures cross the light. Evidently there was a wide door, or else the fire was out in the open.

Duane swerved to the left, out of direct line with the light, and thus was able to see better. Then he advanced noiselessly but swiftly toward the back of the house. There were trees close to the wall. He would make no noise, and he could scarcely be seen—if only there was no watch-dog! But all his outlaw days he had taken risks with only his useless life at stake; now, with that changed, he advanced stealthy and bold as an Indian. He reached the cover of the trees, knew he was hidden in their shadows, for at few paces' distance he had been able to see only their tops. From there he slipped up to the house and felt along the wall with his hands.

He came to a little window where light shone through. He peeped in. He saw a room shrouded in shadows, a lamp turned low, a table, chairs. He saw an open door, with bright flare beyond, but could not see the fire. Voices came indistinctly. Without hesitation Duane stole farther along—all the way to the end of the cabin. Peeping round, he saw only the flare of light on bare ground. Retracing his cautious steps, he paused at the crack again, saw that no man was in the room, and then he went on round that end of the cabin. Fortune favored him. There were bushes, an old shed, a wood-pile, all the cover he needed at that corner. He did not even need to crawl.

Before he peered between the rough corner of wall and the bush growing close to it Duane paused a moment. This excitement was different from that he had always felt when pursued. It had no bitterness, no pain, no dread. There was as much danger here, perhaps more, yet it was not the same. Then he looked.

He saw a bright fire, a red-faced man bending over it, whistling, while he handled a steaming pot. Over him was a roofed shed built against the wall, with two open sides and two supporting posts. Duane's second glance, not so blinded by the sudden bright light, made out other men, three in the shadow, two in the flare, but with backs to him.

"It's a smoother trail by long odds, but ain't so short as this one right over the mountain," one outlaw was saying.

"What's eatin' you, Panhandle?" asked another. "Blossom an' me rode from Faraway Springs, where Poggin is with some of the gang."

"Excuse me, Phil. Shore I didn't see you come in, an' Boldt never said nothin'."

"It took you a long time to get here, but I guess that's just as well," spoke up a smooth, suave voice with a ring in it.

Longstreth's voice—Cheseldine's voice!

Here they were—Cheseldine, Phil Knell, Blossom Kane, Panhandle Smith, Boldt—how well Duane remembered the names!—all here, the big men of Cheseldine's gang, except the biggest—Poggin. Duane had holed them, and his sensations of the moment deadened sight and sound of what was before him. He sank down, controlled himself, silenced a mounting exultation, then from a less-strained position he peered forth again.

The outlaws were waiting for supper. Their conversation might have been that of cowboys in camp, ranchers at a round-up. Duane listened with eager ears, waiting for the business talk that he felt would come. All the time he watched with the eyes of a wolf upon its quarry. Blossom Kane was the lean-limbed messenger who had so angered Fletcher. Boldt was a giant in stature, dark, bearded, silent. Panhandle Smith was the red-faced cook, merry, profane, a short, bow-legged man resembling many rustlers Duane had known, particularly Luke Stevens. And Knell, who sat there, tall, slim, like a boy in build, like a boy in years, with his pale, smooth, expressionless face and his cold, gray eyes. And Longstreth, who leaned against the wall, handsome, with his dark face and beard like an aristocrat, resembled many a rich Louisiana planter Duane had met. The sixth man sat so much in the shadow that he could not be plainly discerned, and, though addressed, his name was not mentioned.

Panhandle Smith carried pots and pans into the cabin, and cheerfully called out: "If you gents air hungry fer grub, don't look fer me to feed you with a spoon."

The outlaws piled inside, made a great bustle and clatter as they sat to their meal. Like hungry men, they talked little.

Duane waited there awhile, then guardedly got up and crept round to the other side of the cabin. After he became used to the dark again he ventured to steal along the wall to the window and peeped in. The outlaws were in the first room and could not be seen.

Duane waited. The moments dragged endlessly. His heart pounded. Longstreth entered, turned up the light, and, taking a box of cigars from the table, he carried it out.

"Here, you fellows, go outside and smoke," he said. "Knell, come on in now. Let's get it over."

He returned, sat down, and lighted a cigar for himself. He put his booted feet on the table.

Duane saw that the room was comfortably, even luxuriously furnished. There must have been a good trail, he thought, else how could all that stuff have been packed in there. Most assuredly it could not have come over the trail he had traveled. Presently he heard the men go outside, and their voices became indistinct. Then Knell came in and seated himself without any of his chief's ease. He seemed preoccupied and, as always, cold.

"What's wrong, Knell? Why didn't you get here sooner?" queried Longstreth.

"Poggin, damn him! We're on the outs again."

"What for?"

"Aw, he needn't have got sore. He's breakin' a new hoss over there at Faraway, an' you know him where a hoss's concerned. That kept him, I reckon, more than anythin'."

"What else? Get it out of your system so we can go on to the new job."

"Well, it begins back a ways. I don't know how long ago—weeks—a stranger rode into Ord an' got down easy-like as if he owned the place. He seemed familiar to me. But I wasn't sure. We looked him over, an' I left, tryin' to place him in my mind."

"What 'd he look like?"

"Rangy, powerful man, white hair over his temples, still, hard face, eyes like knives. The way he packed his guns, the way he walked an' stood an' swung his right hand showed me what he was. You can't fool me on the gun-sharp. An' he had a grand horse, a big black."

"I've met your man," said Longstreth.

"No!" exclaimed Knell. It was wonderful to hear surprise expressed by this man that did not in the least show it in his strange physiognomy. Knell laughed a short, grim, hollow laugh. "Boss, this here big gent drifts into Ord again an' makes up to Jim Fletcher. Jim, you know, is easy led. An' when a posse come along trailin' a blind lead, huntin' the wrong way for the man who held up No. 6, why, Jim—he up an' takes this stranger to be the fly road-agent an' cottons to him. Got money out of him sure. An' that's what stumps me more. What's this man's game? I happen to know, boss, that he couldn't have held up No. 6."

"How do you know?" demanded Longstreth.

"Because I did the job myself."

A dark and stormy passion clouded the chief's face.

"Damn you, Knell! You're incorrigible. You're unreliable. Another break like that you're out with me. Did you tell Poggin?"

"Yes. That's one reason we fell out. He raved. I thought he was goin' to kill me."

"Why did you tackle such a risky job without help or plan?"

"It offered, that's all. An' it was easy. But it was a mistake. I got the country an' the railroad hollerin' for nothin'. I just couldn't help it. You know what idleness means to one of us. You know also that this very life breeds fatality. It's wrong—that's why. I was born of good parents, an' I know what's right. We're wrong, an' we can't beat the end, that's all. An' for my part I don't care a damn when that comes."

"Fine wise talk from you, Knell," said Longstreth, scornfully. "Go on with your story."

"As I said, Jim cottons to the pretender, an' they get chummy. They're together all the time. You can gamble Jim told all he knew an' then some. A little liquor loosens his tongue. Several of the boys rode over from Ord, an' one of them went to Poggin an' says Jim Fletcher has a new man for the gang. Poggin, you know, is always ready for any new man. He says if one doesn't turn out good he can be shut off easy. He rather liked the way this new pard of Jim's was boosted. Jim an' Poggin always hit it up together. So until I got on the deal Jim's pard was already in the gang, without Poggin or you ever seein' him. Then I got to figurin' hard. Just where had I ever seen that chap? As it turned out, I never had seen him, which accounts for my bein' doubtful. I'd never forget any man I'd seen. I dug up a lot of old papers from my kit an' went over them. Letters, pictures, clippin's, an' all that. I guess I had a pretty good notion what I was lookin' for an' who I wanted to make sure of. At last I found it. An' I knew my man. But I didn't spring it on Poggin. Oh no! I want to have some fun with him when the time comes. He'll be wilder than a trapped wolf. I sent Blossom over to Ord to get word from Jim, an' when he verified all this talk I sent Blossom again with a message calculated to make Jim hump. Poggin got sore, said he'd wait for Jim, an' I could come over here to see you about the new job. He'd meet me in Ord."

Knell had spoken hurriedly and low, now and then with passion. His pale eyes glinted like fire in ice, and now his voice fell to a whisper.

"Who do you think Fletcher's new man is?"

"Who?" demanded Longstreth.

"Buck Duane!"

Down came Longstreth's boots with a crash, then his body grew rigid.

"That Nueces outlaw? That two-shot ace-of-spades gun-thrower who killed Bland, Alloway—?"

"An' Hardin." Knell whispered this last name with more feeling than the apparent circumstance demanded.

"Yes; and Hardin, the best one of the Rim Rock fellows—Buck Duane!"

Longstreth was so ghastly white now that his black mustache seemed outlined against chalk. He eyed his grim lieutenant. They understood each other without more words. It was enough that Buck Duane was there in the Big Bend. Longstreth rose presently and reached for a flask, from which he drank, then offered it to Knell. He waved it aside.

"Knell," began the chief, slowly, as he wiped his lips, "I gathered you have some grudge against this Buck Duane."

"Yes."

"Well, don't be a —— fool now and do what Poggin or almost any of you men would—don't meet this Buck Duane. I've reason to believe he's a Texas Ranger now."

"The hell you say!" exclaimed Knell.

"Yes. Go to Ord and give Jim Fletcher a hunch. He'll get Poggin, and they'll fix even Buck Duane."

"All right. I'll do my best. But if I run into Duane—"

"Don't run into him!" Longstreth's voice fairly rang with the force of its passion and command. He wiped his face, drank again from the flask, sat down, resumed his smoking, and, drawing a paper from his vest pocket, he began to study it.

"Well, I'm glad that's settled," he said, evidently referring to the Duane matter. "Now for the new job. This is October the eighteenth. On or before the twenty-fifth there will be a shipment of gold reach the Rancher's Bank of Val Verde. After you return to Ord give Poggin these orders. Keep the gang quiet. You, Poggin, Kane, Fletcher, Panhandle Smith, and Boldt to be in on the secret and the job. Nobody else. You'll leave Ord on the twenty-third, ride across country by the trail till you get within sight of Mercer. It's a hundred miles from Bradford to Val Verde—about the same from Ord. Time your travel to get you near Val Verde on the morning of the twenty-sixth. You won't have to more than trot your horses. At two o'clock in the afternoon, sharp, ride into town and up to the Rancher's Bank. Val Verde's a pretty big town. Never been any holdups there. Town feels safe. Make it a clean, fast, daylight job. That's all. Have you got the details?"

Knell did not even ask for the dates again.

"Suppose Poggin or me might be detained?" he asked.

Longstreth bent a dark glance upon his lieutenant.

"You never can tell what'll come off," continued Knell. "I'll do my best."

"The minute you see Poggin tell him. A job on hand steadies him. And I say again—look to it that nothing happens. Either you or Poggin carry the job through. But I want both of you in it. Break for the hills, and when you get up in the rocks where you can hide your tracks head for Mount Ord. When all's quiet again I'll join you here. That's all. Call in the boys."

Like a swift shadow and as noiseless Duane stole across the level toward the dark wall of rock. Every nerve was a strung wire. For a little while his mind was cluttered and clogged with whirling thoughts, from which, like a flashing scroll, unrolled the long, baffling order of action. The game was now in his hands. He must cross Mount Ord at night. The feat was improbable, but it might be done. He must ride into Bradford, forty miles from the foothills before eight o'clock next morning. He must telegraph MacNelly to be in Val Verde on the twenty-fifth. He must ride back to Ord, to intercept Knell, face him, be denounced, kill him, and while the iron was hot strike hard to win Poggin's half-won interest as he had wholly won Fletcher's. Failing that last, he must let the outlaws alone to bide their time in Ord, to be free to ride on to their new job in Val Verde. In the mean time he must plan to arrest Longstreth. It was a magnificent outline, incredible, alluring, unfathomable in its nameless certainty. He felt like fate. He seemed to be the iron consequences falling upon these doomed outlaws.

Under the wall the shadows were black, only the tips of trees and crags showing, yet he went straight to the trail. It was merely a grayness between borders of black. He climbed and never stopped. It did not seem steep. His feet might have had eyes. He surmounted the wall, and, looking down into the ebony gulf pierced by one point of light, he lifted a menacing arm and shook it. Then he strode on and did not falter till he reached the huge shelving cliffs. Here he lost the trail; there was none; but he remembered the shapes, the points, the notches of rock above. Before he reached the ruins of splintered ramparts and jumbles of broken walls the moon topped the eastern slope of the mountain, and the mystifying blackness he had dreaded changed to magic silver light. It seemed as light as day, only soft, mellow, and the air held a transparent sheen. He ran up the bare ridges and down the smooth slopes, and, like a goat, jumped from rock to rock. In this light he knew his way and lost no time looking for a trail. He crossed the divide and then had all downhill before him. Swiftly he descended, almost always sure of his memory of the landmarks. He did not remember having studied them in the ascent, yet here they were, even in changed light, familiar to his sight. What he had once seen was pictured on his mind. And, true as a deer striking for home, he reached the cañon where he had left his horse.

Bullet was quickly and easily found. Duane threw on the saddle and pack, cinched them tight, and resumed his descent. The worst was now to come. Bare downward steps in rock, sliding, weathered slopes, narrow black gullies, a thousand openings in a maze of broken stone—these Duane had to descend in fast time, leading a giant of a horse. Bullet cracked the loose fragments, sent them rolling, slid on the scaly slopes, plunged down the steps, followed like a faithful dog at Duane's heels.

Hours passed as moments. Duane was equal to his great opportunity. But he could not quell that self in him which reached back over the lapse of lonely, searing years and found the boy in him. He who had been worse than dead was now grasping at the skirts of life—which meant victory, honor, happiness. Duane knew he was not just right in part of his mind. Small wonder that he was not insane, he thought! He tramped on downward, his marvelous faculty for covering rough ground and holding to the true course never before even in flight so keen and acute. Yet all the time a spirit was keeping step with him. Thought of Ray Longstreth as he had left her made him weak. But now, with the game clear to its end, with the trap to spring, with success strangely haunting him, Duane could not dispel memory of her. He saw her white face, with its sweet sad lips and the dark eyes so tender and tragic. And time and distance and risk and toil were nothing.

The moon sloped to the west. Shadows of trees and crags now crossed to the other side of him. The stars dimmed. Then he was out on the rocks, with the dim trail pale at his feet. Mounting Bullet, he made short work of the long slope and the foothills and the rolling land leading down to Ord. The little outlaw camp, with its shacks and cabins and row of houses, lay silent and dark under the paling moon. Duane passed by on the lower trail, headed into the road, and put Bullet to a gallop. He watched the dying moon, the waning stars, and the east. He had time to spare, so he saved the horse. Knell would be leaving the rendezvous about the time Duane turned back toward Ord. Between noon and sunset they would meet.

The night wore on. The moon sank behind low mountains in the west. The stars brightened for a while, then faded. Gray gloom enveloped the world, thickened, lay like smoke over the road. Then shade by shade it lightened, until through the transparent obscurity shone a dim light.

Duane reached Bradford before dawn. He dismounted some distance from the tracks, tied his horse, and then crossed over to the station. He heard the clicking of the telegraph instrument, and it thrilled him. An operator sat inside reading. When Duane tapped on the window he looked up with startled glance, then went swiftly to unlock the door.

"Hello. Give me paper and pencil. Quick," whispered Duane.

With trembling hands the operator complied. Duane wrote out the message he had carefully composed.

"Send this—repeat it to make sure—then keep mum. I'll see you again. Good-by."

The operator stared, but did not speak a word.

Duane left as stealthily and swiftly as he had come. He walked his horse a couple of miles back on the road and then rested him till break of day. The east began to redden, Duane turned grimly in the direction of Ord.

When Duane swung into the wide, grassy square on the outskirts of Ord he saw a bunch of saddled horses hitched in front of the tavern. He knew what that meant. Luck still favored him. If it would only hold! But he could ask no more. The rest was a matter of how greatly he could make his power felt. An open conflict against odds lay in the balance. That would be fatal to him, and to avoid it he had to trust to his name and a presence he must make terrible. He knew outlaws. He knew what qualities held them. He knew what to exaggerate.

There was not an outlaw in sight. The dusty horses had covered distance that morning. As Duane dismounted he heard loud, angry voices inside the tavern. He removed coat and vest, hung them over the pommel. He packed two guns, one belted high on the left hip, the other swinging low on the right side. He neither looked nor listened, but boldly pushed the door and stepped inside.

The big room was full of men, and every face pivoted toward him. Knell's pale face flashed into Duane's swift sight; then Boldt's, then Blossom Kane's, then Panhandle Smith's, then Fletcher's, then others that were familiar, and last that of Poggin. Though Duane had never seen Poggin or heard him described, he knew him. For he saw a face that was a record of great and evil deeds.

There was absolute silence. The outlaws were lined back of a long table upon which were papers, stacks of silver coin, a bundle of bills, and a huge gold-mounted gun.

"Are you gents lookin' for me?" asked Duane. He gave his voice all the ringing force and power of which he was capable. And he stepped back, free of anything, with the outlaws all before him.

Knell stood quivering, but his face might have been a mask. The other outlaws looked from him to Duane. Jim Fletcher flung up his hands.

"My Gawd, Dodge, what'd you bust in here fer?" he said, plaintively, and slowly stepped forward. His action was that of a man true to himself. He meant he had been sponsor for Duane and now he would stand by him.

"Back, Fletcher!" called Duane, and his voice made the outlaw jump.

"Hold on, Dodge, an' you-all, everybody," said Fletcher. "Let me talk, seein' I'm in wrong here."

His persuasions did not ease the strain.

"Go ahead. Talk," said Poggin.

Fletcher turned to Duane. "Pard, I'm takin' it on myself thet you meet enemies here when I swore you'd meet friends. It's my fault. I'll stand by you if you let me."

"No, Jim," replied Duane.

"But what'd you come fer without the signal?" burst out Fletcher, in distress. He saw nothing but catastrophe in this meeting.

"Jim, I ain't pressin' my company none. But when I'm wanted bad—"

Fletcher stopped him with a raised hand. Then he turned to Poggin with a rude dignity.

"Poggy, he's my pard, an' he's riled. I never told him a word thet 'd make him sore. I only said Knell hadn't no more use fer him than fer me. Now, what you say goes in this gang. I never failed you in my life. Here's my pard. I vouch fer him. Will you stand fer me? There's goin' to be hell if you don't. An' us with a big job on hand!"

While Fletcher toiled over his slow, earnest persuasion Duane had his gaze riveted upon Poggin. There was something leonine about Poggin. He was tawny. He blazed. He seemed beautiful as fire was beautiful. But looked at closer, with glance seeing the physical man, instead of that thing which shone from him, he was of perfect build, with muscles that swelled and rippled, bulging his clothes, with the magnificent head and face of the cruel, fierce, tawny-eyed jaguar.

Looking at this strange Poggin, instinctively divining his abnormal and hideous power, Duane had for the first time in his life the inward quaking fear of a man. It was like a cold-tongued bell ringing within him and numbing his heart. The old instinctive firing of blood followed, but did not drive away that fear. He knew. He felt something here deeper than thought could go. And he hated Poggin.

That individual had been considering Fletcher's appeal.

"Jim, I ante up," he said, "an' if Phil doesn't raise us out with a big hand—why, he'll get called, an' your pard can set in the game."

Every eye shifted to Knell. He was dead white. He laughed, and any one hearing that laugh would have realized his intense anger equally with an assurance which made him master of the situation.

"Poggin, you're a gambler, you are—the ace-high, straight-flush hand of the Big Bend," he said, with stinging scorn. "I'll bet you my roll to a Mexican peso that I can deal you a hand you'll be afraid to play."

"Phil, you're talkin' wild," growled Poggin, with both advice and menace in his tone.

"If there's anythin' you hate it's a man who pretends to be somebody else when he's not. Thet so?"

Poggin nodded in slow-gathering wrath.

"Well, Jim's new pard—this man Dodge—he's not who he seems. Oh-ho! He's a hell of a lot different. But *I* know him. An' when I spring his name on you, Poggin, you'll freeze to your gizzard. Do you get me? You'll freeze, an' your hand'll be stiff when it ought to be lightnin'—all because you'll realize you've been standin' there five minutes—five minutes *alive* before him!"

If not hate, then assuredly great passion toward Poggin manifested itself in Knell's scornful, fiery address, in the shaking hand he thrust before Poggin's face. In the ensuing silent pause Knell's panting could be plainly heard. The other men were pale, watchful, cautiously edging either way to the wall, leaving the principals and Duane in the center of the room.

"Spring his name, then, you—" said Poggin, violently, with a curse.

Strangely Knell did not even look at the man he was about to denounce. He leaned toward Poggin, his hands, his body, his long head all somewhat expressive of what his face disguised.

"Buck Duane!" he yelled, suddenly.

The name did not make any great difference in Poggin. But Knell's passionate, swift utterance carried the suggestion that the name ought to bring Poggin to quick action. It was possible, too, that Knell's manner, the import of his denunciation, the meaning back of all his passion held Poggin bound more than the surprise. For the outlaw certainly was surprised, perhaps staggered at the idea that he, Poggin, had been about to stand sponsor with Fletcher for a famous outlaw hated and feared by all outlaws.

Knell waited a long moment, and then his face broke its cold immobility in an extraordinary expression of devilish glee. He had hounded the great Poggin into something that gave him vicious, monstrous joy.

"BUCK DUANE! Yes," he broke out, hotly. "The Nueces gunman! That two-shot, ace-of-spades lone wolf! You an' I—we've heard a thousand times of him—talked about him often. An' here he is *in front* of you! Poggin, you were backin' Fletcher's new pard, Buck Duane. An' he'd fooled you both but for me. But *I* know him. An' I know why he drifted in here. To flash a gun on Cheseldine—on you—on me! Bah! Don't tell me he wanted to join the gang. You know a gunman, for you're one yourself. Don't you always want to kill another man? An' don't you always want to meet a real man, not a four-flush? It's the madness of the gunman, an' I know it. Well, Duane faced you—called you! An' when I sprung his name, what ought you have done? What would the boss—anybody—have expected of Poggin? Did you throw your gun, swift, like you have so often? Naw; you froze. An' why? Because here's a man with the kind of nerve you'd love to have. Because he's great—meetin' us here alone. Because you know he's a wonder with a gun an' you love life. Because you an' I an' every damned man here had to take his front, each to himself. If we all drew we'd kill him. Sure! But who's goin' to lead? Who was goin' to be first? Who was goin' to make him draw? Not you, Poggin! You leave that for a lesser man—me—who've lived to see you a coward. It comes once to every gunman. You've met your match in Buck Duane. An', by God, I'm glad! Here's once I show you up!"

The hoarse, taunting voice failed. Knell stepped back from the comrade he hated. He was wet, shaking, haggard, but magnificent.

"Buck Duane, do you remember Hardin?" he asked, in scarcely audible voice.

"Yes," replied Duane, and a flash of insight made clear Knell's attitude.

"You met him—forced him to draw—killed him?"

"Yes."

"Hardin was the best pard I ever had."

His teeth clicked together tight, and his lips set in a thin line.

The room grew still. Even breathing ceased. The time for words had passed. In that long moment of suspense Knell's body gradually stiffened, and at last the quivering ceased. He crouched. His eyes had a soul-piercing fire.

Duane watched them. He waited. He caught the thought—the breaking of Knell's muscle-bound rigidity. Then he drew.

Through the smoke of his gun he saw two red spurts of flame. Knell's bullets thudded into the ceiling. He fell with a scream like a wild thing in agony.

Duane did not see Knell die. He watched Poggin. And Poggin, like a stricken and astounded man, looked down upon his prostrate comrade.

Fletcher ran at Duane with hands aloft.

"Hit the trail, you liar, or you'll hev to kill me!" he yelled.

With hands still up, he shouldered and bodied Duane out of the room.

Duane leaped on his horse, spurred, and plunged away.

CHAPTER 23

Duane returned to Fairdale and camped in the mesquite till the twenty-third of the month. The few days seemed endless. All he could think of was that the hour in which he must disgrace Ray Longstreth was slowly but inexorably coming. In that waiting time he learned what love was and also duty. When the day at last dawned he rode like one possessed down the rough slope, hurdling the stones and crashing through the brush, with a sound in his ears that was not all the rush of the wind. Something dragged at him.

Apparently one side of his mind was unalterably fixed, while the other was a hurrying conglomeration of flashes of thought, reception of sensations. He could not get calmness. By and by, almost involuntarily, he hurried faster on. Action seemed to make his state less oppressive; it eased the weight. But the farther he went on the harder it was to continue. Had he turned his back upon love, happiness, perhaps on life itself?

There seemed no use to go on farther until he was absolutely sure of himself. Duane received a clear warning thought that such work as seemed haunting and driving him could never be carried out in the mood under which he labored. He hung on to that thought. Several times he slowed up, then stopped, only to go on again. At length, as he mounted a low ridge, Fairdale lay bright and green before him not far away, and the sight was a conclusive check. There were mesquites on the ridge, and Duane sought the shade beneath them. It was the noon-hour, with hot, glary sun and no wind. Here Duane had to have out his fight. Duane was utterly unlike himself; he could not bring the old self back; he was not the same man he once had been. But he could understand why. It was because of Ray Longstreth. Temptation assailed him. To have her his wife! It was impossible. The thought was insidiously alluring. Duane pictured a home. He saw himself riding through the cotton and rice and cane, home to a stately old mansion, where long-eared hounds bayed him welcome, and a woman looked for him and met him with happy and beautiful smile. There might—there would be children. And something new, strange, confounding with its emotion, came to life deep in Duane's heart. There would be children! Ray their mother! The kind of life a lonely outcast always yearned for and never had! He saw it all, felt it all.

But beyond and above all other claims came Captain MacNelly's. It was then there was something cold and death-like in Duane's soul. For he knew, whatever happened, of one thing he was sure—he would have to kill either Longstreth or Lawson. Longstreth might be trapped into arrest; but Lawson had no sense, no control, no fear. He would snarl like a panther and go for his gun, and he would have to be killed. This, of all consummations, was the one to be calculated upon.

Duane came out of it all bitter and callous and sore—in the most fitting of moods to undertake a difficult and deadly enterprise. He had fallen upon his old strange, futile dreams, now rendered poignant by reason of love. He drove away those dreams. In their places came the images of the olive-skinned Longstreth with his sharp eyes, and the dark, evil-faced Lawson, and then returned tenfold more thrilling and sinister the old strange passion to meet Poggin.

It was about one o'clock when Duane rode into Fairdale. The streets for the most part were deserted. He went directly to find Morton and Zimmer. He found them at length, restless, somber, anxious, but unaware of the part he had played at Ord. They said Longstreth was home, too. It was possible that Longstreth had arrived home in ignorance.

Duane told them to be on hand in town with their men in case he might need them, and then with teeth locked he set off for Longstreth's ranch.

Duane stole through the bushes and trees, and when nearing the porch he heard loud, angry, familiar voices. Longstreth and Lawson were quarreling again. How Duane's lucky star guided him! He had no plan of action, but his brain was equal to a hundred lightning-swift evolutions. He meant to take any risk rather than kill Longstreth. Both of the men were out on the porch. Duane wormed his way to the edge of the shrubbery and crouched low to watch for his opportunity.

Longstreth looked haggard and thin. He was in his shirt-sleeves, and he had come out with a gun in his hand. This he laid on a table near the wall. He wore no belt.

Lawson was red, bloated, thick-lipped, all fiery and sweaty from drink, though sober on the moment, and he had the expression of a desperate man in his last stand. It was his last stand, though he was ignorant of that.

"What's your news? You needn't be afraid of my feelings," said Lawson.

"Ray confessed to an interest in this ranger," replied Longstreth.

Duane thought Lawson would choke. He was thick-necked anyway, and the rush of blood made him tear at the soft collar of his shirt. Duane awaited his chance, patient, cold, all his feelings shut in a vise.

"But *why* should your daughter meet this ranger?" demanded Lawson, harshly.

"She's in love with him, and he's in love with her."

Duane reveled in Lawson's condition. The statement might have had the force of a juggernaut. Was Longstreth sincere? What was his game?

Lawson, finding his voice, cursed Ray, cursed the ranger, then Longstreth.

"You damned selfish fool!" cried Longstreth, in deep bitter scorn. "All you think of is yourself—your loss of the girl. Think once of *me*—my home—my life!"

Then the connection subtly put out by Longstreth apparently dawned upon the other. Somehow through this girl her father and cousin were to be betrayed. Duane got that impression, though he could not tell how true it was. Certainly Lawson's jealousy was his paramount emotion.

"To hell with you!" burst out Lawson, incoherently. He was frenzied. "I'll have her, or nobody else will!"

"You never will," returned Longstreth, stridently. "So help me God I'd rather see her the ranger's wife than yours!"

While Lawson absorbed that shock Longstreth leaned toward him, all of hate and menace in his mien.

"Lawson, you made me what I am," continued Longstreth. "I backed you—shielded you. *You're* Cheseldine—if the truth is told! Now it's ended. I quit you. I'm done!"

Their gray passion-corded faces were still as stones.

"*Gentlemen!*" Duane called in far-reaching voice as he stepped out. "*You're both done!*"

They wheeled to confront Duane.

"Don't move! Not a muscle! Not a finger!" he warned.

Longstreth read what Lawson had not the mind to read. His face turned from gray to ashen.

"What d'ye mean?" yelled Lawson, fiercely, shrilly. It was not in him to obey a command, to see impending death.

All quivering and strung, yet with perfect control, Duane raised his left hand to turn back a lapel of his open vest. The silver star flashed brightly.

Lawson howled like a dog. With barbarous and insane fury, with sheer impotent folly, he swept a clawing hand for his gun. Duane's shot broke his action.

Before Lawson even tottered, before he loosed the gun, Longstreth leaped behind him, clasped him with left arm, quick as lightning jerked the gun from both clutching fingers and sheath. Longstreth protected himself with the body of the dead man. Duane saw red flashes, puffs of smoke; he heard quick reports. Something stung his left arm. Then a blow like wind, light of sound yet shocking in impact, struck him, staggered him. The hot rend of lead followed the blow. Duane's heart seemed to explode, yet his mind kept extraordinarily clear and rapid.

Duane heard Longstreth work the action of Lawson's gun. He heard the hammer click, fall upon empty shells. Longstreth had used up all the loads in Lawson's gun. He cursed as a man cursed at defeat. Duane waited, cool and sure now. Longstreth tried to lift the dead man, to edge him closer toward the table where his own gun lay. But, considering the peril of exposing himself, he found the task beyond him. He bent peering at Duane under Lawson's arm, which flopped out from his side. Longstreth's eyes were the eyes of a man who meant to kill. There was never any mistaking the strange and terrible light of eyes like those. More than once Duane had a chance to aim at them, at the top of Longstreth's head, at a strip of his side.

Longstreth flung Lawson's body off. But even as it dropped, before Longstreth could leap, as he surely intended, for the gun, Duane covered him, called piercingly to him:

"Don't jump for the gun! Don't! I'll kill you! Sure as God I'll kill you!"

Longstreth stood perhaps ten feet from the table where his gun lay. Duane saw him calculating chances. He was game. He had the courage that forced Duane to respect him. Duane just saw him measure the distance to that gun. He was magnificent. He meant to do it. Duane would have to kill him.

"Longstreth, listen," cried Duane, swiftly. "The game's up. You're done. But think of your daughter! I'll spare your life—I'll try to get you freedom on one condition. For her sake! I've got you nailed—all the proofs. There lies Lawson. You're alone. I've Morton and men to my aid. Give up. Surrender. Consent to demands, and I'll spare you. Maybe I can persuade MacNelly to let you go free back to your old country. It's for Ray's sake! Her life, perhaps her happiness, can be saved! Hurry, man! Your answer!"

"Suppose I refuse?" he queried, with a dark and terrible earnestness.

"Then I'll kill you in your tracks! You can't move a hand! Your word or death! Hurry, Longstreth! Be a man! For her sake! Quick! Another second now—I'll kill you!"

"All right, Buck Duane, I give my word," he said, and deliberately walked to the chair and fell into it.

Longstreth looked strangely at the bloody blot on Duane's shoulder.

"There come the girls!" he suddenly exclaimed. "Can you help me drag Lawson inside? They mustn't see him."

Duane was facing down the porch toward the court and corrals. Miss Longstreth and Ruth had come in sight, were swiftly approaching, evidently alarmed. The two men succeeded in drawing Lawson into the house before the girls saw him.

"Duane, you're not hard hit?" said Longstreth.

"Reckon not," replied Duane.

"I'm sorry. If only you could have told me sooner! Lawson, damn him! Always I've split over him!"

"But the last time, Longstreth."

"Yes, and I came near driving you to kill me, too. Duane, you talked me out of it. For Ray's sake! She'll be in here in a minute. This'll be harder than facing a gun."

"Hard now. But I hope it'll turn out all right."

"Duane, will you do me a favor?" he asked, and he seemed shame-faced.

"Sure."

"Let Ray and Ruth think Lawson shot you. He's dead. It can't matter. Duane, the old side of my life is coming back. It's been coming. It'll be here just about when she enters this room. And, by God, I'd change places with Lawson if I could!"

"Glad you—said that, Longstreth," replied Duane. "And sure—Lawson plugged me. It's our secret."

Just then Ray and Ruth entered the room. Duane heard two low cries, so different in tone, and he saw two white faces. Ray came to his side. She lifted a shaking hand to point at the blood upon his breast. White and mute, she gazed from that to her father.

"Papa!" cried Ray, wringing her hands.

"Don't give way," he replied, huskily. "Both you girls will need your nerve. Duane isn't badly hurt. But Floyd is—is dead. Listen. Let me tell it quick. There's been a fight. It—it was Lawson—it was Lawson's gun that shot Duane. Duane let me off. In fact, Ray, he saved me. I'm to divide my property—return so far as possible what I've stolen—leave Texas at once with Duane, under arrest. He says maybe he can get MacNelly, the ranger captain, to let me go. For your sake!"

She stood there, realizing her deliverance, with the dark and tragic glory of her eyes passing from her father to Duane.

"You must rise above this," said Duane to her. "I expected this to ruin you. But your father is alive. He will live it down. I'm sure I can promise you he'll be free. Perhaps back there in Louisiana the dishonor will never be known. This country is far from your old home. And even in San Antonio and Austin a man's evil repute means little. Then the line between a rustler and a rancher is hard to draw in these wild border days. Rustling is stealing cattle, and I once heard a well-known rancher say that all rich cattlemen had done a little stealing. Your father drifted out here, and, like a good many others, he succeeded. It's perhaps just as well not to split hairs, to judge him by the law and morality of a civilized country. Some way or other he drifted in with bad men. Maybe a deal that was honest somehow tied his hands. This matter of land, water, a few stray head of stock had to be decided out of court. I'm sure in his case he never realized where he was drifting. Then one thing led to another, until he was face to face with dealing that took on crooked form. To protect himself he bound men to him. And so the gang developed. Many powerful gangs have developed that way out here. He could not control them. He became involved with them. And eventually their dealings became deliberately and boldly dishonest. That meant the inevitable spilling of blood sooner or later, and so he grew into the leader because he was the strongest. Whatever he is to be judged for, I think he could have been infinitely worse."

CHAPTER 24

O n the morning of the twenty-sixth Duane rode into Bradford in time to catch the early train. His wounds did not seriously incapacitate him. Longstreth was with him. And Miss Longstreth and Ruth Herbert would not be left behind. They were all leaving Fairdale for ever. Longstreth had turned over the whole of his property to Morton, who was to divide it as he and his comrades believed just. Duane had left Fairdale with his party by night, passed through Sanderson in the early hours of dawn, and reached Bradford as he had planned.

That fateful morning found Duane outwardly calm, but inwardly he was in a tumult. He wanted to rush to Val Verde. Would Captain Mac-Nelly be there with his rangers, as Duane had planned for them to be? Memory of that tawny Poggin returned with strange passion. Duane had borne hours and weeks and months of waiting, had endured the long hours of the outlaw, but now he had no patience. The whistle of the train made him leap.

It was a fast train, yet the ride seemed slow.

Duane, disliking to face Longstreth and the passengers in the car, changed his seat to one behind his prisoner. They had seldom spoken. Longstreth sat with bowed head, deep in thought. The girls sat in a seat near by and were pale but composed. Occasionally the train halted briefly at a station. The latter half of that ride Duane had observed a wagon-road running parallel with the railroad, sometimes right alongside, at others near or far away. When the train was about twenty miles from Val Verde Duane espied a dark group of horsemen trotting eastward. His blood beat like a hammer at his temples. The gang! He thought he recognized the tawny Poggin and felt a strange inward contraction. He thought he recognized the clean-cut Blossom Kane, the black-bearded giant Boldt, the red-faced Panhandle Smith, and Fletcher. There was another man strange to him. Was that Knell? No! it could not have been Knell.

Duane leaned over the seat and touched Longstreth on the shoulder.

"Look!" he whispered. Cheseldine was stiff. He had already seen.

The train flashed by; the outlaw gang receded out of range of sight.

"Did you notice Knell wasn't with them?" whispered Duane.

Duane did not speak to Longstreth again till the train stopped at Val Verde.

They got off the car, and the girls followed as naturally as ordinary travelers. The station was a good deal larger than that at Bradford, and there was considerable action and bustle incident to the arrival of the train.

Duane's sweeping gaze searched faces, rested upon a man who seemed familiar. This fellow's look, too, was that of one who knew Duane, but was waiting for a sign, a cue. Then Duane recognized him— MacNelly, clean-shaven. Without mustache he appeared different, younger.

When MacNelly saw that Duane intended to greet him, to meet him, he hurried forward. A keen light flashed from his eyes. He was glad, eager, yet suppressing himself, and the glances he sent back and forth from Duane to Longstreth were questioning, doubtful. Certainly Longstreth did not look the part of an outlaw.

"Duane! Lord, I'm glad to see you," was the Captain's greeting. Then at closer look into Duane's face his warmth fled—something he saw there checked his enthusiasm, or at least its utterance.

"MacNelly, shake hands with Cheseldine," said Duane, low-voiced.

The ranger captain stood dumb, motionless. But he saw Longstreth's instant action, and awkwardly he reached for the outstretched hand.

"Any of your men down here?" queried Duane, sharply.

"No. They're up-town."

"Come. MacNelly, you walk with him. We've ladies in the party. I'll come behind with them."

They set off up-town. Longstreth walked as if he were with friends on the way to dinner. The girls were mute. MacNelly walked like a man in a trance. There was not a word spoken in four blocks.

Presently Duane espied a stone building on a corner of the broad street. There was a big sign, "Rancher's Bank."

"There's the hotel," said MacNelly. "Some of my men are there. We've scattered around."

They crossed the street, went through office and lobby, and then Duane asked MacNelly to take them to a private room. Without a word the Captain complied. When they were all inside Duane closed the door, and, drawing a deep breath as if of relief, he faced them calmly.

"Miss Longstreth, you and Miss Ruth try to make yourselves comfortable now," he said. "And don't be distressed." Then he turned to his captain. "MacNelly, this girl is the daughter of the man I've brought to you, and this one is his niece."

Then Duane briefly related Longstreth's story, and, though he did not spare the rustler chief, he was generous.

"When I went after Longstreth," concluded Duane, "it was either to kill him or offer him freedom on conditions. So I chose the latter for his daughter's sake. He has already disposed of all his property. I believe he'll live up to the conditions. He's to leave Texas never to return. The name Cheseldine has been a mystery, and now it'll fade."

A few moments later Duane followed MacNelly to a large room, like a hall, and here were men reading and smoking. Duane knew them—rangers!

MacNelly beckoned to his men.

"Boys, here he is."

"How many men have you?" asked Duane.

"Fifteen."

MacNelly almost embraced Duane, would probably have done so but for the dark grimness that seemed to be coming over the man. Instead he glowed, he sputtered, he tried to talk, to wave his hands. He was beside himself. And his rangers crowded closer, eager, like hounds ready to run.

They all talked at once, and the word most significant and frequent in their speech was "outlaws."

MacNelly clapped his fist in his hand.

"This'll make the Adjutant sick with joy. Maybe we won't have it on the Governor! We'll show them about the ranger service. Duane! how'd you ever do it?"

"Now, Captain, not the half nor the quarter of this job's done. The gang's coming down the road. I saw them from the train. They'll ride into town on the dot—two-thirty."

"How many?" asked MacNelly.

"Poggin, Blossom Kane, Panhandle Smith, Boldt, Jim Fletcher, and another man I don't know. These are the picked men of Cheseldine's gang. I'll bet they'll be the fastest, hardest bunch you rangers ever faced."

"Poggin—that's the hard nut to crack! I've heard their records since I've been in Val Verde. Where's Knell? They say he's a boy, but hell and blazes!"

"Knell's dead."

"Ah!" exclaimed MacNelly, softly. Then he grew business-like, cool, and of harder aspect. "Duane, it's your game to-day. I'm only a ranger under orders. We're all under your orders. We've absolute faith in you. Make your plan quick, so I can go around and post the boys who're not here."

"You understand there's no sense in trying to arrest Poggin, Kane, and that lot?" queried Duane.

"No, I don't understand that," replied MacNelly, bluntly.

"It can't be done. The drop can't be got on such men. If you meet them they shoot, and mighty quick and straight. Poggin! That outlaw has no equal with a gun—unless— He's got to be killed quick. They'll all have to be killed. They're all bad, desperate, know no fear, are lightning in action."

"Very well, Duane; then it's a fight. That'll be easier, perhaps. The boys are spoiling for a fight. Out with your plan, now."

"Put one man at each end of this street, just at the edge of town. Let him hide there with a rifle to block the escape of any outlaw that we might fail to get. I had a good look at the bank building. It's well situated for our purpose. Put four men up in that room over the bank—four men, two at each open window. Let them hide till the game begins. They want to be there so in case these foxy outlaws get wise before they're down on the ground or inside the bank. The rest of your men put inside behind the counters, where they'll hide. Now go over to the bank, spring the thing on the bank officials, and don't let them shut up the bank. You want their aid. Let them make sure of their gold. But the clerks and cashier ought to be at their desks or window when Poggin rides up. He'll glance in before he gets down. They make no mistakes, these fellows. We must be slicker than they are, or lose. When you get the bank people wise, send your men over one by one. No hurry, no excitement, no unusual thing to attract notice in the bank."

"All right. That's great. Tell me, where do you intend to wait?"

Duane heard MacNelly's question, and it struck him peculiarly. He had seemed to be planning and speaking mechanically. As he was confronted by the fact it non-plussed him somewhat, and he became thoughtful, with lowered head.

"Where'll you wait, Duane?" insisted MacNelly, with keen eyes speculating.

"I'll wait in front—just inside the door," replied Duane, with an effort.

"Why?" demanded the Captain.

"Well," began Duane, slowly, "Poggin will get down first and start in. But the others won't be far behind. They'll not get swift till inside. The thing is—they *mustn't* get clear inside, because the instant they do they'll pull guns. That means death to somebody. If we can we want to stop them just at the door."

"But will you hide?" asked MacNelly.

"Hide!" The idea had not occurred to Duane.

"There's a wide-open doorway, a sort of round hall, a vestibule, with steps leading up to the bank. There's a door in the vestibule, too. It leads somewhere. We can put men in there. You can be there."

Duane was silent.

"See here, Duane," began MacNelly, nervously. "You sha'n't take any undue risk here. You'll hide with the rest of us?"

"No!" The word was wrenched from Duane.

MacNelly stared, and then a strange, comprehending light seemed to flit over his face.

"Duane, I can give you no orders to-day," he said, distinctly. "I'm only offering advice. Need you take any more risks? You've done a grand job for the service—already. You've paid me a thousand times for that pardon. You've redeemed yourself. The Governor, the Adjutant-General—the whole state will rise up and honor you. The game's almost up. We'll kill these outlaws, or enough of them to break for ever their power. I say, as a ranger, need you take more risk than your captain?"

Still Duane remained silent. He was locked between two forces. And one, a tide that was bursting at its bounds, seemed about to overwhelm him. Finally that side of him, the retreating self, the weaker, found a voice.

"Captain, you want this job to be sure?" he asked.

"Certainly."

"I've told you the way. I alone know the kind of men to be met. Just *what* I'll do or *where* I'll be I can't say yet. In meetings like this the moment decides. But I'll be there!"

MacNelly spread wide his hands, looked helplessly at his curious and sympathetic rangers, and shook his head.

"Now you've done your work—laid the trap—is this strange move of yours going to be fair to Miss Longstreth?" asked MacNelly, in significant low voice.

Like a great tree chopped at the roots Duane vibrated to that. He looked up as if he had seen a ghost.

Mercilessly the ranger captain went on: "You can win her, Duane! Oh, you can't fool me. I was wise in a minute. Fight with us from cover—then go back to her. You will have served the Texas Rangers as no other man has. I'll accept your resignation. You'll be free, honored, happy. That girl loves you! I saw it in her eyes. She's—"

But Duane cut him short with a fierce gesture. He lunged up to his feet, and the rangers fell back. Dark, silent, grim as he had been, still there was a transformation singularly more sinister, stranger.

"Enough. I'm done," he said, somberly. "I've planned. Do we agree—or shall I meet Poggin and his gang alone?"

MacNelly cursed and again threw up his hands, this time in baffled chagrin. There was deep regret in his dark eyes as they rested upon Duane.

Duane was left alone.

Never had his mind been so quick, so clear, so wonderful in its understanding of what had heretofore been intricate and elusive impulses of his strange nature. His determination was to meet Poggin; meet him before any one else had a chance—Poggin first—and then the others! He was as unalterable in that decision as if on the instant of its acceptance he had become stone.

Why? Then came realization. He was not a ranger now. He cared nothing for the state. He had no thought of freeing the community of a dangerous outlaw, of ridding the country of an obstacle to its progress and prosperity. He wanted to kill Poggin. It was significant now that he forgot the other outlaws. He was the gunman, the gun-thrower, the gun-fighter, passionate and terrible. His father's blood, that dark and fierce strain, his mother's spirit, that strong and unquenchable spirit of the surviving pioneer—these had been in him; and the killings, one after another, the wild and haunted years, had made him, absolutely in spite of his will, the gunman. He realized it now, bitterly, hopelessly. The thing he had intelligence enough to hate he had become. At last he shuddered under the driving, ruthless, inhuman blood-lust of the gunman. Long ago he had seemed to seal in a tomb that horror of his kind—the need, in order to forget the haunting, sleepless presence of his last victim, to go out and kill another. But it was still there in his mind, and now it stalked out, worse, more powerful, magnified by its rest, augmented by the violent passions peculiar and inevitable to that strange, wild product of the Texas frontier—the gun-fighter. And those passions were so violent, so raw, so base, so much lower than what ought to have existed in a thinking man. Actual pride of his record! Actual vanity in his speed with a gun! Actual jealousy of any rival!

Duane could not believe it. But there he was, without a choice. What he had feared for years had become a monstrous reality. Respect for himself, blindness, a certain honor that he had clung to while in outlawry—all, like scales, seemed to fall away from him. He stood stripped bare, his soul naked—the soul of Cain. Always since the first brand had been forced and burned upon him he had been ruined. But now with conscience flayed to the quick, yet utterly powerless over this tiger instinct, he was lost. He said it. He admitted it. And at the utter abasement the soul he despised suddenly leaped and quivered with the thought of Ray Longstreth.

Then came agony. As he could not govern all the chances of this fatal meeting—as all his swift and deadly genius must be occupied with Poggin, perhaps in vain—as hard-shooting men whom he could not watch would be close behind, this almost certainly must be the end of Buck Duane. That did not matter. But he loved the girl. He wanted her. All her sweetness, her fire, and pleading returned to torture him.

At that moment the door opened, and Ray Longstreth entered.

"Duane," she said, softly. "Captain MacNelly sent me to you."

"But you shouldn't have come," replied Duane.

"As soon as he told me I would have come whether he wished it or not. You left me—all of us—stunned. I had no time to thank you. Oh, I do—with all my soul. It was noble of you. Father is overcome. He didn't expect so much. And he'll be true. But, Duane, I was told to hurry, and here I'm selfishly using time."

"Go, then—and leave me. You mustn't unnerve me now, when there's a desperate game to finish."

"Need it be desperate?" she whispered, coming close to him.

"Yes; it can't be else."

MacNelly had sent her to weaken him; of that Duane was sure. And he felt that she had wanted to come. Her eyes were dark, strained, beautiful, and they shed a light upon Duane he had never seen before.

"You're going to take some mad risk," she said. "Let me persuade you not to. You said—you cared for me—and I—oh, Duane—don't you— know—?"

The low voice, deep, sweet as an old chord, faltered and broke and failed.

Duane sustained a sudden shock and an instant of paralyzed confusion of thought.

She moved, she swept out her hands, and the wonder of her eyes dimmed in a flood of tears.

"My God! You can't care for me?" he cried, hoarsely.

Then she met him, hands outstretched.

"But I do—I do!"

Swift as light Duane caught her and held her to his breast. He stood holding her tight, with the feel of her warm, throbbing breast and the clasp of her arms as flesh and blood realities to fight a terrible fear. He felt her, and for the moment the might of it was stronger than all the demons that possessed him. And he held her as if she had been his soul, his strength on earth, his hope of Heaven, against his lips.

The strife of doubt all passed. He found his sight again. And there rushed over him a tide of emotion unutterably sweet and full, strong like an intoxicating wine, deep as his nature, something glorious and terrible as the blaze of the sun to one long in darkness. He had become an outcast, a wanderer, a gunman, a victim of circumstances; he had lost and suffered worse than death in that loss; he had gone down the endless bloody trail, a killer of men, a fugitive whose mind slowly and inevitably closed to all except the instinct to survive and a black despair; and now, with this woman in his arms, her swelling breast against his, in this moment almost of resurrection, he bent under the storm of passion and joy possible only to him who had endured so much.

"Do you care—a little?" he whispered, unsteadily.

He bent over her, looking deep into the dark wet eyes.

She uttered a low laugh that was half sob, and her arms slipped up to his neck.

"A little! Oh, Duane—Duane—a great deal!"

Their lips met in their first kiss. The sweetness, the fire of her mouth seemed so new, so strange, so irresistible to Duane. His sore and hungry heart throbbed with thick and heavy beats. He felt the outcast's need of love. And he gave up to the enthralling moment. She met him half-way, returned kiss for kiss, clasp for clasp, her face scarlet, her eyes closed, till, her passion and strength spent, she fell back upon his shoulder.

Duane suddenly thought she was going to faint. He divined then that she had understood him, would have denied him nothing, not even her life, in that moment. But she was overcome, and he suffered a pang of regret at his unrestraint.

Presently she recovered, and she drew only the closer, and leaned upon him with her face upturned. He felt her hands on his, and they were soft, clinging, strong, like steel under velvet. He felt the rise and fall, the warmth of her breast. A tremor ran over him. He tried to draw back, and if he succeeded a little her form swayed with him, pressing closer. She held her face up, and he was compelled to look. It was wonderful now: white, yet glowing, with the red lips parted, and dark eyes alluring. But that was not all. There was passion, unquenchable spirit, woman's resolve deep and mighty.

"I love you, Duane!" she said. "For my sake don't go out to meet this outlaw face to face. It's something wild in you. Conquer it if you love me."

Duane became suddenly weak, and when he did take her into his arms again he scarcely had strength to lift her to a seat beside him. She seemed more than a dead weight. Her calmness had fled. She was throbbing, palpitating, quivering, with hot wet cheeks and arms that clung to him like vines. She lifted her mouth to him, whispering, "Kiss me!" She meant to change him, hold him.

Duane bent down, and her arms went round his neck and drew him close. With his lips on hers he seemed to float away. That kiss closed his eyes, and he could not lift his head. He sat motionless, holding her, blind and helpless, wrapped in a sweet dark glory. She kissed him—one long endless kiss—or else a thousand times. Her lips, her wet cheeks, her hair, the softness, the fragrance of her, the tender clasp of her arms, the swell of her breast—all these seemed to inclose him.

Duane could not put her from him. He yielded to her lips and arms, watching her, involuntarily returning her caresses, sure now of her intent, fascinated by the sweetness of her, bewildered, almost lost. This was what it was to be loved by a woman. His years of outlawry had blotted out any boyish love he might have known. This was what he had to give up—all this wonder of her sweet person, this strange fire he feared yet loved, this mate his deep and tortured soul recognized. Never until that moment had he divined the meaning of a woman to a man. That meaning was physical inasmuch that he learned what beauty was, what marvel in the touch of quickening flesh; and it was spiritual in that he saw there might have been for him, under happier circumstances, a life of noble deeds lived for such a woman.

"Don't go! Don't go!" she cried, as he started violently.

"I must. Dear, good-by. Remember I loved you!"

He pulled her hands loose from his, stepped back.

"Ray, dearest—I believe—I'll come back!" he whispered.

These last words were falsehood.

He reached the door, gave her one last piercing glance, to fix for ever in memory that white face with its dark, staring, tragic eyes.

"Duane!"

He fled with that moan like thunder, death, hell in his ears.

To forget her, to get back his nerve, he forced into mind the image of Poggin—Poggin, the tawny-haired, the yellow-eyed, like a jaguar, with his rippling muscles. He brought back his sense of the outlaw's wonderful presence, his own unaccountable fear and hate. Yes, Poggin had sent the cold sickness of fear to his marrow. Why, since he hated life so? Poggin was his supreme test. And this abnormal and stupendous instinct, now deep as the very foundation of his life, demanded its wild and fatal issue. There was a horrible thrill in his sudden remembrance that Poggin likewise had been taunted in fear of him.

So the dark tide overwhelmed Duane, and when he left the room he was fierce, implacable, steeled to any outcome, quick like a panther, somber as death, in the thrall of his strange passion.

There was no excitement in the street. He crossed to the bank corner. A clock inside pointed the hour of two. He went through the door into the vestibule, looked around, passed up the steps into the bank. The clerks were at their desks, apparently busy. But they showed nervousness. The cashier paled at sight of Duane. There were men—the rangers—crouching down behind the low partition. All the windows had been removed from the iron grating before the desks. The safe was closed. There was no money in sight. A customer came in, spoke to the cashier, and was told to come to-morrow.

Duane returned to the door. He could see far down the street, out into the country. There he waited, and minutes were eternities. He saw no person near him; he heard no sound. He was insulated in his unnatural strain.

At a few minutes before half past two a dark, compact body of horsemen appeared far down, turning into the road. They came at a sharp trot—a group that would have attracted attention anywhere at any time. They came a little faster as they entered town; then faster still; now they were four blocks away, now three, now two. Duane backed down the middle of the vestibule, up the steps, and halted in the center of the wide doorway.

There seemed to be a rushing in his ears through which pierced sharp, ringing clip-clop of iron hoofs. He could see only the corner of the street. But suddenly into that shot lean-limbed dusty bay horses. There was a clattering of nervous hoofs pulled to a halt.

Duane saw the tawny Poggin speak to his companions. He dismounted quickly. They followed suit. They had the manner of ranchers about to conduct some business. No guns showed. Poggin started leisurely for the bank door, quickening step a little. The others, close together, came behind him. Blossom Kane had a bag in his left hand. Jim Fletcher was left at the curb, and he had already gathered up the bridles.

Poggin entered the vestibule first, with Kane on one side, Boldt on the other, a little in his rear.

As he strode in he saw Duane.

"*Hell's Fire!*" he cried.

Something inside Duane burst, piercing all of him with cold. Was it that fear?

"BUCK DUANE!" echoed Kane.

One instant Poggin looked up and Duane looked down.

Like a striking jaguar Poggin moved. Almost as quickly Duane threw his arm.

The guns boomed almost together.

Duane felt a blow just before he pulled trigger. His thoughts came fast, like the strange dots before his eyes. His rising gun had loosened in his hand. Poggin had drawn quicker! A tearing agony encompassed his breast. He pulled—pulled—at random. Thunder of booming shots all about him! Red flashes, jets of smoke, shrill yells! He was sinking. The end; yes, the end! With fading sight he saw Kane go down, then Boldt. But supreme torture, bitterer than death, Poggin stood, mane like a lion's, back to the wall, bloody-faced, grand, with his guns spouting red!

All faded, darkened. The thunder deadened. Duane fell, seemed floating. There it drifted—Ray Longstreth's sweet face, white, with dark, tragic eyes, fading from his sight . . . fading . . . fading . . .

CHAPTER 25

Light shone before Duane's eyes—thick, strange light that came and went. For a long time dull and booming sounds rushed by, filling all. It was a dream in which there was nothing; a drifting under a burden; darkness, light, sound, movement; and vague, obscure sense of time— time that was very long. There was fire—creeping, consuming fire. A dark cloud of flame enveloped him, rolled him away.

He saw then, dimly, a room that was strange, strange people moving about over him, with faint voices, far away, things in a dream. He saw again, clearly, and consciousness returned, still unreal, still strange, full of those vague and far-away things. Then he was not dead. He lay stiff, like a stone, with a weight ponderous as a mountain upon him and all his bound body racked in slow, dull-beating agony.

A woman's face hovered over him, white and tragic-eyed, like one of his old haunting phantoms, yet sweet and eloquent. Then a man's face bent over him, looked deep into his eyes, and seemed to whisper from a distance: "Duane—Duane! Ah, he knew me!"

After that there was another long interval of darkness. When the light came again, clearer this time, the same earnest-faced man bent over him. It was MacNelly. And with recognition the past flooded back.

Duane tried to speak. His lips were weak, and he could scarcely move them.

"Poggin!" he whispered. His first real conscious thought was for Poggin. Ruling passion—eternal instinct!

"Poggin is dead, Duane; shot to pieces," replied MacNelly, solemnly. "What a fight he made! He killed two of my men, wounded others. God! he was a tiger. He used up three guns before we downed him."

"Who—got—away?"

"Fletcher, the man with the horses. We downed all the others. Duane, the job's done—it's done! Why, man, you're—"

"What of—of—*her*?"

"Miss Longstreth has been almost constantly at your bedside. She helped the doctor. She watched your wounds. And, Duane, the other night, when you sank low—so low—I think it was her spirit that held yours back. Oh, she's a wonderful girl. Duane, she never gave up, never lost her nerve for a moment. Well, we're going to take you home, and she'll go with us. Colonel Longstreth left for Louisiana right after the fight. I advised it. There was great excitement. It was best for him to leave."

"Have I—a—chance—to recover?"

"Chance? Why, man," exclaimed the Captain, "you'll get well! You'll pack a sight of lead all your life. But you can stand that. Duane, the whole Southwest knows your story. You need never again be ashamed of the name Buck Duane. The brand outlaw is washed out. Texas believes you've been a secret ranger all the time. You're a hero. And now think of home, your mother, of this noble girl—of your future."

The rangers took Duane home to Wellston.

A railroad had been built since Duane had gone into exile. Wellston had grown. A noisy crowd surrounded the station, but it stilled as Duane was carried from the train.

A sea of faces pressed close. Some were faces he remembered—schoolmates, friends, old neighbors. There was an upflinging of many hands. Duane was being welcomed home to the town from which he had fled. A deadness within him broke. This welcome hurt him somehow, quickened him; and through his cold being, his weary mind, passed a change. His sight dimmed.

Then there was a white house, his old home. How strange, yet how real! His heart beat fast. Had so many, many years passed? Familiar yet strange it was, and all seemed magnified.

They carried him in, these ranger comrades, and laid him down, and lifted his head upon pillows. The house was still, though full of people. Duane's gaze sought the open door.

Some one entered—a tall girl in white, with dark, wet eyes and a light upon her face. She was leading an old lady, gray-haired, austere-faced, somber and sad. His mother! She was feeble, but she walked erect. She was pale, shaking, yet maintained her dignity.

The some one in white uttered a low cry and knelt by Duane's bed. His mother flung wide her arms with a strange gesture.

"This man! They've not brought back my boy. This man's his father! Where is my son? My son—oh, my son!"

When Duane grew stronger it was a pleasure to lie by the west window and watch Uncle Jim whittle his stick and listen to his talk. The old man was broken now. He told many interesting things about people Duane had known—people who had grown up and married, failed, succeeded, gone away, and died. But it was hard to keep Uncle Jim off the subject of guns, outlaws, fights. He could not seem to divine how mention of these things hurt Duane. Uncle Jim was childish now, and he had a great pride in his nephew. He wanted to hear of all of Duane's exile. And if there was one thing more than another that pleased him it was to talk about the bullets which Duane carried in his body.

"Five bullets, ain't it?" he asked, for the hundredth time. "Five in that last scrap! By gum! And you had six before?"

"Yes, uncle," replied Duane.

"Five and six. That makes eleven. By gum! A man's a man, to carry all that lead. But, Buck, you could carry more. There's that Black Edwards, right here in Wellston. He's got a ton of bullets in him. Doesn't seem to mind them none. And there's Cole Miller. I've seen him. Been a bad man in his day. They say he packs twenty-three bullets. But he's bigger than you—got more flesh. . . . Funny, wasn't it, Buck, about the doctor only bein' able to cut one bullet out of you—that one in your breast-bone? It was a forty-one caliber, an unusual cartridge. I saw it, and I wanted it, but Miss Longstreth wouldn't part with it. Buck, there was a bullet left in one of Poggin's guns, and that bullet was the same kind as the one cut out of you. By gum! Boy, it'd have killed you if it'd stayed there."

"It would indeed, uncle," replied Duane, and the old, haunting, somber mood returned.

But Duane was not often at the mercy of childish old hero-worshiping Uncle Jim. Miss Longstreth was the only person who seemed to divine Duane's gloomy mood, and when she was with him she warded off all suggestion.

One afternoon, while she was there at the west window, a message came for him. They read it together.

You have saved the ranger service to the Lone Star State.

MacNelly.

Ray knelt beside him at the window, and he believed she meant to speak then of the thing they had shunned. Her face was still white, but sweeter now, warm with rich life beneath the marble; and her dark eyes were still intent, still haunted by shadows, but no longer tragic.

"I'm glad for MacNelly's sake as well as the state's," said Duane.

She made no reply to that and seemed to be thinking deeply. Duane shrank a little.

"The pain— Is it any worse to-day?" she asked, instantly.

"No; it's the same. It will always be the same. I'm full of lead, you know. But I don't mind a little pain."

"Then—it's the old mood—the fear?" she whispered. "Tell me."

"Yes. It haunts me. I'll be well soon—able to go out. Then that—that hell will come back!"

"No, no!" she said, with emotion.

"Some drunken cowboy, some fool with a gun, will hunt me out in every town, wherever I go," he went on, miserably. "Buck Duane! To kill Buck Duane!"

"Hush! Don't speak so. Listen. You remember that day in Val Verde, when I came to you—plead with you not to meet Poggin? Oh, that was a terrible hour for me. But it showed me the truth. I saw the struggle between your passion to kill and your love for me. I could have saved you then had I known what I know now. Now I understand that—that thing which haunts you. But you'll never have to draw again. You'll never have to kill another man, thank God!"

Like a drowning man he would have grasped at straws, but he could not voice his passionate query.

She put tender arms round his neck. "Because you'll have me with you always," she replied. "Because always I shall be between you and that—that terrible thing."

It seemed with the spoken thought absolute assurance of her power came to her. Duane realized instantly that he was in the arms of a stronger woman than she who had plead with him that fatal day.

"We'll—we'll be married and leave Texas," she said, softly, with the red blood rising rich and dark in her cheeks.

"Ray!"

"Yes we will, though you're laggard in asking me, sir."

"But, dear—suppose," he replied, huskily, "suppose there might be— be children—a boy. A boy with his father's blood!"

"I pray God there will be. I do not fear what you fear. But even so— he'll be half my blood."

Duane felt the storm rise and break in him. And his terror was that of joy quelling fear. The shining glory of love in this woman's eyes made him weak as a child. How could she love him—how could she so bravely face a future with him? Yet she held him in her arms, twining her hands round his neck, and pressing close to him. Her faith and love and beauty—these she meant to throw between him and all that terrible past. They were her power, and she meant to use them all. He dared not think of accepting her sacrifice.

"But Ray—you dear, noble girl—I'm poor. I have nothing. And I'm a cripple."

"Oh, you'll be well some day," she replied. "And listen. I have money. My mother left me well off. All she had was her father's— Do you understand? We'll take Uncle Jim and your mother. We'll go to Louisiana—to my old home. It's far from here. There's a plantation to work. There are horses and cattle—a great cypress forest to cut. Oh, you'll have much to do. You'll forget there. You'll learn to love my home. It's a beautiful old place. There are groves where the gray moss blows all day and the nightingales sing all night."

"My darling!" cried Duane, brokenly. "No, no, no!"

Yet he knew in his heart that he was yielding to her, that he could not resist her a moment longer. What was this madness of love?

"We'll be happy," she whispered. "Oh, I know. Come!—come!—come!"

Her eyes were closing, heavy-lidded, and she lifted sweet, tremulous, waiting lips.

With bursting heart Duane bent to them. Then he held her, close pressed to him, while with dim eyes he looked out over the line of low hills in the west, down where the sun was setting gold and red, down over the Nueces and the wild brakes of the Rio Grande which he was never to see again.

It was in this solemn and exalted moment that Duane accepted happiness and faced new life, trusting this brave and tender woman to be stronger than the dark and fateful passion that had shadowed his past.

It would come back—that wind of flame, that madness to forget, that driving, relentless instinct for blood. It would come back with those pale, drifting, haunting faces and the accusing fading eyes, but all his life, always between them and him, rendering them powerless, would be the faith and love and beauty of this noble woman.